Borgia and Four Other Novels

KLABUND

BORGIA

AND

FOUR

OTHER

NOVELS

Translated by Jim Doss

LOCH RAVEN PRESS   SYKESVILLE, MD   2023

Cover Art: Cover photo is Klabund in 1928
  Back cover photo is Klabund and Brunhilde Heberle summer of 1918.

Cover and book design: Jim Doss

ISBN 979-8-9905505-3-7

Loch Raven Press
140 Milrey Drive, Suite L
Sykesville, MD 21784
www.lochravenpress.com

Table of Contents

PART TWO: Peter - Novel of a Tsar (1923)

PART THREE: Störtebecker (1926)

PART FOUR: Borgia – Novel of a Family (1928)

PART FIVE: Rasputin – Novel of a Demon (1929)

Borgia and Four Other Novels

Biographical Sketch

1. Introduction: Klabund's Place in German Literature

Alfred "Fredi" Georg Hermann Henschke (1890-1928), known by his pen name Klabund, occupies a unique position in the annals of early 20th-century German literature. His works, characterized by lyrical expression, stylistic innovation, and an ever-present exploration of existential themes, reflect the complex socio-political environment of the time. While other literary figures such as Thomas Mann and Bertolt Brecht gained greater international fame, Klabund's contributions as a poet, playwright, and translator have left an indelible mark on German cultural history.

Klabund's distinctive voice is particularly significant in the context of German Expressionism, a literary and artistic movement that emerged in response to the rapid modernization, political upheaval, and existential anxieties of pre- and post-World War I Europe. His works, while rooted in the Expressionist tradition, often ventured beyond the confines of the movement, incorporating influences from Eastern literature, historical narratives, and personal reflections on mortality.

This brief biography aims to outline the life of Klabund, touching upon his evolution as a writer and intellectual, his engagement with contemporary literary movements, and the personal struggles and health issues that helped shape his worldview.

2. Early Life and Formative Years (1890-1910)

Klabund was born on November 4, 1890, in Crossen an der Oder at 1:00 a.m., a small town located in what was then part of the German Empire (now Krosno Odrzańskie, Poland). Crossen was a small Prussian garrison town with around 7000 inhabitants, loyal to the emperor, provincial and conservative. His family belonged to the middle class. His father, Dr. Alfred Henschke (1858-1936), was a pharmacist at the Adler-Apotheke which was located at Dammstrasse 344/45, and was appointed to be of the magistrate in 1893, a position he remained in until 1930. He was also elected to the unpaid position of first deputy mayor in 1907, which he held for seven years. His mother, Emilie Antonie (1867-1945), a housewife, ensured the household ran smoothly. His upbringing was comfortable yet provincial, and from a young age, Klabund displayed both intellectual precocity and physical frailty.

Despite the relatively ordinary circumstances of his early life, Klabund's childhood was marked by a deep emotional sensitivity, an acute awareness of life's fleeting nature, and a fascination with literature. By the age of twelve, he was a young gifted pianist with larger than average hands and already engaged in writing poems, although at the time, he had no idea that this early passion would shape his entire life. Klabund's delicate health also became a key part of his formative years. He suffered from recurring bouts of illness, particularly high fevers and bilateral pneumonia, which caused him to be hospitalized in Crossen for six weeks in 1907, and would later be diagnosed as "closed tuberculosis" and dominate his adult life. A 1912 letter is the earliest written confirmation we have that Klabund knew he had tuberculosis. Up until the middle of the twentieth century, a diagnosis of tuberculosis was roughly the equivalent of receiving a death sentence that would be carried out at some unknown, unpredictable time in the future. In the early 1900's, there were primarily two ways to fight this disease, and both were rarely successful. The first technique was to attempt to mobilize the patient's immune system through long climatic cures in wooded highlands, through a "healthy diet" and by avoiding strenuous activity. With the second technique, following the research of Berlin doctor Ferdinand Sauerbruch, doctors tried to defeat tuberculosis surgically: through a resection of the ribs. By means of a "pneumothorax," whose noisy effects Thomas Mann so mockingly described in his "Magic Mountain," part of the lung was shut down. This second option was not viable for Klabund since both of his lungs were affected and he could potentially experience a dramatic deterioration in his condition at any time.

His father, a stern but loving figure, expected Alfred to follow in his professional footsteps. Pharmacy, like many middle-class trades of the time, was viewed as a stable and respectable career. However, Klabund's early schooling revealed a different trajectory. His teachers recognized his literary talent, and he excelled in subjects like literature, history, and philosophy, even as his physical health continued to decline.

In 1909, upon completing his early education, Klabund moved to Munich to study medicine, largely due to the expectations of his family. Munich at the time was one of the intellectual and artistic hubs of Europe, home to a vibrant community of writers, artists, and thinkers. The shift to Munich exposed the young student to a broader world of artistic and literary experimentation. Here, he first encountered the currents of modernism that were sweeping across Europe.

Despite his initial dedication to medicine, his attention quickly shifted toward literature and philosophy. He began attending lectures on philosophy, philology, and history, further cementing his interest in these intellectual pursuits. His time in Munich also allowed him to engage with Expressionist artists and writers, whose works reflected the growing sense of existential crisis that pervaded European intellectual life at the dawn of the 20th century.

By 1912, Alfred Henschke had officially abandoned his medical studies in favor of a full-time literary career. This period also marked the adoption of his now-famous pen name: Klabund. As Klabund explains it: "I created the name Klabund one day in a mood of serious self-parody, but I gave it so much of my blood that it began to live alongside and above me, becoming a reflection of my art and worldview... Klabund emerged from Klabautermann – the mischievous sea ghost that appears to sailors on foggy nights as a harbinger of doom – and from Vagabund. The name points to the vagabond-like days of my early student years..." The symbolic weight of this name is significant – it reflects Klabund's itinerant spirit, his status as a wanderer through both physical landscapes and the realms of human thought as evidenced by the many themes and settings within his literature.

> The It of things to which I've pledged my being
> Softens into the You of reverie.
> I will love my soul unceasingly,
> In its peace, in its frenzy.
> Beloved, eternal upon my lips:
> I am and was and will always be Klabund.

As "Klabund," the young writer fully embraced the bohemian lifestyle of the avant-garde literary circles in Munich and Berlin. He became a part of the burgeoning intellectual community that included figures such as Frank Wedekind (1864-1918), Heinrich Mann (1871-1950), and the young Bertolt Brecht (1898-1956). Klabund's work from this time was heavily influenced by Expressionist themes of alienation, urban chaos, and the search for spiritual meaning in an increasingly industrialized and dehumanized world, with the expectations of war and social conflict between the classes always looming large.

3. Expressionism and Early Literary Output (1910-1914)

Klabund's early works – primarily poetry – were deeply rooted in the Expressionist movement, which sought to reject the materialism and realism of the late 19th century in favor of more subjective, emotional, and often apocalyptic visions of modern life. His first major poetry collection, *Morgenrot! Klabund! Die Tage dämmern!* (Dawn! Klabund! The Days are Breaking!) (1913), embodies the key elements of Expressionist aesthetics: intense emotions, vivid imagery, and an exploration of existential anxiety.

In 1912 Klabund wrote to Walter Heinrich, an occasional writer and bank clerk in Crossen who went by the pen name Unus: "To impress you a little, here are a series of numbers and titles. I have written 597 poems, 29 novellas, 13 one-act plays, 1 novel, a collection of aphorisms, as well as fragments and collections of material for dramas and novels of the highest style (Don Juan, Nausicaa, Adam and Eve, etc.), essays, etc." While only Klabund knows if this was a bit of an exaggeration or not, it demonstrates the type of productivity Klabund would maintain throughout his literary career.

In the winter of 1912, inspired by the writer Villon, Klabund sent some verses to the theater critic Alfred Kerr (1867-1948), who published them in the magazine *Pan*. These poems, written in a coarse and cheeky style, caused a bit of a public stir. The Imperial Censorship Committee found grounds to charge Klabund with "the dissemination of obscene literature." They heard the opinions of Frank Wedekin, Max Halbe (1865-1944), Erich Mühsam (1878-1934), and Richard Dehmel (1863-1920), who objected to these charges which also implicated Kerr by arguing the poems had artistic merit. The trial lasted from September 1913 to January 1915. The judiciary ultimately fined Klabund 50 Reichmarks, only to have the verdict overturned a year later.

This period also marked Klabund's growing fascination with death and the ephemeral nature of life, themes that would persist throughout his career. His lifelong battle with tuberculosis, coupled with his intellectual engagement with Expressionist thought, made him particularly attuned to the fragility of human existence. His poems often meditate on impermanence, mortality, and the disillusionment of the modern age.

In collections such as *Morgenrot!*, Klabund's poetic voice expresses a mixture of despair and wonderment. The natural world, in his work, is often a place of both beauty and terror, filled with fleeting moments of grace that contrast sharply with the bleakness of urban life. For Klabund, the modern city represents a place of alienation, where individuals are disconnected from one another and from the natural world. Yet, even in this disenchanted landscape, he seeks moments of transcendence, whether through love, art, or spiritual reflection.

Klabund reflects on the book *Morgenrot!* that: "I have absolutely nothing: no paper, no money, no profession, not even a proper apartment. As a bait for credibility, rhymes are accompanied not by 'hot' but cheerful 'sexual distress,' ensuring that something primal and vivid is not missing from this lyrical portrait of Samuel Klabund – by himself."

Klabund was also heavily influenced by German Romanticism, particularly the works of Friedrich Hölderlin (1770-1843) and Heinrich Heine (1797-1856). Like these earlier poets, Klabund imbued his work with a sense of longing for a lost ideal – whether a spiritual utopia or a pre-modern world untouched by the corruption of modernity. His use of lyrical, often musical language, as well as his interest in myth and folklore, connects him to this Romantic tradition, even as he critiques the very notion of romantic ideals in a modern context. In 1913 Klabund came into contact with Alfred Kerr's Magazine *PAN*, though he continued to publish in the magazines *Jugend* and *Simplicissimus*. Beginning in 1914 he contributed to *Die Schaubühne* (Show Place), which later changed its name to *Die Weltbühne* (The World Stage).

Klabund completed the manuscript of his first novel – *The Ruby – Novel of a Young Man* in May of 1914 and sent it to his mentor Walter Heinrich in Berlin. The novel was intended to be published by the Erich Reiß Verlag, but disputes between the author and the publisher and the outbreak of World War I prevented its release. *The Ruby* was eventually published posthumously in 1929 by Phaidon in Vienna.

By this point in time, Klabund was destined to live up to the "vagabond" part of his pen name as he frequently changed his place of residence from Crossen to Munich to Berlin to Locarno and other cities, and when his tuberculosis began to severely impact his health he sought healing in the Swiss spa town of Davos.

4. World War I and Changing Attitudes (1914-1918)

The outbreak of World War I in 1914 marked a turning point in Klabund's life, both personally and professionally. Like many intellectuals and artists of his generation, Klabund initially greeted the war with a mixture of excitement and patriotic fervor. He saw the conflict as a way for Europe to purge itself of its decadence and moral decay, viewing it through a lens of romantic heroism. However, this initial optimism would quickly give way to a more complex and critical perspective as the war dragged on, exposing the futility and horror of modern warfare.

Due to his poor health, Klabund was unable to serve on the front lines, in spite of his repeated efforts to enlist, but he followed the war closely and responded to its events in his writing. His early war poetry, while still somewhat idealistic, began to take on a darker, more cynical tone as the scale of the destruction became clear. In works like *Kriegsfibel* (War Primer), a collection of war poems written between 1914 and 1918, Klabund grapples with the senseless violence and the moral degradation that accompanied the conflict.

Kriegsfibel (War Primer) stands as one of Klabund's most important wartime works, capturing his evolving disillusionment with the war. The poems in this collection are characterized by their stark realism, eschewing the romanticized depictions of battle that had characterized his earlier works. Instead, Klabund presents the war as a grotesque and meaningless spectacle, in which human life is reduced to little more than fodder for machines and bureaucracies. Klabund's shift from early enthusiasm to deep cynicism about war culminates in his 1918 novel *Bracke*. The novel is a scathing critique of the social and political structures that led to the war, as well as a meditation on the personal toll of violence and destruction. *Bracke* is one of Klabund's most explicitly political works, and it represents his growing disenchantment with both the war and the nationalist ideologies that had initially fueled it. The novel's central character becomes a kind of anti-hero, whose moral confusion and emotional detachment reflect the broader sense of disillusionment felt by many in post-war Germany.

It would take almost three year before Klabund recognized the senselessness of the war and on June 3, 1917 published on open letter to Kaiser Wilhelm II (1859-1941) in the Neue Zürcher Zeitung (New Zurich Newspaper) urging the Kaiser to abdicate with passages like: "Be the first prince to voluntarily renounce his fictitious rights and bow to the Areopagus of human rights. Your name will then be mentioned among the truly great in the new books of history, where the history of humanity will no longer be written in terms of coalitions but in terms of the history of the human spirit. Then you will establish the people's kingdom of the Hohenzollerns on rock; whereas it is now only a cloud formation that, if you do not recognize the time, will soon be vanished in the rising storm." Many believed his future wife influenced his transformation toward pacifism. Needless to say, this letter did not go over well with all citizens, and cause much resentment and hard feelings toward Klabund. In September 1917, Klabund addressed the controversy of his earlier war poetry to Munich journalists: "These poems were written three years ago at the beginning of a horrific war – when no one knew where it was heading, and when everyone was deceived about its goals. I have greatly changed my opinion about the war; my 1915 Chinese war poetry, more like the pack wagon, and later Moreau, show the path that leads to absolute pacifism, on which ground I now stand."

On a personal note, in 1918 Klabund married Brunhilde Irene Herberle (1896-1918) on June 8th, whom he had met in a sanatorium for lung patients. She was a passionate pianist who loved to play the music of Schumann and the tubercular Frederick Chopin. Larngeal tuberculosis also occasionally rendered her voice nearly inaudible. He calls her Irene in his poems because to him that word meant peace. Klabund described her in a letter: "I am married: to a woman who is entirely animal, entirely child, entirely butterfly, like those beings around us." Rumor was that she was pregnant at the time of their marriage. On October 17th she gave birth to daughter Irene Fiete Anny after a seven-month pregnancy, and was operated on due to complications. Klabund's wife survived until October 30th. On February 17, 1919 the daughter also passed away. Klabund sent a telegram to his friend Walter Heinrich: "Irene has called her child to her today." Klabund wrote several books of poetry dedicated to his first wife, such as *Small Verses for Irene*, and *Sonnets to Irene*. Klabund blamed himself for Irene's death.

I was your death. I murdered you.
I am guilty that chaos, like a crater,
Bursts open and spews its fire. I am the father
Of anarchy, red and overflowing upon us.

I was your death. I murdered you.
In vain the pious father warned me;
I desecrated you, dolorous mother...
I killed you with my own child.

The rule you wielded with the lily,
I overthrew in the fever of my caste.
You smiled. You blessed. You loved.

I glared darkly. Threatened. Cursed. Hated.
And while you sifted gold from dust,
I ran to debauchery, bellowed, drank, and reveled.

5. Postwar Work: Cultural Exploration and the Search for New Forms (1919-1928)

In the aftermath of World War I, Klabund entered a period of intense creative output. The political, social, and economic chaos that followed the war deeply influenced his work during the 1920s. Yet, even as he engaged with the traumas of the war and its aftermath, he also began to explore new forms of artistic expression, venturing into drama, historical fiction, and cultural translation.

In early April 1919, Klabund received a telegram that a friend from his Munich student days, Erich Mühsam (who would later be incarcerated at Fortress Niederschönenfeld with Ernst Toller), had been arrested, and Klabund was asked if he could help him. However this raised suspicions about Klabund and the possibility that he might be part of the Munich insurgents so he was taken into "protective custoday" from April 17th to April 26th in the Straubing prison. The "anarchist" Erich Mühsam was one of the leading figures of the Bavarian Soviet Republic. He was arrested by the counter-revolutionary troops of the Reichswehr and sentenced to fifteen years of fortress imprisonment. Klabund became a victim of his own efforts to help his friend, and was himself accused of participating in Spartacist activities. The political ideologies of socialism, democracy and revolution in reality meant little to him. He was merely committed to trying to help a friend. In the end his "help" achieved nothing, and his ten days of incarceration were documented in his book *Tagebuch im Gefängnis* (*Diary in Prison*). Upon release, Klabung writes: "Free! Outside again! Alive again! I am still too agitated and nervous to contain the waves of emotions coursing through me... Today, I plan to visit Nuremberg, the Hirschvogel Hall, and Hans Sachs. At the Hans Sachs House, I will tip my hat for the first time in nine days and pay reverence to the Germany I love."

During this time, Klabund also became active in the cabaret scene in Zurich and Munich at the Cabaret Voltaire, the Bavarian Cabaret, The Beautiful Bird, and other venues. There he met fellow writers such as Bertolt Brecht, Hugo Ball (1886-1927), the founder of Dadaism, his wife Emmy Hemmings (1885-1948), and other German writers and performers. Klabund was an occasional performer and his ballads of love, murder, alcohol and other frivolities made him a popular performer as he shot a few mocking arrows at both himself and the audience, but he didn't come under the Dadaist influence and remained true to his own poetic instincts. During his time in the cabarets, Klabund also met Maria Kirndörfer (1893-1981), aka Marietta di Monaco, about whom he wrote the novella *Marietta – A Love Story from Schwabing*. Marietta became known as the poet's muse and famous through her close friendships with poets like Joachim Ringelnatz (1883-1934), Frank Wedekind, Fred Endrikat, and Klabund. She recited their works on stage.

Like his health, Klabund's finances were on a constant rollercoaster ride with dizzying highs and depressing lows. As a bestselling author of the time, money would come into his pockets based on the popularity of his books, but then it quickly evaporated again as the poet helped those in need and usually picked up the tab at parties and celebrations. He also would occasionally support penniless students until he himself was in need of help again and had to call on his friends.

One of the most distinctive aspects of Klabund's postwar work is his deep engagement with Eastern literature, particularly Chinese and Persian poetry. This fascination with non-Western cultures set Klabund apart from many of his contemporaries, who remained focused on European literary traditions. Klabund's translations and adaptations of classical Chinese poetry, particularly his translations of the Tang Dynasty poets, introduced German readers to a new literary form that emphasized simplicity, natural beauty, and philosophical reflection.

In addition to Chinese literature, Klabund was also deeply influenced by Persian poetry, particularly the works of the Sufi mystic Rumi. His fascination with Eastern spirituality reflected his broader search for new forms of meaning in a post-war world. For Klabund, Eastern literature provided an alternative to the disillusionment of modern Europe, offering a vision of inner peace, harmony with nature, and a transcendence of the material world.

In the 1920s, Klabund began to focus more intensively on drama, producing several important plays that would secure his reputation as a major figure in the German theater. His most famous play, *Der Kreidekreis* (The Chalk Circle), was first performed in 1924 and became an immediate success. Based on an ancient Chinese folk tale, *Der Kreidekreis* tells the story of a legal dispute over a child and the wisdom of a judge who determines the child's true parentage.

Der Kreidekreis was notable not only for its narrative structure but also for its fusion of Eastern and Western dramatic traditions. Klabund's play would later serve as the inspiration for Bertolt Brecht's *The Caucasian Chalk Circle* (1944), one of the most important works of 20th-century theater. Klabund's use of the chalk circle as a metaphor for justice, loyalty, and truth resonated deeply with audiences, and the play was praised for its universal themes and innovative staging.

In addition to *Der Kreidekreis*, Klabund wrote several other plays during this period, including *Karfunkel* (1923) and *Xantippe* (1920), both of which reflect his continued interest in history and myth. His plays, much like his poetry and prose, were marked by a lyrical style, a fascination with moral ambiguity, and a desire to explore human relationships in the face of societal collapse.

6. Personal Struggles: Illness and Relationships

While Klabund's literary career flourished during the 1920s, his personal life was increasingly dominated by his struggle with tuberculosis. The disease, which he had contracted in his youth, worsened as he grew older, forcing him to spend long periods in sanatoriums, primarily in Davos. His experiences with illness and isolation are reflected in many of his works, particularly his later poems, which often meditate on the themes of suffering, death, and the passage of time.

In 1924, Klabund met celebrated actress in Berlin's theater scene Carola Neher (1900-1942), who would later become one of Brecht's most famous collaborators, on a streetcar in Munich near the Café Stefanie. Klabund keep staring at her until she whispered to him: "If you want to stare at me without any shame, you have to go to the theater. I'm playing Hugenberg in Frank Wedekind's play *Pandora's Box* at the Kammerspiele tonight." After the play, he waited for her by the stage exit, hands her his business card and insists on another meeting. In the spring of 1925, severe blood poisoning forces Carola Neher to spend several weeks in the Breslau Friederici Sanatorium, where she must be operated on immediately after admission. On May 7, 1925, she and Klabund were married in the sanatorium. Their relationship was passionate, but troubled, largely due to Klabund's deteriorating health in combination with the demands of their two artistic professions which requires Carola and sometimes Klabund to move to the various cities where the theaters are located for her parts. Klabund writes to Herman Hesse (1877-

1962): "I live, blown here by fate, still in Breslau, the (bulwark of the East), a damp, unfriendly place in Prussian Siberia. How often I long for the warm, tender Ticino." Neher is cast in Klabund's play *The Chalk Circle*, and he creates parts in subsequent plays for her such as *The Burning Earth* and *XYZ*. On May 30, 1928, Carola Neher and Klabund depart from Gottfried Benn's (1886-1956) apartment for their trip to Brioni. For Carola Neher, it is a holiday of one and a half months before starting rehearsal work as "Polly" in the premiere of Brecht's play *The Threepenny Opera*, and for both, it is their last holiday together. During this trip, Klabund completed work on *Borgia*, his last novel. In July, Klabund contracted a fever again, and needed to return to Davos immediately, where the patient, critically ill, arrived exhausted in the middle of the month. The doctor diagnosed pneumonia once again. On the evening of August 13th, Klabund's life began to fade away. His doctor had not expected the end so soon. Carola, the doctor and a night nurse stood by Klabund's bedside, hardly recognizing him, as he gently passed away on August 14th at 4:30 a.m. Klabund described his wish to be cremated: "I would like my ashes to be scattered over the sea. Then I will end up like Jonah in a whale's belly, or a flounder will swallow me, and one day, a fat gentleman from Königsberg will invite me to dinner. But perhaps I will reach the bottom of the sea safely, yes: perhaps I will reach the bottom of all being." The burial took place in Crossen at the Bergfried Cemetary on September 9, 1928 with the poet Dr. Gottfried Benn delivering the eulogy for his deceased friend.

In his eulogy, Benn said: "I knew him in the times when he was nothing, and in the times of the brilliance of his name. The best years were probably those when, shortly after the war, he lived in a small street in southwest Berlin, in a small room with only one window and no bed; he slept on a sofa, and when you visited him in the morning, he was lying on that sofa, completely covered with manuscripts, newspapers, letters, and journals, working tirelessly and feverishly, as he did his whole life. These were the years of the second period of his poems, his novels, and the years when the thought of the 'Chalk Circle' came to him. They were also years of illness, and I often went to him as a doctor. Sometimes I called him in friendship 'Jens Peter,' which were the first names of the great Danish novelist Jens Peter Jacobsen, to whom he resembled physically, and who suffered from the same illness and died. I often saw violets in his room, Chopin's favorite flowers, his other companion in illness. Once we read together the last words of Chopin, which he wrote on his day of death: 'My attempts are completed according to what was possible for me to achieve' – the farewell words of a true artist who had experienced the fragmentary nature of the individual, words of silence and restraint, as Klabund could have written them too, whose fundamental characteristic throughout all the years was one of deep, brotherly modesty."

Years after Klabund's death Carola Neher married Anatol Becker in 1932 and left Germany following Hitler's ascension to power in 1933. She first emigrated to Prague, where she worked at the New German Theater, but went on to the Soviet Union in 1934, where she met Gustav von Wangenheim and worked with him at his cabaret Kolonne Links. In 1936, during the great purge both she and her husband were denounced as Trotskyites, resulting in their being arrested on July

25, 1936. Becker was executed in 1937, while Neher was sentenced to ten years in prison. She eventually died of typhus at Penal Colony No. 6 of the Federal Penitentiary Service of Russia in Orenburg Oblast.

7. Conclusion: Reassessing Klabund's Legacy

Klabund's early death cut short a brilliant literary career, leaving many to wonder what further contributions he might have made to German literature had he lived longer. Despite his relatively short life, Klabund left behind a significant body of work that continues to be studied and appreciated today – 25 plays, 14 novels, numerous short stories and books of poetry. His poetry, plays, and translations are admired for their emotional depth, stylistic innovation, and cross-cultural reach. Klabund's ability to bridge the literary traditions of East and West, his exploration of human fragility, and his engagement with the existential crises of his time make him a vital figure in both German literature and the broader tradition of European modernism.

In recent years, there has been a renewed interest in Klabund's work, as scholars and critics have sought to recontextualize his contributions within the broader framework of modernist literature. His unique blend of Eastern and Western influences, his engagement with existential themes, and his lyrical mastery make him a key figure in the literary history of the early 20th century.

While his works may not have achieved the same widespread popularity as those of Brecht or Thomas Mann (1875-1955), Klabund's legacy remains significant. His ability to capture the emotional and intellectual turbulence of his time, coupled with his desire to seek new forms of artistic expression, continues to resonate with contemporary audiences.

Ultimately, Klabund's life and works offer a powerful testament to the enduring human struggle for meaning in a world marked by uncertainty, impermanence, and suffering. His voice, though often melancholic, is one of hope, suggesting that even in the darkest moments, there is beauty to be found in the fleeting and the fragile.

Part One:

Spooks

The storm
Bends the branches
And the raven sings.
Thus, God's weather wanders
To the stars.
    – Hölderlin

Written in the fever of an illness,
January to April 1921.

(Erich Reiß Verlag, Berlin, 1922)

Spooks

The Underworld

I had a face. The underworld rose up from my subconscious. The Acheron roared. Charon, the ferryman of the underworld, landed with his boat. The boat ground against the sand. Charon leapt ashore. He cursed:

"Here I land in hell – with an empty boat. Not a single damned soul was waiting for the crossing today. Ever since Jesus Christ appeared to mankind, my handiwork and work of hell have been lying idle."

He rummaged through the pouch hanging from his belt.

"My pouch is empty. Not a penny from a single fare. To hell with the virtue of mankind if it ruins me. I hate this Christ, I hate God, I hate goodness, meekness, willingness to sacrifice, truth, and love."

He made the sign of hell and shouted:

"Hey, Pluto, lord of the underworld, appear! Charon, the ferryman of the underworld, wishes to speak to you in dutiful submission."

Thunder rumbled. The mists of the underworld parted. A lightning bolt tore through the darkness as if it were a black velvet curtain, and Pluto became visible on a fiery throne. Charon knelt:

"Full of grief and bitterness, I appear before Your Majesty. Faithfully and tirelessly, I have served you for thousands of years. I have ferried millions of souls across this dark river to you: that they may be your slaves forever. On earth, your dark demons, your furies and spirits ruled, sending soul after soul down here. But then a miracle came over the world: God sent His only Son, accompanied by hosts of silver cherubim and seraphim. They had no weapons in their hands but lily stems and sunflowers. But they drove your hissing furies into flight. God's Son awakened the conscience of humanity. Man, long enslaved to our dark nature, begins to become God's creation. My boat ferries fewer souls each day, and today it was completely empty. Things are grim, Pluto, for your cause, for my cause, for our cause."

Pluto shook his serpent-crowned head.

"I praise you for your zeal, servant of evil."

And his voice shrieked, like a thousand braying mules. "You Furies, you Erinyes, you demons, you devils and she-devils, come forth! Pluto, your lord and master, calls you!"

Amid thunder and lightning, the foaming spirits and fluttering furies appeared.

Pluto raised his scepter: a staff carved from the tree of knowledge, around which a living adder coiled with a small human head:

"Hear what I have to say to you. Charon, the ferryman of the underworld, complains that his boat carries fewer souls each day. I learn with displeasure that your zeal in the service of the plutonic realm has waned." He swung his scepter: "Beware, you who neglect your duty!"

A devil dared to whisper:

"The power of good is all too powerful–"

Pluto exploded:

"Not so powerful that we cannot break them. Go to the upper world. Use any form: become a priest, a king, a philosopher, a member of Reichstag, a general, a stockbroker, a farmer, a coal baron, an innkeeper, an old woman, a whore: spare no means to entice humans to any crime, to murder, theft, robbery, war, lewdness, lies, deceit, hatred, and hypocrisy. Teach them to turn the lowest to the highest, the highest to the lowest. Teach them to degrade the nobles and elevate the basest, so that they perish and their souls tumble to hell... Go forth. But you, chief of the devils, Satan, remain, for I have a special task to give you."

The demons vanished amid howling and hissing.

I, however, approached Pluto's throne, bent the knee, over which the red mantle, the mantle of the executioner, billowed, and said: "What do you wish, lord of hell, from your most obedient servant?"

Pluto spoke:

"I have been told of a girl, sometimes called Maria, sometimes Marianne. She is beautiful and gentle beyond measure. Her will desires good, but her youth is burdened with premonitions, wishes, and thoughts. She is wax in the hand of a determined shaper. My spirits have reported such extraordinary things about her that I have a strong desire to possess this soul and call her entirely my own. I intend to elevate her to be my consort. You, Satan, shall be my suitor."

I bowed, and the red mantle rustled:

"I will spare no seduction or temptation. Pluto will praise his most obedient servant."

Pluto turned to Charon:

"And you, Charon, are you satisfied?"

Charon nodded:

"I am, prince of hell. My ship awaits. I'm ready."

The House with the Donkey Heads

I was born in the house with the two donkey heads. It stands in a crooked side alley of the city, with the gable facing forward.

When I stuck my head out of the attic window and my father happened to be working on the street, he would shout:

"There are three donkeys sticking their heads out!"

I shrugged my shoulders and laughed silently.

I was neither insulted nor offended. From an early age, I had a tender affection for the gray, good-natured, but also malicious equines.

Once, when the dairy's donkey was being beaten, I threw myself between it and its tormentor, and felt the whip whistle past my ears.

"You people should die," I screamed, "all of you should die."

Whether my parents loved me, I don't know. Perhaps my father did. My mother hated me, because she hadn't wanted children, and I was very much unwanted by her. When I sat at the table and she spoke to me, she always spoke and looked past me.

I cannot recall ever receiving a look from my mother, and to this day, I do not know whether she had blue or brown or black eyes.

I had a penchant for the vastness, for the distance, for infinity – and a penchant for the near, for confined spaces, for security.

I was both a warrior and a peacemaker at the same time.

When I was five years old, I went to a toy store. There stood a small donkey on wheels. I pulled it by its string behind me, marched through the city, over the bridge, then along the highway.

The road workers called out and shouted words to me that I did not understand. The sun was blazing.

I marched, the wheels on the donkey's legs clattered.

I was picked up by a farmer who was driving to the city and knew me from my father's shop.

He lifted me onto the wagon along with my wooden donkey and brought me home.

There, I left the donkey in front of the house, went up to the attic, and lay down on the peat that was piled up in a corner. It was as dark as night. I closed my eyes. Now I was connected to the world only by sounds. A dog barked. A tomcat hissed. The wing of a bat rustled. The sound of my father pounding mortar rang out in the yard. Wagons rolled by. Adults shouted all sorts of senseless noises to one another. Children, no older than I, laughed and cried.

I lay outside this world, entirely to myself.

Only the two donkey heads and the abandoned wooden donkey on the street, my proxy out in the world, were privy to my silent secrets.

But they knew how to remain silent – just like me.

The Blood Brotherhood

Who was my friend?

The donkey from the dairy or the dusty chestnut tree in the yard that looked like it had been stored in the attic for a long time because a customer ordered it and didn't pick it up.

Who was my girlfriend?

Some cloud or glittering mosquito or a white wave in the flowing stream.

My first encounter with someone my age went like this: for my birthday, I had received a sailor suit and a sailor cap. Dressed in this outfit, I went over the meadow to the so-called Goose Pond, carrying a small boat carved from bark in my arms. There, I sat in the grass and let the boat float. It didn't take long before a boy my age stood next to me, completely wild and lice-infested, with an evil look in his cat-like eyes. He splashed his bare feet in the water. His eyes roamed over my uniform.

"Give me your cap," he said suddenly and abruptly.

I didn't know how to respond and remained silent.

Then the boy pulled out a knife from his back pocket, just like a grown-up, and came at me.

I was so frightened that I let go of the string and the bark boat, which I had carved with great effort, disappeared in a whirlpool.

I already believed I could feel the knife at my throat when I heard an adult's voice. I must confess that, even though I was practically in mortal danger, I received it with great annoyance. Adults have an insufferable way of meddling in children's affairs with haughty gestures, which, firstly, are none of their business and, secondly, they understand nothing about.

I looked up and saw the cobbler Leidl, a man of ill repute, as he wrestled the knife from the ragged boy and threw it into the river. The boy bit his hand until it bled. But the cobbler only smiled and said the words he always used to say and which the street urchins shouted after him: "Don't be angry...!"

Then he smiled, the first smile I had ever seen on a human face, and said:

"What can the boy do if his father has money and yours doesn't?"

And he said to me:

"You have wronged the boy without realizing it. Shake his hand."

I opened my mouth in astonishment, completely unable to understand what the cobbler meant. The boy had come at me with a knife, and I had wronged him?

But, gnawed by doubt, I offered the boy my hand, which he reluctantly took.

"Now play together!" said the cobbler and went on his way.

We sat next to each other on the sandy riverbank.

I looked at him, then he lowered his head.

He looked at me, then I lowered my head.

Finally, an idea came to me. I took the cap off my head and said:

"Here, take the cap. I'm giving it to you."

He seemed to doubt my sincerity.

"But what if you're lying? – People lie all the time."

"You can have my sailor cap. I don't like it at all."

A bitter taste in his mouth distorted his face.

"So, because you don't like it, it's good for me."

"No, no," I stammered, ashamed. "I like it very much because I got it for my birthday today."

Then the boy took the cap, put it on, and said:

"My name is Munk, and I'm the son of the butcher Munk."

I told him my name, but left out my father's profession, which couldn't compare in weight and importance to that of a butcher and slaughterer, even though he earned more money.

"We shall become blood brothers," said Munk. "Damn," he frowned like an adult, "that pig which needed to be slaughtered, that cobbler Leidl threw my knife into the river. Don't be angry, don't be angry," he mocked the cobbler. "Just be evil! Just be evil!" he burst out. "Do to humans what my father does to animals. Yes, that's right. Then this cobbler, who drank away his business and beat his wife to death, comes and wants to teach us manners."

He said: teach us manners. God knows where he picked that up. He walked along the riverbank, searching.

Reeds protruded from the shallow shoreline water. He bent a reed towards himself and broke it so skillfully that a sharp point appeared. With this, he made a small hole in his upper arm until the blood came out.

"Here, drink!" he said.

And I drank his blood.

It had a bland, sweetish taste.

I wish I had never drunk it!

Then he inflicted a small wound on me and drank mine. "Now we are forever bound, we are blood brothers," said Munk and looked at me strangely from the side. "Come visit me sometime when it's slaughter day."

The Emperor Moth

It is half past eleven in the morning. I am sitting at my table. I have only one table: it serves as my work table, play table, and dining table. The small yellow lamp is burning: my room faces the courtyard at the back and it never becomes day here. In the courtyard stand trash bins that haven't been picked up for many weeks. The garbage collectors are on strike. I can hardly open the window, otherwise, the wind blows a yellow, foul-smelling, sirocco-like cloud into my room. I got up very early today. Otherwise, I usually stay in bed until two, three, sometimes even four or five.

That is to say, I don't have a proper bed. There isn't space for one in this room. It's more like a kind of sofa bed.

It is cold in the room. Outside, the east wind is whistling. The yellow light of the lamp soothes me. It reminds me of a room far down south, where it wasn't cold and where the same yellow lampshade hung over the lamp. Maria herself had cut it from a piece of silk. Since then, I have disliked the sun and this yellow light suits me just right.

Until now, I had kept my eyes closed. Now I open them and look a little bewildered to find myself back in the world. On the wall, there is an engraving: *Spring of Love*. A small-time gentleman in a Roman tunic leans over an Etruscan barmaid. There is a bookshelf with a glass door through which you can read the titles of the books. The cabinet is always locked because the books belong to my landlord.

The room smells a bit like aromatic vinegar, which I rub myself down with in the morning because I tend to sweat at night.

The doorbell rang earlier, and I have the feeling that some telegram or express letter is lying for me on the corridor table. I have forbidden the maid to disturb me. Should I go check? It hardly matters. Sometimes I don't open telegrams for four weeks. Perhaps the house with the donkey heads has collapsed or a fire has devastated it. It's all the same to me. Which is not to say I am trivializing it. Rather: everything – is – the same. I am my fate, and this telegram will unsettle me as little as the death of a loved one or my own death. I am beyond death and beyond myself. I have suffered too much. Everything now exists only to confirm me: the east wind, the aromatic vinegar, the yellow lamp, the beloved woman, death.

When I began to love Maria, I knew from the first day with a painful, bitter, and sweet certainty: that I would kill her. Kill: without intention, without awareness of purpose and goal. Just as Munk had wanted to kill me when he attacked me with a knife because I was at a loss for an answer.

Fate asked me a question, and I killed Maria – because I was at a loss for an answer. I resisted with all my soul's strength the death wishes I had for her, especially in the tenderest moments of fulfillment and completion. As if it had happened yesterday, I remember that summer night at Silver Lake. A heady fragrance of flowers and stars lay in the air. The flowers shone. The stars exuded perfume. The chirping of summer crickets still rings in my ears. We lay on the veranda, wrapped only in the violet-blue twilight. Maria smiled, and I physically felt her smile: "I am so happy that this happiness cannot last." I turned my head.

The gliding wing of an emperor moth had brushed against me.

The Stone Guest

I put on my coat and went out into the street. The first snow had glazed the pavement with a thin white crust. The angels in heaven were picking at lint. There were so many wounds to bandage: in all worlds, for all beings, on this side and beyond. At Hallesches Tor, I bought a newspaper from a newspaper seller nicknamed "Tomato" because of the red rash on her face. I wasn't interested in the latest political events; I just flipped to the obituary section to see if anyone had died who shared my name. I am superstitious like a savage. The day began with a bad omen. Indeed, someone had died: the director of a corporation. Five obituaries were printed: from the family, the supervisory board, the officials, the office staff, and the workforce. Five times I read my name encased by a mourning border. I took off my hat. Tomato chided, "You'll catch a cold, sir. It's snowing." I turned into Belle-Alliance Street. The cemetery lay in the middle of the city, surrounded by a red wall like a medieval fortress. Even in death, people are quartered in barracks. Outside the walls, in life as in death, only the outcasts, the criminals, the murderers, and the Jews have their place. I unlatched the rusty cemetery gate, which creaked on its hinges like an aging dancer. I walked along the main path. The snow had covered all the graves with a delicate, white lace cloth. You blessed ones! You blissful ones! You are resting! I am still reeling, feverish, burning. You heavenly cooled ones! Paradisiacal silent ones! I feel a noose around my neck, a snake coiled like a dervish. The noose has been flung over the horn of the moon – and the Earth must look very low when viewed from up high.

– I sensed a shadow was behind me. The cemetery was deserted.

"Who are you?" I called out.

"Neither friend nor foe," came the answer.

I didn't dare to look back.

"You are following me."

"You are dragging me behind you."

I left the main path and stepped onto a side path that led to the wall. There, by the wall, lay a grave I loved and feared. One I hadn't visited for months. A white marble tablet bore the name: "Maria," nothing else.

I sat on the edge of the grave.

Snow fell on the earth, through the earth onto the coffin, through the coffin onto the heart. Snow fell onto the heart.

The shadow stood menacingly behind me.

Across the street, beyond the red wall, a window was open. A piano teacher was practicing the *Don Giovanni Overture* with a student.

"Here lies Donna Anna, Donna Maria," said the shadow. I felt its icy breath on my neck. "You have put her in the ground. Beware, lest the stone guest invites you to the feast of the dead."

I looked up.

Next to me stood the stone statue of a Roland over a soldier's grave. The stone knight glared at me with hostility. Now he moved his eyelashes. I heard his armor creak. His eye blinked heavily against the snow's light. Then he clumsily lifted his legs and stepped from the pedestal. With the sword raised in both arms, he staggered toward me. Screaming, I jumped up and fled towards the exit. At the gate, I stopped breathlessly. The clanging of a passing streetcar calmed me. How ridiculous I was. That I no longer had control over my nerves. I was feverish. That's probably why I saw ghosts even in broad daylight.

I glanced around cautiously.

The stone guest had followed me.

My heart stood still. I could no longer escape him. He approached me:

"May I trouble you for a light?"

It was the cemetery guard, a short pipe in the corner of his mouth. He wore a white sheepskin coat.

The Transparent Lady

That same evening, around ten o'clock at the "Green Paintbrush" cabaret, I suddenly suffered the hemorrhage that the press had reported on – in a way that didn't strike me as particularly tasteful. The comedian Kontack, a man with a wooden head but a golden heart, was singing the now popular "Shady Deal Couplets" to an audience of smugglers who were behaving wildly, and shouting along hoarsely to the chorus. That's when it happened.

I was sitting in the audience. No one recognized me. I had placed my hands on my forehead and felt my blood pounding when I saw two eyes directed at me, eyes that I knew had been searching for me for a long time. More precisely, I didn't see these eyes at first; rather, I sensed that two eyes in the room wanted to see mine. If you look there, I told myself, something will happen. The ceiling will collapse. The plague will break out in Berlin. Europe will go under. You will have a heart attack. Or you will be forced to exhibit yourself before these eyes, before this audience. Something dreadful, unimaginable would occur. Because these eyes are the only eyes before which I cannot stand. In these eyes lie my entire life. My guilt. My longing. My desperation, my love, my crime.

These eyes are her eyes.

And it sent shivers down my spine when I thought that she was dead – but her eyes must still be alive, for these eyes were sharp, bright, and clearly fixed on me.

Yet, I immediately began to reason: eyes, in and of themselves, cannot live. Eyes do not float in the air like butterflies, although these eyes did have a butterfly-like quality about them. For eyes to see, they must sit in a human head, connected by the optic nerve and tendons to the brain. Eyes do not exist on their own.

This meditation gave me the courage to abruptly meet her gaze – and I had to smile at my fear, my anxiety. The eyes I saw were smiling back at me, lovingly and tenderly. They belonged to a young lady of about eighteen, who was sitting a few tables away from me with a gentleman whose face was hidden from me, obscured by the broad back of a stout leather dealer or clumsy butter trader. Then I heard her say half aloud to her companion, with a quick glance at me:

"That's him."

Sweat broke out on my forehead.

What did this remark mean?

What did this completely unfamiliar woman know that made her dare to say such a thing? Was she a detective? The police had supposedly modernized recently: perhaps the young blonde woman was an undercover detective.

Then the audience began to applaud, the lady clapped enthusiastically as well, her glances brushing against me several times, and now I understood what she meant by her mysterious statement – I was indeed quite nervous, seeking ambiguities and double meanings behind the simplest, clearest events.

Kontack had just sung a song of mine, and it was not so surprising that the lady knew me, perhaps from the cabaret, as I sometimes perform my own songs: that was not so remarkable. Probably more people in the room knew me, that is: they knew me only superficially. No one, however, had the faintest idea or understanding of my real and true life. I had to laugh out loud at the thought that nobody knew me, which prompted some guests to call out "Shh" indignantly. I suppressed my laughter to a smile, which I directed at that blonde lady and raised my wine glass to secretly toast to her.

She noticed the greeting and returned it faintly. A charming adventure, I thought to myself. Totally my type. She's young, slender, blonde, and since she knows who I am, she will be drawn to me. There will be no complications or lengthy discussions. I'm not up for that. All that remained was to figure out how to detach her from the man at her table.

Suddenly she stood up.

Ah! a promising sign. Excellent, this is going well. She cast a glance from her sapphire-blue eyes beneath long lashes and walked – she had been seated at the rightmost table by the stage, in the bright light that lifted her out of the dim audience space – past the stage.

And then it happened.

She had the light behind her.

Now she turned to face me, after I had seen her in profile for a few steps.

And I saw, my blood freezing and curdling in my veins, the lady was completely transparent. I could see through her clothes and flesh, and I could see only a skeleton and a skull, with her eyes burning in the sockets of that skull.

I had originally stood up to follow her, when I suddenly felt the frozen blood in my veins melt, a torrent of fire began to surge through me. In an instant, my mouth was filled with hot blood rising from deep within me, as if I were a volcano. The stream burst over my lips, and I collapsed, as rigid as a log, to the floor of the cabaret.

The Bleeding Heart

When I awoke, I found myself in a speeding car. Could this be a movie scene, and is the car perhaps not really moving but just being rocked back and forth by two men to create the illusion of driving?

I leaned forward a little.

I saw the chauffeur through the glass window. I saw houses and trees and people and tram stops rushing past.

The car was indeed moving.

I leaned back against the seat – then I felt a hand on the back of my head.

I turned to the side:

A completely unfamiliar lady was sitting with me in the car. I wanted to speak, but she put her finger on her lips to signal that I should be quiet.

And then, all at once, I noticed a cloyingly sweet taste in my mouth – just like the time when I had shared a blood oath with Munk – and now it came back to me: I had a hemorrhage in the cabaret – but what happened before that?

I couldn't remember.

I closed my eyes. Opened them again and noticed that there was a third person in the car: a gentleman whose features I could not decipher because he was sitting in the shadow of the lady.

A gentle squeeze of the hand reminded me of her presence. I tenderly returned the hand squeeze. "Who are you, who takes such loving care of me?"

The lady put her fingers to her lips:

"Do not speak! You must rest. Besides, it's none of your business who loves you."

And from the darkness, the gentleman's voice emerged:

"Hyacinth, tell the gentleman to remain silent. If he speaks, he will have another hemorrhage."

I remained silent, for this voice had a tone that almost compelled obedience. It was neither pleasant nor unpleasant, neither kind nor harsh, neither beautiful nor ugly – it was completely neutral.

I looked out the window.

The car was driving through the zoological garden.

Snow lay on the lawns and icicles hung from the trees.

Snow softens the pain, I thought, though I didn't know why.

Snow falls on the heart like earth on the coffin, like tears on the deathbed.

I racked my brain.

At some point, tears must have fallen on a deathbed.

At some point, earth must have been shoveled onto a coffin. At some point, snow must have drifted onto a heart.

Pink veils stretched before my eyes. Red spiders sat at the intersections where the threads were knotted. Everything I saw was divided into delicate pink squares, like a farmer's sheet, like a chessboard. Check to the queen, I thought.

I couldn't think further. I was too dazed from the hemorrhage.

But as I turned to the lady at my side: my eyes widened in horror.

I saw nothing but her black silhouette and within this black silhouette a red, throbbing heart.

And that heart – bled.

Outside the car window, snow fell, seeming to drift into the bleeding heart, where the white snowflakes transformed into blood-red tears.

Was someone weeping for me?

"It's not true," I cried, "your heart no longer lives! It can't live anymore! Since I buried it in the snow on a winter night –."

The heart burned like a red traffic light in the black car.

The snow fell: on the world, on the car, on me.

> Black is the night,
> and red is the heart,

and white, so white is the snow –

The snow reached up to my neck, and then I fainted.

Charité

I awoke with a jolt.

The car had stopped.

"Charité!" the chauffeur shouted.

"I'll take his left side, you take him on the right under the arm," said the lady.

I was so weakened that I just stared straight ahead as I put one foot in front of the other. Who is walking there? I don't want to walk at all. But I am.

"Chauffeur, you wait here!" said the voice, neither kind nor unkind.

In the admissions room, I lay down on the leather sofa.

A resident doctor, his English pipe hanging crookedly from his mouth, approached me with a annoyed expression.

"Since it's five minutes to midnight, meaning still today, you have to pay for today too, understand?"

I understood and weakly nodded my head.

Everyone's hustling today. Everyone wants to make a buck. He'll probably pockets today's fee for himself. He's likely poorly paid. Charité – what does that mean in English again? In any case, it seems to be a kind of medical scam. A night bar with tuberculosis waiters. Ethics or no ethics. In these spermatozoa, there is only one spirochethics.

"You must pay!" shouted the resident doctor, and his pipe almost fell out of his false teeth in anger.

An orderly, with the head of a warthog, who had shuffled over in the meantime, nodded with malicious glee.

"You have to pay, eight days in advance, pay in advance, then you can be admitted.."

Charity! What kind of people are these!

And then I knew what Charité meant:

Charity...

I reached into my breast pocket to take out my wallet and calm these repulsive demanders –

The wallet was gone!

I sat up in agitation.

I searched all my pockets.

Nothing to be found.

The wallet remained missing.

"But I still had my wallet at the cabaret."

"He who has, has," said the warthog,

"and he who had, had."

"But –"

"But but," the resident doctor mimicked, "did you know the gentleman and the lady who dropped you off here?"

Which gentleman – and which lady – oh – I remember – I looked around – they were no longer there...

"No, I didn't know the gentleman and the lady who were so kind as to help me in my misfortune... how long have they been gone... they were just here?"

"They left a few minutes ago... and," the orderly and the resident doctor roared with laughter, "they were probably so kind as to take special care of your wallet..."

"What does that mean?" I could hardly understand in my weakened state.

"That you probably fell into the hands of fleecers and that they stole your wallet...."

"Swiped," said the warthog-headed orderly, "pinched, pilfered, filched."

"That's impossible!" I protested as best as I could, "the lady belonged to the highest circles of society."

The orderly approached the leather sofa.

"If you can't pay, we can't keep you here –"

I weakly got up.

"But I can barely walk..."

Then I saw the orderly right in front of me:

He had a knife in his hand and his white apron was bloodstained.

"Butcher!" I shouted and leaped to my feet.

Butcher! echoed back from the walls.

I stumbled past the reception desk.

The door slammed shut behind me.

Free! free again! not imprisoned! No longer haunted by the image of that blood-spattered butcher who looked like Munk's father when he returned from slaughtering.

I leaned my feverish head against the cool wall.

I breathed deeply.

But this deep breath tore through my chest.

A new torrent of blood gushed out and, collapsing to my knees, I stained the snow with my blood.

It wasn't snow falling on the bleeding heart –

Blood dripped onto the white snow.

The Man with the Handcart

A man with a handcart trotted past.

When he saw me kneeling in the snow, hands braced forward – at a distance I must have looked like a dog – he stopped:

"What's this? Are you drunk? Have you been drinking too much rubbing alcohol at the Charité? Or did you lose a sixpence in the snow?"

Then he noticed the pool of blood in the snow.

He shook his head.

"Dear God, what heartless people there are these days. Leaving a poor consumptive to die in the snow like it's nothing." He took me under my arms, pulled me up, and loaded me onto his handcart.

He covered me with an old overcoat that was lying on the cart, and a cardboard box served as a pillow, clattering and rattling as he slid it beneath my head.

"Where do you live?"

I gave him my house number.

"That's quite close to where I live... here, you must hold onto this sack tightly so it doesn't roll off."

And he placed a rather heavy canvas sack on the cart next to me.

When I held it in my arms like a child, I felt an icy cold human hand through the canvas.

And this hand was delicate and slender like her hand.

I was no longer capable of an exaggeration of feelings like pain, horror, disgust, fear, after the experiences of this evening.

I lay there silent and stiff.

An icy wind blew over my forehead: in sharp, rapid gusts.

It felt as if I were standing in a duel, unarmed, defenseless, and every few seconds my opponent's sharp, pointed blade struck my forehead and cheeks.

But no blood flowed. It seemed to freeze instantly in the ghastly cold.

Who was my opponent? Who was striving to mercilessly destroy me?

God! God!

I had been sent forth by the Devil as a glittering frigate and now landed before God as a derelict wreck.

The man pushed the cart.

The wind subsided.

The clouds in the sky dissipated. More and more stars appeared. They aligned themselves symmetrically in golden facets, forming a giant fly's eye that stared down at me.

At the Reichstag embankment, the man stopped.

He listened into the night.

The fly's eye had disappeared. The stars glittered like frost flowers on a windowpane: behind them, music played, barely audible, as if crickets were chirping in the distance.

The Spree flowed quietly.

Sleepily and shivering, the houses pressed against each other.

With a jerk, the man pulled the sack from the cart and heaved it over the railing of the bridge.

A dull, blunt thud on the splashing water. He listened again for a moment.

"Good riddance!"

He rubbed his frostbitten blue hands and pushed the cart along the tram tracks.

26

"Are you a criminal?"

I asked this wearily, no longer capable of resistance, agitation, or outrage.

He muttered to himself as though talking to himself:

"There lies the old woman laid out in her death shroud on the chaise lounge. It snowed all day, now it's evening, and the sun bursts and storms through the open window with a golden outcry. A young girl, my bride, stands before the mirror combing her long hair, tears in her lashes. The old woman has snow-white hair. It snowed all day. Her whole life long. Her body is that of a young girl: delicate, slender, and of astonishing complexion. The girl at the mirror occasionally turns to the dead one, and depending on whether her gaze falls on the face or chest, she either smiles or grimaces painfully or slightly bitterly One day I will lie there too, having died in a different way, but death is death, she thinks: in a few decades – or years – or months? Who knows? The day after tomorrow there's dancing in the tents, and I will go dance.

"I sit by the bed and think about all the people I've seen die, and that dying must be bitter, but death itself, when the body finally releases itself from the death struggle after hours, must be sweet. Just as the body lets go when you finally fall asleep.

"The girl at the mirror adjusts her hairstyle.

"Then she turns to me and says:

"Come, we must go.

"Her voice falters, because she is afraid.

"I squeeze her hand, very firmly, and I notice that I feel no pity for the dead woman. There are pains so absolute that they preclude any further intensification and render all other suffering trivial in comparison. It's been two years since my beloved died, and what died then: youth, happiness, the future. Here on the ottoman lies an old woman who has fulfilled her destiny and who will be spoken of in memory: the good old woman. But back then they said: the beautiful young woman... What died back then, died under the sidereal sign. The genius extinguished his torch in the earth. The sun went out. –

"A draft blows through the window.

"A few snowflakes fall on the snow-white hair of the dead old woman.

"The girl steps away from the mirror.

"She steps to the bed and kisses the dead woman's forehead, shuddering slightly, and the living man's lips."

He fell silent and pushed the cart.

The cart creaked in the snow.

I opened my eyes, which I had kept closed during the story.

"Aren't you afraid that I could betray you?"

The other shook his head.

"When I saw you lying there in the snow – in your blood – I felt that you were a comrade of mine. I saw your eyes for a moment in the light of the gas lamps."

"And –?"

"You have a left eye that one does not forget once they've looked into it. And this left eye – it is the eye above the heart – reveals to those who can see who you are."

I smiled weakly.

"And what did you see in my left eye?"

"The image of a murdered woman hangs in your pupil..." I made no attempt to refute this bizarre and fantastical claim.

Could I even refute it?

I remained silent.

The cart creaked.

The stars began to ring like small silver bells.

"Who was that that you threw over the bridge?"

He turned his head in a spiral like a ruminating parrot.

"A good old woman. Seventy-nine years old. She lived at Krausnickstraße 23. We waited in her apartment until she came home. Then I shoved the ether-soaked handkerchief into her mouth. She owned a small corner jewelry shop. In the cardboard box on which you are lying are some jewelry pieces that interested me: a leather bag made of black human skin, a necklace made of Javanese children's bones set in platinum, and a golden necklace whose individual links are real, glazed human eyes."

The House of Pain

I had arrived in front of my apartment.

I climbed down from the cart and shook the other person's hand, grateful for taking me this far.

"Unfortunately, I can't give you anything. I've lost my wallet," I said.

"Oh," he lamented with an animated gesture, "we black brothers should at least refrain from harming each other. It's unfair to rob a thief or murder a murderer... Such things must remain the privilege of the rotten bourgeois society, which is already falling apart at the seams. – Besides, I am well-equipped with all the necessities..."

And he pulled out a wallet.

"How much may I lend you, comrade?"

He drew out a hundred-mark note, pressed it into my hand, which closed around it in astonishment, and disappeared around the corner with his cart.

I could still hear his voice echo within me several times. The last time, I recognized it. I hadn't heard that voice in many years.

No doubt about it, the man with the cart was Munk. I walked – or rather staggered – to my front door and pulled out my house key.

I inserted it into the lock.

It didn't fit.

I tried again.

For heaven's sake, they wouldn't have changed the lock overnight, would they?

I examined the key. No doubt: it was my house key.

Then I heard a voice from inside the house:

"Co-ome in. Well, sweetie. Come on, come here and let me scratch your little head"

It was the voice I had sworn never to hear again. The voice that had accompanied the terrible events of my life with its hollow and ridiculous chatter.

I staggered back a few steps and looked at the house number. Unconsciously, I had given the man with the cart the address of my former apartment. It was the House of Pain, the house where I had lived with her.

"Let me scratch your little head ... Maria..." screeched the parrot. With superhuman effort, I turned around and fled, stumbled, crept for half an hour until I reached my current apartment. The entire way, I feared someone was following me: the police, the parrot, the man with the cart, the gentleman from the car, the orderly with the blood-splattered apron from the Charité, the comedian Kontack, Pluto with his snake head and his otter scepter. I threw myself, still in my clothes, onto the sofa bed in my small, cramped room that faces the back courtyard and never sees daylight, after quickly bolting and locking the door.

And I fell into a deep, heavy sleep.

The Picture

When I woke up, the yellow table lamp was still burning. I had forgotten to turn it off the evening before.

The yellow light felt comforting.

Outside, the day was dreary and gray. Only faint traces of daylight seeped through the curtains into the one-windowed back room. The air carried a faint scent of aromatic vinegar.

I looked at the clock: half-past eleven in the morning.

I sighed deeply and felt a sense of relief.

I was at home.

By the clock, the bluish moonstone glistened, and next to it stood the small Indian cat made of yellow marble. And under the lamp: bathed in a pale halo from its lampshade: her picture.

As if for protection, her hand held the white rose against her chest. Her blonde hair was pinned up high. Her lips, half-open, revealed her delicate teeth. But her eyes – her kind eyes looked at me angrily.

What did that mean?

Wasn't it true that she had forgiven me?

Was her forgiveness a pretense?

Had she only seemingly forgiven me, to now torment me all the more cruelly: as in the times of the Inquisition when they let the convicts escape through countless corridors and dozens of doors – and only when the feeling of ultimate freedom began to darkly intoxicate them in the open field behind the last door: did the executioner suddenly rise red from the ground before them like a gigantic poppy? Fragments of memories from the events of the previous night flitted before my consciousness like clouds in the wind.

And I remembered: that her eyes had sought me out last night; that her eyes, the eyes of a dead person, still lived in this world, on this earth... compelling me to look into them, to see myself reflected in them – and wanted to hold me accountable.

Why hadn't I asked the man who had stolen the bracelet with the human eyes to show it to me? Wasn't it possible – that her eyes were among them? Why hadn't I noted down the address of this man?

I should have bought the bracelet from him... Nonsense... of course, that was nonsense... Murderers don't usually hand out their business cards to everyone.

I glanced over at the picture again.

Her eyes gleamed like two moonstones.

The moonstone that she had left me as a talisman had been her secret symbol.

I gazed into the eyes.

They had guarded me faithfully.

I saw myself.

I was everywhere – I – I – I.

Oh, how I hated myself, how eagerly I wanted to erase myself from the memory of others, from hers and from my own.

I reached for the picture.

The lips seemed to move, and it seemed to me that they spoke the words that cobbler Leidl always used to say: "Don't be angry –"

I opened the frame, took out the photograph, and with the small scissors lying on the table, I cut the eyes out of the picture's head.

The Letter

There was a knock.

I jumped, hiding the picture in the bed.

"Who is it?"

It was the maid, Elise.

I went to the door and opened it.

She brought breakfast and the mail.

I crawled back into the pillows immediately.

I felt indescribably miserable.

I checked my pulse. Without a doubt, I had a fever. The most sensible thing was to stay in bed. That damned hemorrhage last night. You just can't handle anything anymore.

Among the letters were business correspondences, one of which asked if I wanted to perform at the "Bat" cabaret in Königsberg for 8,000 marks a month. That engagement was also going to hell, and I could have really used those 8,000 marks. Good Lord, I don't even have a decent suit anymore.

Another letter: a teacher from Schmachtenhagen, Krossen district, asked me for an autograph. The Lessing Society in Braunschweig, the observatory in Mannheim, the Literary Society in Nuremberg, and the Bookshop Esplanade in Hamburg inquired if I would read "from my works" at their venues. From my works. Those little couplets I churn out are called "works." I feel sick. If these societies and organizations only knew what constituted my real work – the things I won't read from because even I can't decipher them.

I write hieroglyphs.

Finally, I found a personal letter:

"To Mr. ......t"

Probably from a girl, judging by the spelling. And I opened it:

Berlin,........Hospital Ward 2, Room 20.

I hereby inform you that Miss Marianne is here in the hospital. Miss Marianne would have written herself, but she has a high fever. Visiting hours: Wednesday, Saturday, and Sunday 2-3 p.m.

Best regards
on behalf of Miss Marianne

The signature was illegible.

My eyes started to mist over in pink again. I racked my brain to recall how I came to receive this letter or who this Miss Marianne could be. I had loved many women, perhaps Miss Marianne was among them. Maybe she remembered me because she was feeling bad. I would send her 50 marks, of course. God, you certainly can't make ends meet with 50 marks these days, but at least she should see my good intentions.

Then, like a premonition, it hit me: Ward 2, that's where the maternity ward is. This premonition did not deceive me – not in the least.

I, a spawn of hell myself, diabolically blessed and consecrated by Pluto, the prince of the underworld, had brought another child into this godforsaken world, festering abscess of a (perhaps existing) true world.

But who was the mother?

Marianne ... Marianne ... I repeated the name senselessly thirty times without it becoming more familiar or recognizable to me. I had loved like never before in my life the last six months.

Because I wanted to free myself from her.

And surely yesterday's hemorrhage was also a result of these insane excesses: because, not satisfied enough with one woman, on some days I embraced two or three women. In the car. In the stairwell. In the zoo. I rarely bothered to take them home. It was impossible to remember their names, even their faces. A few weeks ago at a party, I met a lady who, after dinner, when we retreated to a corner of the conservatory, showed me a familiarity that delighted but puzzled me. Only after a while did I understand – or rather, remember – that I had spent a night with her once, but had completely forgotten.

Who was the young mother in the hospital?

Office clerks, actresses, young ladies of so-called society, maids, laundry workers, cabaret singers, fifteen-year-old girls, married women and mothers paraded before me in a long line: Who was it?

Their figures were shadowy, their faces indistinct, I had forgotten their names, only occasionally did a name flash like: Lotte, Lilly, Anny, Grete – but one thing I did know:

That I had loved them all, not like one loves dolls or glass beads, but like one loves stars and animals and flowers.

The Albino

The doorbell rang.

I startled awake.

The police?

I heard the maid negotiating in the hallway: "Excuse me, but the gentleman is still in bed –"

A voice, whose melodiousness enchanted me, replied, "Oh, what does that matter – please just let us in."

There was a knock, and in came the lady and the gentleman from last evening.

The lady wore a sealskin coat and a small black hat. Judging by her facial features, which were concealed behind a fine veil embroidered with a dragonfly on the left cheek – she could scarcely be twenty years old. She had a bouquet of lilacs in her hand, which she placed on my pillows with a smile.

The gentleman behind her appeared in a proper top hat, which he now removed. He also took off his mink coat, revealing a somewhat old-fashioned frock coat.

He now approached me. I saw his face, his eyes, for the first time.

He was an albino.

His eyes were red like those of certain rabbit breeds. He had a fringe beard reminiscent of the cobbler Leidl.

His head and facial hair were snow-white, although I estimated his age to be no more than forty years.

"We called at the Charité. You weren't there anymore. Well, how are you? Don't speak loudly – you should only speak softly – the lungs must be conserved and kept as still as possible – lie on your back – like this – we will percuss and auscultate a little – as much as I can without straining you."

He pulled back the bed covers.

The lilacs fell to the floor.

The lady indifferently picked them up and put them in the water carafe on the washstand.

The albino tapped my chest, and I don't know why I let him perform his manipulations. Who had summoned a doctor anyway?

"Strong dampening on the right side – that seems to be an old spot – have you had a cavity? That's likely where the hemorrhage originated."

He reached into his breast pocket and pulled out a collapsible stethoscope. He assembled it and placed it on my chest: "Breathe normally – don't strain – whisper: ninety-nine – again – ninety-nine – ninety-nine –"

He stood up.

"You cannot stay any longer in this cramped and dark room with insufficient light and air. You need to be in a sanatorium or hospital – don't interrupt me – you need rest, care, and a nurse" – his gaze brushed the blonde lady – "must always be with you. I've brought the ambulance along. It's waiting downstairs in front of the door."

I didn't know what to say.

The red-eyed one looked at me intensely.

The lady approached the bed and took my hand.

"You must do something for yourself. I cannot in good conscience leave you here so helpless and abandoned."

But when I felt her hand, ice-cold in my feverish one like the hand of a corpse, it overcame me again: "Leave me – leave me alone – you don't know to whom you are offering your help – to whom you are giving your beautiful and good hand. Don't lean too close to me, lest the pestilential breath of my lungs touch you. Don't look me in the eye. Don't look into my left eye, the one above the heart. Horror dwells in my eyes. A handshake from me is as poisonous as a scorpion's sting."

The red-eyed one stood there, hands crossed behind his back.

"T.B. with psychogenic cause. An analysis not only of the sputum but especially of the soul is necessary."

The lady leaned over me, so close that I could feel her breath, and it smelled sweet like oleander or almond or hyacinth. "My dear man, don't worry, fear nothing. And even if you were a criminal, even if you were a murderer, I would still take care of you. I wouldn't love you less and would not be less kind to you. What concern is it of mine who and what you are? I have no right to ask, only the duty to help you."

I had half-risen from the pillows.

My heart raced with joy.

If salvation was possible, it was only because this woman existed.

The albino reached into his frock coat once more.

"Here, by the way, is your wallet. You lost it in the car last night."

The door burst open.

Two paramedics entered with a stretcher. Behind them, the maid Elise, tears in her eyes, wringing her hands.

I was laid on the stretcher.

The red eyes fascinated me. I didn't dare protest and suddenly felt deathly weak.

I was carried through the hallway.

Curious residents, old women, a young girl in a plaid blouse, a lame customs inspector, and some children were already waiting.

The customs inspector raised his walking stick, imagining himself as Frederick the Great, and crowed: "He brought this upon himself with his way of life. Now he has consumption."

Shuddering, the women wrapped themselves in their headscarves and shawls. The young girl smiled helplessly and awkwardly. The children stared at me with open mouths, and one said: "Look, he's dead. Come on, let's play dead."

The Strange Forest

The entire way, Hyacinth held my hand.

The ambulance had frosted glass windows, so you couldn't see where it was going. It also smelled of creosote, Lysol, and carbolic acid, making me feel nauseous at times.

It seemed to me as though the vehicle wasn't moving at all, as if it were rattling in place.

But after half an hour, I had the feeling that we were passing through a forest. I hoped we wouldn't crash into a tree.

With a jolt that threw me from the cushions, the vehicle came to a stop.

The driver opened the door.

"We've broken down. You have to get out."

The albino and Hyacinth got out.

I rose from the stretcher. Dressed only in a shirt, I stepped out of the car.

The albino and Hyacinth had disappeared. I didn't give it much thought.

Darkness was all around.

I took a few steps and felt as if I were walking on jelly or on the skin of an inflated balloon.

Perhaps the earth is a balloon floating in the ether? I looked up and saw a few stars. One – two – three – I started counting them.

The stars reminded me of car lights. I looked for the lights of the ambulance in the darkness.

They were out.

The vehicle seemed swallowed by the earth.

A sultry, oppressive atmosphere prevailed.

The damp heat almost took my breath away.

It was still dark, I groped my way forward, but ahead of me, the rosy hint of the coming day was breaking through a deep cobalt blue.

I felt my way – my sense of touch told me: from tree to tree. But these trees must have been special kinds of trees: they must have been flowing trees, made of a thick, heavy liquid, because my hands always sank in like honey.

Finally, day broke, lightning-fast.

I walked on soft, steaming soil through a strange forest.

Giant fan palms arched above me.

Trees as tall as church towers stood there – wellingtonia and eucalyptus – and from their trunks flowed an incessant stream of golden resin. Cacti clung to the sky and earth.

A dragonfly the size of an eagle hovered over my forehead.

Its head had something maidenly, something Madonna-like about it, and it almost seemed to me as if it were Maria's head.

Madonna immaculata!

Libellula immaculata!

Golden-winged one, stay a moment!

– Before my eyes, the dragonfly shrank back to its natural size and hovered shimmering and iridescent.

I could no longer make out its head.

Now it seemed to me as if it was the dragonfly that was embroidered on the veil of the blonde lady.

I stepped into a clearing.

A wild horse rose from a hollow as I approached. It galloped off neighing, and I saw and heard that it had twelve hooves, three on each foot.

Monkeys swung on lianas.

They didn't notice me at all, for I was marching among the giant animals and trees like a like a deer or a rose beetle.

"The earth," I thought quite arbitrarily, "belongs to you, you are indeed a dwarf, but you have something like a brain, able to think, to draw logical conclusions, and to overcome the giant animals and trees with cunning and shrewdness."

A white, snow-covered mountain shimmered through the trees. It rose like an iris from the swamp. The closer I came to it, the more traces of human or human-like feet seemed to lead to it. Suddenly, like in a cinema, black letters appeared on the white wall of the mountain: Mount Everest, the wonder of Tibet.

Heavenly Father, I cried, let me experience the miracle!

And I walked and walked onward. The landscape revealed itself to me in ever stranger ways. Fauna and flora merged seamlessly into each other, and one couldn't say: this is an animal, or: this is a plant. There were trees whose branches were snakes, and sunflowers that bore the face of rays. Giant caterpillars crawled along the path, from whose scale segments violets bloomed, and flies flew, their facet eyes replaced by cut diamonds. A lion walked on stone feet, its tail made of wheat stalks.

I passed waterfalls where mills of Tibetan design stood. They were not built for grinding grain; they were giant prayer mills, in which the water chattered prayers incessantly. And harps hung in the trees, in which the wind sang.

The higher I climbed, the more unbearable the climate became. It was simultaneously burning hot and ice-cold. I had frostbite on my feet, and my forehead felt like it was succumbing to sunstroke.

Lord, I cried, when will I have reached the summit?

I saw the footprints leading to the mountain: none led back.

The mills chattered.

The winds sang.

A nightingale rose from the bushes in front of me. I saw it singing its dark path through the radiant ether, my heart swelled, and I knew: whoever guides the nightingale's way through impassable airways will also guide my path to a good end.

And I walked and shouted and sang into the sun. – From flint stones lying by the wayside, I fashioned myself a club and a knife by rubbing them against each other or smashing them together.

With these eoliths, I resolved to make my way forward.

A hyacinth smells sweet, and a nightingale begins to sing

I gripped the club tighter. Then I heard a voice, a sweet, familiar voice: "But you're hurting me!"

I blinked against the light streaming into my eyes. I was clutching Hyacinth's hand convulsively. Her hand was the club with which I wanted to crush my enemies.I was lying in a bright, white-painted hospital room in a wide, comfortable bed.I lay softly, as if on clouds in white, freshly laundered pillows.

Hyacinth had donned a nurse's uniform. She wore the white cap, under which her face shone even more seductively, more enchantingly, like the moon under a white cloud. Around her neck, she wore a cross.But no one was nailed to this cross. It bore the words: Light! Love! Life!

A sweet fragrance permeated the room."What smells so sweet?" I asked quietly, thinking it must be her breath.

She pointed to the bedside table at the foot of the bed.There stood a white hyacinth.

I was startled, but differently than before.

It was a joyful, lovely shock. I reached for her hand.

"What should I call you?"

"Just call me as befits my attire, call me: Sister."

"Which direction does my room face, Sister?"

"Do you want to see the sun rise or set?"

I waved off the question.

"I hate the sun. The moon is my companion. The night is my friend. I cannot bear it when the sun reflects in silver knives."

The Sister stroked my forehead.

"The room faces north."

I sighed in relief.

"How wonderful it must be at the North Pole – cold – cold – the world there is as cold as my heart – and then: eternal twilight..."

A nightingale began to sing somewhere.

I listened in rapture, until my delight turned into gentle fear.

It was January – how could a nightingale sing in January?

Hyacinth, too, had lifted her head to listen.

Then she smiled: "You don't need to be surprised or worried: it is the young girl from the second ward who thinks she is a nightingale –"

"A girl who thinks she is a nightingale?"

"She had delusions from childbed fever, and these delusions have not left her. She believes she can lure the father of her child, the nightingale male, with her singing."

I closed my eyes and turned pale.

I remembered the letter from the hospital.

What if it was me the nightingale called?

Hadn't I already met her when I wandered in the strange forest?

The Sister sat in her chair and embroidered a baby bonnet.

"Don't you think she sings like a real nightingale? Professor Ziegelbert, the famous ornithologist who also lives here, claims that she perfectly imitates the nightingale's call, even though she has never left the stone desert of Berlin and could never have heard a nightingale sing..."

Yenkadi

Every morning at exactly eleven o'clock, the albino appeared.

He asked for my temperature chart and either frowned or burped thoughtfully.

"Yesterday evening 38.9, this morning 38. That's much too high. Any digestive issues?" The nurse answered for me: "Yes."

"Pyramidon?"

"0.6."

"Dionin?"

"Three times 0.02."

"Night sweats?"

"Changed the shirt twice."

"The patient is primarily receiving liquid and gelatinous foods in as cold a state as possible: ice-cold milk, Mondamin, chicken jelly."

"Yes."

"Blood?"

"Still present in the sputum."

"If the seizure recurs: apply an ice pack and administer 25 drops of liquid extract three times."

"Yes."

"The sputum has been examined?"

"Gaffky 5."

"Good. – Goodbye."

The albino shook my hand and awkwardly patted my forehead. –

Since I wasn't allowed to read, the nurse got me glue, glossy paper in all the colors of the rainbow, and scissors.

And I started cutting: first, various kinds of ornaments, which I glued white on black, or gray on pink, or blue on gold.

Then I created an African idol, which I hung on the wall above my bed and worshiped, calling it: Yenkadi.

It was a white idol: white on black.

For black people have white idols and white people have black idols.

But Yenkadi is a word from Senegal that means: it's good here! Let's build huts here!

This is paradise!

The albino laughed at Yenkadi when he saw it hanging next to the bell above my bed.

"Just don't accidentally press Yenkadi instead of the bell button. Otherwise, the sky might fall..."

Sister Hyacinth, however, sometimes looked at the idol with questioning eyes, as if she knew more about it or was seeking an answer from it.

And I moved on to more free-form designs with my paper pictures. Gold, blue, silver, black, red, green, yellow intertwined and merged in chaotic patches, triangles, prisms, circles, arabesques, and the shapes that formed resembled fantastic insects, dragonflies, deep-sea fish, or primordial creatures, like those I had encountered on my walk through the peculiar forest. There was an elephant among them, which had sawfish instead of tusks, two enormous jellyfish instead of ears, an eel instead of a tail, and its eyes were two starfish.

I also made a collage consisting entirely of newspaper clippings like: "The Swindling Aunt from America! Ladies Save Money! Yellow Dog Missing! Foot-and-Mouth Disease! We Save Your Hair! Inventory Clearance Sale: Universe 1921."

Such pictures were very strange to look at. I also cut off heads of men and placed them on women's bodies and vice versa. A statesman got the beautiful legs of a dancer. Her head was placed on a hyena's body. The hyena's head, in turn, was placed on a general's body.

That's how I played creator.

That's how the devil played God.

Morphine

The inhaler hissed. White menthol vapor flowed singing from the glass trumpet. It clung to the ceiling of the room in droplets, adorning it with moist stars. On the adjustable bedside table, the nurse pushed the apparatus towards me, after she had placed a pillow against my collapsing back. Irregularly, interrupted by bouts of coughing, I drew the hot cloud into my mouth and exhaled it again. My glasses fogged up. The room dissolved smilingly. The nurse whirled around like a soft cotton balloon amidst a dance of blurred images, staggering thermometers, stemless roses, and empty books from which the printer's ink had been wiped away. Blank pages turned themselves automatically.

"Ten minutes," said the nurse, "that's enough."

I sank back, breathing a sigh of relief.

The door opened mysteriously and silently, like a rose blossom, and the albino appeared. He bent over the bed. His brown suit clattered as if it were made of tin. His white beard hung from his chin like a pointed sugar cone. His red eyes fell on the bedspread like ladybugs.

With a sure hand, he grabbed my pulse.

"How are you?"

The moisture evaporated from my glasses: the world appeared transfigured. The pictures of several beautiful women I had loved reappeared in their frames. One held her head in her hand, as if the earth were too heavy for her to bear without support on her head. Another blinked cheerfully with olive eyes. Yet another held two children in her arms: a delicately dressed girl and a blond boy in a sailor suit. But she, the mother, still looked like a child herself and seemed to be the third sibling.

My gaze fell on the yellow roses. They swayed lively on their stems. The thermometer the doctor pulled from my armpit showed a clear number.

Life was sometimes so painfully clear and precise. "39.1," said the albino to the nurse, who twisted apologetically at her hips.

I looked at the doctor. A good man! How he floated roundly like a balloon in the room! He was surely willing to extinguish the fire, to brace the walls so that the house wouldn't crumble. Now he rolled up his sleeves. Reddish hairs sprouted like heather from his forearm.

He stepped to the table, unfolded a case. Washed the tip of the injection apparatus with Eau de Cologne.

The nurse pulled back the blanket, and the albino said, "Well then, stretch out your right leg."

The needle painlessly entered my yellowish flesh, which slightly bulged over the injected liquid. The albino washed up and departed. The nurse covered me with the duvet. Then she could be heard chirping in the hallway with the assistant.

In the room below me, a gramophone began to rattle. A one-step, accompanied by laughter.

I propped myself up, slid out of bed, and stood with unsteady knees in the room. I had stepped out of myself, and willingly, I joined the circle of things, equal to them. I stepped beside the long-stemmed roses on the washstand, reflecting the same essence. The central heating warmed not me, only itself. I heated myself. The pictures on the walls revealed themselves as sisters: not as real women, as pictures in frames, just as I was a picture in a gilded wooden frame, held and supported above and below and nailed to the wall like a thieves. For every Christ there were always millions of thieves.

The gramophone jingled merrily like a streetcar. I dreamily boarded the vehicle of these tones for a distant journey. I lifted my feet, holding up the trousers of my violet pajamas with my hands so they wouldn't fall and hinder my stride. Higher and higher I climbed, ascending the spiral staircase that led me to the roof of the vehicle. There I sat and saw the city steeply below me. Smoke lay mossy over the factories. The smell of gasoline filled the sunny air. The river gleamed with the blissful consciousness of its goal, towards which it flowed. Cranes moved like iron arms up and down. Sometimes an arm pointed to the sky, sometimes to the earth. Sometimes to the river. Bells rang from all the churches. In the chorus of their songs, I rose from the upper deck, just as the bus conductor handed me the ticket, and strode, head thrown back, radiantly through the air.

The Miracle

I saw Potsdamer Platz and a colorful crowd moving across it. It was the Potsdamer Platz of 1921, but the people who populated it, those who disembarked from cars, streetcars, and subways, wore Greek costumes and togas.

A Dominican monk forced his way through the crowd, raised his voice loudly, and cried: "God bless you!"

Then many people in their Alexandrian garments stopped as if before a street vendor with cigarettes or oranges, and one of them, a young man, spoke: "May He bless you, venerable old man – if it is the same God that you and we mean."

The monk replied: "Which God do you mean?"

The young man spoke: "It is the God whose temple you see there, standing proud and made of stone."

And he pointed to the Wertheim department store and the Café Fatherland.

The monk said: "There is only one true God: the Almighty, All-Good, All-Wise – and there is no other God beside Him."

The young man smiled: "Your age forbids me to instruct you as I would if you were younger. But let me tell you, I know many gods: the one of Berlin, the one of Yokohama, the one of Moscow. The one from Moscow or Yokohama has no power over us; so your God, stranger – for such you reveal yourself by your garb – will also have no power for or against us."

The monk said: "There is only one God, revealed through His Son, who descended from Heaven to Earth."

Then I, who had followed the conversation up to this point, pushed my way through the circle and shouted over to the monk: "Hey, you filthy son of an ape, see that I don't grab your dirty beard and chase you off with your childish lies. You can tell those to the brainless sons of your degenerate people, but not to the young men of Berlin, who have gone through the school of wisdom. Here is the Earth – there is Heaven: well then, let your Son of God descend from Heaven. I see no ladder and no staircase on which such a thing would be possible."

Then the crowd laughed.

But the monk knelt down, right under the standard clock.

"Lord, Lord, see me kneeling before you in fervent prayer. Do not let me become the mockery of your enemies. Enlighten them with the torch of your wisdom and perform a sign and wonder, that your power and strength and the truth of my faith and my speech may be revealed. Lord, Lord, descend from Heaven and enter into our hearts..."

– Then the heavens opened.

A staircase seemed to lead from it down to earth, on which a beautiful youth slowly descended, his arms outstretched in blessing. The staircase reached the earth, where he suddenly disappeared among the people and was no longer seen. And a voice thundered from the clouds: "Satan – depart from here."

And I fled, pressing my hands to my face, sideways.

I still heard the cries and shouts of the crowd: "Where is the God that we may worship him? He descended from Heaven to Earth – and vanished."

Then the voice of the monk sounded like a clapper striking a bell: "He is among you..."

The Moonlit Night

I woke up with trepidation.

The moon shone pale into the room, illuminating the white idol on a black background, so that it glowed like radium. Its eyes, consisting of two matchstick heads, stared, and it planted its arms as if it wanted to leave the picture and descend upon me.

Then I began to fear my own creation. Yenkadi had always been in my soul. Yenkadi had only now come to light – because he wanted to. Yenkadi had witnessed my deeds and misdeeds. Yenkadi came to demand an account from me. Yenkadi spoke: I existed before you were born, and I will exist when you are no more. Do you remember when you were born and opened your eyes for the first time: did I, Yenkadi, not stand there and bend over you? What has become of you that you forget me for years and decades – until one day you cut me out of white glossy paper – and behold, I am revealed again! But I was always within you and was omnipresent. I walked through the forest when you first embraced Maria in the ferns. Why did you not call my name, the name of your god: Yenkadi: much would have been spared you.

I pulled back the curtains to the bridal bed. But again, you did not heed me. And on that night of nights, when the blood began to flow: you were silent and did not call: Yenkadi! Yenkadi! –

I felt cold sweat on my forehead.

I wanted to scream, but I could only gasp: Sister! Sister!

In the moonlight, Sister Hyacinth stood before me and leaned over me, as Yenkadi once did over my cradle. She had let her blonde hair down and stood there in her white nightgown.

And when I saw her standing there: I saw that it was not her.

It was Maria.

She stood there in her burial shroud, pale as silver. She had loosened the band from her chin and was wiping the sweat from my forehead.

"Why do you fear me? And yourself? I am with you all days and nights."

I raised my arms to the moon. The moon and she: they were all one. "Have I not gone mad with longing for you, you radiant one, you gentle ray, you cool child? Are you back to redeem me and give meaning to my love and purpose to my life?

Come! Come into my arms! Come to me in bed! Cool my burning heart with your cool breasts, my burning eyes with your snow lips! Hold the torch of my destiny always firmly in your good hand! Love me! Beloved sister!

She sat by my bed and stroked my forehead.

"I must not, my hot boy: you have a fever! And if I loved you and you had another hemorrhage in my arms – what would the doctor say? And how could I justify this criminal recklessness to myself?"

"Angel!" I cried. "I have tormented you – and you, you love me nonetheless and love me beyond all understanding and measure."

She pressed a gentle kiss to my lips:

"Sleep, darling, you must sleep. You must not speak anymore either. You need to get well." And she began to sing softly:

> Sleep in sweet peace,
> Close your eyes.
> Hear how the rain falls,
> How the neighbor's little dog barks.
> The little dog bit the man,
> Has torn the robber's clothes.
> The robber hurries to the gate.
> Sleep in sweet peace.

A dog barked in the neighborhood.
The cool hand on my forehead felt so good.
Somewhere very softly a nightingale began to sing.

It sang like swaying willow bushes in my flowing dream.

The Festival of the Dead

Today was the Festival of the Dead. Once a year, they leave the realm of the dead at the bottom of the sea, where they dwell among corals, starfish, rays, oysters, eels, and spiders. They rise upward like glassy jellyfish, and when they reach the surface of the sea, they suddenly ascend into the air with wings and fly like flocks of white herons to the mainland, where they descend from the clouds and take on the form they had when they were still among the living. – I, the cricket merchant Hen-Yo, had prepared everything to welcome my lovely wife Ise. The household altar was adorned with white roses. I had lit seventeen candles in front of it, for my wife, my beloved, my friend had only reached the age of seventeen. She died at the birth of our first child: she took the child with her to the realm of the dead. There it slept dreamlessly under a thicket of crystals, and the mother watched over its sleep like a stone. The green waves passed over them both. – Bowls of rice, fruits, and small cakes were placed before the altar. Because Ise would be hungry from the long journey through water and wind. The tea kettle hummed. Three cups were prepared: two larger ones – though they were still tiny enough – and a smaller one. I sat there, my pointed head supported by my broad hand, waiting. Outside on the doorpost, a poem fluttered on a long strip of paper in the wind. I had composed it myself and brushed it onto the paper: silver characters on a black background. Come back Ise! sang the poem. – It had grown dark. The flickering candle cast trembling shadows over the small, clay, green-glazed god sitting in the niche of the altar, legs crossed, hands raised so that the palms faced outward like pale lotus flowers. He wore a stern, rejecting, merciless face and seemed to grin in the semi-darkness. The movement of his hands suggested, or rather meant: Let go of your foolish hope, Hen-Yo! I, the god of your ancestors and your god who knew you before you existed and will know you when you are no more, tell you: Ise will never return. She will never come back as she never existed. She is only an image, a figment of your imagination, which has never lacked colorful movement. You dreamed her. You longed for her. And your longing once gave her a vibrant form. You are too weak to create her again. Dream a new dream! Even better: strike the gong! Wake up! Do not let your being decay! You still have much to do in life. Have you, for example, taken care of your crickets this evening? – I stood up. I approached the rows of delicate wooden cages, where hundreds of crickets sat. Each cricket had its own cage, for no two could be confined together. They hated each other and would devour each other. Even males and females could not be kept together for long. Otherwise, the female, being stronger, would devour the male. I owned only one female, which I had accidentally caught once with a male in the act of mating. Generally, I let the females go. Only the male crickets are marketable. Only they chirp. My method of catching crickets was very simple, by the way. I only needed a blade of grass. With this, I would probe into the cricket holes, and the crickets, unable to stand the tickling of the grass blade, would come out and were easily captured. – From the neighboring houses came dirges and monotonous prayers through the thin bamboo walls. Some of the crickets started chirping. Others joined in. I prostrated myself before the altar. I recited the great prayer for the dead, then the smaller one, then sang the litany to the melody of autumn music. When I had finished, I saw before me in the candlelight a black cricket sitting on a white hyacinth. I must have accidentally left a cage open. I picked up the cricket in my hand. It was the female, but, oh by some miracle, she began to chirp, and as I listened closely, I heard her speak, delicately and softly: "I am Ise. I have always been with you in my second form. We dead can assume two forms: dwell simultaneously in the realm of the dead and in the realm of the living. But the living know nothing of this. Only once a year do we reveal ourselves to them when they celebrate the festival of the white hyacinth with us. I have always been with you. You just didn't know it. Every morning and evening, you brought me food: fresh spring water and tender, green chickweed. I am your only female cricket, and you have tenderly cared for me. Today you shall receive your reward." I saw the black backplates of the cricket lift like the gates of a dungeon and break open: and from the prison of the animal body floated shimmering, light as the wind and transparent as glass: Ise, as I had once seen her when she was still alive. My memory described her as magical as she stood before me. She wore a blue kimono embroidered with sunflowers and held the boy, who seemed to be sleeping, in her arms. We knelt before the altar. Three times we bowed our foreheads to the ground before the glaring god. My heart trembled with bliss like a morning glory in the wind. I poured tea. I offered rice, sweets, candied fruits. I could not speak. My lips were pressed together like stone slabs. The god in the background had withdrawn into himself. His green eyes glistened. He meditated. – After we had silently drunk tea, Ise placed the child in the god's arms. Then she turned to me, embraced me weakly, and drew me to the marital bed; the mats lay in the corner as they once had. Wordlessly, we sank into bliss. The chirping of crickets sounded in our love. Finally, I found words: "Stay with me, Ise! Don't leave me again! I couldn't bear it!" Ise shook her head, the high blonde hairstyle, in which long yellow tortoiseshell combs were stuck, bowed: "I cannot stay with you, Hen-Yo, as a being of your kind. As a cricket, yes, or as a star or cloud. Stay with me, Hen-Yo. Come with me over the rainbow bridge. Find the way that will unite us forever." I spoke: "Is it not the same, whether you stay with me or I with you?" Ise looked at me intently. Her eyes now had the color and greenish glow of the divine eye. She was silent. The candles burned down. Midnight, the hour of the dead's departure, drew nearer. Ise spoke: "Have you prepared everything for my journey home, as is customary since ancient times?" Then I sighed deeply, tears in my eyes: "I have done as the gods and ancestors commanded." And I slid open the door that led to the garden. The garden bordered the river. In an arbor a small white paper boat lay on a mahogany table, with a thin candle as a mast. Already, the river was strewn and starred with such boats, on which the souls of the dead sailed back home, downstream to the great sea. Thousands upon thousands glided in the quiet current. The candles flickered. The dirges from the shore echoed after them. Then Ise spoke: "You have a boat at the dock, which you sometimes use for fishing. Take me back to the dead yourself and stay with me! Take me with you in your boat!" So I let the paper boat drift away without a candle, where it bumped into another, caught fire, and sank. I untied the chain, Ise, the child in her arms, jumped into the boat and sat in the bow. I tied the sacred candle to the mast, lit it, and took the oar. And the boat glided gently downstream, toward the sea.

When the Little Bell Rings. – The Door Without a Latch

I found myself once again thrown back onto the shore of my bed in the morning. Hyacinth held Maria's picture in her hand.

She looked at it with tender attention.

But the figure in the picture and she herself seemed so similar to me that I didn't know: was the picture looking at her – or was she looking at the picture?

Until I remembered again that the picture couldn't see: since it had no eyes.

Because I had gouged out its eyes.

Out of rage. Out of indignation. Out of fear. Out of malice.

And I felt shame and horror at myself.

"What a wonderful woman she must have been!" said Hyacinth, "firm within herself. Harmoniously curved like Michelangelo's dome at St. Peter's in Rome, but richly adorned like a Bernini tabernacle. She smiles seriously: Madonna of Cimabue. She blooms, a white rose on a black ground, sister of Yenkadi. One would have to erect a tomb to her like the colossal tomb of Cecilia Metella on the Appian Way before the Porta San Sebastiane in Rome. She bears the sign of the Holy Trinity on her forehead: was mother, daughter, and beloved to you."

Yenkadi on the wall moved its lips towards me: When the Three become one again, as the Three once were one – then you will be redeemed.

Hyacinth spoke: "I am not rich enough to be all this. But I love you."

I sat up: "When will you be mine as you have sworn to me?"

She brushed her hair from her forehead, which was wildly spilling out of her cap:

"When the little bell rings..."

Then she gently kissed me on the forehead: "You must recover your health above all, dear one."

She looked into my eyes for a long time.

I became uneasy.

"Why do you look at me so critically?"

"Because I like to look into your eyes."

I became restless: "That's not true. You want to discover something. You're searching for something. You're not just looking: you're spying like a hunter on the prowl. Like a bird of prey for its victim."

"But darling, how funny you are!"

"If I'm funny, why don't you laugh like I do at myself?" I had an ecstatic fit of laughter. "I do find myself quite amusing, indeed."

"You must calm down."

"You always look so strangely into my left eye. What do you see there?"

"But I love both your eyes equally."

"No, you always look into my left eye, the eye above the heart. What do you see in it?"

She looked at me intently: "Myself!"

I fell back into the pillows.

"So – you – will – also – suffer – her – fate..."

I straightened up again: "But don't you perhaps deserve it, eh?"

I became angry and spiteful.

"The moonstone, which lies next to the Indian cat and the picture without eyes, has been cloudy for a few days. And the marble cat has a crack. Do you know what that means?"

She shook her head.

"That you're deceiving me! All your declarations of love are lies! You're withholding yourself from me too. You're deceiving me –"

"But dear, with whom?"

I shouted: "With the albino!"

She smiled sadly: "Darling..."

I sat up straighter: "Oh, I have proof. I just discovered it today. Why does the door of this room have no latch? And the window no bolt?

"Let me tell you: I lie helpless here in bed and perhaps you're keeping me artificially ill because you fear that I might follow you and catch you in your shameful deeds. Oh, I see through you. Show me your left hand. Why is it clenched into a fist? No, you don't want to hit me (although your deepest desire may indeed be to hit me, to stab me, to torture me): but the handle of the door is in it – and whoever doesn't have the handle can't open the door from the inside. Defenseless and helpless, I am at your mercy."

A fit of crying shook me.

Hyacinth stroked my hair with a light kiss. I felt her arm.

The hyacinth on the bedside table emitted a fragrance.

"Cry it out, darling, cry it out. You are feverish."

Amor and Psyche

"The psychoanalytic method of healing," said the albino, "is pure humbug. Nonsense. Because it completely ignores the biological foundation. Do you think that a man with a homosexual disposition, if you point out his repressed complexes and truly bring his subconscious to the surface, is then truly cured? Not at all. He remains just as homosexual as he was. He needs surgery. Gland surgery. That's what matters. Eight days later, he's already fathering his first child with real enthusiasm. Look at Professor Steinach's experiments on rats. He transplanted female sex glands into male rats and vice versa. And automatically their 'inner life' adjusted. A male rat adopted female manners and tendencies, and a female rat adopted male ones. I am a Marxist. The psyche corresponds here to culture in general. The psyche is only the superstructure on the physical, culture is the superstructure on the economic foundation."

I dared to interject: "Psychoanalysis no longer seems to me to be indispensable for understanding artistic processes."

The albino frowned. His red eyes became even redder. "Don't talk to me about art. As soon as you can get up – show me your pulse: excellent; and the temperature? Splendid – as I said, then I'll allow you visits to the Roman three department. There you'll find as much as you want on a few square meters of space: Goethe, Schiller, Böcklin, Manet and Monet, Pindar, Hölderlin, Kokoschka, and Picasso. And the entire remaining cultural superstructure is richly represented: Loyolas, witches, monks, sphinxes, devil conjurers, samurais, Wallensteiners, princes of hell – whatever you want. Even dear God is personally present and grants audiences from 2 to 4. Unfortunately, medical science isn't there yet: but one day it will be: all these fellows and ladies just need to be operated on somewhere, then they would become useful people. I'm all for surgery and injections. That's the entire medical wisdom. Surgery! Chemistry! When you're ready, I'll inject you with tuberculin until you lose your hearing and sight."

Sister Hyacinth laughed at his grim face. She knew not to bring up psychoanalysis with the albino: he'd get furious. That was his complex. When he left the room, I laughed too.

"You see," – Hyacinth addressed me informally, as I did with her only when we were alone – "today is a beautiful day. Today, you laughed for the first time! And you are allowed to get up! You'll get a cane with a rubber tip, a push button to open the door, and then you can make visits around the house."

"I still hear the nightingale singing. I must go to her first – see if I can free her from the cage –"

"For now, you're still in the cage yourself," teased Hyacinth.

The vein on my forehead swelled.

"Now, now," she kissed the vein, which disappeared under her lips.

"It wasn't meant to be that bad..."

The Trinity

There was a knock.

Hyacinth opened the door.

And in walked a peculiar procession.

Leading the way was a dignified old man with a white cotton beard and radiantly beautiful eyes. He wore a woman's red flannel morning robe and on his head was a pointed merchant's cap adorned with golden stars. In one hand, he held a cage with a white laughing dove, and with the other hand, he led a handsome young man in a Roman tunic, with a wooden cross strapped to his back.

Following the cross was a miracle rabbi in a black caftan, murmuring secret prayers and ecstatically rocking his upper body back and forth. An old Prussian general, His Excellency, hobbled along with a Frederickian walking stick, supported on his left by a gentleman of nobility carrying a hunting horn and on his right by a harlequin-painted dancer.

Close behind them were a newlywed couple, she wearing a myrtle wreath and he a top hat on his forehead.

He moved forward on crutches.

Her knees trembled.

He was 105, the bride 91 years old.

"Darling," her toothless lips whispered.

"My sweet," echoed the old man.

He adjusted his glasses: "It seems to me you're quite décolleté today. I shall become jealous."

"And you're flirting with the sister..."

"Your enticing figure shouldn't be visible to everyone."

"Your gaze, your heart belongs to me alone."

"Do you long for me?"

"Immensely."

"When will the day of the wedding be, when will the wedding night be?"

"Soon, my angel, soon."

They stepped aside as if into a stage backdrop, and a man in a sackcloth cassock came into view. It was the monk from Potsdamer Platz.

He immediately handed me his business card, which read: Salvatore Ciavolino, Ventriloquist and Devil Conjurer, Member of the Axmadora Lodge, highly recommended and endorsed for summoning devils for the esteemed gentlemen.

A man in a purple velvet jacket approached and handed me a book bound in violet silk. In silver print, I read the title:

A to Z
Conversational Encyclopedia of the Occult Sciences.

I opened the book and flipped through it – white, unprinted pages stared back at me.

The book was empty.

But the theosophist spoke up: "The day will come! Join the 'coming day': D.K.T. Corporation for the Advancement of Spiritual and Economic Values. Soul and business: that's all the same to us. Business is our soul, and the soul is our business. Buy a share! Ten million have already been subscribed. Subscribe for another million! We own a cigar factory, a food factory, an umbrella factory, a first-class hotel where even God the Father himself is known to stay, a shaving soap factory, a sawmill, a printing press with a publishing house of communist and monarchist writings, a temple, an export business, a Trappist monastery... Try our metaphysical shaving soap! You will be fabulously lathered. Try our Nirvana cigar brand. Every trial leads to lasting clientele.

"Nirvana gives you the bluest, the most violet haze you can imagine..."

"Sir," I shouted angrily, "stop it, go quickly to your Trappist monastery!"

The dignified old man with the cap on his head approached me:

"My name is God the Father. This here," he pointed to the young man beside him, "is my beloved Son, carrying his cross to the place of execution. This, my *tertium comparationis*," he indicated the dove, "is the Holy Spirit in person, who is known to be winged and a dove."

The laughing dove in the cage started cooing and laughing, its laughter turning into a fit of giggles.

God the Father frowned: "The Holy Spirit is being cheeky once again. Making fun of creation. But what more can you expect from an irrational animal? The Holy Spirit even... oh, it even excretes."

He looked disapprovingly at the bottom of the cage.

"Still, what can I do? It's the only real, the only true Holy Spirit, with him and my dear son," he patted the young man, with whom he seemed to be in a homosexual relationship, "I am complete as the Trinity. We have come to pay homage to a foreign god who is said to dwell in this room!"

He looked around the room searchingly.

I pointed to Yenkadi, shining white on black from the wall.

"There is the god. Silent, motionless – but mighty and unwavering, he rules his world.

"His name is Yenkadi."

The Trinity bowed reverently.

The dove wagged its tail and poked its beak through the bars of the cage.

God the Father bowed, as if he had once learned it in a dance class: old-fashioned, as if he were wearing a frock coat: and as if Yenkadi were his office manager.

The young man smiled beautifully: "I am the way, the truth, and the life. No one comes to the Father except through me."

The devil conjurer imitated an Ave bell: Ding-dong-ding.

God the Father, holding the dove, God the Son, the theosophist, and the newlywed couple knelt and crossed themselves.

The miracle rabbi danced.
The dancer danced.
His Excellency saluted.
The nobleman blew the chorale on the hunting horn: "Praise the Lord."
Twilight descended into the room.
Even Hyacinth folded her hands.
Yenkadi shone white on a black background.
Then I folded my hands too.

Dictator mundi

Munk visited me one day, to my great astonishment. He seemed to have traveled a long way from Gänselache over Krausnickstraße to my sickroom because he was dressed in an garish, repulsive elegance that stood in strict contrast to his previous proletarian existence.

He immediately addressed me informally.

"I read in the newspaper about your illness. Our shared school memories made it seem like my duty to check up on you."

I thought of a Pentecost outing to the Birch Forest. We shook maybugs: how they fell damply from the trees: the bakers and cobblers and princes and emperors: when we shook the trees – before sunrise.

Munk took off his lemon-yellow gloves. "I shook the World Oak and the Wotan Oak: before sunset. That's when they fell from the stems: the grain barons, the coal magnets, the iron counts, the emperors. I was the first chairman of a revolutionary club. When I pounded my fist on the table, the glasses and the palaces of the mighty began to shake. We rebelled. We sang the Marseillaise. I decreed that the sun should revolve around the earth again. And so it was decided.

"I inaugurated free love by demonstrating *coitus interruptus* on the sofa at Father Grumbkow's on the Green Path with the waitress Maria as the living subject in the late hour. Nevertheless, I impregnated her. So she conceived immaculately and gave birth to Christian, my son and antagonist. He is now seventeen years old and is housed in this institution, where he seems to have a peculiar relationship with a certain God the Father. He has taken the title Son of God."

"I met him a few days ago. He made a very sympathetic impression on me."

Munk neighed.

"Well, well!"

He lit a "Nirvana" cigar without offering me one: "He's a dangerous fellow. Suspect and counter-revolutionary. He is here in protective custody."

I coughed in the cigar smoke: "But what did he do?"

"That's just it: he hasn't done anything. That's his crime in this most active of times. It wants to roll forward: and he falls under its wheels."

"You speak in such grand words. What about you, what have you become?"

Munk tapped the cigar ash on the bed mat: "*Dictator mundi.* Where do you live? Have you never heard of me?"

"Never, since we lost sight of each other back then – although I have dreamed of you, my alter ego. So you are *Dictator mundi* – I've only become a *cursor mundi...*"

Munk opened his mouth like a stingray: "I'm astonished and offended in my innate vanity. There is someone, my alter ego no less, who doesn't know me, to whom the echo of my deeds hasn't reached."

"Forgive me: I don't read newspapers – like you."

"But?"

I remained silent for a moment: "In the stars and from the hand."

Munk extended his butcher's paw to me: "Do you want to read my fate from my hand?"

"Show me your hand – no, not the right one, the left one: it's ungovernable..."

"I control the world – and myself. I am the first servant of my utopia."

"To Mercury – that's the god of merchants – strong lines run. You are rich."

Munk's butcher face glistened with oil.

"I live in the former imperial palace of Sanssouci. I am involved in all state enterprises, whether they prosper or not, with 15 percent stake in the turnover."

"The *mons veneris* shows predominantly male tendencies in strong emphasis."

Munk bowed flattered: "In the side wing of the palace, fifty rooms are reserved for the fifty most beautiful girls from the nations of Europe, one from each nation. None of them is over eighteen years old, and all were virgins before I touched them. Thus, the nations honor the benefactor of humanity. I have effectuated the true League of Nations. I impregnate the virgins, each a symbol of her nation. Italy is pregnant. Russia has given birth to twins. Mother and child are doing well. Germany is already in the tenth month, and still no signs of an imminent birth are diagnosed."

"The lifeline zigzags... intertwines with a hundred other lines, breaks off, re-sumes. Violence and atrocity and murder stain it – like mine..."

Munk let his hand sink. Then he spread both hands: "I love humanity!"

I dared to ask: "And how does that manifest itself?"

"I have forced humanity to its happiness."

"With what?"

"With civil war, famine, plagues, flu, machine guns, military tribunals, protec-tive custody, and gallows."

"You expect an outcry? Horror or hymn? You too are just a... human."

"Twenty million perished in war and revolution. So what? It's about the hap-piness of humanity."

"Who is that? Humanity? I don't know them. I know you. I know myself. You speak of humanity, as if you love them.

"But do you love even one person?"

"The individual doesn't need my love. It's for the collective whole that I or-ganize, regulate, decree, socialize, communicate. I decree: happiness. And a hundred million are happy. I take up the pen: Paragraph 7314 of intermundane legislation: poverty and crime no longer exist. – The regulation is confirmed by the general supreme central legislative and executive committee."

"You play God, poor devil."

Munk buttoned up his lemon-yellow gloves again: "If I can ever be of assistance to you out of old friendship: please. A position as an assistant in the Ministry of Fine Arts: how about it? Six-hour workday. Participation in the great artistic meetings and discussions. Visits to our great political poets. Formulation of topics. Brother Man, the Brotherhood of Humanity, eternal happiness, eternal peace, man is good – these are the most popular ones, which can still be varied *ad libitum*. If you just shout it properly into people's ears, they'll believe it. Man is happy when he – believes."

I disagreed: "There's only a chemical solution to the social issue. It's the only possible one because it's the only natural one. When it comes to eating, drinking, and whoring, you can't approach humans, any more than any other living creature, with ethics or pseudo-ethics. We're already producing nitrogen from the air electrically. As soon as we manage, like plants, to create organic matter from inorganic substances, the social question will be solved..."

Hyacinth entered the room with dinner.

"Allow me, Hyacinth, to introduce you: "Munk, Dictator of the World, a school friend of mine."

Munk stared: "Very pleased!"

Hyacinth smiled: "You must eat dinner now. There are eggs, milk, and ham."

Munk stood up and clicked his heels.

"The appetite is stirring – and perhaps also the libido. I am superfluous here. I'll leave. My state car is waiting at the bend in the road. Don't forget to occasionally report to me about my son Christian, who wants to improve and redeem the world from the inside out and has become a little insane because of it. One can only approach it from the outside. The souls must be organized. I consider 'The Coming Day' to be a rather clever foundation, which I support in principle. The heartbeat must be rationed. I am in favor of a Taylor system of emotions."

He waved his stiff black hat: "My lady!"

And to me: "Get well soon!"

Visit

The dancer, the general, the nobleman, all lived in a small hall next to my room. One day, the albino allowed me to visit them. I had the attendant carry me over in a chair. The dancer marched through the small hall like a Prussian grenadier. One, two. One, two. The nobleman played the Hohenfriedberg March on the French horn. In one corner stood the old white-haired General Excellency, inspecting the parade. He wore a blue frock coat with red piping on the green civilian trousers. He had made the red piping from discarded flag cloth and sewn it on himself. The dancer suddenly stopped, yet his shadow continued to march. The nobleman put down the horn. The general pranced as if he were galloping along the front lines of a division with a horse under him. To enhance the illusion of a fiery Arabian stallion he imagined between his legs, he neighed. Suddenly, he reined himself in and began to critique. "Gentlemen," he shouted, his face glowing as red as his piping, "gentlemen, today's parade march was a disgrace..." The dancer was preoccupied. He pretended to pick up a telephone receiver from the wall and spoke into the wall: "Miss... Miss... could you please connect me with the northern cemetery... Is this the northern cemetery? Oh, would you be so kind as to put the deceased Mrs. Gela Krestinski on the line? Please, yes? Sweetheart, are you there? I love you, love you more than ever... Are you cold? It was such awful cold weather, wasn't it? Shall I send you a blanket ... the colorful silk blanket from Italy?" He sobbed silently. The nobleman, only catching the word "Italy," played "My Sorrento!" on his French horn. Thick tears dripped from the general's lashes. The door, which had no handle on the inside, softly swung open, and a man in a blue and white striped coat appeared with a tray. "Gentlemen, dinner!" The nobleman, as greedy as ever, pounced on the steaming bowls. The general, even greedier but more disciplined, followed suit. Only the dancer remained by the window. He wrote "Gela" on the windowpane with his fingertip. Outside, in the snow, a raven danced. The dancer tried to imitate the hopping and prancing bird. He performed the first steps of his raven dance, which would later become one of his most famous dances after many years. "Mr. Krestinski," said the man in the blue and white striped coat, "dinner is getting cold!" Then he shrugged and left. The nobleman chewed with chubby cheeks. The general crushed a roasted chicken, bones and all, with grinding jaws. The dancer still danced at the window with his partner, the raven.

The Hall of Mothers

Supported by Hyacinth, I set out to visit the Hall of Mothers.

We walked through a maze of corridors as if we had stumbled into one of those carnival booths bearing the name Labyrinth.

Shouts pointed the way.

They ebbed and flowed intermittently.

Finally, we arrived.

Hall 28.

Above the hall entrance, two inscriptions:

> What God does is well done,

and

> Let the little children come to me!

Hyacinth opened the door.

There, in long rows, lay the unmarried mothers, always eight in a row; at the foot of the beds were small crates, where their children lay, squealing and screeching: red like crabs or pale like white mice. Occasionally, two would squabble in one crate. On one side of the hall, an operating room was attached, and on the other, several single-bedded rooms adjoined. In one of these, the nightingale sang.

I quietly opened the door.

In the room lay a girl, barely sixteen, still a child herself.

It was Marianne.

She had closed her eyes.

Two thick, long blonde braids hung from the bed almost to the floor.

The child in the small box slept.

One could hear its regular breaths.

The devil conjurer sat at her bedside.

He paused for a moment in his torrent of Latin phrases flowing from his lips and turned to me: "She is possessed by the devil! The nightingale singing from her is the devil!"

Then he began again, conjuring the devil: "For what reason did you enter the body of this virgin?"

And a muffled voice, seeming to speak from the girl, answered: "For the sake of love."

"By what pact?"

The voice in the girl hesitated: "By an animal."

The devil conjurer pressed on: "What kind?"

"Nightingale."

"Who sent it?"

Again, the voice in the girl hesitated.

"Markus."

I held my breath.

Markus is my first name.

The devil conjurer continued to question: "Tell the surname!"

The voice fell silent. It seemed reluctant to reveal the name.

He repeated the question: "The surname!"

Then, she softly spoke my name...

The devil conjurer jumped up from the bed.

He raised the cross against me: "Ah! May it be revealed at last! Terrible! You are the devil personified! Satan! Pluto, the prince of Hell, has sent you to seduce and corrupt this girl. Do you remember how you stood before his throne, knee bent under the billowing red mantle, and Pluto spoke: I have heard of a girl named Marianne. She is beyond all description beautiful and gentle. Her will seeks goodness, but her youth is burdened with premonitions, desires, and thoughts. She is like wax in the hands of a determined molder. I feel a violent desire to possess this soul entirely, to call it wholly mine. And you bowed, and the red mantle billowed: I will not lack in temptation. Pluto will praise his most obedient servant. – It is you, it is you who possess this unfortunate girl. You sent her the nightingale. Unconsciously, she uttered your name, which shame kept hidden for too long, compelled by the solemn conjuration. And this child, lying here in the cradle, deep asleep, unaware of the fate that awaits it: it is a devil's child, it is your child..."

Hyacinth turned pale from the fanaticism of his speech. He brandished the cross against me.

I collapsed by the bed, in front of the cradle: "Yes, I confess it, I shout my confession: I am the devil. I have murdered both beauty and goodness, defiled chastity and gentleness. I am not worthy of this being's love, not worthy that Maria held me in her hands, that Hyacinth pales and blushes for my sake..."

The devil conjurer brandished the cross anew: *"Adora Deum tuum, creatorem tuum!"*

And I sang fervently: *"Adoro, adoro..."*

Consistency Unlocks the Gate

I prayed by the cradle, lost in thought, as I hadn't prayed since childhood.

When I rose again from prayer – also rising spiritually – the sorcerer and Hyacinth were gone.

I sat on the edge of the bed and took the sleeping girl's hand in mine.

I don't know how long I sat like that.

Suddenly, the child became restless.

It woke up, moved its legs, scrunched its little face as if dipped in vinegar, and whimpered softly.

In that instant, the mother was also awake.

She looked at me with wide astonished eyes, as if wakening from a deep dream.

Spring breezes wafted through the half-open window.

She looked at me again – and recognized me.

Wordlessly, she wrapped her arms around me.

The child cried.

She let go: "Give me the child, my love, it's hungry."

I picked up the squirming bundle from the cradle.

She slipped her shirt off her left breast.

Filled with a magical sense of bliss, I placed the child at her breast.

On tiptoes, I left mother and child, both tired from giving and receiving, asleep.

I passed by the room of the sorcerer, recognizing it by the sign of the cross, the fish, the dove, and an uncontrollable desire tormented me to bid him good night, fearing that the night might otherwise turn sour for me.

I knocked.

It wasn't until the third knock that the door opened, and a voice said:

To one who knocks once, my heart stays silent,
To one who knocks twice, my ear listens,
To one who knocks thrice, they are heard.
Consistency unlocks the gate.
And I said: It wasn't my finger that knocked, my heart knocked on the gate.
The voice replied: step in and wield the hammer, for I shall gladly be the anvil.
I entered fully.

The sorcerer approached me with outstretched hands: "Welcome, brother, freed from the spell, and thank you for coming!"

He led me to his polished table.

There was a second place setting next to his: a pewter plate with bread, a pewter jug with water.

"Sit down, brother, and partake of my meal. I am always prepared for a guest. You wish to know how I became who I am – as you are on the path to becoming who you are – then hear this: my path was once crooked and thorny like yours. My name is Fra Salvatore Ciavolino. I was the son of a Neapolitan confectioner and began by stealing sweets from my father. I was put into a Dominican monastery early, where I was tasked with delivering love letters for the Dominicans. I used the money I received from women to buy love from kitchen maids. When a lover betrayed me with a soldier, I switched from the Dominicans to the Franciscans, became a monk, a father, and finally a fasting preacher. I enchanted all of Naples: with my eloquence equal to Demosthenes', with my youth, my beauty. It was the women especially who fell into the net of my gaze, but also delicate boys to whom I explained the secret meaning of life in the confessional, as I understood it then. I was twofold: by day, a pious and humble monk, and by night, a cheeky and lustful buck who hopped around in brothels and didn't hesitate to prostitute himself as a male whore. My life flowed with vice and lies – until one day I was saved, as you were also saved... Confrater."

I held my breath.

"It was in a brothel in the upper city, on Corpus Christi day, that the Holy Virgin herself, as a harlot, offered me her body and redeemed me by kneeling before me, the lowest of the low, in the dust. A river of tears burst from me, washing away all my vices. I exorcised the devil within me and entered the third monastery: here..."

He knelt before me: "Grant me your blessing and go your way in peace."

On Meaning

Throughout the night, I read an epistle that the sorcerer had given me. He had written it meticulously and accurately in beautiful handwriting, but the title stood out in bold lettering:

On Meaning

The meaning is the father and mother of all things.
It begets and gives birth as one.
It has neither beginning nor end.
It contemplates eternally.

According to its properties:
according to its unity, simplicity, solitude
– its unity is conceived, its solitude perceived,
its simplicity is felt by the faithful – it's not
disposed to desire a second, different one.
It only desires itself.
Thus, it doesn't act.
Thus, it does nothing.
Rather, it contemplates itself eternally.
It contemplates: not after, not before: it contemplates.

The souls participate in meaning.

They are full of meaning. In the sense that their best 'rests' in it, while their worst still 'lives' outside it.

Meaning, mathematically speaking, can be likened to a flaming sphere, akin to the sun.

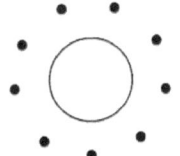

Souls can be compared to smaller spheres that receive their light from the large sphere, akin to the stars.

Just as the stars of a solar system will eventually sink into the sun, so too must the souls, if they wish to be redeemed, someday 'descend' into Meaning.

Figure 1

Soul and Meaning are eccentric spheres, ever approaching more concentric spheres. At first, the souls float, faintly illuminated, outside the large flaming sphere.

This can be mathematically represented as follows: (Figure 1)

They draw nearer as they 'recollect' themselves, progressively approaching the great 'Meaning.' Looking at what we call our existence, through appearances, we find ourselves with the above representation of our soul's relationship to Meaning still in 'pre-existence.' 'Birth' occurs at the moment when one of the small spheres touches the great, immaterial, quasi-gaseous sphere.

From the moment of birth, the soul gradually begins to become conscious of 'its meaning.' It enters the circle of 'Meaning.' At the beginning, its largest part, as a spherical

Figure 2

segment, lies outside the 'Meaning' in semi-darkness (Fig. 2). The more the soul succeeds in pulling this segment into the bright sphere, the more it becomes aware of its itself. It is illuminated by meaning. At the moment of death, the second illumination occurs. The third existence begins, the third physical life (the first physical life lies before birth, the second is this existence). This second illumination is mathematically represented as follows: (Fig. 3).

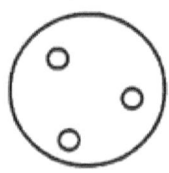

Figure 3

The small spheres float, but still as eccentric spheres, within the large sphere. This third existence ends with a third death (birth is the first, the so-called death is the second death): when the small sphere and the large sphere become concentric, i.e., when they have the same center, i.e., when the soul has merged into Meaning. (Fig. 4).

It follows easily from the above that 'soul' and 'consciousness' cannot be identified. In pre-existence the soul is not yet conscious of itself, which is why we have not brought any memories with us into this existence. Nevertheless, it is already there. Even in this life the soul only becomes conscious of itself gradually and hesitantly. But the largest part of its (mental) life in this life also takes place outside of consciousness, in the superconscious, as it were. At the moment of death, when it enters the circle of the senses, it will become conscious of its full power for the first time. It will reflect on its self, and finally, when it is completely 'sunlit,' it will enter the heart of the world: blissed and redeemed.

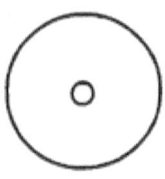

Figure 4

This is the meaning of meaning: the soul is cast out from the center like a boomerang, to have a meaningful effect, and returns to the center – but, like the boomerang, only when it has hit its target!

If it acts meaninglessly, it will float outside in the dark space around the large sphere, faintly illuminated. But since even the most senseless soul still carries a spark of meaning from its origin, it too will one day be allowed to touch the circle.

The aim and upheaval of the soul is meaning.

The small spark is the conscience.

Conscience shows the soul whether it is following its planetary orbit correctly. Only conscience testifies to the fact of immortality, the eternity of the soul. Not knowledge, because this is tied to the brain, to something physical, just as intellect is inconsequential. The essential thing is this: to be enlightened with meaning. But that means: to be good-natured, gentle, delicate, pure: to have great love.

It would be meaningless, and that would be a logical fallacy, because meaning cannot be meaningless, cannot be non-being – (since the soul's goal is bliss: to rest in meaning, in God) – if this painful life were to end with it. This life would be a lie, a blasphemy against God himself, if it were not meaningful in view of the infinite goal. What purpose does the beautiful serve if it is only beautiful enough to rest on the bier? Why should the good be good if it is flogged and whipped for it? Why shouldn't the evil be evil if it earns an easy life and this life sinks into nothingness? No: the good is immanent and the beautiful is immanent. Only evil is repelled by the spheres rotating around themselves.

Just as the spheres of the soul unite with the great sphere, they can also intersect and merge with one another. Their luminous, good aspects attract each other, while their dark, evil aspects repel each other. If two souls completely unite, i.e., if they become concentric spheres from eccentric ones, this can only be achieved through the magic of great love. This love can only be a meaningful love. For with mere affection or understanding, the spheres would only intersect.

Meaningful love anticipates the process of the eventual union of the soul with meaning, and it is the most beautiful and glorious symbol of God, of meaning itself.

Here I let the page fall.
I couldn't hold back a tear.
I thought of Maria, of Marianne, of Hyacinth: of the sweet trinity of Eros.

"The soul becomes meaningful through knowledge.
"Love is based on knowledge.
"The highest love on the highest knowledge.
"Conscience is the measure of knowledge.
"The soul seeks to become good within itself (not outside of itself).
"The soul's purpose is to be—not to do good deeds.
"For the good deed always occurs in the presence of people.
"So that even the best doer gazes at himself in vanity.
"No external temptation: murder or rape: can harm the soul in the slightest."
I had murdered Maria, raped Marianne: but their souls remained gentle, tender, pure, faithful, because they had great love. But I only harbored great hatred.
"The soul is within.
"It is based 'upon itself,' and therefore 'upon meaning.' What surrounds it is its body. And this body is air to it, like how air surrounds the earth. Its core is invulnerable. This body is air to it. Just good enough for it to float like a bird within it. Since it was not there before, it will not be there later either, logically speaking. What has a beginning has an end.
"But the soul is infinite and without beginning.
"The enemy's dagger pierces through empty space as if through an etheric body when he wants to kill the wise one. The tiger's claw finds no flesh on him. The more we gain meaning (the only gain that lasts), the more unconscious we become of our body, the more conscious the soul becomes. Spinoza says: happiness is not the reward of virtue, but virtue itself. The soul is the only real thing about us. And only its works and its effects will endure.
"Conscience relentlessly demands perfection. And whoever does not hear its voice or does not want to hear it, his soul will float with the dark spheres for a

long time.

"The wise man, however, can attain the first bliss even here, if he lives conscientiously. The realm of this life can only be reached in the highest knowledge of meaning: love. When two soul-stars flare up within each other, they rise to a purer fire, to a single star, joyfully shooting toward the 'center.'"

The Day has Come

I spent a sleepless night poring over the manuscript of the mad monk, an odd mixture of mathematics and mysticism, childish folly, and venerable truth. Whether I wished it or not, many of his words deeply moved me. They pierced straight to my fate.

Dawn broke.

I longed for Hyacinth.

When she didn't come to me at the usual hour, I grew restless.

I rang for the bath attendant.

He shrugged his shoulders.

I rang for the maid.

She fidgeted nervously with her apron.

Perhaps the Sister wasn't feeling well...

Finally, right on time, the albino entered. His face ran over like boiled milk, with red eyes floating like tomatoes.

He was completely distraught and speechless.

I approached him – desperation gave me strength – and shook him by the shoulders.

"Where is Hyacinth?"

My voice trembled.

He stared at me blankly: "Calm yourself, she is here."

He walked back and forth, hands crossed behind his back.

I sank heavily into a chair.

I felt that something had happened, perhaps more dreadful than anything I had experienced before.

The albino stopped in front of my chair, as if on automatic reflex.

He absentmindedly checked my pulse.

He stared into my eyes again.

"It's all your fault. You have Hyacinth on your conscience as well, sir."

I turned ashen.

"What are you talking about? Speak clearly, doctor, don't torture me: is Hyacinth – is she no longer alive?"

He remained silent for a moment.

"She is no longer alive – yet she lives."

I couldn't utter a word.

He continued: "Yesterday, she emerged from the nightingale's room with a mad smile. As she passed through the first men's ward where they were serving dinner, she suddenly stopped in the middle and tore all her clothes off, half dancing, half stepping around naked. Her face was divinely transfigured. She spread her arms as if offering herself to everyone and said: 'This is my body! Take and eat of it, all of you!'

"The patients sat stiff as wooden idols in their beds. They held their breaths, and no one dared move. Then she began to walk through the ward and started to sing: Yenkadi! How sweet life is and heaven is everywhere on earth! Come to me, all who are weary and burdened! Cast off your sorrow, your pain, your illness with your clothes. Yenkadi wants you naked! For divinity is naked, beauty is naked, truth is naked.

"Yenkadi!

"The day has come!

"The light has already dawned!

"The night has already vanished

"By the rays of the sun!

"Yenkadi!

"And she strode singing, chanting through all the men's wards.

"And the men threw off their blue hospital gowns and followed her in a long procession like caterpillars in a line, and they all eventually sang the song she sang: 'Yenkadi! "The day has come!"'

The albino had become inflamed by his own account. His eyes seemed to drip blood. Suddenly, he stopped as if a conductor had cut off a symphony midway and stood before me again: "The symptoms Hyacinth displayed sometimes appear in hysterical women after moral assaults on them or attempted rapes."

He stepped closer to me: "Have you tried to violate Hyacinth?"

I rested my head in my hand. It felt as heavy as a lead ball. Oh, if only I had no head, like the scorpion – but a sting like his to defend myself.

Was I insane? Or was he? What did this red-eyed medical fool want?

"Go to hell!" I jumped up. "Or to an exorcist, sir! Don't you know that I love Hyacinth?"

The albino grinned: "I love Hyacinth too, probably longer than you. Your defense is pitiful."

"Go on," I shouted. "What has happened to Hyacinth – what else has been done to her?"

The albino: "She led the procession of the naked through the monastery corridors. You know: our institution is a former Cistercian monastery. The procession looked hideous, I can assure you: all these naked, rickety, scrofulous, swollen, or emaciated bodies – I watched them hidden behind the frosted glass of my office, for I feared turmoil, rebellion, revolt." He paused and chuckled to himself like a leaking faucet: "Well, once again, nothing came of it. The uprising has already been quelled. But, to proceed properly: Hyacinth was heavenly, angelic, divine to behold. It was a mild spring evening. She led the procession into the courtyard, since she found that all doors leading outside were locked. It would have been quite the spectacle – the reputation of my institution and my reputation as *doctor seraphicus psychopathicus* – if the procession had ended up on Potsdamer Platz. In the courtyard, Hyacinth climbed into the Neptune fountain, dusk and darkness descended. She lay in the shell of the fountain like a white pearl. The procession of the naked gathered around her. I observed how her exaltation waned influenced by the night. She fell asleep. And with her, hundreds fell asleep."

He paused.

"Quietly, I stepped over the sleepers and carried her in my arms."

I clenched my fist.

"She slept so peacefully. And her beauty was that of a Greek goddess. I carried her into the hot bath chamber and laid her on the leather sofa there. I gave her another injection of scopolamine for sedation. – We easily regained control of the procession, now leaderless. We herded them back into the wards with whips."

He blew his nose.

"Do you want to see Hyacinth?"

Limping, I followed him through the monastery corridors. He unlocked the hot bath chamber with his master key that fit all locks. In the small white-tiled basin Hyacinth was playing.

She let the water cascade over her shoulders, held her breasts with both hands, then suddenly clapped her hands.

When she saw us, she laughed loudly, a laughter that cut my heart with knives.

Then she splashed us with water: "You fauns! Leave me alone! Go into the forest and play with the centaurs."

The albino whispered: "She doesn't recognize us. She thinks she's a nymph. Well, perhaps it's just an acute psychosis, a kind of nymphomania that will subside. She has dealt with mentally ill people for years. Recently even with you."

We left the chamber.

I had to restrain myself from hitting his vile rabbit-like face.

"I object such a diagnosis for myself."

"Well," he deflected, "I didn't mean to say you're mentally ill – although tuberculous meningitis is also a possibility – but I just said that Hyacinth has recently been dealing with you and has been caring for you. With what success: we see that now. You are healthy – but she has gone mad."

We stopped at my door.

It slammed shut: I was alone again.

The Small Bell Rings

The next morning, the pool attendant brought me a letter written in pencil.

It felt strangely heavy in my hand.

It was a handwriting unknown to me, a woman's handwriting.

I hesitated, then broke the seal –

A metal token from the Police Criminal Investigation Department fell out, with this number stamped on it: No. 13, and on the other side: Homicide Division of the Royal Police Headquarters.

So, my time had come. The police were on my trail. Well, I was ready and prepared.

When the nightingale flew in through the window, when I placed the child on Marianne's virginal breasts, who was still half a child herself, when the exorcist conjured the devil within me, I made the decision: to atone for my crime against Maria, to face the court myself, and to bear with humility and dignity whatever punishment society would impose on me.

And I read the letter:

Dear Human!

I am not who you think I am. I am. When I stood by the bed of the young mother and heard your boundless confession, your will to atone – yes, you were atonement itself: sinless sin – I suddenly felt the burning weight of my own inextinguishable guilt.

I had been your sister, and I had deceived you from the very first day of my sisterhood, yes, even before that. What's more: I had lied to you with my love, feigned and pretended my affection, and committing the gravest sin one person can inflict upon another. I believed I was fulfilling my duty to God and mankind – but I was merely obeying the decrees of a decayed and degenerate society, one that rids itself of the miserable and pitiful criminals it has itself cultivated and raised by unleashing bloodhounds on their trail. Oh, the scum of humanity are those who lead and dispatch these blood and police hounds.

I was such a bloodhound, a bloodhoundess, set on your trail because society, incited by denunciation, demanded your head.

I was supposed to convict you of revolutionary activities and the murder of your wife.

I was to create evidence, circumstantial or otherwise, to spy on your days and nights, your dreams and fevered fantasies. I was to give myself to you if necessary, and with poisoned kisses loosen your lips.

You are a murderer – perhaps – but a murderer without a crime. The murder that happened occurred without a perpetrator. Unless it was God. He allowed Cain to slay Abel and allowed them to nail his Son to the cross.

But I am worse than a murderer.

I betrayed you with my love – until one day I truly learned to love you.

They demanded your head – I found your heart.

I was supposed to play Judith. But I'm sacrificing my own head. Because I played her poorly, and Holofernes will carry his head on his shoulders for a long time yet.

When I recognized my unatoned guilt towards you, I rushed out of the room where a suffering woman lay like me, where the devil conjurer had summoned you, a ridiculous charlatan and profound sage at the same time – like all of us. I rushed out, my heart broke, and my brain was seized by a fiery fever.

The fever has left me today.

I know what I must do.

I was misled.

You set me on the right path.

Thank you.

Come to me one last time in Room 13 tonight when the little bell rings.

Hyacinth

And there was a business card in the letter, torn right down the middle. I put the halves together and read:

> Eva Zumbusch,
> Detective,
> Criminal Division, Dept. III

– The tears I shed were tears of joy.

I had lost a sister and lover – and found her again in a purer, nobler form.

I waited all day for the bell to ring.

In the evening around nine, the little bell began to ring. And I walked through the half-lit corridors.

My body cast threatening shadows that I feared onto the walls: devilish faces, gorillas, giant kangaroos, cavemen, creatures from the strange forest.

I quietly unlocked Room 13, without knocking: there lay Hyacinth, still and blonde and beautiful as ever. An unearthly smile bloomed on her pale face like a white hyacinth. The room smelled of hyacinths.

I tiptoed towards her: "Hyacinth," I whispered, "you called me, here I am..."

She didn't answer. Only her smile answered.

I took her hand hanging over the edge of the bed.

It was as cold as when I held it in the ambulance.

I kissed her lips: for the first and last time.

The little death knell rang incessantly.

Outside, in the park, a nightingale sang.

The Unmasked God

That same night, as I later learned, Marianne had fled from the house with her child.

The guard had carelessly forgotten to lock the window of her ground-floor room with his master key.

Was she the nightingale that sang in the park when the death knell rang?

When I returned to my room in despair, the eyeless picture had regained its eyes.

They were the eyes of Maria and Hyacinth: I could no longer distinguish them, as they both no longer shone in life.

The moonstone, which had seemed cloudy in recent days, shone pure and clear once again.

Even the crack in the small Indian marble cat had disappeared.

My gaze fell on Yenkadi.

And I mocked him: Yenkadi! Yenkadi! We have paradise on earth! How happily we humans live – without pain – without heartache – without need – without death – so blissfully we pass through life. Day and night are one, and the sun and moon are the torches of our festivities. We love each other in innocence. Our lips speak crystalline truth. Our hands entwine in a loose dance, and our song praises the brothers and sisters: the holy Hyacinth and the pious rabbit with its gentle red eyes, the sweet singing nightingale and Maria: the garland of stars.

Yenkadi, I shouted, I created you, God, and you betrayed me on the first day you were supposed to prove yourself. Where is your omnipotence, eh, you boastful idol? Where is your omnipresence? Your omniscience?

Hyacinth has died.

You let her sweet life's breath vanish as if it were thin sacrificial smoke rising to heaven on your altars: ignited from dry twigs by childish sorcerers and ignorant medicine men, your fateful priests. Hyacinth smiles even in death.

But you grin like Prince Carnival on Ash Wednesday. Marianne has fled with her child – my child – you allowed it.

Now I must search for them in the world.

You are exposed, you hollow face, paper braggart.

The Indian cat is mightier than you.

I will hang Maria's picture in your place with Hyacinth's eyes and pray to her: the dual goddess. But you: be cursed and cast out, laughed at and utterly destroyed.

I tore Yenkadi from the wall, lit a match – in a second, he went up in flames.

The Court Session

Only I knew that Hyacinth had judged herself. But her atonement did not absolve me of my guilt, even though she seemed to believe that, like Christ once did, she had taken mine upon herself through her sacrificial death.

They thought I was her murderer.

The motive that guided me was transparent enough: I had discovered who Hyacinth really was; a spy, a stool pigeon, like a tick placed on my neck.

And I had torn the tick from my flesh, thrown it to the ground, and crushed it.

Just before I entered room number 13, the guard had been there, had brought her a hot water bottle, and found her well.

The albino was half-mad with pain.

He had loved Hyacinth.

"Murderer!" he screamed, shaking his fist at me.

Then he rolled his red eyes like marbles, somersaulted like a five-year-old child, and began to walk on his hands.

When he stood back on his feet, he laughed foolishly: "Why shouldn't a psychiatrist go insane once in a while? You just have to remain aware that you're temporarily insane. A specialist in lung diseases can also suffer from lung disease, and a specialist in venereal diseases can be afflicted with *gonorrheic urethritis*. Laughable. Age doesn't protect against folly, nor does life protect against death. You little rascal," he tickled me under the chin.

"Chirp – – – little murderer..."

I was ready to submit to the judgment of any court.

The court convened promptly.

The trial took place in the institution's chapel.

God the Father presided.

It sat before the altar, wearing a pointed sugar cone hat decorated with stars, and to lend himself an air of authority, he had donned horn-rimmed glasses. Above him hovered the Holy Spirit in a cage, suspended by a framework connected to a pillar – the Laughing Dove, which occasionally interrupted the holy proceedings with unseemly laughter.

In a semicircle around God the Father were the assessors: God the Son, Munk's Son, the handsome youth; the demon conjurer, the theosophist, the dancer, the general, the nobleman, the miracle rabbi, the elderly bridal couple.

"Darling," whispered the toothless lips.

"My sweet," echoed the old man.

At first, the demon conjurer wanted to take over my defense. But I was enough for my own defense. It couldn't be an acquittal; it could only be about justice.

The albino represented the prosecution, speaking from the pulpit. He could not find a harsh word that I had not already expressed more aggressively myself, nor an argument against me that I had not formulated more logically and sharply. The flow of his speech dribbled on monotonously.

Only occasionally did it swell into cascades and waterfalls, then I listened with interest.

I sat on a pew in front of the altar.

The sun played through the stained glass windows, through the glass bodies of the saints. The first beautiful day in many weeks.

And the albino raised his voice again: "And so I motion against the defendant for simulating a nonexistent mental and physical state – I also consider his so-called hemorrhage a tasteless ploy, an attempt to evade his earthly judges to seek refuge and protection here in our district – for using a false name, blasphemy committed by worshiping the pagan god Yenkadi, seduction of a minor (the Marianne case) as well as for the double murder: of his wife Maria and of the detective Eva Zumbusch, known as Hyacinth: to be sentenced to death by the executioner's ax, eternal damnation, payment of alimony (Marianne case), and revocation of civil rights."

God the Father nodded approvingly.

The dove laughed.

The sun shone brightly.

The miracle rabbi swayed in prayer.

The demon conjurer looked troubled – even the handsome youth had a tear in his eye.

I rose from the bench.

The Confession

When I, gentlemen of the jury, make a frank and open confession and also try to explain the psychological reasons for my guilt and my fate and to unravel certain threads tied by God or the devil, I do not do this to beg for leniency and mercy from you. I am not entitled to leniency and mercy. On the contrary, I would like to request your incorruptible and unrelenting judgment. I demand justice: for myself, for society, and for the community of people whom I have dishonored and plunged into fear and misery. I demand justice, and when you have weighed everything for and against me – although there is only evidence against me – then you will deliver the verdict which can only be: guilty, guilty, and thrice guilty.

Perhaps everything would have turned out differently, perhaps my life would have flowed in peace and happiness – Spinoza says, happiness is not the reward of virtue, but virtue is already happiness itself – if a butcher's shop had not been established opposite my parental home, the house with the two donkey heads, and if I had not become acquainted with the son of the butcher, named Munk, through a ridiculous coincidence at an age considered the most sensitive and susceptible. I became friends and blood brothers with Munk and, at first, called by Munk and purely out of childish curiosity, went into the butcher's shop, where I felt the dead, disemboweled calves and pigs and, in the yard, watched with more astonishment than horror as a huge ox collapsed under the butcher's hammer. Then one day, as if in play, I dipped my finger into warm blood and licked it. That was my undoing. On that same day, I happened to see a small butcher knife glinting in the sun. It lay, still bloodstained, on a windowsill where a butcher's apprentice might have forgotten it. I hesitated for a moment. My temples throbbed behind my forehead. My heart pounded in my throat. Although I was only thirteen years old, I felt, no, I knew, that the greatest decision of my life was imminent. A circle of sunlight danced like a devil's eye around the knife. I glanced around nervously to see if anyone was nearby. Then I swiftly grabbed the knife and tucked it into my jacket.

My crimes began as I inflicted small wounds on a tame rabbit that I had at home and dearly loved. The convulsions of the poor animal both amused me and filled me with even greater affection for the delicate creature. Often, I was moved to tears by its pain. Then I kissed the wounds, which stood out purplish-red against its white fur, and drank the fresh, hot blood. And one day, I could no longer resist my ultimate desire.

It was a Sunday afternoon. My father and mother were out. I had stayed home, pretending to have a headache. I blinked lazily in the sun – throughout all my misdeeds, the weather was beautiful, and the sun always shone; I find it ridiculous and not true to life when sensation-seeking writers in their meaningless and boring horror novels have their crimes always happen at midnight or during storms and thunderstorms in a romantic setting. The sun shines on the righteous and the unjust alike. This is just a side note. So, I blinked into the sun until my eyes turned red, and there – I saw the knife glinting in the sun again. I grabbed the knife, crept into the rabbit hutch in the yard, pulled the rabbit out by its long ears – it still had cabbage leaves in its gasping mouth – and while tears were already streaming down my face, and my love almost screamed out, my conscience writhed and twisted in anticipated remorse, I plunged the knife into the rabbit's neck. A stream of blood gushed out in an arc, which I tried to catch with my mouth. And I drank and drank the red blood until I was drunk and half-fainted in a corner behind the rain barrel.

The evening dew revived and sobered me. I awoke with a nauseating taste in my mouth. What had I done? Then I saw the dead rabbit next to me and the bloodstained knife. And suddenly, I knew everything. Sobbing, I threw myself over the small animal's body. I hugged and kissed it like a child. Then I secretly carried it to the vegetable garden and dug a grave in the potato field with my bare hands. I stuck the knife in as a makeshift cross and swore never to commit murder again. With sticky, tear-stained eyes, I went up to the house. My parents had not yet returned. I undressed, got into bed, and fell into a fever that lasted for weeks.

When I recovered, I believed that I was also cured of my criminal madness. I looked openly and freely into the sun; there was no longer a knife gleaming in it. I never entered the butcher's shop again, no matter how much my friend Munk (my enemy Munk) tempted me. I studied diligently at school, became what they call a good student, and graduated as *primus omnium*, earning a prize for "Classical Heroism." I studied law without feeling a particular inclination towards any profession and nothing extraordinary happened in my life. I joined the fraternity Teutonia and lived the typical life: studies, dueling, a few relationships, morning and evening beers, occasional theater visits. I held my own in the duels and couldn't suppress a certain sense of satisfaction when I saw my opponent's blood flow. On festive occasions, I showcased my poetic, satirical, and musical talents by performing suggestive songs and couplets, accompanying myself on the piano to general applause. I became a legal intern, earned my doctorate, became inactive in the Teutonia, and was promoted to assistant.

One day, during a mandatory visit to a legal counselor, I happened to meet his seventeen-year-old daughter, a slender, blonde, blue-eyed creature of extraordinary outer and inner charm. I had barely looked into those blue eyes when I knew that fate stood before me for the second time.

I was seized by an unspeakable passion for the beautiful girl, who reciprocated my love. I asked for her hand in marriage, and before a year had passed, we were a couple. Our happiness knew no bounds. We lived in a small house all to ourselves. I joined my father-in-law's law firm as a partner. The work was not overly strenuous; we could enjoy our young happiness to the fullest.

Then one day, I noticed how my young wife sometimes alternated between red and pale and how she (it was summer) began to cough into her handkerchief.

I was very worried and wanted to send for a doctor, but she laughed at me.

One morning, I discovered a handkerchief she had set aside: small, circular red bloodstains.

I grabbed my heart.

My vision went black, then red before my eyes.

I pressed the handkerchief to my lips and kissed the blood droplets.

There was no doubt, my wife was suffering from a pulmonary hemorrhage. I loved – and still love today – my wife more than anything in the world. I held her with fervent tenderness in my arms, and this tenderness was a lie or pretense. I suggested that she consult a doctor, but she laughed at me, dismissing it as a trivial matter – it will pass – and deep down, in my subconscious, I was pleased with this response. She did not want the doctor to come. A terrible thought had taken hold of me, and its tentacles would not let me go. Secretly, I wished that Maria – that was my wife's name – would bleed to death in my arms, that she would, like Christ once did for the faithful, give her blood for me. And I wished to drink her blood like at the Last Supper. It seemed to me that only this could be the ultimate fulfillment of her and my love. And so I became a vampire, a murderer out of love, a murderer without the deed.

In the weeks that followed, I loved her more and more passionately, more and more ecstatically.

"My dearest," she would smile occasionally with her eyes, which were like moist blue gentian flowers, "I am so happy, this happiness cannot last long. I feel I will have to die - and I am happy to die."

So, my death frenzy had already penetrated her subconscious. She desired to die – because I wanted it.

I knew, that is to say, my consciousness did not know it, but my subconscious did, that in her physical condition, my hot sensual love would have to kill her, that her delicate nymph-like body would not be able to endure my lustful leaps – and yet I loved her only ever more wildly, and she surrendered herself to me ever more blissfully.

And one day, it happened.

In the midst of a wild embrace, blood gushed from her mouth in a hot stream, it flowed over my naked body, and I drank her heart's blood from her lips. My lips remained stuck to hers, blood glued them together.

As the frenzy ebbed into blissful fatigue, I realized that Maria's lips were growing cold, I tore my lips away, I looked horrified into her wide-open eyes: I held a dead woman in my arms.

I had murdered Maria with my love.

The doctor diagnosed death by suffocation in the torrent of blood.

I knew better.

I fell into a fever, as I had once when the rabbit died; when the funeral took place, I lay in semi-consciousness, only hearing the bells thundering in my twilight.

Weeks later, I came to.

The doctor diagnosed me with the same disease as my wife: consumption.

I went abroad for recovery.

I gave up my profession and relied on support from my in-laws at first. I also remembered my skills honed at the tavern, wrote topical couplets, and earned laurels and money with them. During the war, I sang war songs, during the revolution, revolutionary songs. I turned like a weather vane with the wind. Consequently, I gained a reputation. Many reputations. A critic once very flatteringly compared me to Bellman, the great Swedish singer. I also let myself be supported by various men and women and disgraced and tarnished Maria's memory. I received anonymous letters addressed to: the pimp... – and the senders were not entirely wrong. But no one knew that I had committed worse, that my conscience was burdened with tons of weight, that I had murdered my dearest in the world, and that my true address should have been: to the murderer...

And now, ladies and gentlemen of the jury, give your verdict. I await eagerly your sentence – and the day when at dawn, my head will roll into the sawdust. My open eyes will with delight see the blood spurting from the stump of my own neck. –

The Judgment

That was my speech.

The jurors retired to deliberate.

After a short quarter of an hour, God the Father, as the foreman of the jury, announced: Not guilty!

He had opened the Bible, adjusted his horn-rimmed glasses, and read monotonously: "Numbers Chapter 35 Verse 25: The congregation shall deliver the slayer from the hand of the avenger of blood."

I collapsed on the bench as if struck by thunder and lightning.

Me – not guilty?

"Godless God!" I screamed, "corrupt scoundrels, bribed by my compelling dialectic, perjurers of your juror's oath, purchasable through an open confession of guilt – who gave you the right to shamelessly bend the law like this? I am a murderer and demand my rights. It is your duty to give me that. I insist on being judged and executed."

The foam of rage came to my lips. But God the Father smiled gently. He closed the Bible, folded his glasses, and looked at me with his beautifully radiant eyes:

"Self rejoices in sin.

"Self is bad.

"Self shuns sin.

"Self is right.

"Self is pebble or glass.

"Self is love or hate.

"Self is pot or potter.

"Self is murderer or creator.

"Self is murky or pure.

"Self is all, but also all alone.

"Self is good.

"Self is evil.

"Self is blood.

"Self is entrails.

"Self can only live for itself.

"Self can only elevate itself.

"Self can only recognize itself.

"Self can only burn within itself.

"Take heart: you Good and Evil ones:

"Self can only redeem itself!"

Weeping, the beautiful youth collapsed on his wooden cross: "So I have sacrificed myself in vain for humanity!"

God the Father spoke: "You have not been of any use to them," and He pointed at me, "nor was this within your power or might – you have done enough to yourself..."

Screaming and gesturing, I was led away, the demon conjurer shook my hand in farewell, the albino patronizingly patted my shoulder: "I always said it, you are a lamb of innocence. All the best and hopefully not goodbye – I hope that for you. Greet the world outside."

Against my will, I was led to the gate and given back my freedom.

The First Attempt

There I stood alone in the immense space, not knowing what to do with my existence. The space arched above me like a dome designed by Michelangelo, gigantic in its proportions, strict in its laws, perfect yet finite. A giant would have had to strike the vault of heaven with his head, making it resound.

Just as there is no eternal time, no eternity, there is no infinite space, no infinity, I thought. We live in a universe that encompasses 999 million solar systems; in one of these systems, we play our pitiful role on Earth: amateur actors dressing up as kings and prophets in golden tinsel and gaudy rags. We should bend over a microscope and observe a drop of water: there, like the stars in the cosmos, infusoria and rotifers follow the same elliptical paths. And every speck of dirt reveals the same oscillatory movement. In plants, the protoplasts wander tirelessly with their nuclei and granules. Likewise, humans wander, just like stars, infusoria, and protoplasts, and each cell within a human follows its own wondrous orbit. Thus, the soul also wanders: it looks down from the star to the speck of dirt and becomes dizzy. Then it gazes up from the rotifer in the speck of dirt to the human, and it grows seasick.

I was once again exposed defenseless and helpless to the wild world.

No walls remained to protect me. No small window that dimmed the light and let it filter softly into my sick eyes.

The sun burned unbearably. I had to close my eyes every moment.

I turned around and rang at the asylum gate.

The head of the white-haired porter, wearing his old, tattered soldier's cap, jutted forward like a fantastical serpent head from the small window.

"What do you want?"

I knelt down: "Take me back to my cell – the one that protected me – from the world – from myself."

The porter smirked.

"Are you crazy? You're discharged. The asylums, hospitals, and prisons are overcrowded. We can't use any surplus and unnecessary boarders." His mouth widened like an ox's: "Steal a bike or kill someone, then come back!"

The window slammed shut.

I staggered through the streets.

People watched me as I groped my way along the houses, afraid to cross an open space.

Some shop girls, coming out of the store, laughed. But then they caught my gaze and were frightened.

What should I do? What should I think? I didn't know.

Dusk rose like gray mist from the pavement.

I reached a public park.

I found the darkest bench and sat down.

I don't know how long I sat there when a soft voice next to me asked: "Do you want to love me?"

I looked up and saw the silhouette of a girl.

I couldn't see her face or age.

"I can't love anymore, girl. I've loved too much."

"Oh," she laughed softly, "if that's all."

She reached out for me and began to play.

Then she sat tenderly on my lap, bounced a little, and loved me as if I were a woman and she a man. I let it happen silently.

A bit of passive, physiological happiness – what next? Did I still have a will for happiness?

She sat next to me and brought her face close to mine: "Do you believe now that you can still love?"

I remained silent.

"Why are you silent?"

She noticed my closely shorn head.

"Where are you from?"

I remained silent.

"Oh, I know where you're from. You come from the gray house. Is that true or not?"

I remained silent.

"You don't need to reply; I know for sure. In this park, those just released from the gray house sit on the darkest benches, which is a few streets from here. They don't know what to do with themselves. They seek the darkness. But – I show them a star in the dark. The star of hope."

I found what she said quite sentimental and still kept silent.

She paused, then: "Are you a pimp? Do you want to be mine? I need a strong guy. And you haven't become weak in the gray house."

She checked my muscles.

I broke the silence.

"I'm a murderer."

I felt her pause.

Then she whistled softly through her teeth.

"Oh la la, I wouldn't have expected that from you. Now I have respect for you. I was once engaged to a murderer named Munk. And I also have a child with him, named Christian, the most beautiful person you can imagine. He's seventeen now and unfortunately a bit simple-minded. How long did you do time?"

"A year."

"Man-slaughter with mitigating circumstances?"

"No."

She paused again.

"Then you bid Father Philip farewell without asking him?"

"No – I was acquitted."

She laughed.

"Boy, oh boy, you're lucky. We should celebrate. Do you have money?"

I shook my head.

"It doesn't matter. I have a few coins left. Let's give them to the 'Blue Monkey' to swallow."

The Blue Monkey and the Green Bird

The Blue Monkey was a basement pub; I can't remember which street it was on.

She had linked her arm with mine, and it was clear she was proud of me, that she was showing me off.

A lover who was an acquitted murderer – that's no small matter.

She whispered with the bartender behind the counter, a guy, fat and tall like a hippopotamus and with tiger paws.

In the little shop, men and women sat, all giving me a sideways glance.

The men all looked like me, and the girls like the one who had hooked her arm through mine.

"Well done!"

The bartender came and shook my hand. He whispered with the guests. They were mostly fences, hiding their stolen goods under their coats: scarves and shoes hanging around their necks on strings.

And in a long line, ceremoniously, they all passed by me and shook my hand.

One, the last one, introduced himself politely:

"Sally the Bagman, also known as Smarty."

The introduction was done with such dignity, he pronounced his name so emphatically as if I should never forget it, that I did him the favor of engaging in friendly conversation, which seemed important to him. Maybe he hadn't made it to being a murderer yet. Maybe he wanted to do a job with me sometime.

"Well, how are you?" I asked.

He shrugged: "Have you read today's newspaper?"

I said no.

He pulled out a sheet of paper and pointed to a note:

Fabulous burglary through two floors with center drills and melting devices.

"Well – and?"

He tapped his chest, which was in a green woolen sweater: "That was us!"

He puffed up like a turkey.

"And the haul?"

He lowered his voice: "Between us: nearly nothing. Three hundred marks were in the safe. A hundred for each of us: There were three of us. Tough luck, huh? Out of spite, I took the green bird with me, who was sitting on a perch in the room where the safe was."

I was puzzled: "What green bird?"

He gestured backwards with his hand: "I gave it to the bartender."

On the cigar boxes behind the counter sat Lora, my parrot.

Sally the Bagman, also known as Smarty, had broken into my old apartment.

I was far from holding it against him.

The enormous technical effort with melting tools and center drills had hardly paid off.

As I approached the parrot and scratched its head, it recognized me; it rolled its eyes so that you only saw the orange-yellow in them and screeched: "Come in. Well, doll. Come on, come on. Scratch my head."

The bird's voice had lost all its terror for me.

He seemed to have forgotten the name Maria because he hadn't heard it in so long.

The girl laughed.

The bartender slapped his belly.

I had to smile. But a tear hung on my eyelashes.

"Maria!" I said to help the bird's memory.

It looked at me askew, rolled its eyes, and fell silent.

The House in Hell

"I have no place to stay."

"Leave that to me."

The girl wrapped herself in her shawl.

I followed her.

We walked through several streets, crisscrossing.

NO was written on some street sign.

We turned into a dark passageway.

The front door was open. The courtyard door.

We crossed three courtyards.

In the third rear building, we stumbled down into a cellar hole. The girl unlatched the unlocked door. Then she took my hand.

"Be careful! Don't wake anyone up! They're lying everywhere here on the ground like corpses. You have to step lightly like a dancer."

An suffocating stench filled the cave.

We passed through two rooms.

In the third, the girl stopped.

"This is my sleeping place."

She began to undress.

I did the same.

Soon I felt her small girl breasts in my hands.

And we sank heavily onto the straw in a corner. –

It must have been morning by then, but the room was still enveloped in an almost impenetrable gloom.

Dirty light flowed through narrow cracks above.

There must have been some kind of window. Eventually, I made out that the so-called window was boarded up with packing paper – probably so no one from the courtyard could see in.

I stayed with the girl for eight days.

The two front rooms were teeming with children and rats. In one corner lay an older man blinded by lead poisoning. A one-year-old child sat on his belly, playing with his red beard. A syphilitic prostitute was decomposing in another corner. She had a game of cards spread out in front of her. She played with the jack of hearts and the king of hearts and called them "sweetheart!" when she noticed me, she read my fortune from the cards: "An engagement is imminent. A letter will arrive. Beware of a dark-haired person. A long journey lies ahead."

The children never saw the light of day, never went outside. They had no shirts, no pants, no clothes. Only rags hung from them. They had never gone beyond the third courtyard, and I had to tell them fairy tales that began:

"Once upon a time, there was a child who had a snow-white, beautiful shirt and enough bread to eat his fill every day..."

"Once upon a time, there was a star that spread light and gentle warmth over the earth, and all the people who walked in its beam shone in gold and silver, and this star was called the sun..."

"Once upon a time, there was a forest, which is an immense army of trees, like the one outside in the first courtyard, but thousands upon thousands side by side..."

"Once upon a time, there was a bird that looked like a sparrow, gray and unremarkable, but it didn't screech like a rusty door hinge, instead, it sang like an angel in heaven itself. This bird was called a nightingale..."

The children widened their inflamed eyes and spread their scabbed lips into smiles.

And the eldest spoke: "What you're telling us isn't true. But they're beautiful fairy tales. Tell us more..."

When I lay in the dark on the straw and the lice and bugs crawled over me, occasionally a rat jumped over my leg too, I thought about the fate of these children.

And I couldn't understand why their parents didn't gather them in a terrifying parade, thousands of them, in their nakedness, and march silently and wildly through the streets of the rich: with Christian leading them, the handsome young man and son of Maria, who had her sleeping quarters in the third burrow: Christian, who believed himself to be the Son of God, yet was only the idiotic son of a murderer and a whore. He had chosen the best profession for himself, for no other profession was open to the children of the hellish house except that of a thief, a pimp, a fence, a robber, and a murderer.

The Chinese Girl

One evening, when I didn't know what to do with myself or the world, I came across strange colored paper strips and lanterns hanging in front of a tavern near Krögel. As I stepped closer, I noticed a pale girl (depicted on one of those paper strips) gazing tenderly up at a fearsome warrior. And between them ran writing I couldn't understand. It was the signboard of a Chinese juggler or actor troupe. I walked through a narrow, damp passage. A hall opened up: and on the primitive, backdrop-less stage, I saw the same play that I had seen on the poster: a pale girl kneeling tenderly before a fearsome warrior brandishing a sword. At that moment, she rose, tiptoed to the footlights, and it almost seemed as if she were speaking directly to me, as she sighed, chirped, and smiled at the audience in an unintelligible idiom. And although I did not know her language, I understood everything: she was trying to convey that she loved the fearsome man with the sword, that he was the executioner who must kill her at the Mandarin's command, but that she would gladly die by his hand, and that she would forever flutter around his brow as a bird in the morning, a butterfly at noon, and a bat at night. Then she tiptoed back, knelt down, and the executioner struck silently – a scream of horror erupted from the audience, and I, pale as chalk, leaned against a column; the head rolled across the boards, blood splattered over them, and the curtain fell.

There stood the little Chinese girl at the stage exit, gazing at the moon high in the sky. She appeared so enchanting, so otherworldly as she turned her head toward me and regarded me wordlessly, like an animal, devoid of thought or feeling. I stepped closer and spoke a few English words to her. She shook her head. I didn't know what to do, my heart was pounding in my throat. I took her hand, and just as she knelt before the executioner, I knelt before her. And I kissed that delicate, frail hand: softly.

Inside, a gong sounded. She slipped away. I was alone. I went home.

Sleepless, I lay in my tar-scented room, thinking of the girl, and in the dark, I saw the little Chinese girl kneeling before the executioner, who was her lover. That night, I composed my first Chinese poem. It was very short, like what the Japanese call a hokku:

> You love the executioner.
> Every day he kills you.
> Your blood flows eternally.
> Yet you smile.

The next evening, I returned. When I entered, they were performing a little comedy: a student loves the shop girl of a perfume store. He can't confess his love to her because there's always a repulsively ugly old woman, the shop owner, present. Finally, he manages to slip a note to the young lady – played by my little Chinese girl – saying: tonight at the temple such and such! She smiles her consent. The second act depicted the temple. The student is drinking with an old monk, waiting for the girl. She does not come. The two drinkers grow weary and fall asleep in each other's arms. Then, with a small paper lantern, the girl appears. She bends over the sleepers. Her face shows no expression. She slips off one of her slippers and places it in the student's lap. She disappears with her lantern like a firefly. The student awakens, rubs his eyes, finds the slipper, and is inconsolable. Curtain. I stepped into the courtyard. There stood the little Chinese girl again. I handed her a bouquet of mimosa that I had stolen for her from a flower shop. She seemed to smile. Then she took my hand for a second. When I came back the next evening, In the hall where the lovely tale of the slipper had played out the day before, clerks, laborers, soldiers, and wild women were dancing.

I went to the innkeeper, who sat heavily behind his counter. "Where are the Chinese?"

"They left early this morning. By the way, are you the one who gave the star of the ensemble the mimosa bouquet yesterday?"

I nodded eagerly.

"I have something for you."

He handed me a small package.

In a corner over a glass of pale ale, I opened it. Two tiny slippers lay inside and a note that read: Mai Lung Fang greets you. Mai Lung Fang dictated these words to a friend for you. Mai Lung Fang loves you as you love Mai Lung Fang. Mai Lung Fang loves art and those who love art. Peace and happiness be with you!

I rushed to the counter.

"Do you know Mai Lung Fang's next address? Where is she?"

The innkeeper frowned: "Mai Lung Fang? Mai Lung Fang? Wasn't that the young Chinese who played the lovely female roles? And so incredibly lifelike. A delightful lad! If you didn't know, you couldn't tell he wasn't a girl. Imagine, there was a young sailor here who fell madly in love with Mai Lung Fang because he mistook her for a girl..."

He chuckled like a seal.

I felt a faint stab in my heart.

The weather had turned dreadful. The rain splattered against the windows. And in the rhythm of the rolling drops, another Hokku formed in my mind:

> The rain trickles down.
> I loved a phantom.
> The clouds drift away –
> Where will fate carry me?

The Boxing Match

As I drifted alone through the streets like a leaf in the autumn wind, I was blown into a corner in front of a billboard. There I read in loud colors, black and white on red:

> Sensational!
> Tonight a boxing match, major event, at the Great Theater on the Weidendammer Bridge!
> The decisive fight for the world championship
> for world domination, between Munk, the European champion, known as *Dictator mundi,*
> and the Asian champion Mai Lung Fang, known as the Chinese wildcat.
> No one should miss out on attending this historic bout.

I didn't want to miss it either, so I entered through a side door of the Great Theater and went into the artists' room, where I found Munk, flexing his muscles, delivering a grand monologue that would have been suitable for the arena itself:

"I personally enter the ring. No one shall say that I am a coward. In me, the continent is embodied and spiritualized. The great hour strikes. The question is: Europe or Asia? The white or the yellow race? Schinderhannes and Schopenhauer, to name two polarities – or Laotse and Lihungtschang? Schnapps or opium? Who will own the future, which will be called eternity? My muscles are honed. I am trained. I have read Laotse. I will defeat him, the Yellow one, with his own weapons. No one can match me. For two months, I have not touched a woman. I burst with generative power. Responsibility strengthens me. Already I hear them singing, the champions of Gleiwitz, Nancy, Warsaw, Czernowitz, Malmö, and Naples: *ave Caesar, morituri te salutant...*"

I stood next to the dressing mirror and remained silent.

Munk paid no attention to me.

The manager burst in, agitated.

Munk asked condescendingly, "How are things looking?"

The manager replied, "Excellent. I came to check the wraps and gloves."

Munk clenched his leather-covered fists: "Fist and blood and heart are one."

The manager beamed, "Victory seems certain."

"Seems?"

"As sure as the sun shines."

"Are bets being made?"

"5:4."

"Too little. Do the people no longer love me?"

Munk stomped his feet.

The manager pacified him, "They love you beyond words. But in boxing, they value the qualities of a boxer. You or him, that's what it is. Not you and him."

"You must knock him out."

Christian, Munk's son, burst into the dressing room.

"Father – I implore you – what are you doing – he will crush you."

Munk looked into the mirror: "Who is this kid? Ah, my son –"

The manager became nervous.

"I beg you not to upset yourself. I have bet a hundred thousand marks on you."

Munk replied, "No fear, my friend. My nerves are as strong as ship cables. What do you want, son? For months, you didn't care about me –"

Christian shook his blond locks: "I have always thought of you –"

"Sentimentality. Whoever truly thinks, acts."

"Your picture hangs above my bed. God the Father knows it."

"Ridiculous. A naked wench would be more fitting and appropriate."

"I love you."

"Nonsense. I don't love you."

Christian raised his hands devoutly: "Let me step into the arena for you. The Chinese will kill you."

Munk bristled like seltzer water: "Nonsense – here, feel my biceps."

Christian spoke softer: "You are strong. But I am weak."

"A bloodless little weakling. I am the strength, the ferocity, and the dignity. I defy. My vitality swells. How I fathered you remains a mystery to me. I had already downed twelve Kulmbachers. And I didn't want you: you were nothing, you barely existed, you oh..."

The youth smiled sadly: "I am the weakness. Weakness prevails. Reeds bend. Oaks – fall. Clouds blow in the storm – towers burst."

Munk frowned: "Symbols don't affect me."

The youth became more insistent: "You only have your life, your position. If you lose, your power ends, your life ends. The laughter of the people will chase you to Tehran. You want to rule. So stay. Ruling is your happiness. I gladly sacrifice myself for you. But it would probably not be a sacrifice: because I cannot lose."

Munk tried a thrust at the punching bag hanging from the ceiling.

"Go to the zoo. Learn to box with the kangaroos. Then come back."

The manager interrupted him with a hoarse, excited voice: "The bell sounds. Are you ready?"

Munk straightened up: "I am."

He walked past Christian and me with large strides, without even giving us a glance.

Deafening applause echoed from the arena.

Christian and I stood like caryatids on either side of the door.

We didn't speak a word.

We knew the outcome of the fight too well.

Mai Lung Fang had also defeated me. He had the ability to assume any form.

After barely five minutes, Munk was brought in on a stretcher, blood-soaked.

The Chinese had knocked both his eyes out of his head.

There was no European worldview anymore.

I still heard the manager screech: "Thank God we have an institute for artificial human eyes in Berlin. Berlin in Germany, Germany in Europe, Europe leading in the world."

I approached the stretcher: "Do you recognize me, Munk?"

Christian stroked him with trembling hands.

I got no response.

I sneaked out of the house as secretly and unobtrusively as I had come.

The Bracelet

After eight days, I left the girl.

She gave me her hand, looked into my eyes one last time, and kissed me softly on the lips.

I walked through the streets, once again unsure where my path would lead. I was covered in lice from head to toe. But I had already developed that camaraderie with lice, bugs, and rats that the poor and destitute have, for whom bedbugs, lice, and rats are better siblings than humans.

I wandered through the streets. A boy whispered in my ear, "Do you want to make your fortune?" I nodded. He pulled dirty scraps of paper from his pocket with numbers scribbled on them in pencil. He said, "A ticket costs five marks. My father runs the lottery. Over there in the doorway. The main prize is fifty marks. Want a ticket?" I had no money to make my fortune.

I stood before the display of a bookstore, checking if any books by me were on exhibit. I read titles like "Proper German for Military Applicants," "German Criminality in its Social, Literary, and Linguistic Development," and "Argot for Beginners." "The New Pitaval" was open. I read the chapter title: "The Confession." It was my confession. It was already printed.

At brightly lit shop windows, I stopped and curiously examined the displays of leather goods and jewelry stores.

I admired a suitcase. Genuine vulcanized fiber.

If I were to travel? A walking stick in a display of canes and umbrellas made me think of wandering.

What if I went on a journey?

I wasn't too old to go tramping.

Dogs barked.

A policeman barked at me, "Don't just stand in the middle of the street like that!"

In the window of a jewelry store, an unusual piece of jewelry caught my eye.

"Attention! Sensation! Bargain! Bracelet made from real human eyes!"

I was tortured by the obsessive thought of finding out the price of this bracelet.

So the man with the cart had managed to sell it after all. Shabby and destitute as I was, I entered the elegant shop.

The manager looked me up and down in surprise.

I stammered, "I would like to know the price of the bracelet made from human eyes in the display."

The manager scrutinized me from head to toe.

"Please leave the premises."

As I left, I heard, "The tramp is scouting out an opportunity for a break-in."

I stopped again in front of the window.

"I wonder," I thought, "whose eyes those are. Maria's, perhaps, or Hyacinth's."

I gave other eyes the names of other women I had loved. I even saw Munk's eyes among them. Only a few eyes were missing: Marianna's eyes.

I knew they were somewhere out there, searching for me amid street dust and starry mist, waiting for me in a dull, blissful peace, with two children's eyes following their gaze into the darkness.

A voice next to me said, "This is nonsense! Fraud! The eyes in the bracelet are not real, but artificial human eyes. I can see that immediately. I am the owner of an institute for artificial human eyes."

I turned around and noticed a small, chubby man wearing a mink coat.

"Excuse me –"

The man looked at me sternly and critically.

"Excuse me," I continued, "I have seen so much misery and suffering, crime and madness on this earth that my eyes ache, and I often wish I could rip them out of my head. Perhaps through your artificial eyes, one sees this life in red and blue and gold and silver, like on postcards. Would you make me a pair of artificial eyes, custom-made?"

The chubby man looked at me in surprise.

"First, get yourself disinfected before you talk to me."

This joke brought laughter and suppressed chuckles from some bystanders who had stopped.

"And for clarification: a pair of custom artificial human eyes costs five thousand marks. Half of the amount is payable in advance when ordering. There are all sorts of unreliable characters..."

He winked, encouraging the surrounding audience to giggle and smirk again.

I looked through the fat man as if he were made of glass. How strange, I had completely forgotten that one needs money to live. The concept of "money" – I had forgotten it.

In the Homeless Shelter

Exhausted from wandering aimlessly back and forth, I entered the homeless shelter late in the evening.

When I looked into the bathroom, a need for cleanliness awoke in me with more than physical force. You must get clean again, I thought, yes, you must: a clean, a pure, a hygienic person.

I joined the line streaming into the bathroom. I undressed. Meanwhile, my clothes were being deloused in a huge, steaming kettle.

Then I stood under the cold shower for fifteen minutes. Ah, that felt good.

At the entrance to the dormitory, I received a bowl for food and a thin blanket. A thick, stuffy warmth filled the room: just like back then when I walked through the strange forest. Oh! How long ago that was! No matter how hard I tried, I could no longer remember.

I lay against the wall of the women's section.

A nailed door separated it from the men's section.

Knocking signals came from both sides.

"Comrade," said someone next to me, mending his shirt in the dim light, "wait for darkness. Then we'll break down the door. There are pretty girls over there."

Someone played the harmonica.

"Early in the morning, when the roosters crow –"

Some sang along.

Then singing came from the women's section.

The harmonica fell silent.

And clearly and audibly through the wall came the words:

> I was a young thing,
> Always fresh and spry,
> Then a man came from Borsig,
> He had money and smarts.
> No one was as handsome as he
> With his red tie.
> He bought me a new hat,
> Who knows what love can do.
> Berlin, oh how sweet
> Is your paradise.
> Our hometown
> Has spirited girls.
> Get over it. Tra la la.

> I always went with him.
> Then the guy disappeared.
> When I was eight months pregnant,
> At night in wind and storm,
> I dragged myself to a meadow,
> Buried the poor worm.
> My heart cried, my blood burned,
> Who knows what love can do.
> Berlin, oh how sweet

Is your paradise.
Our hometown
Has spirited girls.
Get over it. Tra la la.

Now I'm on the street.
I have a pimp.
In a green car
At half-past two at night,
They drove me
To the Charité hospital.
My heart rots, my blood putrefies,
Who knows what love can do.
Berlin, oh how sweet
Is your paradise.
Our hometown
Has spirited girls.
Get over it. Tra la la.

I'm always sick.
I don't care about anything.
The vineyard bears grapes,
And when a young man comes,
I give him something for life,
So he can remember me.
Mercury and decoction,
Who knows what love can do.
Berlin, oh how sweet
Is your paradise.
Our hometown
Has spirited girls.
Get over it. Tra la la.

It became dark and quiet, on both sides.

Rasping, breathing, coughing, snoring, sighing.

"Hey," someone clumsily nudged me in the dark. "Comrade, help, we're breaking into the women's section..."

We pushed.

Someone commanded softly, as if pounding stakes or paving stones: One – hup – one – hup –

The door gave way.

Like bugs, five or six men ran over and soon had a woman in their arms.

I crawled slowly and felt my way to a women's bed, right by the wall, opposite mine.

And as I lean my face close over the woman sleeping peacefully and deeply, holding a child in her arms, I recognized that was Marianne, the one I've been searching for with my heart as a compass and with my longing all these days: Marianne, my girl, and our child.

And silently, I stand guard at her bed like a cherub.

The Way Out

The next morning, I waited for Marianne by the exit of the women's section.

Sparrows and children were shouting and dancing in the sun; overnight, it had turned to spring overnight. Somewhere – wonder of the metropolis – a nightingale was singing.

Marianne walked beside me, skipping, counting the paving stones, and playing the ancient game of heaven and hell as she went.

I carried the child in my arms, who reached for the sun with both hands.

I would and wanted to find work, that was certain. Life had to be taken seriously. Oh, it was only just beginning: in the eyes of this beautiful girl, this cheerful child; never before had this life been lived, the intoxication of love, the fanfare of duty, heaven over a thousand hells. It would begin today with this spring day. A new world epoch would date from today. The first year began. My lungs expanded:

Freedom! No more looking back! The chains were broken. The sun still shone, my lungs still breathed, my heart still beat: like a nightingale.

To have money for today, I established myself as a wild porter at Anhalter Bahnhof. I earned fifty marks.

After we had eaten at a small tavern and were on our way to a cheap lodging in the north, crossing the bridge at the Reichstag riverbank, we found a man lying there under the lamppost.

At first, I thought he was drunk.

I gave the child to Marianne, stepped closer, and recoiled.

I thought I had seen my own face as if in a mirror.

The man lying there was dead. And the dead man bore a striking resemblance to me.

A wild joy, a mystical plan, shot through me instantly.

The dead man was elegantly dressed and could well pass for me in my former worn-out times.

I reached into his breast pocket, opened the wallet: it contained a passport, issued to Andreas Z....., born in 1891, unemployed. I took the passport and placed my identification papers, which had legitimized me until now, into the dead man's pocket.

So from now on, I was called Andreas Z..... and my first self had died, and my second, different self had begun.

With the child on my left arm, my right arm around Marianne's shoulders, her long blonde braids cascading, making her look like a schoolgirl, I went to Schlesischen Bahnhof the next morning, into the first dawn of a mild spring day.

From the ashes of Yenkadi, I rose phoenix-like to a new flight.

The morning papers brought the news that Dr. X....., who recently suffered a severe hemorrhage, known to wider circles as an original songwriter as well as for his performances on stage, was found dead last night on the bridge at the Reichstagufer.

Since the deceased had not been robbed and there were no signs of violent death, a stroke was to be suspected. The press noted with lively regret his unexpected demise.

I don't carry my fate before me on my hands. These eyes burn inward, and this heart beats beneath the skin. Because this forehead is so smooth: is the brain inside all the more wrinkled, and this clear eye has been bought with dark pains. Many tears, unseen by anyone, have washed it so clear. If one looked closely, one would find a few white hairs beneath my blonde hair. The traces of my time in prison, hospitals, and asylums are blurred and blown away like fox tracks in the pine forest of Brandenburg.

Wind and clouds and the world I brush off my eyelashes when I want to. Who can see into my stomach to know it has cracks from hunger?

I stand on the threshold of my thirtieth year, and when I look and listen back, a brown river roars and rages with white foam crests: like the Inn or the Bober in flood. And when I look inward: it is the same river, only illuminated by foreign lights flying from afar like exotic fireflies. And when I listen ahead: it is the same rushing. But I walk over the waters like Christ once did on the Sea of Galilee. I dance, I skip, I jump, and I stride. I fall to my knees, but I jump back to my feet: and stride. And below, the river roars, over which I should ferry the souls of Maria and Marianne to Charon. I hear Charon rowing and cursing. His boat is empty. The river carries me like a moving sidewalk.

Part Two:

Peter - Novel of a Tsar

(Erich Reiß Verlag, Berlin, 1923)

Peter – Novel of a Tsar

Peter was born.

The Don, Dnieper, Volga, and Oka overflow their banks.

Mud rolls over the wheat fields, and many people drown.

Winter flowers bow their broken heads.

The dormice whistle in fear. The wind takes their whistles and with puffed cheeks blows them up into trombone tones until they burst with a shriek.

The trees weep with resin.

Frozen swans sail on dancing ice floes. Their green eyes shine like emeralds.

Frogs drift, their bluish bellies turned upward. Their bodies are pierced by water beetles, which nest inside, dead and bloated: the brown shells of their backs glazed white.

Red snow has fallen.

On the Valdai Hills, foxglove blooms in the midst of winter.

Fire fell out of the heavens from the hands of God. A thousand villages were ablaze. The young storks on the thatched roofs were roasted alive in their nests. The old storks circled through the clouds of smoke and soot, clattering loudly and desperately with their long beaks, as if swords were clashing against each other.

They searched for their enemy and could not find him.

In heaven, he sat and slept on his lapis lazuli throne. He himself looked like a diamond: clear and transparent, shining. His eyes, bright sapphires, his heart a dark red ruby. Draped over his shivering shoulders like a silken scarf was a rainbow. Seven torches burned around his throne.

In his sleep, with his stone arm, he had swept a torch down, a star from the seven-branched golden candelabrum. Hissing and sparking, the meteor whizzed through the eternal space and crashed with its red blind forehead into the earth with a thunderous impact, igniting and ravaging an entire landscape.

The priests sermonized: "Woe to those who dwell on earth! The sun has conceived and given birth to a golden child! It will scourge us with a fiery whip!"

A pack of wolves howls at night outside the windows of the Preobrazhensk Palace. The servants cross themselves.

They whisper: "A wolf-child has been born, a wolf-son. The brothers hurry to greet him."

An old she-wolf reaches the courtyard and howls hungrily up at the windows of the first floor. Natalia Naryshkina, the Tsarina's mother, awakens from her sleep. She holds her breath and listens.

No one dares to kill the old she-wolf.

"It's her child," assures the old coachman Potapov, who thinks much and knows even more.

"If we kill her, we are all doomed."

The next day, the she-wolf is found half-dead in an empty sentry box by seven-year-old Ivan the Fool, the current Tsar. Ivan crawls on all fours and barks angrily at the she-wolf, who gazes at him indulgently with tired, sorrowful eyes. She licks a newborn wolf cub, still blind, but biting at the air as the coachman Potapov takes him. Potapov gives the cub to a dog to nurse and carefully raises it.

The sun breaks through the clouds, looks down on her new little son, looks down on Peter.

His limbs crippled, his eyes smeared, his tiny fists clenched before his wrinkled, old-man's face, Peter lies in the cradle, whimpering like a young wolf. He whimpers, he cries because he is born.

How warm and good it was in that damp, dark cave, which has now spat him into the light against his will. He shivers in the rough air. He fought with hands and feet against being born. The light blinds him. He was a vessel that drank red, hot blood for nine months. His whole body had been a chalice.

He gasps with his mouth like a fish. He is thirsty. He cries.

The midwife hands Peter to his mother, Princess Natalia Naryshkina, who lies pale on the towering, mountain-like blue-and-white checkered pillows.

The midwife lifts her breast from her shirt. Peter grips it with his tiny fingers. Then, with his eyes closed, he begins to swallow, to snort, to grunt, like a young wolf at the teats of the she-wolf.

The midwife sways her hips. Natalia Naryshkina smiles.

Peter is so small, and Russia is so vast – what will become of Peter? Oh dear. What will become of Russia?

Prince Galitzine comes to visit, buttoned-up, in a black coat, as if heading to a funeral.

"Well, Natalia Naryshkina, how are you?"

She has to smile.

His glasses sit on the tip of his nose, threatening to fall off at any moment. He is the only person in Russia who wears glasses. When she is very fond of him, she calls him: Owl.

His blue, watery eyes sparkle dimly and vaguely.

She thinks: The great lover Galitzine. So this is what my lover looks like. The lover of the beautiful Natalia Naryshkina. He is considered the most educated person in Russia. That's why I fell in love with him. He has read Shakespeare and Dante in their languages. I can't even master the Russian language. But I have mastered him. By the way, in his shirt and glasses, he looks hilariously funny. Like a bird. Like a very specific bird. What is that strange bird called again?

Prince Galitzine, who feels that he is being closely watched, shifts restlessly in the wicker chair, which convicts from Siberian prison camps had been forced to weave: "What do you find wrong with me, Natalia Naryshkina?"

"Nothing, my dear, nothing at all... Go over to the cradle – what do you think of it? I had it painted with all sorts of pretty animals: storks, swans, and wolves. – Look at the little barbarian. Who do you think he resembles, I wonder?"

Prince Galitzine walks gravely over to the cradle.

Now she remembers the name of the bird: a marabou stork.

Peter is asleep.

The prince removes his glasses and places them on Peter's soft nose, which bends under the steel.

Peter scrunches up his face in his sleep, about to cry.

"Just like his father, just like his father."

The prince's watery eyes sparkle merrily, like murky ponds in the sunlight. She sighs.

"That Tsar Alexei Mikhailovich didn't live to see his son – how sad. He was a good man."

"Certainly," the prince agreed politely, "certainly. But being a good person doesn't mean much. Here in Russia, we are endlessly moved by good people and toss around the word 'good' on our lips, just as the Prussians do with the word 'duty' and the French with the word 'love.' The demonic force of fate cannot be understood or conquered through goodness."

"And God – is not God good?"

She sat up on the pillows, looking at his narrow lips with eager anticipation.

"God is all-good, all-wise, all-powerful. And that, I believe, means much more."

She sank back into the pillows.

"Let me sleep..." She turned her head toward the wall: "You make me tired when you're so clever."

She turned her head back again: "Prince – I may not live much longer. The birth of this little wild creature, he weighed fifteen pounds and caused me great difficulty even before he arrived, has left me deeply weakened. I've given him all my blood. He has drained me dry like a little vampire. I have named you in my will as regent, Prince. Take care of my three children. Ivan, the Tsar, is a fool. Play hopscotch with him, and if you confuse the tree, you confuse the soul. As for Peter, I know nothing yet except that he will be very tempestuous. But since he's the youngest and has already caused me the most pain, I love him more than Ivan and Sofia combined. Above all, I entrust Sofia to you. She is sixteen and already a woman. You will love her – do not resist. I know you. And Sofia will be clever and vain enough to love you back. But she will need a firm hand."

She grasped the prince's delicate, elegant hand.

"I know this hand is small and slender. But whatever it has grasped, it holds tightly. Hold onto Sofia, hold onto Russia with that tiny hand."

The prince leaned over the bed and kissed Natalia Naryshkina lightly on the forehead.

Natalia Naryshkina drifted on a white evening cloud toward heaven. The cloud seemed to be a swan, like the one depicted on Peter's cradle. It majestically stirred its gentle wings. Its eyes gleamed like green emeralds.

The copper gates of heaven were wide open. At the entrance stood an angel in a sable fur coat, with a white lambskin hat on his head. He bowed, arms crossed over his chest like a serf. A sleigh harnessed to two winged white horses was already waiting to carry Natalia Naryshkina over the snowfields of heaven to HIM, who sits crystalline and bold like an iceberg on the North Star. His chair is made of lapis lazuli. His eyes are bright sapphires, his heart is a deep red ruby shining through his diamond chest. In the cool red light of his heart, everything melts and dissolves like snow in the spring wind: good and evil, hate and love, joy and sorrow.

Natalia Naryshkina wanted to open her lips. But He already knew everything she had done, thought, and willed. He regarded her intentions as fulfilled and her wrongdoings as never committed. That she had betrayed Alexei Mikhailovich – He did not hold it against her. That she had loved Prince Galitzine – He was glad and pleased about it. Fatherly, He drew her to his chest. How good it felt: this coolness after all the fever. This peace after all the restlessness.

Then she remembered the children.

With his stone hand, He parted the clouds: there she saw her three children down on Earth. Peter was sleeping in his cradle, his face twitching in his dream. Ivan lay in a doghouse, barking. Sofia was looking over Prince Galitzine's shoulder, who was thoughtfully working on a Latin mourning ode for the death of the incomparable Natalia Naryshkina. He marked the rhythm of the verses with a goose quill: "These are dactyls. Or would it be better to choose anapests instead: what do you think, Sofia?"

Sofia looked helplessly down at him. Dactyls? Anapests: what did they have to do with her? Were they serfs to be whipped, subjects to be commanded? Ah, dactyls, they flowed lightly and meaninglessly like the waves of the Volga.

"I think, Prince, dactyls suit poor Mama very well. She had something floating, something soaring about her, like these verses you just read to me, which I don't understand. By the way, I didn't understand Mama either. When I die, you can try using anapests for your mourning ode to me. They sound harsher, more masculine."

The prince: "Are you a man, Sofia?"

Sofia defiantly looked up at his forehead.

Peter was being wheeled past in his stroller.

He howled like a wolf.

The wet nurse shrugged apologetically: "He screams day and night and cannot be calmed."

Sofia glanced over at the prince: "Perhaps one day, I'll manage to silence him."

–

She walked away. The gravel crunched under her firm, resolute steps.

The prince watched her, deeply alarmed.

"This child has terrible plans. Will I be able to tame him?"

He looked up to the sky, where Natalia Naryshkina lay at the breast of God, gazing down at him.

"Help me, holy Natalia!"

A tear dropped from her eye.

It began to rain over Preobrazhenskoe.

After two years, Peter suddenly becomes paralyzed. His legs had to be braced with splints.

The old coachman Potapov shook his head gravely. He felt just like Ilya, the mighty son of peasant Ivan, the hero of Kiev. For thirty years, he could not move, neither hands nor feet, sitting motionless in one spot. Until one day, a foreign pilgrim approached him and said, "Get up!" – then he could stand – "Go!" – then he could walk. "Take this sword and fight the brood of dragons and serpents!" And he gave him the sword that the angel Gabriel once wielded against Lucifer. "Fight with it! But never reveal your name to your enemies. Show your face, but hide your heart beneath an iron breastplate. Only the defeated reveal their name. Only a fool shows their heart. The hero fights nameless and heartless. Whoever calls upon the name of his God before his enemies surrenders himself."

Thus spoke the old coachman Potapov.

"Peter may remain peacefully paralyzed for thirty years. I am not afraid for him."

Peter recovered just as suddenly as he had fallen ill. And while he had once been a frail, delicate child, he now grew into a young bear, wrestling with Potapov's wolf. On one occasion, Potapov had to rescue the wolf from Peter's grasp – otherwise, Peter would have bitten its throat. In contrast, Prince Galitzyn once saved Peter from serious danger by sheer luck. He came upon the foolish Ivan standing over Peter's bed as the boy slept, holding a dagger in his hand. The prince wrested the knife from him and examined it closely. Furrowing his brow, he slid his glasses off his nose, as he always did when deep in thought. At last, he remembered where he had seen the dagger before – in Sofia's hands. She had played with it, even pressing it teasingly to his chest.

"Did you steal the knife from Sofia?" the prince asked.

"No," replied the idiot with a malicious glare. "Sofia gave me the knife, so you have no right to take it from me."

"Get out of here," shouted the prince. He trembled with excitement, and his glasses clattered onto the mosaic floor, which depicted the last emperor of Byzantium.

The idiot slunk away with his head bowed. At the door, he stuck out his tongue once more.

The prince went in search of Sofia. He found her in the courtyard as she was just returning from her afternoon ride. She jumped off the horse, tossed him the reins, slapped the animal lightly with her hand, and let the stallion trot back to the stable on its own.

She lightly struck the prince with her riding crop across the shoulder.

He flinched. His soft, childlike face tried to stiffen into a masculine expression. "Stop playing games, Sofia."

"Oh, that wasn't a game at all, Andrei. I struck you because I love you. Do you love me too?"

She pursed her lips like a dormouse and seemed to publicly challenge him to a kiss right there in the courtyard.

The prince grew irritated.

"Yes, I love you too. Ardently, passionately. But not to the extent of indulging the madness you seem to have in mind."

He pulled the dagger from his pocket: "Do you recognize this knife?"

Sofia turned slightly pale: "Show me. – Certainly. It usually lies on my bedside table for my personal protection. Someone must have taken it from me."

"Don't lie, Sofia."

Sofia gritted her teeth. She stamped her foot.

"You've chosen a strange cavalier, one not worthy of you, Sofia. He tried to defend you in a peculiar way. What were you thinking, Sofia?"

Sofia loosened her jaw. She scratched the ground with her foot like a rooster searching for worms. Then she looked at the prince, her eyes flashing. He was startled by the intensity of her gaze.

"I love you, Andrei. You showed me love and life for the first time."

The prince stroked her right forearm, clad in a leather glove.

"Perhaps, Sofia. But more than me, you love something else: power."

"Yes," Sofia exclaimed joyfully, "yes, I love power. I want to rule. I want to be Tsarina. You shall become Tsar. The fool doesn't concern us. But Peter stands in our way. Let him be killed, Andrei, kill Peter!"

She had collapsed before him in tears, clinging to his knees, pleading.

Ivan's mental illness had been declared incurable by a consortium of European doctors. A decree from the Regent, Prince Galitzyn, proclaimed this to the people. However, the people saw it only as the scheme of a court faction and refused to believe in Ivan's madness. Sometimes, the eighteen-year-old was seen walking thoughtfully and dreamily behind the garden gates in the park of Preobrazhensk. He wore an unnaturally pale, angelically beautiful face above a stiffened white collar. The more his mind deteriorated, the gentler his formerly wild manners became, and in the end, even the entire male and female servant staff of the castle, who had once mocked or despised him, fell in love with him.

"You see," said Prince Galitzyn, "how you have deceived yourself, my love. The fool is a much more dangerous rival for you than that surly fellow Peter. Perhaps the idiot is even smarter than the sensible Peter. Perhaps even smarter than us. Who knows? What shall we do with Peter now? It's a pity he wasn't born a peasant."

"Well," Sofia said somewhat slyly, playing with an amber necklace that hung around her neck, a gift from the prince, "let's raise him as a peasant. That will be healthiest for him and do him the most good. What does he, as the future Tsar, really need to learn? I didn't learn anything, and I govern quite acceptably."

"Well, well," the prince smiled, "shouldn't this be resolved so smoothly because I've learned a thing or two? The future Tsar must at least learn to read and write. What else would Europe, whose eyes are expectantly fixed on us, think of us?"

The prince struck a jokingly grandiloquent tone.

Sofia furrowed her brow: "Oh, Europe. Its eyes are not on us at all. For it is a blind, old hen. Yes," she repeated as the prince burst out laughing, "Europe is a blind, old hen. – Kiss me, Andrei."

"And Russia?" he kissed her gently on her unnaturally red lips – "what kind of bird is Russia then?"

"An eagle!" – Sofia spread her arms wide like a bird of prey spreading its wings before it swoops down on its prey.

The prince, half to himself: "Even a young eagle like Peter must learn something: not to fall out of the nest, to hover calmly and securely, to recognize the enemy from afar, to face death in battle, and not to fear the sacrificial death for his kin. He will have to be taught that."

Sofia reluctantly lowered her arms.

"What is it with you and Peter? I believe you love him, not me. So teach me to fly!"

She flew to his chest.

The retired Prussian lieutenant Felix Timmermann was assigned to young Peter as governor. Peter learned rudimentary reading and writing, and stammered in German. He never achieved an orthographically correct style. Arithmetic and geometry were easier for him. In these, Timmermann, a gifted mathematician, was better able to guide him. However, his favorite subjects were military science, navigation, and history, subjects Timmermann himself only mastered moderately well. But again and again, Timmermann had to tell him stories of Hannibal, Caesar, and Alexander the Great. Timmermann, whose knowledge was based on very weak foundations, embellished the biographies of his heroes with his own garish and fantastical ingredients when he saw how his pupil was inspired by them. Alexander the Great, who would have been more deserving of the title "Alexander the Monstrous," in Timmermann's lesson reached far beyond India and China, all the way to an imaginary land where the previously undefeated people of the Giants lived. Alexander personally slew seven thousand giants and, after defeating their king in single combat like a wild boar, married the giant king's daughter, who later killed him on their wedding night with a poison-dipped shirt in revenge for the destruction of her people. Good old Timmermann found himself unthinkingly swept up in the Hercules legend.

But Peter's eyes shone, and his cheeks glowed.

"And?" he asked passionately – "and?" And the good-hearted Timmermann escalated to ever more colossal heroic tales.

Fog lay over Preobraschensk, which Peter now inhabited alone with a small court. Regent Sofia and the imperial regent, Prince Galitzyn, had moved into the city palace in Moscow.

Peter stared out into the autumn. He had become a clumsy lad, unsure where to place his limbs. Sofia and Galitzyn had let him grow wild.

He ground his teeth. Oh, he felt it very clearly; he instinctively knew of his sister Sofia's hatred. He would thwart them when they least expected it. Their plans and his: they didn't add up the same way. They only added. But he wanted to multiply, yes, to raise to a power. He wanted to elevate his abilities to the nth degree. Even if they didn't want that and worked against him: he wanted to make something of himself like Caesar and Alexander the Great. One day they would call him Peter the Great. They would only be Sofia the Small and Galitzyn the Tiny. Alexander had fought giants. Were Sofia and Galitzyn giants? Bah: they were dwarfs, and he stretched his limbs, determined to deal with them.

The bare trees outside in the autumn fog waved their branches like arms. They seemed like skeletons moving in a dance. The wind whistled to them to dance.

Peter pressed his broad, red face flat against the glass: this tree wouldn't be so bad for Galitzyn – and that one for Sofia. If I don't hang them, they will hang me. That's the way of the world. Did Alexander hesitate when he personally beheaded seven thousand enemies?

Peter raised his right arm like a sword when Timmermann stuck his head in through the door.

"Come closer, Timmermann; I don't intend to chop off your head. What do you want?"

Timmermann had two sabers under his arm.

"Come, Prince. We shall begin fencing today. Let's go to the upper hall."

A few French tailors arrived from the capital. Peter was very surprised. Prince Galitzyn had sent them. They took his measurements for splendid and magnificent ceremonial garments made of silk, damask, and satin, and when he asked them for an explanation, they could only shrug their shoulders. His Highness the Prince had deigned to give them this commission. To what end and why – they regretted that they could not provide an answer, as they knew none. Soon, a German shoemaker also appeared, fitting him for fine suede shoes.

Timmermann proved to be disoriented. Peter had various suspicions, none of which satisfied him. Was he to be officially introduced at a court celebration?

The tailors returned for another fitting and, after admiring their own work with many delighted "ahs" and "ohs," left.

One day, Prince Galitzyn arrived in grand style. He chose the finest and most magnificent garment made of gold brocade and had it put on Peter immediately.

He walked around him several times, examining him.

Like the executioner with his victim, Peter thought. What does he have planned for me?

Then the prince ordered him to get into the carriage. Timmermann, also in full uniform, sat in the back. Potapov drove.

Now I am driving Ilya, the great hero of Kiev. Hail! Show your face, but hide your heart under the golden brocade. The journey begins. Good luck!

In the Moscow Kremlin, Sofia welcomed him in white satin. She stood at the top of the grand staircase. He saw her for the first time in years. She descended the staircase. How beautiful she was! The prince helped him out of the carriage. Sofia bowed to him. He blushed, was confused, and didn't know what to say.

They drove in a silver state carriage to the Metropolitan Church. Adrian, the Patriarch, received him, consecrated, and blessed him. Ivan had died. Peter was proclaimed the Tsar at sixteen.

He stood in the bright midday sunlight on the terrace in front of the church and looked down at the surging crowd, which incessantly threw hats, flowers, scarves, jackets, and handkerchiefs into the air and shouted: "Long live Tsar Peter!"

Sofia took his hand and led him to the front of the platform.

Then he suddenly became aware of her.

He tore himself away from Sofia, jumped onto the platform, threw his fur hat into the air, and roared: "Long live Russia!"

Sofia staggered back. The prince swayed his bird-like head from side to side. The Patriarch held his hands folded in prayer. The crowd roared and raged with jubilation. This crowd decided to get to know Peter.

Secretly, at times, he slipped away from Preobrazhensk, dressed as a gardener's boy.

He mingled among peasants, traders, workers, and foreign sailors. He learned from them how to drink and brawl, curse, and seek God and the Devil. He was as strong as a bear. People were reluctant to engage with him.

He got to know the women.

His first lover was a dirty brown gypsy girl who told his fortune from his palm.

"Little brother," she said with a laugh, "you've given me a silver ruble, but I must still tell you the truth: you will one day become a great criminal, a great robber like Stenka Razin, a great murderer like Ivan the Terrible. Yes, little brother, you will even be a murderer. Think of me when that time comes. Poor little Peter, they will one day call you 'Peter the Terrible, Peter the Possessed.' For you are possessed by all good and evil demons, by the holy and unholy spirit, by God and the Devil."

His second love was a young, delicate, fifteen-year-old creature, the daughter of a distiller.

He loved her too intensely. She could not bear his love. She died from it.

Sofia gently caressed the prince's forehead.

"You're starting to get wrinkles, darling. You must do something for yourself, for you and your glory, before it's too late."

The prince adjusted his horn-rimmed glasses and closed the "Iliad" he had been reading.

"My dear child, thank you for your kind reminder of my advancing age: but I prefer to read about heroic deeds rather than engage in them myself. What should an old man like me do with war and military glory? Mars is just a misprint for Mors. I bask in your youth, in your glory. I think the youth should act."

Sofia did not relent.

"Down there in our empire lies the Crimea somewhere. A Khan, who is our subject and owes us tribute, is supposed to rebel against us. You must crush the uprising."

"A ridiculous idea, child. Let him rebel. Russia is so vast that we won't even notice. He or his successor will come to their senses again."

Sofia pouted: "You have no sense of heroism."

"Yes, child, yes, but not for pointless heroism."

"Then I shall go to war myself. Do you want to subject me to the hardships of a campaign?"

She twirled one of his forelocks.

"By the way, you're already getting white hairs, silvery-white hairs like a little lamb."

The prince sighed: "You won't give me any peace until the lamb is torn to pieces by the foxes of Crimea. Very well, I will convert the Tartars."

"Timmermann," said Peter, "today is Sunday, the Lord's day, not the day of the servants. I do not want to go to mass and see a filthy priest defile the holy vessels and the pure liturgy of Chrysostom. I do not want to kneel a hundred times, as the tale goes about my father Alexei, before the colorful icons. I want to stand upright before my God and say:

"Here is Peter, your son, Father. He wants to attempt to live and work in a way not unworthy of you. Listen, Timmermann: to work. Crossing oneself fifteen hundred times and standing in mass for three hours is not work. My dear Russian brothers consider idleness to be the most pleasing virtue to God. This laziness must be beaten out of them. Russia needs craftsmen who understand work of their hands and their souls. The nobility must finally learn something: to ride, to fight, to lead. Recently, my horse lost a shoe on the road. I could not find a blacksmith who could shoe it properly. I had to shoe it myself in a forge. This blacksmith then told the most amusing stories about God and the world over a glass of kvass that I doubled over with laughter. But shoeing a horse: he couldn't do that. Such are the Russians. They can do everything – except what they should and must be able to do. Our peasants don't know how to handle a harrow or a plow; they can't distinguish good soil from poor soil. They grow just enough for themselves and their families in good harvest years. When a bad harvest year comes, of course, they starve and perish, foolish and God-fearing. They sow grain in the woods and plant fruit trees in an oat field. Russia needs workers, workers, workers. But not those who are called such, but those who actually are. Twenty-six hours a day, everyone must work; otherwise, Russia won't rise. Russia needs a fleet and sailors who know how to lead it. The sea lies open before us. We must go to school with the Dutch, the English, and the Venetians. Russia needs an army, officers, and soldiers. Military service must be extended to all classes of the population. France and Prussia must be our models. The earth lies open before us. Now we have a ragtag bunch of armed men, of whom only a fraction carries old, rusty rifles that they don't even know how to use, while most have only clubs, scythes, and knives. Does anyone understand strategy? 'Charge!' is the battle cry in an emergency, with thousands falling uselessly as victims. There are plenty of people in Russia. But as many as we are, what can we do against Sweden? Against Poland? Against the Turks? The Persians? Yes, even against rebellious, poorly armed Tatars? Nothing, because we are nothing."

Peter had worked himself into a rage.

"My father drove the Jews out of the land. I consider that a grave mistake. They were the leaven in the Russian bread. They were like blowflies around us sluggish stallions. But that was as it should be. They didn't let us rest. At least, we struck out once in a while. Now we've forgotten even that and just doze off in the stable. Timmermann, even the Jews had their heroes. Today is Sunday. Read to me from their book of heroes, the Old Testament. Read to me about the Maccabees!"

Peter threw himself onto a polar bear skin on the floor and crossed his arms beneath his head.

Timmermann stood at the lectern like a preacher in the pulpit and read: "And

Judas Maccabeus came to his father's city. He donned his armor like a hero and protected his army with his sword. He was joyful like a lion, bold as a young, roaring lion when he hunts something. And he had luck and victory."

Then Peter sprang up and roared, sounding like a young lion. He roared so loudly that the horses in the stable and the serfs in the servants' quarters became restless and huddled their heads together.

And one person, an old man of many years, whispered: "If only he doesn't go mad like Ivan! Like Ivan the Terrible, like Ivan the Fool! Madness runs in the family, yes," and he nodded with his white head, "Madness and Tsardom: perhaps they are the same."

Then Potapov, the coachman, struck him on the mouth with a wooden spoon: "Even as a child he screamed day and night and could not be calmed down. No amount of rocking, singing, or lullabies helped. That's how Ilya, the hero of Kiev, roared. He will astonish us all. For Gabriel screamed like that when he swung the sword against Lucifer."

Peter entered the State Council at nineteen years of age. Sofia presided. She wanted to assert herself. He pushed her back into the chair.

He wore a small dagger on a silver belt, drew it, and nailed the document that Sofia held in her hands to the oak tabletop with a fist strike.

On the document, Sofia had signed: "Autocrat of all Russians."

"The document is invalid. I do not consent to this charade. Does Russia wish to be ruled by women forever – silence, Prince Galitzyn – making politics from the window of their heart chambers? But a window must be smashed in Russia's wall facing Europe. They have kept me artificially ignorant. But I am not so stupid as to not see through your intrigues, Sofia. Prince Galitzyn, the new Achilles – don't make me laugh. Just look at yourself in the mirror, Prince. The intended campaign against the Khans of the Tartars is a futile arabesque. It will fail because our nobles are arrogant and crude, our citizens cowardly and treacherous, and our peasants dull and foolish. But I still love them the most, for their stupidity has a holy naiveté about it. They are foolish, like goats and oxen and donkeys are foolish. The knights are all Don Quixotes who want to charge with their rusted lances inherited from a long line of ancestors against war-hardened, well-armed, savage peoples. Let us work modestly and humbly on the project that is to be called Russia, respecting the smallest action that brings progress, but cursing and laughing at the empty phrase, the empty head. Anyone who has an empty head can at least lend it as a drum."

"Which could easily turn into a stabbing or knifing incident, Prince. All sorts of things have happened in the world because of a single syllable. In ancient Byzantium, a poor devil was executed because of a single syllable. The emperor told his servants: Take that wretch away! But they misunderstood a syllable, which could be conveyed as: Cut off his head! – and they cut off his head – something that could not be undone. Think of that mistaken syllable, Prince!"

Peter lifted his head and turned it three or four times in different directions: "I disapprove of the campaign. I want nothing to do with it."

He left.

Sofia turned pale.

The gentlemen of the State Council stared after him, mouths agape.

Prince Galitzyn closed his eyes, for he felt dizzy.

All day long, a passage ran through his mind, one that Petrarch had once written to his friend Andreas of Mantua, lamenting over a single syllable: "A grave reproach is mine: for a syllable, though short, I used as if it were long."

The prince began to study the science of war. He delved into the battles of Hannibal, Caesar, and Prince Eugene. But he forgot that they had waged their battles with disciplined soldiers, not with a rabble hastily assembled and whipped into line.

He marched against the Tartars, but the expedition ended in miserable failure. The poorly armed, battle-inexperienced Russians fled from the crossbowmen and spearmen of the Tatars, despite their overwhelming numbers. Almost all their cannons were captured. Since the Russians lacked enough trained artillery personnel, the cannons had not even been brought into action. A single cannon had been fired – backwards. It tore apart its own gunners.

To calm Sofia, the prince sent the most fantastical victory reports to Moscow. Who could verify their truth? No one.

"The entire plain is densely strewn with corpses like the sky with stars," he wrote to Sofia. He omitted that these were the corpses of Russians. – "We have triumphed, the enemy's fortress has been taken, the Khan is captured, the rebels are punished."

Sofia ordered all the bells in Moscow to ring.

Prince Galitzyn made a grand entrance as the triumphant conqueror over the Crimean Cossacks and Tartars. The victorious troops he needed for the entrance were assembled just outside Moscow. Not a single one of them had fought in the Crimea. The dishonorable Crimean warriors had perished, taken down by Tartar arrows, hunger, and pestilence.

Only gradually did the truth seep through.

Peter learned it from his coachman Potapov. Potapov had a nephew in the Crimean expedition who had escaped with his life.

Sofia never learned the truth. She had bronze plaques engraved with the names of the gloriously fallen and placed in Moscow's cathedral: a memorial to the unforgettable Crimean campaign that had enwreathed the ever-victorious Russian arms with fresh, undying laurels.

Peter summoned Potapov's nephew and secretly conversed with him. He was a young, slender, exceptionally handsome man, a pierogi baker by trade, and his name was Menschikov.

Peter pulled him behind a lilac bush. He drew him close and kissed him.

"What is your first name?"

"Alexander."

"Like Alexander the Great. I will make you great like him, so that you too shall be called Alexander the Great. Stay with me. Be my friend. I love you."

The young eighteen-year-old was a bit confused by the unexpected display of affection from the young Tsar. But he reciprocated his tenderness.

Later, he had to give him an unvarnished account of the so-called Crimean campaign.

When Prince Galitzyn, the celebrated commander of the Crimean War, sought an official audience with the Tsar to personally report to him, Peter refused to receive him. He sent Menschikov, whom he had appointed as his chamberlain, to him with a message that he graciously declined his report. The flying wanderer to the moon had already visited him and recounted his journey and how one reaches the moon—namely, by gathering a thousand birds and tying oneself to them. As for himself, Pyotr was sufficiently informed about the conditions on the moon, and those in Crimea, which presumably were not much different, no longer interested him.

Peter selected a thousand strong and intelligent boys from the vicinity of Pre-obraschensk and began to drill with them on his own initiative. He had obtained a Prussian drill manual through Timmermann and followed it. He made the thousand swear loyalty to him until death. He appointed Menschikov, whose extraordinary beauty was accompanied by great intelligence, as his adjutant. Menschikov participated in the instruction given to him by the German Timmermann, as well as the Frenchman Lefort and the Italian Fresini. He even slept in the same room with Peter at night. And the kitchen maid Feodorowna, a plump and pretty girl, they both shared together.

The Streltsy, the old tsarist guard, upon learning of the formation of Peter's personal guard, sent a delegation from Moscow to Preobraschensk.

"Dismiss your personal guard, Father!" urged Colonel Zickler. "It will grow beyond your control and cause you serious trouble. If you need personal protection, aren't we here to protect you, Father?"

God protect me from my friends, who are also the friends of Sofia and Prince Galitzyn, the illustrious warrior of the Crimean War, the new Achilles! thought Peter.

He had his personal guard, led by Menschikov, march past the Streltsy colonel, who twirled his pointed beard and looking sourly at the cloud of dust stirred up by the parade march. This rough fellow knew how to maintain discipline. Impressive! He envied him for his thousand men and thought, with mixed feelings, of his own Streltsy regiment, whose main activities consisted of drinking, whoring, and gambling, and whose officers could hardly tell a crossbow from a pistol.

Peter had the delegation treated to cabbage, porridge, fish, and mead, then sent them back to Moscow without giving them an answer.

Just as they were almost out of earshot, he fired a pistol into the air and shouted after the colonel, cupping his hands around his mouth: "Greetings to Sofia!"

It was past midnight when Sofia crept through the eerie corridors of the Kremlin to Prince Galitzyn's chamber.

She sat on the edge of his bed.

He had a French bed sent from Paris, complete with French linens.

He sat up in his silk nightgown, embroidered with colorful animals, swans, wolves, and foxes.

Tapestries hung on the walls, depicting scenes from the love lives of Greek gods: Leda with the swan, Zeus and Europa, Cupid and Psyche.

Sofia kissed the prince on the forehead.

"I can't sleep."

"Why not, little dove?"

She stamped her foot again, just as she had once done in the courtyard of Pre-obraschensk.

"I can't sleep as long as Peter robs me of my rest. One of us has to yield. For now, I am still regent. The Streltsy are on my side. And you?"

The prince silently kissed her hand. He thought of the insult Peter had dealt him in the council meeting and later, when he had refused to receive him after the Crimean campaign.

Sofia made her soft leather slippers dance on the tips of her toes.

"I will stay in the background. The Streltsy will march on Preobraschensk. His so-called personal guard will flee at the first shot."

"Are you so convinced of that?"

"I am, and Colonel Zickler is too. The Tsar has made himself unpopular with his western ways, his inclination toward reforms, and his associations with for-eigners. Russia wants to sleep and dream. He is trying to wake it. Children who are startled from sleep become irritable. It will be easy to incite the masses against him. They will strike him down. No one will be the culprit. I will rule forever."

Meanwhile, Peter was busy in the park of Preobraschensk, practicing as a bom-bardier. He had a cannon of the latest French design set up under the poplars and was firing into the landscape. Branches splintered, and chickens flew up squawk-ing.

He was blackened with gunpowder smoke. Just then, a monk came walking down the gravel path. No one had announced his arrival. Only Potapov had seen him and let him pass in silence.

The foreign pilgrim comes to Ilya, the hero of Kiev! His great hour has struck.

Peter turned around: "What do you want, monk?"

The monk stepped closer. His eyes shone with authority. He raised the cross.

Peter kissed it.

"Take a seat, holy father –"

And he gestured to the gun carriage.

The monk shook his head.

"Petruschka" – and his voice took on a gentle tone, as if it were anointed and oiled – "Petruschka, what do you see in my eyes?"

Peter looked up.

"Tears," he said softly.

"Yes, tears – tears for you, tears for our beloved Russia. What are you doing, what are you allowing to be done to you? You squander your young life on foolish trivialities: mock wars and dog weddings. You fire shots into the air here and think that God will answer you with thunder. But He sits on His throne of lapis lazuli and does not hear the brazen noise because He despises you. Seven pillars of precious stone are placed around Him: chalcedony, the pillar of mercy; onyx, the pillar of purity; hyacinth, the pillar of humility; beryl, the pillar of wisdom; jasper, the pillar of love; amethyst, the pillar of hope; emerald, the pillar of faith. Is there a single pillar that, if you found it on Earth, you would not topple? You squander your finest feelings on harlots and catamites. Every night you're drunk like a beast, blaspheming God and His devout servants. Did you not recently boast before your drunken companions that you would depose the patriarch, the head of our holy church, from his God-ordained office and ascend the Holy See yourself? Did you not, in your drunkenness, perform a black mass and mock the sacred institutions in a drunken conclave with your harlots and catamites? Is not the Holy Trinity you worship named Vodka, Kvass, and Mead? And who governs the realm in the meantime? Corrupt clerks, vain boyars who flay the living flesh from their serfs and defile Russia's daughters as if they were dogs. Are you surprised, Petrushka, that the Streltsy have conspired against you? I wouldn't be, my son. Instead, I would learn even from my enemies – if they are in the right."

Peter threw the fuse onto the ground. It tore up some flowers and buried them deep in the earth.

"I thank you, dear father, for your good and well-intended advice. You have touched my heart and awakened my mind. I will hang the Streltsy in due time and strive to serve Russia more diligently than before. As thanks for your candor, I will give you a gift, monk."

The monk refused.

"But, pious father, you deserve that I be equally frank with you."

He stepped closer, swiftly pulling the monk's right hand from his cassock. A dagger clattered to the ground.

The monk turned pale.

Peter picked up the dagger.

He examined it. He pondered where he had seen it before. This ivory Venetian handle seemed familiar. Ah, right, with Sofia.

Peter smiled.

"I suspected the Streltsy and – well – that the Streltsy had sent you to murder me."

The monk closed his eyes, trying to look inward. But it was as dark as an underground cave.

He opened his eyes and still painfully felt the light and, in that light, the crude brute before him.

"What I did, I did of my own free will, demanded by no one, hired by no one. I did it from my heart, because that heart hates you and will hate you forever as long as it beats."

Peter barely listened.

"Very well. I will hang and quarter them, my loyal friends and protectors, the Streltsy, as soon as I have the power and opportunity. I will spare your life so you can foretell their fate to them. But you will not go unpunished. Take off your priestly robe. The holy garment must not be insulted and defiled."

The monk took off his robe.

Peter lifted his leather whip, which hung at his belt, and lashed it across the monk's bare back.

The monk stood upright and silent, not flinching a muscle.

When the blood began to flow, Peter paused. He helped the monk back into his cassock.

"Bless me, holy father."

And the beaten and tormented monk blessed him without bitterness or reservation.

"Go, dear father!"

And Peter awkwardly and tenderly patted his rough cheek.

"If I ever need a brave, honest priest, not a clergyman, I will have you summoned. What is your name?"

The monk bowed: "Golovin."

Peter invites Dutch and English sailors, French officers, German merchants, and craftsmen into the country. Refined people, good people, clever people, these Germans. They have manners and morals, slow, measured movements, and their passions are weighed against profits and losses. They dress in simple, plain attire, not in that garish raspberry red, poisonous green, and sulfur yellow like the colorful Russians. They are gray people, clad in their national colors: black and white. They also view the world in these colors. They know only black and white, day and night, good and evil, either/or. They deeply despise the both/and, the partly-this/partly-that of the Russians. In their world, everything presses toward clear decisions. No twilight, no veiling of realities as in Moscow during the long winter evenings. Craftsmen, blacksmiths, gardeners, painters – they are horrified by the clumsy wooden architecture of the churches with their onion-shaped domes. Did those accursed Jews teach you that architecture? It brings tears to one's eyes. Those temples are enough to make one weep. Just as well that you've chased the Jews to hell. Now we have them on our necks. In Germany. What are we to do with them, eh? Burn one or two as sorcerers, hang a few as usurers – but a hundred, a thousand, ten thousand?

At home, the Germans are dominated by Protestant sobriety and clear definitions. The houses of worship are built of stone, bare, unadorned, but durable, meant to last for half an eternity. These Russian painted wooden shacks, resembling carnival booths for jugglers, are laughable. When a storm comes, they will fly up to God along with their believers, if they haven't already splintered or rotted away. These Germans think they'll bring a bit of order to the chaos. Peace and order. That's what we're known and respected for in the world. Peace and order at any cost. Even at the cost of truth.

They are patriots, these Germans, and their mouths are full of boasting when they talk about Germany. By the way, they do so in French. Strange creatures, these Germans. They understand all the world's languages except their own.

Peter ordered his voivodes and boyars to send the most beautiful noble girl from each of the fifty governorates to Moscow. He lined them up in the white hall like soldiers. Then he paced down the row of beauties, stopping here and there, pinching one's cheeks or another on the breast, tugging on the blonde braid of one, and even kneeling on the ground to physically examine feet and ankles. He thinks of a stable full of mares. He sniffs the air. Eudoxia Lopukhina smells the best. He chooses her.

He held the wedding like a peasant. He personally inspected the rye sheaves that are to serve as the bedding for the bridal bed.

During the feast, consisting of pig's head in raspberry sauce and pheasant purée, Eudoxia was groomed at the table by two maidservants. They combed her magnificent blonde hair with golden combs and braided it into two plaits.

Peter himself, already slightly drunk, placed the bridal crown on her head, from which six strands of pearls hang down to her breasts.

"Drink," shouted Peter, "drink! You are doing a patriotic duty. Vodka is the monopoly of the Tsar."

Peter and Eudoxia stepped hand in hand onto the consecrated carpet.

The priest, also somewhat tipsy and supported by servants on either side to keep him from falling, blessed the illustrious couple.

Peter and Eudoxia drank from a single glass as a symbol of their newly established household.

The glass fell to the ground and shattered.

All the guests were shocked.

But Peter composed himself.

He stepped onto the shards: "So may it be for anyone who sows discord between us!"

Girls and women threw hemp and flax seeds at Peter and Eudoxia.

Before Eudoxia ascended into the bridal bed, she was bathed in milk and wine.

The next day, everyone had a hangover. Menshikov staggered. Timmermann couldn't see straight. The priest, who had been searched for in vain late at night, was dragged out unconscious from under the bridal bed.

Eudoxia looked very pale. Only Peter was lively and in good spirits.

He sat at a table laden with pickles and cold, peppered mutton. With this, he lifted a tankard of kvass.

He drank and ate, slapping his thighs with delight.

Then he took a hot bath.

Glowing stones were thrown into a tub. From the hot water, Peter leaps into the snow outside, rolling in it like a snow hare before diving back into the searing water.

The lake of Perejaslawel is covered with a layer of ice. Outside, behind the snow clouds, lay Peter's ship, the one he had sailed with during the summer, now frozen in place.

It was no larger than a big rowboat and was named: "Ivan the Terrible."

Peter stomps in high boots across the ice. He boards the ship.

Leaning his hot forehead against the icy mast, he stares into the snowstorm. He falls asleep standing up.

When he awoke, he could hardly move his fingers. They had frozen to the mast. Bleeding, he tore himself free.

He descends into the cabin.

There lay his notebooks filled with geometric and navigational calculations. He sits down before them and stares at the pages. He begins to doodle.

From the swirls emerges the lovely face of Eudoxia Lopukhina. He crosses it out with two strokes upon recognizing it.

Then he continues to draw: fantastic lines, borders, rivers, mountain ranges, seas: an imaginary Russia stretching far into China and from the Black Sea up to the White Sea, reaching as far as Finland.

I need ships, a hundred ships, a thousand ships, an entire fleet. I will build them; I must build them.

Poor little Ivan, you Terrible one, you instill no fear or terror in anyone.

The pond at Perejaslawel is no longer sufficient for Peter's pirate voyages.

He had "Ivan the Terrible" transported to Arkhangelsk.

The Dutch sailors called the old-fashioned tub "Ivan the Cripple" and swear that it won't make it a single nautical mile across the White Sea without miserably sinking, wobbling, or swaying.

Peter decides to visit the Solovetsky Monastery, located on an island, to pay homage to the relics of the saints buried there and offer them his reverence.

"Ivan the Terrible," swaying dreadfully back and forth like a drunken boatswain, barely makes it to the small island harbor.

On the return journey, a storm sets in. "Ivan the Terrible" spins like a carousel. Peter is desperate. He falls to his knees. He weeps. He beats the sailors. He kisses them. He prays.

He promises the Lord Jesus Christ a cross if he is saved from drowning. He promises to appoint Him as Russian rear admiral.

"Ivan the Terrible" is cast ashore by the surf and crashes against a rock.

Peter and the sailors are washed up on the shore like dead fish.

Peter carves a wooden cross with his own hands and places it at Unskaya Bay, visible from far away to the sailors. In Dutch, he writes this inscription on the cross: *The cross made by Captain Peter, 1694 a.d.*

The summer nights of the North were blue, warm, and bright.

They had captured a ship with southern wine, rolled the barrels across the deck, drank, and sang.

Peter shouted at the moon. He brandished a sword, intending to skewer the moon with it.

Menshikov rolled over the deck like a hedgehog. Peter and Menshikov suddenly embraced each other and exchanged feminine pet names.

They decided to play tug-of-war.

Peter took command of one side, Menshikov of the other.

When the forces balanced out, they dropped the rope and started hitting each other with fists, axes, wooden beams, and spars. Blood flowed, and a young sailor was killed. He had been everyone's favorite and Menshikov's catamite. Menshikov wailed like a washerwoman. Suddenly, everyone was sober.

Four sailors took a sailcloth, rolled the corpse inside, and while a piece was undone and the crew saluted, they let him down into the sea with ropes.

Menshikov fainted into Peter's arms. Peter shook him off like a windblown tree shakes off a caterpillar.

When everyone was already asleep, Peter continued to drink alone. He sang until laughter stifled his voice:

> Lighting the pyre,
> Wheeling, beheading, hanging, sacking,
> Is a merry game for us.
> Cutting off noses and ears,
> That, too, happens with delight,
> But it's not given much attention.

Peter fought with the moon, insulted the stars, cursed heaven and earth until he lay on the ground like a sack.

The next morning, they had to pour buckets of seawater over him before he woke and came to his senses.

He called for the young sailor. They looked away and stood in awkward silence.

Then slowly, the memory crawled toward him like a damp snail.

He wiped his forehead, threw his head back until the sun burned his eyes, climbed up to the command bridge, cupped his hands to his mouth, and shouted to the entire flotilla: "Prepare for battle!"

The campaign is against Azov, against the red crescent, against the Kalmyks, Tatars, and Turks.

The Volga, Oka, and Don are dotted with small ships that float on them like duckweed. Songs ring out, bottles clink, and laughter echoes. At times, two ships rush at and ram each other. One or both capsize. Some people drown. No matter – Russia has plenty more where they came from. Others are fished out with roars of laughter. The journey continues. Downriver. Toward the sea. The sea that is still guarded by yapping hellhounds but will one day serve the Russian bear.

Azov holds firm.

The siege is carried out by Peter and Menshikov like a math problem in school. But it doesn't add up. They've miscalculated.

Peter learns that he can rely on no one but himself –and maybe Menshikov. While Peter stands night watch in the foremost trench, dozens of his soldiers desert from the rear. He is dealing with children playing at soldiers, who cry when it becomes bloody serious and start wailing at the first scratches. Many of his best men have already fallen. Menshikov considers a storming assault. He wants to fill the men with vodka to give them courage and then send them charging at the enemy. Peter rejects the plan. Grinding his teeth, he calls off the campaign. He is defeated before Azov, just as Prince Galitzyn was once defeated in Crimea.

Asov can only be taken from the sea. I was a fool when I trudged across the land. I need ships, regular warships. The noble families must contribute to the cost of twenty-four large warships, while the merchants must provide for the accompanying bomb sloops and fire ships. For the admiral's ship, Adrian, the patriarch, must give church decorations. Why do arrows and spears of pure gold stick in the body of Saint Sebastian? Why do red rubies burn in his wounds? Red glass would do just as well. And his tormentors are adorned with pearls and diamonds.

While the bells in Moscow ring out a *Te Deum*, in the shipyard of Voronezh, the sound of hammering and clattering shipbuilders resounds. Vast oak forests surround Voronezh, along with rich iron mines.

Peter himself fells trees, planes, hammers, and forges iron.

In May of the following year, the fleet is launched, manned in part by Dutch and Germans.

No singing, no clinking of bottles, no laughter as the fleet sets out again for Azov.

Ghost ships silently sail through the fog.

Peter stands at the bow of his flagship, the "Ivan," in a blue sailor's shirt.

"Jesus Christ, I did not appoint You as admiral of my fleet for nothing. Now show what You can do. Help me and all true believers against the pagan Ottomans. Place Azov into my hands, and I will nail it to the cross as You were once nailed to the cross."

Azov fell in July 1696.

The Khan and his two top generals were crucified by Peter, like Christ and the two thieves.

Peter himself performed the Ordeal of the Spear on them.

To the terror of the Turks, a Russian warship with an envoy on a special mission appeared before Constantinople.

Peter had a seal made with the inscription: "I know nothing. I can do nothing. I want to know everything. I want to be able to do everything. Whoever teaches me is welcome."

Europe shall teach me. And there is much to be arranged and rectified in and through Europe. Shouldn't there be European solidarity against Asia? An alliance with Venice and the Habsburgs against Tatars, Turks, and Persians?

Peter's journey through the continent aroused Europe's keenest interest. For the first time, the fabled barbarians of the Volga and Valdai became visible. The journey sometimes resembled a Greek tragedy: evoking fear and terror, sometimes a Molièresque comedy, which could have been titled "The Grand Duke on Tour," sometimes an Italian masquerade, and at other times a coarse Brueghelian peasant farce.

The Russians wore towering fur hats and the thickest furs, even in the hottest summer. They lugged countless, heavy icons of saints with them, before which they performed devotions at every moment. They crossed themselves at every opportunity, three times, and this crossing soon became a comical fashion in Europe at that time. All of Europe was crossing itself – not least in front of the Russians themselves. At banquets, they behaved extremely crudely. They took the meat from the dishes with their hands, skewered it on forks, and only then brought the forks to their mouths. Most of them were unfamiliar with the use of beds. When beds were provided, they threw out the mattresses and slept on the bare floor within the bed frames. The Russians were not overly concerned with the lives of others. Anyone who offended them, even slightly, was immediately threatened with death, though this threat, or even the killing, did not seem to be meant too seriously. There were plenty of people in the world. One more or less: it doesn't matter.

The Russians proved to be shabby, stingy, and exceedingly miserly with the gifts they brought. While they were received splendidly everywhere and lacked for nothing, they expressed their thanks with a few pounds of rhubarb, of which they carried many hundredweight, and a few black fox and sable furs worth only a few rubles. An ermine fur: that was something special and a great exception. Peter only gave it away twice: to the Queen of Holland and to a charcoal-burner girl in the Harz mountains who was willing to be with him.

Peter sometimes traveled incognito as Peter Alexeyevich Mikhailov.

In Riga, he acted foolishly in order to inspect the Swedish fortifications, but was caught spying by the governor himself and chased away.

Grumbling angrily, he said: "I'll have a bone to pick with these Swedes yet."

In Königsberg, he meets the Prussian Elector and trains as an artillery master.

He compliments the Electress in such a manner that she blushes all over in embarrassment and doesn't know how to help herself, except by fainting.

That same evening, he sat with the philosopher Leibniz. He regarded him from all sides, like a monkey performing tricks: saluting, drumming, cracking nuts. He pulled off his periwig and placed it on his own head.

"A philosopher must have a free head when he thinks and speaks."

He had a huge bottle of schnapps standing in front of him: "Drink, Leibniz!"

Leibniz didn't drink.

"You don't want to thin your blood?"

"At your command, Majesty."

"What does that mean: at your command? Can a philosopher be commanded? His thoughts, for example? For what is the special quality of a philosopher? His thoughts, surely?"

"Indeed."

"Well – can they be commanded like serfs? They belong to the soul, don't they?"

Leibniz nervously turned his empty glass in the candlelight.

"The discipline of thought must be as disciplined as the Prussians."

The Tsar burst out laughing: "Tied in a Russian knot, Leibniz, tied in a Russian knot! As for philosophy, I will only say this: I saw it tended by the greatest minds of all times and countries, and yet, to this day, there is not a single point that is not disputed and thus doubtful and uncertain. Descartes said that, another great philosopher. Cheers!"

In Berlin, a court ball was held in honor of the Tsar.

The Elector of Brandenburg commanded the polonaise. The Tsar led the Duchess of Mecklenburg, a tender blonde. When the polonaise dissolved in the Hall of Mirrors, the Tsar and his dance partner were nowhere to be found.

He had pulled her into a side chamber and assaulted her behind a curtain. And he was so strong that she could neither resist nor wanted to.

Then he left her.

Still gasping for breath, she remained in the darkness behind the curtain. A shiver ran through her.

She didn't dare step into the light.

She opened the window behind her, it was on the ground floor, and climbed out.

The window faced the Spree River.

A small boat rocked gently on the waves.

She sat in the boat and looked down into the water.

Death is just as black, and just as wet.

Silently, she slid from the bow into the river and sank. Pike swirled around her, along with perch and sticklebacks.

But the Tsar had long since forgotten her.

He lay in his room, dirty boots in the damask bed, thinking about how he could play the Prussians against the Poles and Swedes. On a console above the fireplace, a pair of porcelain lovers twirled in a minuet. He threw copper coins at them until they shattered with a crash.

Then he fell asleep and dreamed of a field mouse. It had a face like the Duchess of Mecklenburg and whistled softly.

He bit off its head and tossed the small corpse into the field.

Ravens, sitting on a bare willow stump, flapped and cawed as they came down and devoured it.

Two days later, the Tsar climbed through the Ilse valley and past the snow holes at the Ilse Falls to the top of the Brocken.

The sun was shining. The birds were singing. The Ilse River was rushing.

Overwhelmed by an infinite feeling of happiness, the Tsar sank into the grass below the Brocken summit.

Below him lay the vast land, the German land, Russia, beneath him the whole Earth, and even the sky still far beneath him.

Such a mountain should be in Russia. If I could move mountains, I would have faith. From the Russian plain, the mountain should rise. But it is as flat as my thoughts and dreams.

The Tsar spent the night in a charcoal burner's hut. The charcoal burner's daughter helped him take off his high boots.

In Holland, Peter begins work in the shipyard of the East India Company as a shipyard worker. He wants to serve from the ground up. Klaas Wilemzoon teaches him to climb the yards, loosen sails, and heave to.

He spends his free time with the anatomist Boerhaave at the anatomy school. He dissects corpses, assists in surgeries, and eventually learns to operate himself.

One day, a corpse of a young Javanese woman is brought to him for dissection. He throws the knife from his hand and bursts into tears. He falls into a wild passion for the beautiful dead woman, has her mummified, and later takes her with him to Russia.

While he sits in the crow's nest or trepans a dead child, a large woolen doll holds an audience in his place at his apartment.

The Dutch Jews, who had been driven out of Russia by his father, petitioned for permission to return.

The doll remains silent.

With flowing kaftans, like mourning birds, the Jews depart.

It caused offense that the Russians, in broad daylight, had dancers and enticing, easily seduced girls from music halls and brothels come to them, and didn't hesitate to walk with them across the street.

Peter himself did not fuss much when it came to geese or birds of any kind.

He addressed every woman who caught his eye on the street in Russian. If she didn't understand him or didn't want to understand him, he would smile and show her a Russian gold ruble: his usual, imperial fee – a coin bearing his image. He gladly gave this portrait to young, pretty girls if they showed him favor. And they preferred it more than if it had been painted by Frans Hals. One day, Peter saw a young net weaver at the Amsterdam harbor. He wanted to buy her from her father. He was quite astonished when it was explained to him that in Western Europe, women were not commodities and could not be sold like serfs. He kindly remarked that, in general, he was very much in favor of Western reforms and had already implemented many in his country, but as for the question of women's emancipation, he would have to consider it carefully.

The reports Peter sent back to Russia were mere fabrications, embellished for the people and the court, brightly painted and exaggerated. He knew what he could and must present to his Russians in order to maintain their respect for him. Among other things, he had written that Amsterdam had three million inhabitants and was considerably closer to the sun and moon than Moscow. Each of the inhabitants had three eyes: two that looked into the present, but one that saw into the future. The eye that saw into the future had predicted war, victory, and glory for Russia. The greatest sights he had encountered on his journey, and which he intended to bring back to his people – having purchased them for one hundred ermine pelts – were: the knife with which his holy namesake Peter cut off Malchus' ear, a piece of Christ's crown of thorns, with the dried blood of the Son of Heaven still visible on the thorns, a painting of the Madonna made by the Evangelist Luke himself, a fig leaf from Mother Eve, and the hem of Joseph's coat, which remained in Madame Potiphar's hands during his heroic escape.

When the Russians left the houses made available to them in Amsterdam, no one could live in them for weeks after their departure. They looked like pigsties.

Peter had gotten thoroughly drunk at a banquet in Vienna when news of the open rebellion of the Streltsy reached him.

He had a bucket of water poured over his head and became completely sober.

He succeeded in securing a three-year alliance with the Emperor and Venice against the Turks and obtained a declaration of neutrality in the event that Russia became involved in European conflicts. Then he departed secretly.

He traveled through Warsaw, where he had a secret meeting with King Augustus the Strong of Poland, which led to an alliance against Sweden.

Peter sped across the night steppe in a sleigh. The moon sprinkled the snow with green, opalescent light.

Peter cracked the whip.

The horse's coat was streaked with red. Its flanks rose and fell like the waves of the sea.

Peter was breathing heavily.

I cannot arrive too late. Everything is at stake. My life, Russia. Run, little horse, run as fast as you can.

The tormented animal looked back several times during its desperate gallop. It begged for mercy and compassion. Peter covered his face with his hand. He couldn't bear to look into the horse's eyes.

I must not have pity on it. Neither on it nor on myself.

First distant, then closer and closer, came the hoarse barking of hungry wolves.

Peter looked back.

Well, here come my wild brothers.

Black shadows darted across the green snow.

The horse, too, had heard the barking.

With a final burst of desperation, it raised itself. Its nostrils trembled. It ran for another half-mile, then blood gushed from its mouth. It collapsed, just a few kilometers from Preobrazhensk.

A curse escaped Peter's lips. The wolves had come within a hundred meters.

I must reach Preobrazhensk, Lord in heaven, I, the lord on earth, must.

He drew his pistol and removed the reins from the horse.

One last slap on the steaming flanks.

Good animal, thank you.

The wolves had reached him. They smelled the fresh blood. Their dark green eyes glared at Peter with hatred.

Peter retreated twenty, thirty steps.

The wolves greedily fell upon the half-dead horse, which twitched under their teeth.

They had almost devoured it down to the bone when the reins, twisted into a lasso, flew through the air.

Two of the wolves got entangled in the loop. The others scattered. Having satisfied their hunger, they cowardly abandoned their comrades.

Peter approached with the whip. He managed to harness the raging beasts to the sleigh.

He cracked the whip.

With a wolf-drawn sleigh, Peter entered Preobrazhensk in the early morning.

The people who saw him crossed themselves.

"The wolf's son is back," they shouted.

In the courtyard of the palace stood a regiment of the rebellious Streltsy. A shiver of terror ran through their ranks when they saw the wolf-drawn sleigh enter through the wooden gate.

Peter jumped out of the sleigh and cracked the whip through the icy air: "On your knees, you dogs!"

The entire regiment wordlessly fell to their knees.

He walked through the rows, tapping this man and that with the handle of his whip.

"You will be hanged, and you, and you."

"The regiment will rehabilitate itself by hanging every tenth man from among you."

So, they hanged their own comrades, who let themselves be hanged in silence, without resistance.

A delegation of boyars approached him:

"Show us Ivan, where is Ivan, the true tsar? He is the holy sovereign. He has not died. You keep him imprisoned in the palace. He is still alive. Where is he?"

Peter motioned for the delegation to follow him.

They walked through dark corridors. Doors opened and closed on their own. Suddenly, a heavy oak door swung open.

A chapel-like room became visible, with colored lights playing through stained-glass windows.

In the back sat Ivan on a wooden throne, pale, delicate, elegant, with his insane smile on his lips.

The boyars fell to their knees. Tears filled their eyes: "Our Tsar! Our father! Hail!"

One of them crawled to the throne, sliding on wounded knees to kiss his foot. His mouth drooled.

He reached for the foot.

The worm-eaten bark peeled away.

The boyar let out a scream.

On the throne sat the mummy of Ivan the Fool.

Peter motioned to the delegation once again.

They slunk after him with their heads bowed.

He had a gardener bring him large garden shears, the kind used for trimming bushes, and personally cut off their beards, the symbol of the boyar nobility.

Red blood flows on Red Square in front of St. Basil's Cathedral in Moscow.

Peter stands on the scaffold next to the executioner, looking each traitor in the face.

"Who are you? What's your name? Do you believe in God? Why didn't you believe in me? Off with his head."

A head rolls to his feet, one that seems familiar to him. He grabs the black woolly hair and pulls it up. It's Colonel Zickler. A pity. He should have been spared. He had a sense of humor. But the sword doesn't think about whom it kills. When killing, you mustn't think at all, or else you won't get to it – or you'll be killed yourself. Of all the creatures in this world, one devours the other. If astrologers and astronomers are to be believed, the stars themselves devour each other with fiery mouths. The key is to have the biggest mouth and be the creature that devours. That is the meaning of life.

Sofia, veiled, falls before him: "Mercy for Prince Galitzyn!"

"Sofia, little dove, I had completely forgotten about you – how nice that you've reminded me of your existence. Still alive, are you? A dreadful mass dying has begun. For whom are you pleading, your lover?"

"Sofia!"

"Your Majesty," – Sofia bows her beautiful head. He strokes her hair.

"Be honest!"

A shame she was born my sister. She would have made the perfect woman for me. How beautiful she still is.

Peter signals to the executioner: "Prince Galitzyn is granted clemency – to run the gauntlet."

Tears stream down Sofia's cheeks.

"Don't cry, little dove. Don't cloud those clear eyes of yours. Don't ruffle your white feathers."

Prince Galitzyn collapses dead in the middle of the gauntlet, a verse from Homer on his lips.

Sofia screams: "Are you still a human being? Did Natalia Naryshkina give birth to you? Are you not a wild wolf? The Antichrist, whom the people whisper about?"

The Bashkirs and Cossacks had risen up along the borders, joining the Streltsy. Golovin, the militant monk, had incited them: for the Holy Crusade. He stood on a hill, his pale, ascetic face waving like a silver flag, preaching to the people who were gathered around him in terraces: "And I stood upon the sand of the sea and saw a beast rise up out of the sea, having seven heads and ten horns, and upon his horns ten crowns, and upon his heads the name of blasphemy. And the beast which I saw was like a leopard, and its feet were like the feet of a bear, and its mouth was the mouth of a lion. And the dragon gave it his power and great authority. And the whole earth marveled at the beast. Who is like the beast? And who can fight with it? And there was given unto it a mouth, speaking great blasphemies. And it opened its mouth to blaspheme against God and against those who dwell in heaven. And it was given to it to make war with the saints and to overcome them. At its birth, fire fell from heaven, and the rivers overflowed their banks. The poisonous foxglove bloomed and swelled in the middle of winter on the Valdai. Do you know the name of the beast that broke like a wolf into the flock of lambs? That Russia sucks the marrow from the bones to fatten itself: look how thick and fat it is from gluttony. That holy Russia betrays to the Njemzy, the strangers. That it worships an idol, which it brought from abroad: I saw it lying in the dust before a hellish mummy, a woman with eight breasts, called Astarte. Do you know the name of the beast?"

Then they all howled, twenty thousand strong: "Peter, the Varangian! He is the son of Natalia Naryshkina and a wolf. She fornicated with a wolf before she gave birth to him."

Golovin led the rebels forward with a cross in hand. He swung it like a club. It was red with the blood of slain enemies. They marched against the tyrant, the monster, the beast, against the boyars, against serfdom and taxation.

But the rebels were scattered by Peter's guard under the command of Menshikov.

Soon rafts floated down the Don. On them stood gallows. And on the gallows hung the rebels, their arms and legs swaying in the wind, their twisted eyes and torn lips, from which the blue tongue hung down like a dead fish, spoke a clear language.

The Tsar waded in blood, and the legend went that he bathed every morning in fresh, hot rebel blood.

A procession of hundreds of thousands marched, led by Patriarch Adrian, with the Tsar's portrait and many holy images at the forefront, towards the Kremlin.

"Mercy for the sinners! Who among us is without sin?"

The Tsar remained deaf.

Grumbling, the people withdrew into themselves like a snail. Hatred simmered hot beneath the ashes of indifference. Golovin escaped the executioners because the people worshiped him and hid him among themselves. He slept in a different house every night.

Ivan was dead. Golovin had seen it himself. He could be believed. Now all love and secret hope gathered around the boy Alexei, son of Peter and Yevdokiya.

Sofia was taken to a convent.

"Mother Abbess, Mother Abbess –"

The nuns fluttered around Sofia like goats around the lead goat.

During evening prayer, Sofia already noticed strange customs among them.

Some clucked like hens, others bleated, and some mooed like cows while they prayed. The morning mass opened her eyes.

In the holy vessels of the chapel, the nuns relieved themselves.

One consumed dozens of hosts for breakfast, as if they were breakfast rolls. Instead of singing praises to the Lord and the Holy Mother, they sang blasphemous whore songs: "Since he can bear witness to the Lord Jesus, the Holy Spirit must also be a man."

She fell unconscious before the Blessed Sacrament.

Peter had her taken to a lunatic asylum that had been converted into a convent.

From that day on, she spoke not a word more and died after three years, abandoned and forgotten by Peter, God, and the world.

The envoys of Poland and Sweden met at the Moscow court.

"He is a barbarian."

"He is a genius."

"A barbaric genius."

"What will become of him?"

"Of Russia?"

"Of us?"

"He is a noble beast."

"Sable tomcat."

"Glutton. He has a healthy appetite. He will devour Poland."

"He will devour Sweden."

"He will devour Europe."

"When I sought an audience yesterday, where do you think he granted it to me?"

"Well?"

"He summoned me to the port. He was sitting in the mast basket of a ship, which he was repairing, and he ordered me to climb up into the rigging."

"I have the greatest respect for him. He is no king, as we are used to in the West: elegant and capricious, vague and ignorant."

"He is a servant of his work. No task is too small for him. I saw him for half an hour on the way home from the hunt, conversing with a farrier. One of his horse's shoes had come off. He pointed out to the farrier that his method of shoeing horses was impractical and unprofitable. In the end, he shod his horse himself – and the farrier stood by and patted him on the shoulder, saying, 'You're right, little father. You could come work for me as an apprentice.'"

"And the Tsar?"

"He laughed his boyish laugh and said that if the farrier wanted to ascend the Tsar's throne, he would be glad to take over the farriery in return. Then the farrier scratched his head and mumbled that it would be better to leave things as they were..."

"Recently, a girl in the palace fell ill with gangrene. The Tsar cut off her gangrenous leg like an experienced surgeon and carefully and excellently bandaged it."

"If we're not careful, he won't cut off our legs, but he will cut off our heads."

"Sweden must keep its eyes wide open!"

"Poland must keep its ears perked!"

Peter came their way.

"Hey, gentlemen, where are you rushing off to so hastily? Let's drink a little kvass, a little mead together."

"Urgent state business, Your Majesty, unfortunately calls me away."

"The courier to Warsaw is already waiting. I must not delay in sending him my mail..."

Peter grasped the Swede by the buttons of his coat: "Do you have news from Stockholm? How is His Swedish Majesty's health? He has been bedridden for several weeks, as I regrettably heard."

The Swede shrugged: "The doctors are full of hope."

Peter released the buttons.

"How old is young Karl, his son?"

"Sixteen years, Your Majesty."

"Hmm."

The envoys were dismissed. – Peter chuckled as they left.

They are afraid of me. Afraid that they might slip up. I already know what they're plotting. They want to keep Russia ensnared, far from the southern sea, far from the northern sea, sleeping, dreaming, like a good child.

I will tear apart their web.

Peter ran around the room half-naked. His hairy lion's chest bulged out from his shirt.

He pounded his fists against the wall, drumming the general march: "Menshikov, darling, son – what have you done this time? I've tortured Nestarow, hanged Gagarin: can't you come to your senses?"

With tears in his eyes, he stepped before Menshikov, shaking him by the shoulders: "My dear little son, what am I going to do with you? I'll have you beheaded. You'll lose your pretty, clever head."

He stroked the back of Menshikov's head tenderly with his paw.

Menshikov did not flinch.

"Your Majesty has the power to do so. Undoubtedly. But does Your Majesty wish to remain alone in the state? We all steal and murder: one is smarter, the other dumber. – Does Your Majesty have enough money to adequately pay the officials? Well then. We save the state treasury significant sums when we allow ourselves to be bribed... I also see no reason why a judge, who concludes a trial well or successfully, should not take a gratuity."

"Child, my son: you took money from a scoundrel – you brought an honest fellow to ruin."

Menshikov shrugged.

"God is unjust – why should I be just? I, a poor, weak man! Maybe one frees oneself from evil most purely – by doing it..."

Charles XI of Sweden died. Charles XII ascended the throne at the age of sixteen. Peter rubbed his hands together as if he were cold.

That little fellow comes just at the right time. I still have a small account to settle with the Swedes since Riga.

It's night.

A candle, stuck in an empty brandy bottle, illuminates the room.

The Tsar paces back and forth in patched slippers and a shabby, dirty nightgown. The tassels drag behind him. He stumbles every moment.

His eyes shine large and green like wolf's eyes.

The earth must become mine, and the sky and the stars and the moon too.

On the floor lay a crumpled map of Europe.

Russia – how small Russia still is. The Swedes and the Poles and the damned heathens, Persians and Turks constrict my chest so that I cannot breathe.

He huffs.

That Charles of Sweden! A cheeky, vain little brat! He thinks that because he commands a few thousand rum-drinkers and polar bear eaters, he can take me on too. Little brat, little brat: once I get you, I will wash you down for breakfast with a few gulps of vodka. Should I challenge you to a duel, eh? With crooked sabers? Turkish sabers? I would stain your charming white collar and your sky-blue waistcoat badly with your young red blood. You'd need to put on a bib so you don't get dirty.

The Pole is an effeminate fool. He thinks he has me, but I have him. I will send him some lovely Tatar girls and send him after you so that you'll have a hard time with him. And then I will come and give you the finishing blow like a half-dead hunted boar. Halali. And when the Pole bleeds to death fighting you, it will be his turn.

Peter stomped on the map: Livonia, Estonia, Ingria must become ours!

He trudged over to a corner where a half-full bottle stood in the shadows.

He raised it to his lips: Cheers, Charles of Sweden! Cheers, Augustus of Poland! May the cuckoos take you!

He smacked his lips, threw himself onto his straw bedding, covered himself with his Cossack coat, and fell asleep.

He dreamed that he was attending the funeral of the two kings.

He threw three handfuls of earth into the graves, mounted his gray horse, and rode through Poland, Livonia, and Estonia to the sea.

The sea surged at his feet.

He reined in the horse, which stood steadfast in the storm and waves.

The salt wind swept his beard.

He shouted: "The sea is ours, the Baltic Sea, the Russian Sea!"

In 1700, Augustus the Strong marched against Riga, and Peter against Narva. Peter, the man, was struck down by Charles, the boy.

Peter narrowly escaped captivity with Menschikov.

The encircled Russians voluntarily surrendered their officers to the enemy. Charles XII mockingly and arrogantly released all the captured Russians after taking their weapons from them.

Europe laughed behind Peter's back. Satirical coins were minted to ridicule his retreat.

A boy, a child, had teased the bear with a straw, and the bear fled.

Peter gathered new strength while Charles bit at the Poles like a vicious cur. Peter mocked Charles for letting his prisoners go. That magnanimity would cost him dearly. Just as dearly as his easy, cheap victory. We have time, time, time. We didn't capture Azov on the first attempt either. Misfortune will turn into fortune for us: next spring, like a gnarled willow stump. Had we won, we would have become arrogant, lazy, and insolent. Defeat forces us to muster all our strength, to double our efforts, to spur our ambition like a young colt until it bleeds.

During the retreat from Narva, Menshikov found a pretty Livonian maid in a house where he stayed the night. She consoled him over the defeat and stayed with him throughout the night.

Her name was Catherine.

Peter dreamed that he was riding on a winged horse, and before him walked a man with a sack. No matter how hard Peter tried, he couldn't catch up to the man. He called out to him from a distance: "Hey! Stop!" The man stood still. Peter jumped off the horse: "What's in the sack, stranger?"

"Lift it with your hand, foreign hero, and then you will know what is inside."

And Peter lifted the sack, but he barely raised it an inch off the ground. The sack was that heavy.

Then the traveler spoke, his face suddenly starting to resemble Golovin's: "All the heaviness, all the suffering of the world is in that sack; you cannot lift it. You yourself have been the one who helped fill that sack to the top."

Then Peter knelt before him: "Holy man, where can I know the will of God?"

The traveler replied: "Ride to the northern mountains. On the highest of the northern mountains stands the World Oak. Beneath the World Oak is a smithy. Ask the smith about the will of God!"

And Peter rode for three days and three nights: through scorching sun and drought on the first day, through fog and rain on the second, through hail and snowstorm on the third day. There stood the blacksmith on the highest mountain under the World Tree, forging two thin hairs together: one blonde, one black.

"What are you forging, blacksmith? Are you not the blacksmith who was so unskilled the other day and couldn't shoe my horse when I rode home from the hunt and lost a shoe?"

"I am the blacksmith. I forge love to love, hate to hate."

"Whom should I love, whom should I hate?"

"Her father has no name. She lives in the province by the sea. For twenty-five years, she has lain on the dung heap. She has an ugly, gnarled body. Her parents are ashamed of her, and the rooster sits on her body and crows."

Then Peter grew angry that he should love a girl who had lain on the dung heap for twenty-five years and was as ugly as night. And he rode to the capital of the province by the sea, which he had never seen and which was later named Petersburg after him, full of desire to kill the ugly girl.

He came to a shabby house and tied the horse to the garden gate.

No one was at home. Only on the dung heap in the back yard lay a girl. Her body was crusty like pine bark. Peter then pulled out five hundred gold rubles with his likeness from his pocket as a ransom, placed them on the dung heap, swung his sword, and struck it into the girl's breast.

Afterward, he rode out of the city. The galloping hoofbeats of his horse woke him. He rubbed his eyes.

Menschikov unfolded an old Italian engraving: a naked woman resting in an exceptionally alluring pose.

"Come, Catherine."

She looked over his shoulder.

"Look at this woman, study her position. You must lie on the divan like this when the Tsar comes. You don't move and pretend to be asleep."

Peter pulled back the curtain.

He was startled with delight.

On tiptoe, he crept to the bed, carefully removed his spurred riding boots, and approached her, who pretended to be asleep.

She knew how to awaken gracefully, looking at the Tsar with astonishment and confusion.

He kissed her upper arm in clumsy gallantry.

Gently, he fiddled with her Latvian blouse. But when he held her white breasts in tender hands, he was startled once again.

A small blood-red scar ran between them, as if a sword had struck her.

"Catherine," Peter's voice trembled, "who has wounded you with his sword?"

Catherine spoke: "Years ago, an unknown man came to my parents' house by the sea while I was sleeping. Neighbors saw him leaving the house. When I awoke, I had this scar on my chest, and it felt as if it had fallen off my white body like pine bark. I had been the ugliest creature, a sort of tree nymph; it was said that I came from a tree, born from a tree. But now I became the most beautiful of all since the stranger inflicted this wound on me. He also left five hundred rubles behind, with which my parents started a small business."

Peter pulled a gold ruble with his likeness from his pocket: "Were these the kind of rubles?"

Catherine examined the coin attentively.

"Yes, they were exactly those kind of rubles."

"Keep the ruble, Catherine."

He looked deeply into her eyes. A feeling overwhelmed him that he had never felt before with a woman.

"Catherine, from today on you will inhabit an apartment in my palace."

In a colonnade, Catherine and the Tsarina encounter each other.

Catherine is wearing the stylish, rainbow-colored attire of a Latvian peasant girl. She falls to her knees before the Tsarina.

The Tsarina lightly taps her shoulder with a mother-of-pearl fan: "Stand up, girl."

Catherine stands.

Two long blonde braids fall over her shoulder.

"What does the Tsar see in you, girl? Red, healthy cheeks and a firm bosom. Thick blonde strands. Broad thighs. What else?"

Catherine remains silent.

"How often does the Tsar visit you?"

Catherine smiles: "One to two times every day, and every night as well."

"Do you know that it is within my power to have you killed?"

"Certainly – but it is also within the power of the Tsar to have Your Majesty killed."

The Tsarina falls silent.

"What kind of dress is that you are wearing?"

"The dress of a Latvian peasant. I am a peasant's child."

The Tsarina touches the crocheted hem with her slender fingers: "Very pretty, very colorful. It suits you wonderfully. What attire do you think would look best on me?"

Catherine answered without hesitation: "The veil of a nun, Your Majesty."

The Tsarina turned pale.

She lets go of the hem of her dress and walks away.

Catherine fell to her knees.

"Menshikov – Alexei is my son. My heart bleeds at the thought that I will have to have him killed. He has a soul like a white swan. I have read his swan song. A poem: addressed to an unknown lady. But if I let him live, there will be no peace or quiet in Russia. Everything that is dissatisfied and rebellious gathers around him. I believe that he is in cahoots with Golovin and that they occasionally meet in secret. If he were to kill me, if he followed me as Tsar, he would completely ruin my painstakingly built work. He would drive the Germans, the French, the

Italians out of the country, and reduce Moscow to rubble. Do you know what he says about Moscow? That it should not be called the city of the Tsars, but the city of tears. For countless tears have been shed over it. He is a sensitive boy and plays the gusli enchantingly. But with his romances and cantatas, he would completely destroy my work and blow it away with his trumpet, like the walls of Jericho."

Menshikov twisted his beard: "It is the nature and destiny of sons to destroy the work of their fathers. The history of the world consists of these struggles."

"Menshikov, my dear boy, don't chatter, don't philosophize. Leave that to Leibniz and his comrades. By the way, has his response to my plan for a Russian Academy of Sciences and Arts arrived yet? No? How are Lomonosov's alchemical experiments progressing? I need gold, money. The translations of legal, nautical, geographical, and historical works into Russian are proceeding too slowly. I read one. It was written in the most ornate Church Russian. Away with it! I want the living, vibrant Russian language to be heard. Russia, Menschikov, will live by my vision – or it will not live at all."

Peter stepped into the room of the Tsarevich. The later was silently reading the Bible. "What are you reading?"

Alexei read aloud, first softly, then increasingly louder and with growing bitterness: "Lord, how long shall I cry, and You will not hear? How long shall I call to You about violence, and You will not help? Why do You show only horrors around me? Violence prevails over justice. Why do You remain silent while the wicked devour the righteous?"

Peter grumbled.

"Nonsense. The weak will be trampled, and thus it is right. Why do you waste your days reading the Bible, searching for an ethical justification for your weakness? I know that you want to destroy my work. But you do not have the courage or strength to do what you think. Why don't you draw your knife against me like Golovin – your friend?"

The Tsarevich bit his lip:

"I hate murder and war and struggle."

The Tsar raised his eyebrows: "You do not hate all of this as much as you hate me. But you even conceal your hatred from yourself. I will give you an answer from your beloved Bible: 'Let the one who is wicked remain wicked still. Let the one who is unclean remain unclean still.' I know your deeds, that you are neither cold nor hot. Oh, that you were cold or hot! Because you are lukewarm, and neither cold nor hot, I will spit you out of my mouth."

The blood had rushed to the Tsar's head.

He left without a farewell.

A few days later, a closed carriage stopped at a side gate of the palace. The Tsar entered, alongside Patriarch Adrian, into the chambers of the Tsarina: "Eudoxia, my dear wife, I have been told that you are considering taking the veil and withdrawing from all worldly troubles into a convent. What a noble intention! Adrian, the highest bishop of our church, will personally escort you and will consecrate and bless you himself. The Monastery of Our Lady, located on the Solovetsky

Islands, is prepared and adorned to receive you. It is a very picturesque place there by the White Sea, only a bit cold and monotonous in winter. Well, you can keep it well heated. You won't have to endure too many hardships. Our most Christian church is lenient. God bless your decision. The gift of sainthood has always slumbered within you. I am fortunate to awaken it. Come."

The ladies-in-waiting, Feodorovna Shuvalov and Elisabeth Countess Stolberg, a German, sobbed.

The Tsarina opened her beautiful black eyes, which she had kept closed throughout the Tsar's entire speech. She tossed her head back lightly like a noble horse and took the arm that the Patriarch offered her.

In the doorway, she paused once more: "And Alexei, our son, the Tsarevich – what will become of him?"

The Tsar looked out the window at the courtyard, where a group of soldiers was constructing a gallows.

"He is taken care of. Do not trouble yourself about him."

"Moscow, the city of my ancestors, is becoming too cramped for me. I draw a line through the past. The future begins today. I will build my own capital, my fortress, Petersburg, myself. I rode along the Neva. Thirty versts from the mouth lies an island: there Petersburg shall arise. A warning to the Swedes, a monument for myself. Fresini, the Italian architect, shall draft a plan for me within three days – no objections, Fresini – Menshikov will take charge of construction – no objections, Menshikov – you will gather the workers, and if necessary, beat them into submission – within a year Petersburg will stand, my fortress, proud, steep, impregnable, washed by the waves of the Neva."

Menshikov and Fresini bowed.

The audience came to an end.

Fresini sketched day and night. He envisioned a northern Venice, a northern Palmyra: barbaric, yet majestic.

Menshikov sent his recruiters to all provinces. Free bread and fish were promised to the workers, along with a ruble in wages each month.

They came in droves: Russians, Ukrainians, Kalmyks, Tartars: voluntarily and involuntarily.

Menshikov initially needed twenty thousand for preliminary work: for clearing and damming. In fourteen days, he had gathered them. They had to build their own accommodations: damp earthen caves, wind-swept tents. They froze. They starved. They cursed. The supply columns were ambushed and robbed by marauding bands along the way. The equipment was insufficient. Thousands had to dig with their bare hands. Their hands cracked open, bled. The earth had to be carted away in aprons, caftans, and sacks. The overseers swung whips and lashes.

Thousands perished.

They were thrown into the Neva, where their bloated bodies drifted out to sea.

New waves of laborers constantly arrived.

Hundreds of thousands dug, built, stacked, mortared, and toiled in the end.

Menshikov had a stone house with a tower built for himself on a hill in the middle of the island. They called the tower "Tower of Babel." From here, he stood and looked down on the teeming activity.

The Swedes attempted to obstruct the construction. They recognized the threat they faced once the fortress and city were irrevocably established.

From Vyborg, the Swedish General Löwengart marched against the burgeoning Petersburg.

Peter himself charged at them with a few hastily assembled regiments.

He did not flee as he had at Narva. How far Narva lay behind him.

He searched for the general in the battle and thrust his sword into his chest.

The Swedes fled, leaving behind their artillery and baggage. He aimed the Swedish cannons at the retreating enemy.

The work around Petersburg paused for a day. There was a celebration. All the workers were drunk. Peter gifted them the abandoned Swedish camp women and camp boys. Always a dozen or more took advantage of the beautiful blonde women.

One, named Ute, had been requested by Fresini as a gift. She had been the concubine of the Swedish general. He made her his wife.

The next day, the fortifications resumed. On the islet of Kotlin, embankments were dug.

An enemy fleet appeared off Kotlin. They encountered a storm and had to retreat with flapping sails, under the laughter of the Russians. Admiral Apraxin pursued them with a few cogs. Having lost confidence after being so unpleasantly battered by the storm, they fled despite their considerable superiority.

Most of the buildings in Petersburg were still wooden houses and barracks. The transportation of stones posed difficulties. So Peter decreed: anyone traveling to Petersburg by land or water had to pay a toll in the form of stones. He further ordered the richest families in Russia – the princes, nobles, and merchants – to construct two-story stone houses in Vasilyevsky Island, a district of Petersburg, no matter the cost.

Barracks, warehouses, shipyards, factories, and hospitals sprang up, as well as all kinds of promenades. Merchants came from Nizhny Novgorod, Germany, Poland, and France, lured by privileges. Peter promised them tax exemptions. A stock exchange was formed. Tartars were forcibly settled. The Senate was moved from Moscow to Petersburg. A curiosity shop, called a museum, was Peter's pride. At the newly founded imperial theater, the opening performance was "The Hero of Kiev," with the clumsiest allusions to Peter, who saw himself amusingly strolling on stage in a deceptive mask and performing incredible Herculean feats.

1708.

Peter moves to Petersburg.

One hundred thousand people lay dead in the swamps of the Neva, frozen and struck down by toxic fumes. Ten thousand horses had perished: Petersburg lived.

All the houses were decorated with green fir branches.

Peter rode slowly through the city on his white horse, a city he had summoned from nothing by sheer will. He rode bareheaded, in a gray coat without any insignia, wearing high black leather boots.

He wanted to be Russian – nothing else.

Catherine rode beside him: a Latvian peasant girl in a rainbow-colored, embroidered shawl, with red boots: blond, radiant, fresh.

Behind them: Menshikov in a grand general's uniform and Fresini in fashionable Italian attire. Then came the Patriarch: under a blue velvet canopy in golden choir vestments, holding a prayer book close to his freckled face, muttering prayers. Crowds of high and low clergy, monks, and lay brothers followed. The procession was concluded by the Guards regiment: with pipes, horns, and kettle drums, played by a genuine Negro.

Arriving at his new palace, Peter jumped off his horse, knelt down, and kissed the holy Russian earth, which the Patriarch blessed.

The entire crowd, forming a thick line, knelt down: silently, dully, humbly.

Then the singing of the priests resounded, the music of the dragoons, the ringing of small bells.

Incense wafted.

The Tsar and Catherine rode through the main gate of the Winter Palace amid the shouting and jubilation of the people. The retinue followed through various side doors, which were intentionally built so low that one could not walk upright but had to bow humbly to enter the palace.

A feast in the palace.

Just as they are serving pirozhki, a fish dish baked in bread that reminds Menshikov of his youth and is therefore repulsive to him, a courier breaks through the line of servants and attendants.

He has a handwritten note from Admiral Apraxin.

"Charles of Sweden is advancing on Petersburg! King Charles himself at the head of his troops!"

Peter's eyes shine.

He wipes his mustache, which has bits of fish in it, with his elbow.

"We will have a battle as dessert. No interruption of the festivities. You stay, Catherine. Menshikov, you follow me. Musicians, play a dance."

They played.

Peter seized Catherine by the waist and spun her until she nearly fainted.

Then he stopped abruptly and, with a leap, was out of the hall.

By the Neva, the Swedes had set up a fortified camp.

Apraxin believed that the main Swedish force was assembling there.

Peter was not deceived. He noticed how they were building a pontoon bridge further down the Neva and how column after column crossed the river.

Peter gathered a few hundred dragoons and rode against the Swedes crossing over, aiming to seize the bridgehead from them.

In vain. The attack was repelled. He achieved nothing.

The entire Swedish army marched in a long line across the Neva.

Peter retreated. With his cavalry, he devastated the entire region, burned down the homes of his own subjects, set their fields aflame, paid no heed to their misery, cut down their orchards, and slaughtered livestock he could not take with him. The Swede, poorly provisioned and hoping for rich spoils in the conquered land, encountered a desolate wasteland of smoking ruins, charred calves, and blackened meadows. His soldiers began to starve, grumble, and rebel. Winter came. Snow fell day and night. In the forests around Petersburg, the Swedes huddled like half-frozen birds. Hundreds were killed by the peasants. The rest fled back to the sea, exhausted, and boarded the waiting fleet.

At the bow of his flagship stood Charles of Sweden, tears in his eyes.

From the shore, Peter's barbaric laughter echoed through the snowstorm to him.

Catherine wrote to him this letter while Peter was in the field camp: "My everything! My world! Greetings! Kisses! Hugs! May you live a thousand years! You have triumphed over the Swedes! Banner of defiance, fortress of pride: I pray for you: in the morning when the sun rises, in the evening when it sets. My bed lies empty at night. I caress the pillows. Glory to God the Lord for having shown His grace upon you. I was at the monastery of Saint Sergei when your letter arrived. I kissed the saint's feet. You said I should make gifts to the monasteries if you were victorious. I did just that. And I walked to all the monasteries in the area. I had medals struck with your radiant image in memory of your victory. They are not finished yet, otherwise, I would have enclosed one with this letter. God knows how much the dove, the little dove, longs for her dove. My wings are paralyzed. You must teach me to fly again."

At Poltava, Peter decisively defeated the Swedes. Charles lost his hair until he was bald.

Bald, he fled through Ukraine to Turkey. Exhausted and deathly tired, he still managed to incite and rally the Turks, who had not forgotten about Azov, against the Tsar. Charles took command of the Ottomans alongside the Grand Vizier.

Once again, he faced the hated enemy.

At the Pruth, he managed to completely encircle Peter, whom Catherine had accompanied to the field this time.

Three fierce attacks by the Janissaries were repelled with great difficulty.

Peter's fate seemed sealed.

From his camp, he could hear the enemy celebrating their anticipated victory.

For the first time in his life, he felt disheartened and despondent.

He sat, wrapped in his sheepskin coat, on a cracked drum and gazed gloomily into the smoldering campfire.

He had lived too wildly, wanted too much, and had climbed too high. Now, just before reaching the summit, his strength left him. He was tired, deathly tired. He wanted to sleep, to sleep forever, nothing more.

Then something crept along the path. Was it a cat? It was Catherine. She stopped before him and smiled: "Courage!"

He pulled her to him. Then he felt that she was naked under her coat.

Catherine had the Grand Vizier asked for a private meeting through a parliamentary envoy.

The Grand Vizier received her with perfect courtesy.

She returned riding in the morning. When the sentry demanded the password, she called out: "Victory!"

She herself led the troops in the breakthrough against the left wing commanded by Charles of Sweden. Her loose blonde hair fluttered like a golden banner in the wind. Like an icon – radiant, vivid, and inspiring – she led them forward. She stirred the ragged, starving, and dispirited men to action. The breakthrough succeeded.

The right wing, commanded by the Grand Vizier, initially remained passive and only joined the fray after the breakthrough had been achieved.

Charles of Sweden in fourteen days galloped from the Pruth to the Baltic Sea, accompanied only by a small cavalcade. He was preparing for a new battle when he was struck by a fatal bullet on the walls of Frederiksborg.

When Peter heard of his death, he crossed himself reverently three times.

The Treaty of Nystad confirmed all of Peter's conquests: Livonia, Estonia, Ingria, and Karelia were ceded to Russia. Poland was so weakened that it dared not protest when Russia usurped the share of the spoils once promised to Poland.

Sweden was crushed. Denmark dealt it the final blow.

Poland fell into decay and rotted from internal strife. So too did Persia.

The Turk's power was broken. Ukraine fell into Peter's lap like a ripe apple.

The Russian bear stood tall, licking the blood from its snout and paws. Already, it cast a glance toward India and China.

The Senate asked Peter to accept the title of Emperor, which had not been revived in the East since the fall of Byzantium.

At the victory celebration, Peter danced on the table like a child.

Tears of joy stood in his eyes. He laughed and cried nonsensically.

He kissed Catherine, with whom he married on the same day. He deposed Patriarch Adrian, who refused to perform the marriage ceremony, with an air of self-importance. In her honor, he established the Order of Saint Catherine and, on their wedding night, placed around her neck the silver cross that bore, on one side, the image of the saint – it resembled Catherine like one twin resembles another – and on the reverse, an eagle's nest with two eagles holding snakes in their beaks.

When she had fallen asleep, he left her. He went out into the night. He needed to be alone.

He mounted his horse and rode into the darkness. No star shone in the sky. He rode the path he had once traveled in a dream, until he saw the Baltic Sea from a dune.

The salty wind swept through his beard. The sea roared at his feet. He reined in the horse, which stood firmly against the storm and the crashing waves that splashed up to him.

Peter shouted, drowning out the surf, the storm, and the thunder of the spheres: "Our sea is the Baltic, the White Sea! Our sea is the Southern Sea, the Black Sea, ours is the Caspian sea, the Eastern Sea! Ours!"

Then he jumped off the horse, burying his face in its mane, weeping uncontrollably, like a child.

The next day, he wrote to his envoy in Paris: Students usually finish their schooling in seven years. Mine has lasted three times as long. Yet, thanks be to God, it has ended as well as could possibly be.

Peter entered the tavern, filthy and unkempt. His red boots were splattered with mud. His hair was matted. His gaze darted nervously over the sand-strewn floor, like ants. In a quiet voice, he asked the innkeeper to bring him wine for a hundred rubles. The innkeeper, his hands in the deep pockets of his baggy trousers, merely laughed.

Peter cursed.

His gaze sprang from the ground like the devil out of a box.

In the smoky corner by the fireplace sat a group of broad-shouldered revelers – sailors, peasants, dockworkers.

Peter sat down with them.

"Who will buy me a drink? I'm as thirsty as a horse that has eaten a hundred-weight of barley."

The fellows chuckle. One calls out to the innkeeper: "Hey, old man! A glass for our friend!" They drank and sang. Peter sang:

I am Peter, the son of peasant Ivan.
The steppe was my mother.
A falcon perches on my shoulder.
In the cage of my heart, a red nightingale sings.
With my arrows, I've shot down the golden spires of the cathedral of Kiev.
Look at the golden buttons on my vest; they are the tower knobs of Kyiv.
The lineage of creeping serpents is subservient to me.   When I whistle, they dance.   Do you know who loved Princess Nastasja?   The white swan?   Do you know who killed the giant Tugarin?   The gray dog?
I rode from Moscow to Kyiv between morning mass and high mass,
On my dappled horse, with my falcon Sokol.
On the battlefield, I am the last;
With merry maidens, I am the first. –

Thus sang Peter.

The drinkers listened in silence.

One, who smelled of tar, said: "Where do you come from? Old man? Over land? Over sea?"

Peter took a deep sip.

"I come across the White Sea with my ship Sokol. Its sides are the flanks of an aurochs, its strength is that of a bull, its speed is that of a greyhound. It has eyes on the bow like eagle eyes. The eyebrows are made of black sable. It looks dark and brooding. Proud is its soul. This ship foams across the thousand seas and only docks where there is a golden landing pier."

The drinkers marveled. And an old man, who hardly had any teeth left, murmured: "But how did you land in Petersburg then? Where in Petersburg is there a golden landing pier?"

Peter replied, "Last evening – didn't you see how golden the sky was? A golden bridge stretched from heaven to earth. It was on that bridge that I docked."

The drinkers fell silent. They finished their drinks, looked at him wide-eyed, and left. One after the other, they departed.

The last one whispered in the man's ear: "He is a strange man. You must love him or hate him. He doesn't seem to be of this world. It's best to leave him alone. Give him a drink, old man."

Peter sat by the fireplace, warming his hands.

A white cat jumped onto the table and looked at him.

The innkeeper placed a new glass of steaming punch in front of Peter.

He stood there awkwardly, squinting his eyes.

"What do you want, old man?"

The innkeeper said softly: "When you board your ship Sokol again and set sail from the golden bridge to that land lying by the blue sea of heaven: greet my daughter, my little daughter, the slender doe. She stayed with me for only fifteen years. Then a wild man came, who loved her to death. For fifteen years now, she has been grazing in those meadows. Give her this little necklace; she should wear it around her neck; there's a tiny bell on it. When she wears it, I will hear its gentle ringing."

Peter jumped up from the table, embraced the stout, shy man, over whose plump cheeks were streaming with tears.

"I will do as you wish, dear brother."

When Peter had drunk away his money, he drank away his shoes, his coat, his pants, his shirt, and walked back to the palace naked.

It had been a cold summer. Actually, it hadn't been a summer at all. It rained every day for at least a few hours, and at night, one froze under the thin summer blanket, because the thick winter cushions aren't taken out of the linen cupboard before October. Only one hot night was granted to Peter. It burned like a sunflower in the dark. It was the night of the summer solstice. They jumped through the solstice fire, which threw its flickering lights over the distant sea and a thousand sparks into the sky, where they fell back to earth as shooting stars.

"What do you wish for?" asked Ute, whom he held by the hands. "When shooting stars fall, you must make a wish. The wish will come true."

He was startled by the question and didn't know how to answer.

The solstice fire was dying down.

The twigs were a bit sooty.

He had no wish left. If he thought about it, he wished for nothing. God knows, he had grown old. The fire had burned down. It was just smoldering now. Surely that was a sure sign of aging: that he no longer had a wish. Recently, in front of the mirror, hadn't he noticed some white hairs and a bald patch on his head? Didn't he sometimes feel a slight tremor in his knees before going to sleep?

He was stranded.

The waves crashed around his wreck.

"Be cheerful," said Ute, "what's the matter with you?"

"I have you," and he pulled her sideways into a dark garden. By a tree, he embraced her. But strangely: he felt the bark, the tree more than the young woman, who glowed towards him like the Venus of the heavens. He kept thinking about the tree: what kind of tree was this? A tree like the one Catherine had been before he struck her down with the sword to make her human? He reached up into the branches. He felt a fruit. It was an apple tree. He tore down the unripe fruit and bit into its moist, sour-sweet flesh. Autumn and spring have been granted to me once again. God, I thank you. I thank you for this life. Perhaps it will soon be over. What does it matter? It was beautiful and terrible. It was full of pain, full of worries, full of misery and disgust. But it was also full of splendor and happiness, so full of happiness that my heart leaps and dances like a dancer when I think of it. It was good this way, God. You grant me autumn and spring once more, Pomona, golden goddess. The tree here: ripens. And this young creature here: blossoms. It blooms like an apple tree in spring: white and rose-red.

"What are you thinking?" Ute said. "You shouldn't think. Otherwise, I'll become jealous of your thoughts."

Yes, he thought too much. That was devilish. She was right. A bad sign. He began to think. He was growing old. The summer was over. The scabious, the balsams, the star flower had all withered. But the yellow amaryllis, the sign of defiance, remained. I will not be beaten down. Even if in the eyes of this beautiful being the velvet flower, the symbol of deceit, is already blooming – what does it matter? Belladonna: Beautiful lady, that's what the most poisonous of all flowers is called... Meadow saffron, at my feet: you indicate truth and eternity: your seed only ripens in the coming spring. Meadow saffron, my heart.

Ute grew impatient. She wrapped her arms around his neck. He kissed her soft lips. And recalling the old Virgil quote: *Phyllis amat corylos*: Phyllis loves hazelnuts – he pulled her into a hazel bush, which for centuries had lured lovers to tender retreat at the edge of the garden. As he bent the bushes apart, the hazelnuts tinkled like little bells.

Winter came and spring and summer and winter again.

Peter had just returned from a visit to the Olonets ironworks and the salt mines at Staraja-Russ. He intended to inspect the iron hammer and the rifle factory at Lysterbek as well. In Lachta, he saved a boy from drowning. That very day, he was seized by fever chills. He hurried back to Moscow by express.

Peter was writhing in pain. Those cursed kidney pains. This burning in his lower abdomen, as if torches had been ignited within. His bladder also refused to function properly. God in heaven: I praised You too early at the summer solstice festival. You are a gentle, mild, honey-sweet God: You have struck us with pestilence and syphilis, and couldn't care less about the fate of those you've put into the world. Was I not once a strong wolf, a bear, who crushed the girls in his paws and devoured glass like gruel? What am I now? Who would have thought that this little rat Ute's bite would be poisonous? I am helpless as a mole by day, writhing like a worm. Why did you hide the poisonous viper of illness in the jungle of lust, which should not be called the French disease but the disease of God? What have the poor French done to deserve this? But you are to blame.

You allowed it to sting me in the heel. You sit, nameless and heartless, like the hero of Kiev on Your lapis lazuli throne, appearing like a diamond: clear and shining.

But I am so gloomy. I know you have sent a courier to Boerhave in Leyden. He will come too late. I cannot help myself. How could anyone else?

"Fetch my enemy, the monk Golovin."

They brought him.

Potapov met him in the hallway. He made the sign of the cross. It was coming to an end. The foreign pilgrim had come to take the hero of Kiev home. He took the sword from Peter's hand, the one he had once brought to him to fight the brood of serpents and dragons. He had wielded it honorably, like Gabriel wielded the flaming sword against Lucifer. But alas: there were too many serpents and dragons. If one cut off the head of a dragon, two would grow back. If one split a snake in two, each part became a whole new snake.

The monk bowed before Peter.

At Peter's bedside stood, like two archangels, Catherine and Menshikov.

Peter groaned: "Sit on my bed. I'm not feeling well. I want to confess. Grant me absolution and your blessing. I want to confess to you. Five words, brother: it was all in vain. Everything I strove for, lived for, wove like an intricate Persian carpet: it was for nothing. They are already unravelling the threads. What I built is already collapsing like a house of cards. I made Russia great: they cannot bear greatness in any form. It used to be said: Russia lies far behind in Asia, its population is crude, the roads are difficult; it is not worth trading with them. And now? Everyone is clamoring for our products. The posts I established are overflowing. We are respected in Europe and the world. But they scoff at honor and respect if they have enough to eat. What I taught them, they are quick to forget. I built higher and lower schools, spiritual and technical colleges: they go in on one side and come out on the other as if nothing had happened. They learned to read, but they remained illiterate. What has become of the serfs to whom I granted freedom? They didn't know what to do with their freedom, sold themselves again, and drank away their earnings. Who can do anything against God and Novgorod? I have hanged ministers and generals. The ministers and generals still steal and are still corrupt. Even Menshikov, my beloved son, has lied to me, cheated me, and stolen from me. Why did you so urgently and plausibly advise me against the conquest of Swedish Pomerania back then, son, through which I would have become a German prince with a seat and a voice in the German Reichstag? Because you were bribed with twenty thousand ducats by my enemies. Be silent, Menshikov, I speak the truth. But should I perhaps hang you too on my deathbed? I cannot bring myself to do it because I love you, and perhaps it is foolishness. I thought that the culture, which once traveled from Greece to Italy, from Italy to France, and from France to Germany, would now travel to Russia and I could pave the way for it. That is why I called the Germans, French, and Italians to the country. They should help me. People hated the foreigners because they understood more than we did and because they should be learned from. They hated them, like the foolish student at the dull school hates the teacher. I demanded too much: from myself and from others. Monk, monk, I should not have knocked the dagger out of your hand back in the Preobraschenskoe park. Perhaps we would all be better off.""

Peter fell back into the cushions. He groaned: "Recognize in me what a sad creature man is."

The monk murmured Latin prayers.

Peter sat up once more: "Monk, take off your robe."

The monk stood up and silently stripped it off.

Catherine saw his brown back. She liked this monk. She would think of him from time to time.

"Where is your knout, Tsar?" said the monk. "Strike me!" Peter shook his head and smiled: "Put the monk's robe on me!"

Then they knew that his last hour had come. For since the time of the Tsars, they are carried to the grave in the monk's habit as simple, pious pilgrims.

Menshikov and Catherine helped him into the robe. He sighed.

"Menshikov, ink and quill and paper. Sit here: write my will. Or let the monk write it. Are you ready, monk?"

"I am."

Peter searched for words: "I want" – He fell backwards, dead.

Catherine, Menshikov, and the monk knelt down and prayed.

The monk stood up. He wanted to leave. Then he noticed that he was not wearing a robe. He looked around. The Tsar's robe lay over the chair by the bed. He put it on.

As he walked through the palace, nobles came running at him from all sides.

"How are things, Father?"

The monk raised his arm horizontally:

"It is accomplished."

Then they saw the Tsar's robe on his body.

A crowd surged toward him, drawing their swords. "You wear his robe; he has turned to you, he who was his bitterest opponent. So it is his legacy. Be our Tsar, Holy Father, Tsar and Patriarch. Our country has no Tsar, our church no Patriarch anymore."

The monk recoiled. A frantic blush shot to his forehead. There it was, the worldly temptation. The tempter approached him in the guise of that limping nobleman with the crooked, bushy gaze. The tempter said: "You wear the Tsar's clothing; here is the Tsar's sword. Take it, and the realm of the world is yours. Let them pay you homage, Lord."

The monk gripped the ivory cross that hung from his neck. Then he tore off the Tsar's robe. The limping nobleman reached for it like Madame Potiphar reached for Joseph's coat. The monk fled with averted face.

They watched him in bewilderment as Catherine, dressed in a black, high-necked velvet gown, strode down the corridor. Menshikov followed her. She stopped: "His Majesty the Tsar, God's key-bearer and chamberlain, has just entered into eternal rest after receiving the holy sacrament of the dying. I ask the gentlemen from the nobility, from the Senate, and from the clergy to come to the audience chamber."

Menshikov immediately ordered all exits of the palace and the key points of the city to be secured with the guards absolutely loyal to him.

Catherine stood before the throne. Menshikov stood beside her. He held a parchment in his hand and read with a metallic, hammering voice:

"It is my final, unwavering wish and will that my beloved wife Catherine shall take on all my rights and duties as Tsarina and ruler of all Russians.

"Signed, Peter I, Moscow City Palace, in the night from February 7th to 8th, 1725 of the new reckoning."

Menshikov, as the highest magnate, knelt and presented her with the imperial orb, scepter, and crown. She placed the crown on her golden head herself.

The swords of the nobles were drawn from their sheaths, the Senate waved their caps, and the priests raised their hands in blessing: "Long live Catherine, our most gracious Tsarina and mistress!"

In the background, among the clergy, wearing a coat he had borrowed from a gardener, stood Golovin, the monk. His temples throbbed. Was the woman up front on the throne not the one who had been prophesied, the great whore of Babylon? With whom had the kings of the earth committed fornication, and they have become drunk from the wine of her fornication! Woe! The downfall is near for all of us.

Catherine recognized him. She waved him over.

"This is the pious father who heard the Tsar's confession and recorded his last will. Is it not so, holy father?"

The monk stared in horror at Catherine's beauty and murmured, broken like an overly thin glass vessel and unable to resist: "It is so" –

"It was the Tsar's wish that he ascend to the Patriarchal throne of our holy church, which has stood vacant for so long. Long live Golovin, the Archimandrite and Metropolitan of Moscow!"

And again the swords clashed: "Long live!"

Menshikov had stepped to a window. He looked down at Red Square, where, in the snowstorm, the people waited silently and dully for the proclamation of the new Tsar.

As the bearers carried the coffin down the grand staircase, they slipped on the ice that had formed. The coffin slid from their grasp, fell on the edge of a step, bounced up, and the body of Peter rolled down the entire staircase, already swollen and blue. It lay at the bottom, face down, fists clenched in *rigor mortis* pressed into the earth, still clutching the beloved, the hated earth in death.

The cathedral was packed with people. Before the iconostasis with the three doors, the choir singers were grouped. Behind the iconostasis, in the hidden part, seven priests were reading the funeral mass for the Tsar.

Small bells chimed.

In the candlelight, the Gospel book was brought to the people.

Then the Passion took place, the great mystagogy behind closed doors: Life, Suffering, Death, and Resurrection of the Lord.

Incense wafted through the air. Bells rang. Torches blazed.

Golovin, the new patriarch, raised the Christ present in the sacrament high above his head as he came through the central door onto the threshing floor and presented Him to the people.

Everyone fell to their knees.

He desperately lifted the sacrament even higher.

Wouldn't his fingers, daring to carry it, burn? Wouldn't lightning strike his impudently raised forehead? Wouldn't the earth open to swallow him, the traitor to the holy word and holy deed? Had he not once sworn to destroy the cursed tsarist work down to its foundation, like the house of Ahab and Jezebel? Had he not robbed sacred churches of their worldly goods, their jewels and pearls? Had he not stolen silver and golden church vessels and melted them down to obtain means for the battle against the Antichrist? Woe! Did not a storm wind whisper the vows he had once made in his ear? Did not the cathedral's tower crush him with a stone fist? Did not only lies rule the world, violence, lust, atrocities, and wicked deeds?

Weak and powerless, Golovin, the patriarch, collapsed in the midst of the sacred ceremony.

When Golovin awoke, he found himself in the Tsarina's bedroom.

He lay on a bed covered with silk. The Tsarina, dressed in a scarlet house gown with a deep neckline, leaned over him. A sweet scent rose between her breasts, intoxicating him. She held a golden cup, filled with wine, which she offered to him.

He stared at her.

And he remembered the divine prophecy: the woman was clothed in scarlet and pearls and held a golden cup in her hand...

Between her breasts hung the Crucified One, on an ivory chain.

He propped himself up and kissed the crucifix until his lips suddenly turned sideways and clung burning to Catherine's breast.

It was night.

Golovin staggered, drunk on the wine of love, back into the cathedral.

There stood the Tsar's sarcophagus, black in the glaring moonlight. He tore the shroud from the coffin, threw himself over it, clawed at it with his hands, and sank his teeth into the ash wood as if he wanted to tear it open.

"Arise, Anointed One. Return. Help us. Let the Nagaika strike. It is still too mild for us, sons of dogs. We have disregarded and misunderstood you. Forgive us. I am Abaddon, the angel from the abyss. Smoke and sulfur issue from our mouths. We are cast away for all eternity."

Part Three:

Störtebecker

(S. Fischer Verlag, Frankfurt, 1926)

Störtebecker

The wind billowed Marlen's blue and white checkered skirt.

She stood in a niche of St. Nicholas Church, stout-faced and stout-bodied, her bright red hands planted on her hips as she shouted: Plums! Plums! An echo from the houses mocked: Plums! Plums!

The wind swept a cloud of dust over the St. Nicholas Market. At first, it crept along the ground like a glowworm. Then wings grew on it. It rushed up and struck against the painted windows of the St. Nicholas Church like the Phoenix, with enormous wing beats, so that they creaked in their rusty hinges, and the red Saint Sebastian and the green Saint Makarius lost their color, standing brown-dusted like filthy beggar monks or gingerbread men in the glassy oval.

The sky blinked sulfur yellow like a cat's eye at night.

The first lightning flashed its silver whip and lashed the clouds, causing them to roar apart.

Marlen stood in the niche and laughed.

The rain poured down in front of her.

Lightning flashed faster and faster. She placed her broad hand on her belly. The heartbeat of the child she could already feel, and lightning and thunder: that was one blow, one sound, resonating in the same rhythm.

This will be a wild boy, a lightning boy, a thunder lad.

Lightning and thunder crashed and hissed together. A slender pillar of fire rose. The lightning had struck the house of Senator Stollenweber. Windows burst open. Screams. Calls for help. Noise in all the alleys and the watchman's horn from the tower.

Marlen laughed. She clenched her fist.

You rabble, you scum, you vermin! It has struck among you! It was the radiant fist of my son that descended upon your rotting beams! He will come down upon you like the Son of God. He will be no Jesus Christ, no gentle angel, no mild prophet. He will not ignite the light of love until he has smoked you out of the den you have built from our sweat, our blood, our bodies, from our lives, a den that our blood, our life, must again bring down. You have brought Gödeke to the gallows because he wanted to help humanity achieve achieve justice and righteousness. But the dead Gödeke will walk among your houses. He will stand pale behind your chair when you feast, and he will serve you destruction. He will poison your children's souls in the cradle with wolf's milk and rat's milk. Your women will give birth to deformed creatures with goat legs and calf heads, because you have defiled the face and form of man, turning lambs into wolves and lizards into dragons.

You shall choke on my plums!

The rain poured down. The thunder only growled like a distant yard dog.

Plums! shouted Marlen, Plums!

The guard stood immobile like a stone Nepomuk at the gallows. The halberd stuck with its shaft in the damp earth, its point in the sky. A star danced on it like will-o'-the-wisp.

Gödeke swayed in the night wind.

He had hung for three nights and had forgotten life and death. He was dead, just as he had once been alive. A raven, having eaten his left eye, sat upon his bald skull. In the empty eye socket, a lustful glowworm crawled. From Hamburg, the clock struck twelve. Twelve churches chimed in succession. The watchman counted to one hundred and fell asleep standing.

He startled awake.

What was that suspicious noise? He lowered the halberd.

Who goes there?

Marlen placed her hands over his eyes from behind.

Guess who you are dealing with!

The guard cursed. Probably the devil's grandmother. Damn woman, let go. Who are you?

Your friend, said Marlen. And if you want, your lover.

She pulled him toward her so that the halberd fell into the grass and he gasped for breath. When he felt his arms free, he sought her breasts. He peeled them from the coarse linen shirt like fruits. They fell next to the halberd into the grass, which was still damp from the storm.

You're pregnant, said the soldier.

They lay in the grass and looked up at the sky, where the stars blinked sleepily like themselves.

Yes, said Marlen, I'm having a child.

By whom? asked the soldier.

By my husband, said Marlen.

And who is your husband? asked the soldier.

Marlen pointed upward with her sharp knuckle.

That one!

Which one? I don't see anyone up there but stars. So, a star is your husband. He shone like a star and followed his path like the sun.

And who is it?

Marlen raised her finger again: The one who is hanging there.

The soldier straightened up.

The one at the gallows, is he your husband?

Yes, said Marlen, the man at the gallows is my husband.

The soldier shook his head: You should be glad to be rid of him. He was a brutal fellow, a robber and a bandit. He must have beaten you every day.

Marlen thought for a moment: Yes, he did beat me from time to time. That was just his way. But he loved me, and I loved him.

You know how to love, said the soldier.

And to hate, said Marlen.

They fell silent.

The soldier felt as if a cool wind had passed over him. He shivered.

The man at the gallows swayed slightly. The raven had left him. Only the glowworm still shone.

There's a cemetery nearby, said Marlen.

The soldier remained silent.

Yesterday, the son of the cloth merchant was buried. The grave has not yet been filled in.

What does that mean? asked the soldier.

Marlen continued: Gödeke should receive the burial of an honest Christian. For he was a Christian like few others.

Perhaps, said the soldier. Even robbers can be decent people at times. I once played cards with one and took all his loot.

Help me, said Marlen. And suddenly, she had tears in her eyes.

The soldier nervously twisted the edge of his coat.

How could I help you? I'm as helpless as you.

Marlen stood up: We will dig up the son of the cloth merchant and hang him in Gödeke's place at the gallows. The gallows are high. You can't tell from down here who is hanging up there in the wind.

And we will honestly bury Gödeke in place of the merchant's son.

The soldier: I'll lose my head if this ever comes to light. –

The night is dark; it won't see the light of day.

She pulled him close to her. He felt her breasts.

Like cats, they crept the hundred steps to the cemetery.

How much the dead weigh! said the soldier as they carried the merchant's son to the gallows. Well, it doesn't hurt if one of the patricians hangs for once. I wish many more would hang. They're as arrogant as the emperor. To them, we're just a piece of cattle.

They set up a ladder.

The soldier loosened the noose from Gödeke.

He held his nose. Good heavens, your darling doesn't smell too bad.

He let Gödeke slide down the ladder.

Marlen tremblingly took him in her arms and kissed his stinking mouth.

The noose swayed lightly and cheerfully. Marlen looked up.

Oh, look at the cheerful noose! How pretty it curls! Like a snake.

It seeks a new victim. Soldier, show me how to hang people. I'd like to know.

The soldier laughed.

Here, my dove, this is how you hang people, my dove.

He artfully placed the noose around his neck.

When he had his neck in the noose, Marlen knocked the ladder over. He flailed a bit like a frog, twitched a few times, and then hung still.

Marlen looked up at him: This is how it should be for all those who are henchmen.

Her chest heaved heavily.

Gödeke!

She dragged the corpse to the cemetery and buried it. She pulled the merchant's son over the dam and threw him into the Elbe weighted down with a stone.

When the replacement for the gallows guard arrived at six o'clock in the morning, they were horrified to see the guard hanging from the gallows.

No trace of Gödeke was ever found again.

But a tremor ran through the citizens of Hamburg.

The devil is in league with the rebels! whispered the archpriest of St. George and based his next Sunday sermon on these words, painting a picture of the devil that made the Christian congregation shudder as they dispersed at noon, fearing one another in the glaring sun.

A few days later, Marlen gave birth like a dog in a niche of St. Nicholas Church to a boy who was later called Störtebecker.

A young scholar sat before his tankard of wine, drunken and absorbed. Occasionally, he took off his doctoral cap and wiped the sweat from his forehead.

Störtebecker toasted him: To your health!

The scholar looked at him suspiciously through his black horn-rimmed glasses and thanked him grumpily.

Where do you come from? Störtebecker asked without hesitation.

The other remained silent.

He raised the goblet to the light: How clear this wine is! How golden! Liquid sunshine. If only there were a person as clear as this wine. But they are all muddled, unripe, cloudy, too bitter or too sweet. Vinegar or cider. To your health! Are you a warrior?

Störtebecker replied: Something like that, sir. A fighter.

And what do you fight against?

Stupidity, arrogance, and treachery.

The other's eyes sparkled behind the glasses. You are my man. I could show you a worthy enemy. He lowered his voice: I come from Rome.

Störtebecker listened.

There, the trinity you just mentioned reigns unrestrained.

Störtebecker: Come with me to the assembly. Speak to the Frisians! You are one of us!

The assembly took place in a clearing near Bremen. The stranger raised his voice and spoke: Two harlots named Theodora and Varozzia rule. They appoint and dismiss bishops and elevate whom they will to the papacy. Benefices, dispensations, absolutions, judgments: everything is for sale. Justice has become a whore, whose blindfold was long ago removed. The pope celebrates the holy mass without receiving communion, and a seven-year-old child, who plays with the bishop's mitre like a carnival cap, has been consecrated as a bishop. Who knows who the true pope is? One is called Benedict: the Blessed: he is blessed with the French disease. The other is called Innocent, the Guiltless.

He is as innocent as a mercenary whore. In order for them to live their godforsaken lives, they squeeze the Christian believers with tithes and taxes. Doesn't the priest also go around your cottages and dunes with his collection plate, demanding the tithe while invoking the word of God and the Bible? Throw the Bible at his head. What use do you have for the Bible, if it allows such godless children to invoke it? When you didn't yet have the Bible, Frisians, God's word sounded milder and purer to you in the rustling of the winds, in the storm of the sea. No ugly God, who hung twisted on the cross with distorted limbs, oppressed you. Freia, the goddess of beauty, swam over the sea on a dolphin and blessed you! Helpless and defenseless, the Christian allowed himself to be nailed to the cross; likewise, the hypocritical priests demand this of you. They want to nail you to the cross of a thousand contracts and edicts in order to better and more securely fleece you. Do you think it will stop at the tithe? They will demand a third, half, and they will corrupt your wives and daughters in the confessional with Roman vice and Gallic sin. Wodan, the god of battle, still lives! Thor still lives! He swings the hammer of battle and will crush those who stand against him. Down with the priests! Down with Rome! We want to be free Frisians!

Man is free! The sea is free!

The faces of the Frisians flickered with excitement like red torches. They clashed their scythes, knives, and clubs together: Man is free! The sea is free! But the doctor continued: Now the priests have invented a system worthy of the invention of the highest, bloodthirsty devil.

The Inquisition! some shouted.

Yes: it is the Inquisition, the most horrific instrument of torture ever conceived by a human brain! Whoever does not belong to their true faith, as they understand it, they stretch on the rack, cut off their hands or feet, put thumb screws on them, tear their tongues out with burning iron, and cut their hearts from their living bodies. One must not give alms to a heretic. The house in which they are found must be torn down. Criminals, perjurers, and dishonorable people may testify against them. Mutual spying and denunciation is made a duty for Christians. Why all this, my brothers?

I will tell you: they do all this to their fellow men and fellow creatures out of Christian charity.

The roar of the Frisians shook the air. They screamed like animals in heat and bellowed like stags.

The pope, who made such laws, he is the Antichrist described in the Revelation of John. The Albigensians and Waldensians have come to you; they have reported how the priests' sword has ravaged their lands. Truly, the ground of France is red with the blood of the righteous. No grain will grow on it anymore, only weeds and poppies. Enough and more than enough of the murder. We will become the masters of the ravenous wolves. I tell you with Paul: Put on the armor of God, so that you may resist in the evil days and, and, in all things, stand victorious.

Suddenly, with a leap, the bishop of Bremen, who was hunting, appeared in the clearing, accompanied by a servant. Before he knew what was happening, he was surrounded by the Frisians. They stood silently around him, their axes, scythes, and knives sparkling in their hands.

Get down from the horse! Störtebecker shouted.

The bishop obeyed.

Störtebecker gave the horse a slap with his hand. It ran a few steps and began to graze calmly.

Are you are Bishop Ortleb of Bremen?

I am, the bishop bowed his head.

You had yourself appointed as the pope's inquisitor in Rome?

The bishop silently nodded his head.

A murmur went through the Frisians.

You let the peasants pay the tithe through your priests. Who gave you the right to do so?

The law. I gave the farmers the land, they have to pay me for it and pay taxes.

Well, look at that: You gave the peasants the land? Why? Because you needed mercenaries back then. Did you even see the land that you gave to the peasants? Sand, barren sand was the land where only the beach thistle thrived. The sea came every moment and swallowed what months of labor had wrested from the ground. For decades, the Frisians have labored and toiled, built dunes and roads from which you also benefit. And now, when the labor begins to bear fruit: now you suddenly show up, envious and arrogant, wanting to reap where they have sown.

The bishop was silent.

You will never receive even a penny from us. The Frisians shouted: Never! Never! Never!

The bishop raised his voice. He spoke very quietly, but he ground his teeth. I will petition for imperial execution against you.

The tide rose. Störtebecker had trouble calming them down.

Lord Bishop: Is it true what we have been told: that you put the shirt of penance on our brother Hinrichsen, that you had him whipped with a birch rod, that you had his intestines wrenched and twisted out of his body while he was still alive – as a heretic and rebellious traitor?

The bishop had gone pale as a corpse. He remained silent.

It is true, shouted Störtebecker, for – and his voice broke, and tears came to his eyes – I had to see it with my own eyes. You are guilty of the same fate a thousand times over.

Guilty, guilty, guilty! echoed the Frisians.

The bishop fell to his knees, whimpering. He howled like a young dog. Spare my life!

You will immediately grant us an indulgence of three hundred sixty days and an indulgence for all that we will still do to you. Bless us with the church's blessing, or we will do to you what you have done to so many others.

The inquisitor whimpered. He spread his thin arms: I bless you!

Step up to this stone. It is the sacrificial stone of Wodan, pray to Wodan! You are a Frisian from the Stadinger clan! You betrayed your Frisian god for the Roman god. Kneel down. Pray to Wodan!

The bishop stood still. He did not move.

Then some people came up from behind and shoved him, causing him to hit his head against the stone. Others piled sticks and small logs into a pyre. They bound the unconscious man to a young birch tree, arms spread, so he stood like the crucified one. Then they lit the flame. Twilight had fallen. The flame rose into the night. They stood hand in hand, entwined, in a circle around the pyre, and sang:

> Rise flames!
> The Frisian is born free!
> Man is predestined for man.
> Sinner lost in sin,
> Bless us, Thor!

They lay in the heath.

Bumblebees and wasps buzzed around the violet flowers of the heather.

Calluna vulgaris, said Binswanger, bending a tuft of flowers toward him. He sniffed like a dog. He remembered his botanical studies at the high school in Helmstedt. Low, branched and very sociable shrubs with close-fitting, almost scale-like leaves, flowers at the ends or on short branches, whose calyx is longer than the corolla, and a four-chambered capsule.

Then you know what's right.

Anke blinked like a sluggish bird taking a hot sand bath in the sun. The others lay here and there: the green, red, yellow vests stood out from the gray-green expanse like giant flowers. Störtebecker lay on a heath grave and looked down at them. They had buried their heads deep in the heather.

You look like people who have been decapitated. Feel your necks to see if you still have your heads.

Töllessen in his red vest spun around with a jerk.

Be so kind, yes.

Brandes lay on his stomach, eating dirt and spitting it out again.

Binswanger: I don't even need to put the earth in my mouth: I know it's high in quartz. I know. It's all about knowledge.

Brandes rolled over to him like a poorly tarred barrel. He stank. He pulled out his knife and pressed it against Binswanger's delicate, girlish neck: That's what matters. It's about skill.

Without the others noticing, Anke had stealthily crept up to Störtebecker on the hill like a brown lizard. He yanked her toward him by her braids.

They lay silently.

The sun burned.

The bumblebees and bees sang.

Down here lies a dead man, said Anke, and we are in love.

Yes, replied Störtebecker, that's what matters: to be.

To be or not to be, it's all the same to me as long as I'm with you, when you exist, and if I'm not with you, when you don't.

They fell silent and sank into the heather. Störtebecker played with a twig.

People make brooms from these twigs and branches. I will cut myself a clean broom in this heath and whip the fat scum out of Hamburg's gates.

Anke glowed with excitement: Yes, you'll do that! Whip them! Whip them! You must whip them naked out of the city: the delicate gentlemen and the fine ladies who drove so many children out of their wombs before their time that they have no breasts left, only flaps, and who bleed like sows every two weeks. Come, I'll help you cut the broom!

She pushed her hair back from her forehead and tossed her braids over her shoulder. Then she jumped up.

The sun hovered just above the horizon. The heath mist rose, and she looked like a red lantern.

Störtebecker heard a growl from the thicket below his hill.

A wolf! said Töllessen.

They surrounded the thicket.

Just then, the animal broke from the underbrush, leaped at Binswanger with a powerful bound, causing him to fall, and vanished into the heather.

Lupus in fabula, said Binswanger.

Anke laughed so hard that tears ran down her cheeks.

Störtebecker smiled: A sheepdog! Then the sheep cannot be far off, for whose shearing we are summoned. Forward!

The lights of Lüneburg gleamed through the night.

I'm glad to see water again, even if it's the Ilmenau, grinned Töllessen.

What's the deal with the Lüneburg silver treasure, Klaus? Anke clung to him like a sword belt. Are there chains in it, too, to wear around the neck?

Störtebecker grumbled: Shut your mouth. You're beautiful enough as you are. Yes, there are chains among the silver treasure. And we'd do well to watch out that no one locks us into the very chains we aim to break.

Brandes cursed: I'm goddamned hungry.

Störtebecker replied: Wait until Lüneburg. You can gorge yourself on the Lüneburg specialties there.

Waldemar was being carried across the ice in several hand sleds with a small entourage. The east winds whistled. His cracked face turned blue.

He shouted from afar: Where is the captain?

Störtebecker stepped to the railing of the frozen ship: What do you wish, sir? Are you the captain?

I am.

Waldemar jumped from the sled, panting with excitement. He threw his arms into the air like an eider duck spreading its wings before flight.

I offer you an alliance, sir, against the Lübeckers and Hanseatic scoundrels. They've formed a confederation against me. Can you believe it? And holy Cologne, *sancta Colonia*, of course, has to be involved. *Sanctae romanae ecclesiae fidelis filia.* I've brought my scribe and notary with me. Let's get to drafting the statutes: Point one, two, three.

A rattling little man crawled out of the second sled.

Störtebecker laughed: Who are you, sir? Forgive my curious question.

Waldemar's blue face proudly flushed back to rosy. He removed his fur cap, under which his head sweated despite the bitter cold. He was silent but suddenly screamed unexpectedly: Waldemar! I am King Waldemar!

Sailors lowered the gangway from the railing.

He laboriously crawled up it like a plump beetle. The notary behind him: a delicate spider.

Barely had the king reached the top when he shouted coarsely: What's to be done now? Eh? Are you frozen with your ships and your thoughts?

Störtebecker showed him the way into the heated cabin: First, have a hot grog, sir. We'll come to an agreement, sir. Because we have to, sir. With Your Royal Majesty's authority, it's a bit of a tricky matter. Let's not kid ourselves. On the streets of Copenhagen, the children follow you: pardon me: as if you were a carnival juggler.

The plump king looked around helplessly. He collapsed in on himself like a jellyfish that had washed ashore during low tide.

Who's to blame for this? He suddenly blurted out, the words shooting out like bolts from a crossbow: The Papist. The Bishop of Roskilde. He preaches in the cathedral against me, who am a Christian prince, that it is a disgrace. Do I bend the law – like him? Do I torture people – like the Inquisition? Do I do wrong? Do I whore around? I love to eat and drink. Is that un-Christian?

He lifted his glass and downed it. Störtebecker waved.

Food was brought out: lapwing eggs, roasted ducks. A pig's head in raspberry sauce. Fat ran down the corners of the king's mouth.

The little scribe crowed cheerfully.

Störtebecker escorted the king to the gangway, where he got tangled in the ropes in his excitement.

Upon reaching the ice, he still shouted up, cupping his hands around his mouth: No hard feelings!

The sleds glided over the mudflats.

Snow fell.

The king disappeared into a cloud of snow.

Störtebecker turned away.

He went into his cabin.

His furrowed face fell heavily onto the edge of the table.

Anke found him like that.

Klaus?

He didn't respond.

Quietly, she left him again.

The white pilgrim spoke: Do you know the nobleman Rosenkreuz?

Störtebecker made a dismissive hand gesture.

I don't know any nobleman Rosenkreuz. I don't want to get to know him either. I have no longing for nobility. He's probably a Jew, this nobleman.

The pilgrim spoke softly and cautiously, as if to calm himself: What do you have against the nobility and against the Jews?

The nobility are highway robbers and marauding knights. They attack you outside the gates if you don't have a sword to defend yourself. And the Jews deceive and rob you when you're in the towns, when you have no money left and have to pawn a golden chain or a velvet embroidered coat.

The pilgrim spoke quietly: Consider whether it's not your fault if you are attacked and deceived. Why do you go outside the city with gemstones in your pouch and a sword at your side? Why do you own a golden chain if you can't afford to lose it? You only possess what you can do without. One truly lives only in the face of death.

Good God, shouted Störtebecker, is there no justice!

There is, the white pilgrim soothed, yes, and his blue eye shone, but it is not your justice. Just look at yourselves and do only what is yours to do. What others do, why does it concern you? Do you have a right to demand anything from anyone: for good or ill?

I want to help people!

Help! Help! The white pilgrim echoed the word back like a refrain. That word you speak is very grand. Perhaps you cannot help them at all. Perhaps the skill you have learned is like the art of dragon-slaying, which someone studied for four years. And when he finished his studies, he found no opportunity to apply it. Because there were no dragons. And in his rage that there were no dragons, he began to kill men. Perhaps you are of this kind?

Störtebecker groaned.

Yes, I set out to kill the dragon. But it blew fire and sulfur at me, leaving me almost stunned.

And you killed men?

They protected the dragon.

And what did you gain?

Hate, hate, hate – against them – and against me.

Störtebecker buried his bushy head in trembling hands.

The way from hate to love is not far.

The pilgrim gently stroked Störtebecker's head. It felt as if a bird's wing touched him.

When he looked up, the white pilgrim had disappeared.

He sat in his room by the open window, watching a flight of cranes that glided over the city.

Then he heard dull footsteps tapping up the stairs, stopping in front of his door.

In a flash, he turned around, drew his dagger, and positioned himself behind the door, which opened inward.

He laughed and threw his knife to the ground.

Töllessen – brother – how did you find me?

Töllessen's eyes were filled with tears like those of a thirteen-year-old girl who sees her mother again after a long separation.

Störtebecker shook him like a bundle of clothes.

Come, let's go to the tavern. A bottle of Malvasia shouldn't be too bad for this reunion.

Töllessen shook his head.

Leave it, Captain. I have to speak with you. Seriously.

Störtebecker threw himself onto his mattress. Töllessen now stood at the window. The cranes were only visible as small dots.

Störtebecker: Speak, Hans.

Klaus, Töllessen choked, Klaus, you mustn't leave us.

He fell to his knees before him.

The bloodhounds are on our heels. Their barking grows louder and rougher. And the hunters' triumphant cries ring out to us: They have no leader anymore. Störtebecker has fled. He has abandoned them.

Störtebecker closed his eyes. He spoke very softly. It sounded like a bumblebee buzzing: Hans, you know why I left you. I cannot forget the battle against the sea lions. I fought honestly: man against man; I did not stab anyone in the back who wouldn't have done the same to me if I weren't quicker than he was. But that battle, that slaughter of defenseless animals: I cannot forget it, Hans!

We hadn't had a skirmish for eight weeks, Klaus; then it came over us. I no longer understand it today. I would spit in my own face for it. Believe me, Klaus. Forgive us! Forgive me! The crew begs for your forgiveness. We are lost if you do not help us. Brandes is confused and doesn't know what to do. He is cruising restlessly with a galleon and six caravels off Jutland. We have mounted a new figurehead on the galleon, Klaus. The ram's head was shot off in a battle with the Danes.

The ram shot off? A bad omen.

Störtebecker still kept his eyes closed.

Claudius has carved a new figurehead: from a piece of the foremast of a Danish brig: your head, Klaus. You have always been with us, Klaus.

If you have my head, what need do you have for the whole body? Be content with what you have.

Klaus: there's a rumor –

There are many rumors –

– that you have joined our enemies.

He fell silent and looked through his lashes as if through a veil at Störtebecker.

Störtebecker opened his eyes wide.

He sat up on the edge of the bed and laughed.

You have a strange method of regaining my camaraderie.

Töllessen: I will tell you the reason for the rumor: Sita, the daughter of Senator Stollenweber, our fiercest enemy –

What about her?

She is on the man-of-war of the Hamburg fleet sent against us. Yes, it is said that she, the woman, commands the fleet of the Hanse. It is a silly, childish rumor, but I tell you this, Klaus, because it might interest you –

Töllessen lay in wait.

Störtebecker was one step away from him at the window. The crane flock had disappeared. Dusk rose like fog from the streets. He thought aloud: She is looking for me.

She shouldn't search for me in vain. Then to Töllessen: I am yours, Hans. Let's go. Lead me to my people.

Töllessen gleamed with joy.

A boat is waiting at the Outer Elbe. Come, Captain.

The brig turned about.

With sails singing, the enemy frigate charged toward the flagship of the Likedeeler and rammed it sideways.

Grappling hooks clawed into the rigging like vultures.

Small boat bridges sprang from one ship to another like angry dogs, biting into the wooden planks.

With a morning star in her delicate fist, Sita was the first to jump onto the flagship. Her blonde hair flowed in strands and streams from the iron helmet.

Her chest danced beneath the armor.

At the mast, Störtebecker stood, rapier in his right hand, the red flag in his left.

Blood dripped from his neck over the black scarf.

Sita shouted: Likedeeler! Likedeeler! You egalitarians! Death will make you all equal! And it will equalize! You drifters! Driven hopelessly from the current of life into the desolate sea! You stormers! With whom the storm plays! Mors will teach you manners! You shall no longer upend the goblet, reveler, Störtebecker, and drink the blood of your enemies, you bloodsucker! Where is your huge golden chalice? I want to catch your blood and place it in St. Mary's Church in Hamburg as a dreadful memorial, so that tens of thousands will make the sign of the cross before it when the devil sets it raging again.

Roaring with laughter, Störtebecker exclaimed: Girl, girl! Virgin or whore: whoever you are: this blood is immortal! It will forever race through the veins of humanity. It is the blood that Lucifer drew from the angels before he turned away from them. And you seem to be such an angel too, pale and anemic! It is the blood of defiance against God; it ran in the veins of Prometheus when he stole fire from the gods to bring it to mankind. It is the blood that has soaked my red flag – for I have drenched this flag with the blood of my brothers who have fallen so that an honest, bold, and true humanity may rise. I come as the guardian of the holy white grail –

The Grail: it is the gold treasure of the wealthy merchants of Hamburg, extorted from the blood of serving slaves and serfs. You cry Grail and God, but you mean gold and interest.

Then she raised the club and struck him on the forehead, causing him to collapse. But as he fell, he still thrust his rapier into her chest from below.

They sank together as if in an embrace.

Her helmet clattered across the deck. Her blonde hair flowed into his black hair. And their blood mingled together.

When Störtebecker awoke, he shouted: Where is the girl?

He could only open his eyes halfway, as they were glued shut with sweat and blood.

Klaus Toelen, the surgeon, sat by him.

You've only lightly tickled her lung between two ribs. She's alive. She's lying in the cabin next door. Anke Hansen is with her.

Störtebecker closed his eyes again.

The ship rocked up and down.

And it seemed to him as though that girl walked upon the waves of the sea, dressed in a white shift, holding a white flag in her left hand and a lily in her right.

With his eyes still closed, he grinned and contorted his face.

The devil. The god. What silly faces the fever conjures for me. That girl nearly smashes my skull in with a proper, solid morning star, and suddenly I see a flower in her hand. Maybe I didn't even strike her with my sword but merely brushed a Spanish fly from her tender chest with a fan. Did they take off her breastplate? With my hand I long to mend that chest my sword split.

Klaus Toelen smiled: All that's left is for you to become infatuated with the Amazon.

Bockemühl stepped through the cabin door.

I propose we hang her by her blonde locks from the mast. Woman or not, she is our enemy.

Toelen tugged at his yellow pointed beard.

We have a good bargaining chip with her. She is the daughter of Senator Stollenweber in Hamburg. Hamburg will part with some tons of ducats if we send her back to him unharmed.

Bockemühl grumbled: Just so we can have another thorn in our side in five weeks? She's a damned she-devil. I have the utmost respect for her, and that's exactly why I want to hang her. Any ordinary, inconsequential whore we could let go.

Störtebecker tried to open his eyes wide.

He had a bandage around his head and neck.

He rose, and Toelen supported him.

He trudged a few steps, stumbled, and fell against the door.

He reached out, like Samson, to the left and right for the doorposts.

He stomped and swayed into the adjacent cabin.

Anke sat at the foot of the bed, playing with Sita's feet.

She kissed her toes, one after the other.

She gave them names: she called the big toe Grete, the little toe Anna, and so forth, saying: I love Grete, I love Anna, I love them all, all of them.

I love the big toe, I love the little toe. I love all toes.

I love Klaus Toelen. I love Bockemühl. I love Störtebecker –

Störtebecker stood in the doorway.

The ship swayed.

He held on to the wood on the left and right. Anke Hansen was silent.

She let Sita's feet drop.

Sita was sleeping.

Beneath the coarse linen shirt that had been put on her, her small breasts breathed calmly.

Störtebecker took a few steps forward.

Go, he said, trying to give his rough voice a gentle tone, go, Anke, leave me alone with the girl.

He sat down on the bunk and looked at the sleeping girl.

He sat immobile for an hour.

Then Sita awoke, looked at him with wide eyes, closed them again, and went back to sleep.

He cleared his throat.

She awoke.

Why won't you let me sleep? It's the only thing I have left. I can imagine I'm dying. Why don't you kill me?

Störtebecker remained silent. Then he said: Bockemühl suggested hanging you.

Sita looked at him questioningly: And? Why don't you?

Störtebecker held her gaze.

Perhaps you could still be of some use to me.

Sita smiled: Me? Serve? How? If you released me, my first act would be to outfit a new fleet against you, for I could not bear the thought that my first attempt had failed. You will marvel when I tell you quite calmly that I hate you. Because you are strength, and I am weakness. Because you are a man, and I am a woman. Yes: that is why I hate you and strive to destroy you.

Störtebecker: You speak like a professor of eloquence or moral science. All of this is pointless: you are in my power, and I will do with you as I wish.

Doubtless. It would be foolish of you not to do so.

Störtebecker tugged at his eyebrows, which were fused together above his forehead: How much ransom do you think your father would pay if I sent you home to him?

Blood rushed to her pale forehead.

I refuse to serve as an object for such a disgraceful transaction. With the gold you would demand, he could equip an entire fleet against you. What does it matter if I perish? I have dedicated myself to the service of God in St. Nikolai. And because you are the devil incarnate, I fight against you: with the purest weapons and the purest heart.

With the purest heart?

Störtebecker laughed.

Have you never had a longing for a man? Hmm? For me now, for example? I cannot deny that the delicate breast, which moves so gently beneath the rough shirt, tempts me to grasp it and kiss the scar I inflicted upon it.

Sita remained silent.

She crossed herself.

Well – well –

He grinned.

We, too, have our crosses to bear. But we are not Christians. No. Because we wish to cast off the cross that you and your kind have laid upon us and burn it in the midsummer night of our god. Yes, he shouted, his voice breaking, I do not believe in your shameless, submissive, groveling Christian god: I believe in the heathen god of thunder, Perkun, who smashes his enemies with his silver lightning sword. I believe in Wodan. And, he shouted, I believe in the Valkyries. Is there not one lying here before me in the flesh? Resist all you want: you are of the same blood as me, ever since our blood mingled on the deck of the battleship. Unite with me, and I shall become invincible, and the red flag will fly from the St. Nikolai tower in Hamburg. We will tear the Crucified One from his cross, make a fire with it, cleanse our bloodstained hands in the holy water, and at his altar offer sacrifice to the only god worthy of an offering: the god of living life.

He stood with bent knees in the cabin. The ship swayed.

The bandage around his forehead reddened with fresh blood.

Sita had half risen; she supported herself with her right hand and flung her left at him like an arrow: *Apage, Satanas!*

His vision turned red.

Dizziness seized him.

He collapsed before her.

They placed Störtebecker in an iron cage and paraded him triumphantly through the city.

He sat there like an eagle in captivity, proud and silent.

The children in the streets threw horse manure at him, which stuck in his beard.

The women spat in his face. You murderer of our men! Of our happiness!

You bastard of a skunk and a hyena! Where is your pride now? Huh?

They will wring your intestines from your body and hang you with them.

With pliers, they will rip your heart from your belly and hang it in your mouth.

The cage was hung for eight days at the pillory of St. Nikolai Church.

It rained incessantly.

The battle-damaged clothes and boots were washed from his body.

By the fifth day, he stood naked in the cage.

His broad brown chest breathed toward the sky.

One night, the rain began to ease.

Suddenly, it completely stopped.

There was an impenetrable darkness. Suddenly a voice sounded: Störtebecker!

Störtebecker listened.

Störtebecker!

The voice sounded as if in prayer.

Störtebecker replied: Who calls me?

Do not ask me about the who. Who is who? What is what? The darkness calls you. The night. I love you.

Who loves me? I am only hated.

A person loves you. If only one person loves you, then you are saved.

No one can save me.

Yet: you yourself.

How?

Through faith.

In whom?

In me!

Who are you?

Love.

Love is an abstraction.

I am a person who loves.

You are mistaken; you pity me because I hang here in storm and rain.

I have no pity for you. I cannot suffer with you because you do not suffer.

How do you know that?

I feel it.

Then you must love: in deed.

Yes: in deed I want to love you. I want to free you.

You can free me from the cage, perhaps, if you have a ladder, file, and hammer. No man can free me from the cage of my brain and my will.

No God?

No God and no devil.

A ladder was placed against the stone tower. Someone climbed up.

Filing. Sawing. Quiet hammering.

The bars broke.

Sita stood in the cage.

She tore off her cloak and shirt and threw herself naked against the naked man's chest.

They didn't speak another word.

They stood deeply embraced until dawn broke.

Then Sita freed herself from his arms.

You're not following me? A boat awaits at the next creek. I have clothes and – Störtebecker shook his head.

What does it matter? My brothers have been slain. My heart barely beats anymore. I am tired. I am no longer capable of a new deed. Others will come to raise the red flag from the dust, where we, in our ignorance, have cast it ourselves.

She descended the ladder. Threw the ladder, file, and hammer into the water.

Once more she turned her head. The first rays of the rising sun already played around his brow like silver waves.

The excitement among the citizens was great when they discovered that Störtebecker's cage had been sawed through. Even greater was the astonishment that Störtebecker had not fled.

The executioner threw the red shirt of murderers and criminals over him. With his hands bound behind his back, he walked upright and firm amid the guards, who used their spears to hold off the crowd trying to lynch him. Though he had not taken any food for ten days, he walked resolutely to the execution site.

The execution site was filled with a black, bustling, murmuring crowd. When he stepped onto the scaffold, a sudden silence fell over the place. They saw him wave the clergyman away, standing alone in his red shirt, over which his red beard flowed down, bathed in the morning light.

He raised his hand. Instantly, silence fell.

People, he spoke slowly, I have loved you. I wanted to free you from the idols. Forgive me! For I wanted nothing for myself. Even now, I only ask for my imprisoned comrades. After the execution, I want to walk past them, and as far as I can go, they should be free and rid of their bonds.

The judges looked at one another. With a mocking laugh, the chief judge replied: So shall it be! Your last wish shall be granted!

The executioner struck off his head, which rolled into the sand.

And headless, upright, Störtebeker stomped heavily past thirteen of his comrades. Then he fell, stiff and straight, to the ground.

A cry tore through the oppressive silence that hung over the place.

On the balcony of Senator Stollenweber, Sita collapsed unconscious.

On the Hallig Süderoog, atop the highest hill, Anke stood, holding the boy's hand.

The waves lashed against the shore, and sprays hissed like snakes into the front yard of the house, over the hedge of blooming buckthorn, where they hung like dewdrops on the auricles and gooseberry bushes.

The chestnut tree swayed like an ungainly dancer in the storm.

Day after day, Anke Hansen looked out to the south and to the north, to the east and to the west.

She spoke not a word, and the boy was silent too, his left hand clenched in the fur of his favorite goat.

She hoisted the small flag at the mast in front of the house, the one he had carried on the day of their wedding.

She took her red headscarf and waved it over the sea. And only the setting sun waved back.

One night, she awoke from her sleep.

She heard shouting, singing, tin mugs clinking together as revelers toasted one another.

Naked as she was, she leapt from her bed and out of the house.

The sea lay still, blinking like a great eye.

She gazed up at the moon.

She took her two breasts in her hands and offered them to him. Then she sank into the yellow sand, and he leaned over her like a lover, and his love was so radiant and powerful that she had to close her eyes; he dazzled her, he held her tightly in his shining arms.

From that night on, she no longer kept watch. She knew he had gone to join the stars.

One evening, the boy asked: Where is father?

She pointed to the moon: He always sees and knows what we are doing and thinking here on Earth. One day, he will send Töllessen or Bockemühl in a boat to take us to the golden shore. You, Pidder, must become like him: the red flag has been unfurled once, in the cities and on the sea. It will not disappear again. The sea shall be free, the Earth free, humankind free. He showed them the way, and they will not lose it again. Someday, on the towers, churches, and warehouses, on the galleons and caravels of the Hamburg and Lübeck patricians, the red flag will fly: in the leather chairs of the council chambers will sit carpenters, locksmiths, butchers, bakers, and shiphands. After centuries of oppression and injustice, they will have their rights. And where above the mayor's chair, on the wall, once hung the portrait of the emperor – Charles IV, whom they serve – there will hang the portrait of Störtebeker, your father, whom they called a robber because he took back the rights and goods they and their ancestors had stolen from him and his kind.

The boy nodded seriously. Tears stood in his blue eyes.

He raised his hand:

Free is the sea, free is the earth, free is man!

Photographs and Illustrations

Kalbund's Father, Dr. Alfred Heneschke
(1858-1936)

Klabund's Mother Emilie Antonie
Buckenau (1867-1945)

Klabund, 1922

Dr. Alfred Henschke's Pharmacy
in Crossen, Poland

Klábund Lithograph by Orlik, 1915

Klabund with Fran Bruno at Walchensee,
1915

Brunhilde Heberle in 1917
(1896-1918)

Klabund and his first wife Brunhilde Heberle
on a trip to Mergosscia, Switzerland

Klabund with Brother Hans and Two
Cousins

Brunhilde Heberle, 1916

Carola Neher in 1925, (1900-1942)

Klabund in Davos

Klabund, Date Unknown

Klabund Portrait by Eric Buttner, 1919

Klabund, Date Unknown

Klabund, Date Unknown

Klabund with the Actor
Alexander Granach, 1926

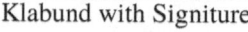

Klabund with Signiture

Klabund, 1925

Klabund, 1928

Carola Neher in 1925

Klabund's New Years Greeting
to Irene and Max Heberle, 1923

Klabund and Carola Neher, 1924

Klabund and Carola Neher, 1925

Klabund and Carola Neher in 1928

Klabund and Carola Neher on the Beach,
Date Unknown

Klabund, Last Photograph, Brioni,
Summer 1928

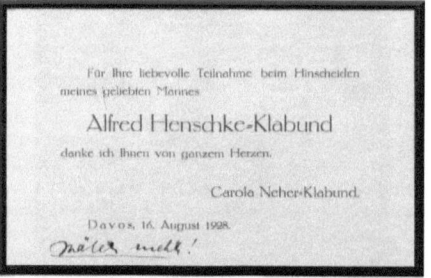

I thank you from the bottom of my heart for
your loving condolences at the passing
of my beloved husband.

Newspaper Clipping: Klabund and Neher in Vienna, 1927

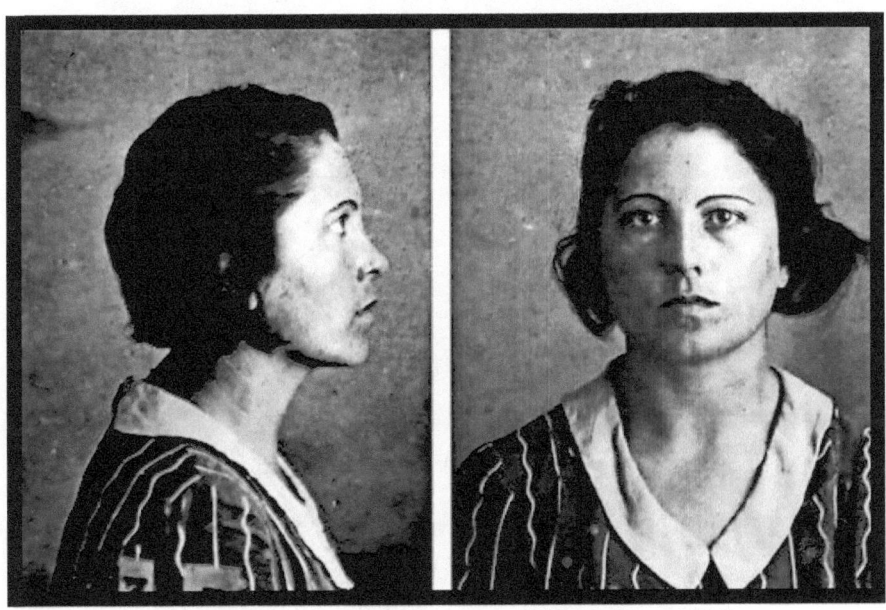

Carola Neher Prison Photo from KGB Archive, 1936

Klabund's play *The Chalk Circle*, 1925

Klabund's play *The Cherry Blossom Festival*, 1928

December 1919 program for the Sound and Smoke Cabaret

Script for Klabund's XYZ play

KLABUND

BRACKE. Ein Eulenspiegel-Roman
5. Auflage / Broschiert M. 6.50, gebunden M. 9.—

Klabunds Eulenspiegelbuch ist das Reichste und Reinste, das Umfangreichste und Bunteste, was er bisher schrieb. Ein ganz deutsches, gutes gotisches Werk; heiter bis zur Ausgelassenheit, schmerzlich bis zur Tragik, feierlich und farbig, Choral und Schwank. Die Sprache ist klar wie ein Waldquell. Ein Buch für die Gelangen ebenso wie für das Volk. Dieser Bracke, dieser saitliche Eulenspiegel, der dem Kurfürsten Joachim und dem Kaiser Karl V. Widerpart hält, mit Tieren und Engeln wie mit Menschen spricht, ein reiner Tor mit Mördern, Henkern und Abdeckern zu Tische sitzt, zu dessen Hochzeit St. Peter persönlich vom Himmel herniedersteigt, um ihm zum Tanze zu geigen, der die Ungerechtigkeit wie die Pest haßt, daran er doch augrunde geht: dieser alte und närrische Mann hat Anrecht, als deutscher Sinnbild zu bestehen neben Götz von Berlichingen und Michael Kohlhaas.

MOHAMMED. Der Roman eines Propheten
Prospero-Druck II / Mit lithographiertem Eingangsblatt von Slevogt und Originalradierung von Hans Meid
Auflage 600 Exemplare / Vergriffen

MOREAU. Der Roman eines Soldaten
Umschlag von Slevogt / 5. Aufl. / Geh. M.5.—, geb. M.7.—

Ein eigenartig packendes Buch ist Klabunds Roman eines Soldaten Moreau. In seinem mit verzückter Knappheit hingeworfenen kurzen Sätzen, die ohne Taschenschnitt ohne alles schmückende Beiwerk geben, liest es sich wie die großartige Antwort auf einer starken Tragödie. Mit merkwürdiger Pathos steht das Leben des bedeutenden Nebenbuhlers Napoleons vor uns wie eine Vision. So müssen historische Gestalten lebendig gemacht werden.
(Kölnische Zeitung)

DER LEIERKASTENMANN
Volkslieder der Gegenwart / Gesammelt und zum ersten Male veröffentlicht von Klabund / Mit vielen handkolorierten Holzschnitten von Szafranski / In entzückendem kolorierten Pappband M. 3.80, in echtem Japanband M. 6.—

ERICH REISS VERLAG, BERLIN W 62

KLABUND

DIE HIMMELSLEITER
Neue Gedichte / 2. Auflage / Geh. M. 3.60, geb. M. 5.50

Diese Verse sind Gelegenheitslyrik im Goetheschen Sinne. Zwanglos aus dem Tag erwachsen, teilen sie die Feierlichkeit großer Worte und wollen nicht mehr scheinen als sie sind. Diese Schlichtheit, die sich ohne Prätensionen gibt, ist besonders erfreulich in einer Zeit, in der jede verschwollene Medisalschrift in einem Tonfall redet, als ob sie Armen zur Verfügung hätte.
(Berliner Tageblatt)

DIE KRANKHEIT
Eine Erzählung / 3. Auflage / Geh. M. 2.50, geb. M. 4.—

Ein seltsames Buch. In dem Kreislauf und Tod auf jeder Seite umgehen. Menschen, die den Todeskeim in sich tragen, zeigt uns Klabund in ihrem Leben, Denken, Haffen und Verzweifeln. (Karlsruher Tagblatt)

»DER MARKETENDERWAGEN«
Ein Kriegsbuch / 2. Auflage / Geh. M. 3.—, geb. M. 4.50

Dieses Buch, das gewinnt, je öfter man die kleinen Skizzen liest, gehört in die Hände aller derer, die, übel und verdrossen von der sogenannten »Kriegslyrik« und der geschwätzigen Kriegsreklamemakulatur, den reineren Wirkungen der Zeit künstlerisch nachleben möchten, die Ernst und Mut und ein Lachen zu würdigen wissen. (Anhaltischen Staats-Anzeiger)

**MORGENROT! KLABUND!
DIE TAGE DÄMMERN!**
Gedichte / 2. Auflage / Geh. M. 2.50, geb. M. 4.—

KLABUNDS KARUSSELL
Schwänke / 2. Auflage / Geh. M. 3.50, geb. M. 5.50

Klabunds Prosa ist von strenger Sachlichkeit. Ereignisse, sonderbare, groteske, doch überaus menschliche. Kunst, die ganz auf Tat und Leben gestellt ist. Psychologisches vermeidet. Diese knappen Erzählungen brauchen auch Psychologie nicht; man fühlt das Seelische heraus, kennt alle Zusammenhänge, spürt Geheimstes und Innerstes, man versteht. (Berliner Börsencourier)

ERICH REISS VERLAG, BERLIN W 62

Klabund's Works Published by Eric Reiss Verlag

Klabund Statue with the Mayor of Crossen, Poland

Part Four:

Borgia – Novel of a Family

(Phaidon Verlag, Vienna, 1928)

Borgia – Novel of a Family

Prologue

I inscribe these letters as a reminder, I write these words for the sake of memory, I think these thoughts for contemplation, I paint these actions for future guidance.

My name is Johannes Goritz, and I was born in Luxembourg in the German Empire. By profession, I am a petitions advisor. My house near the Forum of Trajan in Rome is open to all people of culture and education. In particular, the Germans who come to Rome customarily honor me with their visits. I have had the pleasure of welcoming and entertaining Reuchlin, Copernicus, Erasmus, Ulrich von Hutten, that now quite famous, or infamous, monk Martin Luther in my home. If I remember correctly, the latter was quite a hearty eater, barbarically fond of a sumptuous capon or a fatty roast pork. Indeed, the monastic and the barbaric, the German and the Scythian, oddly mixed in him, providing an explanation for the exaggerated rejection of conditions in the 'sinful Babylon' of Rome. At that time, the earth seemed to spin faster on its axis. People easily lost their balance. Comets trailed across the night sky. Saturn cast its sinister light. Vesuvius and Stromboli spewed fire. There was no end to the horrors of war, to revolutionary and religious strife, and no beginning of true humanity, though everyone spoke of humanism. How, then, could Rome alone maintain its moral equilibrium in such chaos? Was it any wonder that the rock of St. Peter began to tremble and the holy church was shaken to its foundations? With my own hand, I recorded this diary of Roman events during the time of the Borgias in Latin, during the leisure hours afforded me by my extensive official duties. This manuscript was the sole possession I saved from the sacking of Rome in the year of our Lord 1527, that fateful year in which I lost all my belongings except for the strength of my heart and the soundness of my mind. Fate brought me into close proximity with that remarkable giant known as Alexander Borgia. I often had the opportunity to speak personally and intimately with his exceptionally beautiful and graceful daughter, Lucrezia, and His Highness, the Duke of Romagna, Cesare Borgia. From these encounters, I formed my own opinions about three individuals who were both charming and uncharming, in whom the greatest contradictions were united.

Surely, anyone who judges Cesare Borgia solely by his actions and the pamphlets of his enemies, of which he possessed countless, forms a completely false image of his outward appearance and his "public character." Cesare Borgia was always a man of exceptional courtesy, restraint, and rare modesty; in short, the ideal figure of what one might call a virtuous man and courtier. His actions and plans are another matter altogether. His personal charm, indeed his gentleness, was entirely compatible with a factual hardness and cruelty. Without ever being able to love, he was always affable, and I still remember how delighted Machiavelli was to tell me about his encounter with him, which inspired the idea for his treatise on the "Prince." And this was at a time when Cesare Borgia was nothing more than a ruin of himself, as the French disease had terribly affected him. There are also completely inaccurate legends circulating about Alexander VI, the powerful creator of the Borgia dynasty – for that is what it is – especially concerning his visible appearance (every historical figure has many facets, and often a facet that shines through obscures the overall picture). In him, a devil certainly raged – but he was never outwardly recognizable. Alexander Borgia was one of the most beautiful men of his time, strong even into his old age, full of cheerful, harmonious disposition, and averse to all demons of darkness. He loved his children with a fervent passion and was solely concerned with increasing the power of the Borgias with prudence and without any regard for moral prejudices. Whatever he did, he did openly, hiding nothing, and I have never seen anyone so disdainful of the world's judgment as he was. It is far from me to write an apology for the Borgias; I weigh the scales of justice in my hand; may God distribute the weights; it is not my place to pronounce judgment. I am a petitions advisor: I – advise.

I.

In those times, when time did not yet exist, when an eternal sky, the sky of eternity, burned over Hellas, there lived Ixion, a man.

Emerald lizards, angry adders, locusts, crickets, beetles, sheep, deer, and horses lived alongside him. Ringed and Aesculapian snakes hung like precious chains around his neck, and the lizards licked his pointed fingers with their small tongues.

But most of all, he loved a young wild mare, to whom he gave no name. For whoever bears a name already possesses a property that temps gawkers and greed.

Since he gave the mare no name, he hid her from gods and men.

For no one could call her.

One day, however, Zeus, the god of gods, saw the mare at a watering place in a forest clearing.

He soared down to the earth in the form of an eagle. As soon as he arrived on earth, he took on the body of a stallion.

The mare was startled and fled from the lustful god. Her nostrils flared, she stormed shyly through forests and fields, she came to a mountain, she climbed the rocks like a chamois, through chasms and ravines, the snorting stallion close behind her. Thus she galloped straight toward Olympus. At the summit of the mountain, the god overpowered her.

Ixion wandered wailing from early morning until late at night through the groves and meadows.

He did not catch sight of his beloved mare.

And since he had given her no name, he cried out only: Alas! Alas! Alas!

When he had not found the mare after a week, he went mad.

He ran around on all fours, ate grass, crushed and trampled grasshoppers, crickets, beetles, and lizards, and neighed like a horse.

His neighing was heard by Zeus.

He lifted him up to Olympus with a wind, drew him to the table of the gods and took away the torment of madness from him.

He made him his cupbearer. – When Ixion swirled and rinsed his lord's cup at the fountain in the courtyard of the palace of the gods, he suddenly heard a familiar neighing from a stable.

He followed the neighing and discovered his mare, who leaped up joyfully at him like a dog and placed both front hooves on his shoulders.

Filled with anger that Zeus had stolen his mare, he decided to take revenge on the god and cast his eye on Hera, the god's beautiful wife.

One night he crept up to her.

But Zeus, the omniscient, sent a cloud to meet him, which he gave the shape of Hera. So Ixion lovingly mingled with the cloud.

The next afternoon, Ixion, believing he had embraced Hera, approached the table of the dining gods and cried joyfully: I have possessed Hera, the wife of Zeus!

The gods jumped up in horror.

Zeus turned pale and signaled to two servants. They bound Ixion and tied him to the eternally rolling fiery wheel on the northern side of Olympus.

II.

Nephele, the cloud, gave birth after nine months to a son by Ixion, who was named Kentauros.

From an early age, like his father, he was drawn to horses.

He played with the nameless mare in Zeus's stable and soon learned to ride her in all four directions.

One day, he fled on the mare from the realm of the gods and arrived in the lands of men. He gained a wife and fathered seven sons with her. His sons commingled with wild mares, as they could not find enough women in the mountainous forests of Thessaly.

In quarries and damp ravines, the mares gave birth: half human, half horse. The upper body was that of a human, the lower body that of a horse. The hippocentaurs grew into wild, lustful creatures.

They fought with animals, humans, and demigods. Even Heracles had to contend with them in Arcadia.

In their defiance and arrogance, they attempted to storm Olympus, the mountain of the gods. The nameless mare showed them the way. They galloped up the slopes of the mountain, shielded by the morning mist. But Zeus, informed by a startled owl, hurled lightning at them, causing them to flee in panic. They leaped down the rocks, and the rockfall thundered behind them. Many broke their necks and spines, and the eagles and vultures devoured their hearts and entrails.

Some, however, reached the Mediterranean Sea, plunged into the waves, and swam to other lands: to Africa, to Sicily.

Two made it with great difficulty to Spain. And from them, it is said, the Borgia descended.

The Borgia claim their historical origin from the Spanish town of Borja, located not far from Huecha in the province of Zaragoza. Eight knights of Borgia fought under Don Jayme against the Moors, and in 1238, the battle cry first rang out: Borgia! Borgia!

In the Cistercian Abbey of Veruela, located at the foot of Moncayo, west of Borja, the Borgias dedicated their trophies from the Moorish wars to the Holy Virgin: crooked sabers, turbans, belts, daggers, clasps. On one of these clasps hung the Moorish woman Noa.

All eight Borgias loved her in the wind-swept tent by the hot Tagus until the last one, filled with jealousy that the seven other Borgias had her before him, strangled her in his embrace.

A last gasp from her throat sighed: Borgia! Borgia!

III.

In the year of misfortune of 1455, the Spaniard Alfonso Borgia, former private secretary to King Alfonso of Naples, ascended the Holy Apostolic Throne under the name Calixtus III. He was seventy-seven years old, suffering from a chronic stomach ailment, and, like all those with stomach issues, had a gloomy, distrustful disposition, from which only occasionally a whimsical humor flashed like the green moon behind black clouds. More than theology, he was devoted to jurisprudence, studying the Pandects and Decretals more eagerly than the two Testaments. It pleased him to pose intricate pedantic questions and answer them even more pedantically.

Like a comet with its trailing tail, Alfonso Borgia dragged a whole retinue of Spaniards behind him to Rome.

In all the streets, palaces, and taverns, they began to assert themselves, speaking Spanish and mangling Italian. And among the women, the Señores often outshone the Signori. There were dark looks, ill feelings, duels beneath shadowy arcades, and one day the outraged crowd threw a young Spaniard, whom they had caught with a fourteen-year-old beauty from the Ponte district, resolutely over the bridge into the Tiber. He managed to save himself on the opposite shore. It was twenty-four-year-old Rodrigo Borgia, a nephew of the Pope, a strikingly handsome young man who, as it was said, attracted women like a magnet draws iron. He had come from Bologna a few days earlier, where he had received his doctorate in canon law. Still dripping wet, with clenched teeth, Rodrigo Borgia made his way to the Vatican, pushed aside the halberds of the watchful Swiss guards, and entered the Pope's study, where he was currently preoccupied with the legal possibility of a marriage dispensation for the third degree of consanguinity.

He looked up irritably from his parchments.

Listen, Uncle, Rodrigo began, still dripping, your Roman women are very pretty, but your Romans don't understand humor.

They poured water over your head, didn't they? grumbled the old man.

Joking aside, Don Alfonso – you are a Borgia, and I am a Borgia. Everyone else is just scoundrels. It is fitting for us to stick together. I have a proposal for you, which came to me while I was swimming through the Tiber – along with the dirty water I spat out of my mouth and nose. How about you grant me the purple of the cardinals?

The Pope widened his watery blue eyes.

What? he screeched, You want to become a cardinal? Under the table, his belly shook with silent laughter. But it seemed he was afraid to let his mocking laughter escape across the table. For there stood Rodrigo Borgia, unyielding, with no expression twisted on his beautiful face: a Borgia like him, but a man, a desire, a will.

You must show the rabble an iron brow, said Rodrigo Borgia. Whoever yields has already lost. Whoever slams his fist in their face – wins.

The Pope had various legal concerns – he wanted to consult his Commentaries, Decretals, etc., about consanguinity –

Rodrigo slammed his small, delicate, yet rock-hard fist on the table, causing the carved wooden crucifix to bounce up and down like a doll: Only blood relations, Uncle, justify this – and everything else. The kinship of blood is the holiest bond that can bind men. The same blood courses through your and my veins, Alfonso Borgia. So hear it rushing –

And he tore off his wet shirt and pressed the old man's head to his chest, where the elder listened intently, trying to hear the heart of the Borgias beat.

IV.

Calixtus III convened the Sacred College. Cardinals Estruteville, Capranica, and Bessarione attempted to oppose Rodrigo's appointment as cardinal.

It was of no use to them. Calixtus bribed the rest with lucrative benefices and abbeys.

Barely had Rodrigo Borgia taken his seat in the College when he began to dominate the feeble and sickly uncle, and all the weak characters in the College. His first action was to ensure that two more Borgias received high church offices immediately: Don Luis Borgia became Bishop of Segovia and Lea; Pedro Borgia was appointed Prefect of the City of Rome and soon began to cause trouble for the Orsini and Colonna families.

Men and women trembled in Rodrigo's presence, and it was said that even the saints in the paintings of the Vatican lowered their eyes when he passed by them cheerfully and, in good spirits, made the sign of the cross over them.

He celebrated his first Mass, barely knowing the religious customs. But where he lacked a Latin word, he simply inserted: Borgia! Borgia! in its place. He broke the host too early and occasionally let a piece fall carelessly. Throughout his life, he celebrated Mass very reluctantly and did not take the host seriously. Moreover, things never quite went right during his Mass: sometimes the candles were missing, sometimes the singers, sometimes the canopy or the censer, and sometimes even he himself was absent.

Listen, Uncle, he said to Calixtus, it's quite clever of you to support the crusade against the Turks, who, after all, have done us no harm – for you are making yourself and thus the name Borgia popular among Christendom – but don't forget to firmly establish the foundation for the Borgia dynasty. You have granted me the benefices of Benevento and Terracina. Fine. I wear the red vestment. Good. But now I have ambitions for the office of Vice-Chancellor. It is the highest office after yours – you are old; forgive me for reminding you, but something could happen to you – you must secure our position and our influence for all eventualities.

The Pope, who had a glass of a green magenta tincture standing before him which he abhorred, closed his lashless eyes and thought about his nephew. Then he opened them.

You are right. I will sign the appointment decree tomorrow.

Rodrigo Borgia took a step closer to him, so that the Pope almost began to fear: Tomorrow? Today, Uncle, today, right now, at this moment you will sign the decree that I will draft myself, to spare you the trouble of writing. – 'We, Calixtus III...'

V.

During the falcon hunt, Cardinal Rodrigo Borgia and Count Jean d'Armagnac met. They doffed their hats and decided to continue the hunt together.

At the picnic, when the corks had popped from the wine bottles, Count d'Armagnac, who was very heated from the wine, asked the young cardinal, who had also drunk a lot of wine but remained completely sober, for a private conversation. They stepped aside, and leaning against two trees, they were silent for a while before the Count found the courage to speak the first words.

He struck the foliage of the trees with his riding crop.

Had the Most Reverend Cardinal occupied himself in any way with the nature of love – in the free time that his spiritual exercises allowed him? The Cardinal smiled politely: Certainly, more in a theoretical sense, more platonically, as befits a church prelate.

Certainly, certainly. The Count agreed. But it is precisely on the theory, on the principle that I wish to focus. Namely, to what extent is marriage between blood relatives permitted by the Church or – as I would like to express it – possibly tolerated?

The irises in the Cardinal's eyes began to light up. May I ask the Count whom he wishes to marry?

The Count had almost sobered up from the excitement. He regretted his frankness with the impenetrable Borgia. But it was too late to keep the secret. He lowered his head like a schoolboy caught on the wrong path. I love – my sister.

The Cardinal fell silent.

Above in the trees, the wind was howling.

And in the wind, a whiting, a bird of prey, screamed.

Do you hear, said the Cardinal, how beautifully, how strongly, how honestly this bird cries! We humans are wretched liars compared to it.

The Count remained silent. He felt repelled by those burning, black eyes, which he could hardly endure.

The Cardinal turned the ring with the moonstone on his left hand.

A semi-precious stone – but a lucky stone. You should give yourself and your sister – your beloved and soon to be your wife – a moonstone.

The Count felt his face suffused with a purplish hue.

Then you do not insult and despise me because of my unnatural love and passion?

The Cardinal smiled: How can something that is natural be against nature?

And you think you can speak well for a dispensation with His Holiness, your exalted Lord Uncle?

He lowered his brow again: Yvonne is expecting a child in seven months.

The cardinal stepped away from the tree as if he were emerging from the trunk like a forest god: Do not worry. I will personally issue the papal seal with the marriage dispensation for you. You will have the kindness to transfer 25,000 ducats to my banker, of which a considerable portion is intended for the Secretary of His Holiness, Mr. Giovanni di Volterra, and a second co-signing cardinal.

And the signature of the Holy Father?

The Cardinal laughed loudly.

The Holy Father gives his signature for free! Come, Count, our entourage is already missing us.

VI.

Calixtus died at the age of eighty.

The enemies of the Borgia, those accursed Catalan intruders, breathed a sigh of relief and came to life.

In the palace of the Orsini, who had set for themselves the special goal of combating the Spanish nepotism, a feast and celebration took place, presided over by the gaunt and proud Rodolfo Orsini, with members of the Colonna family also in attendance. Late at night, Orsini received one of his closest servants, a Frenchman named Briconnet.

The next morning, Briconnet was found stabbed to death in the Via Giudea.

The assassination attempt on Rodrigo Borgia had failed. Rodrigo Borgia had anticipated it.

Upon hearing of the attack, many Borgias and Spaniards fled Rome, abandoning their homes, which were then looted by the mob. Only Rodrigo Borgia did not retreat. Accompanied by a bodyguard of ten heavily armed Catalans, he went out and visited Rodolfo Orsini, engaging in polite conversation with him about the Greek manuscripts of the Vatican Library.

Pius II ascended to the papal throne.

Cardinal Rodrigo Borgia was still in bed when he was informed of the arrival of a papal courier. Julietta, completely naked, served him chocolate. Corinna, dressed only in a silver veil, sat on the edge of the bed.

The papal courier, an eighteen-year-old handsome boy from Piedmont, stepped over the threshold of the bedroom and hesitated. He tried to squint his eyes.

Then he looked intently up at the ceiling. But even there, he found naked female figures entwined in a sensually provocative dance that made him blush. Come closer, my son, said the Cardinal.

Julietta laughed.

Corinna smiled.

The courier blushed.

Does His Holiness use the baths of Petriolo? The courier nodded.

He seemed to have resolved not to speak a word.

Julietta and Corinna whispered together, unabashedly pointing their fingers at the wiry lad. The Cardinal tore open the letter and read:

Beloved son! Your Eminence!

It has been about a week since a festivity took place in the gardens of Signor Giovanni de Bichi, where a large number of women, notoriously known as loose in character in Siena, gathered to indulge in amusements in Your Eminence's presence, which I am too ashamed to name in detail. Your Eminence participated in this unchristian Bacchanal, paying little heed to your noble office. To further disgrace matters, the husbands, brothers, fathers, and cousins of the young ladies were excluded from the revelry, so that Your Eminence's and a few chosen ones' pleasures would not be disturbed. – I can hardly find the fitting words to express my outrage and disapproval. Here in Petriolo, a bathing spot frequented by both clergy and laity during the current season, Your Eminence's disgraceful and unrestrained behavior has become the talk of the day. The clergy are ashamed of Your Eminence's company, and the laity are generalizing Your Eminence's frivolous ways to the clergy as a whole. Even we, the Vicar of Christ on Earth, are in danger of falling prey to the world's contempt, mockery, and derision, as we seem to tolerate Your Eminence's immoral conduct. The measure of our indulgence, however, is now overflowing, and we ask Your Eminence, for the last time, to reflect and to not only vow penance but also to perform it. Your Eminence holds a seat among the councils of the Holy See, for which your wisdom, decisiveness, and knowledge undoubtedly qualify you. But Your Eminence should consider how much the authority of the Church is diminished when a builder, chosen to uphold it, continuously removes stones from its walls, eventually causing the tower to collapse. Your Eminence is still very young, twenty-nine years, but not so young that your entire day should be spent on nothing but lustful thoughts. We admonish you strictly but fatherly and sign as

Petriolo, June 11, 1460 Pius II.

The Cardinal read with increasing displeasure, which was reflected in the furrows of anger on his forehead. When he finished, he threw himself back into the cushions and pondered what to do. He wrote various signs in the air with his right index finger. The courier followed his movements, seemingly wanting to decipher them.

Finally, the Cardinal's gaze fell on Julietta. He abruptly turned to the courier: Did you ride, or did you bring a carriage, my son?

I rode, Your Eminence.

Good. One of my travel carriages will be hitched. You will return in the carriage –

Very well, Your Eminence.

With my response to His Holiness – God himself has shaped and styled it – there –

And he pointed at the naked Julietta.

Throw a cloak around her – nothing more – and take my response to His Holiness with you – but beware of adding a postscript to her in the carriage. Go with God, my son.

And to Julietta, who could not find a word: Go with God, my daughter.

VII.

The sculptor Umberto was working on a statue of Juno.

Rodrigo Borgia saw it in his studio. He was delighted.

He walked on tiptoe around it. He opened and closed the curtain at the window to study the light and shadow.

He stroked her cheeks and breasts with his hand and tenderly caressed her knees. What do you want for it, Umberto?

Umberto squirmed with embarrassment like a worm.

The statue is commissioned, Your Eminence.

I'll pay double.

It is commissioned – by the original model.

What – Juno is your model?

The sculptor nodded.

I'll pay you triple – and you can keep the statue – if you let me attend a sitting.

Your Eminence –

Behind that tapestry there – up on the loft, or –

There was a knock.

The cardinal jumped behind the curtain.

Vanozza appeared.

Are we alone?

Alone.

She threw off her clothes.

Trembling, the sculptor held the chisel and hammer.

Vanozza became attentive.

What's the matter, Umberto? Are you unwell?

Umberto wiped the sweat from his forehead.

It's hot in the studio today.

The tapestry shifted.

Vanozza turned around.

Naked like herself, Rodrigo Borgia approached her.

May Juno forgive me if Zeus dares to come too close to her without announcing his visit.

And to the sculptor: Umberto – go – you must get new clay – it's time to create a duo in stone: Zeus is courting Juno.

Paler than marble, Umberto the sculptor slipped out of his studio without looking back.

VIII.

From head to toe, the cardinal was splattered with blood. He looked like a butcher who had slaughtered an ox poorly. His plump, oily, yet handsome face twisted between grinning and lamenting.

The soutane is ruined, he thought; the fabric – from Bontempoli in Milan – was good. But too expensive, too expensive. I will try a little Jewish scrap dealer in Via Veneto. They say he delivers extremely cheaply. If I save three pennies per meter, then –

He lost himself in complicated calculations. Suddenly, his gaze fell on Vanozza, to whom he had acted as midwife. On the Piazza Prizzi di Merlo, he had set her up with a house near his palace. Nothing was lacking in the furnishings. Not even a man. He married her off to Giorgio de Croce, a pliant, purchasable gentleman, whom he designated as the father of her children. Vanozza lay on the bed, sunk in deep sleep after the pains of childbirth. The doctor and midwife moved silently like two squirrels back and forth on the carpet. In the background, at the window, a Spanish astrologer sat with his instruments and charts, looking to the sky and casting the child's horoscope.

The midwife had bathed the child. She brought it in a clean swaddling cloth, which she held before the father's thick, freckled nose.

– It's a girl, she said.

Rodrigo Borgia ran his right index finger across the forehead of the tiny being and mechanically made the sign of the cross. A girl! he thought. I was expecting a boy. You can never have enough of those. Heir. Borgia. But so be it. Juan and Cesare have already arrived. They say that a boy comes when the man loves more, and a girl when the woman loves more.

He looked from the child to the mother. What would there actually be if neither father nor mother loved?

He pondered.

The child now contorted its weathered, aged face even more, so that it looked as if an invisible hand were crumpling a package of parchment paper. Then it suddenly opened its glued eyes a crack. It seemed to want to examine and probe the fat, big man standing before it through its eyelids.

You are my father? it asked in astonishment. Did you have any notions of me when you created me? Did you want a human of your impure blood; or perhaps something lovely, beautiful, gentle, delicate, noble – qualities that are foreign to you and your family? Did you want to outlast yourself – blowing a breath of eternity into the storm of time – or did I just slip away from you by chance – like you letting out a puff of steam from your bowels after a meal?

The child's eyes behind the lids asked, receiving no answer. They glimmered with an indistinct, silvery sheen, and it was not yet clear whether they would be blue, brown, or black.

IX.

On Cesare's seventh birthday, Rodrigo Borgia enters his son's room to wake him with a paternal kiss.

Adriana Mila, the aunt, carries a corn cake with seven candles stuck in it, which bear a suspicious resemblance to phalli. Rodrigo rolls a parchment in his fist.

The boy, still half-asleep, reaches out for it.

You shall have it, my little son, you shall have it, along with everything that is written on the paper.

And Rodrigo Borgia unfolds the roll and begins to read: All revenues from the prebends and canonries of the Cathedral of Valencia belong to Signor Cesare Borgia. – The Signor Cesare Borgia is you! the father says proudly, tapping the boy on the forehead. – He is appointed Treasurer of Cartagena. – The Treasurer of Cartagena, that is you. Rodrigo laughs, causing his somewhat plump cheeks to jiggle.

The boy becomes angry.

Don't laugh, Papa. Life is serious. Don Rodrigo pauses, surprised. Then he tenderly strokes his son with the papal seal.

You are right, Cesarino, you are seven years old and so wise, so wise. You will go far. He leaves, leaving the parchment behind.

The boy jumps out of bed. He feels a natural urge coming on. He pulls out a silver chamber pot from under the bed. And since he lacks paper, he tears up the papal seal of Sixtus IV, who has just appointed him Treasurer of Cartagena.

X.

Lucrezia is raised as Primadonna d'Italia by her aunt Adriana together with Julia Farnese, known as 'the Beautiful.'

The two young girls compete with each other in beauty and grace.

Every evening, when their aunt has gone to bed, they stand naked next to each other in front of the mirror.

They watch as their breasts gently begin to round out, as the down between their thighs grows ever thicker.

Each is jealous of the other, and each falsely praises the beauty of the other. Julia says: What beautiful, corn-blonde hair you have, Lucrezia!

Lucrezia says: How delicate the curve of your breasts! It is the two halves of the globe that are bulging out of you.

They glare at each other hatefully.

Julia says pointedly: What do you mean by 'bulging out?' Am I perhaps too fat for you? Lucrezia curls her lips: But Julia! You are as slim as a boy – as slim as Cesare.

Julia turns red like a lobster: So I'm too skinny, eh?

She lunges at Lucrezia and runs the comb of her fingers through her loose blonde hair.

Lucrezia screams and bites Julia on the shoulder, drawing blood.

Julia lets go: You are rude! And you are badly brought up.

Just like you – by Aunt Adriana.

They look at each other with tears in their eyes.

Then they suddenly smile.

They throw themselves into each other's arms and each feels the other's naked, hot body in bliss.

For diplomatic reasons, Lucrezia, without protest and without even having seen him, married Giovanni Sforza *in absentia* at the age of fifteen.

If he is not a Borgia, then a man is just like any other. If he bathes once a week, rinses his mouth twice a day, and fulfills his marital duty three times a night, he can be lived with.

A few weeks after the wedding, she was pursued on a walk along the right bank of the Tiber by a handsome young man whom she could not escape.

She fled into an olive grove.

The young man followed her.

Since she found him attractive, she surrendered to him.

Only later, when he introduced himself, did it turn out that he was Giovanni Sforza, her husband, with whom she had unknowingly consummated the marriage.

This marriage would not last long. The reasons that had motivated Rodrigo to this marriage soon ceased to exist.

The Sforza could no longer be of use to him.

He had been mistaken. He corrected himself immediately.

He had the marriage of Lucrezia Borgia and Giovanni Sforza annulled by a college of cardinals on the grounds of '*impotentia coeundi*' of the husband.

XI.

Cesare is destined by his father for an ecclesiastical career, while Juan, the firstborn, pursues the secular, political path.

Cesare is to study law and theology in Perugia, the capital of Umbria. A Spaniard named Francesco Remolino is assigned to him as a tutor.

Cesare shapes himself into the perfect courtier, into a man of the world.

He rides, swims, dances.

He reads the Greek and Latin classics, especially Caesar, Livy, and Herodotus.

He fences with foil and sabre.

He jumps, wrestles, sings.

One must, he tells Francesco Remolino, live one's life as a beautiful work of art. Ugly things are left for others to do.

His favorite companion was a hunchbacked dwarf named Gabriellino, whom he had picked up along the journey like a nut that had fallen from a tree.

He gave him many things to ponder:

Your Excellency has surely moved to Perugia to find a burial place for your lord father? Perugia is not so unsuitable for burial.

The young man furrowed his brow:

What do you mean by that?

Well, Perugia is the preferred cemetery of the Popes. Innocent III, Martin IV, Benedict XI are buried here in the cathedral. The first two even side by side, meaning dust to dust in the same urn. I have often thought about what a commotion that will cause on Judgment Day when the trumpet sounds. The two will not recognize each other in their dust. Perhaps they will rise as a miraculous Pope, a Pope with two heads.

Cesare laughed: You promised me a pretty girl for the evening. Go, fetch her for me!

The dwarf grinned: I will present to you a female marvel. Two beautiful sisters: two bodies – and no brains, two souls – and no thought. Your illustrious brother, who bears the name Don Juan not in vain, would –

Silence, Cesare interrupted him, burning with anger, speak no more of my brother. I want nothing to do with him.

And without reading, he tore up a letter from Juan that he had just received.

The dwarf waddled away.

XII.

Rome, the Eternal, the Holy City, is pressed into a valley between the Tiber, the Pincio and the Capitol.

The streets are narrow, dirty, and poorly paved. In rainy weather, one sinks into the mud without high boots.

The trading houses are located at Piazza Giudea. The merchants and bankers reside in the Rione di Ponte. In the Rione di Tarione live prelates, booksellers, literati, artists, and courtesans.

There is no street lighting. Suddenly, among the foggy, impoverished houses, opulent palaces and proud churches rise up.

The ruins of the past greet one at every turn.

Geese and goats graze in the Forum. Children play around the Column of Trajan. Rome has fifty thousand inhabitants – one third of Venice.

Through a side gate, Rodrigo Borgia left his palace located between the Angel Bridge and Campo di Fiore, completely unrecognizable, draped only in a few rags, but under the rags, the Toledo dagger. He wandered through the Ponte quarter.

He paused at church doors and begged.

What was the general sentiment of the people – for or against Pope Sixtus IV.?

The Orsini were for him.

The Colonna and Savelli against him.

Hehe – and the Borgias?

He pressed his torn Calabrian hat deeper onto his forehead.

Here in Ponte, on Monte Giordano, the Orsini ruled.

Rodrigo Borgia prowled around the Torre di Nona and Monte Giordano, where Adriana Orsini lived, like a cat around hot porridge.

He must protect Vanozza from the Orsini – but also from the Margana, Falle, Savelli, Cesarini, Barberini.

For her, there could only be Borgia, both great and small. She existed to bear Borgia. For a lineage was to be created, capable of shaking Rome and all the gates of the earth. Apart from him, Rodrigo Borgia, the patriarch of the Borgias and the creator of a new world, Juan, Cesare, and Lucrezia Borgia had already entered this life through their and God's help, destined to make it colorful and magnificent and to rule and guide all lesser human and animal beings: with generosity, boldness, cleverness, beauty, but also with unyielding strictness and severity in the face of disobedient rebellion.

Against God and Borgia, no one may speak ill. Juan! Cesare! Lucrezia! You shall be the standard bearers of the Borgias!

For you, for the glory of the Borgias, I have scraped and clawed and amassed all my wealth. Valencia and Carthage are my dioceses and send me tribute, along with a hundred abbeys in Spain and Italy. Why have I usurped the office of vice-chancellor? To be able to collect ten thousand gold ducats for you each year.

Ten thousand gold ducats, he murmured to himself, turning his hat begging in front of Santa Maria del Popolo.

Then he entered an Osteria – into one of the inns whose innkeeper had long ago been Vanozza.

He drank several quarters of Barberino and then began to shout: Vanozza is a whore. What does she live on, eh? From whoring around with this – and he spat three times – so-called Cardinal Rodrigo Borgia, a damned Spanish intriguer, I swear to God. It will not end well– with her nor with him. Why doesn't her honorable husband, Signor Giorgio di Croce, stick a cold iron between his ribs? Rodrigo Borgia drew his dagger from under the rags and waved it around.

If I ever meet this – he spat again – Borgia alone, I will tickle his guts with this little knife. The bastard should think of me –

From all sides in the tavern came: Psst! Psst! Psst!

He shouted so loudly that it could be heard all the way out to the street.

Everyone shall hear it, he shouted, that Cardinal Rodrigo Borgia is a scoundrel and that Vanozza is a capital whore. Everyone. Do you think she only cheats on her honorable husband with this Borgia? Far from it! We also have the Spanish gentlemen Juan Lopez, Marades, and Taranza, who visit her – heehee, visit her – Also, some male members of the noble families of the Barberini, Cesarini, Orsini, and Torcari may have already planted roots in her...

That's enough, you blasphemer! shouted the huge innkeeper. You're going to ruin my respectable tavern with your disgusting shouting in front of all the honorable citizens. What do I care about Vanozza and Cardinal Borgia? Out!

And he grabbed Rodrigo Borgia by the waist and threw him out onto the cobblestones, where he lay for a few seconds as if dead, then got up limping and only fell into his usual swagger after several street corners.

XIII.

Rodrigo Borgia sits with his fat, firm backside in the chair of the Vice-Chancellor under five Popes.

He cannot be brought down.

He crouches like a brooding duck – brooding the future of the Borgia – he sits and waits.

The humanist Pius II tries to convert Sultan Mohammed to Christianity through letters and dies.

Hehe—

The vain Paul II understands little Latin, collects coins and paintings to not be outdone by the Medici, and dies. Hihi –

The hot-tempered Sixtus IV builds the Sistine Chapel, wages wars, even with Florence and the Medici, who seem invincible, and dies.

Oho!

Rodrigo Borgia begins to take notice. Sixtus is a man who no longer takes the ecclesiastical side of the papacy very seriously. He imprints it entirely with a political stamp.

With seemingly sleepy eyes, Rodrigo Borgia looks around: for fellow cardinals who could help him.

He does this or that favor for this or that person: gives them a pearl, a Persian carpet, a benefice, and promises them a thousandfold.

This Innocent VIII, haha, surely won't live forever! A miserable, cowardly little dog, but he shows how it must be done. He grants absolution and pardon, even for murder and manslaughter, in exchange for appropriate taxes.

He dies.

Rodrigo stands by his deathbed and feels his time has come.

He closes his eyes.

He stands up tall as he walks away from the corpse. It seems to everyone as if he has suddenly grown. His eyes sparkle with fire.

The conclave begins.

Rodrigo Borgia is a Spaniard.

Most of the Italian cardinals believe the tiara belongs to an Italian. They are against the 'foreigner.'

Three scrutiniums have already passed without a positive result.

The decision seems to lie between Cardinal Costa and Cardinal Caraffa. Bets have been placed on them. Even Borgia himself has secretly placed large bets. On himself.

Suddenly, golden, against a black background, Borgia appeared. He goes from one cardinal to another, carrying all the riches of the world on his hands, ready to scatter them among them. He is the great seducer. He leads them over the hills around Rome, shows them Rome, shows them Italy, shows them the world. You, Orsini, will get the Diocese of Cartagena. You, Colonna, the Abbey of Subiaco. Savelli, my friend, Civita Castellana and the Diocese of Majorca belong to you. The Diocese of Pamplona, as lush as its name, is reserved for you, Pallavicini. Riario, Sanseverino, you will all get what's yours! You, Ascanio Sforza, you are the noblest, the most influential, the most worthy; I will shower you with gold and grace – once the tiara adorns my head. You shall have my own palace, my profitable and comfortable office as Vice-Chancellor, the Diocese of Erleu, which brings you at least 10,000 gold ducats – and many other benefices –

So Borgia went from one to the other and gained fourteen votes.

Fourteen votes!

He rejoiced! Just one more, and I am the Pope, the *papa di Roma*, a Borgia, the representative of Christ on Earth; a Borgia will become God!

But as he went to each one – Piccolomini, Zeno, the young Giovanni di Medici, whom he almost loved – they turned their backs on him.

Caraffa and Costa, the most promising candidates at the start of the conclave, were disappointed that the tiara eluded them and wanted nothing to do with him. Finally, there remained only one who was undecided about which side to choose. It was the ninety-five-year-old Cardinal Gherardo.

Rodrigo Borgia stood before him and looked into the eagerly stretched hawk eyes that peered out from a mass of wrinkled skin.

The man is old, thought Rodrigo Borgia, very old. He has already secured his own. What could a few benefices and positions still do for him? Nothing at all. It's not worth offering them. He would laugh at me. Is he an art lover? A nice painting – a statue... He dismissed that thought. This old, half-dead man needed something alive promised to him. Life itself. And who was life itself? Who else but a young woman, a young girl. A blossom of flesh. A mouth like a carnation. Two entwining arms. Two budding breasts. A mossy womb.

Cardinal Borgia drew Cardinal Gherardo closer and whispered in his ear: If you give me your extremely valuable vote in the conclave today, then tomorrow, shortly after noon...

The rest of the words faded into Gherardo's ear, and they only swelled back to hearable volume at the end of the sentence: So help me God.

The hawk eyes of the old man sparkled at Borgia.

Through razor-sharp lips, a whistle escaped like a bird's chirp: Amen.

XIV.

Early on the morning of August 11, 1492, the conclave window sprang open.

Rodrigo Borgia had been elected Pope as Alexander VI.

Alexander VI immediately announced that he would dedicate a new altar and an organ to Santa Maria del Popolo, which had shielded and guided him.

The people applauded. From the benediction *loggia urbi et orbi* he gave the solemn blessing:

> I bless the city,
> I bless the land,
> I bless Italy,
> I bless the world.

At two o'clock, after lunch, the August sun brooded outside, while inside the palace, everyone had closed the shutters and was sleeping.

Lucrezia Borgia, the Pope's daughter, walked through the dark corridors of the Vatican, where green-gold lights flickered here and there, to the chambers of Cardinal Gherardo. She walked calmly, with delicate, but firm steps.

Before the door, she hesitated only a moment and then entered without knocking.

The ancient cardinal rose from his armchair. A purplish hue shot to his forehead, only to be immediately replaced by a deathly pallor.

He strained to lift his eyelids again, to behold the miracle of humanity, the miracle of a girl before him.

She had wrapped only a small brocade mantle around herself, which barely reached her knees.

She opened it and stood naked before him. There she bloomed, the most beautiful blossom of nature: the flower woman. A carnation mouth. Two breast buds. A mossy womb.

He raised his arms once more.

Then his knees buckled.

He fell back into the leather chair.

His head struck the edge of the table with a wooden thud.

Lucrezia's eyes first opened a little in astonishment. Then she closed the cloak and walked toward the dead cardinal. With a light, almost tender gesture, she closed his eyes.

She made the sign of the cross over him, took some delicacies that were laid out in a small silver bowl, evidently intended for her, and left with delicate but firm steps just as she had come.

XV.

Alexander VI is beside himself with joy. He has won the highest game with the highest stakes.

We are on the march, we Borgia. On the march, God, to Your throne. We have already stepped onto the first rung of Jacob's ladder.

Now it is upwards, relentlessly upwards, through clouds and winds, thunderstorms and hail, lightning and stars: up to You, for You are the Father in Heaven, and the Father of the Borgia.

When a son of God ascends to Earth again to redeem humanity, it will be a Borgia.

Rome made Caesar great, but now Alexander boldly elevates it to the summit, the former a man – the latter a god.

Thus the Pope rejoiced and blasphemed.

I will make Juan the secular ruler of Italy. Cesare shall soon receive the cardinal's hat and one day succeed me as Pope. I want to make the papal throne hereditary. It shall belong to the Borgia for all time to come. Cesare must become the third Borgian Pope.

Feed the doves, child, he said to Lucrezia, who stood beside him on the balcony of the Vatican, looking down at St. Peter's Square, where a dog and a bitch, having just made love, could not part and were beginning to hate each other – feed the doves! The dove is the mystical bird of the Holy Trinity! We must give it something to peck at.

The bull is the heraldic animal of the Borgia. Pinturicchio must paint frescoes in the Pope's living quarters depicting the processions of the Apis bulls. Rodrigo Borgia, now Pope Alexander VI, is organizing a corrida in honor of his election and for the joy of the Italian people and the mob.

I am a Spaniard, says the Pope. I no longer want to miss my Spanish pleasures. I have had to do without them long enough. I want to give the Romans a *festa di Borgia*.

Cesare Borgia, his son, strode past the stands in Spanish attire as a toreador, with his sword lowered, and the hearts of beautiful women raced faster as he passed by.

Che bellezza!

Lucrezia threw him yellow roses.

She sat to the left of the Pope in a lavish box lined with red velvet. To his right sat Julia Farnese in her nineteen-year-old beauty, which inflamed him to the point of madness. She still denied herself to him. The Pope had already resorted to mandrake, the love potion, which his personal physician had derived from a mandrake root pulled from the earth by a black dog under the light of a full moon. But the potion had not yet worked.

Lucrezia turned to the Pope: Listen, *papa di Roma and papa di Borgia*, I feel so sorry for the bull. Give him another cow before he dies. It will be easier to die then.

The Pope laughed.

Julia blushed.

Thy will be done – on earth as it is in heaven. He ordered three cows to be driven into the arena, and the raging, rampaging bull mounted all three.

The gallery roared.

Julia kept her eyes closed.

Then the cows were driven out, and the picadors rode into the arena. They teased the bull with short lance thrusts from their horses as it charged them with lowered horns, snorting.

The swarm of banderilleros followed on foot; they drove the barbed banderillas into the already twitching and bleeding flesh of the bull. With the swarm of banderilleros came swarms of flies that clung to the bull's wounds or buzzed around him.

With swinging red capes, the capeadores attempted to distract the bull from a threatened picador.

Too late.

The bull had already gored his horse in the belly and tossed both horse and rider into the air like balls.

With his raised horns, he caught the picador, who had been advancing from behind. Then he hurled him into the sand, which began to turn red.

A scream of horror broke from the audience, and then Cesare Borgia came running.

In his left hand, he carried a stick with a rag of red cloth fluttering from it, which he waved to distract the bull back and forth.

In his right hand, he firmly held the espada.

As the raging bull stood right in front of him and lowered its horns, Cesare suddenly thrust the sword between the horns.

The bull swayed and trembled.

He lifted his head and gazed with glassy eyes into the glaring sun.

He felt the comforting warmth of the divine star once more, then eternal darkness fell over his eyes.

He collapsed, crushed to the ground by the giant fist of death.

Cesare raised the sword and saluted towards the papal box.

Lucrezia was pale with fear.

The Pope had stood up in the excitement of the fight.

Now he clapped his hands obsessively, and all the people joined in applauding.

The next day, against the will of the college, Cesare was adorned with the cardinal's purple, even though he had never been ordained.

Cesare went to the barber: Give me a tonsure! But not too large! So that I can let it grow back soon!

XVI.

Julia, the beautiful, loved Orso, the one-eyed man, the son of Adriana.

When the Pope learned of this, he arranged a magnificent wedding for them and officiated the ceremony himself. He appointed Alexander Farnese, Julia's brother, as a cardinal. The common people soon referred to him as Cardinal Fregnese.

The Pope arranged for the young couple to take residence in the Palazzo San Martinelli, located near the Vatican. A gate led from it into the Vatican gardens.

On a night with a full moon, without mandrake root and black dog, Julia, the young one, surrendered herself to Alexander, the old man.

Orso, the one-eyed, went blind.

Alexander Borgia had Julia Farnese carried as a living saint in a solemn procession inside the reliquary.

Alexander Borgia had lost faith in the mandrake and decided to believe only in himself from then on, renouncing any other faith.

While the people of his time were mired in superstition, Alexander Borgia took pleasure in daring all the demons of the underworld and the upper world.

His bedroom was full of stuffed birds of misfortune, full of owls, cuckoos, bats. A white rose, the flower of death, lay on his pillow every evening.

He loved to dine in the company of thirteen people. The utensils at the table were laid crosswise. At the beginning of the meal, he would, seemingly absent-mindedly, spill wine on the tablecloth.

He enjoyed it when cats crossed his path.

And he was pleased when he encountered a pretty nun.

He often took them directly to the Vatican, or if it was too far, he would go with them to the nearest church, where they would indulge in the side galleries.

The German Doctor *juris et theologiae* Johannes Burcardus from Haßlach near Strasbourg wrote a pamphlet about the new Pope in common German language, which gained wide distribution in Germany and won many friends for the Pope.

'The new Pope is a man of great character and great wisdom. He is the successor of Pope Calixtus, his late cousin, in wisdom, virtue, and upright living. In him, there is grace, trustworthiness, piety, and knowledge of all the things that are fitting for such a high position. We hope that he will be a benefit to the common Christian state and will successfully navigate the dangerous reefs of the sea and reach the heavenly glory.'

Johannes Burcardus was soon summoned by the Pope to the papal court as a scribe in the papal ceremonies and appointed court master of ceremonies.

It is the writers who make the fame, he said to Cesare.

Johannes Burcardus was devoted to the Pope and led a simple, honest German diary of daily Vatican events.

He enjoyed eating and drinking well, especially red wines, and alongside the Pope's favor, he earned himself a dark red Barberino nose and the nickname Johannes the Drunkard.

But in particularly important and discreet matters, the Pope did not trust him either. In such cases, Alexander Borgia would dictate to him two or three letters with opposing contents and left him in the dark about which one he ultimately sent.

XVII.

A few days after his election as Pope, Alexander summoned Cesare and Lucrezia to his castle in Nepi.

He sent all the servants away for an afternoon, leaving only the three Borgias in the house.

They sat in the great hall around the large table, upon which lay a map of Italy, a globe, and a skull.

No one listened to them except the thick walls.

A beam of sunlight fell through the narrow window onto Lucrezia's head, which shone brightly.

Alexander and Cesare gazed at her with pleasure. A green Spanish fly danced in the beam.

When the Pope celebrated the first official mass, the most beautiful women in Rome climbed with him into the seats of the canons of St. Peter's. I don't want to see the priests, those grey ravens, too close to me: they smell bad too, the unwashed saints. More pleasing to me and to God are the fragrant Julia Farnese, my dearest beloved, my Madonna, whom I will have painted, myself lost in adoration before her, Lucrezia, my little daughter, and all the other charming robins, nightingales and hummingbirds.

They chirped, smiled, and laughed into his mass.

They smiled up at him, and he smiled down at them, with Julia Farnese blowing a kiss to his Amen.

Among the audience that filled the church and watched this mass with astonishment and disgust was the Florentine monk Fra Girolamo, who fell unconscious to the ground during the unholy ceremony and had to be carried out into the open by his neighbors. They left him lying between the pillars of the vestibule.

When he awoke and thought he was emerging from a delirious dream, he stood up and leaned against a column.

Tears ran down his face as he came to his senses, and he embraced the column and kissed it.

O column! How glad I am that you are not human! Be glad for that too! You have no eyes to see the shame of Rome and the world. You have no heart to feel the torment of this life. O stone, o cool stone, o dear stone! Cool my burning forehead, behind which fever rages and the longing of Samson, to tear you and all the columns of this church down upon me, so that St. Peter's would crash down upon the Pope and his papists!

But alas – he sighed, pressing the column to his chest – I am too weak.
Too weak and too cowardly.

XVIII.

Audience with the Pope. In a long line, led by the Magister Ceremoniarium,
Court and Ceremonial Master Burkhard, a lean, phlegmatic man who was incapable of wonder and let all the events of life pass him by with the same indifference – so too did this line of people: they passed by and kissed the ground in the
Turkish manner at the feet of His Holiness – clergymen, nuns, knights, peasants,
women, ladies, and prostitutes.

It was upon the latter that the Pope's gaze lingered with particular pleasure.

He whispered a few half-spoken words to one and another, calling each of them
Magdalene and summoning them to the Vatican: one at four, another at five, and
the third at six.

You can't have too much of one dish. Variety makes the meal enjoyable. A
little snipe, a little chicken, a little dove! That's tasty. But three doves – that
spoils your appetite.

As the last of the line, the Pope, who had already intended to retire, the Florentine monk Fra Girolamo approached him. He did not throw himself to the ground
like the others. He did not kiss the hem of his cloak or his sandals.

He remained standing, and in his fiery eyes burned a demand more than a wish.

The Pope cleared his throat: Yes – so – you are the last. What do you want, my
son?

The monk replied: You are the first – and behold – think about what you are
doing.

The Pope: Do you want to have a philosophical discussion with me? I have no
time. My high office – you have no time – and you wish to achieve and comprehend eternity, which consists of nothing but time and time and time? One must
have time to have eternity.

The monk spoke in a singing, melodic tone that began to lull the Pope.

Yes, I hear, said the Pope, I hear. And he heard the Roman fountain of the
Vatican gardens rushing.

Do you know, the monk continued, how deeply you have degraded your high
office?

So deeply, thought the Pope, so deeply – he was strangely moved to agree,
without resistance, to the monk's accusations.

Through shameful simony, you acquired the tiara – through vote-buying – oh,
shame on the Cardinals who sold themselves! You trade in cardinal hats like a
hatmaker, with shepherd's staffs like a carpenter. You court all the whores of
Rome, and at night the devil in female form sleeps with you. You scatter the
cursed seed of the Borgias in all directions. Countless and innumerable are your

daughters and sons. You long to seduce them as well, daughters and sons. You do not satisfy your urges only with women – young boys, monks, goats, and hens are also welcome to you. There is a young mare in your stable, she is bathed in milk and rubbed down with wine. She is your lover.

Borgia! Borgia! Step down from the usurped throne and return the honor to God, the Lord and Ruler, that which is rightfully His. Voluntarily relinquish what your greed for gold and power has seized. Go with Cesare, with Lucrezia, and your kin into exile of your own free will. Then, let an ecumenical council decide on the vacant papal throne and give it a worthy successor to St. Peter.

The Pope had risen from his seat. Then, he knelt before the monk and kissed the hem of his cassock.

Oh – what a glorious feeling surged through him – how sweet it was to be humbled – to taste the bliss of humiliation, to be trampled upon, insulted, and spat upon just like Christ once, when He carried His own cross to the place of execution.

Yes, trample me, he cried up to the monk, spit on me, scourge me with thorns and rods. I will do as you have said: I will leave, flee into the wilderness. Raise your fist and bring it down upon my tonsured head like a hammer. I want to be your anvil. Saliva dripped from the corners of his mouth.

He felt how close he was to salvation – ah – now – now –

Apage, Satanas! the monk cried in horror, made the sign of the cross, and fled.

He did not see how the Pope had risen up and, smiling, shook a clenched fist after him.

In the corridors of the Vatican, Lucrezia encountered the monk as he wandered aimlessly. He could not find the exit – neither from the Vatican – nor from the labyrinth of his soul.

She stopped him: Where are you going? To the Holy Father?

I come from him.

Well, and now?

He fell silent.

Her beauty flared before him like a torch in the twilight.

Would you not also like to pay your respects to the unholy daughter of the Holy Father? She smiled at him.

In that smile, there was offering before he had even desired, fulfillment before the longing, love before the lust.

She glanced quickly down the corridor in both directions.

Come – and she pulled the unresisting monk into a side room filled with clutter: old paintings, dressers, flags, plaster casts.

She bolted the door.

In the half-darkness, he saw a naked white figure before him. It was a plaster cast from a statue Umberto had made of Lucrezia.

Do you want the stone, Lucrezia smiled, or do you want me? You may choose!

Oh stone, oh cool, beloved stone!

And he buried his head in the lap of the stone Lucrezia.

XIX.

On the Feast of the Annunciation, the Pope, in a solemn procession of Cardinals, Prelates, and Nobles, made his way to Santa Maria sopra Minerva.

He conducted High Mass and, following ancient custom, gifted dowries to one hundred and fifty poor girls.

After the solemn ceremony, they had to pass by Alexander: a procession of sorrow, suffering, ugliness, and beauty.

Alexander inspected them very carefully. He summoned the five most beautiful for a private audience in the Vatican.

On the return journey, the Jews waited for the Pope on the Tiber Bridge, crouched and humbly. They had crawled out of the dark corners of their ghetto like moles.

They stood crowded together, whispering and murmuring.

As the Pope rode across the bridge, they all threw themselves before him.

The eldest of the Jews, a certain Ephraim, stepped forward and handed him the Jewish scroll of law, the Pentateuch bound in gold.

He begged, in humble and whimpering words, for the Pope to confirm the Law of Moses for the Jews. The Pope took the scroll, admired the gold for a moment with approval, hesitated, and then said:

Confirmamus, sed non consentimus – and let the scroll fall to the ground.

Then he rode on.

In the afternoon of the same day, the Jews were made to race against each other on horses, donkeys, and buffaloes.

The race track ran from the Arch of Domitian to the Church of San Marco.

Some of the Jews were intoxicated beforehand or stuffed like fattened geese, so that during the race they began to vomit and defecate.

The Pope sat at the finish line by the Church of San Marco, laughing so hard that tears streamed down his cheeks.

The first prize, a piece of red cloth, was won by a Jew who had clung to the tail of a horse and, just before the finish line, leapt onto the horse and over its neck, crossing the line first.

He was graciously allowed to kiss the Pope's feet in a moment of indulgence.

A child was born in the Vatican, of whom neither the name of the mother nor that of the father was publicly announced. In holy baptism, which the Pope himself performed, the child received the pagan name Narcissus and soon became known among the people as the Roman infant.

The child enjoyed the favor and tenderness of all the Borgias.

Lucrezia often carried him in her arms, walked with him around the garden, and played with him. Whenever Cesare encountered him with the wet nurse in the corridor, he would stop and almost tenderly run his slender hand over the child's soft, downy head.

The Pope himself, as the boy grew older, crawled around the floor with him on all fours, let him ride on his back, and carved him small bows and arrows from willow branches, with which little Narcissus shot at the holy images, turning many a Saint Paul and Saint John into a Saint Sebastian.

Soon, a rumor spread among the Roman people that the mysterious Roman infant was the son of Lucrezia, the fruit of her incestuous affair with Alexander or Cesare. For it was whispered that she maintained an unnatural love affair with both of them; that Spanish blood boiled and burned in the Borgias to the boiling point, driving them toward each other like lustful bulls to a lustful cow. And so consuming was their insatiable hunger that they found fulfillment and satisfaction only among themselves. Thus, only a Borgia could truly love a Borgia.

XX.

Around this time, Lucrezia was to be married to the illustrious Lord Gasparro from the House of Procida. Various rumors circulated about how the plan for this marriage had come about and that Lucrezia had thrown a dagger at her father.

These rumors also served as the material basis for the first major pamphlet directed against the Borgias, which was distributed in broadsheets in Rome, Naples, Florence, and even as far away as Germany and France.

The title read:

Idyll in the Vatican
A Merry Tragedy
by
someone who has no ambition
to be named and – hanged

Vatican Garden

LUCREZIA on a swing. Her governess, JULIA. ALEXANDER Borgia sits at a stone table with various documents in front of him, quill in hand, writing, calculating, while eating cherries from a basket at the same time.

ALEXANDER (*looking up*) You shouldn't swing so recklessly, Lucrezia – you're hardly wearing anything – you're practically half naked.

LUCREZIA The nymphs – were even more naked –

ALEXANDER You're right – but back then nudity was something natural, and back then, young girls weren't intent on seducing their brothers, let alone their fathers.

LUCREZIA What do you mean by that?

ALEXANDER That means what it means!

LUCREZIA (*swinging*) I'm flying – flying –

JULIA Up to heaven –

LUCREZIA All the way to hell –

ALEXANDER (*looking up*) What is that supposed to mean?

LUCREZIA That means what it means! –

ALEXANDER Won't you explain it to me?

LUCREZIA Why should I?

ALEXANDER You don't answer a question with another question. –

JULIA (*to Lucrezia*) Your Highness is behaving towards His Holiness in a most unqualified manner – un-qua-li-fi-ed –

LUCREZIA Don't bite your tongue, Julia!

ALEXANDER If you treat me poorly, at least treat your governess with some semblance of respect.

LUCREZIA (*keeps swinging.*)

ALEXANDER What did you mean earlier, about hell?

LUCREZIA That we'll all end up there one day...

ALEXANDER Who – all of us?

LUCREZIA We Borgias – led by His Holiness Pope Alexander the Sixth – (*keeps swinging*).

JULIA This – is – outrageous –. His Holiness must forgive a poor Piedmontese for Your Highness's boundless lack of manners. At times, I am powerless.

ALEXANDER We are all powerless against this... creature.

LUCREZIA His Holiness created me – he should have made me differently.

JULIA Lucrezia – you're a devil –

LUCREZIA All the better, then I don't have to become one – like –

ALEXANDER Like?

JULIA Well –?

LUCREZIA (*jumps off the swing*) Like Cesare. (*To Alexander*) Will Your Holiness give me some cherries – I prefer them slightly overripe – are they poisoned? I hope not! (*Spits a pit in Julia's face.*)

JULIA Your Holiness – I humbly request to be relieved of my papal duties – my dignity is being trampled here in an unacceptable manner! –

ALEXANDER (*glancing at Lucrezia*) With very pretty feet –

LUCREZIA Look, Julia, be sensible and stay here. What do you mean: you want to leave our service? Do you think you'll return to Piedmont alive? You don't know us well. You know too much about us, Julia, to not become dangerous to us with our enemies. His Excellency Cesare Borgia and His Holiness there at the table wouldn't let you get far. At the first Tiber bridge, an unfortunate accident would happen to you – can you swim? Certainly not. Stay with me, Julia. I advise you well. I treat you badly, but at least I let you live. Yes, I even like you. Because I like you, I must torment you. But to torment you, I must keep you alive. (*Strokes her.*) Don't cry, Julia. (*Reaches back into the basket of cherries.*) With us Borgias, it's not safe to share cherries.

ALEXANDER Considering your youth, you speak really presumptuously –

LUCREZIA Should I wait until I'm as old as His Holiness? I hope to be less presumptuous by then.

ALEXANDER To whom should I actually entrust you for taming? A man?

LUCREZIA Your Holiness was man enough to create me. His Holiness should also be man enough to tame me.

ALEXANDER (*takes off his cap and wipes his bald head*) No – no – Lucrezia – back when I created you, I could handle you – but since then, may God punish me, not any longer.

LUCREZIA Yes, God has punished you. With Cesare and with me.

ALEXANDER Have you ever thought about getting married?

LUCREZIA Often.

ALEXANDER With whom, if I may ask?

LUCREZIA With Cesare –

ALEXANDER With Cesare? Are you completely out of your mind? Cesare is your brother –

LUCREZIA Well – and why not? Of all men, he's my favorite.

ALEXANDER Not much of a compliment to me. Beware of even saying such a thing to him. He's already megalomaniacal and conceited enough.

LUCREZIA His Holiness is not without vanity either. I mean, we Borgias should keep entirely to ourselves – we should only have children with one another – Borgias – always Borgias – no drop of foreign blood should mix with ours. I don't even love Cesare – or His Holiness – but the rest of humanity – them – I hate – yes, I hate them – and the more of them that are annihilated, the better. Would His Holiness, for my sake, start a little war? There's money in the treasury, and if there's money – there are always people willing to kill each other for it. Give me a few thousand ducats, and I'll lead a war myself

– I know His Holiness is stingy – lend me the money – I'll repay it from the plunder –

ALEXANDER You are dreadful, Lucrezia – and you don't even realize it –

LUCREZIA Is Your Holiness having moral urges? Oh! Oh! Your Holiness is forgetful. May I remind you?

ALEXANDER (*covering his ears*) Be quiet – (CESARE enters.)

CESARE Did you sleep well, old man? Good morning, Lucrezia!

ALEXANDER Slept poorly – this – child... worries me so much that I lie awake for hours at night.

CESARE Our little Lucrezia? But Lucrezia, you shouldn't give Papa such worries –

LUCREZIA If I don't worry His Holiness, someone else will. It amounts to the same thing. Your Holiness is a hypochondriac.

ALEXANDER She doesn't take me seriously, Cesare. A child who doesn't take her father seriously. Terrible! The world is ripe for destruction.

LUCREZIA We Borgias certainly do everything to make it ripe for that.

CESARE If she doesn't take you seriously, you shouldn't honor her with the courtesy of taking her seriously, Papa.

ALEXANDER (*moaning*) Not taking her seriously – means taking her lightly – and in doing so, one only does her a favor again – because she will do the wildest things under the pretense that it's all meant to be funny. In the end, she will charm or bribe all the cardinals – they will elect her Pope – Pope Lucrezia – my election will be declared invalid – she will send us all underground –

CESARE Unless we prefer to send her underground first.

LUCREZIA (*laughs*).

ALEXANDER Don't laugh!

LUCREZIA (*smiles*).

ALEXANDER Don't smile! That smug smile of yours is making me quite nervous.

LUCREZIA Your Holiness should consult your physician about your nerves.

ALEXANDER Cesare – listen to this – so the supreme shepherd of the Christian flock must endure such treatment from his last sheep.

CESARE Lucrezia – you deserve to be beaten.

LUCREZIA (*flashing, snatches his dagger from its sheath*) I dare you! (*She presses the dagger to his throat, then throws it aside.*)

ALEXANDER She must marry. She has too fiery a temperament.

CESARE You are right. There are only two options: poison her – or marry her off.

ALEXANDER Here – here is the list of Roman and non-Roman nobility – I was just going through it to see if one or another could be taxed more for the papal seat. – Who is a suitable man for Lucrezia? A Barberini? A Malatesta? A Sforza – we've had one already – a Medici – they have fallen from grace – an Orsini – they are at odds with us – a Colonna – likewise – an Este – would have some merit – an Aragon – not too bad, connected to the royal house of Naples – a Rovere – a Proscida –

LUCREZIA (has picked up the dagger again): I have a suggestion for you. Let us invoke divine judgment. Cesare, hold the list of nobles against the tree there –

CESARE Why?

LUCREZIA You will see. *Va bene.* There, now I'll throw the knife at the list, and whoever I hit – that's who I'll marry.

CESARE And what if he is already married?

LUCREZIA Then His Holiness will annul the first marriage with his apostolic authority and bless the second one –

ALEXANDER She speaks of me as if I were livestock –

LUCREZIA Livestock – that's what you are – (*Throws the knife and hits Alexander, who was standing next to the tree, in the chest.*)

ALEXANDER Help! I have been murdered! (*Collapses to the ground unconscious.*)

CESARE Lucrezia!

LUCREZIA (*runs to Alexander, kneels down*) Is he dead? Is he dead? Oh, how I hate him – he who thrust me into this life without asking if I wanted to be his daughter – oh God in heaven – if you exist – and if you hear the cry of a Borgia – and do not plug your ears before him – oh let him be dead – let him not wake up to new atrocities and new horrors – oh, I am already weighed down with pain like with strings of pearls – I am so miserable, God, so wretched, because he is so evil, the one who has made me so – last night he came to me – crept to me on his fat soles – wanted to violate me – his daughter – oh Cesare, brother, how I called out for you and wished that you were my husband, to stab him through his fat belly – Cesare – help me – he is not weak at all – he only pretends to be weak – he feigns his weakness to deceive us – to toy with us – as he toys with all people –

ALEXANDER (*weakly*) Cesare –

LUCREZIA He lives –

CESARE Father –?

ALEXANDER What has happened to me?

CESARE Nothing – nothing serious – Lucrezia will call the physician immediately – the dagger has only grazed the upper chest – above the heart – a few days of rest – and everything will be as it was before.

LUCREZIA And everything will be as it was before –

ALEXANDER How did the knife end up in my chest? Are there assassins in the palace?

CESARE No assassins! Just good friends –

ALEXANDER And who threw the knife?

LUCREZIA I did –

CESARE Yes – Lucrezia – Lucrezia threw the knife.

ALEXANDER Lucrezia –?

CESARE It was a terrible accident that, thank God in heaven, ended without serious harm. Lucrezia meant to throw the dagger at her husband-to-be – and struck you instead. –

LUCREZIA Forgive me, Your Holiness?

ALEXANDER I bless you, my child, with the papal blessing.

LUCREZIA (*kisses the hand that blessed her*).

ALEXANDER And whom shall we give the child as a husband? For she must quickly have a husband – someone she can throw the knife at in the future – when the urge strikes her.

CESARE Yes – shouldn't we ask Lucrezia about her possible wishes?

LUCREZIA Here is a drop of blood splattered on the list – on the name of Gasparro Proscida. I will marry him. For we have become blood relatives.

ALEXANDER Is he married?

CESARE He is a bachelor, twenty-five years old – wealthy in influence and fortune, handsome in face, noble in figure – Lucrezia, you couldn't have chosen better –

ALEXANDER We shall send a secret courier from the Vatican office with our strict command to immediately present himself here and to ask for the hand of our beloved, only daughter Lucrezia. (*To Lucrezia.*) Are you satisfied, child?

LUCREZIA I am. (*To the courier who appears.*) His Holiness has just been saved from grave mortal danger by God's inscrutable decree. Let all the bells of the Holy City ring a *Te deum* in gratitude!

ALEXANDER Amen!
      Bells begin to ring.

XXI.

Lucrezia and her presumptive fiancé meet for the first time. He takes her small, slender hand.

May I hold this beautiful hand forever? Forever is a big word –

For a lifetime –

Which lifetime? There are lives that are very short. Will you not take a seat, Prince?

Thank you, Princess. Will you allow me to remain standing?

You will grow tired.

Not so easily. Principessa, I heard half an hour ago of your wish to marry me.

Will fulfilling this wish be difficult for you?

It will be difficult for me to tell the truth.

Why?

People have become so accustomed to lies these days.

Who?

All of us –

You mean, no one tells the truth anymore?

No, no one –

Not even me?

I do not presume to hold the mirror of truth to beauty.

My name is not Bella or Vera, but Lucrezia.

And do you tell the truth?

Unfortunately, not.

Why not?

Because one is not allowed to tell the truth –

And who forbids you to tell the truth?

Reason.

Do you pray to the goddess of Reason?

I do not practice idolatry.

But suppose I were to lead by good example?

Lead – to where?

The path of truth – would you follow?

If it contains no traps, no pits for wolves – perhaps –

Perhaps?

Lucrezia looks at him for a long time.

He concedes: No: certainly. I would certainly follow you, if I were allowed to trust you –

Well, you may –

You wished to lead the way –

Good. Then listen.

Lucrezia's eyes began to shine. I have chosen you as my husband, not because I love you. I do not know you at all. And I love you as little as any other person. I do not even love myself. But I wanted to put an end to this life here in the Vatican. I wanted to get out of this atmosphere of the Borgias. This is not for weak natures. And I am weak. An opportunity arose. I seized it – and I hold onto you. – She holds his hands, which he tries to withdraw from her.

She presses: Now it's your turn.

He begins hesitantly: Well, then – let me start by telling you the truth – when the message came from your father, I was alarmed – my name and my fortune have long been on the proscription list – my death would only suit him – him and his son. I thought it was the end. I said goodbye to my family at home as if it were for death. I came here and to my astonishment learned that the invitation is no trap, that no daggers and Cantarellas are lying in wait for me – that I am really to marry you. What an honor! But I do not know the reason why I am being honored by you, for I do not believe you. You are a Borgia. The people fear the Borgias. The people hate the Borgias –

Are you one of the people?

And I, I despise the Borgias. Yes, I despise them –

He took a deep breath and looked clearly into her eyes, which were filling with tears.

You are right to despise us. We are wielded like – like scourges over humanity. But we are wielded. You are right – I am not worthy to bear your name –

You humble yourself before me – but I cannot trust your humility. When the Borgias pretend to be humble, there is treachery behind it. Do you even possess the treachery – to tell the truth?

Lucrezia: No – I lied earlier – now I want to tell the truth: I love you. I love you! Because I loved you – loved you long ago – I chose you as my husband – I played this undignified comedy.

The prince was astonished.

But you didn't even know me?

Lucrezia stammered: Yes – yes – I watched you from my window when you rode by every morning.

But I never rode past your window –

So take me in your arms! Why don't you kiss me?

You are lying now – just as you lied before. I am commanded to marry you. Fine. No force on earth can make me love you.

So you hate me?

I pity you. I have compassion for you –

Compassion? I am not that weak. But it is true. I have lied. I have lied all day. And now I want to come clean. I made a joke. A bit of fun, as we Borgias allow ourselves. I wanted to test you. You are conspiring against us. You are in league with the Orsini and the Colonna. You are a rebel.

I do not fear death.

Don't be afraid. We Borgias do not take revenge so easily. You shall remain alive.

Lucrezia clapped her hands. The old, plump nurse Julia appeared. Julia – may I introduce you to your fiancé, Mr. Gasparro Proscida? He has asked for your hand from me. He is eager for you. He can't wait for the wedding night. I myself will prepare the bridal bed for you, and His Holiness, the Pope in his own most exalted person, will bless you with the apostolic blessing.

Julia was deeply flushed and looked embarrassed at the ground.

The prince turned pale: If the devil were to try to possess you, Donna Lucrezia, he would find no refuge. You are full of devilry.

The marriage contract that had already been drawn up between Lucrezia and Don Caspar was declared null and void on June 10th. On June 20th the marriage contract between Lucrezia and Prince Alfonso of Aragon was concluded.

XXII.

Dschem, a very young Turkish prince and brother of the Sultan, fell into the hands of the Pope, who immediately seized and detained him. One never knows when he might come in handy. To extort ransom. To use him as a hostage.

Who knows.

To provide a spectacle for the Roman people, the Pope had the Turk make a ceremonial entrance into Rome.

The prince rode on a noble, splendid camel, ceremonially bowing to all sides where the crowd stood, hurling jests and laughter up at him. Following the prince, led by Turkish guards, were giraffes, lions, and leopards.

A small cheetah ran out of the procession and began frolicking with a dirty white spitz.

In the Vatican, the prince was ceremoniously received.

The protocol had been drawn up by Johannes Burkhard, as there was no precedent for such an occasion.

The prince approached Lucrezia, bowed, and said: *Selam – y aleiküm! – Güselzin!*

Lucrezia smiled helplessly: I do not understand you.

Dschem asked: *Naszyl?*

And, pointing to Cesare: *Bu adam kim dir?*

Cesare did not move, and Dschem muttered something between his teeth, sounding like Aerbijeszis. Then he exclaimed: *Asikar düsman gisli düsman – dan ejidir!*

The Pope, seeing how the prince helplessly swayed between Cesare and Lucrezia, said: I've been informed that the Turkish language has no grammatical distinction between genders. That's likely why Dschem cannot differentiate between men and women. Well, perhaps he'll learn it here in Rome soon enough. After all, he's still young.

XXIII.

After returning to Florence, Fra Girolamo began to preach about the great se-
ductress of Rome, the den of all evil. We must, he proclaimed, start with ourselves. We cannot expect improvement from the world if we do not improve
ourselves. If we want to reform the Church in both head and members, we must
begin the reformation with ourselves, with the Dominican Order. And so great
was his spiritual power that the monastery of San Marco and all the Dominican
monasteries in Tuscany voluntarily undertook a purification of their morals and
customs.

Fra Girolamo first preached in a small alley, then in a square. After that, he
preached in the church of San Marco and, when that became too small for the
multitude of listeners, in the cathedral of Florence.

Among his most fervent listeners was the young Michelangelo Buonarroti,
a sculptor in his own right and an apprentice in the art school established by
Lorenzo di Medici. The apocalyptic sermons of the friar suited his melancholic
nature. He preferred to draw the Last Judgment.

Lorenzo de' Medici, *il magnifico* himself, came one day to hear Fra Girolamo,
squinted his short-sighted eyes, and listened.

A few weeks later, he lay dying in Careggi.

He had Fra Girolamo summoned.

I know no true monk but you. Grant me absolution!

Fra Girolamo said: You must have three things – first, true and living faith;
second, the vision of eternal peace; and third, the unyielding will to realize freedom.

Then Lorenzo, the tyrant, stared at him and turned to the wall.

Without hearing his confession and granting him absolution, Fra Girolamo
returned to Florence.

XXIV.

The vain and sickly Piero di Medici follows Lorenzo in the governance of Florence.

His main pleasure consists of playing ball in the public streets with his cavaliers
and courtesans.

One day, a ball thrown by Piero di Medici flies through a window of the church
of Santa Maria del Fiore, where Fra Girolamo is just preaching.

The friar grabs the ball and crushes it on the stone floor of the church.

Thus will God crush Florence, unless you gather your strength, people of Florence! How long will you allow yourselves to be trifled with? –

Piero cannot hold the reins of governance. They drag along the ground behind him. The Medici bank encounters difficulties. Piero cancels numerous loans granted by his father to respected Florentines.

These are bad times for trade.

Many honorable merchants go bankrupt. The poor and destitute begin to starve.

There had been a failed harvest. Peasants flocked to the city in droves, seeking work they could not find.

The prices of grain rose from day to day. The Stajo climbed from 34 to 60 soldi. Discontent with Piero grows.

When the famine showed no end, Fra Girolamo preached and ordered a 'Day of Alms' to be held: in Santa Maria del Fiore, in Santa Maria Novella, and in Santo Spirito.

In all churches, a special altar was erected, known as the 'Altar of Poverty.' Wealthy citizens and citizenesses, stirred in their consciences by the friar, came to donate at the Altar of Poverty: pearls, diamonds, gold chains and rings, silver bowls, silk dresses, velvet, and woolen fabrics.

But Piero di Medici was not among those who gave alms.

Then the people marched to his palace and shouted:

> Give it up, give it up –
> Surrender your weapons –
> Surrender your crown –
> Surrender your rule –

The apocalyptic sermons and gloomy prophecies of Fra Girolamo had a tremendous impact on the Florentine people.

The girls and women laid aside their colorful garments, and instead of red, green, violet, and yellow, only gray and black were seen in the piazza.

Many men walked in brown linen robes, some with a rope around their necks, to show that they were fundamentally humble in their souls and deserved nothing before God other than to be hanged.

When Fra Girolamo preached in Santa Maria del Fiore, he assigned separate places for men and women. They were not allowed to mix with each other.

Many men also ran to the barber surgeons in their distress, asking to be cured. They had castrated themselves with crude instruments, kitchen knives, and sharp stones, inflicting grievous wounds upon themselves.

XXV.

The Pope, who learned through his spies about the 'prophecies of doom' from Fra Girolamo and his fiery sermons 'against the Antichrist' (referring to Alexander Borgia), and how he was shaking the faith of the believers, nervously drummed his knuckles against the window of his study in the Vatican.

This Savonarola! A liar!

Have I not stood up for the Church? Did I not personally donate an organ and an altar for Santa Maria del Popolo and renovate the cracked ceiling in Santa Maria Maggiore? And have I not fortified the power of the Church by equipping the Castel Sant'Angelo with fortifications, moats, loopholes, and large and small towers?

The Castel Sant'Angelo, the center of the Vatican, is impregnable!

The Rock of Peter, on which it is built, stands unshakable. However, I could make some wealthy bankers and merchants here in Rome, who come from Florence, feel the heat of hell by threatening them with the confiscation of their assets if they do not exert all their influence with their Florentine compatriots to subdue and neutralize this mad Dominican father. –

But then a humorous and cunning thought came to him about how to combat the friar, and he laughed so much that he sank into an armchair.

The people love grim prophecies, whether they come true or not. They enjoy a good shiver. We will send someone to Florence who will predict even more terrible disasters than this well-meaning dog of God.

And he sent a good-natured, stout, somewhat asthmatic Franciscan friar, Domenico da Ponzo, to Florence and obtained permission for him to preach from the cathedral pulpit.

If Fra Girolamo prophesied a flood in the church, Fra Domenico would, with labored breath, immediately foretell a coming deluge in the cathedral. If Fra Girolamo predicted the downfall of Italy and the arrival of a foreign king – a new Cyrus – in Italy, Fra Domenico would go a step further and predict nothing less than the end of the world. The Franciscan was even able to do more: he enlightened the Florentines about Fra Girolamo. Where does Fra Girolamo get his prophecies and wisdom? I'll tell you: quite simply by violating the seal of confession. His fellow brothers tell him about the confessions of their penitents, and then he easily deceives these gullible sheep by claiming miraculous knowledge of their secrets. And so he gains the reputation of omniscience. È vero, no? The people ran back and forth between Fra Girolamo and Fra Domenico, and soon didn't know which way to turn amidst all the gloom and doom, until Piero di Medici temporarily banned the sermons of both preachers.

The Florentines eventually expelled Piero di Medici, who had been their ruler, to Lodovico. Fra Girolamo had castigated his rule as devilish and tyrannical, preaching that Florence must be a free republic, where the people govern and obey themselves. He even drafted a constitution and presented it to the Signoria, who accepted it.

The motto was: People and liberty!

And soon in all the streets of Florence, one echo responded to another: People and liberty!

XXVI.

Fra Girolamo preached: It is only faith that matters, the faith that moves mountains – and gold and precious stones, in order to partake in heavenly gold. Knowledge is a matter of the day and hour. What I know today, I will no longer know tomorrow; science today finds laws that seem eternally valid – and tomorrow it will find other laws that are diametrically opposed to the first ones. Which law applies now? The one from yesterday or the one from today? It is the one from the day before yesterday and the one from the day after tomorrow, my brothers! The law of God: the Christian faith. An old woman who remains steadfast in the Christian faith knows more about the world than Plato and Aristotle combined. An ignorant little child knows more than all the wisdom of the philosophers. Why is that? Because it is pure. For purity is the measure of the earth. When the children have taken control of the world, Christ will return. He will return to you in triumph, guided by the children: led by the three Christian virtues and the four cardinal virtues.

He will come riding in a chariot, drawn by the four mystical beasts. Patriarchs, prophets, and apostles walk on either side. The martyrs and saints follow the chariot, then the priests, and then the countless multitude of Christians.

But last in the procession will stride a black horse, shrouded in black. It will drag the soulless corpse of the Antichrist: the body of Alexander Borgia, whose soul the devil has taken.

We must erect a bonfire in the Piazza della Signoria and burn all the symbols of a decayed and lost time.

But only pure, unblemished hands may receive the indecent and immoral objects and consign them to the cleansing fire: They are the hands of the children!

After Fra Girolamo's sermon, hundreds of children went from house to house and called for 'all the trinkets of the earthly world' to be placed on the bonfire.

They drove in small carts to the Piazza della Signoria: carnival masks and costumes, mirrors, harps, chessboards, playing cards, paintings of naked and semi-naked women, including one of Lucrezia Borgia. Then books of the damned poets: Boccaccio's Decameron, Petrarch's sonnets, Ovid's *Ars Amatoria*, Tibullus' elegies, Catullus' love songs –.

While singing, the children threw everything into the blazing bonfire and danced around in a ring.

Fra Girolamo himself, when the bonfire was already half burned down, threw a portrait of Pope Alexander into the glowing ashes.

Go to hell, Satan!

The image flared brightly.

XXVII.

A young, anonymous Roman called on Fra Girolamo, who was kneeling on his stool in his bare cell, lost in prayer, and urgently wanted to speak to him in private.

Fra Girolamo opened the door of his cell and invited the young man to enter.

The young man waited politely until the friar invited him to sit down.

There was only a stool in the cell. Girolamo sat on the edge of the bed.

The young man, who had an open, clear gaze, a high forehead, and a refined, reserved demeanor, began the conversation: I must first introduce myself. For I know you – but you do not know me. My name is Cesare Borgia. Fra Girolamo jumped up from the edge of the bed. Cesare raised his beautiful, slender hand: Do not be alarmed. I am incognito in Florence. For your sake. I will not eat you. I have no weapon with me.

The priest waved him off.

I am not afraid of you.

Cesare bowed politely.

So much the worse for you. I do not underestimate you.

Fra Girolamo walked back and forth in the cell and stopped before the crucifix and the Eternal Lamp.

The light of the Eternal Lamp flickered restlessly.

Then he suddenly turned to Cesare: What do you want from me?

Cesare: Peace. Peace between you and the Borgias.

Girolamo became agitated: Who has broken the peace? Who has thrown Italy and the world into disorder? Who has upended the eternal laws of morality? Who rules through war and its atrocities? Who incites all people against one another – to profit from their turmoil?

Cesare remained very calm: You are a dreamer, Frater. We Borgias are realists. Morality is a pretty little leash for the weak who need it. But it is as time-bound as fashion. One cannot build a worldview upon it. You yourself, Frater, stand as far outside of today's fashion as the Borgias.

Girolamo pressed on: What is the purpose of your visit?

Cesare laid his glove over his knee: My father sent me. You have deeply wounded and offended His Holiness. If you were not so generous – his voice became hard – he would offer you a gallows. Instead, he offers you – Fra Girolamo looked expectantly at the lips of the Borgia. He concluded: the cardinal's hat.

Fra Girolamo burst out laughing: The cardinal's hat usually costs ten to twenty thousand ducats at His Holiness's discretion. I regret –

Cesare interrupted: You have taken the vow of poverty. You will receive the purple under one condition – What would that be?

You will cease your struggle against His Holiness immediately.

The monk thundered: Never! Never! Never! The conscience of humanity and my own conscience demand this struggle from me. There is only one way for understanding and peace between the Pope and me: The Pope must promise remorse, penance, reform, and must undertake an immediate reformation of the Church.

Cesare Borgia stood up.

He said softly: Never. Never. Never. You have a hard head and a stiff backbone. But consider the following: His Holiness's head is not only hard, but also wise. And his backbone is the Church, while you can only lean against the crumbling walls of a Florentine monastery. But, as you wish –

The Borgia stood up, put on his gloves, bowed, and left.

XXVIII.

Charles VIII, King of France, set out for Italy with a well-armed, well-disciplined army to secure his claims to the throne of Naples. The Pope issued a letter of admonition against him.

The armies of the Italian cities and princes, a hodgepodge of mercenaries and lansquenets, scattered before him like chaff.

Charles VIII entered Florence. And the people remembered that Fra Girolamo had prophesied the arrival of a new Cyrus.

Small, unappealing, red-haired, with a hooked nose, hunchbacked, with drooping eyes and a receding forehead, a giant head on a tiny body, the king sat huddled like a fairground monkey on a dapple-grey horse.

His short, thick, spurless legs hung down like pendulums, swinging left and right. He rode, his lance at his hip, through a corridor of astonished Florentine men, women, and children.

A child, lifted by his father for a better view, shouted into the dead silence: Is this supposed to be a king?

Laughter rained down upon the advancing French.

But the Italians would soon realize that this monstrosity was indeed a king. –

The Pope had declared himself against him. This annoyed him. He had himself briefed on the internal affairs of Florence, ordered white bread to be distributed to the people, and summoned Savonarola. Savonarola appeared.

The king, accustomed to talking while walking, circled and spiraled around him.

It looked as though the little man in his colorful doublet was leading the tall, dark man in a fashionable dance. Yes – well – yes – ch—t— – he had the habit of peppering his speech with meaningless consonants. You are – Fra Girolamo – the uncrowned king – ch—t— – of this – this republic – or so –

Savonarola tried to respond but the king accidentally stepped on his foot. Yes – ch—t— – what are we doing here – Your Holiness – soi-disant – yes – in Rome – ch—t— – placing obstacles in my way to Naples – threatening me – yes – ch—t— eventually – with excommunication – wanted – yes – soi-disant – to hear your opinion on the casus – ch—t— –

He had stopped in front of Fra Girolamo and was looking up intently.

Savonarola's forehead had darkened:

Majesty, are you informed about the nature and misdeeds of this – this devil, who has gained the papal throne through simony?

The king swayed from one foot to the other.

I am – I am –

Well then – Fra Girolamo took a deep breath: You have the power, Majesty, to render the greatest service to Christendom (and to yourself), the greatest service that could ever be rendered –

The king fidgeted: And – and?

Fra Girolamo spoke strongly: Your Majesty, when you enter Rome, depose the Pope, convene a general council that declares his usurped pontificate obtained through simony invalid, and Italy, Europe, the world will cheer you as their liberator!

The king resumed his restless wandering. Yes – well – soi-disant – I thank you very much – will consider everything – act accordingly – ch—t— – you may go.

Fra Girolamo left.

When he was outside, the king jumped onto the windowsill like a child and watched the black monk walk across the square in the bright sun.

He clapped his hands several times in amusement and was uncertain whether he was applauding the monk or himself. Yes – ch—t— –, he thought, I have also received letters from some Roman cardinals, especially from a certain – ch—t— Giovanni Battisti Orsini – that are moving in – ch—t— – a similar direction as this – this monk – yes – one must consider everything – and – then do the right thing – ch—t— –

Fra Girolamo knelt in his cell before the crucifix.

Lord, Lord – I thank you for your grace and your glorious help! O illuminate the mind of the King of France with your eternal light! The temple of the Antichrist in Rome is wavering – it will fall – I sense it, I know it from your heavenly signs! O let me be Samson, who brings down the pillars of the temple! His face shone with glory.

I feel a great trembling of the earth – the red devil on Saint Peter's throne turns pale as chalk – he falls – he collapses – I will place my foot on his neck –

XXIX.

In triumph, Charles VIII rode through Italy. He arrived at the gates of Rome. In great haste, Alexander barricaded himself in the Castel Sant'Angelo. Now it served him well that he had spent thousands, tens of thousands of ducats and indulgences on its fortification.

Charles VIII besieged the Castel Sant'Angelo and planned an assault.

He had to realize that he stood little chance against the strength of the bastions. He had also underestimated the power of the papal symbol. His soldiers were grumbling.

They did not want to fight against the 'Vicar of Christ.' Both parties had no choice but to negotiate a treaty.

Johannes Burkhard, the papal master of ceremonies, rode out to meet the King of France to arrange the ceremonies for his reception.

The king shook his head: Let's – ch—t— – skip the pomp. I come as I come.

Johannes Burkhard looked at his well-groomed fingernails, the only thing he tended to, as he considered washing unhealthy and cleaned himself only with ointments and powders: His Holiness requests Your Majesty to surrender a person close to His Holiness's heart, who by an unfortunate accident fell into Your Majesty's hands during a ride –

The king grumbled: By a – ch—t— – fortunate accident. I ask for a straight three thousand ducats, and you can – soi-disant – take the person with you.

Johannes Burkhard pulled out a bag of money that the Pope had given him and began to count the ducats.

The king eagerly counted along.

It's true. – He rubbed his knobby hands together. You can take Madonna Julia Farnese with a letter of recommendation to His Holiness. She has already cried her eyes out. Those beautiful eyes!

Charles VIII demanded the Pope's son Cesare and the Turkish prince Jem as hostages for the strict fulfillment of the treaty for six months.

At first, Alexander was outraged.

After a private conversation with Cesare, he smiles and gives his consent.

The Pope and the King stand in the Vatican gardens, both bareheaded, facing each other and measuring one another up. The King kneels three times and tilts his pumpkin-shaped head back to look up at the Pope, who kisses his own hand instead of the King's.

This smile, Charles thought, I don't like it. I must be on my guard.

And Pope Alexander sees the King grinning unpleasantly.

And thinks the same.

Your Majesty will, the Pope said slowly, choosing his words carefully, acknowledge me tomorrow at a public consistory in the presence of the cardinals as the true Pope and legitimate vicar and successor of Peter, and swear an oath of allegiance to me.

The King hesitates for a moment.

In the name of the three devils, he grumbles.

Cesare Borgia, the handsome one, rode in cardinal purple on a mule beside Charles VIII, the ugly one, down the road to Naples.

But after just a few miles, he let the King ride ahead, seemingly full of devotion. He felt slightly nauseous because Charles VIII had bad breath.

Following the Borgia cardinal were thirty mules loaded with baggage and nineteen wagons full of suitcases and boxes.

In Marino, they spent the night for the first time. Cesare Borgia wished the King a blessed night and politely declined the card game that the King offered him.

The next morning, when an adjutant of the King wanted to wake the cardinal in his tent, he was nowhere to be found.

He had fled before midnight in the guise of a stable boy and galloped back to Rome.

Charles VIII struck the officer who brought him the news in the face with his riding whip out of rage.

And he leaves behind so many suitcases and boxes, all his precious luggage, just like that?

He ordered the suitcases and boxes to be opened. They contained only straw and field stones.

XXX.

Without encountering resistance, Charles VIII marched into Naples.

King Alfonso II of Naples had fled.

The French king triumphed.

He stood on the Posilip, looking down at the city of Naples at his feet, with the blue sea to the west dotted with the islands of Capri and Ischia, and Mount Vesuvius to the south, its peak wreathed in a cloud of smoke.

He ran his small, thick hand, covered in numerous warts, flat over the landscape.

I have reached the pinnacle of my power.

All this – is mine.

This beautiful landscape is subject to me, the ugly one.

And strangely, he, the unloved, the loveless, felt stirred to love.

He had some fisher girls from Santa Lucia brought to him and enjoyed himself with Laura, the most beautiful, a young sixteen-year-old girl from Capri, until early morning. Half faint with disgust, she staggered back to Santa Lucia, took a tiny boat over to Capri, and plunged into the beloved native sea by the Faraglioni from her cherished homeland.

Dolphins danced around her sinking, phosphorescent corpse in the green water.

A sawfish mercifully cut through her chest, and a young shark tenderly devoured her right arm.

Then the peaceful depths embraced her. Sea spiders moved lightly yet heavily over her. Crabs made themselves at home in her eye sockets. An octopus rested, having had an indecisive battle with a lobster, beside her.

Cesare Borgia stormed into his father's arms.

Saved!

The Pope gently stroked the back of his head: I have not been idle. We are forming a 'Holy League to uphold the dignity of the Holy See.' Wait half a year: the Emperor in Germany, the King of Spain, and the majority of the Italian princes and cities will join our alliance in exchange for special indulgences, tax exemptions, and the provision of subsidies. Trionfo Borgia! Trionfo Borgia! repeated Cesare, grasping the dagger in his scabbard.

Charles VIII was not happy with the possession of Naples.

With the fleeing Borgia, his good fortune had abandoned him.

Prince Djem, the Turkish hostage, died a few days later, officially reported to have succumbed to spoiled tuna. However, there were not a few who suspected that the Borgia had poured a white powder into his evening drink just before his hasty departure.

Doctors and nurses surrounded his deathbed, perplexed.

No one understood Turkish.

The king shouted at him with agitated gestures.

Helpless as a dying animal, the Turk opened his inflamed eyes wide.

His last words were: *Hajwan ölür Szemeri Kalyr, inszamölür ady Valyr –*

Under the influence of the hot Neapolitan climate, discipline in Charles's army gradually loosened alarmingly.

The French soldiers fell into a frenzy of debauchery. In broad daylight, one stumbled in dark alleys and on stairs over entwined and contorted couples.

An epidemic broke out in the French army, known as the French disease, which claimed thousands of soldiers.

Charles was desperate.

He received news via mounted couriers of the formation of the 'Holy League to uphold the dignity of the Holy See' and of the Pope's refusal to invest him with Naples, despite the contract.

They want to uphold the dignity of this papal seat! Ch—t—! It did not matter to this... he could not find a term of abuse low enough to describe it.

Charles began the retreat from Naples: with a decimated, depressed troop. The Pope had prudently left Rome and was hiding in Orvieto. Charles did not find him there.

At Fortenuovo, the army of the League stood ready to completely destroy Charles.

Through a deceptive march, he managed to avoid battle and cross the French border.

Upon arriving in Paris, he collapsed. He wanted to see no one anymore.

A raven, a monkey, and a black dog kept him company in his dying moments. Louis XII ascended the French throne.

XXXI.

The Pope said: The Florentines are constitutional fools. They give themselves a different constitution every moment and yet always find themselves in a bad state. They do not base things on living life, on humans, but on a fiction called 'politics' and construct purely mathematical parliaments, councils, voting rights, and whatever else. This Fra Girolamo is nothing but a constructor. He wants a rule 'of the best.' Of the sixteen districts of the city of Florence, each should elect 'the best' of its district, the sixteen best then elect the best among them. Who, do you think, Cesare, will finally come to power?

Cesare smiled his polite smile: The very best one who has the other fifteen hanged.

His Holiness, Pope Alexander VI, to the Prior and the Brothers of the San Marco Monastery of the Dominican Order in Florence:

My beloved sons!

Greetings and apostolic blessing beforehand! We have been horrified and deeply saddened to hear that a certain Fra Girolamo Savonarola from Ferrara, who comes from your midst, has taken it upon himself to proclaim devilish heresies, schisms, and seditious aspirations. He blasphemously claims to be illuminated by God himself. But it is the devil's torch that burns above him, and he will be the first to cast it into the pyre that a just court will erect for him. For the devil knows no gratitude and mockingly abandons the souls he has seduced.

I have waited and endured with apostolic patience, hoping that he would become aware of his imagined prophethood and crawl back to the cross of Christ, which we eagerly extended to him. Not at all! I have been mistaken. Commissioned by God the Lord to preserve the building of Christ from all shocks, I find myself, with a torn heart, compelled to restore to the Church the longed-for peace and harmony by entrusting the resolution of this vexatious matter to the Vicar General, Brother Sebastian of Brescia, to whom, under threat of immediate excommunication in case of insubordination, unconditional and unconditional obedience must be rendered. Given and sealed Rome... etc.

The Pope received some letters from Fra Girolamo. He did not open them and did not read them.

He twisted paper balls from them and with a blowgun shot at the sparrows from a window of the Vatican.

XXXII.

The Pope's letter had its effect.

Soon the rumor spread through the streets of Florence that the Pope had placed a ban on Fra Girolamo.

There were also reports that the Pope had been victorious in the struggle against Charles VIII, who had come to depose him from his high office.

Doubt and despair began to seize the citizens of Florence.

The Pope, no matter who or what he is, is still the Pope. He derives his power from the Lord God. And all priests have received their authority from him, the Pope.

He may be a great sinner – but are we not all sinners, as Fra Girolamo himself preaches? And if he fails as a man, does that mean he must fail as Pope? Is he not as Pope the vessel of God – into which He pours His wisdom and knowledge? Can a priest speak against the papal priesthood? Was not perhaps the sudden onset of the plague in Florence a punishment from God for the blasphemous and heretical actions of Fra Girolamo?

No sooner had the Pope cast the ecclesiastical ban upon him, publicly announced from the pulpits of Santo Spirito and Santa Maria Novella, than the plague broke out a few days later, first in the Borgo di Ricoboli. Sixty people died on the first day, eighty on the second, and two hundred on the third. Many wealthy people fled.

Fra Girolamo stayed, visited the sick, and preached, disregarding the excommunication: Through God's counsel, the adults who have partaken in the sins of this world die.

But God allows the children to live, so that a new generation may grow up, unburdened by the sins of the fathers. And in fact, no child and no young person under twenty years of age died from the plague.

But the Florentines no longer believed his prophecies.

The Pope's spell was stronger than the spell cast by Fra Girolamo's personality.

In the streets, passersby fell dead, and bearers with litters came and carried them away in silence. In July, the sun suddenly darkened, and it became dark night in the middle of the day. And when it became light again, the streets were strewn with corpses. At the doors of houses stood several who had died while standing. On the Mercato Nuovo, at a money exchange, sat an old Jewish moneylender, his head supported by his hand, bent over a roll of ducats.

He seemed to be sleeping.

It was said that the devil roamed the streets of Florence at night. Every day someone claimed to have seen him: with glowing red eyes, in the shape of an upright walking fox, its long bushy tail elegantly draped over its right front paw like a train.

Even the youth, so dearly loved and praised by Fra Girolamo, began to be seized by confusion and rebellion.

One afternoon, a group of children aged ten to twelve marched onto the Piazza della Signoria.

They dragged a cross with them, along with a hammer and nails, and would have crucified one of their own, a small idiot of seven years, if two city police officers had not come along and stopped them.

But these two policemen, two sturdy Tuscan fellows, had a hard time, as the idiot bit them and the children beat them with the cross like mad. Only with great difficulty could the children be subdued.

Fra Girolamo was shaken.

He presented his theses once more and nailed them to the door of the cathedral:

God's one and only Church requires complete internal and spiritual renewal.
God will chastise it,
God will renew it.
Florence will be chastised,
Florence will be renewed.
The heathens, Turks, and unbelievers will convert to Christ.
All of this will happen in our times.
The excommunication pronounced against Brother Fra Girolamo by His
        Unholiness, the Antipope, is null and void.
Whoever disregards it does not sin. –
Handwritten and signed. Florence, Monastery of San Marco
Fra Girolamo.

In his desperation, he wrote letters to Emperor Maximilian and the kings of Spain, France, England, and Hungary, imploring them to take a stand against the Antichrist and convene a council. He would deliver a well-founded indictment against the false pope before the council. The pope would then answer to him and the council.

Against the express order of the Signoria, Fra Girolamo dared once more to ascend the pulpit of San Marco.

He had hardly opened his mouth when a deafening outcry arose against him.

He did not get a word in.

His friends no longer dared to speak up for him, and one by one, they slipped out of the church, ashamed. The children in the street unwillingly withdrew from him when he attempted to stroke their foreheads and pet them. The little idiot who had wanted to be nailed to the cross spat in front of him. And some others threw horse manure at him, which clung to his robe.

XXXIII.

The papal envoys were the Venetians Giocchino Turriano, General of the Dominican Order, and the Spaniard Francesco Remolino.

Listen, my son, said the Pope, taking aside the small, maliciously charming Francesco Remolino, the former tutor of Cesare, as he was taking his farewell. I speak to you as a Spaniard, from Spaniard to Spaniard. You are, like me, a lover of the corrida, the bullfight. There are small, barbed spears that one thrusts into the bulls to incite them to blood. Thrust such spikes into the belly of Frater Girolamo. Play the picador. Torture him until he confesses what you want. He must die, even if he were to rise again as John the Baptist.

If it cannot be done otherwise, you must lure and seduce him into confession. Promise him that if he confesses, he shall only stay a week in prison. You will keep your word strictly, let him out of prison after a week – but only to hang him. Also, calmly promise him life – another will pronounce the death sentence. One must always adhere to the truth. A naive person would call such methods cunning and treacherous. But what does the Apostle Paul mean when he says: 'When I was cunning, I caught them with guile.' –We must be cunning, Francesco Remolino.

The Spaniard bowed with an oily smile. Your Holiness will be satisfied with me.

As soon as the Spaniard arrived in Florence, he ordered a thick rope with a pulley to be set up in the armorer's guild. He arranged the torture instruments and tortured him in the proper sequence. First, he applied the thumbscrews, then the hand screws, then the Spanish boots, then the Spanish donkey. Next came the ankle torture, the rod torture, the toe torture, the binding, and the rope torture. The Spaniard himself tied Fra Girolamo to the torture rope and pulled him up and down by the arms fourteen times. His feet were weighted with stones.

Confess, smiled the Spaniard, confess!

Muscles and tendons creaked and tore. On the thirteenth time, as blood gushed from his mouth, nose, and ears, he confessed everything that the torturers wanted him to confess. The spiked hare and the stinging cradle were no longer needed. It was also unnecessary to bring in those judicially appointed goats, which were supposed to lick the artificially wounded soles of the delinquent's feet, into which salt had been sprinkled.

Turriano himself documented the friar's statements, in which he freely confessed all heresy and devilry: So help me God!

He had only served the devil, and all his prophecies had been inspired by the devil, who had also incited him to revolt against the Holy See with a scourge of fire.

When the people of Florence learned that Fra Girolamo had confessed to his seven deadly sins under torture, they turned away from him with contempt.

If he were a true prophet, he would not have recanted. Not even under torture!

One by one, his friends abandoned him. Those who had been closest to him kept their distance the most.

And when they were asked: You were on familiar terms with this Fra Girolamo, weren't you? – they opened their eyes wide and said: What? That heretic Girolamo? That must be a mistake. I only know him very slightly and from afar – from his accursed, heretical sermons.

In the Piazza della Signoria, the pyre was set up, along with a spectator's stand with comfortable seats. The first row cost one lira, the second row two quattrini, the third row five denari. The executioner's assistants walked through the standing areas collecting donations with plates.

A large crowd from Florence and the surrounding areas had gathered, including many men, women, and children who had loved him but had become unfaithful to that love during the time of trial.

But no one raised a hand for him. Only a few women sobbed, and a small eleven-year-old boy threw stones at the executioner.

Fra Girolamo was led to the execution site, adorned with all the insignia of his order.

Canons, priests, councilors, officials, and captains awaited him.

The General of the Dominicans approached him and tore off one insignia after another, saying: *Separo te ab ecclesia militante, non triumphante!*

Fra Girolamo calmly replied: *Militante, non triumphante: hoc enim tuum non est!*

The executioners bound his hands behind his back and led him to the pyre, where he was tied to a thick tree in the middle.

On the way, a hunchbacked man, an intrusive member of the Compagnia di Santa Maria del Tempio, pushed himself towards him, whose duty it was to comfort and bury those condemned to death.

Do you want comfort, Frater? That costs one lira. – A small comfort? That costs only a few soldi.

They ignited the pile of twigs. A storm had gathered in the sky. It began to drizzle, thunder, and lightning.

Fra Girolamo burned and was enraptured in the flames: I see an angel descending from heaven, clothed with a cloud, a rainbow bound around his forehead. He carries God's fiery sword in his right hand and will swing it fearfully over mankind, and his voice is thunder, and it sounds mightily over the earth, and his left hand carries the bowl of wrath, to pour it out over the earth.

Woe, woe to the great city of Babylon! The judgment is coming soon!

Gold, precious stones, silk, purple, ivory, marble, ebony, wine, wheat, cattle, man, everything will perish in an hour.

O Angel of the Lord, rescue me from destruction!

Thrust your burning sword into my heart that beats for you!

I am on fire! I am burning! I shine in the love of God! Oh I, the torch of God! I shine over all seas and lands into the darkness of the earth!

And he began to sing:

Let me die!
And what would you want
to comforts me
from such a harsh fate
in such great martyrdom?
Let me die!

The Frater burned for two hours.

First, his left arm fell off, then his right arm.

When he was burned, the executioners took the ashes, collected them, and poured them into the Arno so that not a speck of him would remain to serve as a relic for posterity.

That boy, who had thrown stones at the executioners, jumped into the river and swam to a piece of coal, took it in his mouth like a dog fetching a stick, and swam back to the shore, where he soon disappeared in the maze of streets.

In the following June, a strange kind of black caterpillars, never seen there before, infested the meadows of Florence.

They had human-like heads, whose facial shape seemed to resemble the features of Father Savonarola.

They only ate the lowest and most useless weed: the thorn bush.

There was an excellent grain harvest, and the Stajo fell to thirty soldi.

XXXIV.

My little son, said Alexander, who had returned to Rome, to Cesare, now that we are rid of this Charles VIII and that foolish Dominican Fra Girolamo, we have time to deal a bit with our internal enemies, the barons of Romagna, the Orsini and Colonna. Juan, the Duke of Gandia, my beloved son and Captain General of the Papal States, will take command against the unruly knights. Grant him your blessing as a brother and cardinal!

Cesare left the room without a word.

Juan set out to the field and suffered a pathetic defeat against the Orsini, who maintained all their castles.

Vanozza hosted a small celebration in her vineyard in Vincoli near St. Peter's for the grape harvest and the granting of the fiefdoms of Benevento and Terracina to the Duke of Gandia.

The Pope had arrived, along with Lucrezia, Juan, Gioffredo's beautiful wife Sancia, Cesare Borgia, and some Roman nobles from the Borgia circle.

For the amusement of the table, some monkeys, jesters, and gluttons were brought in. One of them began his meal with thirty hard-boiled eggs, only to immediately follow it with an entire salami, which he had to wrestle for with a monkey.

The monk and jester Arlotto told lewd jokes. For instance, he claimed, known for his lechery, that the Pope and he knew the same way to triumph. The Pope asked amusedly, With what? With the papal bull! But I could also take on Demosthenes. In what way? With the tongue. Juan fell backward laughing.

Lucrezia amused herself by plucking grapes from the vines and throwing the berries one by one into the mouths of the guests.

The Pope laughed and coughed, having choked on a berry.

Cesare bit his lips together, and the berries fell to the ground.

Sancia looked at him sideways.

Juan snapped up the grapes with great skill.

He managed to catch thirteen berries and was declared the winner in the 'grape toss' by Lucrezia.

Later, she sang Spanish songs and danced the Tarantella. The Pope tenderly followed each of her graceful movements.

At midnight, they set off.

The Pope and Lucrezia rode with torchbearers and servants in one company.

Cesare and Juan, the Duke of Gandia, formed the second group.

At the palace of Ascanio Sforza, Juan bid a cheerful goodbye to his companions to pursue a little adventure.

The next day, he was fished out of the Tiber near the mouth of the main sewer.

His swollen body showed a dagger stab right above the heart.

The Pope locked himself in his room, and here, where no one could see him, he let his tears flow freely.

He wept for the first time in his life. Juan Borgia, the general captain of the Church, the future king of Naples, of all Italy – extinguished like a torch in the sand.

I will do penance, he cried. Lord, I deeply regret my cursed life. Pour your grace over me one more time. I will reform your beloved Church, I myself. I will...

He did not eat, drink, or sleep for three days, fevered, and meditated.

On the fourth day, Cesare visited him.

The Pope snapped at him like a dog: Who killed the Duke of Gandia?

Cesare did not respond.

Who stabbed Juan Borgia and threw him into the Tiber?

Cesare replied with a question: Who forced me into the spiritual profession, although I was the elder and more suited for worldly dignity than he, who has covered himself with shame and ridicule in the campaign against the Orsini? And who made me a cardinal, although the cardinal's hat fits me no better than a nightcap? Who wants to make something of me that I am not?

Alexander stepped toward him and placed both hands heavily on his shoulders.

He wanted to press them down, but he could not.

The slender, thin man stood immovable.

The Pope sighed: What am I to do with you now, huh?

Cesare shrugged his shoulders: Are you going to spit in my soup? The saliva of the Borgias is already poison enough. You don't need to use the Cantarella.

Alexander walked back and forth in silence. After ten minutes, he stopped again in front of Cesare.

They're causing me the greatest inconveniences. The death of poor Giovanni ruins all my plans.

Cesare said calmly: Make new plans.

Alexander exclaimed: I loved him. Do you know that?

Cesare replied: He is dead. God rest his soul –

He made the sign of the cross.

The Pope swatted his hand away.

Cesare continued: He is dead. I live. Cast the love you had for him into the love you have for me. Then I will be happy. Love me! Father!

Alexander's face brightened: For the first time, you call me Father. Come to my breast. Son! Son!

The Pope allowed Cardinal Cesare Borgia, who had never received the ordinary priestly ordination, to lay aside the cardinal's purple.

Cesare threw the cardinal's cloak out the window into the street, where the mob began to fight over it. In no time, the cloak was torn into a thousand pieces. They tore the cloak and thought they were tearing the one who had worn it.

XXXV.

From then on, the Pope no longer concerned himself with Vanozza.

She had given him, as was her duty, the Borgias and had thus fulfilled her mission.

One day, when he learned that she was seriously ill with malaria, he sent her his personal physician Torella.

He administered an injection that caused her to fall into a deep, lasting sleep. She slept for thirteen years until her death, awakening only for a few minutes each day and night, during which she was only half-conscious.

She completely forgot the language and could finally remember only one word: Borgia.

The Pope waved a parchment in his hand.

Trionfo, Borgia! The new King of France asks me to annul his first marriage and allow him to enter into a second! I have agreed – under one condition –

Cesare: Don't put me on the rack.

Alexander: We have already done that with this Savonarola. Joking aside, Cesare: on the condition that you marry a French princess.

Cesare grinned with pleasure: And he has agreed?

The Pope rejoiced: Yes! He proposes Charlotte d'Albret, the sister of the King of Navarre. – My dear son, continued Alexander Borgia, you must appear noble in France. We need carriages, traveling wagons, pages, runners, riders, velvet, silk, gold, brocade, pearls in abundance!

And where will we get what will amount to two to three hundred thousand gold ducats? Cesare smiled modestly.

My dear son, the Pope affectionately patted his cheek, you must do something about your freckles; they only mar your pretty face. Yes – what I wanted to say is that there are some wealthy individuals suspected of heresy, such as Pedro de Aranda, Bishop of Calahorro. If we don't prosecute them, they will gladly and willingly pay a sum. And what are the Jews for? We condemn them for ungodly usury to severe prison sentences, which they can then pay off with money. Calm down, my son; we will have the two hundred thousand ducats together in a week. By the way, I will also establish a Borgia bank. A bank where one can obtain indulgences for fixed fees. Murder will cost, let's say, five hundred ducats, while theft, embezzlement, and even abortion and defamation will cost correspondingly less.

Cesare joked: You yourself have enough operating capital to contribute.

Alexander Borgia ignored the remark: Twenty percent of each deposit goes directly to the papal chamber, that is, to us. We can significantly fill our coffers with this, as sinners, thank God, do not die out.

Cesare smiled: And neither do fools.

Alexander chuckled: Amen. By the way, what I wanted to mention: a prince of Aragon, of Naples, cannot be of much use to us after our recent successes. Lucrezia's marriage to him was folly. We must make amends.

One evening, when Alfonso wanted to visit his wife in the Vatican, he was ambushed by masked men and stabbed repeatedly.

Bleeding from his head, arms, and thighs, he fled to Lucrezia's chamber, where she fainted at the sight of him.

The Pope granted him absolution. But contrary to expectations, Alfonso recovered.

He was carefully and tenderly nursed by Lucrezia, who prepared all his drinks herself and tasted all his food first before handing it to him.

One afternoon, in the mild evening sun, now already on the mend, Alfonso stood at the open window and saw Cesare Borgia walking through the garden.

His vision went red with rage. He snatched the dagger from its sheath and threw it at him.

The dagger fell to the ground in front of Cesare.

Cesare picked it up without looking at the window. He examined the coat of arms of Aragon on the hilt for a moment.

Then he threw it at an olive tree, where it became lodged in the trunk.

That same evening, Cesare visited Alfonso and kindly inquired about his condition. During the night, Michelotto, one of Cesare's creatures, secretly entered Alfonso's room and strangled him in his sleep. Cesare played a game of chess with the Pope that night.

While he was putting the Pope in check with his queen, he casually remarked: The way is clear for a marriage between Lucrezia and Prince Este of Ferrara.

The Pope dropped the king he had drawn.

I'm tired, he said, let's go to sleep.

Lucrezia was beside herself when she heard about Alfonso's murder. For the first time, she lost faith in her own family. Her lips refused to utter the name Borgia, and she vomited it out in disgust with green bile.

She refused to see Cesare and would not allow Alexander to appear before her. She wanted to be alone and never see a Borgia again.

She covered all the mirrors in her room so that she wouldn't have to see herself. At night, she walked, deeply veiled, to the convent of San Sisto and pleaded for admission.

XXXVI.

Cardinal la Grolaye had told Lucrezia about the young, twenty-three-year-old Florentine sculptor Michelangelo.

One day she invited him to her convent.

She looked at him curiously, like a child observing Turks and Indians.

You are a sculptor?

Yes, Madonna.

Noble?

From the noblest lineage –

Do you understand your craft?

I hope so, Madonna.

Do you make a living from your art?

I make art from my living.

Can you create horses – or better yet: horse-people, centaurs?

The battle of the centaurs and Lapiths? I will try, Madonna.

A dying Adonis – I will ponder that –

Are you interested in ancient excavations? Beautiful statues, a goddess, or a Silenus are found all the time. You can learn a lot – if you wish.

It is the content of my life, Madonna.

What have you accomplished that is remarkable?

A group, Madonna.

What does it represent?

The Pietà –

You must show it to me!

I beg you, dispose of me as you wish!

Lucrezia entered his studio, accompanied by the abbess of San Sisto. She was in very good spirits and kept nibbling on dates.

She saw a centaur started in clay.

It bore the features of Alexander Borgia.

She saw a dying Adonis.

He bore the features of Alfonso of Aragon.

She turned to Michelangelo, smiling melancholically: And what do you want to make of me?

Suddenly she stood before the Pietà. And all her cheerfulness shattered in an instant, the moment she exchanged it for the Pietà. This Pietà is not a painfully aged Mater Dolorosa – it is a very young, suffering woman who resembles me, and Christ – does he not bear the features of that Fra Girolamo who was burned in Florence – of that wretched heretic –

She said aloud: You knew Savonarola?

The sculptor nodded silently.

He is not dead at all, it seems. He is merely sleeping –

Yes, said Michelangelo, he is only sleeping.

My God, she thought, I must cry. I feel the tears welling up. I must leave at once.

But it was already too late.

Tears poured from her eyes.

Michelangelo, after she had left him, fell into an ecstatic frenzy. He threw aside the chisel and began painting a series of passionately sensual works:

Leda embraced by the swan.

Venus embraced by Cupid.

Leda and Venus bore the features of Lucrezia Borgia. He began to write verses to the *Donna aspera e bella*.

And called her: *La donna mia nemica* –

My beautiful enemy.

He dreamed of her nakedness.

And began to sketch a Christian painting in which the Madonna, the Savior, Saint Peter, and Saint John, all in pagan nakedness, wandered through a Florentine landscape.

Lucrezia returned to the Vatican, tenderly summoned by the Pope.

She told him about the sculptor Michelangelo.

The Pope thought for a moment.

He should make a design for my tomb. For a tomb that will be destined to unite all the Borgias one day. He sent Michelangelo to the quarries of Carrara to break the suitable marble.

Michelangelo encountered a mountain on the coast, visible from both land and sea.

I will carve a colossal statue from the mountain – why carry Carrara to Rome? The bodies of the Borgias must be transported from Rome to Carrara and rest beneath this colossal stone block, which I will give the form of a gigantic centaur.

XXXVII.

The sky arched cloudlessly over the Borgias.

The sun shone only on the wicked. Cesare Borgia married a French princess.

When she saw him for the first time without his helmet and headband on their wedding night, she was startled and nearly fainted.

The Borgia unmistakably bore the mark of the French disease on his forehead.

Madame, smiled Borgia, this mark on my forehead is from God and France. You won't hold it against me. I am ready to consummate our marriage, for the time being, only in effigy.

And he sat on the edge of the bed, took a lute, and began to sing Roman folk songs to Charlotte d'Albret until she clapped her hands and laughed, singing along with the chorus.

Cesare, who returned to Italy, never saw his wife again.

The French allied with the Borgias. The Colonna submitted willingly.

After the death of Djem, the Turks invaded Italy and seized Venetian ports.

The Pope preached a crusade, planning to secretly negotiate peace with the Turks soon.

Meanwhile, Cesare, with the backing of the French king, waged his war against the Italian cities and princes of Central Italy.

One city after another fell into his hands.

One prince after another fell in battle or fled.

He was on the path to the Italian crown. On the path – to himself.

His motto, engraved on his sword, read: *Aut Cesare aut nihil.*

Cesare Borgia loved to dress elegantly and correctly in the latest fashion when marching into battle. He was dissatisfied with his tailor.

You dog of a Tuscan clothes maker, he roared at him, you ruined the whole battle at Forli for me. You dressed me in five glaring colors, making me look like a harlequin. Do you think this war is a carnival, huh?

The tailor gathered himself to respond: War isn't much different. It's just that blood flows here, and wine flows at carnival.

Spare me your figurative philosophy. You are not here to think, but to cut skirts, and if you ever deliver such a miserably botched costume again, like the last one, I'll cut off your nose and whatever hangs between your legs and resembles it – with your own dull scissors. – Keep your mouth shut! Take measurements! That's enough!

Cesare laid siege to the fortress of Forli.

Inside, he besieged Caterina Sforza. Caterina Sforza had lost her father, brother, husband, and lover to murder and poison. She wore chainmail and had an iron heart. She fought for her little son, Ottaviano.

She stood on the castle wall and challenged Cesare to a duel. She mocked him and threw a stinging nettle at his face. He desired her, but he did not let it show. He sent word to her that he was ready to fight her – in the olive grove outside Forli – but without witnesses.

She laughed: she was not afraid.

The next morning, they met in the grove. In the first exchange, he struck her rapier from her hand, threw his own rapier into the grass beside hers, embraced her, and forced her to submit to his will.

Thus, she became his captive, in body and soul.

Cesare played marbles with little Ottaviano.

When Cesare won one of the colorful glass marbles, in which the universe swirled fiery, the little boy cried out in anger and struck him in the face with his clenched fist.

Cesare rubbed his slightly flushed cheek: You are the only man who has made Cesare Borgia blush. I will give you back the glass sphere. And later, when you are grown up, even Forli –

Cesare leaned over a map of Italy. He traced the rivers and mountain ranges with nervous fingers.

He struck at the individual cities – and his finger curled like a vulture's beak. Siena! Navarra! Genoa! Naples! Everywhere others hold power.

He thought 'others,' for, in truth, there was only one kind of people destined to rule: the Borgias. Those others – the flat-headed, empty-brained, potbellied, trembling beanpoles – were born to serve silently and obey without question.

The Riaris of Imola and Forli had been vanquished.

Soon, like ears of grain bending before the wind, all the princes of Italy bowed before Cesare Borgia, Duke of Valence, Standard-Bearer and General Captain of the Holy Roman Church.

Colonna and Orsini bowed down, and even the Este and Gonzaga fell to their knees.

Cesare returned to Rome because he needed money, money, and more money for his military campaigns.

He entered Rome as a triumphant victor, in the style of Caesar's triumphs.

On a chariot, he brought with him a beautiful naked woman who flailed like a fish in a net.

It was Italia.

From the Loggia Beneficione, the Pope blessed the entrance of the victorious son, and his right hand, raised in blessing, trembled with pride.

XXXVIII.

Pesaro, Rimini, Imola, and Forli had fallen.

The Gonzaga and Este families, although not vassals of the Papal States, sought the favor of Cesare and Alexander. Now Cesare faced Faenza. Faenza was the key to Ravenna and Venice. The city defended itself heroically.

When the men's resistance began to falter, it was the seventeen-year-old Diamante Jovelli who reignited their spirit. She walked along the walls, bringing one man a cup of water, another a word of encouragement, hauling ammunition and fascines. Her example inspired the other women, and after a week, Diamante Jovelli became the captain of a women's battalion. She had a white flag raised on the ramparts, depicting a girl in chainmail stepping on a skull.

What Diamante Jovelli, the black-haired, delicately built daughter of a tanner, did, she did out of love for the eighteen-year-old Astorre Manfredi, the prince of Faenza, whose mother, Francesca, had stabbed her husband, Galeotto Manfredi, to death for his infidelity.

For seven hours a day, Cesare Borgia's artillery bombarded Faenza. The sixty-pound stone cannonballs rained down on the walls and ramparts.

The breaches in the walls made during the day were repaired at night under the leadership of Diamante Jovelli.

The siege was directed by Cesare's chief engineer, a certain Leonardo da Vinci, an remarkable inventor of various cannons and ballista, who eagerly studied the flight of birds before Faenza, as he intended to invent a machine that would enable humans to fly. In his leisure hours, he painted pictures, which were well received by connoisseurs of the fine arts. –

Cesare Borgia made no progress. He offered the city of Faenza a very favorable treaty for both it and its prince.

Astorre Manfredi entered Cesare's headquarters unarmed at night.

Diamante Jovelli had tried in vain, with tears, to stop him: You are walking into your doom, Astorre! Do you trust the oath of a Borgia?

Astorre smiled his beautiful boyish smile: He is a lord like me. He will not break his word.

Cesare was astonished when he saw Astorre in the light of the torches.

A wave of emotion struck him, like the brush of a moth against his forehead.

He is the most beautiful young man I have ever seen. What strength in his gait and what grace in his movements! What fire in his dark blue sapphire eyes! How imperious and yet childlike he tosses his blond hair back. And that high, intelligent forehead!

Cesare granted Astorre everything he requested: every citizen of Faenza was guaranteed life and property, and the city would not be occupied by Cesare's troops. The family of Astorre was promised safe passage wherever they wished to go.

Astorre returned home elated.

That night, Diamante Jovelli surrendered herself to him, for her heart almost burst with joy when she saw him return and finally held him in her arms.

Astorre Manfredi kissed her tenderly.

You see, one must have trust! The truly noble return kindness with kindness.

Who is 'truly noble?'

Cesare.

The Borgia?

Yes –

Her face darkened. She wanted to say something, but fell silent as she looked into his shining eyes.

Cesare Borgia had invited the young Astorre Manfredi to visit him in Rome. A few weeks later, Astorre accepted the invitation.

He stayed in Cesare's palace, and rumors circulated that an unnatural love connected the two. They were often seen embracing as they walked on the Monte Pincio. In honor of Astorre, there were various festivities, including a crossbow shooting, during which a regrettable accident occurred.

A careless marksman missed his target, and the bolt struck the Prince of Faenza in the neck so unfortunately that he, after having received the holy sacraments of the dying, passed away a few hours later. His last words were: Borgia! Borgia!

These were interpreted to mean that he wished to thank the Pope, who had hurried to administer the Last Rites, for his caring kindness.

Carnival.

On the Campo Fiore and at the Banchi, thousands of masks swarmed and frolicked like swarms of mosquitoes.

Arlecchinos, Colombinas, Turks, Blacks, soldiers, stilt walkers, peasant girls. Many wore hideous, terrifying masks, as if for one day the evil demons of their souls had come to light and taken on form and shape. Some wore enormous phalluses as noses. Fiddlers and trumpeters played lively tunes. The drummers artfully struck the calfskin, sometimes softly, sometimes forcefully.

During a solitary walk, Alexander Borgia, the Pope, found himself among them. They did not recognize him and mistook him for someone dressed as the Pope.

You, fat man, they shouted, come dance with us! And they formed a circle, dancing and rhythmically singing: *vinum bonum, vinum bonum,* and the Pope danced along with them, laughing, until the circle broke, the chain dissolved, and Alexander Borgia was left alone in the square.

He felt hot.

The spring sun was piercing.

He dried the sweat from his forehead with a small cloth.

And he nearly reached up to tear off his wig, before remembering that it was his real hair.

Yes, he puffed, everything about the Borgia is real, everything is real!

XXXIX.

Niccolò Machiavelli, hailing from a humble popolano family and educated in humanism, was sent on an extraordinary mission to Cesare Borgia as the secretary of the Florentine 'Council of Ten.'

Florence, too weak to resist an impending attack from the prince, sought to come to an amicable agreement with him.

Niccolò Machiavelli lived on a small estate near Florence.

He woke early in the day, hunted for finches, worked as a woodcutter in his little grove, spent half the day in the tavern chatting with the innkeeper, the farmer Gismondo Buonarotti (a brother of the sculptor Michelangelo Buonarroti), butchers, bakers, carters, and brick makers, playing backgammon or tricktrack. He quarreled with them over every quattrino, and their shouting could be heard echoing up and down the country road for half a mile.

In the evening, at dusk, he trudged home, took off his farmer's smock, and in just his shirt sat at his desk reading Dante and Petrarch, Tibullus and Ovid.

He read Ovid's *Ars Amandi*, and sighing, he thought of his own past romances. That was all over.

He had a wife and four children, and only occasionally did a favorable wind lead a farmer's wife or maid into his grove.

When he grew tired of Ovid, he closed the book, opened his writing case, and continued his studies *sul arte del stato*: on the 'art of statecraft.'

He could hardly manage his rural estate, but his mind ruled sovereign over republics and monarchies: The mind of a clever, preceptive, insightful, and incorruptible man – corruptible neither with gold nor flattery, unyielding to sympathies and antipathies.

He was moved by 'politics itself,' its methodology. And the measure of his standards was given solely by the man who makes politics and history.

What was the nature of the lowly man? He was stupid, cowardly, selfish, treacherous –

What was the nature of the higher man? He was intelligent, brave, selfish, and true to himself. His intelligence dictated using the stupidity of others, his bravery, subjugating their freedom, and his loyalty to himself could manifest as treachery towards others. Foolish was he who kept faith with the faithless, stupid was he who was outsmarted by the clever, cowardly was he who recoiled from assassination – when others had already prepared the poison and erected the gallows. The key was to be first: with a woman, in politics.

Go to bed early – and rise early: by the time others awoke, half the day's work had to be done.

By then, he had already caught seven thrushes – and Cesare Borgia had ensnared seven treacherous condottieri.

The Florentines knew what they were doing when they sent Machiavelli to Cesare Borgia. It was not the first time that the peasant with the soul of a statesman served them on important missions.

In the palace of Cesare Borgia, that memorable conversation took place between Cesare and Machiavelli, which would inspire the Florentine for his treatise on *The Prince*.

It was still very early in the day. Dawn hung dimly in the room. Cesare had summoned Machiavelli to an audience at six in the morning. For months, Borgia had not shown himself in daylight.

Illness had increasingly ravaged his face. It was covered all over with festering pustules. His nose was eaten away. Only his bright blue eyes sparkled intact and imperiously.

"Please take a seat," said Borgia. He positioned his guest so that his face was in the light while he himself remained in the dark.

Machiavelli took a seat in a deep armchair, in which the small, corpulent man almost completely disappeared.

Cesare laughed:

Yes, here you have an immediate example of my political method: I always force my guests to sink deeply below me into a soft armchair. This makes them submissive to me and their minds soft and pliable. I myself prefer to sit on a hard, high wooden chair.

Machiavelli looked up from below and spoke toward where he suspected the Borgia was in the darkness:

I admire you, Your Highness.

The Borgia asked: How does Florence fare? They are not particularly well-disposed toward His Holiness and me, are they?

Machiavelli tried to wave the question aside.

Cesare continued: They don't like to see me establish myself in Umbria and the Romagna, nor that I am in accord with Louis XII of France. They call me cruel. But this cruelty has held the Romagna together, while the much-lauded mildness of the Florentines has brought about the destruction of Pistoia. Which is truly crueler? My cruelty has perhaps killed fifty people in the Romagna. But the Florentine mildness in Pistoia – two thousand!

And he quoted Virgil: *Res dura et regni novitas me talia cogunt / Moliri, et lati fines custode tueri.*

Machiavelli: Florence must strive to assert itself as an autonomous state amid the chaos of the times, so long as –

Borgia: Well, as long as –?

Machiavelli cautiously continued: As long as these times do not change.

The Borgia laughed softly.

Well, these times are an abstract concept. They will not change themselves. We are called to change them. We humans.

Yes, Machiavelli flattered. You humans, you great men! You Borgia!

Cesare turned away for a moment, disgusted: Has Florence sent you to shower me with incense and sugar cubes like a dancing fairground bear? I detest both.

The Council of Ten from Florence sends me to express its respect for you – even if there is an abyss between your political convictions and theirs.

Borgia: What kind of abyss?

Machiavelli: We Florentines are republicans.

The Borgia smiled: I am not. I am Borgia.

Machiavelli: Whether republic or monarchy – good laws are the foundation of the state.

Cesare: Good laws cannot exist without a good army.

Machiavelli: A good army requires discipline above all, and thus again – on laws.

Cesare: A good army consists of good soldiers. Good soldiers are essentially just natives of the land, meaning people who love their homeland, who go out to defend their own land, their livelihoods, their wives, and their children.

Machiavelli: But you have often relied on mercenaries and foreign soldiers –

Cesare: Necessity compelled me. The ideal army is the national army. For this very reason, Charles VIII of France was able to overrun Italy so quickly because his disciplined French army was unmatched by our unruly hordes of mercenaries and servants from all countries.

Machiavelli: But how can a national army be established without a nation?

Cesare leapt to his feet, and his pale face suddenly shone brightly in the intensifying morning light: You are right. Here lies the cardinal point of Italian politics. Italy must become a nation. That is my most fervent goal and that of my illustrious father: a united Italy, a united Italian army.

Machiavelli politely interrupted: And a king?

Cesare now stood at the window, watching a blackbird shake the morning dew from its feathers: Indeed. –

Machiavelli asked hesitantly: And who is to be this king?

Cesare: A— a— he broke off the thought – it will be a beautiful day today. –

Machiavelli stood up: A Borgia, Your Highness, you meant to say.

Cesare cut off the conversation with a swing of his riding crop, which he let fly through the air: We will see, time will tell –

Machiavelli: A Borgia will come –

Cesare: To Florence.

Machiavelli: I have the honor, Your Highness, to offer you an alliance with the city of Florence. It would consider itself fortunate to secure Your Highness as condottiere, as a military leader. Florence offers Your Highness an annual salary of thirty-six thousand gold ducats.

Cesare escorted the envoy of the Florentine Republic to the inner door: I ask you to present me with a draft of the contract in the name of the Signoria. I have enjoyed our conversation immensely; do visit me again sometime. Machiavelli bowed deeply.

Machiavelli walked away through the early morning shaken by the conversation. He aimlessly roamed the alleys and then climbed the Monte Pincio to view the city of Rome in the glow of morning.

He thought: A monster – if one chooses to see it that way – and if one focuses only on one side of the coin. But turn it over, and you see: a genius – a political genius, like his father. They do everything solely for themselves, driven by a fanatical *sacro egoismo*. Yet look: their thoughts and deeds flow seamlessly into the grand course of world events.

He wants the unification of Italy – for himself – to become king – but is it not the greatest and most worthy goal of a modern Italian?

His thoughts are sharp as Spanish blades.

Even what his father does and plans – the hypertrophic elevation of the power of the Holy See – is conceived purely in the interest of the Borgias. But one day, his successors will still benefit from the fact that he has laid a solid political foundation for the papacy itself. Where are they now, the Orsini, the Colonna, who for generations condemned the Pope to impotence in his own city? No, these Borgias are not fools; they are – they are –

As he searched for a word, he heard a blackbird.

They are geniuses of amorality. They do not know what is evil or good. They only recognize the utility of a thing, as far as it pertains to themselves.

The centaur Chiron has been their teacher: half man, half beast, and they themselves have become centaurs.

They receive their destiny and their light from the constellation of the Centaur.

It takes four years for light to travel from the Centaur to Earth.

It takes an eternity to receive light and warmth from the Borgias.

They have armored their hearts a hundredfold. –

He bent down to the ground.

Look there! A flower of the Centaurea! What do the centaurs, the Borgias, have to do with it? – There is a species of Centaurea whose bitter root is used as an antidote against – poison.

And he began to jot down notes on a few scraps of paper he rummaged from his coat: The Borgias excel at using both natures, the human and the animal, because one cannot long exist without the other. They excel at being beasts, taking from the fox and the lion what suits them. The guise of the fox is necessary to recognize traps; the mask of the lion, to drive away wolves. He who only plays the lion does not understand his craft.

XL.

We need a saint among us, a holy Borgia. Don't you know one? asked the Pope as he flipped through the *Legenda Aurea*, addressing his son Cesare.

Cesare laughed heartily but quickly composed himself.

I beg forgiveness for my inappropriate behavior. One must never neglect form, said the bell founder, but by then it was already too late, and the bell was botched. So – who should I recommend to you? Calixtus doesn't cut much of a figure. The Duke of Gandia is dead, true, but we can't make a saint of him. Lucrezia – she'd make a beautiful saint – but she's still alive. And so is that boy Narcissus. Let's wait a few hundred years, *Papa di Roma*. Once we Borgias have run our course, we'll manage to produce a saint. And he will be just as holy as we were unholy. Because a Borgia does nothing halfway. Addio, Rodrigo!

He only called his father Rodrigo in particularly tender moments.

The Pope watched him fondly: A clever head, this Cesare –

He rubbed his hands together.

For the first time in his life, he felt cold. I'm getting old.

Outside, it was June. June 27, 1500.

He ordered a fire to be lit in the fireplace.

It was an ancient fireplace, where even Calixtus III had once warmed his Borgia body.

When had that been?

About fifty years ago, the Pope thought in astonishment.

That was fifty years ago!

He leaned against the fireplace.

And suddenly it seemed to him as if the fireplace were a fire-breathing crater.

The earth began to tremble.

With a thunderous crash, the ledge of the fireplace collapsed over him.

Lucrezia found him and cried out loudly for help. Her maid and some soldiers from the Swiss Guard pulled him out from under the rubble. For the fraction of a second, she wished that the old man there, her father, who had dragged her into this life – would be dead, completely and forever dead. But he was bear-strong, bull-strong. The fireplace had only grazed his skull. It hadn't been able to crush him.

Lucrezia tended to him.

After his recovery, he celebrated a High Mass in the Church of Santa Maria del Popolo.

In his still trembling hands, he held a chalice filled with three hundred ducats and poured it out before the altar of the Virgin: Three hundred, three—hun—dred ducats I offer you in thanks for my recovery, most holy, most virgin, most gracious Madonna! –

The ducats rolled down the steps of the altar.

But that night, suddenly, he was overtaken by remorse.

He woke abruptly from his dreams, especially since he had eaten a heavy lobster pâté that evening.

Three hundred ducats! he thought. The Madonna would have been satisfied with two hundred. Or – one hundred fifty.

Sweat stood on his forehead. He rang the bell.

But the officer of the Swiss Guard on duty in the anteroom was asleep.

The Pope tied a knot in his prayer shawl and resolved to have two hundred ducats retrieved from Santa Maria del Popolo the very next day.

As he tossed and turned sleeplessly from one side to the other, he lit the lamp again, grabbed his notebook, and began to jot down various thoughts:

My goal is to make the authority of the Papal States unshakable under my scepter.

Anyone who opposes me among the princes will be crushed. My enemies are doomed to destruction. I curse them with the papal curse. See Charles VIII and Fra Girolamo.

The Orsini and Colonna, my inner enemies in Rome, will have an eternity in the afterlife to think of me.

The submission of the Este in Ferrara isn't succeeding? Fine, then Lucrezia will marry an Este, and we'll win them that way and Borgia-ize them in the process.

One must play people against each other: the Italian princes and cities against foreign powers and vice versa. Internally steadfast, but outwardly noncommittal. That is politics. Cast the line in clear water and fish in the murky. Promise everything and keep only what serves your own benefit. Let Italy grow thin; we Borgias will grow fat. Italy must be brought into disorder so that we remain in order.

And he got up, slipped into his slippers, and trudged down to the cellar, where he had arranged a cell for himself as his treasury.

No one was allowed to enter it – not even Cesare and Lucrezia.

The cabinets on the walls were filled with bags full of ducats, boxes full of gemstones, emeralds, rubies, sapphires, golden bowls, crosses, and figures. Altar vessels and communion chalices stood on shelves. The Pope poured a sack of ducats onto the table and rummaged through it.

Saliva dripped from his lips. His eyes opened greedily like those of a hawk spotting a rabbit.

And in the ecstasy of possession and greed, he spilled his seed into a golden vessel.

Alexander summoned Leonardo da Vinci, the renowned military engineer and inventor who served Cesare.

Leonardo, who was currently sketching a pen drawing entitled 'The Hanged Man,' arrived reluctantly.

The Borgia made himself heard: Yes, I now know the earth, mountains, valleys, cities, villages, men, women. You have made me a globe, it stands on my desk, and sometimes my hand tenderly glides over the curvature of the sphere, as if it were a woman's breast.

All of this is tributary to me, pays me respect, honor, wealth, and money: Italians, Spaniards, and as I hear, even Germans and Moors.

But now I want stars around me. Build me a planetarium!

And when the planetarium was built, the Borgia sat among the stars, under Uranus, Neptune, Saturn, the sun, the moon, among planets and fixed stars.

He reached out with his ever-so-slightly sweaty hands, and they allowed themselves to be held, like fledgling birds.

Then he let them go again: Fly, sun! Fly, moon!

And they orbited in noble ellipses around his forehead.

XLI.

Before Lucrezia departed for Ferrara, she summoned the Roman infant, who had now turned five years old.

With tears in her eyes, she bid him farewell.

I cannot take you with me, my dear child. I must leave you here with the Holy Father and the unholy brother, Narcissus. They will protect and care for you, and an archangel will watch over you.

The boy looked up at Madonna Lucrezia with wide eyes and did not understand why she was crying.

I will never return to Rome. God protect you, if He wishes to protect a Borgia. The Holy Father has appointed you Duke today at my request and granted you the fief of Nepi. Narcissus, Duke of Nepi. But you do not understand all of this yet, and you will only comprehend it later. – Farewell, my little duke!

She lifted the boy to her breast and kissed him passionately on the mouth.

It was three o'clock in the afternoon when Lucrezia left Rome.

She rode a gray horse. Her gown, trimmed with ermine, was made of red silk and flowed shimmering down the flanks of the horse.

Her blond hair fluttered in the wind.

She had torn off her travel hat and held it pressed against the horse's neck with the reins.

All the cardinals, many nobles, and a large crowd accompanied her to the Porta del Popolo. To her left, Cesare rode on a bay horse.

At the gate, he straightened himself in the stirrups and offered her his hand.

She did not take it and merely looked at him darkly.

He remained behind with the other Romans, and for a long time, he watched her blond hair glimmering in the afternoon sun.

Like autumn threads, he thought. The autumn threads of the Borgias.

They foretell an early winter –

Twenty miles from Ferrara, before the Bentivoglio castle, Lucrezia encountered a hunter on horseback. He had rabbits hanging from his saddle, and she had one of the knights in her retinue ask him if he would let her have a few rabbits for supper.

The hunter was very courteous and readily agreed.

He lifted his hat.

They introduced themselves, and it turned out that the hunter was Don Alfonso, the heir prince of Ferrara, her husband whom she had just married *in absentia*. Surprised, but then quickly composed so as not to lose face in front of her retinue, the spouses regarded each other, having never seen one another before.

Lucrezia had been forced into the marriage with the heir prince of Ferrara for political reasons.

Ten minutes of polite, superficial conversation were enough, and he was enchanted by Lucrezia just like every man before him.

Lucrezia's entry into Ferrara provided one of the most magnificent spectacles of its time.

Leading the procession were seventy-five mounted archers dressed in the colors of the House of Este: white and red. Following them came a hundred trumpeters and pipers. Behind them rode, all alone, Don Alfonso, the groom, dressed in red velvet, wearing a black velvet cap adorned with a gold clasp, black velvet leggings, and black boots.

Next came the nobles of Ferrara on splendidly adorned horses, followed by pages, Spanish grandees, bishops, and the envoys from Rome.

Three of Lucrezia's court jesters capered about at the head of a procession of thirty dwarfs, all of whom somersaulted continuously and performed other antics.

Then came ten exquisitely beautiful pages, dressed in the colors of the rainbow. And then –

Lucrezia, the bride, on her favorite gray horse.

She wore a sleek black velvet dress trimmed with gold borders, over which she draped a cloak of gold brocade.

Her full blond hair was enveloped in a veil-like net of fine gold, so that the strands of hair and gold could not be distinguished. A sunburst blazed upon her forehead.

She rode beneath a purple canopy carried by the tenured professors and doctors of the University of Ferrara, as there was a shortage of servants.

The envoy from France followed behind her, riding beside the Duke Ercole of Este. Princes, nobles, and pages came after them, and then, in fourteen gala carriages, were the ladies-in-waiting and court ladies of the Ferrara court.

Eighty mules, including two white ones, carried the bride's wardrobe.

With many Ahs! and Ohs! the gawking women of Ferrara admired the precious garments, carpets, and jewelry. Yet some peasants and townsfolk stood by the roadside, thinking:

These are the taxes and tributes extorted from us by a holy church – for the Borgias.

There – there – on the backs of the mules they carry away: my and your 'St. Peter's pennies.' From pennies come guilders, from guilders ducats, and many ducats make that wide-sleeved Camorra of green velvet or that fivefold chain of rubies and pearls wrapped around the neck of one white mule. Next to the two white mules walked a red bull, the emblem of the Borgias.

The crowd mocked and jeered at it, as they dared not target the Borgia themselves. But proud and unapproachable, it passed by with its head lowered, refusing to see or smell the people it despised.

In the cathedral square, where tightrope walkers performing between two church towers greeted her, Lucrezia dismounted.

The rector of the university, Professor Nicolò Leoniceno, a senior professor of mathematics, an elderly, nearsighted gentleman, held her stirrup.

Pipers, trumpeters, drummers, timpanists, and trombonists began to compete with the ringing of the church bells in a cacophony of sound.

Lucrezia, who loathed all loudness, tightened her mouth slightly but then let a smile play about her lips, enchanting everyone present.

In the reception hall, Lucrezia and Alfonso took their seats on the rose-adorned throne.

According to ancient custom, the bride was allowed to make a request, which was to be fulfilled immediately. Lucrezia asked for the release of all prisoners in the city of Ferrara.

Spanish jesters began to sing to her. The poet Ariosto was the first orator to greet her:

> O Rome! O poor Rome, plunged into night,
> When the Borgia's sun abruptly left you,
> And now kindles its light in Ferrara:
> Lucrezia, most graceful star, chosen
> To bestow upon us flame, warmth, and future joy –
> O pour the vessel of fire upon us,
> And burn us into torches, O Queen!
> That we might burn divinely in your honor
> And, even as ashes, still confess our devotion to you!

The unnaturally pale twenty-seven-year-old poet bowed and stepped back with awkward grandeur.

Lucrezia sent him a gentle glance – out of her *occhi bianchi* – her bright blue eyes.

That very evening, having returned to his lonely chamber, he wrote the lines:

> The woman is a dangerous, great child,
> She has the eyes of a dove and the grip of a panther.

The court theater of Ferrara, located in the hall of the Podestà, could accommodate three thousand people.

On the evening of the gala performance in honor of the heir prince's marriage, it was packed to capacity.

Before the performance began, all the actors stepped forward to the footlights and presented themselves to the audience with utmost deference. The director announced the play to be performed.

Ariosto had submitted his Cassaria, but it had been rejected as too modern. The duke and the audience were in favor of 'the classics.'

The performance began with Plautus himself appearing and expressing particular joy that one of his comedies would be performed.

They performed *Epidicus.*

Most of the audience grew bored and only perked up during the ballets interspersed between the acts.

Ten black dancers appeared with candles in their mouths. A gladiatorial combat raged. A fire-breathing dragon and a beautiful, naked maiden on a unicorn received special applause.

At the end, however, there was a clumsy early Christian morality play about the courtesan Thais, which deeply moved Lucrezia to her very core.

XLII.

Thais

Marketplace of Alexandria

THE PIOUS FATHER PAPHNUTIUS (*enters*) I have heard from various travelers that there is a maiden in Alexandria who is incomparably fair and enchanting, such that all the young men of Alexandria swarm around her like bees around their queen, unable to resist her seductive charm.

> *The young men present initially remain silent, feeling embarrassed. Then one speaks.*

YOUNG MAN You are right, virtuous elder, to reproach us young men of Alexandria for our frivolity and debauchery. And we know whom you mean: it is Thais, the courtesan, who has bewitched us so that we are no longer masters of our senses. She has set all of Alexandria ablaze. Men abandon their wives for her, and beardless boys steal their fathers' treasures to please Thais and adorn her forehead with the golden circlet.

PAPHNUTIUS Where does she live? I have a message for her.

YOUNG MAN Her house is nearby. In that alley over there. If you wish, we will guide you, for we know the way all too well.

PAPHNUTIUS I prefer to go alone. God be with you, young men.

YOUNG MAN God be with you, most venerable father.

House of Thais

The DEVIL in the form of a youth.

DEVIL Pour me a glass, Thais. I'm thirsty. When the red blood of the vine trickles down my throat, I'll imagine it to be human blood.

THAIS I shudder when you speak so blasphemously.

DEVIL I was jesting, my sweet.

THAIS These are dreadful jests you indulge in.

DEVIL Embrace me, and we shall indulge in better ones.

THAIS I am not in the mood for jesting, of any kind, today.

DEVIL Why so coy, my little dove?

THAIS I had a dream last night, and it has made me reflect.

DEVIL You make me smile, Thais. Do you believe in dreams? You let your mood be ruined by fantasies you created yourself, perhaps because you ate too much or too richly the evening before, or drank too quickly. I would have thought you wiser.

THAIS I dreamed of a forest where I once dwelled, back when I was still good and happy.

DEVIL Good – good – what does that mean? It's not about being good, but about enjoying life, savoring it like I savor this drink now.

THAIS Too often and too easily have I always been tempted and enticed by you. Shame burns in my cheeks when I think of how I gave the child, the fruit of our immoral relations, to an old woman in the suburbs to raise and care for, so that I wouldn't be hindered here in my life of debauchery and wild ways. How might the child be faring? I dreamed of it.

DEVIL You should not concern yourself with the child. Be glad it's not here running around your legs and driving away your visitors with its cries. *Vestigia terrent.* It would spoil the desire of many a delicate young man to see so tangible a reminder of delightful carelessness.

THAIS I dreamed that the forest uprooted itself and came walking like a man – towards me –

> *There's a knock at the door.*

THAIS (*startled*) Who is it?

DEVIL This interruption is most unwelcome.

A VOICE Good friend, fair Thais, open without fear.

> *THAIS opens the door: PAPHNUTIUS enters, with the hood of his pilgrim's cloak pulled over his head, concealing his face.*

THAIS Who are you? I breathe pure, clear air now that you are in the room. There is the scent of pine about you. What is happening to me?

DEVIL I can't bear the stench. This fellow seems familiar. (*Steps closer, then recoils.*) It is that accursed Christian...

> *PAPHNUTIUS makes the sign of the cross.*

DEVIL (*hunched and crooked as he exits through the door*) Beware of him, Thais – if you remain true to me... but fear me, if you fall to him.

PAPHNUTIUS Who was the man who just left you, beautiful Thais?

THAIS A youth from Alexandria and my friend. – You seem to be a stranger in these parts, are you not?

PAPHNUTIUS I come from far away, through the desert, from the forests of Thebes.

THAIS My dream!

PAPHNUTIUS Oh Thais, oh Thais, what long and arduous journeys I have undertaken to reach you.

THAIS You longed for me – and for me alone – even though you did not know me before?

PAPHNUTIUS The roads of the world are filled with the fame of your beauty.

THAIS Since you show such desire for me, I will no longer hide my face from you and unveil myself. (She does so.)

PAPHNUTIUS Thais, Thais –

THAIS Then cast back your hood as well, so I may know with whom I speak – whether it is a young man or an elder who seeks my love.

PAPHNUTIUS (*clutches his heart*).

THAIS What's the matter with you? You are trembling?

PAPHNUTIUS I shudder because I think of your fate, and I weep for your ruin.

THAIS What a voice... The tears of a stranger move my deepest heart... You do not know my fate. Why do you weep, stranger, for someone you do not know? I am a stranger to you. You are a stranger to me. An hour ago, you did not know me, nor did I know you.

PAPHNUTIUS I have always been with you, Thais, through the strength of my prayer. You have never left me – I have never left you.

THAIS I have not prayed in years. I have nearly forgotten the name of God.

PAPHNUTIUS You just spoke it. But tell me, of which God did you speak?

THAIS Of the one true God.

PAPHNUTIUS So, you believe in Him?

THAIS (*lowering her head*) I believe in Him.

PAPHNUTIUS Then you also believe that He is all-knowing?

THAIS My deeds are not hidden from Him.

PAPHNUTIUS And do you believe that He judges with righteousness and justice?

THAIS I believe He weighs our deeds with a just scale...

PAPHNUTIUS O Jesus Christ, how infinite is Your patience, how boundless Your mercy and forbearance, and You show the path of repentance even to the most condemned. (To himself:) Let the hood fall from my head.

THAIS (*crying out*) My holy father...

PAPHNUTIUS Have you suffered, daughter?

THAIS Suffering upon suffering.

PAPHNUTIUS Who has deceived, seduced, and betrayed you?

THAIS The one who deceived Adam and Eve, causing them to lose Paradise.

PAPHNUTIUS Where is the angelic purity you once lived by?

THAIS Gone, gone.

PAPHNUTIUS Where is your virginity? Your discipline and virtue? Where is the golden chastity?

THAIS Faded from my mind.

PAPHNUTIUS Has any human lived without sin except the Son of the Virgin?

THAIS Never.

PAPHNUTIUS It is human to sin. But it is diabolical to remain in sin. Do you repent?

THAIS (*kneeling*) Woe is me, wretched as I am. I repent.

PAPHNUTIUS With words? With your lips?

THAIS With deeds. With my soul. With my entire being. I will atone. I will atone. I am not worthy to kiss the dust of your feet.

PAPHNUTIUS Rise, my daughter. It is never too late to turn back.

THAIS I am crushed under the weight of my sins.

PAPHNUTIUS Arise. In the name of the triune God – the Father, the Son, and the Holy Spirit – I release you from all your sins. Arise, my daughter, and walk in the Lord.

THAIS May it please the Lord to restore me as an honest child of man and of God.

PAPHNUTIUS The essence of the Most High is unchanging, but it is a small matter for him to change ours. Be comforted and believe!

XLIII.

On the same night, after the bride and groom had long since retired to their chambers and a notary had officially recorded the union, Duke Ercole of Ferrara wrote a letter to the Pope in Rome:

Most Holy Father and most venerable Lord,

Your Holiness's illustrious daughter has arrived safely in Ferrara. She has consummated her marriage with my son and has won, with ease, the hearts of the difficult-to-win Ferrarans and Ferraran women: through her charm, grace, virtue, and wisdom. Rest assured, Your Holiness, that my son and I will cherish her as the most precious thing we possess on this earth.

When the Pope held this letter in his hands, his eyes lit up, only to soon become glazed with moisture.

Tears, one after another, began to drip onto the letter.

For the second time in his life, Rodrigo Borgia wept.

My child, he sobbed, my dearest child! You are happy! I am happy if you are. My Borgia heart! May you find bliss even here on earth! I have done everything to prepare this happiness for you. I laid carpets before your feet so you wouldn't have to tread on stones. I have shielded you from cold and heat, you cool, noble gem. *O bionda, mia bionda, biondinella d'amor!*

The Pope exempted Ferrara from paying church taxes, which amounted to a remission of two hundred thousand gold ducats, and assured the Duke of Ferrara of his special favor.

Cesare received this letter from Alexander:

> My dear son, I follow your endeavors with constant attention. Though they may not have recently turned out as well as hoped, do not let this discourage you. Try instead to let others be discouraged. There is no doubt we must deal with that accursed Orsini family, who bear most of the blame for your recent failures. They have been our enemies since the beginning of the world, were so before, and will be again afterward. We will encounter them again either in heaven or in hell. The condottiere Paolo Orsini has most disgracefully betrayed you, along with his nephew Fabio Orsini and Vitellozzo and Oliverotto. You must try to seize them by trickery. At the same time, I will write a tender letter to Carlo Orsini and Cardinal Giovanni Battista Orsini, who fled Rome in fear of me, to convince them to return.
>
> Once we have them all in hand, we will close that hand, and they may all suffocate and perish. Henbane, belladonna, water hemlock, foxglove, and mandrake are useful plants, and arsenic, lead acetate, and mercury are minerals worth studying. I hold little regard for a poison with a delayed effect.
> God's blessing upon you!
>
> Your loving old father.
>
> P.S. Lucrezia is well. Cardinal Giovanni Borgia is no longer able to perform his duties, as he is suffering from the *malum gallicum*. I always warned him about that Neapolitan *sciantosa*.

Cardinal Giovanni Battista Orsini accepted the Pope's gracious invitation. He was all the more hopeful of being received and reinstated in full grace since Paolo Orsini had once again placed himself at Cesare Borgia's disposal and seized Sinigaglia by force for him.

Believing he carried a message highly welcome to the Pope, Cardinal Orsini rode into the Vatican on a white mule. Without ever being brought before the Pope, he was dragged from his mount and taken by armed guards to the Castel Sant'Angelo. It was the same day Cesare Borgia lured Condottieri Paolo and Fabio Orsini, Vitellozzo, and Oliverotto into a trap and had them strangled on the spot.

As soon as the Cardinal Orsini's mother heard of his arrest, she requested an audience with the Pope.

The audience was denied. However out of sheer humanity, the Holy Father allowed her to visit her wayward son once daily. He added that if she wished, she could personally bring him lunch. The Cardinal, he noted, had expressed (unfounded) distrust of the Vatican cuisine, which he deemed too simple and unseasoned for his refined Orsini taste. The Pope said he understood; even his own son Cesare and the young cardinals were reluctant to eat at the frugal papal table.

Every day at noon, Madonna Orsini, the most distinguished lady of the Roman aristocracy, carried food to her son Giovanni in prison with her own hands. She passed it through the bars where he sat on a cot, reading a breve or playing chess with himself.

Giovanni, she pleaded, what is your crime? The Cardinal looked into her eyes: that I am an Orsini, mother.

One day, the prison guard took the dish from Madonna Orsini at the gate and poured the minestra into the gutter.

Your son, old lady, doesn't need anything to eat anymore. He peacefully passed away last night from a digestive ailment. The Pope himself gave him the Holy Host yesterday evening – but it did not agree with him.

He tried to hand the dish back to her. It slipped from her hands onto the tiles and shattered with a loud crash.

She ran through the empty midday streets screaming. At every window, blankets and shutters were drawn.

The sun burned unbearably.

No one saw, no one heard the old woman dressed in black.

In the glaring sun, she staggered back and forth like a butterfly – a mourning cloak.

XLIV.

Upon hearing the news of Cardinal Giovanni Battista Orsini's death, all the Orsini in Rome and the surrounding area rose up against the Pope.

Giulio Orsini set out with an army from Ceri, and Giovanni Giordano Orsini from Bracciano.

Cesare quickly returned to Rome to assist his father.

Once again, he succeeded in decisively defeating and humiliating the Orsini.

Cesare's victory led the French King Louis XII to enlist Cesare and his army for the reconquest of Naples.

The money needed for the campaign was obtained by the Pope through the appointment of new cardinals, each of whom had to pay between fifteen and twenty thousand ducats for the cardinal's hat.

Furthermore, the Pope and Cesare invited themselves to dine with the fabulously wealthy Cardinal Adriano. It must have been a pleasure to inherit from him.

The Pope, usually indifferent to culinary pleasures, took a lively interest in the menu.

He personally went into the cardinal's kitchen. He tied an apron around himself, and he was seen preparing a pheasant. The pheasant was cleaned, and the Pope carefully separated the skin from the breast. Then, he chopped a quarter pound of lard, a truffle, and fifty grams of pork, and stuffed the mixture between the breast and the skin. Next, he wrapped the entire pheasant with bacon.

The cardinal had prepared a delicate meal: fresh asparagus, trout fillets in brown butter with crayfish patties, pheasant on snipe croutons with a cream-dressed salad, pineapple in currant sauce, and warm cheese pastries.

The Pope, who led a meager kitchen out of stinginess in the Vatican, heartily enjoyed the food. He and Cesare were in excellent spirits. Things were going splendidly for the Borgias, always moving forward, always progressing, sometimes only like in a jumping procession: two steps back, then three forward; God was with them, the devil and Fortuna, the goddess of fortune.

The Pope was just considering whether he should build a temple or at least an altar to the pagan goddess Fortuna, and whether she could be made a Catholic saint, when Cesare stood to make a toast. He took the glasses from the cup-bearer standing behind him, exchanging a quick glance of understanding with him, handed one glass to the Pope, one to the cardinal, and one to himself, swirled his glass, and said, turning to the cardinal: To the health of Your Eminence!

They all emptied their glasses to the bottom. No sooner had they drunk than the Pope and Cesare were struck by violent vomiting.

They had to be brought back to the Vatican in haste.

The cupbearer, a creature of Cesare, had switched the cups.

Diamante Jovelli, the young tanner's daughter from Faenza, the mistress of Astorre Manfredi, had persuaded him to do it with the promise of a night of love.

XLV.

Alexander attempted to say Mass the next morning. His head fell sideways onto the shoulder of a cardinal who supported him.

In his bed, Alexander writhed in pain.

He felt a burning sensation that ran from his throat down his esophagus into his stomach.

His skin began to flake.

Blisters appeared.

He vomited greenish-yellow bile.

He had his personal doctor inject him with the blood of a young man who had died from blood loss.

It did no good.

Poison, he thought – he has poisoned me – he himself, Cesare, my little one, my son, has poisoned me – or – who else?

Cesare must come to me!

The servant brought word that the Duke himself was lying gravely ill.

The Pope thought: he lies, he's pretending.

The fever spread over him in pink, then fiery red clouds.

Suddenly, in a long black coat and a starched white ruff, looking half like a doctor, half like a judge, Death entered the room through the red mist.

The Pope leapt up from the pillows: *Quid mors seva petis?* Death said: *Te. Me – quis jure? Quod hora en properat. Heu mihi – Quid luges? Parum vixisse.*

Lucrezia – Cesare – he had suddenly forgotten her.

Where was Julia? Julia, *me miserum non defendis*: I loved you if I loved you more with my heart. Julia, I had Pinturicchio paint you as Madonna – me lost in worship before it. So help me now, Madonna Julia!

Nemo potest te juvare.

So must I die?

Yes.

I want to confess to you –

Stop, you need a new, second life to confess. I do not have that much time. Confess to the devil.

A woman, the Pope cried as he awakened from a long faint, a woman will make me well!

Lying on a woman, in the mirror room, the Pope was struck by a heart attack.

The mirrors reflected his final glance a hundred times back into the room.

His last lover, a young laundress who had been introduced to him by her mother, fled screaming.

The powerful body of the mighty old man did not want to die.

Even as his soul had already left him, his mouth was still foaming like a cauldron over the fire and his belly was swelling enormously.

His feet twitched as if they were preparing to step onto this earth once more.

As long as it was uncertain whether he was still alive and would rise again, no one dared approach his bed, for good or for ill.

But when the doctors irrevocably confirmed his death, there was no more hesitation.

XLVI.

The people of Rome cheered, and like during Carnival, masked figures roamed through the streets.

The news of the death of the 'Antichrist' spread like wildfire through the holy city.

People ran into the streets.

Strangers embraced one another.

Mothers brought their children out into the sunlight: the light is pure again since the monster no longer illuminates it.

Crowds of people broke into the homes of the various Borgias and looted them.

The rabble of Rome was completely drunk on Chianti and delight over the Pope's demise.

They organized a joyous funeral procession.

A butchered pig, symbolizing the body of Borgia, was dragged in an open coffin adorned with paper garlands by two Jews and two mules.

Howling, gurgling, squeaking, roaring, the mourners followed: beggars, chestnut sellers, retired mercenaries, whores, brickworkers, astrologers, musicians, vagabonds, and pilgrims to Rome.

Among the procession walked a leper bearing the name Cesare Borgia and a beautiful blonde whore with the name Lucrezia Borgia written on her forehead.

Also, a kind of goddess of peace was carried in a handcart: a half-naked woman who waved a lily in her hand and placed her unwashed foot on rusty armor, halberds, and helmets.

The city police turned a blind eye and let the mob rampage.

Thousands passed by the corpse of Alexander Borgia, unhindered by the Swiss halberdiers: clerics, peasants, mercenaries, workers, citizens openly expressing their hatred. Indeed, when the Swiss guards were not watching, one or another spat in his face, where the slime forever glued his eyes shut. However, not a single woman passed by his corpse. The women had loved him and did not want to disgrace the memory of the handsome, well-formed man with the sight of the disfigured corpse.

Julia Farnese learned of his death while sitting in the bath. She fainted and would have drowned if a young Moorish woman, her maid, had not happened to check on her.

She had herself splashed with Cologne water and sat motionless in the bay window all day. Below, the mob surged by, and now and then someone threw a mocking kiss up to her.

The devil has taken him, shouted a shoemaker from St. Peter's Square. He had made a pact with him that brought him to the papal throne: he could be Pope for twelve years and four days – after that, his dirty soul belonged to him, to Beelzebub, so the contract stated. Yesterday, his term had expired. A pack of black dogs had been howling in the corridors of the Vatican since the day before yesterday. Those were the chief devil and twelve subordinate devils.

The poet Ariosto also passed by Alexander Borgia's bier. Someone had attached a note to it.

Ariosto read:

> Quis jacet hic?
> Sextus.
> Quis funera plangit? Erynnis.
> Quis comes in tanto funere obit?

Vitium.

He stopped and gazed at the misshapen colossus for a long time, trying to elicit its secret.

Futile, he sighed, it is futile.

Perhaps, he mused, he will burn in purgatory. But the fire will do him no harm, for it is his element. Regret? No, he did not know regret. He will not repent in purgatory either, and when we must descend one day, he will still be burning – and many thousands of generations after, until perhaps one day or night God the Lord redeems him and sets him as a star in the sky: there he may continue to burn and, burning, be purified for the service of light and warmth.

But that will be the only regret we can expect from him.

And he placed a white rose between the swollen lips of the dead Borgia.

The white rose that Lucrezia had commissioned him to place. No priest blessed the burial. No litany was sung.

The grave diggers struggled to fit the swollen corpse of Alexander Borgia into the coffin. They stuffed the mass of flesh inside with their rough fists like stuffing a goose into a plucked goose.

XLVII.

It became clear that even Cesare's empire had only been held together by the authority of the papal father.

Piece by piece, Cesare's crown was breaking apart. The princes who had been driven out by Cesare returned to their capitals, greeted with jubilation by the populace: Sforza to Pesaro, Guidobaldo to Urbino, Varano to Camerino – and so on.

Cesare still lay in bed, gravely ill, paralyzed and hindered in all his decisions and actions. Machiavelli paid him a visit.

I have thought of everything, sighed Cesare, but that I would be gravely ill at the moment my father dies – I did not think of that. I am powerless; I am completely helpless.

Only Romagna still stood by him.

In Ferrara, Lucrezia worried for Cesare.

Her position was unassailable due to her beauty, intelligence, and caution. She managed to have the Duke Cesare send troops to preserve Romagna for him.

Piccolomini was elected Pope as Pius III.

Cesare rejoiced. Piccolomini was favorable to him. Cesare had bribed several cardinals in his favor.

Just three weeks later, Pius III died. Cesare collapsed.

The end was near for the Borgias. They had no more luck. Fortuna, who had smiled upon them for fifty years, turned her face away from them. From where they had come: from the darkness, from nothing, there they returned again, to nothing, to darkness.

Cesare rode through the city, choosing his own grave. He was still feverish. But he did not take the fever medicine that his physician prescribed. He poured it under the bed.

Whom would they choose as Pope? He cursed himself for having so easily laid aside the cardinal's purple back then.

Today, he could have used it.

Perhaps the Rovere was still the most useful Pope for the Borgias?

He secured the votes of the Spanish cardinals.

The Rovere placed the tiara on his head as Julius II.

Julius II said: I do not want to live in the rooms where the Borgia lived, the one who has defiled the holy dignity of the Church like no one before him. He did not rightfully hold the papal throne but usurped it with the help of the devil. And I forbid, under penalty, the name Borgia to be spoken in Rome from now on. His name shall be crossed out, erased, and forgotten. All images of the Borgias shall be covered with black cloth. All the tombstones of the Borgias shall be turned over, and the inscriptions carved out.

Julius II demanded that Cesare Borgia surrender the fortified places in Romagna. Cesare realized that resistance was useless. He fled. In Ostia, he boarded a sailboat.

When he landed in Naples, he was arrested and thrown into the castle of Ischia.

He escaped and made his way to Spain. Ragged, like a sailor, he set foot on Spanish soil, the land that had given birth to him and all the Borgias.

Julius II had confiscated his possessions.

In a dive in Seville, where he was involved in illegal gambling with all sorts of dubious characters, he was arrested again and taken to the castle of Medina del Campo. He called for help from the King of France.

There was no reply.

He wrote to Lucrezia.

The letter was intercepted.

He did not know that she had since become the Duchess of Ferrara.

Ercole had died, and Alfonso had ascended to the throne.

Cesare managed to escape once more.

He harbored a deadly hatred for Julius II in his heart.

Hatred is good, he thought. But it must not be based on emotion. It must be systematic hatred, a sober mathematical one. I hate Julius too passionately.

News of his flight reached Italy and frightened the Pope:

A terrible man, this Cesare Borgia. We must guard against the boldness of his ventures. His name alone is enough to raise armies.

A mystical power still emanates from him.

He decided to offer him resistance.

At Pamplona, ambushed, Cesare, thirty-one years old, fell under the daggers of assassins. Seven had attacked him.

He mortally wounded six before the seventh dealt him the fatal blow.

This seventh was a Moor. With great respect, he regarded the dead enemy.

Brave man, brave man. But good that he is dead and I still live.

A thousand ducats beckoned him and the return to Africa to his black wife.

Full of longing, he licked his thick lips as he wiped the bloody knife on the robe of the Borgia.

XLVIII.

Lucrezia received the news of her brother's death, which they had tried to keep from her while she was in labor.

She cried out once to the heavens,and then never uttered another complaint.

She healed from the death of a son.

The Borgia's life is over, she thought. The thread has been cut forever. I, too, am weary and sated with this life.

In the fever of childbirth, she wrote one last letter to the Pope in Rome:

Most Holy Father and most dearly revered Lord,

The soul of a dying woman bows before You and kisses Your holy feet with all due reverence. This dying woman is a sinner and a Borgia – and thus a sinner doubly and many times over. All the sins and vices of this world have entered into my wretched, pitiable body – now, as I near death from childbirth, they have surely all flowed out with my blood. Oh, have mercy, and pray to God for mercy for me and all the Borgias. They were endowed with the greatest gifts of mind and body. They were destined to lead the world. But they allowed themselves to be led by devils and demons. Their souls were not focused on petty matters. History will remember them, in awe and disgust, but not without recognition of their fate and their talents. Oh, grant me the Holy Benediction, Most Holy Father – I am Your faithful and humble child, the last and most inconspicuous branch from the tree of the Borgias, destined to wither and decay.

Written in Ferrara, in the penultimate hour of my human life.

Your Holiness, the lowest maid, Lucrezia Borgia.

Twilight in the room.

Lucrezia dreams the fairy tale of the withered almond tree, which begins to bloom again under the gaze of a pure person.

She blossoms.

She gains a new virginity and chastity of being.

Those who see her are touched by so much sweet grace and soulful humility.

She inspires poets, who dedicate verses full of passion and reverence to her. Ariost, Giraldi, Antonio Tebaldeo, Marcello Filosseno compare her to Minerva, Helen, and Venus.

She becomes the ideal of a faithful, virtuous wife.

Michelangelo raises her on a pedestal and carves her as a Pietà.

All lusts and vices have long slipped away from her. Like Anadyomene, she rises reborn from the sea of life.

She has burned all the letters from her father and brother – even her once-precious clothes.

She wears a simple gray robe.

She lives in reverse.

She suddenly remembers:

Back then, when Alexander –

Back then, when Cesare –

Back then, when Alfonso –

From the graves rise the Borgias.

Many carry a dagger in their chest, some have their heads under their arms.

She dances a Spanish dance in their honor.

A monk beats the tambourine of the moon.

The dead Borgias watch her.

She dances until she falls down unconscious.

When she awoke, it had grown dark in the room.

The darkness spat out ghosts.

Ghosts within her –

Ghosts outside her –

A sulfur-yellow flame struck from the sky into her heart.

A small, hunchbacked man suddenly danced in front of her, and she found it disgusting to see him not walking, but wiggling and dancing in an affected and obtrusive manner with an exaggerated rump.

Suddenly he vanished into the wall, as if there were a door there.

But there was no door.

Only a small hole, in which a toad sat, staring at Lucrezia with golden-brown eyes.

The sun had long since set, draped in a violet cloud mantle.

Now the stars rose.

It became light, ever lighter.

A rushing sound surrounds her, a rushing of light. A stream of brilliance.

She smiles.

Then her smile freezes, turning to horror.

The brilliance begins to burn. Every pore of her body burns.

It becomes hot, ever hotter, she is in purgatory.

On her tombstone, this inscription was found, which remained legible for three days until the rain washed it away: Here lies Lucrezia – by name. She heaped atrocity upon atrocity and disgrace upon disgrace. She was her own father's wife and whore, Her husband's murderer, her brother's whore.

Epilogue

Luis was the father of Rodrigo.

Rodrigo was the father of Pedro.

Pedro was the father of Alfonso.

Alfonso was the father of Juan.

Juan Borgia was the Chief Huntsman and Chief Stablemaster at the court of Charles V.

He loved Isabella, the Queen of Spain, and when she died, he escorted her coffin to Granada for burial in the royal crypt.

According to old custom, the coffin was opened once more, and Juan Borgia stepped forward to swear that the body lying there was that of the beautiful and noble Queen Isabella.

He raised his hand – but the hand remained motionless in the air.

This piece of flesh, already in decomposition beyond recognition, was supposed to be Isabella, the beautiful Isabella, the miracle of woman?

He refused to take the oath, and his clenched fist seemed to curse God.

He rushed away and came to the castle of Tordecillas.

He encountered a mad old woman dancing the Tarantella grotesquely before him.

It was Joanna, the mother of Charles V.

He fled and encountered Charles V in Jarandilla, who had renounced his throne in disgust.

Then Juan Borgia went to the Jesuits and became their General in 1565.

To remove the curse and shame from the name Borgia, he was canonized by the Curia after his death as the best of the Borgias.

San Francesco Borgia!

Poor saint – who calls upon you in their distress, who dedicates wax hearts and candles to you? Who wears your medallion on their chest?

No one calls upon you.

No one prays to you.

Alone you stand, apart from all other saints, at the throne of God.

A tear glimmers in your seraphic eyes when you hear the songs of praise for the other saints roaring and resounding. Poveretto Borgia!

You bear a black name, which even God's grace could not polish clean.

You Borgia!

That was once a term of abuse like 'rascal' or 'scoundrel,' and even a murderer could not be called Borgia without punishment.

One day, San Francesco Borgia approached God and asked: Take away the halo that your holy church has placed upon me. No one believes it. Not the people, and not even your angels. Let me go to the devils in hell, where the Borgias belong. –

And God saw the holy seriousness in the face of the Saint, sighed deeply, and said: Go – go to your own.

And the Borgia bowed, took off the uniform of the Jesuit General, and slowly descended the nine hundred ninety-nine steps to hell.

And he knocked on the gates of hell. Lucifer himself opened the door.

Who are you?

A Borgia!

The devil's face brightened: Ah, very good. Ninety-nine Borgias are already inside. You are the hundredth. Welcome! Pay the entrance fee, and you may enter!

The Borgia was astonished: The entrance fee? How much?

Because it is you: a thousand ducats!

The Borgia: I don't have a thousand ducats.

The devil: Well, let's say: five hundred!

The Borgia: I don't have five hundred either.

The devil: By God, what do you have then?

The Borgia: Not a penny. –

The devil erupted in outrage: What, you, a Borgia, have no money? You're lying. You are just a filthy miser or have invested your fortune in heaven because God has promised you better interest rates. Hundreds of thousands of ducats have arrived here from your illustrious relatives. When Alexander Borgia came, my servant devils carried boxes of gold for eight days. Get yourself to heaven if you cannot or will not pay the hellish toll. And he slammed the gates of hell in his face.

> Between heaven and hell, with no home
> anywhere, the last Borgia
> wanders restlessly.

Part Five:

Rasputin – Novel of a Demon

(Phiadon Publishing House, Vienna, 1929)

Rasputin – Novel of a Demon

Prelude

Hehe, there was a man, let us call him Yefim.

He didn't have a proper, respectable name like the nobles and bourgeois bore, a proper name that was his own and belonged to him alone. He was a peasant, a muzhik, his father had picked up the name from an old, yellowed and tattered calendar. "He is to be called Yefim," said the father grumpily and sullenly, for he had a difficult time spelling it on the calendar.

"Fine," said the priest, and wrote the name in the church register.

"Good," said the commissioner and later wrote it in his passport, which he carried with him as requited.

No, no one could say anything against him. Perhaps someone, a policeman or the like, might come along and suspect him of something evil or illegal. Immediately he would pull his greasy passport out of his green woolen jacket, tobacco leaves and pink, sticky raspberry sweets fell to the ground. Well, Your honor, everything is fine, isn't it? and he winked his cunning polecat eyes, and his grayish green straw beard bristled like the tail of an irritated tomcat.

No one could harm him. No policeman, no officer – not even the Tsar himself.

If the Tsar came along the way and confronted him: Hey, you there, what's your name? – he needn't tremble. He wouldn't have to move an eyelash. He presented the passport to the Tsar with a slight, cavalier bow:

Here, dear sir, everything is in order, my name is Yefim Alexandrovich, born here and there, at such and such a time, please feel free to verify –

And the Tsar saluted and apologized:

Forgive the inconvenience, my dear Yefim Alexandrovich – stepped back and cleared the way. Then Yefim strode confidently and boldly. He panted a bit because he suffered from a fatty heart and asthma.

But that would sort itself out in the healthy Siberian climate. Despite his thick feet, he hopped lightly like a bird into a train car on the Petersburg-Tyumeny railroad line.

The cunning polecat eyes blinked playfully at his fellow passenger, a young peasant woman from the Tobolsk province. They had seven hours to travel together – hehe – all sorts of things could happen – a friendship was forged – for life, or what one thought was a friendship – perhaps a bit of love would come his way, Yefim Aleksandrovich, thirty-three years old, quite vigorous and, aside from a few rotten teeth, in splendid shape, a postal coachman by nature, an imperial Russian postal coachman, stationed in Pokrovskoye, situated on the Tobol River in the Tobolsk province. But Yefim Alexandrovich was tired from the long journey.

He fell asleep, dreamed of a black iron stallion and a silver mare, and when he woke up, the peasant woman was gone and a soldier with a face like a tomato was sitting across from him. His eyes weren't visible at all. But his breath reeked terribly of onion soup and bad vodka.

Yefim Alexandrovich worked up an appetite and unwrapped half a blood sausage and a hearty piece of rye bread from newspaper. He had to pack it himself; he, Yefim Alexandrovich, was all alone in the world. He had no mother, no father, no wife, only an old, hard-of-hearing uncle in Nizhny Novgorod, and with whom there was no way of getting along.

A tear fell from Yefim Alexandrovich's gray-green beard.

The soldier suddenly had eyes that looked like small shooting targets, for some unknown reason. "Someone died for you, I suppose? Well, take comfort. Death is death. Any one of us can die any day. I'm a warrior, and that's a tough profession. God save the Tsar."

"May He protect him," said Yefim Alexandrovich, taking off his cap.

He was puzzled by the soldier saying "warrior." What a grandiose word for such a lowly profession. Warrior! Then he must be called a postal councilor or a horse warden, hehe. But then he started to tell the soldier at length about the bereavement he had suffered in his immediate family. He wove such a web of lies until he himself believed the truth of his falsehoods. Did the sergeant know Petersburg? No, he did not know it. However, Moscow, Riga, Lodz, Warsaw—those were familiar to him.

"All right," Yefim Alexandrovich interrupted him brusquely, "I have a story to tell. Was it your niece Feodorovna who died, or was it mine? Feodorovna, the wheat-blonde, angelically beautiful child of God? At the tender age of fourteen, she was lured into a dark alley off Newski Prospekt by a fine but brutal gentleman and there –"

"And there?" – the soldier's tomato face reddened even darker with excitement.

"Well," said Yefim Alexandrovich, "you can imagine what happened there –"

"Not possible," the tomato-faced soldier exclaimed in surprise, "and she died because of that?"

"She was as delicate as a lymph," tears beaded on Yefim Alexandrovich's eyelashes –.

"Like a lymph," echoed the tomato. "I haven't heard that before. And the fine gentleman?" he inquired curiously.

"He stabbed himself with his swordcane on the spot –"

"Swordcane?"

"Yes: a walking stick with a sword inside it."

"Imagine that!"

"The unfortunate creature!"

"The poor thing!"

They both suddenly began to cry together, rose to their feet, and embraced each other. They kissed each other on the cheeks and mouth with smacking sounds.

"God's blessings be upon you, brother!"

"God's grace, little brother!"

The train chugged into Tyumeny smoking.

Yefim Alexandrovich tearfully said goodbye to the soldier, forcing the rest of his blood sausage upon him.

"Take it, take it, little brother, you're a good, decent man, you must eat your fill, you're a warrior, yes yes, eat, eat, little brother." And he stuffed the blood sausage between the soldier's teeth.

Then, with his short, thick legs, he plopped onto the platform. He had the feeling that someone would pick him up – but that was a nonsensical, foolish feeling. Who would bother to pick him up, the postman Yefim Alexandrovitch, transferred to Pokrowskoje?

Perhaps the governor himself?

Or had a carriage been sent for him?

He looked around the dirty train station square. It had rained. An old, rickety rental carriage was stuck sideways in the mud. A few children had startled a rat, which squeaked and ran into the station's outhouse.

"How far to Pokrovskoye?" Yefim Alexandrovich shouted to the coachman.

The coachman took a clay pipe out of his crooked mouth, "Would Your Excellency wish to make use of my services?"

Yefim Alexandrovich laughed.

"Ha-ha, I am a coachman myself, I am the new postal coachman of Pokrovskoye."

The coachman disappointedly put the pipe back between his lips.

"Well, push off before it gets dark. It's a good three hours for a fat man like you."

Yefim Alexandrovich set off and shouted back to the coachman:

"You scoundrel, shut your dirty mouth!"

The coachman scolded back:

"Get lost, you postal fart!"

Yefim Alexandrovich trudged into the dusk. He passed by some oil lamps. Then it became pitch-black night. He walked along a straight avenue of poplars that helped him orient himself. He mechanically put one foot in front of the other and mechanically thought the same thought:

In three hours I'll be home. In three hours I'll be back. I'll know where I belong again. I'll know what I have to do again. I'll groom the horses. They'll be named Jakob and Anna. Maybe even Pavel and Alexandra. I'll breathe in the good smell of the horse stable again. And press my sagging cheek against the warm, steaming flank of a mare. Oh! –

In the roadside ditch, behind a poplar tree, lay a fat, awkward man playing with a jagged stone.

Yefim Alexandrovich couldn't see him in the darkness.

The man thought: Should I? Shouldn't I? The first one who comes along –

Yefim Alexandrovich was the first one to come along.

The man in the ditch shot up like a fat, poisonous sand viper, straight at Yefim Aleksandrovich and smashed his skull with the stone.

Yefim Alexandrovich was still thinking: in three hours I'll be home – in three hours I'll be home.

Then his eye shattered like a cheap carnival mirror. The man bent over him. He took a small lantern out of his jacket and shone it over him. He reached into the green jacket. Twenty rubles – and the passport, in the name of Yefim Alexandrovich, born here and there, at such and such a time – and the request from the postal authorities to report to the Pokrovskoye post office as a postal coachman.

The man softly whistled the first bars of the Tsar's anthem. The next day the postal coachman Yefim Alexandrovich began his service at the Pokrovskoye post office. It was the same day they found the body of an unknown, paperless man in the roadside ditch between Tobolsk and Pokrovskoye.

Since he obviously belonged to the lower classes, the police didn't delve too deeply into investigating his identity and the causes of his death. He was buried in the suicide corner of the Tobolsk cemetery.

Rasputin

Yefimy, the father of Grigory, who would later be called Rasputin, was a servant at the state horse postal service, which operated in a railway-poor region of inner Russia, in the Tobolsk administrative district.

Snow in winter, a white, vast expanse, called the Troika, often pursued by wolves to the first houses – grey-green steppe, grey, wide expanse in summer – Yefimy drove the rickety carriage over hill and dale, and the passengers often looked out of the windows in horror, as the rickety crate ran away with them.

Grigory, with a peasant's head like his fifty-year-old father was twenty years old and helped his father with watering and grooming the horses, and sometimes took the reins of the post when it galloped along too wildly.

Yefimy was not averse to a good drop of vodka. Grigory, the boy, also loved vodka, the horses, dancing and the girls.

He flirted with the peasant girls with their colorful headscarves, they mocked him: *Rasputnik*: which means lecher – which is where he got his name from, and sometimes he looked longingly at the distinguished ladies traveling in the postal carriage.

His friends were Ossip and Porfiri. But his carefree nature did not stop him from naively crossing himself before every image of Christ, kissing the hands of the priest, and going to Mass every Sunday, dressed up, looking more at the pretty girls than at the clergyman.

Grigory was then a true muzhik, a peasant, like fifty million others in Russia: gullible and reckless, cunning and cheerful, depraved and pious. He believed in God. He believed in the Devil. He believed in the Tsar, the intermediary between God and man. And he believed in himself.

For centuries, the muzhik's longing has been for "land," for their own property. For centuries, they have been the servant of the large landowner who owns the land.

Near the village of Pokrovskoye, where Grigory lives, lies the Pokrovskoye estate, which belongs to Baron Akim.

The Baron has a young, now ten-year-old daughter named Irina, who is visited during school holidays by her twelve-year-old cousin Felix Yusupov.

They play together. They enjoy each other's company.

They row together on the castle pond. Irina leans out of the boat towards the water lilies – she leans further and further – she falls into the water –.

Grigory, who was leading his horses to the watering place, notices the child struggling with the waves. He jumps into the water, he rescues the little girl. He carries her in his arms to the castle. He's dripping wet. Now he stands dripping in the parlor. Irina's mother is indignant. She looks at him through her monocle – He's ruining her entire parlor, that muzhik. The child is saved, after all. He can leave.

Oh, but perhaps he should be given a certain reward – she hands him a ten-kopeck coin. Grigory first looks at the money – then at her – throws the money at her feet, leaves without a word. – Yefimy, Grigory's father, loves a good drop of vodka. One day he drank one too many glasses again. He had received a handsome tip from a wealthy passenger, and drank a glass at every stop.

He nodded off on the coachman's seat on the way home, and when Grigory met him at the home station, one of his horses was missing. Robbers had unhitched it along the way.

Yefimy was charged with "embezzlement of state property" and sentenced to prison.

Completely broken, he went to prison. Grigory took his place as a postilion. Singing, cracking the whip, he drove the fine gentlemen and the beautiful ladies across the countryside. One day, he felt a longing to see little Irina again, who for him embodied the essence of higher life. He went to the park gate looking for her. He picked flowers, a bouquet. Then the estate owner, Baron Akim, comes along the path:

"What are you doing there?"

"I am picking flowers –"

"This is my land: peasant louts! And everything that grows on it is mine! Throw the flowers away!"

He hesitates. The Baron snatches the bouquet from him, the individual flowers fall to the ground. Grigory watches them. He has kept a single flower. The landowner walks away, beheading the buttercups along the path with his cane. Irina comes. He lifts her onto his lap. He gives her the only flower, he has left. She picks it apart. She smiles. He laughs. He laughs grimly. She stops smiling. She is frightened of him. He puts her on the floor. The little cousin, Felix Yusupov, comes running over. He pulls Irina away with him, who steals glances back at Grigory.

Yusupov: "Leave the dirty peasant!" Grigory shakes his fist at him.

One day there is a great commotion in the Pokrovskoye post office: an extra mail service is requested at the Tobolsk station for a high-ranking person. Who should be sent to the station?

Grigory, the son of a convict, is deemed unfit to be presented to a person of high standing. The postmaster himself, though he hasn't driven horses in a long time, dresses in his ceremonial attire.

Grigory hitches up the horses, the postmaster drives to the station. From the train at the small station Anna Vyrubova steps out, the Tsarina's lady-in-waiting, who has come to visit the monastery of Pokrowskoje and to engage in pious exercises. The postmaster drives her to the monastery, the horses run wild, he can't control them – Grigory comes along the path, he takes hold of the reins, he has saved Anna Vyrubova.

As sing of gratitude and a token of remembrance, she gifts him a Byzantine icon of Christ. Rasputin remarks that the image looks like him –. She inquires about his name:

"What is your name?"

Anna Vyrubova

"My name is Grigory Rasputin –." She writes the name down in her little notebook.

"Drive me the rest of the way!"

He drives her to the monastery. The postmaster is left behind. – From that day onward, a transformation begins in Rasputin. He paces thoughtfully in his chamber. He pushes Lisaweta, the peasant girl who loves him, away:

"Go away! You filthy thing! I'll have completely different lovers than you! –"

He looks at the image of the saint that the lady-in-waiting gave him. He presses it to his lips. He goes to the Abbot of the monastery:

"Father, you know how to read and write – teach me! I'll give you rubles!"

The Abbot recognizes the boy who brought the lady-in-waiting to his monastery. The lady-in-waiting told him about Rasputin. Rasputin could become her protégé, a favorite at court – who knows?

The Abbot gives him lessons, teaches him to spell using the Bible: G-o-d. Eagerly, Rasputin reads the Bible. Rasputin's sharp mind learns quickly. Soon he writes his first letter, with awkward characters, to little Irina:

"Have you forgotten your loving Uncle Grigory? God's blessings upon you!"

Rasputin catches a dove from the estate, which Irina often plays with. He ties the letter around its neck and releases it. It flies to Irina, who reads the letter in astonishment – looks around for Grigory – then her mother arrives, sees the letter, reads it, tears it up, drags the child away with her. Old Yefimy returns from prison. No one wants to acknowledge him. Grigory meets him in the steppe, while driving the mail carriage.

Grigory: "Now I am the postillon! I don't know you anymore! Get lost!"

He cracks the whip. The old man wanders on. Several years pass. Irina goes to a boarding school in Moscow. Felix Yusupov joins the army as a cadet. Rasputin carries his mail. He waits for his moment.

The government, seeking to win over the peasants in the upcoming Duma elections, sends the high priest Vostorgow as an agitator to the most remote parts of Russia. Thus he also arrives in the Tobolsk province, where Rasputin picks him up with the horse-post from the railway station and takes him to Pokrovskoye.

In the school building Wostorgov speaks about the goals of the government. Many peasants are present. They sit on the low school benches. The blackboard from the last class still stands, covered in chalk marks.

The lord of the Pokrovskoye estate, Baron Akim, is also present. He nods approvingly at Wostorgov's remarks. The peasants try hard to follow him. Then a voice interrupts the speaker:

"When – will – the – poor – peasants – get – land?" All eyes turn to the speaker. The Baron is outraged. The speaker smiles awkwardly. It was Rasputin who interjected. He repeats the question. The peasants cheer. The speaker responds:

"Obey the Tsar and give to the Tsar what is the Tsar's – and the peasant will receive what is the peasant's."

The Baron applauds. The peasants are dissatisfied. Rasputin steps forward from the crowd and climbs onto the platform. With a sweeping motion, he pushes the high priest aside and begins to speak – haltingly, ungracefully, but with lively movements and gestures.

He declares that God gave the earth to all people for their use – not just to a select few.

The baron is indignant – the peasants listen intently – And he continues speaking:

"If the Tzar loves the peasants as the peasants love the Tzar: then he will give them land and earth, earth and land, taking it from the few and placing it in the calloused hands of the many –" The baron jumps up angrily – . The peasants cheer: they carry Rasputin in their hands to his apartment:

"Bravo, Grishka, you're right! You shall go to the Duma! You are one of ours! Give it to those up there!"

Rasputin, early 1914, with admirers

Grigory Rasputin has become famous in his village. The peasants gather around him, they shake his hand. Only Baron Akim gives him a wide berth.

High Priest Wostorgov has returned to Moscow and reports to the election committee.

"To succeed, one needs agitators from the peasant class itself!"

And he reports on the quick-witted peasant Grigory Rasputin in the Tobolsk district, who was uneducated and crude, but a persuasive speaker. He said that all one had to do was to teach him that, what he should say – then he would be an invaluable help. The chairman of the committee laughs:

"You tame an elephant to catch the whole herd!"

Wostorgov: "Exactly!"

A telegram is sent to the Tobolsk Governorate, ordering the postman Grigory Rasputin from Pokrowskoje to be sent to Moscow immediately.

The police are aware of Rasputin's public appearance at the assembly against High Priest Vostorgow.

Grigory Rasputin is arrested at night from his bed by police officers who, like the peasants, believe that he should be tried in Moscow.

He is shackled. Peasants, both men and women, kiss his hands. He is transported for many days in a cattle car between calves and pigs, accompanied by soldiers with fixed bayonets. He drinks from the same filthy bucket of water as the animals With a scruffy beard and disheveled appearance, he finally arrives in Moscow –

At the train station, Vostorgow awaits him, along with some ladies from the committee, to whom Vostorgow has been telling stories about the peculiar muzhik

– like a martyr, Rasputin steps out of the carriage – unkempt – shaggy – dirty – Vostorgow greets him. The misunderstanding about his arrest is cleared up. The chains are removed from him. He is triumphantly escorted to a carriage. Rasputin slaps the horses on their flanks with his hand –

"I understand something about horses," he looks around the circle, "and people!" He rides through the streets of the big city. Rasputin looks around in astonishment at the elegant stores, the tall buildings, the many people, the magnificent cathedrals, the wealth, the poverty, the hustle and bustle. Twilight. Lights flash on, ten, a hundred, a thousand. Amidst Vostorgow's crowd.

Vostorgow surveys him from head to toe: "I can't present you to the nobles like this." –

He leads him into the bathroom, which Rasputin regards with distrust. A bath is prepared, Rasputin is placed into the tub. Wostorgov himself scrubs him down. A maid brings a silk Russian shirt, pants, a long coat, high black boots – Rasputin dresses. Wostorgov hangs a cross around his neck. "Now you look very dignified, Grigory Rasputin! Come!"

Tea at Countess Ignatiev's. Many distinguished ladies. Also Anna Vyrubova, lady-in-waiting to the Tsarina. Tense anticipation of the peasant announced, the muzhik, the son of Russian soil, from whom, as Dostoevsky once prophesied, the salvation of Russia shall come.

Rasputin is announced. Wostorgov goes ahead, Rasputin waits alone in the antechamber. There hangs a life-sized painting of the Mother of Mankind, Eve, a naked female figure. Rasputin first regards the painting with wonder, then with delight, but suddenly pulls a knife from his boot and cuts a cross into the naked chest of the figure.

Countess Ignatiev comes to fetch him –. Rasputin points to the painting: "It is not proper to expose the Mother of Mankind, Eve, naked to all lustful gazes," and he makes the sign of the cross over the painting.

The Countess is moved by such naive piety: "I will have the picture taken to the attic tomorrow." Rasputin, with a grand gesture: "No – now – today – immediately!"

The Countess, fascinated, rings the bell. Two servants enter. She gives the order. The servants lift the picture – then they notice the cross-shaped cut – the countess steps closer – where Rasputin made the sign of the cross over the picture, there is a cruciform cut into the picture: a miracle, a miracle has happened and a miracle-worker, a holy one, has arisen among us!

There is tremendous excitement in the Countess's salon.

The Countess's salon erupts in tremendous excitement. All the ladies examine the painting. Even Anna Vyrubova. Then Rasputin approaches her, places his hand on her arm: "Do you recognize me?" (He addresses everyone informally, as is the peasant custom.) She hesitates – "Can't you remember? I once saved your life!" And he produces the icon that Anna Vyrubova had once given him – Anna Vyrubova: "So it was you, the holy man, who in the guise of a post driver seized the reins of the runaway horses?" She kisses his hand. Everyone gathers around him. "Bless us, dear Father!"

Among the ladies is also Irina, a relative of Countess Ignatiev. She has just turned sixteen. Beautiful, radiant.

Rasputin approaches her: "Irina – little dove – I once saved your life too – in the pond." Irina blushes. She feels his mesmerizing eyes fixed on her. She feels dizzy. She steps back.

Wostorgov is entirely overshadowed. The plan with the "peasant agitator" is no longer mentioned. For instead, a new saint has emerged, of humble origins, like Christ himself. The distinguished ladies of the capital compete to have him for tea at their homes.

A strange, mystical power emanates from him. He begins to preach at these gatherings, in simple, easily comprehensible, suggestive words, which find fertile ground among the corrupted Moscow society.

Thus Rasputin preaches: "Did Christ not say, I have come to call sinners to repentance – not the righteous? To repent – one must first sin: And how does one free oneself most sacredly from sin? By committing it! How does one quench the blazing fire of desire? By extinguishing it!"

Spellbound, the ladies' gazes are fixed on his lips, as he utters such blasphemous words.

Grigory Rasputin returns home, to the small apartment furnished by his female admirers. He approaches the mirror. Looks into it. Wants to see himself, to recognize himself. Who am I? A good person? A saint? A devil? He makes faces in the mirror. His own eyes fascinate him. Then he hears music rising from the courtyard. He goes to the window. Choir singers are performing a Russian song. He smiles, he laughs. And suddenly, he begins to dance. Wildly – Wilder and wilder, until he collapses, exhausted, onto the sofa. There is a knock at the door. Repeatedly. The maid brings tea. He embraces her so vigorously that the entire tray crashes to the floor. She yields to his embrace without resistance.

Irina meets with Yusupov. They go riding together. Irina talks about Rasputin. Yusupov disdainfully swings his riding crop:

"He is a charlatan! A fraudster!"

Irina accidentally encounters Rasputin in the park during a morning ride when she is riding alone. She intends to pass by him, but Rasputin shouts a few words to the horse. And the horse stops trembling and cannot be driven forward even with the whip and spurs.

Rasputin smiles: "Irina, little dove, you must come to me sometime to confess – or are you not a sinful person?"

Irina: "You are not a priest! You have not been ordained!"

Rasputin: "But the grace of God has bestowed the priesthood upon me!"

He gives the horse a light stroke. The horse gallops away. Rasputin watches Irina as she departs.

"Physical purification," Rasputin preaches, "must go hand in hand with spiritual purification."

A Russian bathhouse. A dozen women are gathered around Rasputin. He preaches. It is hot in the bathhouse. He removes his overcoat. All the women fall into ecstasy. He baptizes them anew. He sprinkles water over their elegant dresses, which they then begin to tear off. They dance frantically, half-naked, around him, as he blasphemously blesses them. Then, the door is flung open: the police. The priest Vostorgov, disgusted by Rasputin's actions, had contacted the authorities. The half-naked women, wearing only their fur coats, are ironically escorted through the snow by the policemen to their sleds. Rasputin himself is arrested and sent to a remote monastery on the White Sea. A monastery of the Skoptsy sect.

Rasputin in the Skoptsy monastery. He diligently participates as a lay brother: mass and liturgy, learning much about their sacred rituals.

The Skopzen try to persuade him to join their community and undergo castration.

Rasputin: "No – God created man and woman – he did not create the eunuch..."

The "Rasputin scandal" that stirred up such a storm in Russian society, seems to be over.

Irina breathes a sigh of relief.

Irina and Yusupov, who has been promoted to lieutenant in the Volhynian Equestrian Regiment, love each other.

Prince Felix Yusupov with wife Irene

He confesses his love to her. Petersburg – the northern Venice – canals – arched bridges – a magical dream –

The Tsar lives in a happy marriage with the Tsarina, the beautiful Alexandra, the *Niemka*, "the German." Four daughters, each more beautiful than the other, were born of the marriage: Olga, Tatiana, Maria, Anastasia. But the longed-for son, the heir to the throne, was denied to them by Heaven.

The doctors are consulted. They have no advice to give.

In desperation, the mystically inclined Tsarina summons all sorts of miracle workers and magicians to the court: the witch Darya, the doctor of Tibetan medicine, Badmaev, the "holy fool" Kolya: a deaf, mutilated, hunchbacked dwarf. Each promises her, through their pious magic, "the son." In vain.

The Empress falls into deep melancholy. Anna Vyrubova, the lady-in-waiting, stays with the Empress. Anna Vyrubova, who still believes in Rasputin. Anna Vyrubova speaks to the Empress:

"There is a person in the world, a saint, who is able to help Your Majesty –"

The Tsarina smiles agonizingly. "Name him!"

Anna Vyrubova: "Rasputin!"

The Tsarina: "I have heard of him. He is an unholy man and has been banished to a monastery because of his blasphemous life."

Anna Vyrubova: "Unjustly! Summon him! He will help you through the power of his prayer!"

The Tsarina spends a sleepless night. The Tsar at her bedside in the morning. He rides to a parade of troops. The four princesses bid good morning to the mother. Hadmayev, the Tibetan doctor, Darya the witch, Kolya, the cripple, appear – She dismisses them. She has them thrown out of the palace, whipped, chased away like dogs –

Anna Vyrubova appears. The Tsarina: "Summon Rasputin for me!"

Anna Vyrubova rejoices. She sends a telegram to Rasputin, boasting to Rasputin in the monastery –

"The Tsarina summons you. Prepare yourself!"

The Tsar's Family

An airplane arrives from Petersburg. It lands in the monastery meadows. The monks rush over in amazement, gazing at the iron bird – The pilot is tasked with bringing Rasputin to Tsarskoye Selo as quickly as possible.

Rasputin blesses the airplane, blesses the monks. Then he climbs in. The airplane takes to the skies. It lands in Tsarskoye Selo, gets caught in treetops, crashes, splinters. The pilot breaks his neck. By some miracle, Rasputin escapes death. Like a phoenix from the ashes, he emerges from the wrecked airplane, walks through the park, up the poplar-lined avenue, and arrives at the rear of the palace, at the Empress's chamber, where a giant Ethiopian guards the door.

Anna Vyrubova hears Rasputin's voice. She opens the door, lets Rasputin enter, who walks with dignity to the Empress's bedside. He strokes her hand casually. "What do you desire? You summoned me."

The Tsarina, anxiously: "They say you are a saint and have the gift of seeing into the future. I have been deceived so many times. Tell me: will I have a son?"

Rasputin waves to Anna Vyrubova:

"Leave us alone! Ensure that we are not disturbed!" Alone with the Tsarina, Rasputin looks at her for a long time with his large eyes, then he strokes her forehead with his hand:

"You – will – have – a – son. You – will – have – a – son –"

After a few weeks, the Tsarina feels like a mother. There is great excitement in the palace. The Tsar is tenderly concerned.

Rasputin lives in seclusion in Petersburg. Only sometimes does Vyrubova lead him to the Tsarina, who begins to believe in him as in a starost. After nine months – a back and forth of doctors and midwives in the palace – everything is done quietly – the hour of birth approaches – The Tsarina gives birth to a son! The long-awaited heir to the throne. Jubilation in the palace. Everyone embraces. Rejoicing among the people. Illuminations light up the night streets. The blissful Tsarina holds the son close to her on a cushion – she weeps with happiness – The Tsar is ecstatic – for the first time, he receives Rasputin, takes him by both hands and appoints him as the imperial "Keeper of the Eternal Lamps." Even the Tsar now believes in Rasputin's supernatural powers, while among the people here and there rumors surface that the Tsar is not the father of the Tsarevich – Even Irina, now advanced to the position of the Empress's lady-in-waiting, hears of the rumors, tells Yusupov about them – and how she once, behind a column, accidentally happened to see Anna Vyrubova secretly leading Rasputin to the Tsarina.

Yusupov covers her mouth with his hand: "The walls have ears! Be quiet! And keep Russia's shame to yourself."

Tsarina, Children, Governess, Rasputin, 1908

Rasputin's opponents are defeated by the arrival of his prophecy, that the Tsarina would give birth to a son. Rasputin rises in favor with the Tsar and the Tsarina, despite the attempts of some Grand Dukes, such as Nikolai and Dmitry, try to warn the Tsar. Their words fall on deaf ears.

The courtiers try to win Rasputin's favor, and he, lulled into safety by the grace of their Majesties, gradually resumes his old life. For nights on end, he spends time with drinking companions "among the Gypsies" in the infamous Villa Rhode, drinking, dancing, and clumsily declaring love to the Gypsy women. He preaches: "You shall love your neighbor as yourself.—I love myself very much.— So I must love all of you very much, too. You, my neighbors—"

The Tsarina strolls through the park with the heir to the throne. Irina is with her. Rasputin appears. He plays with the child. The Tsarina notices Rasputin's interest in Irina, "the little dove." Jealousy stirs within her.

Rasputin now has an apartment, where he is besieged by petitioners of all kinds. Half of Petersburg meets in his anteroom: officials seeking career advancement, alone or accompanied by a pretty woman, bankers trying to bribe Rasputin, officers, students, peasants, workers, priests, women of all classes, prostitutes, and society ladies in search of adventure.

Many hold petitions in their hands. Others pray the rosary. Now and then, the door in the background opens, and Rasputin appears.

Rasputin has two secretaries, his childhood friends Ossip and Porfiri, refined drinking companions. Proud of his power, he gladly helps out of vanity. He scribbles his wishes on torn-off slips of paper, instructions to the ministers. He makes ministers. He topples ministers. He, the simple peasant, has risen to the highest level of power. The Tsar and Tsarina heed his advice. The heir to the throne, Alexei, is growing up. The sailor Derevenko carries him in his arms. The Tsar and Tsarina adore the Tsarevich – who is of the frailest health.

The little Tsarevich clings to "Uncle Grigory," to Rasputin, who tells him all sorts of fairy tales, plays with him, lets him ride on his back.

The European sky clouds over. A clear sky, under which a storm is brewing.

Lightning and thunder.

The Austrian heir to the throne has been assassinated in Sarajevo by a Serb. Extra newspaper editions are being announced on the streets, which peo-

Prince Alexei Romanov, 1916

ple snatch eagerly from each other's hands. Paralyzing horror and fearful anticipation of what is to come.

Council of Ministers in Petersburg.

The Tsar stands at the window of his study and looks up at the sky, which suddenly darkens.

Servants bring candles. The ministers gather.

Minister of War: "We must not avoid war! We are prepared."

Minister of the Interior: "We have needed the war to prevent the outbreak of internal unrest. The peasant issue still has not been resolved."

The Tsar, undecided, bites his lips. Tsarina enters, "What will you do?" The Tsar shrugs his shoulders. He stands at the window and watches the thunderstorm.

Tsarina: "Ask the miracle man, ask him, who has so often foretold the truth to us!"

"Rasputin?"

"Yes!"

"Where is he?"

"He is waiting outside."

Tsar: "Let him in—"

Rasputin with Officers

Rasputin enters. He pushes aside the ceremonial master and the servants, stands upright in the room, he examines each in turn with his large eyes, approaches the Minister of War: "You are a fool!" The Minister of War is embarrassed. Rasputin moves to the Minister of the Interior: "You are a fool!" The Minister of the Interior is outraged. Rasputin steps up to the Tsar: "You are" – he smiles – "the lord over war and peace! Choose peace! War will destroy Russia! Love your enemies! War offends God! And remember one thing that I tell you now: If I should perish, you will perish too!"

He leaves, standing upright, slams the door behind him. Everyone remains frozen in place.

The Tsarina: "The people have spoken! It was the voice of the people!"

The Minister of War takes the Declaration of Mobilization out of his briefcase, asks the Tsar to sign it – the Tsar takes the document, reads, takes the pen, throws the pen away, leaves.

Rasputin is with Ossip and Porfiri, his companions. They are drinking.

Ossip: "You advised them to choose peace? There are all sorts of business deals to be made in war."

Rasputin: "I pity the blood of poor, innocent people that will be shed – for nothing."

Rasputin rests his head on the table. The other two quietly rise and leave.

Conference of ministers.

Minister of Police: "Shall we stage an assassination attempt of the Tsar by a German?" The War Minister and Minister of the Interior brighten up: "A splendid idea!"

The Tsar receives threatening letters daily – they're tucked into his coat pocket early in the morning, at noon under his napkin at table. They are smuggled in by the Okhrana, the secret police, themselves.

The secret police – Okhrana – recruit a wretched German fellow from a dive bar, offering him 500 rubles and a guarantee of release to carry out a revolver attack on the Tsar.

He is smuggled into the park of Zarskoje Selo by the police themselves, hidden behind a bush.

The Tsar comes walking along the gravel paths on his usual morning stroll with the little Tsarevich –.

Then a suspicious individual jumps out from behind a bush – takes aim, the Tsar shields the Tsarevich with his body. The individual fires several times, misses, and is overpowered by the approaching palace guards.

The Tsar is in the palace. The Tsarina with him, beside herself, report of the palace commander: "The assailant is a German!" The Grand Duke Nikolay arrives:

"There you see how the Germans behave against you!"

The ambassadors of England and France to the Tsar, Grand Duke Nikolay, the ministers, the generals. The Tsar, still undecided, plays with the dice left over from a game with the Tsarevich – The Tsarina arrives.

Tsar: "If I roll eighteen, it shall be God's verdict!" He throws the dice: Eighteen!

He signs the declaration of war, which Grand Duke Nikolaj almost snatches from him, still wet from the pen.

Grand Duke Nikolay is appointed Supreme Commander.

The newspapers carried the news of the assassination attempt, of the declaration of war. War sentiment and enthusiasm in the streets. Processions are forming. The Tsar's anthem is played in the taverns. Flags. Reservists marching in. Tearful farewells to the wife and child, to the bride. Irina bids farewell to Yusupov, who is going to the front.

The heir to the throne Alexei is ill as a result of the excitement during the assassination attempt. He suffers from severe, barely controllable bleeding.

Great excitement at the palace. Doctors come and go, the mother is in despair, the Tsar is depressed. The doctors shrug their shoulders. The situation is very bad. The Tsarina sends Anna Vyrubova to Rasputin. Rasputin answers the telephone, gets himself connected with Tsarskoye Selo, calls the Tsarina on the telephone:

"Are you there, Mammuschka? Listen, take the sick boy out of bed and hold him to the telephone so that he can hear my voice."

The Tsarina herself carries the boy to the telephone: Rasputin: "Are you there, Alyosha?"

The boy, smiling, languidly: "Yes." Rasputin: "Do you hear me?" The boy: "Yes."

Rasputin: "You will sleep now – immediately – sleep – you will sleep twenty-four hours – and then be healthy –"

The boy begins to smile and fall asleep during the conversation. Blissfully, the mother carries him to bed. The boy slowly recovers.

The huge sailor Derevenko carries the convalescent boy in the park in his arms to his favorite spots.

A Saint Bernard, his favorite dog, always accompanies him. The sailor carefully settles the boy on a bench. The Tsarina and Rasputin approach. Rasputin goes to the boy, sits down next to him, he takes his hand, he begins to tell a story:

"Once upon a time, there was a little Tsarevich who was always good and obedient – and followed his dear mother and his dear Uncle Grischa..."

The boy smiles. He plucks a blossom branch from the tree above him and hands it to Rasputin, who hands it to the Tsarina. Rasputin and the Tsarina walk away. They walk through dark leafy paths of the park, the Tsarina falls down before Rasputin, she kisses his hand.

Rasputin: "God has seen your tears and heard your prayers! Your son will live!"

The first wounded from the front arrive.

The Tsarina walks, followed by ladies of society, including Irina, dressed as a sister, through the hospitals, speaking here with one, laying her hand on a blanket there, distributing cigars and cigarettes, sweets, flowers. Rasputin makes peace with the war. He sells army supplies to the highest bidder.

Bankers, smugglers, and spies crowd his antechamber, to whom he allocates weapons, zwieback, shoes, and powder supplies for the Russian army.

A wax candle manufacturer asks him for help. Rasputin: "The Tsarina will donate ten candles for each church in Russia. Participation fifty percent?"

The black marketeer, delighted: "It's a deal." And while at the front, in the trenches, the muzhik heroically fights and dies, corruption spreads in the rear, fueled by Rasputin, in its grim circles.

The shoes delivered to the soldiers contain cardboard soles. A train with food departs from Petersburg for the front, but never arrives. Thousands of ammunition crates are unloaded at the front – everyone jumps cautiously aside – caution is unnecessary: ten centimeters of powder at the top, everything else dust.

In the restaurants, "collections for those blinded in the war" are held, Porfiri and Ossip go to collect, the money flows into their hands. While the muzhik is torn apart by grenades, the machine guns rattle, and in the entertainment restaurants in Petersburg, champagne corks pop. Begging wounded and crippled war veterans are thrown out. They disturb the guests' appetites. Rasputin squanders the bribes in questionable establishments, with gypsies, black women, Chinese women – sometimes he also preaches, drunk, from the music band's podium, and all the guests, as drunk as he, roll around laughing. He has set up a chapel in his apartment, with a confessional, before him the noble ladies and even the less noble ones come, he intoxicates them with incense and phrases. Occasionally, one sees a carriage driving through the streets, stopping at a corner, a deeply veiled lady walking through narrow streets to Rasputin's apartment and disappearing through the back entrance. (It is the Tsarina.)

The initial mood of victory among the people has given way to doubt and depression. You can hear people whispering covertly in the cafes and the small streets. They no longer believe the army reports. They see the corruption in the hinterlands and clench their fists. Many a fist clenches against Rasputin, as he walks through the streets. The Tsar plays on the floor with the Tsarevich. Wooden soldiers are lined up. They play, shoot with small cannons, soldiers fall down. A courier is announced, enters. The Tsar looks up from the floor, kneeling, irritated, "What is it?"

"Your Majesty has lost the battle of Lodz – eighty thousand dead."

At that moment the Tsarevich shoots. An entire row of wooden soldiers falls over. He claps his hands in jubilation: "Victory!" The Russians are retreating in storm and rain.

Rasputin's unholy life is increasingly causing scandal, especially since he uses the mask of a monk, although he never received priestly ordination. The highest synod of the Russian Church deals with the Rasputin affair.

Rasputin is summoned before the Supreme Synod, and appears, since he knows no fear. The highest-ranking clergyman, an ancient gentleman, curses him: "You disgrace Russia, you desecrate the Holy Church, you desecrate the name of the Tsar and the Tsarina, who are under your terrible influence. You are the Antichrist!"

All the clergymen stand up in agitation, shake their hands at Rasputin, spitting at him – and he doesn't defend himself.

"You pretend to be a monk! But where are the three monastic vows: chastity, poverty, obedience, in you? You obey only the devil, you take bribes and live in luxury, you're a *Rasputnik*, a lecher, as your name says!"

Antimonarchist Caricature around 1916. The Tsar couple in the power of the devilish Rasputin.

Rasputin: "Your Reverence, you are mistaken: I am called Rasputin because I stand at the *Raspute*, at the crossroads of two ages – God loves me – and to his favorites God forgives much."

The highest clergyman brandishes the crucifix, and all the clergymen advance upon him with crucifixes, as if they want to beat him to death with the crucifixes: "Swear on the crucifix to repent and never enter the palace of the Tsar again!"

Rasputin cornered, swears! The clergymen release him.

Rasputin wastes no time breaking his oath and telling the Tsarina about the incident, who sees him as a martyr: "Saints are always slandered."

He succeeds in getting the Tsar to dismiss the highest clergyman of the Synod, "for extortion," and banish him to Siberia.

In his place, Rasputin suggests the Abbot of the Pokrowskoje monastery, who once taught him to read and write, and whom he has not forgotten.

Meanwhile, the displeasure with Rasputin's favoritism is spreading. In the Duma, Deputy Purishkevich speaks of the "mysterious powers that dishonor Russia" and of a certain "despicable person," the "Antichrist personified." In the gallery, Felix Yusupov, ardent patriot, listens to him, who has come on leave, The misfortune of Russia burns in his heart. He enthusiastically applauds Purishkevich's words, as does the entire audience in the gallery. The gallery is cleared for disorderly conduct.

Yusupov visits Deputy Purishkevich at his apartment. He pours his heart out to him – his plan the disaster of Russia: Rasputin, to eliminate Rasputin.

A mere peasant should no longer rule Russia, a wild animal, an untamed, uncontainable beast.

Purishkevich listens to him thoughtfully. He shakes his hand: "We will find a way out of the swamp in which we are in danger of sinking."

In the evening, Yusupov goes to dine with Irina in an elegant Petersburg restaurant. They take a seat, speaking tenderly to each other. After a while, Rasputin arrives with his followers: Ossip, Porfiri, and the former Abbot of Pokrovskoe. He orders champagne. They drink, they drink heavily. Music plays! The gypsy fiddler steps close to Rasputin, playing melodies in his ear. Rasputin stands up, dances.

He dances closer to Irina, circling her until he falls before her. He reaches for her hands, her breasts. Yusupov pales, stands up, and punches Rasputin in the face, causing him to stumble back. All present are horrified. The police arrive at once. Yusupov is dragged away – Irina stands, stunned.

No one remains in the restaurant but Rasputin and Irina. She seems utterly passive. He looks at her intensely. She recoils in terror.

"Irina, my little dove," he say. He approaches her. She faints in terror.

Rasputin catches the fainting woman in his arms.

Yusupov in prison, angrily beats on the bars.

Irina, still dazed from the night's events, goes to Rasputin. He receives her in his finest embroidered silk shirt: "What do you wish, Irina, little dove? You know I love you, your wish shall be granted in advance!"

Irina, crumpling her handkerchief, with a tear-streaked face: "I beg you: forgive Felix Yusupov! He was drunk!"

Rasputin, smiling: "For your sake – he shall be forgiven."

She, smiling softly: "May I hope – that he will be released from custody?"

Rasputin scribbles a note: "Immediately! Give this to the police chief! He knows me!"

Rasputin strokes his beard.

"One more thing, Irina, my dove. Send me your Yusupov. I have to talk to him!"

Happy, Irina rushes to the prison, hands Rasputin's note to the director. The director bows, calls for a jailer who immediately unlocks Yusupov's cell. Irina and Yusupov sink into each other's arms.

Imperial Theater, gala evening.

The Tsar and several Grand Dukes are in the royal box, the audience rises when the Tsar enters. The famous imperial ballet. Pavlova dances the "Dying Swan." She collapses.

Tsar Nicolas II and General Brussilow, 1916

Grand Prince Nikolay to the Tsar: "This is how Russia will sink!" The Tsar leaves the theater.

As the war progresses German agents venture into Petersburg. The financier Manus, a German agent, organizes lavish banquets with champagne and women, to which he invites Rasputin. Rasputin gets drunk and in drunkenness reveals his conversations with the Tsar.

Rasputin is fed the idea of a separate peace with Germany. Much is promised to him.

Rasputin convinces the Tsar to appoint the pro-peace Prime Minister Stürmer.

And the Russian troops are defeated again and again. In the hinterlands, the population grows restless. Bread and meat become scarce. Famine threatens. There is a shortage of coal in Petersburg, everything is freezing. Only in front of Rasputin's house are coal deliveries made. Already at dawn the women queue up at the baker's and butcher's stores. In the suburbs the first looting begins! Curses of the mob resound against the war, against the Tsar, against Rasputin.

On vast parade grounds, reservists practice – with clubs, because rifles are in short supply.

A meeting of the grand dukes.

It is decided to open the blinded Tsar's eyes to Rasputin's treacherous schemes.

Grand Prince Nikolay, the Supreme Commander of the Russian army, requests an audience with the Tsar.

Grand Duke: "You must abandon Rasputin. He is a traitor, the disgrace of Russia. Already in the Duma people speak openly of his irresponsible regime, as if he were the ruler of Russia, not you! They also speak disrespectfully of the Tsarina – yes, they are not afraid to..."

The Tsar, agitated, "Silence!—Do you speak only for yourself?"

Grand Duke: "I speak in the name of all the Grand Dukes – and in the name of Russia."

The Tsar telephones Rasputin.

The Tsarina picks up the receiver at Rasputin's house, to hand it to Rasputin. Rasputin: "It is father!" The Tsarina is startled. Rasputin: "'All right, I'll come to you immediately." The Tsar receives Rasputin. He nervously smokes one cigarette after another. Tsar: "Our army is defeated."

Rasputin: "I always advised you against war. You did not listen."

Tsar: "What should I do?"

Rasputin: "Consult the spirit of your father, Tsar Alexander, in prayer. Summon him tonight at midnight! He will answer you."

The Tsar, praying at night. The clock strikes midnight. From the drapes in the background of the room the ghost of Alexander II emerges, approaches the pale Tsar. "You have summoned me, son! What do you want?" Tsar: "How am I to carry on the war?"

The spirit: "You have an incompetent Supreme Commander, Grand Duke Nikolai. He is losing all the battles. Dismiss him! Take command of the troops yourself. Assume supreme command! And negotiate a favorable peace with the Germans – before it is too late. Win over the peasants! Give them the 'land' that has been promised to them for centuries!"

The spirit vanishes – behind the curtains, then into a side corridor. Rasputin's face appears demonically illuminated in the moonlight. The spirit: Rasputin. The Tsar's decree relieves Grand Duke Nikolai of supreme command. The Tsar himself takes over. A proclamation from the Tsar to the people:

"I offer you my greetings, O my brave people! I will lead you! Hang in there! Without victory, there will be no peace! You peasants shall have 'land' after the war ended victoriously!"

The proclamation is met with mockery, contempt from the people: "No peace without victory! Quite right! The question is, who will win?"

Secret meetings of the workers take place. A munitions factory is blown up. The emperor hears the explosions in his palace. The Tsar travels by special train to the center of his troops at the great headquarters. Farewell to the Tsarina, to the Tsarevich, to his daughters, on the platform in Tsarskoye Selo. At last Yusupov contacts Rasputin. He asks him for forgiveness for that embarrassing scene.

Rasputin dismisses it:

"I have here a letter – with a seal – to the Tsar – which I may entrust to no one but you – go to the grand headquarters – deliver it personally!"

Yusupov is amazed at Rasputin's kindness, tries to conceal his astonishment.

Rasputin: "I have forgiven you – for her sake."

Yusupov meets Irina. Tells about Rasputin's mission. She advises him to be on guard. He travels to headquarters. He is brought before the Tsar. He delivers Rasputin's letter. The Tsar unfolds it and reads: "This brave officer is eager to fight in the front line. Give him the opportunity! – God's blessings upon you! Grigory."

The Tsar: "You are a patriot! Your wish shall be granted." The Tsar crumples up the letter and throws it toward the wastebasket, the letter falls next to it – The Tsar leaves the room. Yusupov remains behind, standing at attention, then he moves. Discovers the crumpled letter on the floor, quickly picks it up, smooths it out, reads it, and quickly pockets it. A

Prince Felix Yusupov and his wife, a niece of the Tsar.

courier orders him on a dangerous patrol ride. It's impossible to resist. He kisses Irina's picture. He rides. He is shot from his horse. Medics find him. He is put on a medical train bound for Petersburg, is admitted at a military hospital, where Irina works as a nurse. Only when she folds back the cloth covering his face does she recognizes him. She nurses him with tender devotion. Slowly he recovers. He shows her Rasputin's letter.

Irina, horrified: "He wanted to get you killed!"

Yusupov: "What does it matter to me! He wants to murder Russia!"

The Tsarina is left alone at Tsarskoye Selo, with the heir to the throne and the princesses. Rasputin arrives to see the Tsarina. Rasputin: "Mother! I need money!" The Tsarina looks up.

Rasputin: "For pious deeds! I want to build a chapel in honor of little Alexei, the heir to the throne. Prayers for him shall be offered there forever!"

Tsarina: "I have no money, holy father –"

Rasputin: "But you have the Romanovs' crown jewels! – Show them to me!"

The Tsarina, fearful, leads Rasputin into underground catacombs – into chambers to which only she has the key – they enter a room, filled with precious stones, gold, crowns. Rasputin's eyes gleam greedily. He takes the crown of the Romanovs, places it on his head, then pulls it off, tears out the most precious diamonds, emeralds, pearls from the crown with raw fingers, stuffing them into his pockets like pebbles. –. The next evening at the Villa Rhode with the gypsy girls, Rasputin drinks, dances, laughs, throws pearls and diamonds from the Tsar's crown to the girls, who fight over them.

Yusupov has recovered. One day Rasputin comes to the hospital, to bless the soldiers and look for Irina.

There he finds Yusupov.

Rasputin: "You're alive?"

Yusupov: "Pious prayers have protected me!"

Yusupov has arranged his wedding with Irina.

He meets with Purishkevich, where he also meets the Grand Duke Dmitry. He shows them Rasputin's letter to the Tsar, which almost cost him his life.

The three agree to eliminate the beast Rasputin, the scourge of Russia. No one must know about the plan.

The three swear allegiance to each other. They decide to poison Rasputin: with poisoned wine, poisoned cake, which Purishkevich will arrange.

The conspirators also agree that the Tsarina will be banished to a convent, that the Tzar should abdicate in favor of his son Alexei, and that Grand Duke Nikolai must assume the regency, so that Russia may rise again.

The conspirators decide to assassinate Rasputin on the day of Yusupov's wedding with Irina at Yusupov's house.

Yusupov takes it upon himself to invite Rasputin. Yusupov invites Rasputin to the wedding.

Rasputin: "I have a special wedding gift for you – if you grant me the *ius primae noctis*, which is the right of holy men –"

Yusupov hesitates, "I will give you Irina for one night – as a gift."

Rasputin rejoices.

Yusupov: "And what will you give me as a present?"

Rasputin: "The Tsar is here" (motioning with his finger to his forehead). "I will make you the Tsar! I have the power! You are a Russian! The Tsar is not truly Russian at all. He has more German than Russian blood."

Rasputin takes several glasses – pours red wine into one, water into the others –.

"The red wine, that's the Russian blood! See, this is how it's diluted in the Tsar!"

He pours half of the red wine into a water glass, then half of that into another water glass, and once or twice more, holding the last glass up to the light:

"This is the Tsar's blood!" It is transparent like water.

Rasputin tells the Tsarina that he will attend Irina's wedding.

The Tsarina: "Beware of her!" Rasputin: "She is so gentle!" Tsarina: "The gentlest cats are the fiercest tomcats! – At least don't go to the wedding alone!"—

Rasputin: "I fear no one –"

Tsarina: "Take the sailor Derevenko with you as your bodyguard! My most faithful servant! I fear for you!"

Rasputin agrees. The Tsarevich arrives with Derevenko. Rasputin tenderly greets the Tsarevich, lifts him up, kisses him on the forehead. The wedding of Yusupov and Irina. The couple is blessed by the priest in the church. The arrival of guests in front of Yusupov's house. The banquet table, including: Purishke-vich, Grand Duke Dmitry, the conspirators. Rasputin has not appeared at the table yet. The conspirators are already getting restless. Rasputin is at home. He's wearing his finest silk shirt, embroidered by the Tsarina. He sits at the table with Derevenko, the giant sailor, and throws dice. They both drink vodka. Derevenko grows tired, falls asleep. A sled arrives at Rasputin's, Yusupov emerges from it, climbs the stairs to Rasputin, knocks: Rasputin opens the door. Yusupov: "I've come to get you! Irina is waiting." Rasputin embraces him, kisses him. Derevenko snores. Rasputin initially wants to wake him up, but decides to let him sleep. He follows Yusupov into the sleigh. The guests at Yusupov's have already left. The table has been cleared, but not yet properly set. Overturned wine bottles. Yusupov leads Rasputin through the halls to his study, invites him to a armchair. In front of him is a table with port wine, small white and black cakes. The black cakes are poisoned, the port wine is poisoned. Yusupov: "A lit-tle glass of wine?" Rasputin: "You drink first!" Suspicious. Yusupov drinks: one of the glasses without poison. Rasputin drinks: one of the glasses with poison. Yusupov: "A cake?" Rasputin eats from the poisoned black cake –. Nothing hap-pens. Yusupov turns pale. Rasputin: "Where is Irina, the little dove?" Yusupov: "Soon." He starts playing a gramophone record: a Russian song that Rasputin hums along to. Yusupov goes out, up one flight of stairs, where the conspirators are waiting. Yusupov, pale: "A miracle! The poison doesn't work!"

Purishkevich: "He must not escape us! Russia's salvation is at stake. Here –" He hands Yusupov his revolver, which Yusupov hesitantly takes. "Go downstairs, otherwise he will become suspicious! You must act!"

Yusupov returns to the room with Rasputin, who nervously paces back and forth. Rasputin: "Where's Irina?" He stops in front of Yusupov, takes him by both shoulders, looks him openly in the eyes, Yusupov can only endure this gaze with the utmost concentration.

Rasputin: "Felix Yusupov – I love you – you and your wife – I am lonely – alone with my soul – the Tsar is here" (taps his forehead) – "he is weak – effeminate – foolish. You, Felix Yusupov, are young – handsome – proud – clever. You shall rule in his place. The war is a folly – and a crime – it makes the heart of Christ bleed every day – I will make you a Tsar – I have the power – and you will make peace!"

At this moment in the background Irina passes under the colonnades, in her wedding dress, Rasputin sees her, spreads his arms – at this moment, when Rasputin stands there like the parody of the crucified Savior, Yusupov raises the revolver and shoots at him –.

Yusupov: "Die! Traitor! Disgrace of Russia!"

Rasputin falls, pulling the tablecloth and the lamp on it down with him. It immediately becomes pitch dark. Yusupov cries for light. Servants come running through the corridors of the house with lights – when the room becomes bright again – Rasputin has disappeared – Yusupov stands aghast. He runs out into the corridors. Rasputin has escaped. Irina is seen fleeing through the palace corridors – Rasputin after her – Yusupov after him. Irina manages to mislead Rasputin in a colonnade –. Rasputin suddenly finds himself in the courtyard – moonlight – Rasputin takes a deep breath – He spits. He spits blood into the snow. Slowly he walks in the moonlight across the courtyard, towards the exit gate. There at the last moment Yusupov sees him from a window. He shoots once, twice, three times. Rasputin collapses at the gate he has just reached.

Yusupov, Purishkevich, Grand Prince Dmitry come running.

Purishkevich checks the pulse of the dead Rasputin. The three of them wrap him in his own fur coat, carry him to the waiting sleigh, which Yusupov himself is driving.

At the moment Yusupov climbs into the driver's seat, a policeman appears at the gate, who heard the shots. Saluting, "What's going on, gentlemen?" Yusupov: Pointing to the dead Rasputin with the whip handle: "We have shot Rasputin – the scourge of Russia. Do you understand?"

Rasputin's body after it was recovered from the Neva.

Policeman, saluting: "At your command! – Served him right!"

Yusupov drives the sleigh to the Neva River, where the conspirators chop a hole in the ice and dump the body in it.

The news of Rasputin's assassination spreads like wildfire in Petersburg the next day.

There is jubilation among the citizens, in the higher circles, who light candles in the churches, before the image of Saint Dimitri, in gratitude for Rasputin's removal – While in the officers' clubs, champagne flows freely – the Tsarina weeps – blaming Sailor Derevenko fiercely for allowing Rasputin to go to Yusupov alone.

Derevenko shrugs his shoulders. She holds her fist under his chin, which he grabs and lowers. Derevenko: "Your time is over." He stomps away. The workers, especially the peasants, have different thoughts about the murder of Rasputin. He was – despite everything – one of their own, a muzhik, from the very bottom of society, and he rose all the way to the Tsar's throne. Through him, the Russian people had the ear of the Tsar. He made the voice of the people heard before the throne. The lowest had mystically joined the highest.

And there were rumors: Rasputin was murdered by the aristocrats so that the Russian people no longer had the Tsar's ear – he died because he wanted peace –

and because he had always advised the Tsar to "distribute land" to the peasants. The "elites" do not want to give the "land" to the "commoners."

The fermenting discontent among the people, starving at the front, where they are dying senselessly, is increasing.

Enormous amounts of snow fall, the food trains get stuck in the snow. Wolves come into the cities. It is minus forty-three degrees Celsius. Street riots.

One regiment refuses to obey the officers' order to shoot into the crowd. They throw away their rifles.

Tsar Nicholas II and his son Alexei shoveling snow.

The people carry the unarmed soldiers on their shoulders, cheering. The conspirators had miscalculated. They, who wanted to strengthen the monarchy, were overrun themselves before they could carry out their further plans. The soldiers in the trenches, the sailors of the North Sea Fleet, the sailor Derevenko, who had carried the Tsarevich in his arms, they rose up, they no longer wanted to wage war, they overthrew the Tsar. Rasputin's prophecy came true:

"If I should perish, you too, Tsar, will perish as well!"

The Tsar, who was returning to the capital from his headquarters on the parlor train, where he had received reports of unrest, was stopped on the open track by revolutionary peasants, workers and soldiers. One of them, Sailor Derevenko, waved the red flag, just like the signalman used to wave the track flag, and there the train stopped. The Tsar looked out of the carriage.

With rifles slung, revolvers in hand, the revolutionaries entered his compartment. He is forced, at gunpoint, to sign the abdication document. Russia no longer has a Tsar.

He is taken prisoner. The entire imperial family is held captive in Tsarskoye Selo: Tsar, Tsarina, Tsarevich, the four princesses. Their chief guard is the sailor Derevenko.

The body of Rasputin was buried in the park of Tsarskoye Selo, the funeral procession was followed by countless women, and frequently the Tsarina performs her devotions before the grave of the "holy man."

The Tsar plays soldiers with his son as before. Or they go for a walk in the park, or build a snowman from snow in the park and throw snowballs at him. The Tsarevich laughs. One night they were all, the entire imperial family, rudely torn from their beds. The "Whites" are advancing, to liberate them all, under the command of Yusupov, who managed to escape during the revolution. Advice from Derevenko and the revolutionaries:

"We must put an end to Tsardom once and for all!"

By torchlight the entire imperial family is led to Rasputin's grave. They walk upright between their executioners, the princesses weeping, the Tsarina tearless, the Tsar leading the Tsarevich by the hand. They stand in front of the grave. The firing squad takes aim! Then the little Tsarevich throws his cap into the air:

"Long live Russia!" The volley resounds. Around Rasputin's grave the legend is already beginning to sprout. Crowds of believers come, to pray, at the grave of the muzhik who foresaw Russia's downfall.

The revolutionary government has Rasputin's grave opened to dispel the legend.

His body is exhumed, burned on a funeral pyre. The ashes are collected and from the tower of the Kremlin are scattered to the four winds.

Once again, Rasputin's face appears on the arch of the sky, his features fade, they merge into Lenin's features, who stands on a platform in Red Square in Moscow and speaks to the people.

Vladimir Lenin

Part Six:

Open Letter to Kaiser Wilhelm II

(Published on June 3, 1917 in the "New Zurich Newspaper")

Open Letter to Kaiser Wilhelm II

Published on June 3, 1917 in the "New Zurich Newspaper"

Your Majesty!

More than you may suspect in your political and human isolation and solitude: the eyes of the whole world are upon you pleading, imploring, demanding. While the hostile press may still paint you as a vandal and barbarian, incompetent and insipid diplomats and statesmen, who would be better described as state cripples, may still harbor the crazy plan to drive out the devil militarism with Beelzebub imperialism, the lower devil mechanism with the upper devil rationalism: in every country, the eyes of people who remain human, as well as the eyes of the Muschiks, Poilus, Tommys, Hecht-grey and field-grey soldiers, and those in olive green, are all fixed on you. For you, Majesty, have it in your hands to offer the world a prompt peace...

You claim that you were ready for "peace" last November. Indeed, you extended your hand to the enemy in peace – but the hand was clenched into a fist and was not a human hand pulsing with blood. It was the iron fist of Götz von Berlichingen.

Your Majesty: recognize the time! Within it: the blossom of eternity! Recognize that all ideas of power, no matter what they are, have suffered a shipwreck in this war. Power is a clay idol if spirit, goodness, and justice are not connected to it. The principles of power and its "subordinates" must finally be over: lust for power, pride, police spirit, idolatry, Byzantinism, Mammonism... (the latter two always grow parasitically alongside each other).

Your Majesty, your Easter message has enlightened the hearts of the Germans and touched their foreheads with a faint glimmer of future light. But understand that one should speak to a people who want to be free and who one honors and respects – as a free man to a free people. Yet you spoke in the tone of nobility. Still lingering in the public and secret cabinets of Berlin is the "principle of subordination." And you were ill-advised when you tuned your Easter message to the tone of grace. Rights, Your Majesty, are not bestowed. They are originally present, are essential and exist.

Abandon the belief in divine right and walk as a human among humans. Cast off the purple of singularity and cloak yourself in the mantle of unity: of brotherly love. Establish the true people's monarchy of the Hohenzollerns. Free yourself from the ancestors; free from the delusion that you could rely on a small capitalist-junker clan, which "recruits" its civil servants and senior officers from itself, blaring trumpets to drown out the cries of the people. They, in truth, will erode the throne and torment the blinded Samson until he eventually topples the pillars of the state.

Now, Your Majesty, you are a shadow emperor! For you stand in the shadow of the autocratic barons and plutocratic munitions manufacturers. Be yourself: reveal yourself as an illustrious Christian by granting the people, whose servant you wish to be (forget your inscription in the Munich Golden Book: *regis voluntas suprema lex:* you shall atone for it willingly...), the freedom of their will and soul from a heart overflowing with love. Grant it freely.

Not as grace: as from a level of justice and cooperation equal to the people. Of mutual trust. Of brotherhood. What indescribable heavenly joy would pass through the lands if it were said: Wilhelm II. renounces the outdated, harmful, inhuman right to unilaterally decide on war and peace.

He requires the cooperation, the approval of the people for such crucial decisions concerning the welfare of the people. He no longer wishes to be the master, but the servant of the German soul. The army will henceforth swear allegiance to the name of the fatherland. For it is a people's army. Immediately, the House of Representatives and the Reichstag should convene to prepare the restructuring of the constitution: so that under the same, direct, and universal proportional electoral rights – where majorities can no longer be violated, minorities no longer suppressed – a parliamentary and democratically governed empire will emerge, in which ministers are appointed and supported by the people's will, and are accountable to the people, not to an individual.

For the German people have matured in years of unspeakable suffering and outgrown their infancy: they no longer need paternalism. They are fed up with it.

Your Majesty! Does not the feeling of boundless responsibility sometimes weigh heavily upon you in sleepless nights? How easy it would be to bear the burden if the people themselves helped you carry it, sharing in the responsibility because they participate in the government.

Your Majesty, you have it in your power to summon peace without delay. The peace of such a war cannot be concluded: between the freely elected and publicly accountable leaders of democratically governed nations, on one side, and between a single authoritative man, on the other, who is constitutionally the only one authorized to make peace, and who receives his power not directly from the people but from the supernatural, superhuman idea of divine right. The new Russian government and Wilson in America – the most peace-friendly of your enemies – they are merely waiting for you to walk the path of freedom for your people, which would enable them to hear the voice of that people and negotiate with its elected representatives.

For this is what matters: finding a basis where man can speak to man. Not: Prince to subject. Not: Lord to servant. Not: enemy to enemy anymore.

Republic is just a word: Wilson and Kerensky are not thinking about promoting it for Germany. They only want to make peace with a government accountable to the people: a peace that represents the will of the whole people.

The domestic political question in Germany - do you recognize this, Your Majesty! - is the most important one for achieving a near-term peace. Far more important than any probable or improbable victory in the West, which the German military leadership may still consider possible. For in a future world empire – there will only be an imperialism of humanity – military successes will no longer matter. The military age, in which wars could still be decided by weapons, is coming to an end. Today, it is no longer armies but nations that fight against each other.

More important than military power is economic power: cultural power.

Be the first prince to voluntarily renounce his fictitious rights and bow to the Areopagus of human rights. Your name will then be mentioned among the truly great in the new books of history, where the history of humanity will no longer be written in terms of coalitions, but in terms of the history of the human spirit. Then you will establish the people's kingdom of the Hohenzollerns on rock; whereas it is now only a cloud formation that, if you fail to recognize the times, will soon be vanished in the rising storm.

I am Your Majesty's most devoted Klabund

Part Seven:

An Appeal to Wilson

(Published on October 25, 1918 in the "New Zurich Newspaper")

Appeal to Wilson

Published on October 25, 1918 in the "New Zurich Newspaper"

Wilhelm II has not risen to meet the demands of his era. History will bypass him and march towards its goals. Now, Wilson's hour has come. The heaviest responsibility ever borne by a single individual now rests on his shoulders. It lies within his power to call heaven down upon the hell of the earth to transform people into angels, to summon eternal peace as a joyous present and an even more joyous future. Let him sweep away the clouds sent by the European continent to darken his brow and obscure his vision. The German people have risen; they are on the verge of casting off their clinking chains and stretching their eternally youthful limbs for the first time in newly won freedom. Wilson will have to muster all his intellectual and moral strength to prevent this people from being shackled anew, to thwart blind chauvinism and deaf vindictiveness from turning his best intentions into shame and disgrace. He must not let a misguided, but noble, people suffer and atone for what a ruthless tyrannical government has inflicted upon them and the world. He must move away from the standpoint of unconditional surrender, which his note of October 15th seems to demand. Such a stance is apt to drive a proud, undefeated people (for the people cannot be defeated: only states, only governments) into a desperate fight if they see that their opponent demands all guarantees while offering none in return. The submarine warfare must be halted immediately as one of the preconditions for an armistice. But will England, in turn, commit to lifting the hunger blockade? Should the German people lay down their arms and offer their exposed, defenseless chests to a terrible enemy, – an enemy who has not committed itself to cease hostilities and can raise his hand to strike a death blow at any moment? The clay idol of German autocracy has been toppled from its pedestal, and no power in the world will prevent its complete destruction. The German people are only half-awake, like a child rubbing the sleep from its eyes. Give them time to fully awaken: once their vision clears, they will hold a relentless reckoning with the guilty. When Wilson declared war on German militarism, he demanded violence against it: violence, violence to the utmost.

German militarism lies on the ground. Now the call must be for justice for the German people: justice, justice to the utmost! Wilson's lofty principles must be applied and realized with equal justice on all sides, or Germany and the world will perish. The hyenas of the battlefield are already stirring, and their hoarse howls shake the night.

Wilson insists on a referendum in Alsace-Lorraine and the provinces of the German Reich claimed by the Poles. He will not allow a German irredentism to flare up in the East instead of a Polish one, which would be no less powerful than the former. Is Wilson aware that in Danzig, claimed by the Poles, only two percent of the population are Poles – compared to ninety-eight percent Germans?

Wilson's domestic political demands align with those of the young German democracy.

The enemy of German democracy is Entente imperialism. – Will it find in Wilson the ally it has hoped for, one who will protect it against the execution that the followers of Clemenceau want to stage against the German people as if it were a criminal?

The German people are no better and no worse than other peoples.

The rejection of a far-reaching peace offer, extended in good faith, or the imposition of extreme armistice conditions will lead only to one outcome: the outbreak of proletarian revolution first in Germany, then throughout Europe. Indeed, "if the democratic bourgeoisie, most purely embodied in Wilson, fails to rise to the occasion, it will signify the open bankruptcy of the bourgeois-democratic ideal." It would prove powerless against imperialist-capitalist challenges and incapable of realizing its lofty ideals. The path would then be clear for proletarian democracy to dominate the world – to what end, whether good or bad, remains to be seen.

Part Eight:

Sermon of Repentance

(Written June 1917, published in *The White Sheets* 5 (1918),
Quarter July – September)

Sermon of Repentance

Written June 1917, published in *The White Sheets 5* (1918), Quarter July – September, pp. 106–108.

What have I done, that I sang you beautiful words and hung Aeolian harps into the wind? I am so weary of my being, so weary of the tulip bells and the green shepherd's flute... Repent! Repent! For the kingdom of hell has drawn near. Your hearts have become nests of serpents. Your eyes, murky puddles of the bloodiest vice. Your hands, once meant for loving embraces, grasp only empty air.

The ice sea has overflowed its shores. Erratic boulders crush the blooming garden. Comets drag fiery tails like mourning veils through the streets, and the city stands steep in flames. Strike your crumbling breast—once a divine cathedral, now a bony ruin overgrown with every kind of weed: hatred, malice, envy, fornication, lies, cowardice, arrogance. Cry out, roar, kneel in the filth of your own corpses; scream: I, a sinner. I, walking filth. Festering spit of a decayed dignitary.

Once blessed at the edge of the world; now slothful, sighing in the South, tear-stained in the scent of carnations—like a butterfly, its wings breathing softly on the orange-colored breasts of the fairest woman.

> The rain bleeds from my wound.
> The sun nails me to a fiery cross.
> I foam: a red sea. I cry out:
> I, the nameless, I, the dream—am guilty of this war.
> Each one: I. Millions of I's... are guilty, are guilty.
> The scourge of God explodes.

I know, I confess: to duty, to obligation, to truth, to admission. We must drum, blare, ring, whisper, wail our guilt into the world, so that we, the intellectuals, or at least those willing to strive for intellect, are no longer seen as mercenaries of a power-hungry idea, of the bandit's revolver. This war would never have become such a repulsive colossus had it not fed on certain festering abscesses of our own souls.

Tear your shirt open. Strike your breast. Confess: I, I am guilty. I will atone. Through word and deed. Through good words and even better deeds.

Let No One Think Themselves Too Low to Confess Their Guilt. No One Too High. We remain silent about the warriors of all nations who still exist today; one cannot appeal to their conscience, for they have none.

But you, who, like me, have long since awakened—awaken now from a dreadful dream that pressed upon you like a nightmare—confess, having so far remained silent out of false shame, that this dream was a deception, that you were fools (and some of you, who advocated war as war, were worse than fools) when you believed in the baptism of steel for the soul, which became a bloodbath; when you believed in the ideas of power, night, and bayonets, in war as an ethical reformer, in the German, French, or English cause, when you should have believed in the idea of humanity! Whether you defended your former opinion in writing or in speech makes no difference. You thought this way; it resonated in the chorus.

Renounce the frenzy of 1914! The resignation of 1915! The skepticism of 1916! Commit yourselves firmly to 1917! Rise up! To the new will of a new era! Leap from your passivity, like a long-drawn bow snapping into action: into accusation, repentance, and improvement. Our present position must be made clear—so that many more may step onto the platform with us. And let them be thousands, ten thousands—and more.

At the thought of another such war, the whole world crosses itself. Mothers collapse into unconsciousness and madness. Children turn into criminals.

There is a powerful party in Germany that dares to speak of the next war even as this one rages. Their talk is blasphemy, high treason against the spirit, an outrage against God and humanity.

The disorganization of the intellectuals also bears blame for this war. We are all guilty of this war—because we saw it coming and did nothing to stop it, and because, once it began, we allowed ourselves to be deceived about its true nature.

A raging protest against the war mentality and the war system throughout the world is urgently needed.

We will not remain silent. We will not become guilty of a second world war.

If we do not achieve our goal, then we have remained alive in vain—and would be better off lying, peacefully guarded, among the dead at Ypres and Kovno, at Gallipoli and Gorizia.

It is a matter of the nobility of the earth. The eternal Empress—Nature—has been dethroned. The original sin of abstract humanity—the rift between idea and reality—is spreading wide, threatening to tear the earth apart. This must not happen: for the intellectual to float in high clouds while, in reality, power is placed before justice, the bayonet before the pleading, uplifted hand. This must not happen: to hold and understand the good in principle, yet act wickedly, to be wicked. Until the idea of goodness is put into action, until we strive not merely to think good thoughts but to be good, we have no right to hope for the true victory—the victory of the sun, the moon, the blue mountains, and the red heart.

It is dreadful to see how small military successes immediately intoxicate nations with a superficial triumphal euphoria, drawing them away from what truly matters. As if it were of any ethical significance for ending the war to conquer a few thousand more square kilometers—at the price of a hundred thousand slaughtered human beasts. As if a military victory for one side could resolve the moral and legal questions at stake!

It is a sad sign of our militarized age that politicians take their directives from generals—when it should be the other way around. There is a lack of renewal in spirit and will, a lack of spiritualization in goals and means. To hell with Realpolitik! Let us practice the politics of ideas! Instead of allowing themselves to be driven by reality, as Realpolitik does, let people create reality through the power of ideas.

At the train station entrance, the Salvation Army soldier stands at his post, obedient to the general's command. Thousands run, race, sneak, stumble past him. He holds the War Cry in his hand.

> Silent, teeth clenched, the Salvation Army soldier waits.
> He may not cry out: God! Goodness! Justice!
> For the police have forbidden it.

Thus, it is our duty—the duty of those awakened from a murky dream, the contemplative, the prudent, no longer deceived (not: disillusioned), those uplifted to the spirit—despisers of power, of darkness, and of predatory frenzy—to stand at the gateway of the future, with the cry of peace, the call for eternal peace and a new humanity on our lips, soldiers in the army of the only true salvation.

Today, only one hears the call. Tomorrow, a dozen. The day after, thousands.

We must wait, teeth clenched.

One day, the mythical fire will descend and illuminate all those who still err and waver, enkindling them with understanding and inflaming them to decisive action.

Let laughter or vileness hail down upon us like a storm today—

Soldiers of the soul, we must stand firm. One day, the red flag, soaked in our blood, will flutter in the spring light.

You sybarites of blood—then be cursed!

You hypocrites, you unawakened, you sluggish—away, down into the cellars of eternal death with the toads!

But you, immortals, infinite ones, legionaries of the sacred army—rise, to the drums, to the flutes! Swing your weapons: the lily stalk, the willow branches still bearing catkins, the mimosa clusters, the sunflower.

God beckons! To us, his silver sons!

Part Nine:

Open Letter to the National Socialist Freedom Party of Germany

(From *The World Scene 21*, 1925)

Open Letter to the National Socialist Freedom Party of Germany

From *The World Scene 21*, 1925

Gentlemen!

You do me the honor of concerning yourselves with my humble person in a petition. A poem of mine, *The Three Holy Kings*, has, as you declare, offended your religious sentiments, and in response to this poem—like firing cannons at a sparrow—you call upon the state prosecutor. I must say, I am delighted that in these dull and dreary times, there are still people who can be deeply moved and shaken to their core by a poem, a work of art.

The very purpose of art is to stir and unsettle the soul. To stir, like the wind moves the blossom. To unsettle, like the storm churns the sea. While modern man is easily stimulated by all sorts of mechanical excitements—radio, racial hatred, boxing, theosophy, world war, and jazz—his inner self hardens and becomes encrusted, and it takes quite a lot for him to react to a work of art, whether positively or negatively, in an electric or explosive manner.

Thus, gentlemen of the reactionary faction, I am quite pleased by your reaction to my poem. However, as for the conclusions you choose to draw from your agitated state, I must first express my utter astonishment. You, gentlemen of the swastika, who advocate for the old Germanic Wodan cult, who believe paradise lies in Mecklenburg, and who have often openly mocked the feeble Christian faith—you, heathens who at most would have jurisdiction over blasphemy against Wodan—you, of all people, now rise in defense of the Christian God, whom you have always regarded with disdain, and lament blasphemy?

And what exactly is this supposed "blasphemy?" I fail to find any trace of blasphemy in the alleged offending poem. What I do find, however, is an astonishing ignorance—especially from those who consider themselves the most German of Germans—of German folk customs. The poem *The Three Holy Kings* does not, as you seem to believe, refer to the Three Wise Men from the East, but rather to a tradition practiced in many parts of Germany on Epiphany. On this day, three young men, dressed in caricatured costumes as the Three Kings, roam the villages, reciting rough and boisterous verses to the farmers in exchange for beer and schnapps. These verses are coarse, cheeky, witty—but blasphemous?

Dear God! I believe you must take great, divine joy in them. After all, you are not a National Socialist representative. You even created the devil because, in your eternal goodness, you felt uneasy and needed some kind of counterbalance. Yes, without the devil, you would hardly be conceivable, hardly imaginable. God and devil, day and night, man and woman—one is only truly visible through its opposite. Just as the National Socialist Freedom Party is necessary to prove that there are indeed intelligent people in the world.

I trust that these intelligent people—which hopefully include the state prosecutor—will make it clear to your party, if clarity is even possible for the dim-witted, that if a poem as rough yet harmless as *The Three Holy Kings* is to be considered blasphemous (what is God to one may be the devil to another), then Goethe's *Faust* positively overflows with blasphemy. In fact, Goethe himself wrote a poem about the Three Kings, titled *Epiphanias*, which perhaps should be included in your petition for blasphemy as well.

To sit beside Goethe on the defendant's bench—I would consider that a very special honor.

Yours sincerely,
Klabund

Postscript

To prevent further misunderstandings: I am not a Jew! I have no Jewish grandmother! I am not a "Mischling!" My name is not Krakauer, nor am I from Lemberg. My full legal name is simply Alfred Henschke. And my grandfather, as the tutor of the former Kaiser, did his very best to ensure that we lost the war—yet instead, we gained the National Socialist Freedom Party. Next time, hopefully, the outcome will be reversed.

Part Ten:

Letters to Brunhilde Heberle

Letters to Brunhilde Heberle

Klabund met Brunhilde Heberle in 1916, they married on June 8, 1918, and on October 30, 1918, Brunhilde, whom he calls Irene (which means peace), dies after giving birth prematurely in Locarno, Switzerland.

Rorschach, Cafe-Konditorei Baier, May 26, 1917

Dear Irene,

I have fixed my gaze on the ship that took you away from me: now it looks like a cloud, now like a swan, and now like a beautiful white mermaid, who raises her arms once more and, with the incomprehensible cry of a strange being on her lips, vanishes into the blue depths. – The lake is a silvery gray, smooth plate – one could serve fruits and God knows what else on it, it lies so metallically smooth – I can no longer see the ghost ship, the pirate ship. The ship was called St. Gotthard, and with the name of the ship, I sail the long route back that we were allowed to travel together: from Rorschach... via Zurich... the Gotthard to Locarno. The emerald lizards, your pretty sisters, once again walk fearfully and gracefully along my path. Crickets chirp, and nightingales incessantly sing... even during the day. Be that as it may – do you know the words of Lynceus, the watchman? – they were so beautiful... Always yours, Klabund

Locarno-Monti, after May 26, 1917

Saturday morning

My dear, dear girl,

I should not leave you for a minute, angel, I love you as I have never loved a woman before you – and I deprive myself of you to spend the whole night in the company of a silly fool, an awkward Portuguese, a German card cheat, whom you wouldn't even suspect, and have the whole night go by in misery. I came home at 6 a.m. and haven't slept yet due to all the excitement of smoking and playing cards. It should no longer comfort me that Dostoyevsky also played (and Casanova, who stole more skillfully, if I'm not mistaken), I give you my word of honor, that from today, I will not play poker for half a year. I am so disgusted by the game, I can't even begin to tell you.

By the way, you must be "avenged." By merit and worth. I lost about 500 francs, almost everything I had on me. And I already telegraphed home to my parents for money early this morning, which I have never done before. But otherwise, it is impossible for me to pay Pöschel even a centime. My poor, but honest father!

Be good and hug your Fred

From the cursed smoking all night long, my stomach is tightening like a swing in a bath and then loosening again. It is rather uncomfortable. "Donkey" is a compliment for me.

Unknown location, June 2, 1917

Dearest (I have but a fountain pen that works excellently),

Girl! That is, it sometimes works strangely: just now I twist it open, and it immediately squirts a huge stain onto my dearly beloved checkered suit. How do I remove this horrible mess? I'm hopeless. The sun casts swirls on my table (because I am writing in the garden), birds are chasing each other in the bushes, the lawn glows "wildly" – and I have a stain on my knightly jacket... But, like Jean Paul, I'm bouncing from one thing to the next. I wanted to write you a letter, through the enclosed returned letter, which I must send you by mail, a single unofficial letter: I love you a thousand times a thousand times a thousand: your most beautiful picture hangs above my bed, and I look at it day and night. If only I had the desired passport! This will be decided in the next few days! (Why: you may see from a printed matter that will reach you today: a newspaper...) – I received your letter. I am grateful to you for it. And happy. Joyful, as your father would telegraph. "Most joyful." You haven't received my second letter and the Hodler card yet? From now on, I will number my mailings to avoid such questions. This is No. 5 and 5a. (For 5 is "Mohammed," which I sent yesterday.) Be embraced, my slim beautiful girl, *bionda, o mia bionda, o biondinella d'amor!* to speak in Tessinese. Always yours, Fred

Unknown location, after June 2, 1917

Darling –

This is the 6th (!!) letter I'm writing to you in three days. If it depended on the number of letters, my love, then I love you 3 times more than you love me. By the way, have you received the identification papers? We're going to Lugano together. I think I will go to Lugano on the 25th – you expect me in Bellinzona – I've already bought a timetable today – I'm so longing for you – and we'll spend two days all alone in Lugano (if we have the money, the blessed money!) – But I want to love you, love you, love you, and I don't ask for a whole collegium of doctors. Enclosed is a letter I received today. You see how disgusting the slander is everywhere, whether in Davos or Locarno, working against me. It would never occur to me, even in my wildest dreams, to discredit the lady poetically. Be warmly embraced by your Fred

Unknown location, before June 21, 1917

Dear Irene,

You have surely received my letter from yesterday by now. Thank you for yours from Zurich. I just wanted to let you know that I will still be giving a reading in Zurich on the 23rd, which suits me best – at the Literary Club of the Hottingen Reading Circle. So, I would arrive in Locarno around the 25th.

Mrs. Visscher wrote a very kind and motherly letter to me in which she fully agrees with my views on Anny. One cannot be angry with her; one must always be good to her – she is like a sick child. Your dress arrived and was paid for.

Yesterday, I attended a hypnotic soirée. The mysterious gentleman with white hair named Krause performed astonishing experiments in mind control. Reiner, who offered himself as a subject (among others), was out in a quarter of a minute, despite resisting and sitting down on the chair with extreme skepticism. Send my regards to the Behns and a big hug from your Fred.

Zurich, June 21, 1917

Dearest girl,

A strong wind is blowing. Sunlight and shadow fall alternately on the letter I am writing in the garden under the trees. I'm not feeling well; I can hardly handle this intense heat. I might go to the high mountains for two weeks in the coming days, because I must be well when I come to you. Maybe I've overworked myself. I sleep little at night, and in the mornings, I feel half-dead. I have so much to do right now: poetry and politics – I'm quite worn out. A long novella (as long as *Mohammed*!). A play. Things are rather tumultuous in Switzerland as well: you've surely heard of the Hoffmann affair and the incidents in Geneva and Lugano, about which I briefly commented in the Bern Bund. All of which shows that, despite... or precisely because... Klabund is also a German. My eyes are closing; it's only half-past two in the afternoon. I started this letter to hug, caress, and kiss you. Come into my sleep, dearest girl!

Your Fred

Basel, December 31, 1917

Dear Irene,

Did you not remember that on the 24th the festival of love was celebrated? Humility suits us all better than pride, and that's why I'm writing you this letter: on the last day of a year that has brought our hearts so much joy and so much pain. I cannot and will not believe that those harsh words you gave me – so-called love, scorn for my "sacrifice," and that I am worse than the worst human being – came from your heart. You were confused and clouded when you wrote them, weren't you? And you were breathing in a poisonous atmosphere as far as my opinion was concerned. Because Thea and Hilde and Mrs. Poeschel, however sweet and kind they may otherwise be, are like dragons that spit poison at me. When I received your letter, I raged, and in this frenzy, I wrote a letter to your mother. I hope she understood it correctly. It is, after all, the way of mothers to understand, not only their own daughters but perhaps also other people's sons. Why didn't you stand firm against all accusations, as would have befitted your love: "I love him, I know him – everything else is half-truth or outright lies?" When have I ever humiliated you? Because I thought a marriage under the circumstances and from the standpoint you suggested would not be good? Reflect on this and, above all, get well. I don't want to drag myself around with a girl's corpse, even if I'm innocent, and only guilty, as we all are.

All the best for the new year: above all, health, peace, and clarity.

Yours, Klabund

Basel, after January 4, 1918

Dear Irene,

"– quarrelsome fishmonger's girl" – you know very well when I wrote this: it was when your first letter from Davos had driven me mad.

Everything will, everything must, be made right between us again. Let us merely meet again, see each other, hear each other – feel each other.

Did you receive *The Organ Grinder*? I sent it to you three days ago. Isn't it charming? The colored woodcuts?

Your Fred

Basel, before January 12, 1918

Dearest Irene,

Let these flowers be a sign to you of how much I am thinking of you! After a sleepless night, I am sending these lines with someone traveling to Davos. I beg you: believe in me and don't let yourself be unsettled by this brood of vipers who have separated us and fill me with unspeakable disgust! We must talk! A letter will follow. In haste.

Speak of me to no one anymore – except to your parents, whom I revere despite everything.

Basel, Grenzacherstrasse 13 – January 12, 1918

Dear Irene,

I will be leaving here next Sunday, as I will have finished my work by then. I have a question for you – I wouldn't call it a request: could I not meet you to talk before I return to Ticino? I believe it would be good for both of us to speak in person. I would come wherever you wish, to Davos or Klosters. You could travel early to Klosters and be back in Davos by evening. Zurich is too far for you, isn't it? Of course, this time you will want to undertake nothing without your parents. I understand that and ask you to send a telegram to Passau. In Davos, no one needs to know about it. Write to me by express mail to let me know what you think. In haste.

Always yours, Fred

Zurich, Confiserie Huguenin & Cie., January 16, 1918

Dear Irene,

Please, please: don't misunderstand me so easily. I didn't want to ask you because even asking seemed too much of a demand on you. I wanted to leave it entirely up to you to decide whether to meet me. Since you were just at Rüedi's, you are probably still offended–it's probably best that you rest for a few days first, and then we meet in Klosters. I'll telegraph you the day. – But one thing already seems most urgent to me: you must leave Stolzenfels, where you've been treated so cruelly. I only found out today just how much they tormented you, and I am stunned.

As for how much I am misunderstood in Davos: an overwhelming disgust and an unshakable contempt for people has taken root deeper and deeper within me. That they succeeded – even unknowingly, yes, even your parents, whom I deeply respect – in separating us, separating us so violently that heart's blood flows between us like between two fighters when we were once lovers – I will never, ever forgive the world for that. That I count people like the Poeschels among my enemies, people I once thought brave enough to stand up for me. Oh, what a disgrace. And that they parade around with a broken promise of marriage – Irene, you remember the first evening of our love – when we still addressed each other formally, and I said: I love you. But I will not seduce you. I will not make you a promise of marriage. I ask you, openly and honestly, and I beg you to answer openly and honestly: do you want to be mine? – That's what I said. And you raised your beautiful head and simply said: Yes. That shook me deeply at the time. – Should everything between us now be sullied? – If not for the peculiar circumstances in Basel with the Romang family, who are also embroiled in conflicts, I would offer you everything and anything now. As it is, I cannot, and I beg you, I implore you: leave Stolzenfels for a quiet boarding house.

When I telegraph, come to Klosters. Don't forget your papers (ID) just in case, and bring all the money you have with you. A trusted friend of mine will take you to Klosters by sleigh. I'll telegraph him to arrange for the sleigh; you only need to get in. I trust in your complete, absolute discretion with everyone. Otherwise, further communication between us will not be possible.

Yours, Fred

Please take good care of yourself!

Address: Basel, Grenzacherstr. 13 remains!

Unknown location, March 2, 1918

Dearest girl,

Tomorrow, I'll be with you again. Perhaps this letter will reach you before I do. That's why I'm writing it. It's just two o'clock now. And school has started next door. The boys and girls are screaming like storks and making such a racket that I can't even hear my own thoughts. But I can still think this much: that I love you. – The bread and fat ration cards (now comes the prose) have arrived. And (poetry) so has your letter. Letters from your mother and a friend also came, which I'm enclosing. Your mother's letter took 18 days (!) again. There's no longer any hope for normal communication. If they want to announce their departure, they'll have to do so three weeks in advance. To your dismay, you'll read in your mother's letter that yet another wardrobe, regulator clock, or who knows what has been purchased for a thousand marks. I sigh. How well we could have used that thousand marks ourselves. I saw a sunset-colored dress for you at the silk spinner's for 37 francs on sale! I saw a gray suit for myself for 67 francs! – Let it go... Nicholson will be getting his suits soon. They cost 135 francs. He'll send me a selection to choose from. That's the most sensible thing to do, isn't it? I'll also bring you something – but what, you don't know?!

Hugs for you, Your Fred

I wrote a letter and a poem to your mother.

Arosa, Restaurant Quellenhof, September 20, 1918

Darling,

Arosa is shrouded in fog, and it's raining. After days of glorious warmth (I mostly hiked naked, even down from the Weisshorn), an unpleasant, damp cold has set in. I keep hoping the fog will dissipate, and then I plan to walk via Langwies and the Strelapass to Davos. In Davos, I absolutely need to restore myself a bit – I need to get into different clothes and shoes and have the opportunity for a (externally...) proper "lifestyle." That's why I asked you to send me laundry, clothes, etc. Having to sit around in mountain gear for days in bad weather is not pleasant for me.

How have things been for you in the meantime? For you? The house? Hasimauz, Pio? Have you received all my cards, packages (apples! Gravensteiner wine!), poems, telegrams? Has the money arrived? I don't think I'll need any until I return. (I plan to be back with you by October 1st at the latest.) I might still climb a few mountains from Klosters or go from Seewis to the Schesaplana – provided the fresh snow doesn't persist. (Today, I wanted to go up the Rothorn, but the weather made it impossible.)

I find that Arosa hasn't changed much since my time here: a few hotels have been added, and the new Kurhaus – that's all. But the "life," as it's called here, is the same. The evening before last, I attended a small celebration at the Forest Sanatorium: held in honor of the art critic Meier-Graefe, who had previously given a talk on French art (German cultural propaganda...). He has a lot of intellectual skill and temperament, but personally, I find him rather unsympathetic. I visited Felix Moeschlin, the editor of Schweizerland (who published your little verses). I liked him very much. I also paid a visit to a charming yet brusque Prussian nobleman-turned-painter, Baron von Alvensleben, in his studio.

Now you have an idea of my stay in Arosa, which, incidentally, is quite boring today (yesterday, I was still at the Schwellisee).

Greet the newborn of the house, and be embraced with love and kissed on forehead, eyes and mouth by your Fred

Davos-Dorf, Sanatorium Davos-Dorf, September 22, 1918

Dearest Irene,

I was very alarmed by the letter that was included in the suitcase (I didn't get the letter from Chur). Please, please stay entirely calm: let Gina and Geka handle trips to town, and don't leave the garden or the house. Telegraph me if you feel worse – I would come to you immediately, of course.

You must have received my letter from Arosa by now. Regarding my telegram from Arosa, I hope you kept the envelope: it's outrageous that they didn't deliver it to you immediately. I'll lodge another complaint with the postmaster, as it was a so-called "D" telegram (urgent, with double postage! And the messenger was paid by me!). The postal service can really drive one mad.

Do you need money? You must write to me immediately – I'll find a way to get it to you. You mustn't lack anything!

It's pouring rain today. I just managed to get over the Strela Pass yesterday without getting wet. The bell is ringing for lunch now. I'm writing in haste so you'll have news from me again (the porter is heading to the train). Please write back to me immediately. Greet Frau Jung, the Süffels, the hare, Pio, and the cat.

And let your Fred give you a hug.

Davos-Dorf, Sanatorium Davos-Dorf, September 25, 1918

Darling,

Your letter from the 23rd hasn't exactly reassured me, and I'm very worried about you. You mustn't speak at all: it might be best if you traveled to Davos to consult Rüedi. I'm always thinking of you and am always with you. I love you and don't want to love anyone more than you.

On the 29th, I'll leave here, either on foot over the Bernardino Pass if the weather is good, or by train via Zurich if the weather is bad, since the Oberalp Post, the next connection from Chur to Göschenen, stops running as of September 21st.

The Levys are very kind to me. The weather is icy cold: I shiver half the day. The other half, I'm warm–because I'm thinking of you... Have you received my packages from Davos? The apples? The red chalk drawing? A Ukrainian painter has made a portrait of me. He saw me "with his soul." (If I look at myself with my own soul, I appear a bit different...)

I spoke with Thea. She invited me to dinner and, indirectly, passed along Poeschel's regret over their past behavior. People (all of Davos) are, of course, still talking about me, about us. And the wild stories outweigh the rest.

Your father writes very kindly. I'll respond to him from here. – I also saw the large *Brache* advertisement in the Börsenblatt. So it should appear soon. Have no new corrections for Villon arrived yet? Your book, Irene, has been widely discussed here and is also on display.

Hilde has written from Germany: she too has come around to a calmer and gentler view of our relationship and wishes the best for you and me.

As much as I may have accumulated wrongdoing and malice otherwise, here in Davos, in love, and toward all of you, I was right. And it's a small consolation to me that, little by little, everyone recognizes their own wrongs: Thea, Hilde, the Poeschels – you were the first, of course... and you surely won't regret your regret?

Be firmly embraced and kissed by your Fred

P.S. Aren't the illustrations in the art journal for my poems excellent?

Locarno-Monti, October 16, 1918

Good morning, darling,

Are you doing well? I send you my most heartfelt greetings and hurry to at least make my presence felt for breakfast. If only the weather would improve! How quickly I would run down to you in the morning!

Let yourself be embraced by your Fred.

I just read Wilson's reply. As the newspapers here put it, it truly is terrible: dreadful! It seems the world won't be spared the world revolution.

Locarno-Monti, October 23, 1918

Darling,

If at all possible, I'll send Gina to you this morning so I can quickly find out how you're doing. Don't hold the letter too close to yourself, and throw it away after you've read it. After all, one can't be sure whether it might carry infection. I'm so sorry I can't receive Mother today, but the doctor's wife, who is so kind in taking care of me, will go to the station. And there's already a bouquet of roses waiting for her in the living room. It's better if I stay in bed a little longer; the quicker it'll pass. I'll ask Franzoni to come up today and examine me. I'm so happy that you're doing so splendidly. Forgive my handwriting. The electrician is here right now; hopefully, everything will work. It's always such a complicated matter, which annoys me every time. (You know: the bouillon...)

Send my regards to the head and assistant nurses and give the little one a kiss from me (from a distance, so it doesn't catch any germs).

Give Gina any telegrams if there are any. I assume Mother will telegraph you. – Ceka will go.

A thousand hugs, kisses, held close to your heart, loved by your Fred

Please give Ceka the Hölderlin book you have with you!

Locarno-Monti, after October 23, 1918

Dearest Irene,

Just make sure the child doesn't catch a cold at the baptism! I don't care about anything else: whether a brown, black, or checkered cleric gives his blessing. Later, the child will know where it belongs. I understand that it's better for you and the child at the moment if it manifests itself as Catholic. But I already have your agreement to allow it to be re-baptized Protestant, Lutheran, etc., later according to its wishes. I regard the hospital baptism as an emergency baptism.

I'm glad you're making progress.

A thousand hugs, and send my regards to Mother.

Your Fred

Is it a monk from Madonna del Sasso baptizing the little one? I think that's quite charming.

Locarno-Monti, after October 23, 1918

Dearest Irene,

I am happy that things are steadily improving. The beautiful sun will also do its part: I can feel how much it benefits me as well. – I had to take Ettore Balli as my doctor; when I called for Franzoni, I was told he was ill himself. But this illness doesn't seem all that serious if he can still visit you in the hospital. Yesterday, a telegram arrived from my parents asking about you. Hugs, and best wishes for the baptism.

Your Fred

Locarno-Muralto, before October 30, 1918

Dearest Irene,

Always, always, I think of you! How much it pains me that I cannot see or speak with you, that I cannot hold your hand and touch your forehead! Oh, if only we could soon be together again, and if only you could make quick progress now. May God grant it. I am always so worried about you. – I am doing very well. I am now under excellent care, and I hope to be fully recovered in a few days.

A thousand hugs and kisses from your Fred.

Part Eleven:

Letters to Irene and Max Heberle

Dr. Max Heberle

Brunhilde and Irene Heberle

Letters to Irene and Max Heberle

Irene and Max Heberle are the parents of Brunhilde Heberle, whom Klabund married on June 8, 1918, and who passed away on October 30, 1918.

Zurich, Elite Hotel, October 3, 1916

Dear Mr. Heberle,

I would be very happy to do so. It would be best if you ask your wife to send me the poems intended for "Youth," so I can pass them along. I am only in Zurich for a few days and will soon return to Stolzenfels.

With the most devoted regards and recommendations to your wife,

I remain yours, Klabund

Davos-Dorf, Villa Stolzenfels, November 26, 1916

Dear Madam,

I take the liberty of informing you that "Youth" has accepted one of your most charming poems upon my recommendation. The payment will reach you in the coming days. I would be delighted if you remained in regular contact with "Youth." However, I would advise you not to send verses too frequently. Perhaps you might also try your hand at "short prose."

With the most sincere greetings, also to your husband, Your Klabund

Davos-Dorf, Villa Stolzenfels, January 3, 1917

Dear Mr. Heberle,

I warmly return your kind New Year's wishes. I hope I will soon have the opportunity to visit Passau. When that time comes, I shall take the liberty of seeking your advice, guidance, and support.

With the most sincere greetings,

Your Klabund

Telegram: Locarno-Monti, October 18, 1918

Irene was suddenly operated on during the night of the seventeenth and awoke with a healthy little Irene. Both are doing excellently. The happy parents,

Irene and Fred Klabund

Telegram to Irene Heberle – Locarno-Monti, October 18, 1918

Your immediate arrival to care for the child is absolutely necessary, otherwise the child's life is in danger as there is no wet nurse available.

Klabund

Locarno-Monti, October 19, 1918

Dear Father,

I would like to give you a faithful report about Irene's illness, which we are all suffering from so painfully, and I hope it will pass censorship immediately. (I've noticed that you haven't received two of my recent letters.)

Upon my return from Davos, I found Irene already feverish. I immediately consulted four doctors: a lung specialist, a gynecologist, and two surgeons. They unanimously agreed that Irene could not survive a normal birth in her condition. We decided on an operation to be performed by an expert, Dr. Hermann, in his private clinic in Lugano. Unfortunately, Irene's condition deteriorated to such an extent that I could no longer justify keeping her here in our solitude, either to you or to myself.

On Sunday, I drove her to the hospital by car. Here, against all expectations, labor began the night before last (in the seventh month). She had to be operated on immediately, at half past two in the morning, and a healthy little girl, whom we want to name Irene Fiete Anny Tony, was born.

Because the operation had to be executed so hastily, it wasn't possible to maintain the necessary two days of preoperative diet. Irene was operated on with a full bowel, which has still not emptied and is causing the high fever (over 104°F) that is now tormenting her. I have rented a room in a small hotel near the hospital and am constantly by her side. You must be assured that I am doing everything possible to ease her situation and lift her spirits. However, I find it absolutely imperative that her good mother comes immediately, not least for the child's sake.

I won't waste empty words on describing my own condition. You will feel in your own heart how it is with me. We are powerless against fate. May it be merciful to us!

Your Fred

Irene sends her regards to you! She is always thinking of you and finds it painful that she is unable to write to you herself.

Locarno-Monti, Villa Neugeboren, October 24, 1918

Dear Father,

I hope you have received my letter reporting on Irene's condition. I wrote that letter to you from bed, where I have now also been laid up, to make matters worse. I've been sick with the flu for three days, which significantly complicates our already complex situation.

I cannot visit Irene at all, and I can only communicate with your dear wife, who arrived yesterday, from a distance across the balcony. So, in these difficult hours, the two women are entirely without male support and guidance, entirely on their own.

The little one is thriving splendidly. However, it seemed to us that the best thing for both mother and child would be to separate them for now. Irene above all needs rest. Unfortunately, we've not yet managed to place the child anywhere. Neither a wet nurse nor a caregiver has been found, and the Zurich infant home had no one available to send. Our last hope now is the children's sanatorium in Ascona. One feels so powerless against the thousand snares of fate.

Irene herself is somewhat better, though of course very weak and drained.

I am sending you two of my publications: *Appeal to Wilson* and *The New Germany*. Perhaps you could acknowledge receipt. Sending you the warmest regards, Your Fred

P.S. The two publications, *The New Germany* and *Appeal to Wilson*, appeared in the *New Zurich Newspaper* on October 20, 1918.

Locarno-Muralto, Villa Maria, around October 28, 1918

Dear Mama,

The night before last, I had a very bad night; the fever rose above 104°F. Since I've been dragging myself around like this for eight days now, I thought it best to consider a quick and radical recovery, which wasn't so easily possible up there, as I had to do everything myself. The constant getting up has completely worn me out. – Since I've been here (a small private medical clinic), I already feel excellent due to the rest. The nurse taking care of me, a Frenchwoman, is very kind, and in a few days, everything will hopefully be better.

Today I called the hospital and inquired about Irene's condition. I'm quite depressed that there hasn't been any improvement since yesterday. Could you please be so kind, perhaps around midday and evening when you go to eat, to always call here and tell the nurse (she speaks German) exactly how Irene is doing? If there's anything urgent, of course, you'll call right away. How is it that such a sad autumn had to follow this somewhat beautiful summer! We always seem to pay dearly for our happiness...

Your sad Fred

Locarno-Muralto, before October 30, 1918

Dearest Mama,

Your phone messages today have filled me with such dreadful anxiety. I am therefore sending a messenger with this letter to the hospital and urgently request a short, clear answer. If the situation is very bad, I ask to be allowed to come for a few minutes. During that time, no nurses or others should be in the room. I could stand outside at the veranda door in the open air. I promise I won't infect anyone.

Your deeply distressed Fred

Locarno-Muralto, October 31, 1918

Dearest Father,

I no longer know where to turn in this world. I have no home anymore. The heart inside her is no longer beating. The earth, shaken by all its dreadful eruptions, could not bear such a high and sacred joy as ours: for it smiled and was always good. But the earth can only grin and snarl now. And even the gods above do not love it when humans bring heaven down to earth. So they tore us apart – granting us only one brief, blissful summer. That summer was the purest and richest fulfillment of my heart. I will not experience another like it. You knew what Irene was to me. But you never heard me speak to you about her. When you asked me about it during that unforgettable journey to the Bavona Valley – I faltered and could only utter a few gruff words. We Henschkes, as Nordic people, have always been deeply hesitant to speak to anyone but the beloved themselves about our love for them.

Today, now that this being no longer lives, my love must overflow. It surges boundlessly and searches for a channel in which to find rest. Irene was my wife, my beloved, my mother, my child – she was everything to me, but she was even more. I fled to her as the true and spiritual image of my soul's peace from a pestilential presence. She was the goddess of my finest verses. Only she could smile upon them and grant them their fulfillment.

Soon, the bells will toll for her funeral. I will not stand at her grave, for I am still lying here sick and wretched in bed. But even if I were well, I could not throw those three handfuls of earth onto her grave – for this earth is too dirty for her.

God will cast a handful of stars upon her, and the sun will darken.

Keep me in your hearts as your son. And if I don't know where to go – may I come to you? There, we can speak of Irene – the only joy we have left.

Your Fred

Locarno-Muralto, Villa Maria, November 2, 1918

Dearest Mother,

Your letters are placed before me. I read them over and over again, as they are the last that speak to me of Irene. The letter from the 29th, so full of hope; then the two brief lines, and the letter after the visit to the cemetery. Day and night, Irene is in my thoughts, and God knows how gladly I would die. Her last and most beautiful image is always with me: she holds a flower in her hand and smiles. And that smile (she could smile so divinely) will forever bring me to tears of joy.

Oh, certainly, one should be strong, strong like a man, but I cannot; I am utterly weak with grief. As soon as the nurse leaves, I weep. Sometimes I am full of resentment: did they do everything possible that last night to overcome her weakness? Her heart responded so strongly to alcohol – this I know from experience. Aside from the camphor injections, was champagne given to her? Such thoughts are childish, I know, yet in my despair, I grasp at every possibility: what if...?

That she could not leave me any final words, that her last smile was given to the priest – this tears my heart in two. I cannot open my eyes without them starting to bleed.

When I look out of this window, I see the church where we were married. From the other, I see the Madonna del Sasso and the Monti streets we so often walked together. One summer. Only one summer. It was, in climate and landscape, an unbelievably, even otherworldly beautiful summer – unlike any I have ever experienced and never will again. The more beautiful the summer became, the more passionately we loved each other. And we loved each other more and more deeply.

Such a love as ours, in such a summer, surely existed nowhere else in the world. Once, Irene was sleeping on the balcony. It was night, and only the stars shone. She said, "I think our happiness is too great. It will be taken from us. I am so afraid of that."

And it was taken from us. It is so hard to be the one left behind.

Think how long the blessing of togetherness has been granted to you: over twenty years of shared joy. And us? Only six months of purest happiness were given to us... and we were still so young, with an eternal youth of many years that could have blossomed before us.

> "Whoever wishes to see a living angel
> Must go to my wife.
> Whoever wishes to be in paradise
> Is invited to my home."

That is what I wrote this summer. Now, Irene speaks the last two lines from on high. Perhaps a kinder fate than before will soon allow me to follow her.

Greetings to Father, I send him my heartfelt thanks for his telegram, he will have received the letter by now, and let me give you a hug from

your Fred

Locarno-Muralto, November 7, 1918

Dear Mother,

Today I got up for an hour. I sat by the window, looking westward. It is raining. The mountains are shrouded in mist. I am entirely gray as well. Irene's picture is my joy. Day and night, I gaze at it again and again. When I do, I hear her breathing and see her smile.

In her presence, I wrote the "Lament for the Dead," which I will send to you once it is complete. The sonnet – the most beautiful, strictest, and hardest poetic form – shall pay her tribute. These poems will always stand closest to me among all my writings. Whether they are good or bad, they are the tears I wept for her. If you wish to have a copy made for yourselves and the child, perhaps on a typewriter, please make three or four additional copies for me. I would like my handwritten version returned; I want to place it on Irene's grave. I cannot write it again, and I don't want to give it to anyone here for transcription or sensation.

The rain will wash the verses from Irene's grave; the wind will scatter them and carry them to her.

Dearest Mother, in a week, I will be back up in Monti. I don't need to describe to you the emotions that flood my heart at the thought. For now, I have decided to stay here. Where else could I go? I will be equally lonely everywhere. The long winter evenings are already announcing themselves. I will sit alone in the dark,

like a child waiting for Christmas gifts. And I will wait for my gift.
Greet Father and receive my heartfelt love.
Your Fred

Locarno-Muralto, November 10, 1918
Dear Father,

Yesterday I went out for the first time, and my first visit was to Irene. It had rained for many days, so the wreaths and flowers were still fresh. She rests in the sunniest part of the inner cemetery wall – beside another Irene. The neighboring grave bears the same name. I thought: if it becomes possible later, we should bring Irene to Passau or Crossen, to our family burial site, and reinter her there. These Italian cemeteries, despite all their sunlight, feel so cold. They stack grave upon grave with little care, hardly bothering to raise a mound. The grave monuments are distressing to see: marble and tin in dreadful compositions. Wouldn't we rather have Irene near us? If she could have been buried in our garden in Monti, she would have rested in the earth of our happiness. I don't like seeing her so isolated among strangers. In any case, I plan to lease the grave for 30 years. I will fence it in and have it cared for by the gardener Schäppi. Once the situation stabilizes, we can make a final decision.

The work of my days is carving Irene's memorial. It will not be made of marble – only words and verses. But with all the strength of my heart and the power of my love, I will strive to make it worthy of her.

I am as shaken as on the first day of her death. My conscience wavers so much. When I look clearly into myself, I must confess: murderer. I killed her with my child. When I embraced her then, was it not the destructive instinct – so often suddenly flaring up like a sulfurous flame in human life – raging wickedly within me?

This is man's fate: that he cannot live without death. He dies – and kills.
Your unhappy Fred

Locarno-Muralto, November 10, 1918
Dear Mother,

I was just at Irene's grave again, and met two nurses from the hospital and the young girl who was sometimes with Irene. They told me about Irene's last hours, how she kept waiting, wondering if I might come, and how every time the door opened, she believed it was me.

My heart nearly stopped. Why wasn't I called that night? I wasn't so ill that I couldn't or shouldn't have come under those circumstances. It wasn't right that they only telephoned you, and then too late.

I will try to go on with life. But I am utterly broken. If I fail, I hope the few people who love me won't hold it against me.
Your Fred

Locarno-Monti, Villa Neugeboren, November 12, 1918

Dear Mother,

Today, I am sending you all of my manuscripts that belonged to Irene – for you and later for the child. Among them is an unpublished sequence of scenes that will especially interest you today: written in June 1917, reflecting so much of October 1918. The manuscripts are:

1) Eulenspiegel
2) Sleepwalkers
3) François Villon
4) The Harp Girl
5) The Front
6) Poems
7) Mohammed

I've written you many letters.

Your Fred

Locarno-Monti, Villa Neugeboren, November 14, 1918

Dear Father,

I have sent you at least ten letters and manuscripts, but have received no reply. Naturally, I am entirely in the dark about the postal situation in Bavaria, so I am sending this letter into the wind as well, hoping it will bring an echo.

I just returned from the stonemason. I have commissioned him to frame Irene's grave in granite and place a simple white marble plaque above her head. On it, there will only be her name, the two dates, and the first line of one of my sonnets. I could not bring myself to give her any other, time-bound name. "Irene:" it sounds of eternity, of eternal peace, and it should sing so through the spheres. Beneath the plaque, I am having a coffer mounted on a pedestal, and in it, I will place all my writings that wholly belonged to her: Irene, The Lifeline, The Elegy – and also Mother's beautiful book, which I read again these days with passionate emotion: *My Child.*

I also read all your letters to Irene, which you sent her in Switzerland, with a thousand emotions, and I thank you from the depths of my soul for bringing Irene into the world, for surrounding her with your warmth and ever-verdant love, for brightening her life. And most of all, I thank you for giving her to me with such trust.

The more deeply I grew together with Irene, just as trees entwine, the clearer and more unshakable it became to me that I held far more in my arms than just a dearly loved woman. (If only a wife had died, I'd grit my teeth and bear it...)

In Irene, after a lion's battle, I found what 99 out of 100 people on this earth never encounter: the mystical, the cosmic beloved. And because of that, I also found in her the paradisiacal muse: the most perfect bliss. When we were together, we had no further wishes, no desires—we had each other, and with that, the earth, and with that, heaven.

I remember the last 14 days before Irene went to the hospital: we could no longer surpass our love, and surely our senses had been sanctified and utterly transfigured, for Irene was no longer capable of physical love. I know how much I owe her: she transformed me as much as I transformed her. And if I ever find grace at the seraphic throne, it will be for her sake, not mine.

Give my regards to Mother, and be warmly greeted by
Your Fred

Locarno-Monti, November 17, 1918
Dear Mother,

It always calms me a little when I can speak with you. I don't even know if all my many letters, cards, and manuscripts–which I'm sure I've sent as often as days have passed since her death–have always reached you? Even after her death, I live off her kindness and foresight. The household brought her such joy, and she organized it so magnificently. I barely need to buy anything besides bread; Irene took care of everything else. For many months, there are supplies of potatoes, eggs, fruit, both preserved and fresh (apples and grapes), condensed milk, canned vegetables, meat preserves, jams, rice, flour, spreads (pâtés), and meat (tongue, bacon, smoked meat, and sausages).

It always feels as if she's handing everything to me across the table. Irene's pictures surround me: the one with the flower, the one with the cat (the Madonna with the flower, the Madonna with the cat), the one where she's sitting beneath the column in Mergoscia in the Verzasca Valley, and the little picture in the snow. I'm always speaking with her.

It's dreadful, waking up anew each day and having to face the day once again. Its gaze is so bright – it blinds me. I always want to remain in darkness. Sometimes, I leaf through Goethe or Hölderlin. Do you know this quatrain by Hölderlin? It feels as if it speaks directly from my soul:

> I've enjoyed the pleasures of this world.
> The hours of youth – oh, how long, how long they've passed!
> April and May and June are far away.
> I am nothing now. I no longer wish to live.

Your Fred
I wrote this in bed; forgive the pencil!

Locarno-Monti, November 24, 1918
Dear Mother,

When I think about what pains me most regarding the circumstances of Irene's death, it's always that I wasn't allowed to be with her in her last days or at least her final hours. Yesterday, I heard from Soffel (bit by bit, I learn more) that Franzoni came to see me on the evening of the 27th – when I had just gone to the Villa Maria – to speak with me about Irene and to tell me that there was no longer any hope. That day, I had such a peculiar feeling: when the carriage arrived to take me, I wanted to pay for it and stay rather than go to Villa Maria. Only after much deliberation did I go. If only I had followed my dark feeling! I would have spoken with Franzoni, and I could have been with her on the 28th. We would have had a whole day together. But Franzoni believed I was too unwell to hear the news. Their reasoning was, of course, entirely wrong: nothing affected me more than being so helpless and unprepared for what had happened. If only I had been able to speak to, hold, and kiss Irene, I would feel infinitely better. Perhaps her death in my arms would have redeemed me as well. Instead, I am now a wretched soul, hanging alone on the cross of my torment. I count every one of my days against the day of her death – and my own.

Your miserable Fred

A few nights ago, I had an apparition: I lay awake in bed when suddenly the entire room was filled with a storm wind that raged around me for seconds before subsiding. Then an icy, cold draft swept across my forehead. Simultaneously, I heard, quite faintly and very close (as if from within the wall, it seemed to me), a clock striking. It struck (I counted) eleven times. (I then checked my watch – it was half past two.)

Are you familiar with the book *On Life After Death* by Fechner (published by Insel)?

I was afraid to send the manuscript of "Lament" due to the current state of the postal service, but I've had it typed up here after all. It's already on its way to you. Given the uncertain state of things in Germany, which I view very pessimistically, it's impossible to determine when it might be published as a book. Perhaps it would be nice to have the sonnets privately printed and given as a keepsake for those who loved Irene. Two sonnets per page would make one sheet, and a print run of 100 copies might cost around 70 marks.

Locarno-Monti, November 26, 1918

But, dear Mother, I could have made it in time to see Irene once more, to hold her, to feel her – just read my last letter about Franzoni's visit. If I had had the memory of one last embrace, perhaps I could even have become joyful again. But the lightning struck me out of a clear sky. I was so unsuspecting – and then so helpless. Every day, I must fight anew for my life. It's now been a month since her death. Oh, how it has passed in tears. If I could ever calm myself, I would be calm. What do I want anymore? What can I do in this world?

At night, I have auditory hallucinations: it feels as if someone is chiseling at the wall to break through it. Sometimes, the house shudders faintly, like an earthquake. In the kitchen, plates and pans rattle. And amid it all, I hear two tones, minor, always the same, as if played on a cello. When I try to recall them during the day, I can no longer find them. Of course, these disturbances are merely the result of my shattered nerves. Irene has nothing to do with these confusions.

Sometimes I feel her blissfully, almost tangibly, within me: it's as if my pores open and absorb an indefinable essence that sends a shudder of bliss down my spine. When I die, I will dissolve into her, ascend, and be redeemed. If only it would be soon.

I fear the man chiseling at the wall at night might one day begin to chisel into my brain.

Today, I will visit the child. Warm regards to your husband, and a heartfelt embrace.

Your Fred

I'm sending you two rare booklets: in the second, a longer cycle of poems by me from 1915-16; in the first, a poem about a rabbit.

Locarno-Monti, November 28, 1918
Dear Mother,

Aren't you happy about how well our little one is doing? For the past eight days, it has been thriving; they switched its food, and since then (I could see for myself), it has been positively blooming and radiant. I am so relieved that yesterday was the first light day for me after returning from Ascona. I had become so pessimistic, and 14 days ago, when I was over there, no one knew what would become of the little one, and because of that uncertainty, I couldn't send you any news. But I wanted to give you good news.

What yesterday's visit also meant for me, you can imagine. The thought that Irene's sacrifice, her surrender to death, might have been in vain would have driven me to the brink of despair once again. And there have already been so many moments when I was half on the verge of crossing over myself.

Regarding the manuscripts from the first shipment, please don't misunderstand me. I didn't send them all to you because they were especially beautiful, but because I want them to be kept safe. Among them are some unpublished works, like *The Front* and *The Negro*, which will have value for the child in the future.

The *Lament for the Dead* rises above all these works like a white tower with a black flag flying. You must have received it by now. When you read it, Irene and I, and the unity we shared, will become vividly present to you in a special way.

Irene is entirely within me. I feel it more and more strongly. She inspires my thoughts and makes my forehead shine. Everything I do and think comes from her, from the awareness and the sacred conviction that our fates, our souls, can no longer be torn apart – neither here nor there.

Yours, always, Fred

Locarno-Monti, November 28, 1918
Dear Father,

At the end of your last letter, I noticed some material questions, and I will answer them here: The 1,500 marks = approximately 1,000 francs arrived safely.

Hospital (everything)	577.00
Dr. Franzoni	90.20
Coffin	184.00
Burial plot	60.00
Funeral a) carriage	79.50
b) priest, monks, bell ringing, etc.	270.00
Gardener (approx.)	50.00
Dr. Hermann (approx.)	20.00
Dr. Rusca (operation) (approx.)	300.00
Tombstone (granite and plaque) (approx.)	150.00
Total:	1480.00

The expenses thus amount to around 1,500 francs. Whether and how much you wish to contribute beyond the 1,000 francs you have already sent is entirely up to you.

Yesterday, I visited the child. I am delighted that it is doing so well. (I telegraphed you about this.)

The weather and the landscape here continue to enchant me. I haven't even turned on the heating yet. (Admittedly, this is partly due to laziness.)

Warm regards to you both,

Your Fred

Locarno-Monti, December 1, 1918

Dear Mother,

It has been eight days now since I last heard from you. I don't even know if you are reassured about the little one. I sent you a telegram and a detailed letter about it. Miss Mendwyler also wrote to you. I hope you received the *Lament for the Dead.*

I spend my days (and nights – often I don't sleep until five) pondering the wisdom of the "Old One" (Lao Tzu). "Mind" is his term for the highest being, for God. Were it not for him, and for the comfort I derive from Spinoza's Ethics and, cautiously sipped, some of Fechner's and du Prel's ideas, I might have already despaired.

This sense – this word to express it – is what keeps me alive. Reason proves to me that her soul is immortal, that my soul is immortal, and that one day we will both rest in the great Sense, or, in Christian terms, in God. God will one day be the bridal bed for our souls.

Even though my heart sometimes seems ready to burst with the pain of longing– especially when I look up at the starry sky during these magnificent autumn nights – I know that not only will we have each other again, but that we will one day be entirely one.

I am translating and clarifying Lao Tzu's teachings anew for myself. I want to write them down and send them to you. Perhaps I can even make you "disciples of the Tao." The mindset of the Tao, I believe, is the only one that can help humanity overcome these times. Especially Germans should embrace it entirely and understand that they will become victorious in the "Mind" as soon as they are truly "weak" and truly "gentle" (these are Taoist terms).

"Whoever fights with mind fights without hatred. Whoever seeks to defeat the enemy with mind does not wage war on him. This is the essence of peace. This is the way to serve and be served. This is how to become heavenly, as the ancestors envisioned."

Be embraced and send my regards to Irene's father.

Your Fred

P.S. In the November issue of *The Dame (No. 3)*, there is a picture of Irene.

Locarno-Monti, December 4, 1918

Dear Mother,

I have just returned from Irene's grave. It has been arranged so beautifully now, as simple and delicate as she was. A narrow stone border surrounds it, with three rows of boxwood shrubs inside. At the head, there is a pedestal. On the pedestal rests the casket with her books, and atop the casket, a bowl of moss adorned with the colorful branches of autumn: hawthorn, vine leaves, and ivy. Between the leaves, the inscription on the red and violet marble plaque reads:

IRENE

October 18, 1896 – October 30, 1918

No one knew you but God and me – Klabund

I know the inscription might seem a little arrogant, but you won't hold it against me, will you? I plan to have the grave photographed and will send you a picture. The other photos aren't ready yet, so I haven't been able to send them.

I sometimes play piano in the mornings now. Dr. Jung's wife left me the key. I've also resumed one of the first artistic activities of my childhood: composing. I've been working on "I must prepare everyone..." (the Dschinnistan song from *Hafiz*), *Dialogue* (*The Organ Grinder*), *The Sorceress*, and the little song of yours that ends with: "A God and a mother are your life's blessings."

Would you consider sending your songs to the publisher Reuß and Itta in Konstanz, the editor of Timebooks? They would be a lovely addition, and if I were you, I wouldn't lose courage with publishers either.

I'll send the books Father requested. It's possible I might travel to Zurich for a few days. The central library there has an unusually valuable Chinese-French book (side-by-side dual text) that I need to consult to deepen my understanding of Lao Tzu. I'm unsure whether they would send it here. The postal service in Monti has deteriorated again; train routes have been cut, and mail arrives only once a day.

Sending you all my heartfelt greetings,

Your Fred

Among the things Mrs. Drach is supposed to send is my small typewriter. It's probably covered in dust. Would you be so kind as to have it cleaned? By the way, is there a ban on exporting used typewriters?

Locarno-Monti, December 6, 1918

Dear Father,

I know you've taken an interest in such matters, so I want to share my recent "occult" experiences with you. I put "occult" in quotation marks not out of mockery, but to express my skepticism about the occult nature of these experiences – except for one I already described to Mother.

It happened when a cool mist passed over my forehead. I had the distinct feeling I was near death and called out to Irene! The winds and clouds dissolved. I also believe in Irene's inner presence (within me); she always announces herself with the same peculiar shiver in my body, sometimes even a momentary paralysis.

All other "manifestations," however, I consider products of my overstimulated and agitated brain. My strongest objection remains their foolishness, which makes them unlikely to be spiritual. There's the clattering of dishes in the kitchen, hammering on the house wall, and an incessant dull step – along with other muffled noises.

As a conscientious observer, I've measured my pulse to find a correlation but failed. Music of various kinds also sounds, and if I fall asleep (which often doesn't happen until 5), something always wakes me with a sense of dread at precisely midnight. Then, something seems to "call me back to life."

Hallucinations, like those I had at 17, are now rare and faint – just faint veils or airy visions in the dark. The strangest vision occurred twice: the room was lit, but it suddenly dimmed, though the light burned steadily. Twice, something invisible brushed against my bed's wall (in light).

Lastly, something you might find intriguing: the house here has a reputation for being haunted. It's built on the foundations of another house. Many people from Ascona, for example, refuse to enter. I haven't discovered why.

While walking down to Locarno, there's a shortcut past a brook and a bridge. Three acquaintances have encountered the same apparition there at night: a white, woman-like figure with a long train seated on the bridge stone. One of them, a woman, reportedly fainted into Mr. Soffel's arms out of fright. I've passed the spot at night twice recently but saw nothing.

Warm regards,

Your Fred

P.S. Today, another bill arrived: 90.40 francs for the pharmacy.

The most important scientific task for occult studies would be a systematic examination and translation of the vast Chinese occult literature. The Chinese have been spiritualists for millennia. They have produced a so-called psychographic literature for thousands of years. But, sadly, spiritualists often understand everything except Chinese...

Locarno-Monti, December 6, 1918

Dear Mother,

A dark wave is washing over me again, and I must fight not to sink. Ten days ago, when I visited the child's resting place, the sunset eased my heart for the first time in a while. Now, the weight has returned. The clear blue sky feels like an iron plate pressing down on me, and under the stars' fire, I begin to crackle like kindling.

Please don't tell me more about Irene's final days – I fear it will drive me mad. You're probably right: I was still a boy not long ago. But this boyishness has carried me across a thousand chasms. Otherwise, the life I've lived so passionately would have long since broken me or consumed me from within.

Is it arrogance to say that I came to Irene just as she came to me? I believe so, despite everything. Your boldest dreams couldn't imagine the adventures I've survived intact –especially my soul. If I hadn't known hundreds of women, I wouldn't have been able to appreciate Irene as I do. I measure them all by her standards.

Imagine this: the forest is still burning! And with it, my heart burns anew. Kind words won't douse these flames – only God's rain or a flood could. The world seems ripe for such a deluge.

I can't leave Irene's grave yet. Each walk, retracing her steps, pains me, but this pain is my only solace.

Your Fred

Regarding the *Sonnets*, I've inquired with several publishers about when they could be released. I'm unsure about the current state of publishing. Reiß would print them, of course, but the question is when.

Locarno Monti, December 9, 1918

Dear Father,

Yesterday I was in Ascona. I visited the child again and found it very lively. In the evening, in a smoke-filled osteria, I had a (very interesting) conversation with a friend of Lenin and Zinoviev. We sat by the fireplace, where logs were burning, and our thoughts seemed to ignite as well; yet, I felt as though only my outer, superficial self was speaking. It was as if I were standing behind my chair, looking over my shoulder and listening with a certain tender indulgence to what "the other" (namely me...) was saying.

I sent you Lenin's writings, among others. Hopefully, you've received them. I committed a certain stupidity: when I returned to Monti, feeling a need for "cleansing" and "closure," I burned a huge amount of manuscripts and papers, including the private dispatches from the Russian Soviet mission in Bern. I should have saved them for you – if only for their curiosity value. We've already spoken in person about how the entire rest of the world is intent on smearing the Bolsheviks as darkly as possible. I find it outrageous that German revolutionary troops, together with their own executioners, the Allies, are advancing from Ukraine against the Bolsheviks, as demonstrated by a decree from General Denikin. In doing so, they make themselves complicit in the atrocious barbarities perpetrated by the Allies in Russia. (They have, medievally, declared the Bolsheviks out-laws and have already hanged them by the hundreds. What this may mean for the western proletariat remains to be seen. It will not be forgotten; and should the western proletariat ever rise, it will summarily "hang" all the bourgeoisie.) The times are as wild as the civil wars of the Middle Ages: the Peasants' Wars, the religious wars. (What "religion" was then – "Catholicism and Protestantism" – is now "democracy" and "Bolshevism.")

As I walked home that night, shooting stars fell, and what else could I wish for but death? What can I, a poor, miserable human being, do to help others? If Irene were still alive, I would certainly have been in Germany long ago. But I cannot fly: my wings always collapse. The same passion with which I once clung to life I now bring to death. And I can almost understand how a gentle person like Zinoviev became a mass murderer and had the bourgeoisie shot by the hundreds. Did I need pain to mature? What I needed was the happiness I had in the summer; never have I thought and worked so easily as during that summer.
Your Fred

I am sending you a copy of the Russian constitution today. This is the only basis on which the Bolsheviks should be attacked. It is their Achilles' heel.

The German mark is at 58 (!). I need 500 francs a month, which is 1,100 marks!!

Locarno-Monti, December 11, 1918
Dear Mother,

Today, I sent you two photos: one of the child and one of the grave. Your verses are here; they continue to sing within me. We share the same tone. The heartstring in both of us has snapped. I am tired and completely drained; my hands tremble as I write this. Six weeks of ecstatic exertion are taking their toll physically. The "body" can no longer keep up. For four days now, I haven't been able to think at all. I am just tired—dead tired. My work on Lao Tzu has stalled midway. And precisely when I received an extremely valuable book: a Chinese-French edition of the Tao Te Ching, with the Chinese text alongside a French translation. Here I have the source I've been seeking, yet I sit before it, weak and overexhausted, like a wanderer who has traveled too far. The spring flows by, but I am too weary to drink.

I cannot comprehend your optimism. Be thankful you still have Eisner. Revo-lutions always tend to radicalize. Would you prefer Mühsam instead of Eisner?

German money is plummeting due to the coups in Berlin; even the leading German banks in Switzerland have had their credit revoked. This shows that faith in any quick stabilization of German conditions has vanished. Ten days ago, the value of German money was 69; today, it is 52.50! Should the Entente's demand for the surrender of Germany's gold reserves be implemented, German money will be virtually worthless (since its value is based on gold backing). I fear it will drop to 30. What I would do then is a real puzzle to me. Things are already precarious now, as I have countless bills – over 1,100 francs – still unpaid, despite living as sparingly as possible. (1,100 francs is about 2,500 marks!) I calculated everything today: 6,000 marks! That's what the six weeks cost for the two of us!

Today, I had a heated argument with a well-known German Bolshevik, a supporter of Liebknecht. He will soon appear in Germany. It is absurd that just as Lenin, according to recent reports, is moving closer to the Mensheviks (moderate socialists), Liebknecht might take offense at him. You should at least familiarize yourselves with the possibility of a dictatorship of the proletariat!

Your Fredi

Enclosed: 8 photos.

Locarno-Monti, Sunday, December 15, 1918

Dear Mother and Father,

What more can I do to convince myself of the necessity of preserving my life? Verses are only frozen tears, and to me, they are like momentary intoxicants. I might as well take opium or morphine. Last night, I lay awake until half-past five again. An idea and a feeling for a drama came to me, and I worked on it for six and a half hours straight. Naturally, I could hardly sleep afterward. I tossed and turned until nine and then drank strong coffee. The short one-act drama, which I finished writing this morning, is, of course, about Irene and me. It is called *The Gravedigger*. The setting is a cemetery on an autumn afternoon. The characters are: the old gravedigger, the young gravedigger, the young gentleman, and a few pallbearers. I'll have it copied and will send it to you right away. I intend to dedicate it to you if that would please you (though "pleasure" is a poorly chosen word when everything speaks of death). I'll also send it to the 3 Masks publishing house. Perhaps it can be performed alongside a one-act play by Strindberg or Hofmannsthal. It's in verse, and I've incorporated the elegy for Irene into it.

The Soffels are very kind; they cook for me. I hide my state of mind as best I can because I dislike sentimentality. I am sorry to hear that your wife is also down with the flu. I hope you are fully recovered, dear Mother, by the time this letter reaches you. I would gladly take it upon myself to bear your flu – and all the world's flu's – so I wouldn't have to torment my mind and heart with anything else.

I plan to go to Lugano for two days to attempt a change of air and mood. These days, I often think of Cecile's ecstatic visions, where her "God" enraptured her. I too am driven to a frenzy every day, though not by a God, but by a goddess. Spirit and Eros live close together and are one in their highest sublimation. But since, alas, we are still plagued by a body, the impossibility of complete dissolution is a constant torment.

Have you received the newspapers, Bolshevik brochures, etc.? Does censorship still exist in Germany? Have the photos of the child and the grave arrived?

317

With heartfelt greetings,
Your Fredi

Locarno-Monti, December 18, 1918
Dear Mother,

The so-called life is approaching me. Should I follow its not very inviting call? A large Swiss publishing house has asked me to take on the publication of a larger bibliographical catalog, which is to be based on an entirely new foundation: only books with a certain human/political/ethical direction are to be included, books that point toward the "new era." This would involve a lot of work, months of it, but it could be a cultural achievement. Of course, I am pleased that I was thought of, as it shows that I am regarded as somehow important. But I, myself, can only accept this (the feeling of importance...) with all sorts of sophistry, I feel so unimportant – a glance from Irene would be more important to me than ten thousand cultural catalogs. Yes: such a heretic, such a believer am I.

Now Christmas is approaching. We will roast a goose, but that will be the only festive thing. I will go out into the night, as I do every evening, and talk with the moon and the stars. Every night, I go over to Orselina or down the road to Locarno.
Yours, Fredi

Lugano, December 19, 1918
Dear Mother,

I have now gone to Lugano. I could have spared myself the trip. One cannot run away from oneself. I am returning tomorrow. It was pointless and purposeless. It is cold here. And there is snow on the Generoso.

May I recommend two small books for Christmas? Both were published in the Inselbücherei: Fechner, *On Life After Death*, and Meister Eckhart's *Book of Divine Consolation.*

I am trying to console myself with them. I have squandered and lost this life – without really knowing it, like a child playing ball and throwing it too high. There it lies on the roof, how is the child to get it? Yours, Fred

Locarno-Monti, December 24, 1918
Dear Mother, dear Father,

It is Christmas Eve, I have just come from Irene's grave. The basket is now filled with colorful greenery. Between the boxwood, there are small branches with red berries, and in front of the casket, there is a large wreath of yellow roses.

It is beginning to rain outside. I am sitting here in the Swizzero – the billiard balls are clinking. The Italians are shouting, and I don't know what to think so as not to shout myself – but in a way different from their cheerfulness and laughter. So reluctantly, I let myself be drawn into life: all kinds of correspondence from political and artistic directions have come to me in the meantime. Whether I would like to participate in a conference in Geneva. Whether I would like to join the political council of the workers there, and whether I would like to inaugurate this. If I do not avoid the various businesses and ideas, I would probably have to go to Germany in February. But I don't want to go into the unknown. Only if positive work is possible (both for me and in general).

I had a meeting in Lugano, during which I wrote to the councils in Munich, Dresden, Mannheim, where I have connections. I believe, apart from all questions of guilt and completely disregarding Entente imperialism: everything should be done to support Wilson. Unfortunately, this has not been recognized by the "government" in Berlin, which one can only put in quotation marks. What a logical short circuit to make Count Brockdorff the Minister of Foreign Affairs! One should form a provisional peace commission from the "Wilson people" until the National Assembly, people who have Wilson's trust and against whom the Entente can find no objections. (Note: the Entente will not negotiate with a purely socialist commission.) I heard from a well-informed source that Wilson is just waiting for such a commission. Only unencumbered people are possible in it: from the diplomats: Lichnowsky, Schlieben; from the bourgeois: Dr. Muehlon, Prof. Foerster, Prof. Nicolai, also Harden and Gerlach; from the socialists: Eisner, Dittmann, Bernstein; from the intellectuals: Heinrich Mann. These are all, aside from the sympathy America has for them, also good Germans.

What do you think of this suggestion? But you are probably an opponent of Eisner?

– I of course agree with your suggestion that you take on a third of the child. Both of you are embraced by your Fred

Locarno-Monti, December 29, 1918
Dear Mother, dear Father,

I sincerely thank you for your Christmas gifts. The picture did me so much good. At that time, everything was still a dream, something that was later to become reality. The eyes beautifully veiled and dreamy. I thank God that I was allowed to lift the veil: in all her last pictures, the eyes shine so clearly and transcendentally, so fulfilled. In this way, I was able to carve a little bit of her statue in the good.

The article "To a Political Poet" has brought me all sorts of attacks. It has also been misunderstood in some parts. In a certain sense, I myself am "a political poet." What I was railing against was only that extreme view that, favored by the Revolution, rises up: as if only the thesis, the appeal, the call (in whatever poetic form: e.g., Hasenclever's "Son," Rubiner's writings, Becher's poems, etc.) is poetry. Everything else is "Tandaradei." Despite all the pretended spirituality, this programmatic narrowing of poetry is related to the naturalistic program of the 80s and, as a narrowing, should be fought against.

What do you think of Berlin? This development was as certain as $2 \times 2 = 4$. For the whole government under Scheidemann etc. was, from the beginning, a product of fear without any idea or energy.

I have tried to speak several times (in the *Berlin Daily* for example), but the German press as an expression of public opinion has a deathly fear of any radicalism of thought. I have tried to present my view in the sense of Lao Tzu: but they don't want to hear that. The confirmation of my ideas unfortunately always comes quicker than I myself have to fear.

How is it with a residence permit in Passau for me? (I read that one needs it in Bavaria now.) I would like to come over in February and, if possible, do some readings here and there.

Provided that I am not on the blacklist... of the new government by then. This farce could still happen. If a cabinet of Liebknecht – Ledebour comes to power, which seems quite certain, then my most intimate enemy, Franz Pfemfert, will certainly be part of it. (He recently attacked me in a whole column.) I will send father the latest counterpapers against Bolshevism: Kossowski, a Russian socialist, is their author; Greulich, the chairman of the Swiss Social Democracy, wrote the preface. Have you read the great discussion about Bolshevism in the Bunde "New Fatherland" Berlin? Greiling (the author of *J'accuse*), Nicolai, Pfemfert, Ströbel spoke. When a socialist who had just returned from Russia attacked Bolshevism and wanted to speak, they were shouted down. This is the political struggle in Germany under this sign. Whoever has the loudest voice has the better opinion. (By the way: you know this already: I don't lightly judge Bolshevism, as so many do. But one can only fight it "from the inside." It is very strong as a thought.)

Warmly yours, Fred

Locarno-Monti, December 31, 1918

Dear Mother, dear Father,

For the past few days, I've been sleeping like a dead person until noon – only to wake up again. I am moving these days: to Soffe's living room with the two balconies. I no longer need a kitchen, and what should I do with three rooms? I only live in one. Also, I save half the rent, which is something, especially since I want to keep my apartment in Monti permanently, even if I return to Germany. I want to spend a few months a year where I was blissful.

I have not heard from you for a long time. I wrote and sent you a lot. If Reiß allows it, I will have the *Sonnets for Irene* published in a special edition by the Rarität Kiel publishing house. The copy will cost 2 marks, and you can get the few copies you need much cheaper than if I had printed them at your expense.

I visited the child yesterday. An old woman was sitting by the cradle, looking at the small growing being with a face wrinkled and weathered. Upstairs, on the first floor, her husband, an old man, was dying. She then brought a few flowers from the garden and took them upstairs. When you are that old, death only brings comfort and is taken for granted. I hate him and still bear a grudge against him.

Today is New Year's Eve – the last day of a year that has made me the happiest and unhappiest of all people. I think of a word from the young Goethe: (I quote only approximately from memory:) "Give me, God, all the joys, the infinite ones, all the sorrows, the infinite ones, completely..."

The year has given me much in poetry: the completion of *Bracke* in January, *Silvia* in spring, *The Harp Girl*, the work on Hölderlin and Lao Tzu in the summer, and in the winter: *The Lament, The Gravedigger, Hafiz*, and a small volume of ballads (Lao Tzu – Francis – Montezuma, etc.), which you have not yet seen. But everything, everything is little compared to one of her moments and is worth nothing when measured by her value. Her last picture is the one with the flower, of which I sent you the enlargement. The other, which you wish, I will send you later. Warmly embraced, your Fred

Locarno-Monti, January 2, 1919

Dear Parents,

I kept Irene's linen, clothes, stockings and shoes, everything that is still in good condition for my grandmother and her granddaughter, and sent only a few items like the red jacket and a pair of shoes to Vienna: the shortage of raw materials will continue for a long time, you will need them. If you come here in the summer, which I hope you will, you can take them with you.

Did I already tell you that I moved? I have taken Soffe's room with the huge two balconies: the sun burns in there like a torch that is close by. I am so glad for the child that we have such a warm winter. She is doing well; yesterday I was with her, she has large blue eyes like Delft porcelain plates, and her hair is now reddish-brown like a deer's. It will probably turn blonde. The sister told me you suggested something about nursing milk. She spoke with the doctor: he thinks either/or. He considers a mixture dangerous for digestion. I think it will be best to leave the child with the sister until spring and perhaps give it to the nurse for a few months in summer, before you take it.

It hurt me to tear apart Irene's small work on our home. Now the walls upstairs are bare and cold, as they were when she arrived. I find it so hard to manage in the material, and if Soffel, Mendwyler, and three "Migratory birds" hadn't taken care of everything, I wouldn't have moved at all. But now: where I am now: I will never move out. And when I travel to Germany, as I hope in February, I will keep the apartment. I will still send you brochures about Bolshevism, etc. Please keep them for me: they are often so hard to come by because Switzerland has also banned them at the moment.

Radek is said to be in Berlin? One must distinguish between Bolshevik ideas and Bolshevik methods: I am totally opposed to the latter. The former is marching through the whole world. Even Werfel has already become a Red Guard...

If only there were a spark of spirit, energy, or purpose in bourgeois democracy! None of it. You would be very interested in a book because it is probably written entirely in your spirit: it is based on your standpoint–that human nature cannot be changed. It is by an American millionaire – who almost becomes a Bolshevist! It is called *John Kay, The World Alliance*, published by [gap in the text] and was the last work (translation) of Countess Reventlow.

Both of you are warmly embraced by your Fred

An almanac has been published by Reiß (*The Decade*) that will interest you. It costs, I think, 2 marks.

The considerations of the masses are indeed the following: the old economic order gave us war and chaos. It can't get any worse with the attempt to establish a new economic order.

Locarno-Monti, January 6, 1919
Dear Mother,

Yesterday and today were such painful days; I was only half alive. Last evening, I had everything arranged, I thought, now it's done, now I want to do it. The revolver lay on the nightstand, next to it a glass, filled with... water. On the pillows in the bed before me lay her picture, I held her letters in my hand, and the small bundle of blonde hair. Then I cried. And then my courage was gone, for I didn't want to pass over in despair, but calmly, proudly, and blissfully. I don't toy with the thought; I think it over again and again. And I think that it might be right to pass over with will and knowledge: when the transcendent subject lets the realization shine in us that we can no longer progress on Earth. That our time here is fulfilled. I am convinced of this, that no one escapes their fate, i.e., that one cannot escape any duty through death. But what earthly duties do I still have that should not yield to my heavenly duties? I cannot replace the mother for our little one: you must do that. And will I be able to write better books, manifest myself nobler than before? A child of fortune once – now I am nothing but a child of death. I am only "ash in the wind...." I want to reverse Spinoza's saying, "Virtue is happiness:" happiness makes one virtuous. I felt it, how good I became in our happiness. Should suffering make me bad again?
Fred

Monti della Trinità, January 9, 1919
Dear Parents,

I think my last letter was quite childish, I regret today that I sent it. I haven't heard from you in nearly two weeks. Your Christmas letter was the last news. I sent you many letters, manuscripts (*Gravediggers, Ballads*, etc.), newspapers, and brochures. Could you send me some issues of Eisner's *The New Journal*? And whatever other new publications come out, just some sample issues for review. – I'm going to the little one today. The sun is shining again today, the rain is over. A few days ago, I thought I had to lie down again. That's over now.
Hugs from your Fred

Locarno-Monti, January 10, 1919
Dear Father,

A few words about Bolshevism:

There is a lot of mysticism in the idea: early Christianity wants to realize itself: as in the time of the Peasants' War: "we, the poor and the wretched, are called and chosen." Sermon on the Mount: Blessed are the poor and the poorest, for the kingdom of heaven is theirs... This kingdom of heaven, they want to bring down to Earth in their own way, whereby the mysticism then dissolves into naturalism, namely: the angels become prostitutes, and God... a people's commissar... In any case, one cannot dismiss the movement from above, as the bourgeois press likes to do. Its practical goals might be achievable if one were to learn from Lenin. That is, two things are absolutely necessary, or else the German Revolution will die like the Russian one: strict compulsory labor for the workers (not just like in Russia for the bourgeois), and secondly: preservation and increase of capital (because how should the workers live later, if they live off the interest of capital, as happened and is happening in Upper Silesia, etc.), and the destruction of capitalism. That is two things. And the identification of capital and capitalism was Lenin's gigantic mistake. Now he realizes it – too late. The Ultras are supposed to have already arrested him for – counterrevolution. Lenin a reactionary!!! That is how far madness, hunger, and stupidity have taken people!

Please greet Mother. She wants to send me one or two corrected copies of her entire poetry collection to Irene: I want to get in touch with a few publishers. I don't know Schulz's *Euler*, but if he wants to publish the book without you having to pay anything, that could be discussed.

Warmly, your Fred

I sent a letter to my friend Kaufmann in Munich, asking him to send it to you for review. Did you receive it?

Locarno, Confiserie & Patisserie E. Scheurer, January 15, 1919

Dear Mother, dear Father,

I am writing to you with a heavy heart. I was just with the little one. She is not doing well at all. There has been a sudden change in the weather, and it has not been good for her. The doctor has been here several times. He believes that there is nothing wrong with her lungs, heart, etc.; the temperature has affected her digestive organs. She is digesting poorly and is reluctant to take what is given to her: milk, tea, porridge, I don't know what else. I have agreed that if the doctor thinks it necessary and possible, she should be given a wet nurse immediately. That is: she cannot be given to just any wet nurse, because she requires all possible medical supervision and care, which the local wet nurses are not familiar with; a nurse would need to be brought into the house. The costs would naturally amount to about three times the current amount, and I could not bear it alone. I took it for granted that I had your approval when I authorized the sister to do whatever the doctor deemed necessary. We want to do everything to keep the little one. The thought that Irene's sacrifice might be in vain in this life is horrifying and enough to tear me apart and rob me of my spirit. And just eight days ago, the child was doing so wonderfully! She was already laughing.

The trip to Ascona has made me so tired again. I passed by the cemetery on my way back. I wanted to ask Irene to leave her child with us – because what earthly future is left for us? – but the cemetery gate was closed, and I stood outside in front of the iron bars, as if I was in a prison.

Yours, Fred

Locarno-Monti, January 16, 1919

Dear Father,

I sent you all the Bolshevik literature I had. Since some of it is banned, and some is no longer available at all, I ask you to keep it for me: I intend, as soon as I have some peace, to write a small "Psychology of Bolshevism" and will need these writings for it. Please confirm their receipt. I sent you:

1) Lenin and Trotsky, War and Revolution
2) Trotsky, From the October Revolution to the Brest-Litovsk Peace
3) Trotsky, Work and Discipline will Save Soviet Power
4) Lenin, The Struggle for Bread
5) Lenin, The Struggle for Soviet Power
6) Viator, The External Situation of Russia
7) Tchitcherin, The Red and White Terror
8) Kossowski, On Bolshevism
9) Burzew, Damn You Bolsheviks
10) Experiences of Russian Swiss in Russia

Since the Soviet mission was expelled from Bern, its publisher (Promachos) has ceased operations. So, the books have quickly gained not only practical, but also bibliophilic value. I now send you Kropotkin's anarcho-communist program (he is said to have been murdered by the Bolsheviks); he is even further left than the Bolsheviks, as far as I can judge so far.

Lenin's last cohesive work, a whole book containing his system: "State and Revolution," was just announced when the Bern Mission had to leave. It would have been the most interesting: Lenin has shifted rightward over the course of the year. (A natural historical necessity: every government gradually becomes conservative.) – It's a pity I wasn't at the meeting where Unterleitner spoke. I read your comments with great interest... perhaps I would have spoken as well. (Probably, I would have spoken too abstractly for the audience.) – By the way, the *Spartacus Program* has been printed with counterarguments by Hermann Bousset's publishing house, Reading Youth Verlag, Berlin S.W. 61.

Your help with my book catalog is much appreciated: I am sending you my "work program" and you will see that there is also some way you can assist. How painfully I miss Irene, especially materially, I need not emphasize. My clothes, etc., are all mixed up, and I will probably appear as a beggar, half-ragged, when I come to you. (Yours are well packed with the help of Miss Mendwyler.) In March. For I would like to finish the catalog in its rough form and, above all, not get sick at your place when it is cold: not for my sake, I would be fine, but for yours. I don't want to burden you with a sick Fred.

Locarno, January 18, 1919

Dear Parents,

I was with the little one: she is better. I can breathe a sigh of relief and hope again. She is drinking again and crying again. For one day, she was completely silent and wouldn't take anything. – You might be interested to know: The commander-in-chief of the Spartacists in Berlin was none other than Drach. According to the *Berlin Daily News* and *New Zurich Newspaper*, he is said to have behaved very charmingly. I spent months with him in Davos. I now remember with particular fondness a conversation I attended between him and Grimm – the Swiss socialist – in Lugano in the autumn of 1917

Sincerely, your Fred

Locarno-Monti, January 20, 1919

Dear Mother,

I thank you for loving me a little. There are so few hearts that beat with mine. Only those who love me truly know me. (I rested so gently in Irene: she knew me to my deepest depths and highest heights, for she loved me.)

You would raise your hands in horror if the image of me, drawn by my kind enemies, came before your eyes: cyclical writers, mammonistic literary hacks, extortionists, swindlers, and pimps – these would be the mildest epithets dedicated to me. Are you not startled – by me? Or – by them? Today I received telegraphic and written invitations to speak in February "over there:" in Mannheim, Munich, Berlin, perhaps also in Kiel, Essen, Breslau, Dresden. Often I am fired up for it—and then again, I am ashes and soot. Am I robust enough to be a "popular speaker?" I will raise my arms – and suddenly there will be a stone wall and I will speak into the stone. Werfel would blow this wall down with his breath. Lenin would hack it apart with his fist. But I: I will stand helpless, the foreign doubt in me will make me despair. I will give credit to anyone who wrongs me. I often stand – how often! – on the side of my enemies. I allow them the mildest of excuses. Yes: it is easier for me to love them than myself. Belief in the Tao makes one gentle and humble. I used to be a roaring lion, now, by God, I have become a sheep...

In Frankfurt am Main, a new series of pamphlets on the Revolution is being published (Tiedemann & Uzielli). I hope that one of mine will appear, on the question of guilt. They wrote to me, and I sent the manuscript today. Sometimes, when I read my opponents, I think I am entirely to blame for the war, because I wrote the war volunteer song on August 4, 1914.

I believe that "one" in Germany generally misjudges the situation: simply because one expects this coming capitalist "peace" to last. Germany and Russia are, however, finished, done, finished – but I also see the Entente facing collapse. They ignored the omen of the Brest-Litovsk peace – and now they will perish from a peace of the same sort. What a wild world we poor gamblers have been born into! While we suffocate in the swamp, Irene may blissfully smile over it, among the stars. I will be happy when your poems to her are published anew. Perhaps the few words a friend of mine dedicated to her could serve as an introduction. (They were supposed to appear in the *Berlin Stock Exchange Newspaper*, but did not; I copied them and am enclosing them here, but would like them returned after transcription.) They do, however, mention my name. – I often read Irene's letters to me. They are so beautiful that I thought one day, when I am dead, they should be published like a small Bible of love. Embraces from your Fred

Locarno-Monti, January 23, 1919
Dear Mother,

I have often been with the little one lately; today I found it much better than the day before yesterday, also rounder in the face, and its eyes widened when it saw me. Surely its little brain worked hard to figure out who this could be, leaning over the crib. I don't yet know what will happen with the wet nurse. As for the costs, I gratefully accept your suggestion to share the surplus with me. (I don't want to approach my father again for now: he recently wrote to me twice that he would send me what he could, and he is quite honest with me, and not at all a mammonist, but he cannot send more.) I will also try to write something for the newspapers again. (In German money, they pay very well: for the small New Year's poem of 12 lines, the *Berlin Daily News* sent 35 marks, and the *Vossische Newspaper* sent 100 marks for the advance print of a chapter from *Bracke* in four feuilleton columns. In francs, it always melts away considerably.) – Today seems to be the first cold day. I have heated well. But the stove was smoking, and at first I sat there as if in a chimney. When I look at the landscape, I can hardly believe that it has been or will be winter. It still looks exactly as green, brown, and violet as in September. – I carry Irene always within me. In the evening, I speak to her in our language. Sometimes there are moments when I feel there is no wall between us: heart to heart. Your Fred

The philosopher Bloch, the poet Else Lasker-Schüler, and the poet Bruno Frank wrote so passionately and lovingly about Irene, I must send you their letters. All bills, except for the grave rent, have now been paid.

Locarno-Monti, January 28, 1919
Dear Mother,

I hope the little one will continue to do well. The weather, however, has changed again: winter now seems to want to arrive: today there was snow on Monti, snow on the grave. – I want to travel to Lugano in the next few days and inquire about my journey. There are probably no difficulties from the German side this time – but perhaps from the Swiss. Switzerland has recently tightened its entry regulations twice in a very short period. Even the sick are only allowed in after a very thorough examination of their reasons. "The best connections with Swiss dignitaries are of no help:" (This is how the wife of an acquaintance of mine has been waiting for her passport to Switzerland for six weeks: her husband earns his income in Switzerland, pays taxes here, and his wife is ill. They are friends with the Swiss consul!) I must, therefore, make sure if I can return to Switzerland: because I have my work, my manuscripts, books, etc. here – and the child, and I cannot take all of this with me at the moment. (Also, working on the catalog is hardly possible over there if the publisher is in Switzerland.)

The idea with the ballads is certainly nice: but I don't yet know how publishing will develop now. Reiß is quite skeptical. I have a huge number of unedited books lying around. Some are even in print (*Sleepwalkers, François Villon, The Gravedigger*), but I cannot say when they will be published. (*The Gravedigger* is the most likely to come first. It should serve as a memorial to Irene.) – I've been spending the last few months working a lot on China again. One fruit of this (it fell from the orange tree...) you should soon taste. – Why are you so angry with Eisner? I find the Scheidemann government the most arrogant and foolish that has ever ruled Germany. Compared to these people, Wilhelm II. was, God knows, by the grace of God... (I am also curious about the deeds of the National Assembly. The fact that they want to make the old Naumann president: already rotten: as the Berliner would say.) Best regards, Your Fred

It is rather disappointing that the National Assembly turned out so "bourgeois." A whole 24 men in opposition! At least 70 should have been included!

Locarno-Monti, January 29/30, 1919

Dear Mother,

It feels again as if I have taken an opiate: today, in one go, scarcely after receiving it from the library, I translated the main work of Taoist literature (the epigone of Lao Tzu), called *The Book of Retaliation*. (There is no German translation yet, and I am especially proud that I managed it entirely without a dictionary. (Now, while refining it, I naturally need one.)) I will send it to you as soon as I have had it typed. I am completely immersed in China again. Even Su Tung-po and the other great lyrical masters of the Chinese are again close to me as if they were brothers. In particular, I was captivated by Su Tung-po's (he lived around 1000 A.D.) *Flower Ship*. I consider it the most beautiful love poem in all of world literature, not excluding Goethe and Platen. I have written an article just about this ten-line poem, and you will receive it. I am happy that you take part in my thoughts. Who else should I tell them to? The world only sees the image. Perhaps that will suffice. I will send the reviews of *Bracke* to you as well; with the exception of the *Berlin Daily News*, they are excellent. – Suddenly, I feel tired. My head is already tilting to the left (the bad side: according to the definition of Taoism – by the way, also in Christian mythology – it is because left... is where the heart sits?)

January 30, 1919

You surely don't yet know the latest news: that the Berlin government has appointed me as a general, that is, as the commander of Greater Berlin. I must send you the newspaper clippings about it sometime. Unfortunately, I carelessly threw away the first ones, although I had a vague suspicion. But yesterday a newspaper arrived, and I read, no longer surprised: The Poet as General. And then: Klabund as Revolutionary General (parallel: Moreau...). Hugs from your Fred

Locarno-Monti, February 2, 1919

Dear Mother,

I am overwhelmed with work like a day laborer (only the outward reward for the effort barely corresponds). The catalog. Constant collaboration with the critical journals such as *The New Book Show*, *Bookworm*, etc. Replies and attacks here and there. Poems in *Switzerland, Wieland, New Review, White Leaves, Rarity, Young Germany,* and so on, and so forth. My translations from Chinese – French. The pamphlet. A plan for an annual of pure philosophy, pure poetry (antipolitical, antipolemical, as far as the *a priori* soul is concerned). Plus corrections of all kinds. *Villon* is in print and will appear soon. *The Gravedigger* is being typeset. I suggested *The Cherubim* to Reiß for Christmas: as a lyrical work of the greatest extent, containing: the sonnets, the odes, the distichs, small songs, the ballads, and the Chinese love poems. Irene should not be allowed to complain about the temple built in her honor. Everything, everything, everything is dedicated to her. – You will receive the books you requested, and some more.

I am sending you *The Poetry*, a publication from Roland Verlag (with which, by the way, I have nothing to do). – Do you like *Katharina*?

Enclosed for your autograph collection is a little something. – I haven't understood the new regulation for money yet. If one is only allowed to send 150 marks (= 75 francs!): one cannot live on that! – The wet nurse situation will take a while for now: first, one cannot find one, and second, according to the doctor's view, one is not necessary at the moment. I was over there today again; the concern remains with us. A cold cannot be overcome by a wet nurse either. – I myself am once again in an unbearable mood for the past three days. Therefore, do not expect any revelations in this letter. Your Fred

Locarno, 5 February 1919

Dear Mother,

I assume you agree that you will allow *The Dame* to use four of your poems, which I have selected, for a fee of 100 (one hundred) Marks? They are the poems: *Passion, Last Song, Fulfillment, My Child, My Spring,* under the overall title *Poems of a Mother*. You only need to reply to me. In haste, warm regards for today, your Fred.

Lugano, Huguenin, Confectioner – Glacier, February 11, 1919

Dear Mother,

I am writing to you amidst the smoke and music of a café. I am in Lugano due to my passport. I have been treated very attentively and courteously and have immediately been granted a three-month passport with a return visa to Switzerland. Now only the return visa from the Swiss authorities is missing – and I can travel on the first of March, and perhaps already be with you by mid-March. I had a half-hour meeting with the Legation Councillor of M., a charming representative of Prussia. He seemed to trust me with various things and only asked that I not take over the Spartacist (!) leadership. He had attended the Brest peace talks and spoke with respect of the Bolsheviks. I explained to him that I am absolutely opposed to the Scheidemann-Ebert government, but equally opposed to the methods of the Spartacists, to which he then dared to assume responsibility for my passport. I will speak in Mannheim, Karlsruhe, Frankfurt, Munich (Galerie Caspari), Berlin, Elberfeld, Breslau: at least I have arranged the program this way. I will read from my poems, but in the working-class town of Mannheim, I will talk about... Chinese state philosophy...

The accompanying card should be read with attention: I was effectively in Italy today... But this trip to Italy cost me in one day what a week-long trip to Venice or Milan usually costs. Joking aside: in Campione, on Italian soil (it's forbidden in Switzerland), a luxurious casino was opened on the first of February for peace, with the same attractions as in Monte Carlo. Upon seeing the green cloth, my old passion for gambling was revived: I played an extremely high-stakes roulette game and, unfortunately, not knowing when to stop (I had already filled my bag with hundred-franc pieces!), I lost all the cash I had brought with me. That was a foolish thing to do, or more than foolish: I should have been more sensible by now, especially now when it's so hard to get money out of Germany, when the currency is so bad, and when talk of "earning" is out of the question. Are you angry with me?

You are right. Irene was missing here too. But I will promise you that I will not gamble any more: instead of her. I even have the unpaid bill for her grave (160 Francs) in my pocket (the only thing I haven't paid, it only arrived yesterday). So, I've gambled away her grave – and mine as well... (All in all, I still have 500 Fr., apart from my debts). And someone like that wants to teach others Chinese state philosophy. They should start with themselves...... Your miserable Fred.

Locarno-Monti, 14 February 1919

Dear Father,

But – but! – how can you believe all the nonsense that's being spread in the Bavarian hate press about Eisner! Eisner never spoke of the colonies, and the story about the wretched servants is really laughable. The German press continues to lie so terribly that the sky darkens. Already, the shadow of Ludendorff rises again over the wall, and how soon will he be back in person, or at least his reincarnation, if no one takes heed. I find the German National Assembly pitiful in its first utterances: they made David (!) president, Ebert Reichskanzler, Scheidemann (!!) prime minister! Hopefully, we'll soon have a chance to argue about it in person. – I have been very tired and down for the past five days. But I hope to be back on my feet by the first.

I look inside myself like a burned-out volcano. The verses, the scenes, the short stories: they are like the last pieces of lava flying out of the crater. In them is my last ember. I am like the fencer who wants to raise his arm with the sword: but he cannot anymore: the tendon is severed. I am glad that I can be a little for you. And I thank you for bringing me warmth: I am freezing despite the South. I was so spoiled by love. In love and mutual love, the circle turned. Now it's so empty around me. Desolation and wilderness. Jackals and vultures. And I can no longer find the oasis. – If I am to awaken to life again, I must be placed in the incubator like a five-month-old child.

I sent you a lot of printed material. The new regulations about sending money are still unclear to me. With 150 M. (75 Fr.) no one can live! However, I have not yet received the February payment from Reiß, nor the January and February payments from the Roland Publishing House. That adds up to about 800 Marks. This uncertainty is, of course, not reassuring for someone who lives hand to mouth. It would be bitter for me to have to leave here. Warm hugs from your Fred.

Locarno-Monti, February 19, 1919
Dearest Mother,

Today is the first spring day, and today I must bury the child. In your name, I will place a small wreath of lily-of-the-valley and carnations on the little coffin, and a bouquet of flowers on Irene's grave. The little one will be laid next to her mother, in that grave which I had actually intended for myself.

When I was in Ascona on the 15th, I had very little hope left. When I went home that night, I prayed to the moon and the stars. When I was in my room and almost swept away by an inner storm, I did not interpret it as a good sign. Is it not enough of the suffering that I, like Job, have been burdened with? What terrible guilt must I atone for? Guilty, innocent, we stagger through life.

Why am I condemned, oh without blushing, to kill those beings I must love?

In a moment of passion, I murdered the dearest person, and a second, and myself along with them. The Trinity of Death. But this passion was a holy passion – how inextricably entangled we are in heaven and hell at once. And from the holy passion became a bitter passion, in which I now miserably drag myself along.

I am not entirely sure what the child died of. Probably from its delicacy and weakness. The digestive system and blood circulation had not been working properly for a week. In addition, there were swallowing difficulties, which it visibly suffered from. I almost fear it had laryngeal tuberculosis, although the doctor denies tuberculosis. It had become so charming recently, one could see it beginning to become a person. It already distinguished people, looked from one to the other, and when someone entered the room or opened the door, especially when the nurse came, it made itself known by sounds. You, poor mother, have now lost your child for the second time – and I have lost the hope of a second Irene. Let your Fred give you both a hug.

Locarno-Monti, February 20, 1919

Dear Mother,

Today I sent you a whole series of the latest literature that might interest you. (Not for reviewing!) I always receive a huge amount at home. (I like Hülsenbeck and Hardenberg: the rest: dubious and unattractive.) A volume of mine will also be published soon in the collection "The Newest Poem." At first, I thought of sending the odes to Irene. But in the end, they seemed too precious for that: I do not want to tear apart the cherubim, I hope it can be published in autumn by Reiß. So I submitted Montezuma and a grotesque poem, *The Feathered World*, for selection, also including drafts for cover pages, which I "drew" myself. – I sent an article today to the *New Zurich Newspaper*: "The League of Nations of the Allies." I find the "League of Nations" program ridiculous. – In *The Revolutionary No. 1*, an article of mine appears (written November 18): Hear it, German!. In the Breslau political journal *The Earth: The Man with the Black Mask*. In *The New Mercury* and the *Munich Papers*, poems, and in *The People* – Dresden a justification: Pro domo (in response to various attacks). You see: the young literature is stirring again – and I within it.

(This is the fourth letter in three days!) Hugs to both of you, your Fred.

The German currency is so weak (49!) that I can no longer send letters by registered mail!

The Dark Ship (Gryphius) is appearing in a new, probably shortened edition: If you don't have it yet, get a copy of the first edition (Roland Verlag).

Locarno, Casino Kursaal, February 25, 1919

Dear Mother,

aren't I practically covering you with white paper, considering how much I write to you? Now spring is here: I walk around again in a shirt and trousers, but I almost feel as if I'm in a masquerade. The evenings are already so bright, and we eat again on the stone terrace in front of the house. I go down to Locarno every evening and then home through the absolute darkness all night. The darkness feels so good. I don't feel nearly as lonely and isolated as I do in my room. It was at this time last year that we arrived here.

– I am still very inhibited: in thought and gesture. Sometimes I catch myself making a gesture or step that I don't know what to do with. I am so scattered and so uncertain of myself. Minutes ago, I stood on the path by a blackberry bush: not knowing why, and only later did I remember my helplessness and that such weakness already borders on psychopathology.

The excellent reviews of *Bracke* give me much joy, I will send them to you soon. They are a small confirmation that I am not here by chance, but necessarily here.

I hope you also authorize me to publish your poems (of course, only in respectable reviews). I think publishing in *The Dame* will bring you some pleasure. Always yours, Fred.

Just now in the cafe I was reading a *Bracke* article published in the *Berliner*

Newspaper on the 21ˢᵗ.

Locarno-Monti, March 7, 1919

Dear Mother,

I haven't heard from you in three weeks. I've written so much to you, and I don't even know: are you ill, or is Spartacus or someone else ruling in Passau, making the mail system not work? I loved hearing you speak, Irene spoke through you. You also haven't replied to me about the poems I wanted to submit to *The Dame*. The grave is now being prepared for the summer: blooming flowers are being planted, and ivy is climbing the wall. Should I have a small plaque put up for the little one? I don't think it's necessary: it wouldn't look nice since the space is so small, and we know who rests there. The doctor said it died due to atresia, meaning an incomplete development of some internal organs (stomach, intestines), and it was never likely to live long. Even the most unshakable scientific facts don't bring comfort: whether or not he's right, it lived – and doesn't anymore... this is our experience...

The Gravedigger will arrive in April. I'll dedicate him to you in the public edition–if you don't object. A grotesquely sentimental poem *The Feathered World*, half parody, will also be published soon. Also, *Villon*.

I'm still waiting for the visa from Bern. It's been six weeks. I have several opportunities to read in Germany. Yesterday, I heard about the collapse of the armistice negotiations, which didn't surprise me. The Entente had long been unmasked as an imperialist-capitalist-sadistic band of robbers. Now, their own Bolsheviks will present them with a bill they hardly suspected. Be embraced, your Fred

Bellinzona, March 21, 1919

Bavarian Brewery (!!)

Dear Mother,

In Bellinzona, in an old brewery. I've been away from home for 8 days now. Again and again, I try to escape from myself. The body rebels against the mind. But it's a senseless and pointless endeavor. Today I'm going home. Hopefully, I'll find lots of mail: letters from you as well.

I would have rather come to Germany today than tomorrow. But in Bern, at the Foreign Police, they've become rude and inconsiderate: out of pure Bolshevik fear. Every traveler to German Revolutionary territories is suspicious. And now: the literati! They didn't answer me for 6 weeks – and then gave a wrong response. I've telegraphed, I've written express: nothing has moved so far. The Swiss have become Prussians – and the Entente militaristic.

The National Assembly: pitiful. Rational Assembly. Soulless. The old Reichstag and Seichstag. I'm writing a pamphlet against it.

I recommend to you: (sending it to you): *Captain Deutschle: A German War Book*, which seems far better and more exceptional to me than the usual Latzko's and Frank's. Always your Fred

I recommend to you...: Karl Zimmermann (i.e., Käthe Zimmermann-Jatho). *The Captain Deutschle*. Book for grandchildren. Zurich: *Rascher*, 1919; Andreas Latzko, *Men in War*. Zurich: Rascher, 1917; same author, *Women in War*. 1918; Bruno Frank, *Stanzas from War. A pamphlet*. Munich: Langen, [1915]

Locarno-Monti, March 21, 1919

Dear Mother,

I have one of your new poems, *The Golden Web*, which I liked very much, and I've sent it to the *Orchid Garden*. The others I've enclosed again here: they somehow seem unfinished. You must still think and refine them. *The Dame* has accepted the 4 poems, but hasn't sent the honorarium yet. You'll receive it as soon as it arrives. I had Irene's grave renewed: ivy has been planted along the wall, and pansies between the stones. At the base: hyacinths.

Today, strangely delayed, the first real snow of this winter has fallen on all the blooming almond trees and mimosa. It has settled and is still snowing.

Yesterday, Reiß wrote to me. *The Sleepwalkers* will appear in the fall, and either *The Cherubim* or *Silvia* (the second part of Irene). Also, Silvia... is Irene. I leafed through *The Sleepwalkers* again today and was once more deeply shocked by my uncanny premonitions, which I had back in 1917. They all came so inescapably true that I must also believe my own premonition of death is more than a dark wish and a dark game.

In *The Revolutionary*, a second article of mine appears: *The Anabaptist*. Also, a pamphlet against the National Assembly, which you will probably dislike. It's written, moreover, in Berlin jargon.

I've received the 100 francs. Many thanks. When will I be able to visit you? They've become terribly unfriendly toward foreigners, and I've been telegraphing and writing express for 6 weeks to Bern, almost to death. Always your Fred

Locarno-Monti, March 27, 1919

Dear Mother,

You can get an idea of the rudeness of the Swiss authorities, as they seem to practice it more recently, when you hear that I have been waiting for a response from Bern (Federal Foreign Center) about my travel for 7 (!) weeks. All the telegraphing and express letters are of no use. This is the only reason I am not yet in Germany. I will probably have to give up my lecture tour: it will be too late in May, and I let it go with great pain: I had already planned Hamburg, Mannheim, Coburg, Munich, Karlsruhe, etc. – The bad winter weather has now arrived in spring here. It is cold and wet. For a few days, I didn't feel well either, and one day I was in bed. I haven't done anything reasonable or beautiful in the last few weeks. I've only sifted through and polished the *Sonnets to Irene* and almost think about publishing them as a small special edition: my literary friends believe they contain the richest poetry I have written. (There are now 22.)

What do you think about that? *Montezuma* will appear as a small special issue in *Latest Poems*, *The Gravedigger* in a presumably one-time edition of 500 copies from the publisher "The Beautiful Rarit'" – Kiel, Preußerstr. 19. I can give you two copies. If you want more, it's a good idea to preorder them. (They cost only 2.50.) *Around the Flower Boat* is being contested by Inselverlag and Rolandverlag. I don't understand where all this paper comes from with the evident paper shortage. – As for the reviews: you only need to review briefly what offers positive value. – Recommend me to Kubin. – The German money rises and falls like the waves of the sea. In 4 weeks, the current government will have been overthrown – or do you think differently? I can already see the gray shadows of the Independents appearing on the cinema screen of the National Theater. (I wrote a pamphlet against the National Assembly: this will probably create new "friends" for me...)

Hugs from your Fred

Locarno, March 31, 1919

Dear Parents,

A short heartfelt greeting from a Birraria, where I am drinking a bad Americano out of sheer melancholy (and in thoughts of Wilson...). I am so happy to rest spiritually with you for a few days (weeks?). I miss home so much. I miss Irene. Today I read the corrections of *The Gravedigger*. The wound still bleeds fresh. Again and again, I must bury my life alive. Your Fred

Regensburg, before April 20, 1919

Dear Mother, dear Father,

I was taken last night by car, on the orders of the 3rd Army Corps, to Regensburg Brigade. I ask you to immediately take the necessary steps that could contribute to the clarification of the matter. Do not be afraid! Hugs, your Fred

Nuremberg, April 20, 1919

Dearest Mother, dearest Father,

I was admitted to the investigative prison in Nuremberg yesterday. Everything else, all the bitter details, will be told in person. I don't know what will happen. I am completely helpless and powerless. I may not write any more.

Your unfortunate and innocent Fred, who hugs you

Nuremberg, April 21, 1919

Easter Monday, Nuremberg Detention Prison

Dearest Parents,

I am only allowed to write about facts, nothing that goes beyond a bare report. I will postpone what weighs so heavily on my heart for later (when will that be?), and report the following facts to you:

In Passau, contrary to the statement of the arresting officer, I was placed in a completely dark, damp, and cold room that contained nothing but a cot with a straw mattress. No pillow, no blanket, no light – nothing.

In Straubing, I was placed in the detention room of the Cheveauleger: cold, damp, containing nothing but a cot with a sack and blankets. The food – gray soup and smelly stockfish – was inedible. A soldier managed to get me a pancake.

In Straubing prison, I was put in a so-called sick cell, which contained nothing but a bed on the ground. At least it was warm (heated). There was good soup, some potatoes, a piece of bread.

In Nuremberg, I was placed in the detention room of an infantry regiment. In the evening, I was moved to the investigative prison. For food, from early at 5 a.m. until evening, I received nothing but: 1 glass of schnapps at 5 a.m. and a piece of bread at 6 p.m.

My northern cell here looks like this:

A very small window at the top. Spittoon, chamber pot, fold-up table, fold-up cot, very hard, thin blanket.

Fold-up chair.

For food, there is coffee at 7 a.m., soup and potatoes at noon, and a piece of cheese in the evening. The judges, the doctor, everyone has Easter vacation. Hugs from your Fred.

I think of my paradise in Monti. If the matter is not settled soon, within eight days, my return is at risk: my apartment, my work, my health, my existence are at stake.

Nuremberg, April 22, 1919

PLEASE DEMAND URGENT RELEASE AGAINST BAIL OR GUARANTEE. YOUR FRED

Nuremberg, April 23, 1919

Dearest Father,

Every day I have to stay here costs me nerve and soul power that I do not want to waste on matters of heaven or hell. I am feverishly waiting for a resolution. I can hardly believe that, based on this telegram, any reasonable justice system would press charges against me. If one wants to arrest someone for "relations with the Soviet Republic," then they would have to arrest all the officials, soldiers, workers, etc., who actively participated in the proclamation of the Soviet Republic – there are nearly one hundred thousand of them. And I had nothing to do with the Soviet Republic itself. You very well remember my statement made in the presence of Kubin: "It's a shame I didn't come to Munich three days earlier. Perhaps I could have prevented the proclamation of the Soviet Republic." – Now, that may be an overestimation of my reputation and name: yes, it surely is, but the statement alone characterizes my position sufficiently. – I am utterly disheartened that I have not heard from you. From tomorrow on, there will be no passenger trains. I also have various doubts in my mind about the legal grounds for my arrest (I am still in the military detention prison, I, a civilian!). It feels as if the old militaristic Ludendorff dictatorship is playing tricks on me. As though some scheming power wants to torture me. – If you do not see any quick possibility of my release, please send: money, books, clothes. Irene, the deceased, keeps me alive. Embrace Irene, the living. Tell her how grateful I am to her.

The lecture tour has fallen through. I intend to file a lawsuit for damages. I read you the last evening's Platen. Do you remember? *Exoriar aliquis...* Your loving Fred.

I don't want to write to the Crossner parents until I see things more clearly. Have any corrections come in?

Nuremberg, April 24, 1919

Dearest Mother, dearest Father,

I have written you many, many letters, but I could not send them. However, my thoughts have always been with you. I truly feel you are my second parents, since you are Irene's parents. When I was cold, I warmed myself with the warmth of your hearts. I have written a "Diary in Prison," which will bring you closer to the time I have spent here, more endured than lived, my suffering and endurance. Mr. J. N. Zilcher is very kind. Today, he brought me cakes and headcheese. Until today, I had always been hungry. I immediately ate my fill. Finally, I managed to arrange for a restaurant to send me food in the evening: I didn't have any ration cards. Mr. J. N. Zilcher also helped with that. Please thank him very much! If only it were possible to get me released soon! From today on, there are no more passenger trains. It is a chaotic time.

My parents in Crossen have not heard from me for about six weeks, apart from the telegram. Can't you write to them diplomatically? I would like, for the sake of Switzerland, that my arrest does not become public for the time being; otherwise, I may be turned back at the Swiss border due to the Swiss fear of Bolsheviks. I hope the German press has not reported anything yet. I will speak for myself later.

I asked you, dear father, through Mr. J. N. Zilcher, to send him all my things immediately, just in case: above all, the wallet with all the ID cards, also my suitcase, and all the money, minus the expenses you have for me, in a check made out to my name, so that I can take it with me to Switzerland. That is my hope: to get permission to return to Switzerland. Yes, if necessary, they can place me at the border, but my feelings for this Germany are naturally not the rosiest. I would be overjoyed, extremely happy, once I'm back there, in my Monte Paradise. Embrace Mother. And thank you a thousand times for all the trouble you've taken with poor me. Always your most grateful and devoted Fred.

Please send my mail to the address of Justice Councilor Zilcher! – If only I could be back in Switzerland in about ten days: you know that a Swiss residence permit, like the one I have, expires after a certain time. Switzerland no longer issues new ones!! So I couldn't return!

The diary is also intended for my Crossen parents. Please announce it to them, but do not send it yet!! Or perhaps you should wait with the announcement.

One more thing: there is a small bottle in the nightstand labeled Pyramidön (because of border control), but it contains cyanide, the most powerfult poison. Please keep it safe so nothing happens to it!

The identification papers: passport, residence permit, etc., I ask that you send separately, not in the suitcase.

Nuremberg, April 25, 1919

JUST RELEASED, A THOUSAND THANKS TO YOU TOO. PLEASE SEND ALL MY BELONGINGS EXPRESSLY TO JUSTICE COUNCILOR ZILCHER. MONEY IN A CHECK MADE OUT TO MY NAME, AND THE IDENTIFI-CATION PAPERS SENT SEPARATELY, REGISTERED EXPRESS. PLEASE CALL ME WITH MOTHER BETWEEN 8 & 10 OR 2-4 TOMORROW AT HO-TEL KOENIGSHOF. I AM STILL VERY NERVOUS AND EXCITED. I WANT TO GO HOME TO MONTI IMMEDIATELY. HUGS, YOUR FRED.

Nuremberg, May 5, 1919

Dearest Parents,

I think with longing of the beautiful days in Passau, full of such tender yet secure protection. Now, the wild world rages around me again, in which I once felt very comfortable, but now it disgusts me again and again.

I have moved out of the hotel. I was only there for one night. This time, I was too annoyed with the director and a scoundrel from Boy. I am now staying at Dr. Graf's, Sulzbacherstr. 80. Today, I received a letter from Coburg, urgently inviting me to come there. I still don't know what I will do. I also thought about meeting Fiete here for a few days. (I don't know if Irene told you about Fiete? They were very fond of each other, and perhaps spending a few days with her would have done me good. Irene knows that I am not taking anything from her.) I am still unsure. If I accept Coburg, I would have to start over with Mannheim, etc.

Thank you again, a thousand times, for your love and kindness. Despite all the noise and commotion around me, despite all my worldly years, I have always been a lonely person. In Irene, I found my salvation. My heart spoke openly and freely. If it weren't for you, and a few others, very few people, it would fall silent. Hugs from your Fred.

Nürnberg, Sulzbacher Straße 80, May 7, 1919

Dear parents,

Last evening was a great success. The house was sold out! People were stand-ing and sitting on the most impossible devices and shelves. I read poems, I-hi-wie, Hölderlin, and *Bracke*, and I had the impression that I was being met with open hearts, and I just had to pour it all in. Of course, I don't know what the reviews will be like. Critics, after all, are not always – people. However, members from other literary clubs were present, from out of town, and they immediately booked me for a new "tour" in the fall: I am supposed to read in Gera, Weimar, Jena, and Altenburg. (Unfortunately, I don't have time now. However, I will still travel to Coburg today, where they promised me special travel discounts if I came right away and read on Thursday evening.) – If there is urgent mail, please send it to Lederer, Augusta Anlage 9, Mannheim. – Imagine this: the club even made a deal with me! I brought them three times the revenue that Edschmid, who recently read here, made. Naturally, this delights the second, Mammonistic heart of these people. Warm hugs from your Fred

How Irene would have beamed with happiness on such an evening. She was always far happier and more heartfelt in her joy over my successes than I was.

Mannheim, May 13, 1919

Dear parents,

A warm greeting in great haste! I am always on the move, running, writing autographs, shouting, speaking, roaring, attacked and worshiped. I will write to you soon in peace. Your faithful Fred

Locarno, May 24, 1919

Dear Mother,

Please help me with my animal anthology as well. If you know or find something, please let me know or send it to me immediately. – I arrived here last night, quite diffuse and nervous. The incredibly accumulated work will lift me above a state of exhaustion and the endless old pain. I was still at Irene's grave at eight in the evening.

– I am thinking that, if there is even some peace, I may return to Germany in August, after completing my contracted work. Your Fred

Locarno-Monti, June 2, 1919

Dear Mother,

I don't know if you, for example, read Kaufmann's letter: I hope you did. The "liberation of Munich" must have been a very strange liberation. I also spoke with a good friend of mine in Heidelberg, who had stayed in Munich until the last day and was then arrested. The "Prussians" have become exceptionally popular. (That the "murder" of Stuck and Dall Armi was a provocation lie, I, the old fool, who still occasionally falls for a government telegram, realized far too late. The murder of the "hostages" also took place differently than the press liars would have liked to portray. I read the official protocol of the Munich police headquarters on this case in Nuremberg.) The fact that all the significant leaders of the radical opposition in Germany have been murdered, from Liebknecht, R. Luxemburg, Jokisch (not the Silesian Jokisch), to Eisner, Landauer, Dorrenbach, etc., speaks volumes. But a Lieutenant Vogel escapes – under the protection of the gracious patron Noske (the ____ protege of your husband...). In today's Germany, it is already considered suspicious to be a "revolutionary." It is dreadful how this poor Germany is being torn apart: externally by jackals and internally by the vultures of the old system. How much longer until the monarchy is re-established? It seems the time is nearing when one will seriously ask the question whether, despite all the principled differences that separate us from the official party program of the KPD, we should join Spartacus out of revolutionary protest. Your Fred

Locarno-Monti, June 3, 1919

Dear Mother,

I have sent you a number of journals in which there were again contributions from me. *The Front* appears serially in *The Revolutionary* under the title *Awakening*. It will also be published as a book, also by the Revolutionary Verlag. There too: Tao (my political and ethical essays). The Dresden publisher has printed the *Ode to Montezuma* especially lavishly. The *Animal Book*, which I am working on with Soffel, is progressing – less so the calendar, against which there are many external and internal obstacles. I have received all the letters. Many thanks. My opinion on "peace" is found almost verbatim in an article by the *National Newspaper* from Ragaz, which I am sending to Father today. (Ragaz is a pastor, but a radical socialist.) The *National Newspaper* had also reported on my arrest. I was at the editorial office and allowed myself to give some clarification about the conditions in Bavaria. This clarification has not been without effect on the editorial pieces, as I have already noted. – The first letter I found here was from the South German Concert Agency in Dresden about a lecture tour in the fall!! I would love to go back soon. Germany has revived me from my passion into action, and I am now, precisely because of the Sleeping Beauty peace here, nervous to the fingertips. I even feel like drinking again (drinking would be too weak an expression) and doing all sorts of unholy things, and with Ulla Weinblatt you know the lover of the Swedish poet Bellmann – I would like to dance once. Don't you get a little scared by my suddenly breaking vitality? Once I am alive again, I will be very alive. – Both of you, a hug, perhaps and hopefully we will see each other very soon, Your Fred.

Angel is for your autograph collection: the well-known literary historian.

I have just received an inquiry from the large publisher Dürr and Weber if I would take over a volume for their economically political library. What do you think? It would interest me to write a monograph, for example, Revolution and Revolutions, fully grounded in history. But this would again take time away from my poetic work. I haven't had time for months now.

Locarno-Monti, June 5, 1919

Dear Mother,

It is a quarter to three, actually still early for me, because I have already worked several times until five or six. I have a headache and feel cold. I have taken on much, perhaps too much. I could really use a secretary, and if it weren't so expensive, I would hire someone by the hour to type at my house. But given the current currency situation, I dare not indulge in extravagances. I am sending you some reviews, as far as I already have them. Please keep them with the other *Eulenspiegel* reviews. The fact that a lieutenant of the government troops slept in my bed has irritated me. My sympathy for the white guards, who unjustly carry the color of the lily and innocence, since they are heavily covered in guilt, has always been minimal. I now read the German newspaper *Berlin Daily*, and I would also recommend to Father that he read it carefully. It is the paper of the Pan-Germans, and there he will learn what these gentlemen are allowed to do without being disturbed by the white Noske guards: quite simply, because Noske is their boot-polisher. They openly preach the fight against the government and talk about the restoration of the monarchy. The Kaiser is glorified. The resumption of war, his recall, is demanded, and the revolutionaries of November 9th (i.e. Scheidemann etc.) are already called "traitors." It is generally forbidden in revolutionary Germany to be a revolutionary. (Digestive) rest is the first civic duty, and the new capitalist order is the sign under which victory is periodically achieved. As Crown Prince Wilhelm said in 1914? "Victory will be achieved in any case..." (In America, bets are already being placed on the restoration of the monarchy in Germany...) The bourgeoisie, which so gently observed the entry of the "government troops," will likewise gently watch the new monarch being installed, and no hand will be raised when the few hundred real revolutionaries (not just Spartacists) are lined up against the wall. That Levine is to be shot I find horrendous. He is certainly completely innocent of the hostage killings; he is a lamb (Lamb Levine was his nickname among his friends). Will Toller also be shot?

Despite the late hour, I have talked myself into a rage. (Father and I would clash more than ever now.) I actually wanted to tell you about my work. Another time. Warmly, Your Fred

Locarno-Monti, June 16, 1919

Dear Father,

I read today in the *Frankfurter* that the left-wing parties in Munich have gained tremendous support due to the events that led to the execution staged against Munich. A very significant manifestation. If the generals had a little more psychology, they could have foreseen this. You are unfortunately still thinking in terms of Bismarckian politics. "After all, it all comes down to success." No, dear Father, that is entirely not my opinion. Success is a relative concept: as relative as the duration of our human lives. Bismarck had 40 years of "success" – and then? Hoffmann will have 6 weeks of "success" due to an iron cure, to which he was not morally and politically entitled. There is a great difference between the hostage killings of the 9 and the summary executions of the 186. The hostage killings were a retaliation for the summary execution of 12 people at Starnberg, which is already the subject of protest even by the majority socialists, and were carried out independently by inferior organs of the council government. The summary mass executions in Munich were official bloodbaths of the Hoffmann government, which identified with them. I am glad that even some bourgeois people are protesting firmly against this, including Lujo Brentano and Thomas Mann. I have absolutely reliable people who spoke about Munich, who were there until the end. It sent a chill through me. All those with insight claim that the fault for the fighting lay entirely with the Hoffmann-Schneppenhorst government, which wanted to "set an example." Toller was always ready to negotiate. Nothing would have been lost: on the contrary, it would have been reasonable to negotiate. People like Frank and Kaufmann, absolute opponents of the council republic, have become downright radical since the experiences they had with white terror. How childishly mild the council republic's court-martials were has already been shown by the trial against the leaders of the Revolutionary Tribunal. – I have also protested against Levine's execution in a telegram to the Hoffmann government. – That they arrested Mrs. A. away from her three young children I find appalling. But thousands have been senselessly murdered to the greater glory of military god. What can be done for them? Please orient yourself! – Do you know that I have a feeling of shame for walking freely while all decent people in Bavaria are arrested? Had I known what kind of resurrection militarism would celebrate in such a short time: I would have refused to participate in my protocol and simply demanded my release. Against this Beelzebub, all thoughtful men must declare solidarity: and although I was no supporter of the council republic, I will always side with Levine against Schneppenhorst-Hoffmann. To him, I am his "comrade." Greet Matthes and tell him that the visit to Aberham has now left a bitter aftertaste in my mouth. I read that the Hoffmann government has broken its original promise to treat the Red Guards as prisoners of war, and that the imprisoned Red Guards have been sentenced to 1 to 3 years in fortress detention. Matthes had promised these people their release within a few days. Now they will probably still be up there. If this is true, I hope that he throws this government's trash at their feet too: they lie just like the old Pan-Germans (as the Bamberger smear reports in the press have already shown) and are just as much in the hands of the military as the old one was. – But of course, you don't want to see that.

Today I read in the National Assembly that all the parties have concluded a new truce until the peace question is resolved. I would only have agreed to such a truce under the condition of the immediate amnesty of the Munich political prisoners and the immediate abolition of the court-martials. Warm greetings to you and Mother, Your Fred.

Yes, I will take my Easter experiences as a warning: but in a different sense than you mean. I will henceforth reject every compromise, however small, with the partisans of Noske-Lützow-Schneppenhorst.

Zurich, Elite Hotel, June 28, 1919

Dear Mother,

I am in Zurich for a few days. A publisher from Leipzig had telegraphed me in Locarno, saying he wanted to speak with me. After being assured of reimbursement for travel expenses, I came here, and we had a conference. It concerns ongoing collaboration on a series of books for public education in political, economic, and literary fields. I will probably write a history of German literature for him. Additionally, I might write a children's *Bible* (the *Bible* for children aged 10–13). These are tasks that certainly appeal to me. But time, time, time!

Yesterday, I was at the central library. It's the one thing I miss in Locarno: delving into old, beautiful books and exquisite prints. I held the first edition of the *Wandsbecker Messenger* (1774) and Gessner's *Idylls* in my hands. For all my respect for modern German publishing, they can no longer produce books like these. I also rummaged around for my animal book and found some interesting material in old Latin writers (Flavianus, Romulus) and also some unknown fables by Aesop and Phaedrus. (The German fabulists of the 17th and 18th centuries–Lichtwer, Goeckingk, Pfeffel–are really just imitators of Aesop, paraphrasing him skillfully.)

I'm returning to Locarno tomorrow. The big city exhausts me. If I am to accomplish everything I need to by winter, I will have to (at the very least) adopt a thirteen-hour workday.

The "peace" treaty was signed yesterday. No one here paid it any mind, sensing rightly that this "peace" does not even represent a stage along the path of suffering we have embarked upon. The many uprisings in Germany are all spontaneous, localized actions–I see that quite clearly. They only harm the true revolutionary movement. But the masses, underfed and fanatically agitated, no longer obey their leaders: neither the Majority Socialists nor the Independents, and not even the Spartacist leaders anymore.

I have occasionally brought fresh flowers to Irene's grave, but they don't last in the scorching sun. The gardener Schäppi has placed a tasteful artificial bouquet, brown and silver. In summer in Locarno, it really can't be any other way.

Here in Zurich, it's cold and wintry; you could almost heat the rooms. Both of you are hugged by your Fred.

What about Mrs. Anny? Tell Father that I'll send him the money from Germany!

Unknown location, July 3, 1919

Dear Mother,

I sent you a copy of your poems so that you might send them to some publishers again. Have you inquired with Reuß and Itta (Constance, Time Books)? Or with Eugen Salzer (Heilbronn)?

Today, I want to share with you a plan that is becoming more and more tangible. I want to build a small house, perhaps near Heidelberg, or maybe somewhere in Bavaria. Very small: just a kitchen, bedroom, living room, and guest room.

Just large enough that it would remain entirely mine, even in the event of house communalization. If you haven't sold the furniture yet, please wait a bit longer – I'd buy it from you.

I plan to stay here until September 1st. Whether I'll stay longer, I don't know yet.

Warm regards,

Your Fred

Unknown location, July 3, 1919

Dear Father,

1.) This is not about a "Starnberg hostage murder" but about the summary execution of captured Red Guards near Pöcking. This is not some "Red Guard hoax" but is officially documented in the list of summary executions in Munich (185) in the *Munich Latest News*.

2.) The scandalous complicity of the Hoffmann government in the Soviet Republic is becoming increasingly evident through the trials (Levine, Niekisch, Sauber, etc.). Witnesses belonging to the government are either not summoned or are questioned privately to prevent the Hoffmann government from being compromised. But this won't last much longer. The Schneppenhorst trial against the *New Journal* will hopefully bring clarity. The government is deliberately obscuring the truth.

And you support such a government? For "peace and order?" And you still believe the blatant lies served up by the "government press" (including government-socialist papers)?

It's no wonder that, after the experiences of recent months, people are turning ever further away from such nonsense, and that the boundless bitterness among the masses will one day find no peaceful outlet. I find this entirely understandable, as I feel myself electrified by the events of recent months. The storm flashes more fiercely than ever. Will the thunderstorm pass over? Or will it strike?

Your Fred

Locarno-Monti, July 10, 1919

Dear Mother,

Thank you for your faithful collaboration! It has been very useful to us. Wouldn't it be easier for you to simply send me the *French Lyric Poetry*? I believe it's a book, and then you wouldn't have to copy things out, which must be quite a hassle for you. (But Maupassant and Souvestre are prose, aren't they?) In any case, the French authors are very important to me. I also miss your spider poem. I absolutely want to include it. The manuscript must be finished by August 1st, as per the contract. And by September 1st—the literary history. (I haven't written a single line yet...) I gave your books to Miss Mimi Simon, Karlsruhe, Bismarckstr. 41. I've written to her several times, asking her to send them immediately.

I've already received more invitations for lectures. Allegedly, they now want to stage *The Gravedigger* in Mannheim too. But I've grown quite suspicious of the theater. It's the only thing that has consistently disappointed me. The *Sleepwalkers* is supposedly published now. Also *The Feathered World* and *Heavenly Vagabond*. I don't have a single copy myself, of any of them. I'm sending you the pamphlet and two magazines with this same post. – Really, it's sheer recklessness on my part to try to write a literary history up here on the mountain with almost no resources, no library, relying solely on my good memory. I feel like Harras, the bold jumper.

Both of you are embraced by your Fred.

Locarno-Monti, July 15, 1919

Dear Mother,

The newest plan occupying my mind is this: to write a national epic. While working on the medieval epics for my small literary history, I was reminded of the beauty and immediate popular appeal of these old legends. Then, when I happened upon Goethe's fragment *Ahasver*, it became clear to me how one should shape the old German legend to revive it anew. In terms of subject matter and ethics, the legend of Robert the Devil appeals to me the most, and I want to attempt to approach it. If you have the sections I send typed in five copies each time, I'll gladly send you the work as it progresses. I hope it doesn't end up as a fragment like *Ahasver*. I'm enclosing the first chapters.

Warm regards to you and Father Max.

Your Klabund

Mrs. Wend, Nürnberg, Spittlertorgraben 19/1, took excellent photos of me (the ones with the hat!). Didn't she send you any? I asked her to, but she should send the bill to me.

Locarno-Monti, July 28, 1919

Dear Mother,

I went to bed at 6. Out of eighteen hours, I spent twelve writing the literary history. I have to be done by September 1st, as per the contract (the book is supposed to be out by Christmas). September 1st hangs over me like a Damocles sword, as the catalog and three anthologies I've taken on in addition must also be finished by then. (*Along with The Zodiac*, a lyrical anthology titled *The Drunken Song*, and another anthology *Loyal Women*... love stories from Indian, Chinese, Old German, etc. literature.) Zacharias Werner wrote a fate drama titled *February 24th*. I'll write one titled *September 1st*.

After September 1st, I absolutely need to rest properly. I must spend months just lazing around. My nerves do give out occasionally. I'll likely just manage to get past September 1st.

The exchange rate is still horribly low (34!). That's really the reason I took on the anthologies. But what are 1,500 marks? Not even 500 francs.

Did you receive all the books? (I've shelved politics for a few weeks...)

Always your Fred

Locarno-Monti, August 10, 1919

Dear Mother,

I was away for a few days. In Basel. For a wedding. I had a beautiful yet painful experience that moved me deeply. Since Irene's death, even the sweetest draught has a bitter gall mixed in. Perhaps I'll write to you more about it someday when I've come to terms with it.

I'm sending you some brochures on affordable housing with the same post. These brochures have just been published to help alleviate the housing shortage, and they show that you can have a lovely home of your own for 2,000–3,000 marks. Father should take a look at the plans and tell me what he thinks. I would really like to have one built for myself. (The furniture can be built in: one doesn't need much – two beds at the very least, a wardrobe, a bookshelf, etc.) Maybe he'd contribute to it, and we could build it a bit bigger so you could spend your summer holidays there.

With warmest regards, Your Fred

Enclosed are the autographs of Johst, Henckell, and Harbeck.

Locarno-Monti, August 13, 1919

Dear Mother,

Every day brings inquiries, and I'd need to be twelve people to fulfill everything being asked of me. The Dreiländer Verlag wants a book, a publisher in Hanover another, as does E. P. Tal in Vienna and a newly founded Berlin publisher. Reclam wants me to prepare an edition of *Gessner*, and they'd like me to advocate for a Heine selection. Since my return from Basel, I've been poorly inclined to work and must force myself to complete the essentials – which is already more than enough.

The experience I had in Basel weighs on me more than I first realized. Medically speaking, it's affected my heart. What should I do? Should I return to Basel in three weeks? I suppose I'll have to; otherwise, I won't find peace. I hesitate to form a clear idea of what might happen, should happen, or must happen. That my senses are reawakening is all too understandable and natural. But is it more than that? Or am I just restless because my feelings haven't yet found their natural release?

The girl, a charming creature, is barely more than a child – 16 or 17 years old. How should I define her feelings for me? General, vague infatuation with the world, of which I happen to be the object? A poet's allure, mixed with respect and a touch of vanity at being loved by him? Or is it simply: love? I don't dare decide so easily in favor of the latter. She is the daughter of a highly respected Basel family, all living within the most conventional and constrained circumstances. Perhaps she was only intoxicated for an evening by the breath of freedom that blew over her?

I can't include *The Gravedigger* in the poetry book. I've already promised it to the Dresden publisher for the new edition. I reread it yesterday with particularly strong feelings, right after receiving a letter from the young girl in Basel. The psychological interpretation of this instinctive reaction I leave to the psychoanalysts – or to you, if you prefer.

Warmest regards to you both,
Your faithful Fred

Crossen/Oder, October 5, 1919

Dear Mother,

To be honest, I'm growing anxious about the long delay with the five (!!) crates as well. Enclosed are the shipping receipts – please file a claim. The crates contain all of Irene's belongings, blankets, etc.; two are full of books and manuscripts, and there's also a small suitcase. I didn't insure the items; it costs a fortune–a couple of hundred marks – and is entirely unnecessary, as the railway is still liable. I remember reading an article in the *Vossische Newspaper* by a Berlin lawyer explaining in detail how redundant such insurance is. Most of the contents are irreplaceable, though I still hope they'll arrive.

I'm enclosing the key to my suitcase in case I need something.

You're quite right about Fiete: she is a kind-hearted person, but trapped in a thousand illusions, none of which I am to blame for, as I've always been brutally honest with her. She created a terrible scene in Berlin, and I barely stopped her from attempting suicide. I care for her deeply, but she's always overestimated our relationship. I thought I'd made everything clear, but a few days ago, she sent me a letter with a marriage proposal – in an almost dictatorial tone: "I will marry you, I will give you children, I am essential for your development," and so on. The letter was so psychologically off the mark that it alarmed me. My firm "No" will likely bring the Fiete chapter to a close.

I have more work than enough. The corrections for *Zodiac* are consuming a lot of time. I'm supposed to write a foreword for a Heine selection. I'm working on a Gessner edition for Reclam – Gessner is one of my favorite poets. Hopefully, I'll also come to an agreement with Reclam about a small volume of my own–poetry and prose. I'm still undecided about the final arrangement of this year's poetry collection. I've now grouped *Silvia* and the *Sonnets to Irene* together for stylistic reasons.

Other plans are floating around, including a personal appearance with Reinhardt. What do you think?

The parents send their warm regards to you both. Can we ship the typewriter? It's so practical, especially since the printer can never read my handwriting.

The latest *White Leaves* is full of atrocious printing errors that distort both meaning and sound, as is the case with *Orchid Garden*.

Always yours, Fred

Greetings to Kubin!

Crossen/Oder, October 10, 1919

Dear Father,

Of course, I will come to visit you; it's just a matter of when. How could you think that I wouldn't come at all? Would I be sending you all those boxes otherwise? Enclosed is a power of attorney that will hopefully suffice. When I visit, I hope it will be warm at your place. It's dreadfully cold here. Could you at least heat one room properly? And will the clatter of my typewriter bother you? I already type like a seasoned office clerk. Mother should gift herself one of these machines for Christmas. It's a special system from AEG Berlin. The model my father has is even simpler: Latin script. He only gave me this machine because it was too cumbersome for him. He bought it out of patriotic reasons: German script. Back then, he purchased three machines at 100 marks each. They would undoubtedly cost much more now. You can take a look at mine. It's a very small machine.

I already wrote to Schäppi some time ago, asking him to prepare the grave nicely for October 18th. I'll write him again, though. I had ivy planted along the wall earlier. The Sant' Antonio cemetery itself is indescribably bleak. The only beautiful thing about it is its location in the southernmost sunlight.

Today I applied for a long-term visa at the Swiss embassy. That way, I could at least spend 14 days in Switzerland every few months. I noticed several affordable houses or properties in Bavaria being advertised in the *Munich Latest News*. I regret not having purchased a small house in Solln back in 1915, which was offered to me then for just a few thousand marks.

Warmest regards, also from the parents here,

to both of you,

your Fred

Crossen/Oder, after October 10, 1919

Dear Father,

It seems you didn't receive my last letter. The conditions at the post office are scandalous. Today I learned that two registered letters to Berlin have gone missing – one of them contained a foreword to a small Heine edition.

I am returning the power of attorney to you here. Please do keep the room for me; you can say it's my permanent residence, which is true since all my belongings are with you, and that I am just traveling. I had written to Schäppi long ago, and he will arrange everything beautifully. Please feel free to take anything you want from Irene's belongings. Just let me know beforehand if you plan to give something to others, as there are items I'd like to keep. If you go to Locarno next year, take me with you. I'm already longing for the mountains, the lake, and the sunshine of Monti.

Shall I describe the view from here to you? Restaurant Blue Angel, Restaurant

Otto Grenzius, Wine Tavern Auguste Kopsch, Widow Jaensch...

Regarding your request about corrections: unfortunately, I can't comply, as Irene has already been printed in its second edition, and a new edition of this challenging verse book is unlikely anytime soon. As for the distichs, I don't think I'll incorporate them into book form. On the other hand, "Max" has been excommunicated from *The Sleepwalkers*.

I'm glad Landauer means something to you. I agree with him on so many points. He was more of an anarchist than a communist, after all. If you want to read something reasonable about Russia, read Paquet's *Spirit of the Russian Revolution*, published by Kurt Wolff. It ought to be distributed to all citizens free of charge, instead of the silly pamphlets of the Anti-Bolshevik League.

Warm regards to both of you,

your Fred

Crossen/Oder, October 15, 1919

Dear Mother,

I'm feeling somewhat better, but I still won't be able to travel to Basel for the premiere of *Hannibal* on the 20th. I'll probably have to stay here for another eight days. Hopefully, I can then start my lectures.

A few days ago, I received a letter from my old landlady in Munich, who always took such good care of me. It would be nice if I could arrange to stay in her room again. That way, I could divide my time between Passau and Munich as I please. Is the connection already passable? The express trains have been canceled here, but I hope to leave by car.

I'm enclosing a card from Schäppi; he will surely arrange everything very nicely. We often talk about Irene. My parents have had a beautifully enlarged photo of her made, which I'll bring to you. My mother still cries every day before Irene's picture and always places flowers in front of it.

I feel like the restless wanderer I once was before I had Irene–unable to find peace, neither here nor there. Work numbs the pain, but it shouldn't; it should inspire and uplift.

The Zodiac is now finished: a book of over 500 pages. Also, *The Intoxicated Song*. The corrections for *Threefold Sound* – that's what I'm calling the new poetry book now – are almost done, too. It will be published together with *The Sleepwalkers*. I had a massive task with the *History of Literature*: it had become too long – imagine that, I had to cut 130 pages, including many important ones.

Warm greetings, also from the parents here,

always your Fred

P.S. Please include the poem *Poor Konrad* in your next letter.

Crossen/Oder, after October 15, 1919

Dear Mother,

I am very clumsy: now I've gone and lost the copy of *Poor Konrad*. Would you complete the measure of your kindness and write it out for me again? Yes: the ballads will be published separately, also by Reiß. *The Gravedigger* was published by the Dresden Verlag in 1917. But of course, I will come to visit you: a parable – back in 1909, I wanted to travel to Lausanne. I passed through Berlin and ended up staying an entire year there. Then I traveled to Copenhagen, to Holland, to Venice – and, through the Simplon, to Lausanne. So, in the end, I did get to Lausanne...

Do you enjoy preserved seafood, like eels, flounders, crabs, and the like? I can provide you with an address where you can order them directly at very moderate prices. We've been sourcing from there for years. I don't know if you are as fond of fish as we are. By the way, I'm speaking entirely *pro domo* – for myself: when I visit you, I would really enjoy eating smoked fish and so on.

Yes, this is what brotherly love looks like,

your faithful Fred

Crossen/Oder, October 18, 1919

Dear Mother,

Today is the 18th. I think of the one I will never forget, who was the most beautiful and best part of my life. If I have ever hurt you, I ask your forgiveness. Sometimes I'm cruel without meaning to be.

Yours,

Fred

Crossen/Oder, October 21, 1919

Dear Mother,

I am returning Frau Jung's letters to you with this. They are very kind. I am also supposed to give a reading in Jena, so I will see her there. Every day I intended to leave, and yet I am still here; I didn't dare travel with my cold. But I will definitely leave the day after tomorrow.

Today, a telegram arrived from the theater in Basel, and it seems that *Hannibal* was a great success. Well, we have gradually become devout skeptics: let's wait for the reviews. Here, I've been rummaging through old letters and manuscripts. I found entire boxes I had completely forgotten, and long-buried memories blossomed anew.

I found my first "drama:" a treatment of the conflict between Napoleon and Metternich, written in 1903... I was twelve years old at the time. Then I found my first poems. A novel: *The Journey into Life*, written during my senior year in school, and fragments of that dreadful book titled *Peter*, which I wrote during my early days in Berlin – a work of such cynicism and contempt for humanity as could only emerge from the image of Berlin itself. Indeed, that's what Berlin is like: the book is horribly current. Hopefully, I'll rediscover the whole thing.

The package has just arrived. Many thanks.

When you write, and mention the little envelope labeled "Poems 1904-1906," saying how much my mother must have delighted in them: you touch on a dark point in my relationship with her. Even now, my mother cannot comprehend why I write poems, which "are entirely unnecessary." She understands me only instinctively, only maternally.

That I sometimes have intensely antagonistic feelings toward her (perhaps even feelings of hatred...): this may stem from her inability to grasp what is most essential about me. In and of herself, she is a truly good-hearted woman.

Always yours, Fred

Berlin, Late October 1919

Dear Mother,

Reclam wrote to me today: they are going to publish a small selection of my work–prose and verse. Isn't that very nice? With that, I'm now somewhat of a minor classic and on my way to true popularity. – You probably already know that I am editing Geßner for Reclam. For two new major projects – new editions of the classics – I am supposed to serve as editor. My literary history is being printed in ten editions at once. The man has courage. – Unfortunately, printing takes an eternity under current conditions. *The Sleepwalkers* was supposed to have been published six months ago. I'm still working on *Triad*; it probably won't come out until spring. Reiß is also putting together a special book of ballads. – Then I have another idea (in fede): *Image and Poetry*. A monumental work. It's supposed to be ready here by March 1st. Price point: 40 marks. With many pictures. I have more than enough work. The provisional state of housing, etc., is, of course, paralyzing. Life here is insanely expensive in the long run. Without entertainment tax, without housing – in other words, just for food, drink, transportation, etc. – I need 50 marks a day. In this regard, it's good that Reinhardt is here. He can pay... I've been sick with a cold ever since I arrived. – In Hamburg, as I read afterward, they ended up butchering *The Gravediggers*. Well, you'll read the reviews yourself. I protested. But what good are protests? (Just look at Germany!) – I'll be glad if I can escape this witches' cauldron somewhat unscathed. – The French lyric poetry is here. On the other hand, I never received *The Songs of Venus*, which I actually need. A censorship official surely stole it.

Hugs to you both,

your Fred

Berlin, November 1, 1919

Dear Mother,

At 1 a.m. on the 30th, I stood at Potsdamer Platz. It was Irene's hour of death. An endless cacophony raged around me. The street vendors shouted, the cars rattled, the prostitutes hissed like snakes. Above, the electric arc lamps glared down like a thousand evil moons. Far away, high above, Irene's star softly glimmered.

Dear Mother, please don't send me anything for my birthday. I can get all the books I want. I don't need anything, and anything I do need – clothing, etc. –

I can buy for myself. Hopefully, I won't need a tailcoat at Reinhardt's. That now costs as much as a teacher's annual salary used to. In such matters, Berlin is unaffordable. – I'm reading in Rostock on the 6th, in Berlin on the 7th, in Hamburg on the 9th, in Kiel on the 11th, and in Königsberg on the 13th. Hopefully, the trains will run as expected. Today I'm going to the Deutsches Theater again – most likely, my contract with Reinhardt will be finalized. Then I'll move out of here into a good boarding house. You can get one for 20 marks. Even the film people are beginning to take an interest in me. They're asking if I want *Moreau* adapted into a film. Five-figure sums are being thrown around like nothing. Here, everyone talks in numbers.

Basel was a very big success. I just read the reviews, which you'll receive. Anny Romang must have been delightful as the American Miss. – My new poetry collection is finished, and the brochures have already been sent out. It looks entirely different now compared to *The Cherubim*. But it has gained a great deal in coherence; Reiß, Dr. Kayser, and others consider it my best book by far. How do you like the title *Triad*? The middle section, Coelia, contains the Sonnets to Irene. Dr. Kayser wrote that it represents a "pinnacle of modern German lyric poetry." It's become very slim and thin – only 83 pages. You'll receive it right away.

Hugs to you both, your Fredi

The girl from Basel wrote a charming letter. Should I send it to you?

Berlin, November 10, 1919

Dear Mother,

It's so unpleasant that the suitcase with my clothes still hasn't arrived. The weather is terrible – snow and storms. If I didn't have my grandfather's fur coat, I'd be lost. I only have summer clothes here. November 9th passed unnoticed in the snowstorm. All the rumors about communist coup attempts were (of course) nonsense. It wasn't "celebrated" at all. I didn't see a single red flag or ribbon. An incredible "revolution." – On the 7th, I read here as part of the Reiß publishing evenings. I still haven't recovered from that evening. I had asked Reiß in vain to leave Resi Langer out that night – she's more of a literary operetta diva. The discrepancy between the two parts was unbearable for my ear and my heart. She read pieces from *The Carousel and Dawn*, which suit her, but have almost nothing to do with what I'm doing today. I read *Francis* and some ballads. – Of course, it's my fault alone: why was I so weak and let myself be persuaded by Reiß? – Most people surely didn't notice, but the few I care about certainly did. And so, for me, the evening was an absolute failure.

For people here to pursue pleasure, Berlin must seem enchanting. But if you have work to do, even the smallest task requires an enormous effort of willpower, nerve, and organizational skill just to be where you need to be at the right time. You have to know all the transportation options by heart, rush from the subway to the tram, from the tram to the city train. Here, you're always rushing. Walking doesn't get you anywhere.

Hugs to you both, your Fred

Berlin, November 25, 1919

Dear Mother,

The package just arrived. Many thanks! Yesterday, I attended the dress re-hearsal of *Orestie* at the Grand Theater. The theater is magnificent. The lighting system is unbelievably beautiful. (There are no lamps: the columns and the dome glow!) It was after midnight when I left the theater feeling rather dissatisfied. The second part wasn't even over. I had the impression of something antiquated: in previous years, I was much more deeply moved by *Oedipus*. They should have performed *Antigone* in Hölderlin's translation.

The books are terribly delayed. Everything should already have been pub-lished, and yet nothing has appeared: neither *Triad* nor *Sleepwalker*, neither *Drunken Song* nor *Zodiac*, neither *Hafez* nor the *Literary History*. The publisher of the latter played a nasty trick on me. I explicitly asked for a final text revision. They didn't send it and went ahead with printing the book. I'm honestly dreading its publication. The sonnets will appear in a particularly beautiful edition from Reiss: only 300 copies. *The Dance Anthology* refers to a lyrical anthology.

Warm regards to you both. I'm writing this in bed. I'm quite tired. Your Fred

Berlin, December 10, 1919

Dear Mother,

Schall und Rauch opened its doors the day before yesterday: the reviews in the *Daily Paper, Lunchtime Newspaper*, and *8 O'clock Evening Paper* are glowing. I don't share that view–I find the whole thing dreadful. If I had known earlier about the how and what, I wouldn't have taken part. I was lured in by Reinhardt's name, blindly walked into the trap. Well, now it's a matter of gritting my teeth and getting through the month.

Monti surrounds herself in my memory with an ever more golden halo. If only I could return. You'll be glad to hear that Reiss plans to publish the sonnets in an especially beautiful edition, with accompanying etchings or lithographs.

Warm embraces to you both from your Fred

Berlin, December 15, 1919

Dear Mother,

Thanks for the letters. I don't wish for anything for Christmas. And what I do wish for, I can't be given anyway. Please tell the housing office that I absolutely need a permanent apartment somewhere. Where else am I supposed to keep my things? They're deteriorating beautifully in the meantime–especially the laundry and clothing here. I can't take care of it. I don't even know how.

I've received a new and favorable offer from *Schall und Rauch*: starting January 1st, I'm to join the management (and it's sorely needed with that literary mess). I wouldn't need to stay in Berlin for it; I'll make that a condition. And I'd receive an annual salary of 15,000 marks. I really should accept it. Then I wouldn't need to earn money for an entire year. What do you think? What's your opinion on this? (I'm sending you the two latest very amusing Dada magazines.)

Warm embraces to you both.

Your Fred

Berlin, December 20, 1919

Dearest Mother,

A thousand thanks for the rich, colorful package! You bestow so much upon me, but what is most precious to me is your love, which I ask you to carry with you into the new year and all the coming years that are, shall I say: are granted to us or are yet to be imposed upon us? I am indeed a broken person, and I do not mean that in a sentimental sense, but: the rays of my being, which somehow come from the sun, are fractured; I am no longer at one with myself. The tree has a fracture above the root.

Have you read about Einstein? The world is full of his fame and his research results. And yet, if humanity were truly insightful, it should have understood the theory of relativity in science, in the sciences, long ago. It is the simplest truth when approached from a spiritual standpoint. I remember having a long dispute with Levy in Davos in 1917, where I literally put forward the same thesis as Einstein without having conducted or needed scientific experiments: because there is an absolute truth that has nothing to do with experiments; it must be abstracted from fundamental spiritual facts. Levy disputed my view back then, but the next day he came to me and said: I believe you are right.

But what will people do with Einstein now? They will, as with Newton before, stop short, instead of recognizing the relativity of all sciences, including mathematics – and not only the sciences, but all domains of practical reason, including moral and economic areas. We must talk about all this in person.

Please, have the songs marked in red copied! But don't do it yourself! It is mortally boring. Both of you are warmly embraced by your Fred.

Berlin, December 26, 1919

Dear Mother,

These days and nights have hurt me deeply again. I searched everywhere for Irene. I wandered through the streets, hoping to encounter her somewhere. What reason has long since understood: heart, eye, and ear still refuse to accept.

I had far too much to do even during these days. The new program is under my direction. I also directed for the first time, and you, as a layperson, may not understand the enormous mental energy it requires and how completely drained one is after just a few hours of rehearsals. I am sending you the new program and all the texts. To give you a hint: the announcer is a Spanish miracle-theater director, then there is a singer with a lute, a dancer, a Finn with the kantele, Gussy Holl with songs, H. v. Meyerinck with a scene from *The Gambler*, Mady Christians as a dancing girl, Twardowski with parodies, Graetz as a newspaper boy, and a political film from Trier. All the texts of the songs and scenes are by me, currently under a new pseudonym: Pol Patt.

I have committed for a year now, as I probably already wrote to you. Thank God I explicitly arranged not to stay in Berlin. Another position has been offered to me by a German-American newspaper conglomerate. However, I am undecided and seek your advice. I am inclined to decline it, despite the excellent financial terms: I am to take over the editorial management of a new daily newspaper being founded with a capital of 10 million marks. I would receive 40,000 marks. Adding Reinhardt's 15,000 marks: a total of 55,000 marks, so that, including income from my books, I could estimate an annual income of 70,000 marks – if I stayed in Berlin and worked myself half to death. What do you think?

Berlin is entirely Americanized. The few people needed are paid exorbitantly. If I were to join a film company, an additional 15,000–20,000 marks a year could be added, making 100,000 marks the balance of a second Berlin year – in which I might already be worn out. Because 8, 10, 12 hours of work: it wouldn't suffice.

If someone gave me 1,000 francs a month, I'd leave everything behind: and return to Monti.

The trip to Passau has also become quite expensive. A first-class sleeping car – there's hardly another option since there's only the night train, and I can't stand for 14 hours – will cost 200 marks! Hopefully, we'll see each other soon, around the 15th or 20th of January.

With heartfelt greetings and embraces,
your Fred

Berlin, January 22, 1920

Dear Mother,

I have heard nothing from you at all. I've sent you so much: letters, books, magazines, *Triad*. I don't even know if everything arrived. Did Father, for instance, receive the Buddha? I just remembered: You gave him *The Decline of the West* by Spengler in the spring at my suggestion. I'd love to hear his opinion on it. To me, it seems the only historical-philosophical work of our time. But hopefully, we'll be able to talk about it in person soon.

It's fate that something always gets in the way: I would have liked to be with you long ago. Suddenly, there's a new restriction. And now I'm a bit unwell (nothing serious, not my lungs). I've, as the French charmingly say, *attrapé quelque chose*. It doesn't affect me emotionally at all: Since Irene's death, I've gained great equanimity toward all external events and appearances.

Anny Romang was here until yesterday for a few days. We spent a lot of time together. She's getting married this summer.

What do you think of *Triad*? If I abstract from the personal aspects – which goes without saying for us – I see it as a typical book: perhaps the first poetry book of the post-expressionist and post-activist era. And (in some way) aligned with: Spengler, Keyserling, Bloch.

I'm writing this letter in bed, so please excuse the handwriting.

Both of you are warmly embraced by your Fred.

"I've become a member of various societies, including the Kant Society, heartily applauded by Vaihinger, its chairman, the as-if phenomenologist. I've already published my first anti-Kantian essay, titled: *Lao Tzu and the Kant Society.*"

– From a letter by Klabund to Ernst Levy, [Berlin], February 15, 1920

Berlin, February 4, 1920

Dear Mother,

Here is the slip, I have filled it out. I am thinking of heading to Munich later from your place: "to study" (I'm old enough for it, after all...). Otherwise, it seems that it's not easy to get a residence permit. The reactionary tumult in Munich is said to be appalling. – Here, I am stepping in – temporarily – again. Holl is ill, and Christians too. The flu is rampant. In Rostock, Jena, Meiningen, Braunschweig: in the provinces, so to speak, I will be reading in the coming days – unless something gets in the way again. Did you read about my matinee in Mannheim? – In the *New Zurich Newspaper*, I was attacked as a "Jew" (!!!): unbelievable! Anti-Semitism is such a nice thing when it's directed at non-Jews. – Berlin is getting more and more unfair. You wouldn't believe it. I paid for tailoring repairs twice recently: 125 and 50 marks! Ironing costs more now than an entire suit used to. Berlin has made me bitter and malicious again: I think my next work will be a tragicomedy. Otherwise, everything is available here, but the prices are as follows: smoked eels 20 marks per pound, pickled goose breast 30 marks, liver sausage 15 marks, American meat 10 marks, butter 25-30 marks per pound. Honey 12 marks, coffee 26 marks. Those are the delicacies for supper. Excellent marzipan 30 marks, chocolate 30 marks, cakes 22 marks. – As a housewife, this must interest you, though the quality is admittedly very good. Still, a modest dinner costs 10 marks. Breakfast, honey, etc., not much less. I spend around 50 marks per day. For the main meal, I have pork chops, veal roast, or omelet – all without ration cards, with soup and dessert, for 12-15 marks, and it's very good. In Munich, they say it's half as expensive.

Warm regards to you both,

your Fred

Berlin, February 14, 1920

Dear Mother,

Would it trouble you to look among the recent newspaper clippings for one containing my protest about the Hamburg performance of *The Gravedigger*? I need it soon. In the *New Zurich Newspaper*, I was subjected to anti-Semitic abuse... they thought I was a Jew... me, of all people. In *Schall und Rauch*, Mady Christians had a sensational success with a revolutionary rag of mine in the February program. I am thinking of coming over around the 25th. Hopefully, nothing will get in the way this time.

Warm regards to you both,

your Fred

Meiningen, February 22, 1920

Dear Mother,

Sending you warm greetings from Meiningen. I am utterly charmed by this little town: I spoke at the theater this morning and received the kindest reception. The audiences are better, more enthusiastic, and easier to engage – and deeper – than in Berlin. Not being in Berlin: that alone is happiness... If only I could free myself from *Schall und Rauch*, I would be so content. But, unfortunately, I am still too financially tied to it.

I'm getting closer and closer to you both. If I had packed my things already, I could be with you tomorrow, as Meiningen is closer to you than to Berlin. However, it will likely take another ten days. I'm planning to be with you on the 15th at the latest. – Frau Wesselsky visited me earlier and brought greetings from you. I'm glad to hear you are both well.

With heartfelt embraces,

your Fred

What one can still eat and drink here well – and cheaply! In Berlin, there's nothing but vinegar.

Berlin, March 12, 1920

Dear Father,

Your telegram: "...no hurry for you to come..." sounds so harsh, as if you no longer want me at all. And you can't imagine how long I have been longing for you: for a little peace, quiet, home, and intimacy. Something always seems to come up: it's so typical of Berlin: here "something always comes up." – By the way, you Passau people are looking sharp: respect: hand grenades, bombs, rubber truncheons: these are not mere delusions. What the unleashed soldiery has accomplished in the past 14 days: it's unbelievable. The reaction is not marching: it's already here. And Hungary is only a few steps away. The events have made me quite reflective, and I am contemplating whether, despite all the fundamental differences, I should join the U.S.P.D. or the K.P.D.: just to stand in line against the reaction. – The following telegram will certainly interest you: *The Gravedigger* was performed in Mannheim the day before yesterday. Yesterday, I read with great success at the Lessingbund in Braunschweig. Both of you are warmly embraced by your Fred.

Hannover, May 2, 1920

10:45 p.m.

Dear Mother,

In a hurry, a few lines quickly written in the office of the chief director. They are playing the third act of *Tristan* outside. In the past few days, I have experienced many things and met many people. The boy is quite charming, a lovely guy, a nice mix of cheekiness and contemplation. He always called me Klabünterle. Of course, I brought him chocolate and won his heart that way. No surpise that Mrs. D. is quite frazzled with her nerves. Her husband is now in prison in Berlin. I also met the little stenotypist in Berlin, and the lady in blue, whom you don't like, but who has a very provocative effect on me. She goes to the blood like (at least) peace champagne. To quickly summarize everything in haste: there was a row at *Reinhardt* and *Schall und Rauch*. It was very good that I went to Berlin; that way, I saved a few thousand marks for myself and immediately resigned from *Schall und Rauch* as of May 1st. That's no shame. On the contrary. Maybe I could have saved more materially if I understood legal tricks and had threatened lawsuits, etc. I didn't, though, and accepted the compromise. It seems that *Schall und Rauch* is being kept afloat through some kind of manipulation (New Society, etc.). Hollaender, Herald, and Theobald Tiger have also left. – Now I am here. Yesterday, 2 acts of *Abduction from the Seraglio*. I am staying at the Hindenburg Inn (!!!), Bödekerstr. 79, where Küppers, whom I spoke to, is very ill in bed (flu or something: suddenly: wife and child are sick too). Tomorrow, I'll attend the rehearsal. This morning there was a lecture. In all haste, you are both warmly embraced with longing for Passau's peace from your Fred.

Greetings to the good people: Hingsamer, Kieffer, the school inspector and his wife.

Hannover, May 7, 1920

Dear Mother,

A few words in all haste. Tonight is the performance. I have attended rehearsals daily from 10 to 4:30. Every evening, I've been invited until deep into the night or early morning: you can imagine that I sometimes had a great longing for Passau's peace. I have eaten (and I must say it like this) and drunk here in Hannover like I haven't in years. The chief director here, Dr. Roenneke, is very competent; I'm very pleased with the performance, it's everything that can be pulled from the resources and means of a former court theater. I very much regret that the Intime Theater Nuremberg performed *Hannibal* recently, without me knowing. Friends wrote to me that the performance and direction were of the lowest quality and that the audience hissed extensively at the end. If I had known, I would of course have gone to Nuremberg and taken over the direction myself. The 4th act should not be played at all: it's for the book. – Tomorrow, I'm leaving. Both of you are warmly embraced by your Fred.

Hannover, May 8, 1920

Sleepwalkers launched with an excellent performance, a bitter theater battle like Hannover has never seen before. In the end, the enthusiastic and raging youth defeated the organized resistance of a court theater clique and called the poet, director, and performance to the stage 20 times before the proscenium and the iron curtain. – Greetings, Fred

Heidelberg, before May 15, 1920
Dear Mother,

Thank you for your letter. I think I will be with you again in the week after Pentecost. Then I will rest, do a few small things like the anthology, and finally eat properly and well again. (In Hannover it was very good, but in Heidelberg and Mannheim, there is no food, it's more like slop.) I've made many friends everywhere. Roenneke, the director of the theater, critics Frerking and Havemann in Hannover, Dr. Küppers, the founder of the Kestner Society, poet Schiebelhuth, publisher Steegemann: all in Hannover; here in Heidelberg, art historian Fraenger, the old Philips, I'm only naming people to whom I feel a certain closeness. Spending time with the lady in blue and Mimi has undoubtedly done me good. The world maintains its balance by the law of the scales. Peace must be fought for. The press agitation against me does not affect me. I stand too firmly and securely on my own to be thrown off balance by a newspaper clamor. – Congratulations on your candidacy. Maybe Sternheim's candidate is the right reading for you now? – I am sending the Reclam contract herewith. Please give it to Father. – I am writing these lines under the green trees of the Stiftsmühle on the Neckar. In the evening, we want to return to Heidelberg by boat. You are both warmly embraced by your Fred.

My money is running low. I will probably have to ask for a wire.

Heidelberg, May 15, 1920
Dear Mother,

Just a quick greeting from Heidelberg; I am sitting by the Neckar, staring at the red walls of the castle. Clouds are racing across the sky, and it's getting bright and dark alternately. Just like in me. Yesterday, there was a wonderful celebration in Wolfsbrunnen; we sang the songs of the old immortal Bellmann, and at the end, also songs by Werfel and me. Tonight, the original *Hamlet* is being performed here. I can only hint at everything to you. Mimi is here. She wore a hoop skirt yesterday because she played Ulla Winblad, the lover of the Swedish poet. Did you receive my telegram? I am running out of money. You are both warmly embraced by your Fred.

Nuremberg, Sulzbacher Strasse 80 at Graf, May 25, 1920
Dear Mother,

I wanted to call you today, but they said: disruption in Passau! Surely you haven't: either declared a Soviet Monarchy or a Wittelsbach Republic, have you? I'm coming on Sunday with the fast train from Nuremberg to Passau (I don't know when it leaves). I'm still reading here on Saturday. I feel very comfortable. I partly traveled the Heidelberg-Nuremberg route by car, along the Bergstraße to Frankfurt, and in this way, I got here incredibly fast (Heidelberg-Nuremberg about 7 hours!).

To my horror, I just realized that I forgot the main thing of the entire trip: the very reason I was traveling: I forgot to bring the National Assembly stamps... I don't know if I can face Father now... By the way, I ask Father to have me listed on the voter rolls so I can vote. (U.S.P. or K.P.D.: the murder of Paasche, this barbaric atrocity, has made me furious again.) I read yesterday that you made an alliance with these dogs in Bavaria, you democrats with these autocratic butchers; I could hardly believe it. The Democratic Party has forfeited its right to exist by aligning with the Center Party. It should and must perish.

For the time being, I'll stay with you, at least for four weeks, unless you send me out, though the air is now more than lukewarm: here, a tropical heat is brewing. You are both warmly embraced by your Fred.

Munich, Saturday, July 24, 1920
Dearest Mother, dearest Father,

It's a shame you won't come to Munich while I'm here. By the way, I don't understand the sentence in Father's letter: Have you postponed the trip, or are you not going at all, in light of Poland? – I've already had enough of Munich, or rather, of myself, and I would immediately return to Passau. Pleasure doesn't last in the long run. Frank and Fredi have welcomed me very warmly: Frank held a lecture evening, the proceeds of which he is giving me, which I completely don't think is right: don't you think I should refuse it? Tonight, there is a big garden party at Mannheimer's: all of Munich will be there, and I will go too. What else I've encountered in these days – dealers, film divas, acrobats, writers, painters, girls, singers, unhappy widows, publishers, etc. – I can't distinguish. Now and then, there was a person among them. I'm, of course, already dead tired. I've also thrown money out the window. Please send me some to Mittenwald. I'll give you the address later: temporarily, for mail from Tuesday: Mittenwald, post restante. You are both warmly embraced by your Fred, who really longs for you.

The card is for Mother's autograph collection. My handwriting is terrible. I can hardly write anymore.

Mittenwald, August 11, 1920
Dear Mother,

Hans has invited me to stay with him in August and September. Now I am happy to be invited from three sides, and it's hard to decide. The studio is also still reserved for me; what could I, what should I, what would I – what must I do! – Mimi is still my star. But a second star has risen beside her, above the Karwendel.

I lead quite an untragic life here. I am terribly lazy. I always think I should do something again. But I don't know what. Sometimes I read a few pages of Dostoevsky, but then it's already too much for me. I am neither happy nor unhappy. Existence hangs in the balance. In Munich, I met dozens of people, and I believe

I will spend the first part of the winter in Munich and only the spring in Italy. – Today I hoarded potatoes from a peasant woman. I also have to wait for Hans's boy sometimes. Recently, there was a Ganghofer memorial celebration here: Almenrausch and Edelwoaß. In the end: living pictures: the poet surrounded by his brave mountaineers, writing. – The weather changes: rain, sunshine. I would like to go to Innsbruck. Unfortunately, it's so far to Füssen from here: from 9 in the morning until 4 in the afternoon. The stretch from Garmisch to Reutte (45 kilometers!!) alone takes about 4 hours – it would have been half an hour by express train! – Hugs to you both, your Fred.

Munich, August 21, 1920

Dear Mother,

I am writing to you in great haste with a short pencil to wish you and Father a good Sunday. I am back in Munich, staying a few days or maybe longer. Mimi is leaving for Karlsruhe on Monday. She was very sweet. But it is definitely time for her to leave. I can't tolerate women for long. Unless they are like Irene, whom I often thought of with sweet longing. Fannerl cried. During the trip, I leafed through the Karamazovs. Mimi always said I resembled Dimitriy. Maybe... Today I strangled her, and that was surely not right. Ah, the most beautiful thing is freedom: to throw your head back and look at the stars. – Please send my mail here. The publisher wants to print a very large edition of the history of literature, which is continually being bought. This would make me – for material reasons as well – very happy. I had to ask Hans for 1000 marks, and in total, I've probably spent about 4000 marks. Please send me a receipt or confirmation that the office has sent the 1000 marks to Hans, as I requested (I sent back the postal orders I signed).

Both of you are tightly embraced: life is still worth living: despite devils, death, and tears. Your Fred.

Munich, Schwindstr. 29/IV. I., before September 2, 1920

Dearest Mother,

It's one o'clock at night, and I'm quickly writing to you before I go to bed. I've just corrected the *Holy Legends*. Please (the publisher missed it) send me the source references from the *Holy Legends* – the manuscript is probably in Father's safe. If you could also send some bread coupons and a little sugar, it would be very kind. I live wildly, like in a robber's cave. I have to do everything myself.

I live a lot, but I also work a lot. In the last two days, I've written twenty poems. – Today I met the philosopher Ernst Bloch. Yesterday, I met Professor Kutscher, with whom I drank until late at night. The day before yesterday, I was with Johst. I saw Jagerspacher: the best is still the green-pink cushion on which the one act lies: enchanting. His latest works are too virtuosic, too sweet. You are embraced by your Fred.

Munich, before September 14, 1920

Dearest Mother,

Your letter has reassured me again: you are still fond of me after all. I have no inclination for sentimentality, but in my feelings for you, it seems to be sometimes intensified: I am so attached to you. – Read the enclosed card and be so kind as to look for the critiques of lecture evenings (Nuremberg, Meiningen, Mannheim, Braunschweig, etc.) and send them to me. I will then go through them. – At the moment, I am in financial disagreements with Reiß. I want to ask him for ten thousand marks for Italy, and I think he is obligated to give them to me, don't you agree? Imagine: *Moreau*, *Carousel*, and *Taverner*: all three are currently out of stock! He is terribly boring with reprints. – The sonnets are finished and will appear in 14 days. *The Holy Legends* will be out in early October. Also, the Lao Tzu. – In Meyer's newest *Conversations Lexicon*, I am already listed!! Also in the Herder edition! *The Munich Medical Weekly* has published an extensive review of my Davos books. (Issue of August 7th.) I met Kubin yesterday by chance. – Jagerspacher is a great experience when you first see his works (the best: the act with the green-pink cushion, which he himself plagiarized three times, since he liked it so much, the violinist, the Christ-like figure). Gradually, this impression fades, and you notice how much sentimentality and affectation are in many, especially his latest paintings. He is a good academic, and as such, naturally better than all the bad expressionists. The *New Secession* is generally quite weak this year: I liked: *Erbslöh, Der Desenberg, Jawlensky, Improvisations*, Th. Th. Heine, *Under the Willow*, Kanoldt, *still life*, Kokoschka, *Portrait of a Gentleman*, Lichtenberger, *Ludwigstraße*, Pechstein, *Women's House*, Pascin, *Weihlicher Akt*, Seewald, *Waldlandschaft*, Werefkin, *The Red Door*, Doerner, *Pilsensee*, and a *Davringhausen*. That's all. There's nothing really devastating. – Kubin is a hero against most of the scribbles and nonsense there. – I'm rather fond of Pascin (only sparsely represented), who illustrated Heine very charmingly (for Cassirer). – Yesterday I attended the festival of the international free socialist youth. (Tonhalle.) It was the first World Youth Day. – The U.S.P. cannot accept Moscow's dictatorial demands as a party, or it is no longer a party.

I don't like this tone at all: what does Moscow know about Germany? (Maybe I'll go there next time. But I believe I'm not quite right for the Bolsheviks either, since I am, after all, a homo sapiens, a thinking being, and I won't give up thinking, even for Lenin, whom I greatly admire). You are embraced, your Fred.

Munich, September 14, 1920

Dear Mother,

Please send the following books immediately to the Schauspielhaus Bad Pyrmont, Director Dr. Ulbrich for Klabund: *Mohammed* (hand copy: corrected), *Villon, Fire Worshipers, Epigram, Bracke, Ladder to Heaven*. – I have nothing here and will probably also read in Oldenburg and Hanover. – Also send a Klabund brochure to: Konzertbüro Bernstein, Holzgraben 6, Hanover. (The one with the Oppenheimer drawing.) – The reviews are too random: the most important ones are missing. – Warm regards, your Fred. – Mrs. Kaufmann appears to be dying.

Munich, September 21, 1920

Dear Mother,

Dr. Ulbrich writes, "I am happy to inform you that *Hannibal* was a strong, heartfelt success. At the end, people asked for you, and I had to thank the audience on your behalf..." Isn't that nice? – I am terribly cold, coughing and wheezing, taking codeine and plantain tea, but it's not helping. I am supposed to go to Berlin, Reiß telegraphed today, to read on the 28th and negotiate with him, we are by no means in agreement. I don't know yet what to do. –

Yesterday we buried Frau Kaufmann. I had a fit of weeping at the cemetery – not in regard to the certainly very good Frau K., but because, in that moment, the whole atmosphere of Locarno became so vividly real. It's exactly this time now – two years ago – the wound still burns. Hugs, your Fred.

Feldafing, by the Lake, September 25, 1920

Dear Mother,

I have not received the letter you mentioned in the card! Nor have I received two shipments from the Dürr and Weber publishing house that should have had the corrections. I don't understand this at all, it is very annoying because the book is supposed to be published for Christmas – but maybe I am already "under police supervision" again. In Munich, there are lively conditions in this regard. I hope to be able to leave on Monday: my cough seems to be subsiding. If I receive money from Reiß, I may go to Merano in 14 days. Maybe not. I can never say anything definite. But please defend my room with lion-hearted courage! I have to be able to have a home somewhere, if I don't have a home anywhere, I will get sick.

> Peach Blossom
> How sweet you smell
> Colorful comforter
> When the rain fairy
> Bends over you
> And moistens you
> With her tears.

How do you like this improvisation? It's from Li Tai'pe (and me). Hugs for both of you, and think of your Fred sometimes.

Munich, after September 25, 1920

Dear Mother,

It's half past two in the night. I just came back from Feldafing, where I was with Frank and Fredi: I've worked until now: read corrections, wrote letters to theater directors, concert agencies, now I'm writing one more letter, which I like far better than the others: to you. I have endured so much, in every regard, that I wonder how my nerves haven't snapped yet. In addition to everything else, Reiß is causing me the greatest concern: you can imagine that Munich is not exactly cheap, even with modest demands: my money is slowly going the way of all earthly things, I absolutely need a larger sum, if I am to go to Merano, which I probably really need: 10 or 20 thousand, I will have a tough fight with Reiß on Tuesday. On Monday, I am going to Berlin, despite my cold. How I will speak on Tuesday evening: is still a mystery to me. (Sorry for the handwriting.) I also want to try to speak to Wegener about a film. I will definitely come to see you before Merano: I think in 14 days, after Mannheim (12th October).

If only I had the money: it's seriously troubling me. – Oh, the wrong towel, that's horrible. – Maybe I'll have a child from a beautiful blonde (married – separated) woman, but for God's sake: I don't want it. – Always yours, Fred.

Munich, before October 12, 1920

Dear Mother,

A few days ago, I wrote to the *Basler National Newspaper*, sending them some manuscripts and asking them to send the fee directly to Locarno, to the gardener Schäppi, so that he could decorate the grave for the 18th. I also wrote to Miss Mendwyler. I think of Locarno so often, and when I think of Merano, I actually also think of Locarno. Yes, hopefully, Reiß will provide the money. I am thinking of going to Berlin on Sunday; I don't feel really unwell: I may be slightly feverish, but the worst is the cough, because I won't be able to fulfill my lecture commitments.

On the 12th, *Hannibal* is in Mannheim. I really want to see him on stage at last. I am negotiating with the theater here, which had a great success with Hidalla, about "Poor Kaspar." Hopefully, something will come of it. Yesterday, I had an examination. But lung doctors are always much more anxious than necessary. According to them, I should already be long gone. Yes, love and loving is quite a thing: man and woman here will only understand each other – if they love each other… The physical and mental constitution is too different. Yesterday and today, the sun is shining. It feels so good. My mother is also ill. She never takes care of herself. And my father, besides his profession as a pharmacist, is still (I believe in the 5th year!) an unpaid mayor! I find this a scandal. Both of you, embrace each other from your Fred.

Berlin, before October 14, 1920

Dearest Mother,

I hope to come very soon: please stop sending post etc. for now. On the 14th, *Hannibal* takes the Mannheim stage: it is truly sad that something always comes up when I want to see my plays. I don't feel well enough to travel (Berlin from 8 a.m., arriving at Mannheim by midnight!!) – Of course, I have mostly settled my business matters here: I made a new contract with Reiß, which is not entirely in my favor; he has almost too many "rights," and I had to lower the percentage to 15%. In return, he has committed to paying me 12,000 marks in four installments, starting immediately: and that was the most important thing to me, to get money for Merano. I may even receive Lire from him, though I could be taken in – he might also be. The risk is on both sides. – I also had bad luck with my lecture: it was sold out, but the newspaper strike began the same day, so only brief reports appeared in *Forward* and the *Börsen Courier*: the big newspapers didn't come out.

Tonight, I am at the Munich Christ, visiting Eugen Klopfer. I am utterly exhausted. I would like to go to Crossen as well, but I don't know if I will have the energy. I ran into Benn here and some other acquaintances. For the Rakete, I should write some couplets. It would be useful financially. Embraces to you, I have a slight fever, which also makes me feel weak. Your Fred

Berlin, October 18, 1920

Dearest Mother, Dearest Father –

Today is October 18th, and in memory of Irene, I embrace you warmly. I went to the bookbinding shop and arranged for them to bind a copy of the *Sonnets* in advance and send it to you for today. I hope it has reached you by now and that it tells you how unchangeable my heart is in its attachment to Irene, how inextricably I am bound to her. All the women I love or create: they are only her and always her. The Miss in *Poor Kaspar* – Gonhild in *Francis* – Maria in *Mohammed*: her and always her. I have asked Miss Mendwyler to decorate her grave for today. There will be dahlias and asters. – I must stay in Berlin for the next few days because many things are being decided. I tried to write a film, transferring the legend of St. Gregory to today's Russia. I'm always with you, your Fred

Berlin, before October 21, 1920

Dearest Mother,

Yes, something like that must of course happen in Berlin! And not only has my coat gone missing, but also a silk shawl, my suede gloves, and a lorgnette. –

I am working a lot. I have written three short one-act comedies: *The Strange Guest, The Eternal Return, The Solution of the Social Question.* I will include them in the volume of my collected dramas, which is to be published by Kaemmerer-Dresden. Reiß will collect my large poems. And a special edition of my Li Tai Pe poems is also in the works. – Do you still have a second copy of your poems, just as we had selected them? Please send it to me!! By the way, I also pressed Kaemmerer on your behalf, and I have not yet given up hope with him. – I am always sleeping badly, coughing a lot, but mentally I feel as alert as ever. I have also written a lot of new poems. Warm embraces from your Fred

Crossen/Oder, October 21, 1920

Dear Mother, dear Father,

I have been in Crossen since the day before yesterday. Generally, I feel quite well, though something seems off. I have pain in my pleura and keep coughing. I hope that this will ease by the first of November: I have – don't be alarmed – taken a double engagement for *Rakete* and *Schall und Rauch* in November – of course, solely for the financial aspect and in consideration of my mysterious trip to Italy. I will receive for the one month about the same as I did last year for five months. Also, I want to use the reprieve I've been granted in Berlin to establish film connections. Berlin has become even more expensive, and I've already spent a considerable amount on laundry, shoes, etc. I've also paid off some debts and, of course, was immediately approached by "good friends" asking for loans. Of course, I don't count Frau D. in that group, to whom I was happy to help. By the way, has anything come in for me from Passau? Dürr and Weber wrote something about 600 marks. Please send my mail to Berlin: I will be back by the 28th. Have you received the sonnets? Soffel wrote to me that he could house me for five francs, but that's still 70 marks. And it's still quite primitive. Meran would probably be more appropriate.

My parents, who are very kind to me, send their warm regards. I have to go to the dentist later: I'm terribly scared. Reiß will probably feature my collected Chinese poems. You're both hugged by your Fred.

Crossen/Oder, after October 21, 1920

Dear Mother,

Thank you so much for your letter. However, I really don't understand why the housing commission can take my room away. I spoke to my father, who is also involved and vehemently denies this. I have a profession that requires frequent travel: it's not right for them to take away my room during that time; for example, a traveler wouldn't have any place to stay if he were away for months. I'm still registered with you, so don't let them push you around: what would I do in the inn near the train station? I might as well live anywhere. I would even go to court over this. Of course, I can't come before December 1st or 2nd: we will see what happens afterward. I'll send you the favorable reviews again here: add them to the others. I'm composing like mad: Valetti, Kürschner, and Adalbert (in *Rakete*) will sing my works. In *Schall und Rauch*, I sing... myself. A bold move with my rusty baritone. You're both hugged by your Fred.

The parents here send their warmest greetings. My birthday wish? That I can keep my room!

Berlin, November 11, 1920

Dearest Mother,

What should I say? Staying in a hotel was, of course, quite cumbersome; perhaps Father will be kind enough to have the lights switched off and buy the mattresses at my expense. While you're at it, please ask him how much money I still have with him, and especially, I'd like to know if the publisher Dürr and Weber sent around 600 marks at that time. I'm working a lot, maybe too much, but mostly on things at the periphery. I've now translated Tartarin anew: it's supposed to be released by Christmas with illustrations by George Grosz. (He would also be a fabulous illustrator for my *Whore Songs*.) The Insel Verlag has behaved foolishly, but I think Reiß will now bring my new Chinese poems. The Lao Tzu has been published. The *Legend of Saints* as well. I haven't received any copies yet. I'm now trying to write a film; hopefully, it will succeed. A new cabaret wants to hire me as an artistic advisor. I'll only do it if I'm not committed to Berlin. How gentle and beautiful were the days in Munich compared to this! Here, everything is always in turmoil. People rush, run, and when there's a traffic strike, they are completely desperate. It's all about speed. Please don't forget to send me my bread tickets! That's the only thing I absolutely need. I'm still registered with you. Also, send me some of my sugar occasionally. Everything else is available here, but it's even more expensive than last year. I don't think I can get by with 4000 marks a month (I have 9500). But maybe I'll manage to save about 5000 from Berlin. That would be something. Yesterday, my brother was here. A piece of Tartarin himself. But much more likable than the last time. A really nice boy again. You're both embraced by your Fred.

Berlin, November 30, 1920

Dearest Mother,

Thank you very much for the two packages. They just arrived. I'm so sorry I always have to trouble you, and such unpleasant work! The manuscripts seem to be all the ones I need. (The French manuscript should be among them as well.) There's one more I need for the poems: the diary from prison, of which please send me two copies. Today, I will speak for the last time in *Schall und Rauch*, thank God. The day before yesterday, I was asked to speak from a box where a Mr. Matthes was the Grandmaster.

Father, I ask you to keep the money for me and to send me the bookseller's invoice, which I need to review. I'm working a lot. I'm – relatively – happy, though the cough is particularly bad this year. What would you like for Christmas? Hans Adler has published a very charming (and well-printed) poetry book with the E.P. Tal Verlag, Vienna: *Monkey Business*. My new poetry book will be quite curious: it contains so much that could only have been born on the Berlin asphalt. Maybe you won't like it at all. The title *The Gallows Ladder* or *The Gallows* leaves room for all kinds of speculation! Hugging you both, your Fred.

Berlin, after December 1, 1920

Dear Mother,

I could not find a copy of *Eros* with Reiß either. Please take another careful look, maybe in a suitcase, to see if it is there. I clearly remember that I did not take the folder with me. Today I received a telegram from Vienna asking if I would speak in January, possibly also in Graz, Linz, and Salzburg. Maybe I will do it. I am not entirely sure yet. If I go, I would travel via Passau and spend Christmas with you.

Please send me all the poems you have written so far again for review. Yesterday I spoke with a well-respected publisher here who has published books by me and with whom you would be a good fit. I believe I can promise with 90% certainty that your songs will be published in the spring. We have even already chosen the typeface. He will write to you directly.

Warm hugs from your Fred

Berlin, after December 1, 1920

Dear Mother,

You are very unfair: I can only confirm the packages once they have arrived! For example, the fur, which was surely sent later than some other things, arrived a few days ago – as I immediately informed you. Today, only the sugar, Martha Burkhardt, and your kind letter have arrived. Yes, the "Negro" has also arrived, you are relieved of him. And I sincerely thank you again for the cigarettes. (You are just like my mother: when she sends me a package, I have to confirm expressly that even the envelope and string arrived...) The book by M. B. is lovely. I am happy to write about it. The day before yesterday, I performed for the last time at *Schall und Rauch*. Thank God. Unfortunately, Berlin has become incredibly expensive: I need about 6000 marks per month. I cannot sustain this much longer. (Right now, I am still living off past earnings.) It is exactly as expensive as last year. I am supposed to give lectures in Breslau, Münster, Duisburg, Mannheim, etc., but I do not know if I will do it. Where is the *Eros*? I need a few poems for the new poetry collection. And the *Nothing*, *Le Baladin*, and the *Prison Diary*: I must trouble you about these. I believe in lonely nights you curse me and the fate that blessed you with me. If I ever come to Passau – I will surely come – we will finally work on the two anthologies together. Reiß is already getting angry. And it is not possible here.

Hugs from your Fred

Berlin, December 19, 1920

Dearest Mother, Dearest Father,

I send you my warmest Christmas greetings – and wishes! The little gift I have for you, dear Mother, you should receive in time for Christmas Eve. It weighs no more than 20 grams... but perhaps it weighs more: for you... What do I wish for? That your love and affection may remain with me, just as I will always carry you in my heart.

I am currently working on a selection of my entire poetry, which I would like to call *The Chime*. I am curious if you love the same poems I do. I choose carefully. For example, from Li Tai Pe I selected 3 poems, from *Chinese War Poetry* 3, from

The Geisha Osen 4, from *Fire Worshippers* 6, from *Villon* 7, from *Dawn* 12, from *The Ladder to Heaven* 15, from *Irene* 5, from *The Triad* 18, etc., and then 30 new ones. I find this plan nicer than the *Gallows Ladder*, which I have set aside for now. In February, I am supposed to go to Königsberg. For 8000 marks. Should I? I would only do it for the money. In itself, I am already disgusted by all this: performing in the cabarets. But how else is one to earn money? I do not know. Both of you are hugged by your Fredi, who is now (Sunday, December 19, 1920) still in bed at 4 p.m.... (and is not ashamed...)

Berlin, December 23, 1920

Dearest Mother,

The package has just arrived, which I hereby confirm for the moment: I have already confirmed the manuscripts to you long ago, and since then I have written at least three letters. And my Christmas gift – has it perhaps not arrived either? And my Christmas letter? I thank you sincerely for everything that will be in the package (I have not opened it yet). And even more for the love that you are supposed to preserve for me. My second home is, after all, with you.

I have had so much to do in the last few days: also excitements of all kinds: yesterday was the premiere of the new cabaret, of which I am on the literary advisory board. I am curious about the press. Tonight I didn't get home until 4 a.m. Anyway, this Berlin. Despite everything, I feel good this year, which is purely a psychological and emotional matter. I truly came to life only this past spring with you and then in Munich. Last winter, too much sorrow and fog hung over my heart. Hugs from your Fred

December 31, 1920

Dear Mother,

It is completely mysterious to me that the 20 grams have not arrived yet. You really can't rely on anything anymore today. Not even on yourself: I saw that yesterday. After I had coughed up quite a bit of blood yesterday morning, I had a regular hemorrhage at the cabaret in the evening. Today I am lying flat on my back and am annoyed that I am forced to stay in bed: I would have liked to do so voluntarily. The blooming dreams of the cabaret have thus (which is not really a pity) come to their temporary end. Farewell Königsberg! And so many other things. I will have to leave Berlin as soon as possible: to the south. In the spring, I will be with you again. All the best in the new year, which for us should mean the same as the old year: we want to remain the same. Always yours, Fred.

Did you read the article "Applied Expressionism" in the *Journal*?

Berlin, Sanatorium Dr. Weil, Viktoriastr. 46, January 4, 1921

Dear Mother,

Actually against my will, my friends here – partly also at the insistence of my parents – have brought me to a sanatorium, where I have been lying for three days, cared for day and night by a nurse who watches over me with eagle eyes like a policeman. They have also severely restricted my visitors. I feel quite good so far. I have hardly any temperature since the hemorrhage (between 98.6 and 100°F). Before, I sometimes had up to 102°F. Maybe the bleeding did me some good: the filth is coming out. It's also better with the cough. I will probably have to stay lying down until there is no blood in the sputum anymore. A lot of people have behaved very touchingly, including people to whom I have never done anything good.

The sanatorium is of course very expensive (I estimate 150-200 marks per day, they haven't told me yet). But all kinds of people are offering me money. (By the way, regarding the question of anti-Semitism: almost all the people showing this real nobility are Jews. Later, in peace, I will tell you more.) Drach has also proven to be extraordinary, having done much for me, and I have not always been kind to him. To my surprise, I have seen how many people care for me and love me. And that is nice. Be embraced by your Fred.

Irene's picture is on the nightstand. I look at it often.

Berlin, Sanatorium Dr. Weil, Viktoriastr. 46, January 8, 1921
Dear Mother,

I believe I already wrote to you that I have been in the sanatorium since the 1st. A nurse is with me day and night. They take very good care of me: I get to eat and drink whatever I want. A lot of milk, butter, eggs, chicken, ham, etc. I just have to order. The prices are, of course, in line with Berlin standards. (The first weekly bill was 1200 marks! So nearly 200 marks a day.) I wouldn't be able to stand this for long, but it seems (I say seems, because I am lying here as an object and have mainly learned about my benefactor through the newspaper) that the director of the Berlin cabarets "Rockets" and "Black Cat" wants to cover the costs of my stay in the sanatorium. I expect I will need 15,000 marks for a three-month recovery stay, perhaps and hopefully less, because I haven't gathered that much money yet. So far, I feel quite good. Since today, no more blood has come, and hopefully that will continue. I probably won't be allowed to get up just yet. I still don't feel like it.

Hugs to both of you. Say hello to Kubin and your friends from your Fred.

Berlin, after January 25, 1921
Dear Mother,

The second poem is especially very original and funny. I like the old man. Please send the picture of Kubin directly to the publisher. Why don't you like it? – The Paris conference has really dealt me a bad blow. I wanted to go to Meran. When I tried to buy lire yesterday, it turned out that a catastrophic currency crash had started again. I wanted to buy 2500 lire. From one day to the next, I would have had to pay 1000 marks more. (And it keeps falling.) I have developed a direct hatred for this "currency." Isn't there a place in Austria, up near Innsbruck, where mountain railways go up to some health resorts? The crown is doing so poorly. – I am feeling better and better. In 8-10 days, I hope to leave this sanitary penitentiary. Be embraced, both of you. Your Fred.

I am supposed to write a history of world literature. What do you think?

Meran, Pension Burgund, Franz-Ferdinand-Quai, March 14, 1921
Dear Parents,

I have now been here for 4 days. The sun is shining incessantly, I am lying on the balcony, but although I feel physically quite well, a general feeling of well-being has not yet set in. I am once again very out of sorts with myself. Well, that will be resolved. Such depressive states also pass. – I ask Father to please send me 3000 marks as soon as possible, preferably by transferring them through a bank in Passau to the Banco di Roma, Meran, in my name (Alfred Henschke Klabund). I think it takes long enough. The money that was sent to me from Berlin before my departure here has not arrived yet. – Life here costs about the same as in Berlin. It is certainly not more expensive. What acquaintances do you have here that you mentioned? I am thinking of going even further south (Capri? Positano?). Maybe I will go to Vigiljoch this afternoon. Hugs from your Fred.

Meran, March 21, 1921
Dear Mother,

You say: it's a matter of mood – but this depression must have some reason: I've been paddling in this frog swamp for a week, and everything is so gloomy around and within me. I am a wandering vagrant by nature, but somewhere I must have a fixed point around which I swing: somewhere there must be home, house, and hearth. Lately, I've often thought of Irene. I also read the corrections to the little songs. And all sorts of dark wishes came back to me after many months: to no longer be here anymore. Since the stay with you last year, since Munich and Berlin, I had regained balance. Now I am wavering again. Perhaps I will return via Switzerland (Locarno), if it's not too expensive. – I'll send you the corrections: please keep them for me, as well as the excerpts. – The Italians behave very nicely and obligingly here in the occupied area. They often turn a blind eye. (The German newspapers here are extremely pro-German: and their attacks against the Entente and Italy are not exactly restrained.) Germany has gained many friends everywhere through the attitude of the Entente: its position in the world is strengthening every day: but no foolishness must be made, like Bavaria's stance on the civilian militia issue. Otherwise, the old opinion could quickly return.

I have dealings with Poles here. It will interest Father that they are for Germany: Upper Silesia will become German, I am certain of that: but not because the Germans there are German, but because the Polish workers, enlightened by Rosa Luxemburg, will be organized in the German union sense, voting for Germany: against Polish reaction, against Polish militarism, and military service. This is the opinion of the local Poles, and they are undoubtedly right. Because if it were based on statistics, Upper Silesia, which has 60% (or more) Polish-speaking population, should vote for Poland. Hopefully, Germany will immediately adopt a policy of reconciliation and balance with these masses of Poles and Polish workers, and not make the same mistakes as in past Polish politics. – I was very sorry not to be able to meet you in Munich. Unfortunately, it was two days too late. Both of you are embraced by your Fred.

Has Father received the contract with Kaemmerer, based on which I will probably have to sue?

I am reading: Vehse, *History of the Prussian Court*: and I am filled with hatred and contempt for this scum called Hohenzollern. (The book is meant to be completely different!!)

(How many handwritten pages does my *Literary History* have in manuscript? 300?) Write soon!

Isle of Capri, Villa Giulia, Postmark: April 1, 1921

Dear Parents,

I am sending you warm greetings. It is wonderfully beautiful here, Ithaca and Orplid, but it all reminds me painfully of Locarno. I don't know how long I will stay here. Perhaps a few days, perhaps a few weeks. *Forse sì, forse no*. This landscape has too many emotional and sensual charms to be endured without the presence of a loved one. Your Fred

Positano, Provincia di Salerno, Albergo Roma, April 15, 1921

Dear Irene,

The word "Irene" came to mind and pencil so suddenly that I want to leave it as it is. I am sitting on the terrace of my hotel room, with the vast, vast sea before me. Somewhere far back there, Africa must lie. The clouds hang heavily over the mountains I drove over this morning in a small carriage. Positano has no railway or ship connections. It lies a bit wild, a bit grotesque between the rocks, a Saracen nest. There are two or three inns, all in an old-fashioned style. When I drove up with the carriage and the innkeeper shook my hand and introduced me to his wife and personally showed me the very large room, I felt transported to another time. If you read Goethe's *Italian Journey*, you can have similar impressions. The vast sea calms infinitely. Only the evenings will be long: there is only candlelight. I think I will stay here until around the 25th, then go via Amalfi, Salerno, Paestum, Pompeii to Naples, and from there to Rome, where I expect mail starting around the 28th: Via Sardegna 34, Hotel Victoria. Perhaps you can write to me here again, and please send me a bunch of discarded *Berlin Daily News, 8 O-clock Evening News*, and *Munich Latest News*. I absolutely don't know what's going on in Germany, haven't known for weeks. The local newspapers in Naples say nothing about Germany. For them, only a scandal trial or the lottery matters. Will your verses be published soon? Both of you are embraced by your Fred.

Amalfi, May 23, 1921

Dear Parents,

I am walking this road tonight from Amalfi to Positano. I saw so many of the most beautiful things just yesterday: Ravello and Amalfi. Ravello, the garden and the view from the Norman Palazzo Ruffo, is indescribable. In general, I feel most deeply connected to the old Norman architecture (from around 1000), more than anything I have seen in Italy. Yours sincerely, Fred

Positano, May 27, 1921

Dear Mother,

It is getting so hot here that I will probably leave in the next few days. Where to, only heaven knows: for the moment, Rome, but since it won't be any cooler there, I'll go further north. I can tolerate heat well, but there must be a garden by the house and the possibility of walking around completely naked. I always go to the sea at 4 in the afternoon, swim, and return home after sunset. I can hardly eat anymore. Soffel has invited me to come to Ascona. It would tempt me for many reasons, but I can save that for the fall. I must also confess that I have a second reason for leaving Positano, and that is (you will say, of course!) a woman. I've had a flirtation with a Neapolitan girl for the past three weeks: a young girl from a respected and wealthy family. She was in Positano, is now in Amalfi, and will return to Positano next week. Of course, her parents are with her – an affable, plump glutton and a sleepy, sluggish lady, who is not at all "mobile." There's also a maid, a horse, and a carriage. The integrity and virginity of a young girl in southern Italy is a matter of canon law. It is watched over with eagle eyes, and any attempt to break it is punished with the dagger of the Camorra or with marriage. In short, I fear that if I stay here, I will wake up one morning as the husband of a very pretty and charming Neapolitan girl, have to take her for an afternoon stroll on the Corso in Via Caracciolo, and otherwise lose all my senses in the heat of Naples. I can already feel how weak-willed I am becoming here and how anyone can do anything to me if they just start energetically enough. So, like Casanova from the lead chamber of Venice, I will try to flee from the oven of Naples. Always yours, F.

Munich, June 24, 1921

Dear Parents,

I am temporarily staying with Fredi Kaufmann, Widenmayerstr. 45/IV, telephone 21154. – Please bring me La Rochefoucauld, *Maxims*, in my translation (*Thoughts on Love*) if you have it. I look forward to seeing you soon. Your Fred

I've already worked all day in the library. At the theater, I want to see *Nestroy* (Kammerspiele) and *From Morning to Midnight* (New Theater) with you.

Nestroy: On June 17, 1921, his play *He Wants to Have Fun* premiered at the Munich Intimate Theater under the direction of Paul Kalbeck, with Elisabeth Bergner, among others.

Munich, July 5, 1921

Dear Mother,

Your book is delightful. Congratulations. Please send me 10 copies, each in an envelope. I will arrange reviews for you. (Subscribe to Schustermann!! By the way, send me all of Schustermann clippings: it might be that I'll need one someday or have to polemicize. You'll get them back afterward for safekeeping. Enclosed is the draft. Deadline: about 3 weeks.) The Russian clipping interested me. But that's not Russian poetry, it's Italian Futurism in Russian language. A translation (partly literal) of a manifesto by Marinetti. If people weren't so stupid, they'd diagnose something like that correctly right away. Both of you, hug each other for me, greet Kubin. Always your Fred

May I ask you for a table of contents of my grotesques and small sketches (*Small Diary & Night Book*) in the safe? Also, include the article Prussianism and Socialism. Where are my political essays: with you?

Munich, July 8, 1921

Dear Parents,

The evening was a sensation for Munich. The hall was packed, so I will have to repeat the lecture on Tuesday (today I am reading at the university's literary-historical seminar). *Munich's Latest News, Munich Daily,* and the *Southern German Press* wrote very nicely about it. Did you read the shameless enthusiasm of the *Augsburger*? Is there nothing we can do about it? Yours sincerely, Fred

Munich, July 10, 1921

Dear Mother,

I have another request. Please send me my prison diary in typed form. I am making it so hard for you – please don't be angry with me! Where are the 10 Echo's I asked for? It is truly a delightful book. And please write me a dedication in one of them! Both of you, hug each other from your Fred

Munich, July 27, 1921

Dear Mother,

Thanks for everything: please don't send the novel until I write to you again. I just wanted to make sure. – I am working a lot lately. By August 1st, I have to submit the manuscript of *World Literature*. The heat is terrible. I am naked all day, unless I have to go out. I will probably go to Gauting on Friday for a few weeks. Maybe I'll go back to Italy in August (but then on assignment for a newspaper). Does Father need the thousand marks? I can return them to him in August. Please send back the 50 marks from the Inselverlag. That is not a fee, but a dog's wage. – Affectionately, your old, or rather young, very cheerful Fred

Gauting, September 25, 1921

Dearest Mother,

You wanted to send me a table of contents for the Kaemmerer Verlag collection! Please do so! – Would you like to read my new novel? I'll send it to you: just please forward it to the editorial office of the *New Review* (Dr. Rudolf Kayser), Berlin, Bülowstr., S. Fischer Verlag. Both of you are embraced by your Fred

Autumn has been so beautiful these last days. Fiery red apples lie in the green grass of the garden, and in the evenings, blood-red streaks stretch across the blue sky.

No Location, Saturday, October 8, 1921

Dear Mother,

I'm going to Partenkirchen today, Hotel Gibson, for a week. I'm a little tired, physically and emotionally. To make matters worse, I've been tricked again, my belief in the decency of mankind is wavering dangerously. I had saved 1000 lire for a trip to Italy. When I was tidying up today before leaving, I saw that someone had stolen the thousand-lire note from the locked drawer... Who, I don't know yet. God help me, I hope it's not another "good friend." – It's so depressing; how long must one work again, how mechanically on must work, to make up for this, and actually, my planned trip to Italy this year is now definitely canceled. There are good people, God knows. Both of you are embraced by your Fred

Partenkirchen, Hotel Gibson, October 10, 1921

Dear Mother,

A warm greeting from the summer-like hot autumn. From Merano. (I am here as a guest, otherwise I couldn't afford the Gibson. I mention this in parentheses so that you don't think the gold ship has arrived from India.) A question for Father: is there a promissory note from Drach for about 2000 marks among the papers I entrusted to him? I want to collect it now. I believe I've already written that my lire were stolen? Yes, the art is cheerful – to steal. You shall read the novel as soon as it's somewhat finished. Both of you are embraced by your Fred

Berlin, November 15, 1921

Dear Mother,

I would be happy to give your poems back to *The Dame* once you've worked on them again. (Attached with comments.) – I feel quite comfortable here, although I live quite improvisationally: my clothes, shoes, etc., are partly with Fredi, partly still in Gauting. – I spoke about your poems with Heyden, they seem to be doing quite well. (I believe he's sold two thousand.) My Lao Tzu is already in its 13th thousand, *The Geisha* and *Epigram* in the 10th thousand, and *The History of Literature* in the 30th thousand: I hope this continues. The three novels are with Reiß. Now there's also a grotesque volume coming (Roland Verlag): titled *The Colorful Decline of the West*. *World Literature* (unfortunately, I don't have a copy yet, but you will receive it) has been published. Also the Reclam edition, which I am enclosing, is once again a greeting to Irene, whose parents are embraced by your Fred.

Berlin S. W., Halleschestr. 21/1. r., after November 15, 1921
Dear Mother,

I was in Hamburg and Kiel. I'm sending you (some very good) reviews. Do you have the reviews of *Hannibal* there? If so, I ask you to send them: I must promote it. The *Comedy Theater* should perform it. I'm thinking about a time comedy. Berlin is as lively and interesting as always. (Munich, on the other hand, has the atmosphere of a night watchman.) Furthermore: Gotha wants to perform *The Gravedigger*. I no longer have any copies. Please send me some (2-3). – I wrote to Soffel's on around October 20th, asking them to place asters on Irene's grave. The currency situation is so bad that soon no one will be able to go to Switzerland. Davos is said to be deserted by Germans. – Much has been published these days: the 3 little novels, *World Literature*, *The Little Songs for Irene* (in the *Small Klabund Book* Reclam edition). Hugs from your Fredi.

Berlin, December 10, 1921
Dearest Mother,

All I wish for Christmas is your unchanged love. Have I already sent you the 3 novels? They are, of course, yours. Please write to me about them (to Crossen, where I will go in a few days). And – now comes something a bit unpleasant for you – I am once again preoccupied with the Peasants' War.

I still have some books and brochures at your place. Would it be a problem to send them to Crossen? Please do! Be embraced by your Fred.

Crossen/Oder, December 24, 1921
Dear Mother, dear Father,

We send our warmest Christmas greetings and New Year wishes to you. We think of you often. Irene's picture is adorned with fir branches from the Christmas tree. She looks down on us, blessing us, like the Madonna with the fir branch. I still live with her: you have seen it in all my recent books. She is also at the center of the great new novel: *Agathe*, she is none other than Irene. And in *Francis*, the *Letter to Giuletta*: it was once directed to her. And just as Faust searched for Helena in every woman, so I search for Irene in every one. This longing is indelibly burned into me. The girls and women I love or who love me know it too. I deceive no one, neither them – nor Irene.

My parents also send you their warmest regards. They have so much to do: Father at work, Mother with household chores, that they don't have time to write. They both should take a good rest. My brother, the pharmaceutical student, has also arrived, with his fiancee from Jena. Be embraced by your faithful Fred.

Crossen, January 3, 1922

Dearest Mother,

Thank you for your letter. Carossa, whose poems I am very fond of, also made little impression on me with his childhood memoirs. But let's wait and see how it all turns out. On the other hand, I would like to draw your attention to Bert Brecht, a young, somewhat awkward man from Augsburg who had a poem in the last *Merkur* and a novella in the previous one. I have placed him with Reiß. I consider him unusually talented. – I was delighted by *The Sleepwalker*. Felber is a skillful man. And Sinsheimer was as kind as he could be. – In Berlin, I lived and worked a lot. Yesterday I finished the final editing of my selected poems. It took me exactly a year to choose 100 from about 2000 poems, the ones that seem to me the relatively and absolutely best. I'm curious if the selection corresponds to your taste. – I've been working on a time comedy for a long time. I think I'll finish it soon. The new novel also occupies me strongly. – My parents send you both warm greetings, and embrace you, your Fred.

The new postal and railway tariffs are catastrophic.

Berlin, after January 3, 1922

Dearest Mother,

Berlin is completely covered in snow. How much I would have liked to be in the mountains. I long so much for Davos sunshine. But what's the use? One must trudge through the zoo and think that the houses behind the trees are mountains, and the streetlamp there is the moon. – I have (yet another) request. I am preparing a new edition of *The Organ Grinder*. I am cutting it down and expanding it at the same time. (For example, I'm cutting The Mother-in-Law...) Please send me corrections for the Bavarian songs, namely: *Hatschier, On the Drum, The Buddy*, which I would like to keep. Also, please lend me *Dragoon and Hussars*. I would like to include some excerpts. – How are you otherwise? I still hope for a performance in Berlin. (Even at the grave, hope is planted.) – The *[Munich] Latest* is pouring strange amounts of oil on my agitated waves. They have also praised *Moreau* again. On the other hand, my paper (the *Morning Post*) criticized *The Sleepalker*. – Be embraced, also greetings from my father, who was here for a few days for a chamber meeting and left today. Always yours, Fred.

Berlin, February 8, 1922

Dearest Mother,

Once again, I must bother you with a request: please send me something, urgently: namely the corrections to my *History of World Literature*, which, as you know, had to be slightly shortened at the end. Imagine, I am supposed to become a lecturer at the Lessing School and am to start my lectures on February 10th: World Literature in Outline. I also need the Chinese books I have (at your place), as well as Egyptian ones, etc. I trust you will send me the right items. I regret always troubling you, never giving you joy, but this is extremely urgent for me: I need the materials right away. I send you a thousand thanks and a big hug, your Fred.

Berlin, February 8, 1922

Dearest Mother,

It is kind of Ceka to still think of us. But of course, we cannot help her. What would 100 Francs be for us! A fortune! I am still dreaming my Italian dream. A few days ago, someone brought me a mimosa bush. The scent made me very melancholy. For weeks now, there has been a bitter Russian cold here. (I cannot recall such a winter.) Recently, during the strike, when there was no light, no coal, no gas, Berlin seemed completely like Moscow to me, especially at night when only meager candles burned in most restaurants, the stove was cold, food was expensive, and outside, in the dark, the pickpockets were having a rich harvest. – Overall, this winter has been very good for me, health-wise and spiritually, especially spiritually (unbelievably: three times knocked under the table). I have felt and feel as happy as the watchman in Faust:

> Whatever your eyes have seen:
> Be it as it may,
> It was still so beautiful. –

On Monday, I am to begin my lectureship at the Lessing School. Actually, this makes me a little nervous. I have never spoken in public like that before. – I am also reflecting on the fact that I promised to translate a French operetta, for which I am to receive 10,000 Marks and have already received 4,000. I am quite tempted to return the 4,000, as urgently as I needed them, and to leave the project behind. It really is a terrible waste of nerves.

Please give my regards to Father, and with the hope of seeing each other again, I send you a big hug, your Fred.

Berlin, March 3. 1922

Dearest Mother,

My father, who has resigned from his position as city councilor, has been made an honorary citizen of Crossen. Please write him a few lines; he will be very happy about it. He is such an exceptional person. – I am deeply immersed into work. A few days ago, there was a bit of spring. It's already gone again. It's cold once more. Unfortunately, foreign exchange rates have risen significantly again. (I'm only concerned about this because of my hope for Italy.) Everyone here fears that the dollar will rise to 400. And this seems very likely. The inflation here is unimaginable for you. With 5,000-6,000 Marks, one can barely exist.

Prices have risen by 100% since I arrived in November. – Today, I received the first corrections for my new poetry collection. Do you have any title suggestions? It consists of ballads, myths, and odes. Hugs to both of you, your Fredi.

Berlin, March 29. 1922

Dearest Mother,

Thank you very much for your letter along with the ballads. I don't know if I already wrote to you that I had to take to bed. I've been lying down for three weeks now, but for the last two days, my temperature has been below 100.4, so things are slowly getting better. I'll gladly come to visit you in May. Afterward, I want to head to the mountains. If I can get up soon, I'll spend a few weeks in Crossen. A trip to Italy has become impossible. I'm toying with the idea of a trip to Serbia, but I first need to know exactly how the dinar stands, etc.: it seems relatively inexpensive and certainly adventurous enough. It's also far enough south in the coastal towns. I saw a brochure for a Grand Hotel Imperial in Ragusa, which I found very appealing. But that's still a mirage. – I read your ballads attentively. They are, with the exception of the completely botched Marian legend (impossible ending!), all very charming in their themes and already quite detailed in many parts. Much is weak, not well thought out, and not fully developed. I've underlined those parts. The best is *The Black Death*. Send it to *The Youth*. – *The Doll* needs a lot of work. They're all interesting, but you must work much harder on all of them. Don't let that discourage you. Hug both of you, your Fred.

Heidelberg, Scheffelhaus, May 15, 1922

Dearest Parents,

I have been wandering around the world history for weeks now, or perhaps it's almost a month. I was in Tangermünde – Magdeburg – the Harz – Halberstadt – Goslar – Hildesheim – Mainz – Koblenz – Wiesbaden – Darmstadt – Mannheim – and I ended up here. Next week, I plan to go to the Black Forest, then finally to Munich. It is wonderfully hot. The Neckar gleams like a mirror. I sit here half-naked in the garden. In the evenings, I sit with friends, I have many in the area, and we drink (still cheap here) wine that clears the mind and purges it of the dust from Berlin. I am so lazy, it is indescribable. I had to submit a large manuscript on July 1st, and I think I will breach the contract. I let myself be spoiled (by myself), and yesterday I played the grand seigneur in the Schloss Hotel opposite a pretty and charming woman from Alsace. The mood towards the French in Alsace has turned very cool, almost hostile, and even in the occupied areas (Mainz, etc.), one gets the impression that the (originally warmly received) French have completely failed in making any moral conquests. In Mainz, there are now 25,000 French civilians alone, yet there has been no integration with the local population. They live side by side, the surest proof that the French occupation cannot be sustained. This may last a few years, but no more. – I have a request for you, dear Mother: Among my books is an older Greek mythology with steel engravings that does not belong to me and is constantly being claimed from me. Please send it to Mr. Paul Nikolaus Steiner, Hebelstraße 9, Mannheim. – Unfortunately, I cannot report anything about my work because I am as lazy as sin. I try to imagine that I will soon intend to write a novel again, and I shudder. I just saw in bookstores that the second volume of *The Decline of the West* has just been published. Thank

God it is only a book. Paper. And printer's ink. The West, thank God, is still very much alive. One notices this in oneself. – How is the Bavarian tourist scam going? Hopefully, the Munich people have been taken in. The prices I heard are a strong imposition even for foreign visitors with good currency. And the whole design of Bavarian tourist advertising had something unreal, fraudulent, slimy, and sentimental about it. – (The Bavarians are, like the French, terribly sentimental. They confuse sentiment with sentimentality. Their "coziness" has little to do with actual warmth.) – These are the "psychic abysses" between North and South. Even the exploitation of the Fechenbach trial is rather childish. He really only achieved a local success. That Germany is solely to blame is something no reasonable person, especially no German, would claim, but that Germany bears a considerable share of responsibility for the war, just like the others: denying this is historical falsification that seeks to clear the former rulers. Where are the bigger falsifiers? Who, for example, forged the Ems Dispatch? (1870?)

Greetings from your Fred

Unknown location, May 1922
Dear Mother,

Thank you very much for your letter. You must think I have been unfaithful to you, not in thoughts, but in reality, because I was supposed to be with you in May: but things have been delayed, not only in terms of the weather. But I will definitely come soon. At the end of May, I will go to Munich, where Harich is once again offering me his apartment, which is very tempting, and I intend to take advantage of it. I have several plans for the summer: especially working on two major prose pieces, one a Berlin affair and the other a study of 14th-century Germany (the Hanseatic period), for which I have already made hundreds of notes. Unfortunately, there is also a deadline looming: a translation due by June 31st – from Hungarian (with a Hungarian collaborator). You will have seen all sorts of entertaining and enchanting things in Munich. The Berlin winter was rather bleak in terms of artistic experiences. The theater is stagnating. I have gotten along quite well with the people. My Munich address from the 14th day onward: Elsenheimerstr. 16/1, p. A. Harich.

My new poetry collection will be titled *The Hot Heart*. Do you like the title? Warm hugs from your Fred

Munich, after June 24, 1922
Dear Mother,

I'm back in Harich's apartment. It is very far out in a desolate area, at the end of Landsbergerstraße. rear building, sparse trees, factory chimneys, poor people, the end of the city, the end of the world. But it's a wonderful feeling to have my own apartment again. That's why I'm happy to be here. Health-wise, things are so-so. Before winter, I must do something for myself. I had planned to go to the

Black Forest, but then other things got in the way, and now I especially want to finish a new novel of mine (about 15th-century Germany, the Hanseatic League, and the pirate era). When are you going to Berchtesgaden? In August, I will probably have to leave here. Munich is as beautiful as ever. The Munich people are becoming more unbearable year by year. (Probably under the influence of the *Munich Latest News*, which I would unreservedly call the dirtiest, most indecent paper published in Germany. *The National Observer* is a clean affair compared to it. Anyone who only reads the *Latest* must become stupid and brainwashed.) The trade fair is very tasteful. That the police and organized scams drive the tourists away: that's good. Everywhere in Germany, one is treated decently. I have been in about 30 German cities in the last 7 weeks: North Germany, South Germany, the Rhineland: nowhere is the foreigner so openly exploited as here. (Wiesbaden maybe excepted, which is only for foreign exchange holders.) In Heidelberg, a tourist town like few others, I paid 40 marks for a hotel room in the Scheffelhaus with a balcony (living room and bedroom). Fabulous wine 10-15 marks. Lunch 35 marks. The same quality in Munich costs double or triple. Only a healthy bankruptcy of many hotels, etc., will help. Then their minds will be cleared. And this bankruptcy is perhaps to be wished for Bavaria in a political sense as well. The university celebration here was a scandal (like everything that officially happens here). Black, white, and red flags that have made us nauseous since the Kapp Putsch, everywhere. (By the way, you remember how I characterized the core group of the Kapp Putsch: the Ehrhardt Brigade: the murderers of Erzberger, Gareis, and Rathenau: they are all Ehrhardt people. The Organisation C is just a continuation of the Kapp Putsch with other means.) Ludendorff as the honorary guest of the university! (The freedom of science under Ludendorff...)

Attached is an excerpt you might be interested in. Warm hugs from your Fred

Munich, August 1922

Dear Father,

Thank you. I accept your proposal. In mid-August, I will have to leave here anyway. The Leixner is safely in Berlin. Do you need it urgently? Then I must write to Berlin. – The prices in Northern Germany are certainly high (like everywhere), but no comparison with what was demanded in Bavaria until recently. I have been in about 30 cities lately. The most expensive were Wiesbaden and Magdeburg, where I paid 80 marks for a bed, otherwise about 30-40 marks everywhere. Boarding at the Scheffelhaus in Heidelberg (which is flooded with foreigners, especially the English!) costs 120-140 marks including room! – The worst thing about Bavaria (and the current Bavarian situation) is not the inflation itself, but the hypocrisy, the deep untruth upon which everything is "being rebuilt" here. In Berlin, they don't deceive themselves or others. The Berlin "scam" is honest. – Here, they make huge advertisements, lure the tourists in, and then treat them – in the police, the theater, the hotels – miserably. The slogan "Avoid Bavaria!" was quite justified. Politically: the same thing. The *Munich Latest News*, a reactionary revanchist paper, as the guardian of the republic! The democracy! Herr v. Kahr, the type of Machiavellian politician. I found the people here far more unpleasant than last year. I have no sympathy for the type of person that is beginning to crystallize here: spiritually arrogant, though there is no spirit, "German" in that sense of inner untruth that makes any unity of idea and being impossible. The isolation into which Bavaria is withdrawing is the same that Germany found itself in 14 years ago in the world. It will only harm it. For the outside world of Germany will hardly rally around Bavaria as an "orderly cell."

Give my regards to Mother. Attached are two autographs for her: Paul Hindemith is the composer of the most modern opera (performed in Frankfurt and Stuttgart), Franz Dornseiff, professor in Basel, is the most important contemporary scholar of ancient philology (Pindar researcher).

Always your Fred

Munich, August 1, 1922

Dear Mother,

Please arrange the room in Schellenberg for me. I will come right away.

Dr. Harich is coming tomorrow. I will go to Tegernsee for a few days to visit friends. My address remains the same. Write to me at your Schellenberg address. I would like to arrive on the 13th or at the latest on the 14th. I will bring the novel corrections and various work that you can help with if you like. The new poetry book has already been printed, and perhaps I already have a copy. If you want to bring books to read, I recommend Döblin, Wallenstein, Bertram, Nietzsche, Schaeffer, Helianth, Ulitz, Ararat. That should be enough for 4 weeks. Have you ordered a newspaper (*Berlin Daily News*)? I am really looking forward to seeing you. Yours, Fred.

Carossa's new book is very beautiful. I will send it to you.

Books to bring for reading: Alfred Döblin, *Wallenstein*. Berlin: S. Fischer, 1920; Ernst Bertram, *Nietzsche. Attempt at a Mythology.* Berlin: Georg Bondi, 1920; Albrecht Schaeffer, *Helianth*. Leipzig: Insel, 1920; Arnold Ulitz, *Ararat.* Roman. Munich: Langen, 1920

Munich, August 29, 1922, Krumbacherstr. 7/111.

Dear Parents,

You're not angry that I haven't come yet, are you? Two things got in the way: first, I'd just immersed myself in a major new work and have been in the library every day since then, browsing through Old Russian books. Secondly, about 3/4 years ago, I invested all my little savings in securities and foreign currency, and I must now be very careful. You must have heard in Schellenberg that the critical time has arrived for the German economy. In the last 14 days, all prices have increased by an average of 100-300%. Shoes, which were 800, are now no less than 2400; coffee, which was 120, is now no less than 400; a suit is now 20,000, a dress now 25,000-40,000, and so on. The crash of the mark has gone much faster than the crown collapse in Austria. Everything depends on tomorrow, Wednesday: either the dollar will rise to 3000, or it will fall to 1000 and below. The more likely scenario, given Poincaré's whole policy, is the first. In any case, I haven't sold my lire and crowns. If you come through Munich, please wire me! We should be together then. We can go to the theater, I will get you tickets. Enclosed for Mother is an autograph from the poet Carl Zuckmayer, from whom the Berlin State Theater performed The Stations of the Cross last year. I really need a rest. Hopefully, as I've planned, I can go to Passau for another 14 days. Always yours, Fredi.

Mother must have been so shocked by the poetry book that it left her speechless? I can't sweet-talk anymore when it's storming all around.

Berlin S. W., Halleschestr. 21/1. r., October 30, 1922

Dear Parents,

Here I am back in Berlin, in my fox and dragon's den. The week in Munich was a lost week, wasted and squandered time. I shouldn't have gone. I hurt people without wanting to and without being able to do otherwise. I went under autumn stars (the new book by Hamsun, I will try to send it to you). Berlin is exciting as always. A hundred letters were waiting for me. The cost of living is catastrophic. Everything is twice as expensive as in Munich, three times as much as in Passau. (Except for clothes and shoes: they have the same price.) Coffee: one cup costs 60 M, cake 45 M, meals 200-400 M. A pound of coffee is 1300. Butter 600-700. Rolls 12. It's a good thing I earn crowns (and Swiss francs; the Swiss national newspaper reports something). I'm going to Reiß today to check on the books. I've received the printed materials, etc. I won't answer them.

There are 2 postal orders and 1 insured letter that I sent to you, please send them back soon.

All the best, I've bought my hundredweight of coal, I'm somewhat prepared for the cold. Yours, Fred.

Heyder must have already sent you the new, very beautiful calendar?

Berlin, December 18, 1922

Dear Mother,

I wholeheartedly return your Christmas wishes. This year will be a gloomy holiday for many. I've been wandering through the north and northeast of Berlin these days. Wherever you look: decay, rot, collapse. The houses look like they are about to cave in. The people too. Of course, in the west, on Tauentzienstraße, there is splendor and magnificence. The shop windows are lavishly decorated. And the prices are often in the six-figure range. A modest meal now costs 700-1000 M. It's supposed to get better now (allegedly). A billion loan or something like that. I'm still skeptical. (I still have my few dollars.) The novel has been published. Too late to be considered for the Christmas table. Like everything else, except in luxury shops, sales in bookstores are also sluggish. Prices have climbed too quickly. The publishers are in a crisis. They don't have enough working capital anymore. A page (16 pages) of typesetting now costs 40,000. A printed edition of a novel now costs the publisher around 3 million! Be glad that your little poetry book has been published. Nowadays, you wouldn't risk it anymore. Berlin is always interesting and exciting. I'm thinking of a continuation of the ghost story: *Spooks...* I was recently in Potsdam, bought a few porcelain figures for a few hundred marks, and am quite proud of the purchase. All the best, also in the new year, always yours, Fred.

Berlin, January 10, 1923

Dear Mother,

Thank you very much for your letter. I don't think this affair is particularly destined for success. People prefer cozy things, where things go along pleasantly, "so that we can forget the gray worries of everyday life," which are soon going to grow over our heads. Because inflation is marching faster than the dollar (which had been fairly stable for two months, but during those two months, prices have risen dramatically). I would like to go somewhere for winter sports. However, the prices they are asking are 5-10,000!! per day, room and board. I don't earn that much. The bread here now costs 570 marks. And a modest lunch costs 1,000 marks. And everyone is talking, just like in the third year of the war, about prices, food, coal, etc. One becomes quite disheartened by the hustle and bustle. And in a new book I just finished, I unleashed all my sadism and hatred of mankind. So, it has not turned into a friendly idyll. The time for gentle books seems to be over. I don't think I will be able to create something like Saint Francis anymore. One becomes malicious. And to avoid becoming evil, one has to release the evil: by doing or writing it. – Huts to you both, your Fred.

Berlin, after February 26, 1923

Dear Father,

Please send me a detailed list of your Japanese collection as soon as possible. I now have several interested parties for it (for example, a Dutch collector). I still believe it could sell well. Could you give the collection, with this list, to someone trustworthy who is traveling to Berlin? That would be the best option. The international market for these things is very "strongly" positioned. – I hope you are doing well. The fall of the dollar has caused a stir here. Unfortunately, the prices have not yet dropped: the same development is also appearing here as in Austria. If the dollar manages to hold steady (which I sadly don't believe), one could go back to Italy. The prices there are currently lower than those abroad. It would be cheaper there than here. (At least here in Berlin.) I have taken on a new large translation project. The affair was a failure. It came out at a very unfavorable time. No one is buying fiction now. That it is still being printed surprises me. I have several things in preparation. Two luxury prints of Chinese poetry (from Insel Verlag and Reiß) have just been published. This is something that still works. Although I think one copy costs 80,000 marks.

Give my regards to Mother. The Soffeis are currently in Berlin. Always yours, Fred.

Enzklösterle, Black Forest, Hotel Waldhorn, March 21, 1923
Dear Mother,

If it suits you, I will come on Wednesday (perhaps earlier, please keep the mail there!), by express train from Nuremberg, I believe it arrives there around half-past four. I will then stay over Easter. – The sun finally seems to be shining here, but it is still quite cold. In a few days, I will be done with a very unpleasant task: revising, reworking, and stylizing Soltau's translation of the *Decameron* based on the Italian edition. I had imagined it would be easier, but I've already been working on it for 4 weeks, 6-7 hours a day. – My new novel is supposed to go to typesetting soon, supposedly to be published in May, but I think it will be Christmas. Otherwise, I don't know yet what I will publish this year. There is enough ready, but the circumstances are not favorable. – How are your ballads going? Warm regards, also to Father, your Klabund.

Around April 1923
Dear Father,

By now, you must have received my postcard. As far as I remember, I have already confirmed the arrival of the Japanese pieces earlier. I am continuously working on them. I also spoke with some experts about them. A Japanese person showed me 17 sheets that he considered top quality. (By the way, not including the Matahei!) Also, a beautiful Utamaro (Mother and Child) has been trimmed. One expert (whose opinion I kept to myself) quietly doubted the authenticity of the great Sharaku. (The gray background is not the usual Mikadruck.) Others exalted it to the highest heavens. In general, it is always the same 20-30 sheets. Would you give them to someone trustworthy to take to America? – I also have a lot to do besides that: corrections to *Peter, Boccaccio, Goethe.* – As I said before, the Reichsbank could not continue its support action. In one day, they spent the entire dollar treasure bond. I would consider a larger use of the gold reserves to be madness. The final collapse of the mark would only be delayed by a few months. I believe we are marching confidently toward a dollar rate of 100,000 (so beyond Austria). – Attached is an autograph for Mother. Warm regards to you both, your Fred.

Berlin, July 3, 1923
Dear Father,

In great haste, I want to inform you today that (in my opinion) two serious buyers have expressed interest in the pictures. (In total, at least thirty people have seen the prints. You can be sure that I have done everything within my power.) After deducting luxury tax and commission (10%), 4000 Swiss Francs could be considered for you, payable in foreign currency (dollars). Would you agree to this? I would appreciate it if you could reply immediately (by telegram). The other offers are much lower. In my opinion, the prints are worth 10,000 Francs, but one will not get that value here in Germany, certainly not. (It is a German collector who is keen on them.) The foreigners (the Japanese) did not offer more either. Perhaps I can still get 4500, but that would be the utmost. Since the Goldmark is weaker than the Franc, the difference between your demand of 5000 Gold Marks and 4000 Francs is not large. (The Gold Mark is currently 27,500 Paper Marks, the Franc 29,000. This means if you ask for 137 million you would receive 116.) I think the bank could settle for 4000 Francs. They should understand. – I hope I haven't promised too much; skepticism is always necessary today, but the buyer who just visited me seemed serious. He will make his final decision by tomorrow. He is only interested in the 30 best prints and all black-and-white ones. Please consider giving me the rest as a memento of this affair. – Warm hugs, your Fred

Guben, en route to Crossen/Oder, September 19, 1923
Dear Father,

I have just heard that my brother wrote to you about a major mistake he made (apparently in a kind of dazed state). The situation is not as bad as I first thought. The main buyer has agreed to return the sheets since they were sold without my authorization.

Sharaku, Utamaro, Harunobu, Koryusai, etc. will likely return to us. An Englishman paid 100 dollars for lesser sheets. I hope to get those back as well. I know his address. If, against expectations, that doesn't work out, the 100 dollars are available to you, so the sheets will at least not be underpaid. I was very upset for a few days due to all these affairs. But I believe the sky is clearing again, and everything will be alright. – Warm embrace, your Fred

Crossen/Oder, September 29, 1923
In bed in the evening
Dear Mother,

I wanted to use the last inexpensive postal day to send you a greeting. I don't know how the political situation in Bavaria will develop or whether I will even be able to travel through Bavaria. I am not going to Davos with a light heart, rather with strong inner reluctance, and I am only going because of Rüedi, since I have already experienced enough of the sensations of Davos in the past... I will have to severely limit myself; in total, I will have about 1000 Francs available. I hope this will last me three months. I will hardly be able to stay in a pension like Stolzenfels, which costs 10 Francs a day. I will probably have to rent a room. Although there are many reasons against this. Especially: I won't have proper care. But the dilemma between what I need and what I can afford is definitely there. My voice, which still barely functioned in Munich, is now almost gone. You and Irene have already gone through this once. It will all seem strange enough to us, starting the sad game again. And perhaps, who knows, it will end just as bleakly. Only I seem to be too tough a weed to be easily uprooted, unlike a delicate flower.

I will travel to Berlin on Thursday and hope to bring the main prints (Utamaro 161, 158, 160, 159, Koryusai 65, 38, Sharaku 71, 368, Harunobu 43) back into our possession. I had to negotiate for a long time about the conditions for their return, especially because I had to raise the money. The enclosed letter informs you. Please keep it until the transaction is complete.

Then there will still be 9 sheets missing, which I have already claimed as well. It seems that political conditions are preventing Griffith, the correspondent of the *New York Herald*, who is probably in the Ruhr region (I read something about it today), from responding yet. Griffith paid 100 dollars, which, if the return doesn't happen, will be available to you in Francs – though I would strongly advise you not to throw the few hundred Francs (about 550) into the jaws of the Chur bank. Keep them as a reserve for yourselves instead. I still don't understand how the bank can pressure you like this. You have tried everything. They must know how poor we Germans have become. I am happy to speak with the director in Chur (as long as I can still speak), but he must understand that, where there is nothing, even a Chur bank director has lost his right, and it is not bad will preventing you from paying, but inability. – Prices are rapidly approaching the gold price. Perhaps, in a few years, you will be able to pay back the 6000 Francs. But right now, during this transition period, nothing can be said for certain. –

The people in Munich have to have their political carnival again. Kahr is to-day's Eisner, and Hitler is the Levien – with different signs. Hopefully, it stays a masquerade and doesn't turn into sharp shooting. Ludendorff will, to quote Kraus, once again get away with a blue lens, as he did after Sweden. Once again, it's all "foreign-blooded" outsiders or unbelievers: Kahr, the Protestant; Hitler, the Austrian; Ludendorff and Roßbach, the Prussians. (Ehrhardt is probably there as well.) –

Best regards, your Fred

Berlin, October 26, 1923

Dear Mother,

It seems you did not receive a detailed letter from me, nor a postcard. But there is supposed to be censorship in Bavaria again; I'm no longer surprised by anything... as the Berliner says. The Japanese are back in my hands except for 7 sheets; an Englishman took the 7 sheets to London with him. He said he would bring them back as soon as he comes to Berlin again. He has not arrived yet. It is Griffith, one of the most famous American journalists. As soon as I speak with him and have the remaining sheets, I will make the entire collection available to you again. Should the remaining 7 sheets no longer be available (which I don't believe), you will receive – as I said before – 100 dollars in dollar treasury notes. I have postponed my trip since I am working on a play for Elisabeth Bergner. I would love to write more, to visit you on the trip – but Bavaria has become "enemy" territory, who knows what they would do to me... Hugs from your Fred

Davos-Dorf, Villa Stolzenfels, November 20, 1923

Dear Mother,

I have been in Davos for ten days. I immediately went to Dr. Rüedi, who, on the second day, cauterized my larynx. I will have to undergo this unpleasant procedure several more times. (You are familiar with all this from Irene.) I can't speak right now. My book *Peter* will appear shortly. You are on the list, please welcome him kindly. Talking about Germany, especially Bavaria, is pointless. There is censorship again, just like during the war in May. Even the black lines are appearing again. The times are getting more wonderful every day. One thing remains the same: the stupidity of people and the disgusting lies they tell each other. I plan to stay here until spring and then go to Austria. The Japanese folder is with Heyder. I am still trying to get in touch with Griffith. The 100 dollars are always available to you. Warm greetings, your Fred

Zehlendorf, December 31, 1923, written in Davos

HAPPY NEW YEAR, dear parents! All the best!

I visited Rüedi again today, and am already able to produce some low notes. He is excellent both as a doctor and as a person. I hope that when I come to you, I think in the fall, I will be able to roar, shout, and sing properly again. There has been about ten days of snowfall here, which even the so-called oldest people cannot remember. One couldn't go outside for days. The snow is 6 and a half feet deep! I have transferred the equivalent of 100 dollars (with a heavy heart: for you) in Swiss francs to the Cantonal Bank, on December 31st, to the account of Justizrat H. Passau. The receipt will be sent to you as soon as it arrives. The Rentenmark was quoted today in Davos at 1.27 francs, so above the peace parity, a good sign, but my distrust remains. (500 Rentenmarks would therefore be about 614 francs.) I am writing this card on the deck chair. The air is quite mild. I don't know if this is the same Griffith, but what strange people one encounters, it's almost like a fairy tale. Warm hugs from your Fred

Zehlendorf, January 27, 1924, written in Davos

Dear parents,

I have regained my voice! And, aside from the eternal financial misery, I am very happy. The bank has probably already sent you the receipt. I would advise you to pay the annual interest. At least now that should be easy for you, and then my deposit would be the first interest payment, so to speak. Griffith wanted to get me 5 of the 9 missing sheets. We still don't give up hope. It seems I was wrong about my Rentenmark pessimism. Thank God! Warm greetings, your Fred

Davos, March 4, 1924

Dear Mother,

Thanks for your letter. I'm glad to hear that Germany is progressing economically. We are all quite interested in that. Thank God, the horrible inflation period is over: hopefully for good. How much things have changed, I see from my fees at the *Berlin Daily News*. On November 23rd, the fee for an article was 1 (one) franc, now it's at least 40 (forty) francs. In that respect, unfortunately, the 100 dollars from Griffith has depreciated greatly – they were once worth at least ten to twenty times as much. I still regret deeply that my brother's scoundrel behavior destroyed the Japanese, but if anyone wanted to hold him accountable now, he would only commit another questionable act to cover up the old issue. I wouldn't encourage that. I still hope that Griffith, whom I'm writing to again today, will provide the 5 promised sheets. (He's not the criminal G., but an English correspondent.) Health-wise, I'm doing quite well. My voice is back. Only I still have throat pains. Regarding your Graubünden debt, I would just consider it a loan and start paying interest regularly from now on, which should be easy for you. Or you could demand a significant reduction in payment. By the way, of the two Sharaku portraits, the large one is undoubtedly fake. I've verified it. I haven't worked much lately. I've been as lazy as sin. Warm greetings, your Fred

Montreux, poste restante, June 4, 1924

Dearest Mother,

I must go to Germany to settle my publishing affairs. I am definitely parting ways with Reiß. My latest book, titled *Reader*, will be published by our publisher Heyder. You should help with this; look through the manuscripts stored at your place and see if any good small prose pieces can be found. I want to collect all my little prose. – Have you written new ballads? Send them to me: to Munich, Herzogstr. 42/in. p. A. There, I will be living. Let's meet in Munich. I am also negotiating with Meyer and Jessen about taking up a senior position. Kind regards, in haste, your Fred

Have you read my article *Mascha* in the *Berlin Daily News*? I've become friends with Mascha.

– Perhaps you could lend Roda Roda the carousel with a sacred oath of return. (He lives at Elisabethstr. 14. Write to him first. It concerns a collection called World Humor?)

Lugano, Café Brasserie de la Ville (Hotel de Ville), June 8, 1924

Dear Mother,

Thank you for your letter. I am currently reachable at Lugano poste restante. I was in Italy, invited by friends, visiting Genoa and Milan. In a few days, I will return to Milan to see the sensation at the Scala, the opera *Nero* by Boito. (The main thing is supposed to be the fantastic staging.) – The weather was beautiful for 14 days; now it's raining again and cold and unfriendly. – I visited Locarno.

I thought the grave would be overgrown, but it wasn't. It seems that someone (I don't know who) has taken care of the grave. If you want, I can inquire about a plaque, although in its current form (the ivy frames the inscription, the grave itself is filled with some grass) it doesn't give an unpleasant impression. I wouldn't plant flowers; they wilt too quickly in the Ticino climate if not cared for daily. – I send my warmest belated wishes to Father for his sixtieth birthday. What can one wish him that he doesn't already have? A magnificent character, a magnificent wife, and the memory of one of the finest and best people who came from his blood: what more does he need? – The environment, of course, is drearier than ever. At times, I feel very, very depressed and more pessimistic than ever. To quote Sternheim: "I find Europe disgusting..." As soon as I have enough money (I've actually been living the last few months by begging on the streets, i.e., from friends. I'm completely done with Reiß. He behaved too despicably: after 14 years of collaboration, a particularly strong piece...) – I plan to go to the Orient. I'm also toying with the idea of a world trip. For now, I've already rented a place in Constantinople, I can go there any day, but I'm still hesitating, to use a Bavarian expression, to "make the leap." – I've written a lot of small pieces: *Berlin Daily News, Frankfurter, Youth, Simpliz., Merkur, New Review, Dame* will bring them. All the best, be embraced by your Fred

Say hello to Frau Kahn-Gehrke!

Munich, August 14, 1924
Dear Mother,

Thank you for your card from the Wachau, it must be wonderful there. I'll be going to Berlin for a longer stay next week. I'm staying at the Hotel Adlon, Under the linden trees. I have much business to attend to and hope that it finally works out, as I'd like to be in Lugano in September. Whether and what will be published of mine in the winter is still uncertain. I've written many small stories and poems. I also need to see how things go with Reiß. – How is your business going? I have to complain about the slow payments, and every month I end up in a tight spot, which is not a pleasant position. If you read *Simpliz.*, Bauz, that's me too. Wishing you happy holidays, all the best, your Fred

Frankfurt/Main, Excelsior Hotel, Early January 1925
Dearest Mother,

Among my books, there should be two volumes of *Puppet Shows*, bound in violet. Do you remember? Please send them to me at the following address: Fritz Heyder, Berlin – Zehlendorf, Königstr. 1. – *The Chalk Circle* was the biggest theater success in Frankfurt in many years. Countless curtain calls. Hanover, Hamburg, and Prague have also reported great success. Cologne and Vienna seem to have postponed the performance.

Kind regards to both of you, your Fred

Breslau, Heiligegeiststr. 20, Before May 3, 1925
Dear Parents,

I send you warm greetings. You will hopefully see *The Chalk Circle* in Munich or Vienna, as it has now been accepted by 40 stages. In the meantime, I've written a new play: based loosely on a medieval puppet play, a new tragicomedy about Dr. Faust, which will have its premiere in Hamburg and Hanover in the fall. Currently, I am working on a translation of the play *Aiglon* by Rostand, which has already had its 2000th performance in Paris. – At the time, it was a star role for Bernhardt. I've also worked on a Shakespeare film (*A Midsummer Night's Dream*). So, I've had a lot to do. Health-wise, I'm doing so-so. The Breslau climate and the city itself are highly unpleasant to me. But what can one do? Fate. Fatum. Ananke. Best regards to you both, your Fred

Breslau, May 3, 1925
Dear Father,

Thank you for your letter. In Vienna, the *People's Theater* and in Munich, the *Playhouse* have accepted *The Chalk Circle* for the beginning of the next season. It's a pity that you didn't see the performance in Frankfurt. It was of the highest quality and could hardly be improved upon: direction-wise. – Unexpectedly, I have temporarily slid into drama. *The Lessing Theater* in Berlin will see my adaptation of Rostand's *Aiglon*, the famous French Napoleon drama, in October. Hamburg and Hannover will see *Christoph Wagner*, which Munich rejected because of the (sent to you) 4th Act – fear of clerical objections – Pope Jutta, etc. – Warm regards to Mother and you, your Fred

Frau Neher is still in the sanatorium, still very ill, has been operated on for the second time, but hopefully is now out of danger.

Breslau, Heiligegeiststr. 20, May 6, 1925
Dear Mother,

Thank you for your card. I would also love to see you again, and hopefully, it will happen soon. I have had a very exciting and hectic year. In the end, the person in question was struck by a severe blood poisoning and was lying in a critical state, and in my desperate fear, I made a vow that if she recovered, I would marry her. Frau Neher is now on the road to recovery. I am enclosing some pictures for you so you can get to know her. She is an unusually charming and lovable girl, also a highly talented actress (she has now played Saint Joan here 50 times, also the leading role in *Hannibal*, the *Miss*, and will also play *Haitang*). The concerns I had about marriage – and which are still not completely dispelled – are primarily external: an actress is tied to the city of her engagement, and that can be a dreadful city, which will matter less to her as she has her artistic work. But a city like Breslau, for example, greatly gets on my nerves. I have been here for 6 months and sometimes can hardly breathe. I already hate long stays in cities – and then this one! A city that has grown immensely since the war, (larger than Munich), without any musical brilliance, without any, even the slightest, natural beauty. On top of that, a horrible climate: few discussable people: that's Breslau. Other concerns lie in the two artistic professions. (No one can give up their own.) And finally, the "professional hysteria" of the actress. – So, with all love and affection, I enter this marriage with mixed feelings. But miracles happen. A miracle saved her life. Perhaps a miracle will also save our marriage. A thousand greetings, also to Father, always yours, Fred

Breslau, Heiligegeiststr. 20, Quisisana, May 16, 1925
Dearest Mother,

I just opened your letter and read the first sentence: "Now you are getting another mother ..." No, dear Mother, I am definitely not getting another mother: there are no other mothers as lovely as you and my mother in the world, where would the third one come from? I don't know her; she belongs to the bad mothers of fairy tales, I've hardly heard anything good about her. So my bride is actually an orphan. (Her father is dead.) She is still very ill. The danger to her life has been removed, but her recovery is terribly slow. The wound is still open. I will send your dear regards to her. I embrace you as your grateful and loving Fred

Breslau, Sanatorium Friederici, Parkstr. 2, July 8, 1925
Dearest Mother,

Thank you for your dear letter. It has been three weeks today since I had the bleeding, but I'm already feeling better and hope to go to Davos with my wife – we got married yesterday here in the sanatorium – in 8 days. Whatever happens, we want to leave to the future. Unfortunately, we are both very much in need of rest and still ill. You are right, the last few months have taken a tremendous toll on me emotionally: I spent two and a half months sitting by the bedside of a dear person, morning and afternoon, 8 hours, and only came to work, which I had to deliver contractually, *Aiglon*, late at night. In one month, I saw the sun rise 15 times at my desk. Plus the constant worry about a person constantly in danger of death – it was too much for me. So the collapse was much more emotional than physical. –

You will be interested to know that I just received the news that the *Burgtheater* has accepted my *Aiglon* adaptation for production, so hopefully, you will be able to see both *The Chalk Circle* and *Aiglon* in Vienna. Or do you want to come to Berlin? Both will be released in Berlin in October: with a fabulous cast: *The Chalk Circle* directed by Reinhardt! *Aiglon* at the *Lessing Theater*! – Unfortunately, I am having serious problems with Kiepenheuer: money issues, which are ruining some of my days. I embrace you, your Fred, and heartfelt greetings from

Carla.

Breslau, Höfchenstr. 87/111., September 9, 1925
Dearest Mother,

I wrote you a long letter – still from Breslau – in August: why have you never responded to it?

I've been back in Breslau for a few days and found quite a nice apartment, three rooms. Carla is now performing *The Chalk Circle*: the *Haitang*: my God, how bad the Munich performance was! The Vienna one will surely be interesting, as Martin is a very original director. The local one will also be very good. Hopefully, the Berlin one will be soon. – You are embraced by your Fredi.

P.S.: Dearest Mother,

I've also received reports from Vienna and hear consistently from those who know something that Martin has "directed" *The Chalk Circle* into the ground. He is a very talented but very vain director, and in the case of *The Chalk Circle*, he seems to have gone mad with delusions from Tairoff. The drama is a fairytale and must be played as such: delicately, lightly, cloud-like, floating, even the grotesque parts should not be taken too heavily. The Frankfurt performance as a whole, for example, was an ideal performance. Very good, under my supervision, also the Breslau performance with Carla as *Haitang*. Here – and everywhere where the play was performed meaningfully – it has become a very big success, and they are expecting months of sold-out houses. – I'm glad I wasn't in Vienna, I would have surely been half-dead from frustration. It's funny that Vienna and Munich offered such dreadful and poorly-directed performances. – Now Reinhardt is rehearsing, and I'm curious to see what will come of it. The performance is between October 5th and 15th. Can't you come to Berlin? – A thousand thanks for your report. But I sent you a long letter from the sanatorium, many pages, full of content. – I'm sending the reviews and pictures from here, which I request back. Warmly embracing you, your Fred.

Davos-Village, Villa Stolzenfels, December 30, 1925
Dearest Parents,

A blessed New Year to you! As you can see, I'm back again in old Davos. It's the same, but also many things have changed. Of the Davos people you, dear Mother, knew, the sculptor Modrow has died. He wrote to me shortly before his death. He died with his eyes open. The records of his daily diaries accompany his slow demise. It is moving to read them. I wrote a little essay about him and hope it will appear in the *Berlin Daily News*. In the meantime, a new poetry book has been published, that is, a selection from all my poetry books. I will send it to you, or perhaps the publisher Spaeth has already sent it? Warm hugs from your Fred.

Berlin, Passauerstr. 18/111., June 6, 1926

Dear Mother,

Do you know any sources about the *Peasants' War*, do you have any? I have been meaning (for a long time now) to write a novel based on it, with the central character being a woman, the so-called "black court woman." Do you know anything about her? A very interesting woman! –

Enclosed for autograph collection: Goetz (author of *Gneisenau*). Warmly embraced, both of you, your Fredi.

Vienna, June 19, 1926

Dear Father,

On June 26th, I will unfortunately no longer be here. I must hurry back to Berlin on matters regarding the revue, as it must be finished in the next fourteen days. – You love Vienna very much. I still have a mixed impression and am not sure whether I like it or not. The people are sometimes incredibly charming (journalists), sometimes incredibly rude (drivers and waiters). Theater is played very badly, worse than the average German province. Only the theater in the Josefstadt is outstanding, where I recommend you see *The Prisoner* with Helene Thimig and Ernst Deutsch in the lead roles. That is top-notch theater. I have been interviewed every moment. The Viennese seems more interested in the person than in the work. This obsession with indiscretions, the lack of objectivity, the slow pace – these are all traits of the Viennese character that I do not find sympathetic. But if one stays here for a while, perhaps one also falls asleep and adapts to the romantic sloppiness.

Be warmly greeted and embraced by your Fred.

No location, December 7, 1926

Dear Mother,

A thousand thanks for your letter. Oh, I am not at all a socialite, and neither is my wife. She goes out here and there for reasons of "representation," which an actor needs within certain limits, but in general, we don't bother with all that. An actor who works seriously, and she works fanatically on her roles, has no time for such things. It is actually a terrible profession, terribly beautiful – rehearsal from 11 to 4, food, sleep, 7 o'clock at the theater, 8 o'clock performing, 2:30 am removed from makeup, food, then sleep. I think only miners have it as strenuous. I, for one, am quite lazy, exceedingly lazy. I do nothing anymore. – We do not want to "relocate" to Vienna. My wife has indeed been offered a position at the *Burgtheater*, but she doesn't fully trust that calcified institution, and wants to go only as a guest for a few months. She is such a modern, aggressive, irritating actress that I really can't be sure how the Viennese audience and critics will react to her. They are so fond of intellectual pastries, nonsense, and Gugelhupf. – Both of you are embraced by your Fred.

Do you read much? I read little. A strange, interesting, and also debatable anthology: *Borchardt, Eternal Supply of German Poetry.*

Thomas Mann, *Disorder and Early Suffering* – delightful.

Debatable Anthology: *Eternal Supply of German Poetry.* Edited by Rudolf Borchardt. Munich: Verlag der Bremer Presse, 1926.

Thomas Mann, *Disorder and Early Suffering.* Novella. Berlin: S. Fischer, 1926.

Vienna, April 2, 1927

Dearest Mother,

A warm greeting from Vienna! (Park Hotel, Schönbrunn.) Vienna is not presenting itself kindly. Storm, rain, April. – In the coming weeks, two new books of mine will be published, which you will receive immediately – *The Novels of Passion* and *The Harp Girl.* – I am very tired, exhausted, drained. The attached card for your autograph collection is from Arco, the great radio engineer. – Didn't you know Hans Adler in Davos? He wrote a charming Austrian novel, *The Small Town* (published by Ed. Strache, Vienna). I find it magnificent (apart from the title). Both of you are embraced by your Fred.

Vienna, after April 22, 1927

Dear Mother,

I am glad that dear Father is already better, and I hope this improvement lasts. I do not know what advice was given for Father's condition on the Yugoslav coast, but I hear so much about the wonderful climate, the splendid scenery, and the extraordinary cheapness of places like the island of Rab or Dubrovnik, Cirkvenica, etc. –

My wife had a great success here, with the audience and in the press (Newspaper, Journal, Morgen (Polgar), General Release, etc. – except for *The Hour*, but that has a completely private background. In Vienna, everything is so terribly private, personal, and subjective. Liebest, is considered an absolutely corrupt guy. Not through money, but sexually – corruptible. At least that's what they told me immediately.)

I was from the beginning not entirely convinced of her suitability for the *Burgtheater.* She is too modern an actress. And in *Cleopatra*, it looks as if a cat is playing with a rat (Caesar) and a number of mice. She plays so wonderfully aggressively, not at all cozy, and lacks the usual Viennese "charm." At the end of August, she will also perform in Munich. Hopefully, you can see her then. – Warm greetings to both of you from Fred.

Munich, Herzogstr. 42/111.1., May 14, 1927

Dearest Mother,

Your deeply moving letter has only just reached me today in Munich. I left Vienna on Friday. I feel the deepest sympathy for the terrible misfortune that has befallen you, and for the bitter suffering that, already endured once, now returns to you. But when you are on the verge of breaking down – think also, in your pain, of your happiness: Think of how happy you have been all these years, in marriage to Father, whom I also love and admire so much, one of the noblest and best people the Earth has ever produced. How few people were blessed with such a marriage: such a husband – and such a daughter. Irene's image rises painfully sweet before me, and I kiss her delicate ghostly hand in the realm of shadows. As we met in this life, on this Earth, we will meet again in another life, on another star, for such grace, such goodness, such love cannot perish. Be embraced and kissed most tenderly by your loving Fred.

If I can assist you in any material matters, etc., please let me know without hesitation. I will stay about 4 weeks in Munich, where I have some work to complete. Where will dear Father be laid to rest? In Karlsbad? Will you then return to Passau? If you need my advice, should I come to Passau? Please write to me soon.

Davos-Dorf, Villa Stolzenfels, January 2, 1928
Dearest Mother,

I was very happy to receive your letter. I am also glad that you are moving closer to Munich, as this way we will surely be able to see each other more often throughout the year. Although Munich has not experienced the rapid and interesting rise that Berlin has, which is becoming more and more the heart of Europe, the old, culture-laden city, with its theaters, museums, and exhibitions, is still significant enough to provide you with plenty of stimulation. And Dachau is just a stone's throw away. I also love Dachau very much for its scenery. Which area near Dachau is the Rennweg located? Only in midsummer, in some years, are there many mosquitoes. But you can protect yourself in the apartment with mosquito windows, etc.

Even though I don't write often, the three of you – You, Irene, and Father Max – are always present to me. Irene was my greatest happiness, and I often think of her, of Locarno, and the summer evenings on Monti Trinità. There comes a time in everyone's life when one no longer lives forward, but backward. The memories almost become stronger than the present. Sometimes I think that I am not far from that time.

On Saturday, the premiere of *XYZ* will take place in Munich, the play in which my wife played the lead role at the Vienna *Burgtheater*. The Munich cast is nowhere near as good as the Vienna one. I also feel that the lead role has been wrongly cast with Rühmann: for the play must be funny through the dialogues, characters, and situations. But it must not be played as funny. Otherwise, it becomes farce. And I almost fear this from Rühmann (who, otherwise, is a fine actor, but a comedian).

Would you like to see the play? There are two tickets for the premiere in my name for you at the box office. If you don't use them, please call the theater!

Hugs, kisses from your Fred

Berlin, April 28, 1928
Dear Mother,

I am sending you four copies of the opera today. Please send them to the An-bruch for the prize competition. I've written to the Schott publishing house and sent it to them.

In haste, a thousand greetings, your Fred

Davos-Dorf, Villa Stolzenfels, July 23, 1928
Dear Mother,

Yes, please send me the newspaper clippings from the *Prison Diary*. I promise I will return them to you. I have come to Davos because the heatwave that had come over Europe had particularly strong effects in Italy. Here, it is, of course, cool. I plan to stay about a week. Then I want to go to Munich for a few more weeks and certainly hope to find you in Dachau at that time. The Russian comedy that I read to you a little back then has been accepted by the *Berlin State Theater*.

Give my regards to the Hingsamers, and be warmly greeted yourself by your Fred

Davos, July 27, 1928
Dearest Mother,

Thank you very much for the "diary." As soon as I have used it, I will return it to you. I plan to write the story of a murderer who spends 18 years in prison. I am in bed again, as I suddenly developed a fever, over 100.4°F, as I have unfortunately had many times recently. I dislike being in bed, that is, when forced, but willingly when necessary. In September, a novel of mine will be published, and I will send it to you immediately after. Yes, the Amperbad must be wonderful. The simplest pleasures of life are the greatest.

We were in Brioni for about two months. I enjoyed it extraordinarily once again. It is one of the most pleasant places to live. Unfortunately, it is very expensive. My wife is already back in Berlin. The rehearsals for the new season begin in August.

Much love, greetings to the Hingsamers, hugs from your Fred

Part Twelve:

Diary from Prison

(April 18, 1919–April 26, 1919, Military Prison at Nuremberg)

Diary from Prison

April 18, 1919.

It's eleven o'clock. I am sitting on the cot in the ice-cold detention cell in Straubing and writing this letter. In the evening, I am supposed to go to Nuremberg, to the 3rd Army Corps, but perhaps not until tomorrow. When I think that I have to spend the night here in this ice-cold damp hole, without even a straw mattress, it makes me shudder. And I already have a terrible night behind me. I was thrown into the detention cell in Passau, on the ground floor, damp and completely dark. (This cell also has no light...) Only a cot with a straw mattress inside. Do you remember what the officer who arrested me promised? He also falsely promised that I would be handed over to the civil authorities in Passau the next day. (Have the officers changed their profession? Have they become policemen?) At half past two in the night, an open car came and raced with me through the night to Plattling. Frost lay on the fields like snow. The wind howled. I was freezing to my marrow. In Plattling, I boarded the train to Straubing, a guard with a loaded rifle next to me. – I have just been interrogated for the first time; it was about the telegram you are familiar with. That's the whole story. Based on that, I was accused of participating in the Soviet Republic. You know, dear father, how I stand on this matter, and you also know that I do not lie. And you know that it was precisely my sense of responsibility that kept me from getting involved in the affair. And that telegram, which I wrote in private, is now supposed to make me an official emissary of the Soviet government?

Imagine this: during the interrogation, I was even confronted with an accusation of *lèse majesté* from 1917 (there were portraits of three princes hanging in the examination room)! By an officer of the Socialist Republic! What I endure in the cells and from the concept of "cell," I don't need to describe to you, I, who love internal and external freedom above all and, as a student of Lao Tzu, hate all power, which is why I am also against the dictatorship of the proletariat, because it breeds the same arrogance of power in them as once existed in the ruling classes under imperialism.

Holy Saturday, April 19, 1919

Dear Mother, dear Father, today marks the third day that I am imprisoned, and there seems to be no end in sight. I am being dragged from cell to cell, and I have the impression that a person is valued even less than in imperial Germany. Those who have interrogated me so far have shown no sympathy for me. I was simply snapped at. They feel entirely in the role of the judge and, as a matter of principle, only attribute *mala fides* to the "accused." What am I to do when they simply say: That's not true, that's not true. It's an extremely simplified judicial process reminiscent of the Tsarists courts. What do these "rulers" care about a prisoner who wants freedom – not out of a whim, but out of his inherent sense of justice? At the Nuremberg Garrison Command, the court officer (or whatever he was) addressed us informally: "Guys, you're now simply being put into protective custody!" (Protective custody, a euphemistic term for what is happening to us.) And a plump, rosy-cheeked civilian standing behind him shouted, free, satisfied, and happy: "There's no rush with the interrogation..." I couldn't help but turn around and shout: "There is indeed a rush, because we are human beings deprived of the noblest human attribute – freedom, personal freedom – and have been dragged back and forth for days and nights now." – Tonight we were housed in the Straubing Penitentiary. At least it was warm, but the procedures they subjected us to are among the most degrading things one human being can do to another – they even looked at and dug right into our rectums to see if we were hiding anything... I would like to know how criminals are treated if "protective detainees" are treated like this, or rather, I know: no worse, no better, just the same. Because today, a female convict from the penitentiary who was sentenced to years of imprisonment for aggravated theft traveled with us.

I'm writing these letters out of the blue, just to be with you. To at least be loved and well-treated in thought by people. By the way, the ordinary people, the soldiers accompanying us, the prison guards, etc., are by far the most humane and friendly. The authorities are just as conventionally harsh as before. I am becoming increasingly disappointed in revolutionary Germany. What the imperial authorities would have liked: protective custody: the socialist authorities managed to impose it on me. I feel like I'm in an unlimited military dictatorship, as if Ludendorff were back. – Did you receive my telegram yesterday? They promised to send it from Straubing. But I wasn't allowed to add any information to it. Can't you do anything for me? Can't you vouch for me? After all, you're a well-known Old Bavarian? Of course, my sense of cleanliness is violated at every turn. My two handkerchiefs are gone. Yesterday's meal: stinking stockfish and a black soup, was inedible. At least the soup was decent in the penitentiary in the evening, and there was water and good bread with it.

I have just now come from the so-called interrogation at the Justice Commissariat of the Third Army Corps. They half-listened to me, didn't even read the entire report (especially not the one I attached), and simply said: "I don't believe that. You are to be transferred to the investigative prison in Nuremberg until the situation is further clarified. The files now go to Passau." So I ask: why was I dragged through all of Bavaria, tormented, and tortured, only to then be judged in Passau, where I come from? How long can this take? Ah, weeks, I fear. When the six weeks are up, I will not be able to return to Monti, to paradise.

> First, I ran headlong into the wall
> And shook the bars.
> I cursed both death and life
> And set the whole prison on fire with my fiery gaze.
> The barred window above was blind and small.

I never knew if the sun was shining or if it was raining.
I was starving and had a thousand stomachs,
And I wanted so badly to be my own grandson.
Then I threw myself onto the cot.
A bowl of soup floated through the door.
I trembled like a hungry zoo lion.
Once a woman's step passed by in the hallway.
The step of a queen.
Eventually, I became convinced that I'm
A criminal, and that I had been rightly rendered harmless.
I endured being mocked by the guard,
And I feel that he is something like a cherub
With a flaming sword and the avenger of my deeds.
One day the door will open, as if by grace,
Noble freedom will be granted to me again by God.
I will rush straight to a first-class hotel and bathe
And go to the riding school and mount my favorite horse.
I believe it was called Mimi, like the delicate girl in the
Famous Bohemian novel,
And I will race through the English Garden and ride
Through fields of corn and poppies,
And I will gallop and wave the red flag of the sun
And I will lead the heavenly revolution.

Nuremberg, April 20, 1919

I was brought to the prison here yesterday evening. The officer who brought me consoled, saying, "the rooms are quite nice..." Naturally, I was looking forward to my room. To sleep in a bed again, how wonderful that would be. However, the preliminaries were so strange that I became suspicious. Everything possible was taken from me, my money, even my watch, and then I was led into a cell that differed from that of Straubing penitentiary only in that it had a small foldable bench and an non-folding table.

At least in the Straubing penitentiary there was a flush toilet in the cell. Here, the old bucket doesn't close properly and stinks up the air. All I had to eat for the entire day yesterday was: a shot of schnapps at 5 a.m. (nothing to go with it) and at 6 p.m a piece of bread and a small bottle of beer. No lunch, no dinner, not even a cup of warm coffee. I said I would arrange for something on my own expense. They said that wasn't possible. So far, I have been treated like a convicted prisoner. My two cellmates are here for embezzlement and theft. One called to me softly last night: "Comrade," he said, "Comrade, do you have a cigarette?" I didn't have any left, as I had already given them all away in Passau to the soldiers of the guard, who had been so friendly to me. "Comrade," he continued, "I tried to steal a goose at Christmas, they caught me, shot at me, I got five bullets, I lay in the hospital for two months, and now two months here." He fell silent. Then, thoughtfully: "You know, the lieutenant who was here the last few days, the one from the Spartacists, he had cigarettes."

I was very cold last night. I dreamt about... Irene, but I can't remember what. I kept my underpants and my thick woolen vest on, and still, I was freezing. At 6 a.m., the prison guard shouted – I pity these creatures for their job as prison guards. That people can even be found to do such things to each other. The prison guard shouted: "Get up, Henschke!" Then the trap window in the door opened, a hand slid in: "Here's a towel." I had to wash myself, make the "bed," then the trap window opened again and a cup of black coffee floated in. – At least it's warm. – Today is Easter Sunday. Today the Lord rose from the grave once more. I was laid in the grave on the night of Maundy Thursday. When will I rise again? Break these walls? Bend these bars, have wings again, and fly into the light?

I wanted to send you a telegram yesterday, you haven't known where I am for four days, and your anxiety must be great. But the guard wouldn't accept it. I have to wait until the "sergeant" comes. Will he come today? It's Easter after all, and everyone, including the examining judge, is on Easter holiday. I'll probably have to sit here for days before I'm called again. Outside, the sparrows are noisy. They sing like angels.

A large lump of bread is tossed in to me. I have nothing to cut it with. I am not allowed a knife (I don't know why, maybe because I could go after the guard?). I try to cut the bread with my toothbrush. My only precious possessions are: a cigar and an orange. I wouldn't dare smoke the cigar or eat the orange. I just smell them. When I smell the orange, Monti, my Ticino paradise, rises before me. The almond trees are in bloom, the green lizards are shimmering, and today Soffel, the good man, has surely caught a grass snake. The sun is shining, the Maggia river resounds, Rio, my dog, is barking because the garden gate is creaking – and freedom – freedom is everywhere!

The guard shouts: "I need the coffee mug!" I can't gulp down the drink down like this, otherwise I'll get sick. I tell him: "Just wait a moment!" He is immediately becomes angry, maybe now he won't report me to the "sergeant," then another day and more than a day will be lost. I want to ask him to send the telegram to you, and will also request a medical examination. –

> Can I still sing verses,
> While I'm sitting behind bars?
> Thunder rumbles, lightning flashes,
> And the wall refuses to crack.
> If only the door would open
> And a female figure enter,
> Who would take me by the hands,
> Whether she is a girl or an old woman.
> If only the table would come to life,
> If only my coat would embrace me!

This pillow would cling to me,
This effigy – if only it were alive!

Nuremberg, April 20, 1919

One of the prisoners, who is cleaning the corridor outside, slips me two small booklets through the window to read. They are the 14th and 15th installments of "The Violinist's Daughter or the Mystery of the Blue Mountains." On the cover it says: "This novel deals with the mysterious enigma and truthfully recounts the strange fates of the girl Klara Herzfeld, endowed with wondrous beauty." I look forward to being initiated into the strange fates of the girl Klara Herzfeld, endowed with wondrous beauty. Will her fate be as strange as mine, and will it be of such wondrous beauty as you, Irene?

Lunch: a bowl of good soup in which two pea-sized pieces of meat float, a bowl of decent potato salad, and a piece of green, moldy bread. I am brought to the "sergeant" and ask him to send a telegram to you. He doesn't know if it's possible; actually, all mail must be presented to the examining magistrate, who, of course, isn't here today or tomorrow since it's a holiday! The doctor won't come until the day after tomorrow either. Finally, he promises to let a short letter containing only my whereabouts be sent to you. When will it reach you? Probably not before the day after tomorrow. The days pass. The room disintegrates. Time passes. And nothing happens for me. Everything: in itself and for itself. I am completely outside the earth. In hell, I rotate around myself.

A board hangs on the wall, and I can see what my poor brothers, the fellow prisoners, receive for their work in the prison: sewing letters onto cards, a dozen cards 5 pfennigs; making backpacks, 1 piece depending on size 1 to 2 pfennigs; making toys, daily 2 to 25 pfennigs; sewing, embroidery, and crochet work, daily 5 to 10 pfennigs; writing work, for 500 addresses or similar, 25 pfennigs; tailoring, shoemaking, locksmithing, carpentry, saddlery, plumbing, painting, masonry, daily 25 pfennigs; knitting, mending stockings and socks, daily 3 to 10 pfennigs. I can understand how a not particularly robust person, forced to dwell for weeks or even months in this makeshift chamber-turned-toilet, might begin to doubt themselves, crushed by the hammer of fate, considering themselves the most wretched of all creatures and readily willing and capable of accusing themselves of all mortal sins and confessing to whatever is demanded of them. I force myself to hold back my bodily needs as long as possible because I am disgusted by opening the bucket, and the stench that lingers in the room for minutes.

What time is it? 5? 6? Dinner comes: A white hand reaches through the trap window with two small pieces of cheese. That is all. The moldy bread from lunch is apparently intended as an accompaniment.

April 21, 1919

Last night I dreamed of Irene again. She was sitting in her silk wedding dress in a corner of a tearoom, embroidering a child's shirt. It is six o'clock. The warden: "Wake up! We can't wait for you! Take your slop bucket and empty it outside!"

Sometimes I feel like getting angry, but I realize it's completely pointless. I'm not a person who deserves respect. I don't look wild or romantic; who would be afraid of me? Not even the shyest child. I have a boyish face, and people think I'm an impulsive high school student who participated in the Spartacist turmoil just for fun.

I gave the cigar to the soldier who was so kind to me yesterday, and I ate the orange last night. I couldn't resist the urge any longer. My two wonders from the outside world are gone. I'm saving the orange peels for myself. They perfume the cell so sweetly, and if I soak them in water, I might use them as a tooth tincture. I have a north-facing cell. Earlier, when my shutter window was open, I looked across to the cell opposite. It was open. The sun was shining in there, lying on the bunk like a beautiful blonde woman. How I envy the man across from me for his sun. He was also arrested in Passau, a telegraph operator who allegedly worked as a telegram censor for the Soviet Republic in Passau.

A vague twilight always wanders through my cell, as if it were just before sunset, as if evening were about to begin. It may be that the red terror reigns in Munich, which is occupied by communists. It is certain that the white terror rages all the more blindly in Bavaria, which is ruled by the Hoffmann government. Dear father, you always boast proudly that we have the freest right to vote in the world. What use is the freest right to vote to you if you yourself are so unfree that the government has the power at any time to have you, a civilian, arrested by the military and taken into protective custody. Protective custody still exists in revolutionary Germany; an institution of truly medieval barbarity. Is this the new Germany? Wasn't it always one of the very first demands of freedom-loving men, whether they be democrats or socialists, that protective custody must first and foremost be abolished? And yet it still exists! Private censorship is also still maintained. What use is the most beautiful freedom of thought, dear father, if you cannot freely express your thoughts? Letters to you and from you are intercepted, telegrams are monitored, there is a spy sitting at your table in the café: this, dear father, is the new Germany, which only differs from the old in that others have taken the place of Wilhelm II and Ludendorff. Just now I read in the "Nuremberg Gazette," which a soldier slipped through the door for me, that the Third Army Corps has temporarily banned all assemblies in Nuremberg.

Is this the so-called freedom of assembly? Changing personnel achieves nothing: unless the spirit changes, unless the soul rebels. The citizens are already bowing down again, as they were accustomed to bowing down in the past. And already, I see the shadow of a princely figure rising over Bavaria.

> Outside, a bird sings in the world.
> Outside, a blue spring field blooms.

Outside, a girl dressed in Easter finery
Walks arm in arm with the policeman.
Outside, instead of in a restaurant,
Citizens sit listening to music and clinking forks.
At Nuremberg Castle, a child plays
With clouds and the wind from heaven.
And the examining magistrate is perhaps
Stroking his wife's blonde hair.
Outside, they smile at each other:
The old man and the infant, girl or boy.
Outside, they love each other deeply:
Deer and meadow, sunshine and sea...

Nuremberg, April 21, 1919

Lunch: a bowl of good soup, a bowl of less good spaetzle. Dinner (brought in at the same time for convenience): a tiny piece of cheese (like yesterday). I've already eaten the cheese by 4 o'clock because I am hungry. I fold down the bed because I don't feel well and lie down. I slept a little. I walk along the walls and see all sorts of mathematical numbers and formulas. I approach more closely and notice that they are calendars created by the prisoners. From the day of admission to the day of release. And some number sequences are endlessly long. A line through the date means: another day passed. Another day closer to life, light, dance, and laughter.

Should I also create a chart?

I'm hesitant. I'm afraid of the numbers.

Yesterday, the sergeant said: "Just wait, in a few days you'll be released." The people are all so nice, but the same thing was said by the driver in the car: "Just wait, in Nuremberg they will let you go immediately." It was not true. People are mistaken about the sluggishness of the judicial system and the brutality of the military machinery.

Today, to my amazement, I learn that I am being held in the military section of the detention prison. How is that possible, me, a civilian? A bad sign. Not for me. For Germany. According to law and justice, I should have been handed over to the civil authorities immediately. It seems the civil system has already been sidelined again.

If you weren't my sun,
And if this image didn't illuminate me,
Ah, I would freeze to death in this barren cold
And this wilderness would not see me alive.
I am still bound to you as once before.
You, the dead, keep me alive.
And many of my darkest hours

Sing under your violin's bow.

Now it grows dark again.
No star enters my cell
With its sparkle.
The walls grow pale,
And green hands reach out
For me, as if to join in a ghostly dance.
What will tomorrow bring?
(No heaven here on earth)
The night ripples in such gentle waves.
Shrouded by black flowers,
I sink as if lost
Into a river that carries me away.

April 22, 1919

I am always hungry. And I am always freezing.

I just reported to the sergeant: I asked for permission to read newspapers and to refill my fountain pen, which was graciously granted. I also handed him a telegram with the request to expedite it.

"Please urgently request release from custody on bond or bail."

The sergeant said, "We'll see what can be done, dear Henschke." I don't know what else to do, now I'm waiting for the doctor. Will he be able or willing to help me? I've been in custody for a week now. I recall from reading the "Crossen Local Newspaper" that men were sentenced to a week's imprisonment for minor theft. So, I would have already served the punishment for a minor theft.

The guard shouts through the peephole, "Do you want to take a walk, Henschke?" I decline. I'm waiting for the doctor. I know all prisoners have to line up in formation, and then we silently go out to the courtyard. "Without cadence, march!" I hear the supervisor's voice fade away and the footsteps of the prisoners. What kind of weather is it? I can't tell through the dirty, half-blind window; every day, the sky reflects the same gray.

What feelings animate me? Oh, nothing "animates" me. I'm freezing and hungry.

They've just taken me to another cell, which at least has the advantage of being warmer. The central heating is on.

The doctor prescribed anise drops.

I found the following story neatly written on an old notebook page in the new cell: Who could have invented it?

A father and a mother lived with their two children on a rugged island in the vast ocean, where they had ended up after a shipwreck. Roots and herbs served as their food, a spring was their drink, and a rocky cave was their dwelling. Often, terrible storms and thunderstorms raged on the island. The children could no longer imagine how they had come to the island; they knew nothing of the large, solid mainland. Bread, flour, fruit, and all the other delightful things found there had become unknown to them.

One day, four Moors landed on the island in a small boat. The parents were overjoyed and hoped to be relieved of their suffering. However, the boat was too small to carry them all to the mainland at once – and the father wanted to make the journey first.

Mother and children wept as he climbed into the fragile wooden vessel, and the four black men began to carry him away. But he said, "Do not weep! It is better over there, you will all follow soon."

When the boat returned to pick up the mother, the children wept even more. But she also said, "Do not weep! In the better land, we shall all be reunited!"

Finally, the boat came to fetch the two children.

They were very afraid of the black men and quaked in fear at the terrible sea they had to cross. They approached the land with trepidation and trembling.

But how joyful they were when they saw their parents standing on the shore, reaching out their hands to them, leading them into the shade of tall palm trees, and welcoming them with milk, honey, and delicious fruits on the flowery grass. "Oh, how foolish our fear was!" said the children. "We should not have feared but rejoiced when the black men came to take us to the better land."

"Dear children," said the father, "our voyage from the barren island to this beautiful land has a deeper meaning for us. Another journey awaits us all to an even more beautiful land. The entire earth on which we live here resembles a desolate, rugged island. This magnificent land here is a weak image of heaven for us. The crossing over the stormy sea represents death. That little boat reminds us of the bier on which black-clad men will one day carry us away. But when that hour strikes, when either I, your mother, or you must leave this world, do not be frightened! Death is nothing but a transition to a better land for pious people who have loved God and done His will."

Nuremberg, April 22, 1919

The guard brought anise drops. I sipped them like Hennessy or Benedictine, savoring their taste in my mouth for a long time. Thirteen years ago, when I was bedridden with pleurisy and the fever refused to subside, I had to endure a starvation cure. I was given nothing but tea and watered-down cocoa. I starved so long that I wept and dreamed at night of the vending machine, where you insert a ten-pfennig coin into a slot and receive a ham roll, a salmon sandwich, or an egg sandwich – oh, oh, what wonderful things there were to eat in this good world! The meager fat-free lunch doesn't last, and besides, there's only a cup of coffee in the morning and a bit of cheese in the evening. By 4 o'clock, I've already eaten it all, and then there's nothing left for the evening.

It's terrible to be hungry. Hunger robs you of all other thoughts, and all you think is this: eat, eat, devour, devour. If only it would get dark! Then I could sleep! Shut off the stomach. Close the eyes. Let the heart speak in dreams. Be with Irene.

April 23, 1919

Due to a coal shortage, passenger traffic on the Bavarian State Railways must be suspended starting Thursday, the 24th. If I am released today or at the latest tomorrow morning, I can no longer leave Nuremberg. Should I believe this? Should I hope? Why haven't I heard anything from Passau? Someone must have written or telegraphed to me, right?

Whenever the guard rattles the keys in the hallway, I perk up my ears like a hare. I am considering sending a telegram to the Prussian Ministry of Justice.

Time creeps like a snail. It moves like a crab, backwards. It's just now striking 9 o'clock.

Today we had soup, beetroot, and a small piece of meat for lunch. In the evening, artificial honey and tea. All quite palatable; just too little to be satisfying. The guard promised to get me dinner.

Justice Counselor Z. was with me. He showed me a telegram from you. My hope flared up. If he could manage to get me released soon, very soon. Everything depends on that. I asked him for books. Klara Herzfeld, the beautiful girl, didn't quite satisfy me, and I am numb from staring into the wall. Writing is also becoming difficult for me. I just "ate" dinner, but I'm already ravenously hungry again. If I eat the piece of bread that's still there now, I won't have anything to eat tomorrow morning.

I am fighting a battle of conscience.

Hölderlin, my great, holy brother, how I long for the land of Hyperion, for a verse from you, dripped into my wound like balm. What would beetroot, artificial honey, and army bread mean to you? It would all be the same to you, which, I admit painfully, means so much to me in my situation. Schubert was imprisoned in Hohenasperg for thirteen years. I am horrified. I feel quite pathetic compared to the masters of the past. But they felt like martyrs, that they were enduring something for a greater cause. What am I enduring? Because an ass sent me a telegram, a second ass intercepted it, a third ass deemed it suspicious. No reason to theatrically display my suffering.

April 23, 1919

And tonight
I awoke,
A hand wrote on the wall.
And the writing was red,
As red as blood,
And the hand was white as wax.

And I saw it and forgot

My fears and read
What the hand, the silver one, wrote.
Do you need me?
You are not alone,
And I will love you forever.

Do not forget the feast,
The Holy Three,
The cry, and the endless kiss.
The prison is breaking
Judgment draws near,
And the river flows upward to its source.

The night and the day,
The moon and the hedge,
We love each other anew.
You kiss my forehead
Like the sun kisses the snow,
And the straw covers us as beggars.

If you stay, I'll stay,
then sing, then speak,
Did I speak appropriately, did I say you, did I say thou?
I grasp the silver hand
On the wall,
And it drew me towards the stars.

Every evening, the medical sergeant comes and takes my temperature. Then he prescribes anise drops for me. Downstairs, someone is always playing the piano. It seems that a permanent prisoner in the civil department has rented it. The oldest operettas. *The Zampa Overture*, which I know so well from the carousels and fairgrounds of my childhood. I think of my last hours on Swiss soil. In the locked ward of a private mental sanatorium. A billiard hall. The windows can only be opened with a key. An attendant in a niche. The dancer Nijinsky, Anna Pavlova's partner, plays billiards with short, hard strokes against a petty bourgeois man without a collar. Herr von Waldkirch appears on felt soles and stutters as he praises his violins.

He has a collection of violins. He fetches one with a magnificent tone. A virtuoso from Constance who accompanied us takes it out of the case, examines it, and begins to play. The gentlemen at the billiards table listen, stiffly. Herr von Waldkirch's face melts away, like spilled milk. They hand me "The Boy's Magic Horn." I read a ballad. Dr. Levy, my good friend, recites the last poem from "Irene."

I hadn't been with such reasonable people in a long time as these madmen, who suffer from severe paranoid delusions.

"Monsieur," I say to Nijinsky, "is it not true that you were in Berlin seven years ago?"

"Monsieur," he replies, "I don't remember anymore. Berlin or Petrograd, it's all the same, like Jesus and Jehovah."

Were these all premonitions, that I was in passageways in a house where the windows could not be opened and the doorknobs could be unscrewed? Rooms with small barred windows in the house? Upholstery on the walls? Those fools were better off than I. They can empathize with a state of voluntariness. They are boarders. Guests. Was this a premonition of my current state, that the morning before my arrest I began a mystical poem:

"The Prisoner?"

Nuremberg, April 24, 1919

The event of the day is your letter, dear Mother. Yes, if only all people were like you and thought like you! Please don't forget that an ancient legal custom demands that the accused be assumed to be the worst and most guilty *a priori*. What did those who interrogated me know about my verses, my work, my intentions? They didn't know I was a poet, but according to instructions received, they considered me a "Spartacist." The interrogation by the squadron clerk in Straubing was utterly farcical, and in Nuremberg at the 3rd Army Corps, it lasted half a minute. The man glanced briefly at the record and said: "No one believes what you're saying, do they?" and "Put him in pretrial detention until the matter is clarified." That was all. Dearest Mother, I was dragged through Bavaria for four days because of that. If they had interrogated me the next day in Passau, as the officers had promised, everything might have been resolved soon. Now the affair has taken on a mystical aura: due to the car ride, the penitentiary, and the infinitely numerous escorts (with loaded rifles, of course). I believe that since Thursday of last week, fifty to sixty people have been unnecessarily troubled because of me. In my statement, I had assumed that my good faith would not be dismissed outright. If I had seen through the malice of the entire apparatus from the beginning, I would have only given one sentence for the record.

April 25, 1919

Yesterday, I read *The Serapion Brothers* by E.T.A. Hoffmann. In the composition of his stories, he is probably unmatched by anyone in Germany. The happiest blend of three talents: that of a painter, a musician above all, and a poet. And a fourth talent that guides and restrains all the other three: he was a visionary.

> Like the arctic fox of the polar night
> I wander through life alone,
> Not devoted to anyone in the future,

Because only solitude makes things true.
Didn't I falsify my brother's footsteps?
Does he seek my advice to achieve his goal?
Let each find their own path,
And already the vulture's wings are fluttering.

Yes: forgive the poor fool,
For he fought for his brothers.
Here, he lays down his weapons,
For you did not choose him.
The moon stares paler and yellower,
Rocks follow its glow.

And forgive me for my tears,
For I wished nothing for myself.

Last night I dreamed so vividly of returning to Monti that when I woke up, I believed I was in Monti.

April 26, 1919

Free! Back outside! Alive again! I am still too excited and nervous to be able to control the waves of emotions surging through me. An old acquaintance from Munich, formerly a dramaturge here at the theater, and Miss Z..., the daughter of the justice councilor, took care of me. We went to the festival grounds, watched "Faust's Descent into Hell" at the puppet theater, performed in the most beautiful Bavarian dialect, and rode the carousel. Between the stalls, sailors with rifles walked around, and it was said that a new communist coup was being prepared in Nuremberg. What coup! What revolution! I just want to breathe again and be able to smile.

I took an elegant room at the Königshof and immediately ordered a bath. My clothes look terrible. Dirty and torn. I was so excited that I didn't sleep the whole night. I want to call you to let you know I won't be returning to Passau. The trains are canceled, it would take considerable effort to return on freight trains in a matter of days. And then my passport will expire soon. Should I risk it? I need rest, rest, rest. And I have that in Monti. With the current situation in Bavaria, I would feel very uncomfortable in Passau again. There's another train to Württemberg. Send my papers and things here as soon as possible, express.

Today I want to visit Nuremberg, the Hirschvogel Hall, and Hans Sachs, and in the Hans Sachs House, I will tip my hat, for the first time in nine days, and reverently greet the Germany that I love.

Sonnet on Nuremberg

You German city, the most German of cities,
Your walls protect me, a wavering soul.
You are tender to the tender, rough to the rough.
I pray your prayers of stone.

Oh time, when even tools were good and pious!
I feel moved by noble tremors.
God, who became image and gable, will endure,
After we have long become fertilizer for cemetery beds.
Were these trenches created for war?
Broom and lilac bloom around the embrasures.
Did the goldsmith take gold to hoard it?
Time was eternal. The songs of larks.
Let our souls strive for simplicity
And give us Dürer, give us Hans Sachs again!

About the Translator

Jim Doss is a founding editor of the bi-annual journal *Loch Raven Review*. He was born and raised in the foothills of the Blue Ridge Mountains, and is a graduate of the University of Virginia. His work has appeared in numerous publications, both on the Internet and in print. Doss has published three books of poetry: *Learning to Talk Again* (2011), *What Remains* (2017), and *The Long Goodbye* (2024). He has also translated Georg Trakl's complete poems, *The Last Gold of Expired Stars,* Ernst Toller's autobiography, *A Youth in Germany*, and *Letters from Prison* in addition to a number of Ernst Toller's plays, and a poetry anthology entitled *Nine Holocaust Poets* (2024). He is a retired software engineer.

www.ingramcontent.com/pod-product-compliance
Lightning Source LLC
Chambersburg PA
CBHW021845010726
47493CB00005B/1553